PRAISE FOR KAY HOOPER'S NOVELS

Amanda

"Don't miss a story that will keep your reading light on until well into the night."
—Catherine Coulter

"Kay Hooper's dialogue rings true; her characters are more three-dimensional than those usually found in this genre. You may think you've guessed the outcome, unraveled all the lies. Then again, you could be as mistaken as I was."
—*Atlanta Journal-Constitution*

"Keeps you reading." —*Philadelphia Inquirer*

Haunting Rachel

"She keeps me guessing until the very end."
—Linda Howard

"The pace flies, the suspense never lets up. It's great reading." —*Baton Rouge Advocate*

"A stirring and evocative thriller."
—*Palo Alto Daily News*

BANTAM BOOKS BY KAY HOOPER

The Bishop Trilogies

Stealing Shadows
Hiding in the Shadows
Out of the Shadows

Touching Evil
Whisper of Evil
Sense of Evil

Hunting Fear
Chill of Fear

The Quinn Novels

Once a Thief
Always a Thief

Romantic Suspense

Amanda
After Caroline
Finding Laura
Haunting Rachel

Classic Fantasy and Romance

On Wings of Magic
The Wizard of Seattle
My Guardian Angel (*Anthology*)
Yours to Keep (*Anthology*)

KAY HOOPER

Amanda

—

Haunting Rachel

BANTAM BOOKS

AMANDA / HAUNTING RACHEL
A Bantam Book / August 2005

Published by
Bantam Dell
A Division of Random House, Inc.
New York, New York

0-553-38384-1

These titles were originally published individually by Bantam Dell.

Printed in the United States of America
Published simultaneously in Canada

www.bantamdell.com

OPM 10 9 8 7 6 5 4 3 2 1

Amanda

Prologue

July, 1975

*T*HUNDER ROLLED AND BOOMED, ECHOing the way it did when a storm came over the mountains on a hot night, and the wind-driven rain lashed the trees and furiously pelted the windowpanes of the big house. The nine-year-old girl shivered, her cotton nightgown soaked and clinging to her, and her slight body was stiff as she stood in the center of the dark bedroom.

"Mama—"

"*Shhhh!* Don't, baby, don't make any noise. Just stand there, very still, and wait for me."

They called her baby often, her mother, her father, because she'd been so difficult to conceive and was so cherished once they had her. So beloved. That was why they had named her Amanda, her father had explained, lifting her up to ride upon his broad shoulders, because she was so perfect and so worthy of their love.

She didn't feel perfect now. She felt cold and emptied out and dreadfully afraid. And the sound of her mother's voice, so thin and desperate, frightened Amanda even more. The bottom had fallen out of her world so suddenly that she was still numbly bewildered and broken, and her big gray eyes followed her mother with the piteous dread of one who had lost everything except a last, fragile, unspeakably precious tie to what had been.

Whispering between rumbles of thunder, she asked, "Mama, where will we go?"

"Away, far away, baby." The only illumination in the bedroom was provided by angry nature as lightning split the stormy sky outside, and Christine Daulton used the flashes to guide her in stuffing clothes into an old canvas duffel bag. She dared not turn on any lights, and the need to hurry was so fierce it nearly strangled her.

She hadn't room for them, but pushed her journals into the bag as well because she had to have *something* of this place to take with her, and something of her life with Brian. *Oh, dear God, Brian . . .* She raked a handful of jewelry from the box on the dresser, tasting blood because she was biting her bottom lip to keep herself from screaming. There was no time, no time, she had to get Amanda away from here.

"Wait here," she told her daughter.

"No! Mama, please—"

"Shhhh! All right, Amanda, come with me—but you have to be quiet." Moments later, down the hall in her daughter's room, Christine fumbled for more clothing and thrust it into the bulging bag. She helped the silent, trembling girl into dry clothing, faded jeans and a tee shirt. "Shoes?"

Amanda found a pair of dirty sneakers and shoved her feet into them. Her mother grasped her hand and led her from the room, both of them consciously tiptoeing. Then, at the head of the stairs, Amanda suddenly let out a moan of anguish and tried to pull her hand free. "Oh, I *can't*—"

"Shhhh," Christine warned urgently. "Amanda—"

Even whispering, Amanda's voice held a desperate intensity. "Mama, please, Mama, I have to get something—I can't leave it here, please, Mama—it'll only take a second—"

She had no idea what could be so precious to her daughter, but Christine wasn't about to drag her down the stairs in this state of wild agitation. The child was already in shock, a breath away from absolute hysteria. "All right, but hurry. And *be quiet.*"

As swift and silent as a shadow, Amanda darted back down the hallway and vanished into her bedroom. She reappeared less than a minute later, shoving something into the front pocket of her jeans. Christine didn't pause to find out what was so important that Amanda couldn't bear to leave it behind; she simply grabbed her daughter's free hand and continued down the stairs.

The grandfather clock on the landing whirred and bonged a moment before they reached it, announcing in sonorous tones that it was two A.M. The sound was too familiar to startle either of them, and they hurried on without pause. The front door was still open, as they'd left it, and Christine didn't bother to pull it shut behind them as they went through to the wide porch.

The wind had blown rain halfway over the porch to the door, and Amanda dimly heard her shoes squeak on the wet stone. Then she ducked her head against the rain and stuck close to her mother as they raced for the car parked several yards away. By the time she was sitting in the front seat watching her mother fumble with the keys, Amanda was soaked again, and shivering despite a temperature in the seventies.

The car's engine coughed to life, and its headlights stabbed through the darkness and sheeting rain to illuminate the gravelled driveway. Amanda turned her head to the side as the car jolted toward the paved road, and she caught her breath when she saw a light bobbing far away between the house and the stables, as if someone was running with a flashlight. Running toward the car that, even then, turned onto the paved road and picked up speed as it left the house behind.

Quickly, Amanda turned her gaze forward again, rubbing her cold hands together, swallowing hard as sickness rose in her aching throat. "Mama? We can't come back, can we? We can't ever come back?"

The tears running down her ashen cheeks almost but not quite blinding her, Christine Daulton replied, "No, Amanda. We can't ever come back."

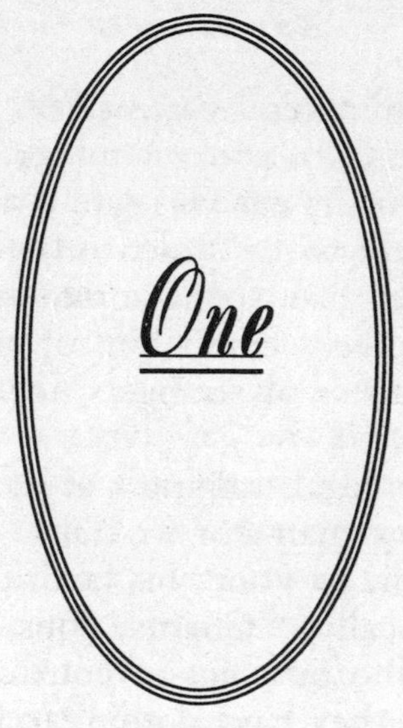

One

Late May, 1995

"STOP THE CAR."

It was more a plea than an order, and as he pulled to the side of the private blacktop road and put the car in park, Walker McLellan was already probing the three small words for a deeper meaning.

"Lost your nerve?" he asked in the practiced neutral tone of a lawyer.

She didn't answer. As soon as the car was stationary, she opened her door and got out. She closed the door and walked along the side of the road a few yards until she could cross the ditch and enter the pasture through the gap of a missing board.

Walker watched her move about thirty yards into the lush green pasture until she reached a rise. He knew that from where she stood the house was visible. He wondered how she had known that.

After several minutes, he turned off the car's engine and got out. He didn't forget to take the keys with him, even though the car was safely on Daulton land and most unlikely to be stolen or even disturbed in any way. Walker had spent some years in Atlanta, which had effectively cured him of any tendency to rely on the kindness of strangers not to steal his belongings.

Of course, his legal training had left him with little trust in his fellow man—or woman.

"People will lie to you," his favorite professor had stated unequivocally. "Clients, cops, other lawyers, even the man who puts gas in your car. People who sincerely believe they have nothing to hide will still lie to you. Get used to it. Expect it. Assume you are being lied to until you have proof of the truth. Then double-check the proof."

Words to live by.

Walker swung himself easily over the three-rail fence rather than go through as she had, and joined her at the top of the rise. "How did you know the house was visible from here?" he asked casually.

She glanced aside briefly to meet his gaze, her own smoke-gray eyes unreadable. Obviously not deceived by the dispassionate tone he had used, she said, "You have no doubt at all that I'm a liar, do you?"

"On the contrary. If I didn't doubt that, you wouldn't be here."

She looked across acres of lush green pasture, her gaze fixed on the tremendous house still nearly a mile away. "But you don't believe I'm Amanda Daulton," she said.

He replied carefully. "I've been unable to prove you aren't. The practice of fingerprinting children was virtually unheard of twenty years ago, so that proof is denied us. You have the right blood type—but that means only that you *could* be Amanda Daulton, not that you are. You've answered most of my questions correctly. You seem to have a thorough, if not complete, knowledge of the history of the Daulton family as well as some familiarity with living family members."

Still looking toward the distant house, she smiled slightly. "But I couldn't answer all your questions, and that makes you very suspicious, doesn't it, Mr. McLellan? Even though it's been twenty years since I was . . . home."

It was just that kind of hesitation that he mistrusted, Walker reflected silently. This woman *was* quite familiar with details concerning the Daulton family, but most of those were a matter of public record and available to anyone with the will to dig for them. She could have easily enough. And if she had, she wouldn't be the first; Walker had disproven the claims of two other women in the past five years, both of whom had sworn they were Amanda Daulton.

With Jesse Daulton's estate valued in the tens of millions of dollars, it was no wonder women of the right age and with the right general appearance would turn up hopefully claiming to be his long-missing granddaughter—especially now.

But this one, this Amanda Daulton, Walker thought, was different from the two earlier pretenders he had discredited. Not at all eager, bold, or emphatic, this woman was quiet, deliberate, and watchful. She hadn't tried to charm him or flirt. She had not floundered for answers to his questions, either replying matter-of-factly or else saying she didn't know. *I don't know. I don't remember that.*

But was it lack of memories? Or merely holes in her research?

"Twenty years," he repeated, turning his head to study her profile.

She shrugged. "How much does anyone remember of their childhood? Fleeting images, special moments. An odd mixture of things, really, like a patchwork quilt. Do I remember the summer I was nine? I remember some things. How the summer began. It was hot even in May that year, the way it is now, today. The honeysuckle smelled the way it does now, so sweet. And the air was still and heavy nearly every day, like it is now, because there's a storm nearby, maybe just over the mountains. If you listen, you can hear the thunder. Can you hear it?"

Walker refused to allow himself to be swayed by the dreamy quality of her voice. "It frequently storms this time of year," he said simply.

A little laugh escaped her, hardly a breath of sound. "Yes, of course it does. Tell me, Mr. McLellan, if you're so doubtful of me, why am I here? You could have said no when I suggested it, or advised the Daultons to say no. You could have insisted we wait a few more weeks for the results of the blood test. They might be conclusive, proving or disproving my claim beyond doubt."

"Or they might not," he said. "DNA testing is still an infant science, and the courts are still divided as to how reliable the results are—especially when establishing a familial connection between grandparent and grandchild."

"Yes, it would have been simpler if my father had lived," she murmured. "Do you think it's true? That there's a strain of madness in the Daultons?"

The question was no non sequitur, Walker knew, and he replied imperturbably. "Brian Daulton was unfortunate—not insane. We should go on to the house. Your—Jesse's expecting us."

She hesitated, but then seemed to stiffen a bit before she quickly turned and headed back toward the road. Walker paused a moment himself, his attention caught by several horses that had noticed the visitors to the pasture and, curious as horses usually are, were moving up the rise toward him. He frowned, then made his way back to the road and got into his car.

"You're afraid of horses?" he asked as he started the engine.

In a slightly vague tone, she said, "What? Oh—I don't like them very much. Did you say all of my family would be here today?"

Walker wasn't sure if the change of subject meant anything beyond her probable—and natural—preoccupation with what was to come, so he didn't comment. Instead, he merely replied, "According to Jesse, they will be. Kate is always at Glory, of course; Reece and Sully both moved back home after college."

"None of them are married?"

"No. Reece came close a few years ago, but Jesse—took care of the problem."

She looked over at Walker as if she wanted to ask another question, but he turned the car off the paved road and onto the gravelled drive just then, and she turned her attention ahead to study the house looming before them. Walker wondered what she thought about it. What she felt.

One of the most magnificent mansions ever built in the South, it had originally been named Daulton's Glory—with a conceit typical of its owner—but no one had called it anything except Glory in more than a hundred years, probably because the name was so apt. It was massive, with an extraordinary presence. Two very old and very grand magnolia trees flanked the circular drive in front of the house, their waxy ivory blooms magnificent. In addition, there were several huge old oak trees near the house, as well as a scattering of smaller flowering trees: dogwoods and mimosas. Numerous neat evergreen shrubs and azaleas provided perfect landscaping for the house.

But the house itself was the centerpiece, as perfect in its setting as a gem surrounded by gold. A striking colonnade stretched across the front, with ten tall, fluted columns of carved wood—four of them set forward under a pediment so that the house seemed to step boldly out to greet anyone approaching. The columns were painted white and stood out against the sandy facade, while the side walls of the house were unpainted brown brick.

"Know anything about architecture?" Walker asked.

"No."

He stopped the car just to the right of the walkway and shut off the engine, then looked at her. She was gazing toward the house, and he could read nothing from her profile. Conversationally, he said, "Glory is a type of Southern mansion that uses columns as a symbol of wealth and pride. It was said at the time the house was built that most rich people could manage four columns, a rare family six—and the Daultons ten."

She turned her head to look at him, and though her delicate features remained expressionless and the smoky gray eyes were hard to read, Walker had the sudden impression that she was scared. Very scared. But her voice was calm, mildly curious.

"Are you an expert on the Daulton family, Mr. McLellan?"

"Walker." He wasn't sure why he had said that, particularly since he'd been at some pains to keep his attitude toward her both neutral and formal since their first meeting. "No, but local history is a hobby of mine—and the Daulton family is responsible for most of that history."

"What about your family? Didn't you say both your father and grandfather had been attorneys for the Daultons?"

She doesn't want to go in. "Yes, but we're relatively new to the area. My great-grandfather won a thousand acres of Daulton land in a poker game in 1870, and built a house about a mile over that hill there to the west. He was a virtually penniless Scottish immigrant, but he ended up doing all right. In time, the Daultons even forgave him for naming his house after that winning poker hand."

Still mild, she said, "I suppose I should remember all this, shouldn't I? But I'm afraid I don't. What was the house named?"

"King High. Both the house and the name stand to this day, but the animosity's long forgotten." Without commenting on whether she should have remembered Glory's only neighboring house for miles around, Walker got out of the car and walked around to her side. She hadn't moved, and didn't when he opened her door. He waited until she looked up at him, then said, "Now or never."

After a moment, she got out and stepped aside so that he could shut the door. Her gaze was fixed on the house, the fingers of one hand playing nervously with the strap of her shoulder bag, and she didn't budge from the side of the car. She had obviously dressed with care for this first meeting, and her tailored gray slacks and pale blue silk blouse were flattering as well as neat and tasteful.

Walker waited, watching her.

"It's . . . big," she said finally.

"No bigger than it was, at least from this angle. Don't you remember Glory?"

"Yes, but . . ." She drew a breath, then murmured, "I've heard it said that things from childhood are always smaller than you remember when you come back to them. This isn't."

Unexpectedly, Walker felt a pang of sympathy. Whether she was the real Amanda Daulton or a pretender, she was about to face a group of strangers, all of whom would be waiting for her to betray herself with some mistake. It would be an ordeal no matter who she was.

He took her arm in a light grip and, quietly, said, "We'll leave your bags in the car for the time being. If this—interview doesn't work out, or you feel too uncomfortable to stay, I'll take you back to town."

She glanced up at him with a curious expression, as if he had taken her by surprise, but merely nodded and said, "Thanks."

They went up the walkway that was bordered by low, neat shrubs and climbed the wide, shallow steps, passing between the two central columns to reach the portico. Several pieces of black wrought-iron furniture were placed here and there in the cool shade, breaking up the expanse of pale stone, and two planters on either side of the massive front door held neatly trimmed miniature trees.

Walker didn't ring the bell, but simply opened the right-hand side of the double doors and gestured for her to precede him. If she hesitated, it was only for an instant.

As they stepped into the cool quiet of a spectacular entrance hall, he said somewhat dryly, "Jesse isn't overly fond of antiques, so you won't find many original furnishings in Glory. Some of the bedrooms still have theirs, but most of the house has been thoroughly modernized in most respects. Except for air conditioning."

She gazed at the curving staircase broken only by a graceful landing as it swept up to the second floor, looked down at the beautiful gold and cream tapestry rug spread out over the polished wood of the floor, then turned her attention to Walker. "Does the house stay so cool all summer?"

"Not really," he replied. "By mid-July, it tends to get pretty stuffy in here—especially upstairs. But Jesse prefers fresh air, no matter how hot and humid, and Jesse is very much in charge here at Glory." He wondered if she heard a warning in his voice. He wondered if he meant to warn her.

Before she could respond, their attention was caught by the sound of voices raised in argument. One of a set of double doors opposite the staircase was wrenched open, a harsh, furious voice shouted, "Sully!" and a big, dark-haired man in jeans and a dirty tee shirt erupted from the room. He slammed the door behind him with a vicious thrust, then caught sight of the visitors and froze.

Even though they weren't touching, Walker felt the woman beside him stiffen. He didn't blame her. The fury emanating from Sullivan Lattimore, Jesse's youngest grandson, was so strong it was visible, like heat shimmering off sun-baked pavement. And since he was a physically powerful man who looked like he wanted to destroy anything he could get his hands on at the moment, even Walker—who knew for a fact he could take Sully one on one—eyed him warily.

For a long moment, Sully didn't move. He was staring at her, his gaze fierce, and she seemed unable to look away.

In the silence, Walker shifted his gaze between them, waiting to see what would happen. All they had in common, he thought, was black hair and gray eyes, both Daulton family traits. There the resemblance ended, though they were supposedly cousins. She was petite, only a few inches over five feet tall, and delicate, with small bones and finely textured fair skin; he was big, well over six feet tall, with the heavy bones and robust build of most of the Daultons. His skin was darkly tanned and his strong hands were calloused. Her exquisite features were still, composed, giving away nothing of her feelings; his handsome, surly face was so expressive it held all the subtlety of neon.

Though his thinned lips writhed in a snarl, Sully didn't speak. He merely stalked past them and out the front door, slamming it behind him.

She didn't turn when he passed them, but Walker saw her let out a little breath after Sully had gone. Then she looked up at him and said steadily, "Not a promising beginning."

Walker hesitated, then shrugged. "Don't let Sully throw you. He likes to think he's as mean as a junkyard dog, but it's mostly bluff."

"Mostly?"

Her wry tone made Walker smile. "Well, I wouldn't advise making him mad for no good reason, but his temper usually takes the form of yelling and cussing rather than hitting or throwing things. He'll probably spend an hour or so riding through the woods and pastures until he calms down, and be relatively civilized by suppertime."

"He doesn't want me here."

"No, he probably doesn't." Walker hesitated, but decided not to comment on the subject further. She would find out soon enough—if it hadn't already occurred to her—that the arrival of Amanda Daulton had put more than one nose out of joint in the family, and that it was likely only Jesse *wanted* her to be who she claimed to be.

The door Sully had slammed opened again to reveal a tall, dark-haired woman who stepped briskly out into the entrance hall, shut the door quietly behind her, and stopped when she saw them. She might have been any age between forty-five and sixty-five; her mahogany-brown hair, worn short and stylish, had no more than a few threads of gray, but her face bore the deeply tanned, leathery appearance of someone who had spent a great deal of time out in the sun for many years. She was slim and trim, handsome rather than pretty, and her brown eyes were completely unreadable.

Without a smile or a glance toward Amanda, she said, "Are you waiting for an invitation, Walker?"

"No, Maggie," he replied imperturbably, accustomed to the brusque manner of Glory's longtime housekeeper. "Just pausing a moment to recover from Sully's charge through here." He was about to add an introduction when he realized that the only name he had for the silent woman at his side was one he didn't believe to be the truth. Christ, was he supposed to preface every introduction by saying "She *says* she's Amanda Daulton"?

Taking the matter out of his hands, the housekeeper turned her attention to the younger woman, eyed her shrewdly, and spoke in the same brusque tone. "Just so you know, I don't plan on playing guessing games about what you do or don't remember. Twenty years is a long time no matter who you are. I'm Maggie Jarrell, and I run the house."

"I'm Amanda Daulton." Her voice was very quiet, matter-of-fact rather than defiant.

Maggie pursed her lips and nodded. "Okay. How do you take your iced tea?"

"Sweet, with lemon." The response was prompt and offered with a smile.

Maggie nodded again, sent Walker a glance he couldn't read to save his life, and headed toward the back of the house.

"Walker."

He looked down, too conscious that it was the first time she'd used his given name. "What is it?"

"I realize it must be difficult for a man trained in the precision of the law to accept something he doesn't believe to be the truth," she said evenly, without looking at him. "But just to make the situation easier on all of us, I would appreciate it if you could bring yourself to at least *call* me Amanda. You don't have to worry. I won't be stupid enough to think it implies any admission on your part. You think I'm a liar—fine. Even liars have names." She looked up at him, gray eyes steady. "My name is Amanda."

Until then, Walker hadn't realized that he had managed to avoid calling her anything at all, at least while he was with her. He hadn't intended a deliberate slap in the face, but it seemed obvious she had—with reason—felt slighted.

"I'm sorry," he said, and meant it. He gestured toward the room both Sully and Maggie had left. "Shall we—Amanda?"

Squaring her shoulders visibly, she nodded. They walked to the door, Walker knocked briefly, and when there was an impatient reply from inside, he opened both doors so that they could enter the room side by side. It was a half-conscious gesture on his part, impulsive, and he was glad he had done it when she glanced at him with the flicker of a grateful smile.

The room they entered was very large and looked even more so with its high ceiling and oversize windows. The furnishings were comfortably modern without shouting about it, the colors were pale and soothing, and the floor was covered with a thick, plush wall-to-wall carpet. There were three people in the room: two men on their feet near the fireplace, and a woman seated on one of two long sofas at right angles to it.

Walker didn't hesitate this time. Taking her arm in a light grasp, he led her across the room to the taller and older of the two men, and said simply, "Here she is, Jesse."

Jesse Daulton could have been taken for a man fifteen years younger than his seventy-five. A couple of inches over six feet tall, powerful and big-boned, he appeared robustly healthy with few signs of age and none of frailty. His face was a romantic wreck, startlingly handsome features ruined by a lifetime of temper and indulgence, but he was still a very attractive man. His black hair was only now beginning to gray around his tanned face, and his eyes gleamed like lightly tarnished silver.

"Amanda," he said, and seemed unable to say anything else.

His normal speaking voice was deep and usually harsh; Walker had never heard it quite so soft and unsteady as it was now. He watched the slim, pale hand she extended be gently engulfed in both of Jesse's big, leathery hands, and he thought that if she had given the old man any sign of encouragement, he would have swept her off her feet in a bear hug.

But she was reserved, polite, and watchful, and showed no desire for any gesture of affection. "I seem to remember that you wanted me to call you Jesse when I was a child," she told him as she gently drew her hand free of his grasp. Her voice was quiet, her smile slow and curiously charming.

Before Jesse could respond, the man on the other side of the fireplace did.

"All of us call him Jesse, even Kate," he told

Amanda, and when she looked at him he offered her a smile that was only a little strained. "I'm Reece. Reece Lattimore. Welcome to Glory, cousin."

From that last statement, Walker drew two conclusions. One, that Jesse had made it plain to his family that he considered this Amanda the genuine article until proven otherwise and expected them to behave accordingly. And, two, that Reece was too smart to openly betray—as Sully would—the hurt, frustration, and bitterness he had to feel about the matter.

Amanda took a step away from Jesse and offered her hand to Reece with that slow smile of hers. "Reece. I think . . . didn't you offer to give me your horse one summer?"

Jesse gave a bark of a laugh that was more than a little derisive. Color rose in Reece's face, but he continued to smile as he shook hands with her. "Yeah, I think I did. Never was as horse-crazy as Sully, I'm afraid."

Unlike his younger brother, who was indisputably a Daulton physically and emotionally, Reece took after their father's family. He was tall enough, nearly six feet, but lacked the heavy bones and imposing physical strength of the Daultons. He was fair and blue-eyed, not especially handsome but with pleasant features, and the laugh lines fanning out from the corners of his eyes indicated he was quicker to smile than to frown.

He and Sully were too dissimilar to be close, but differing ambitions at least kept them from destructive conflict with each other. Most of the time.

Walker touched Amanda's arm to draw her attention, and spoke to the other woman in the room because he knew Jesse wouldn't. "Kate? Come and meet Amanda."

Immediately, Catherine Daulton rose from the sofa

and stepped forward. Youngest and only surviving child of Jesse and the wife he had buried just days after her birth, Kate was five foot eleven in her bare feet and built on noble lines, voluptuous without an ounce of excess flesh. She had the Daulton coloring, and at forty her smoothly tanned face was still astonishingly beautiful, with hardly a line to mar its perfection.

In all honesty, Walker had never seen a woman more beautiful than Kate. Heads turned when she walked by, and mouths fell open in shock. He had even once seen a man literally hit by a car because he'd been staring mindlessly at Kate as he stepped off the curb. She could have made a fortune as a model, and might well have brought princes to their knees if only she had left Glory and ventured out into the world.

But Kate had spent her life here, and though many men in the area had been—still were, in fact—eager to court her, none had been successful. In fact, she had never shown interest in marrying, and rarely dated. Her secrets hidden behind the tarnished-silver eyes she had inherited from Jesse, generally calm and self-possessed, she acted as Jesse's hostess when necessary and filled her time with volunteer and charity work.

Extending a hand to Amanda, she said politely, "How do you do? Welcome to Glory."

Amanda looked up at the older woman for an instant with no expression, then smiled as she shook hands. "Thank you, Kate."

Jesse, who had rarely taken his eyes off Amanda, urged her now to sit down, and took a place for himself beside her on the sofa facing the one where Kate had been sitting. His voice was still quieter than normal for him, and Walker had never seen Jesse's face so softened.

Kate had resumed her seat, silent once more, and Reece sat at the other end of her sofa. Walker took up a position at the fireplace, leaning a shoulder against the mantel. He was as comfortable in this house as he was in his own, and accepted by the family to the point of having long since abandoned any attempt to be businesslike except when he was going over legal documents with Jesse.

Strictly speaking, his part in this little drama had been completed. He had conducted the preliminary interviews with the woman claiming to be Amanda Daulton, had obtained the most thorough background check possible, had sought and arranged the necessary blood tests, and had reported all information available to Jesse. He had relayed her suggestion that she spend some time at Glory, and had counselled the older man to wait until all possible evidence was in before meeting Amanda. Overruled on that point, he had delivered her to Glory, where she was to remain at least until the DNA test results were provided by a private laboratory sometime during the next few weeks.

There was no reason for Walker to remain. No legal reason. And it wasn't as if this were an off day for him; there was a stack of paperwork on his desk, a series of meetings he needed to schedule, and no doubt a dozen or more phone messages requiring his attention. Despite all that, he had no intention of leaving just yet. He told himself it was merely that he was absorbed in the drama and, naturally, concerned that his client's interests be protected.

He ignored the little voice in his head that insisted he remained because he didn't want to desert Amanda. That was absurd, of course. He was far too skeptical of her claim to feel in any way protective of her.

She glanced over at him as Jesse sat down beside her, and Walker could have sworn there was a flicker of relief in her eyes. But it was a fleeting thing; as soon as Jesse spoke, she turned her attention to him.

"So—you grew up in the North?" What might have seemed an inane or awkward gambit was made less so by Jesse's tone, which was as intent as his gaze. He was half turned toward her, and though his hands rested on his thighs, his upper body was just slightly inclined, so that he seemed to lean toward her.

"In Boston," she answered readily, but offered nothing more.

Reece gave a little laugh. "You don't sound it. In fact, you don't have much of any kind of accent."

She looked at him, smiled slightly. "I'll probably sound more Southern after I spend more time here."

"Deliberately?" Kate asked almost absentmindedly, as if she were only half aware of the conversation, but she was looking at the younger woman.

"No, not really." Amanda shrugged, unoffended. "But Mother's accent was pretty strong, and since I had that in my ear for so many years, I'll probably take the path of least resistance once I hear it all around me."

There was an odd little silence, and then Kate spoke again in that same detached tone. "I don't remember Christine having much of an accent."

"Don't you?" If she was nonplussed, Amanda gave no sign of it. Instead, she shrugged again. "Maybe it just seemed stronger to me, living in the North."

"Natural," Jesse decided with a nod. Having reclaimed Amanda's attention, he held it. With a vengeance. "Walker tells us you don't remember the night your mother took you away from us. Is that true?"

Watching the two of them, Walker decided that Amanda would make a good witness and one he wouldn't hesitate to put on the stand. She didn't blurt out a response to Jesse's abrupt question, and when she did answer after a deliberate pause, her gaze met his steadily.

"There's a lot I don't remember, including that night. Before then, the time I spent here seems almost . . . dreamlike. I remember just bits and pieces, flashes of scenes and conversations. I think I could find my way to the bedroom I had here, but I didn't remember how to get to the house from town. I remember a litter of kittens in a barn loft, but I can't recall the games I must have played with my cousins. I remember kneeling at a window to watch a storm . . . seeing a foal born . . . hearing my father laugh . . ." She tilted her head a little and her voice dropped to something just above a whisper. "But I don't remember why we had to leave Glory."

Damn, she's good. The voice in Walker's head this time belonged to the cynical lawyer trained in suspicion. He glanced at Jesse's face, unsurprised to find that the old man was visibly moved. Even Reece seemed affected, his ready sympathy stirred by Amanda's wistfulness. Neither of them apparently realized that her "memories" were so vague they could easily have been created out of thin air and shrewdness.

"Give it time," Jesse urged, one hand reaching over to cover hers.

"You're bound to remember more now that you're here," Reece agreed.

Only Kate appeared impervious to the younger woman's appeal, her enigmatic gaze moving among the others as if she were watching some performance staged to entertain.

Walker slid his hands into his pockets, forcing himself to remain silent. Christ, she was winning them over already, the men at least. That hesitant, pensive voice . . . He was torn between the professional urge to remind Jesse yet again that nothing had been proven and the increasingly personal urge to find some way of penetrating Amanda's smooth and deceptive mask of self-control to find what lay underneath. She was hiding plenty, he was sure. He could feel it. Every time she opened her mouth, all his instincts tingled a warning for him to beware of what she said.

Jesse was patting her hand with the slightly awkward touch of an undemonstrative man, and when she stirred and smiled at him, Walker could have sworn there was a flash of something calculating in the smoky depths of her eyes.

"I'm sure I'll remember more eventually," she said, as if reassuring herself more than them.

"Of course you will," he said, giving her hand a last pat. "It'll all come back to you."

Maggie came into the room then, carrying a tray which she set down on the coffee table between the two sofas. She handed out tall glasses of iced tea, unsmiling, then took one for herself and sat down in a chair opposite the fireplace.

"Have I missed anything?" she asked.

In a colorless tone, Kate reported, "Amanda doesn't remember the night Christine took her away."

"Am I supposed to find that surprising?" Maggie slumped in her chair and propped sneaker-clad feet on the coffee table. She was wearing jeans and a crisp white man's shirt, hardly the usual housekeeper attire but standard for her. "It was twenty years ago, for God's sake, and she was a child."

"Nobody expects her to remember everything," Jesse said, reaching out to pat Amanda's hand once more and giving her a smile. "We were just curious." He hesitated, then said, "It must have been hard on you and your mother all those years."

It wasn't precisely a question, but she accepted it as one and nodded. "Yes. Mother held down two jobs most of the time while I was in school, and even then there wasn't much money."

As if the question had long haunted him, Jesse said, "Why did she cut us off like that? I would have helped her even if she'd felt she couldn't come back to Brian. And, later, after he was killed . . ."

Amanda was shaking her head as she leaned forward to set her glass on the coffee table. "I don't know. She didn't talk about any of you or about Glory, and all she ever said about—about my father was that she had loved him very much."

"She changed her name, your name," Jesse said, and it was an accusation of betrayal.

Again, Amanda shook her head. "I don't know why she did that. I don't know *how* she did it. Until she was killed last year and I found my birth certificate among her papers, I didn't even remember being Amanda Daulton."

"How could you forget your name?" Maggie asked, the question honestly curious.

Amanda looked at her for a moment, then gazed off at something only she could see. Her eyes were wide, almost blank, and her voice was oddly distant when she spoke. "How could I forget my name. It was . . . what my mother wanted. She insisted, over and over, that I was Amanda Grant. I had to forget the rest, that's what she told me. I was Amanda Grant."

"Did she hate us so much?" Jesse asked in a voice that ached.

With a blink, Amanda returned from that distant place and looked at him. Focused now, she said, "I don't know. Try to understand . . . she didn't want me to ask her questions, so I didn't. It was like . . . she had a wound she couldn't bear to have touched. Maybe we would have talked about it one day if she hadn't been killed in that car accident, but I can't know that. It seems to me that for my mother, all of you and this place just stopped existing the night she left."

There was a stricken expression in Jesse's eyes. "She must have heard about it when Brian was killed. She must have *known.* Didn't his death matter to her?"

Watching them, Walker thought that Amanda almost reached out to the old man, almost offered a comforting touch. But in the end, she clasped her fingers lightly together in her lap and merely looked at him gravely.

"That's a question I've asked myself. Among her papers, I found a newspaper clipping about his death, but it happened so soon after we left here and that time is fuzzy in my mind. I don't remember if she seemed different then, more upset than she had been. I just don't remember."

"She didn't tell you he was dead?" Reece wondered in surprise.

Amanda frowned slightly. "I . . . don't know. I have the feeling I knew, but I don't remember her telling me. I know I wasn't surprised when I found the clipping, except—"

"Except what?" Walker spoke for the first time, watching her intently.

She met his gaze, her face utterly without expression for a split second before she smiled sadly. "Nothing, really. I was just surprised he was so young, that was all."

She turned her attention back to Jesse, and Walker didn't say a word. She had just lied and he knew it. The question was, what did it mean?

"*J*ESSE—"

"Don't say it, Walker."

"I have to say it." Walker watched as Jesse went to the compact wet bar tucked away in a corner of the big room and poured himself a scotch. He wasn't supposed to drink, but that hardly mattered now. "Somebody has to say it. There's not a shred of evidence to support her claim. No proof."

"She has her birth certificate."

Maggie had taken Amanda up to her room, with Reece going along to carry the luggage, so only Walker and a silent Kate were left with Jesse. And the old man's features were set in a stubborn expression that would have been familiar to anyone who had ever known him.

"She has a photocopy of the birth certificate,"

Walker said, trying anyway. "Which anybody can get. And the notary dated that photocopy barely more than a year ago—shortly before Christine supposedly died."

"Supposedly?"

"I haven't been able to confirm it, I told you that. I checked in Boston and then the entire state, and found no record of any traffic fatality by the name of Christine Grant—or Daulton or her maiden name, for that matter."

Quietly, Kate asked, "And what did Amanda say to that?"

"She was vague," Walker replied. "Damned vague. She said her mother was cremated, the ashes scattered—okay, fine, I'll buy that. But what about the accident itself? Various state and local officials like to keep track of things like that, and why couldn't I find any record? It happened on a highway somewhere outside Boston, she said, and she's not sure where the death would have been recorded. Rhode Island, maybe, or Connecticut. Or, hey, how about New Hampshire?"

"She didn't put it that way," Kate decided with a faint smile.

"No," Walker agreed, "but almost."

"For God's sake," Jesse said impatiently, "she was probably in shock when Christine was killed, and it's been months since then. Maybe she just doesn't remember where it happened."

"Maybe," Walker said. "But I can take you to the precise curve in the road where my parents were killed—and it's been nearly ten years."

There was a moment of silence, and then Kate said gently, "You travel that road almost every day. How could you ever forget?"

Walker offered her a slight smile but changed the

subject quickly, annoyed at himself for having dragged anything personal into this discussion.

"The point is, precious little this woman claims can be verified." He stared at Jesse and added deliberately, "I don't believe she's Amanda Daulton."

"She's got the right coloring," Jesse said.

"She doesn't look like Brian or Christine."

"Christine was delicate."

"She was tall. She also had blue eyes."

"Gray eyes are dominant in our family," Jesse snapped.

"So is unusual height and heavy bones," Walker reminded him evenly. "Genetically, the real Amanda is far more likely to be tall and imposing."

Jesse frowned down at his glass. "Her blood's AB positive, and that's rare."

"Three percent of the population. In a country with a quarter billion people, that's quite a few possibilities. About seven and a half million if my calculations are correct."

Jesse shrugged. "If you say so. But still rare, and what are the odds for someone claiming to be Amanda to just happen to have that type? Slight, wouldn't you agree?"

"I don't play odds," Walker reminded him. "I'm interested in what I can prove. Her background's full of holes, Jesse. Maybe Christine *did* somehow manage to get them new identities twenty years ago—by claiming that a hospital fire had destroyed records of Amanda's birth and that her own birth certificate was somehow lost during the chaos of World War II, something like that. Stranger things have happened. But I can't find elementary-school records for an Amanda Grant in Boston, where she supposedly grew up, and high-school records are incomplete and—

oddly enough—missing photographs of Amanda Grant."

Impatient, Jesse said, "So maybe she's camera-shy or just happened to miss school that day."

"All four years? Eight years counting college, because she isn't in those yearbooks, either. And here's another odd thing; Amanda Grant minored in architecture, but when I casually asked the lady upstairs if she knew anything on the subject—she said no."

"Probably misunderstood you," Jesse decided.

"I don't think so."

"Well, I do!"

Walker sighed, but didn't give up. "Okay, then what about medical records? She claims they didn't have a family doctor, that there was a clinic in their neighborhood, but it was rather conveniently closed down a few years ago and I haven't been able to find out where the paperwork went."

"Who the hell cares about medical records? Do you think it matters when she got her vaccinations or how many times she had the flu?"

Walker held up a hand to stem the old man's irascibility. "That's not the point. The point is what's normal. People leave a paper trail, Jesse, a trail of photographs and documented facts. But not her. In twenty years of living, even under a false name, she should have accumulated documents in different areas of her life. School records, medical records, bank records. But all hers are either remarkably incomplete or unavailable. She has a checking account less than a year old. She signed the lease on her apartment in Boston just six months ago. Before that, she'd 'rather not say' where she lived. No credit cards or accounts. She's never owned a car, according to the DMV, and claims she's misplaced her driver's license."

"Well, so what? Hell, Walker, I have no earthly idea where *my* license is."

Walker didn't bother to point out that since Jesse hadn't driven himself in thirty years his license had long ago expired. "Look, all I'm saying is that her story looks suspicious as hell. There are too many questions. And whoever she is, I'm willing to bet she's fabricated a background with just enough information to sketch in a life. She can't prove she's Amanda Daulton—but I can't prove she isn't. Maybe the DNA tests will be conclusive, but it's doubtful since there's nothing distinctive enough about the Daulton family —genetically speaking—to show up in the blood. And having to use your blood for comparison instead of the parent's makes it even more difficult. At best, we may be told there's an eighty percent probability that she is who she claims to be."

"I'll bet on eighty percent," Jesse said flatly, his eyes fierce.

Walker didn't have to have that explained to him. As the only child of Jesse's only son, Amanda occupied a very special place in the old man's heart. He had loved Brian so much that his two other children had been all but excluded from his affections, and Jesse was as ruthless in his paternal feelings as he was in everything else. He had seemed virtually unmoved when Adrian died with her husband, Daniel Lattimore, in a plane crash in 1970, leaving her two boys for Jesse to raise, and Kate might as well have been invisible for all the attention her father gave her.

But Brian had been different, and his daughter was all Jesse could have of that favored son.

If Jesse convinced himself the woman upstairs was indeed his granddaughter, he was entirely capable of leaving no more than a pittance to his daughter and grandsons and bestowing the bulk of his estate on

Amanda. Never mind that Reece worked hard as a junior VP of Daulton Industries, that Sully had done an excellent job raising and training the Thoroughbred hunters for which the Daulton family was justly famed, and that Kate had spent her entire life as the gracious hostess of Glory.

None of that mattered.

"Jesse—"

"It's *her*, Walker, I know it. I knew it the minute she walked into the room." Jesse's eyes were still fierce. He downed his scotch in a gulp, grimaced briefly at the liquid fire settling into his belly, then nodded decidedly. "Amanda's come home."

"You can't be sure, not so quickly." Walker knew he wasn't making much headway, but he had to try. "At least give it a little time, Jesse. Wait for the test results, and in the meantime talk to her, question her about her life, her background. Don't jump the gun on this."

Jesse laughed briefly. "You're as cautious as your father was, boy. All right, all right—I won't change my will just yet."

"I'm glad to hear it." Actually, it was more than Walker had hoped for. "Now, if you'll excuse me, I need to get back to the office and try to work a couple of hours today."

"Come for supper tonight," Jesse said, more command than invitation.

Too curious to invent other plans, Walker merely accepted with polite thanks.

"I'll walk out with you," Kate murmured, rising to her feet.

From the front window of her corner bedroom on the second floor, Amanda watched the lawyer stroll to his car with Kate Daulton at his side. They made a striking couple. He was a little above six feet tall and built athletically, which made him a good match for Kate's height and impressive figure, and his dark, hawklike good looks complemented her flawless beauty.

They paused by his shiny Lincoln for a few moments, talking intently, and Amanda wished she knew what the conversation was about. When he had spoken to Kate downstairs, his voice had been oddly gentle, and something about his posture now indicated a kind of protectiveness Amanda would have sworn was alien to his nature. Walker McLellan was not a man given to macho protect-the-little-lady impulses, Amanda thought.

But Kate, it seemed clear, occupied a special place in the lawyer's affections. Were they lovers? It was possible, even probable, given the circumstances. He was clearly at home here at Glory and seemed to be treated virtually as one of the family; he and Kate had known each other all their lives; both were single; and it was doubtful Jesse would have objected to the relationship.

Walker was a good seven or eight years younger than Kate, Amanda thought, but he didn't seem like a man who would give much consideration to the age difference if he loved her. Odd, though, if they were lovers and hadn't married. With passion as well as affection, what would prevent them? It certainly appeared a good match, and since both were prominent citizens in a small Southern town where reputations still mattered and sex out of wedlock was still eyed askance, they would have found it troublesome if not downright unacceptable to conduct a discreet affair for any length of time.

Amanda waited to see if Walker would kiss Kate before he left, and she was a bit unsettled to feel a pang of relief when the lawyer got into his car with no more than a casual wave of his hand. Probably not lovers, then—or else extremely undemonstrative ones. And she wasn't *relieved,* she told herself, just . . .

Just what, Amanda? Just glad the sharp-eyed, lazy-voiced, and suspicious lawyer who thought she was a liar wasn't having an affair with her aunt?

Shaking her head a little at her own ridiculous thoughts, Amanda watched Walker leave and then turned from the window with a little sigh. He hadn't exactly been on her side in all this, but she felt oddly alone now that he was gone. Natural, she supposed, since he had been her sole contact during all the interviews that had preceded her arrival here.

She could clearly remember him rising from the big leather chair behind his desk when she had walked into his office for the first time a few days ago. Still see his impassive face and the vivid green eyes weighing her.

"Mr. McLellan. I'm Amanda Daulton."

And his cool response.

"Are you? We'll see."

With an effort, she pushed that wary meeting out of her mind and stood for a moment looking around the room. Maggie, true to her word, hadn't played guessing games; she hadn't hesitated to explain that this had not been Brian and Christine Daulton's bedroom, nor Amanda's as a child, but had always been used for guests. It was one of the larger available rooms, and Jesse wanted her to have it.

Modernization during the last thirty years or so had given the room a private bathroom, spacious and lovely in shades of blue, as well as plenty of closet space, but the furnishings were some of the few remaining antiques left in Glory.

There were two tall chests, a long dresser with numerous drawers and a wall-hung oval mirror, and a marble-topped nightstand with a small lamp beside the bed. The bed itself was stunning, queen-size and custom-built by a famed New Orleans cabinetmaker. It was a half-tester, or half-canopied, bed, designed with curved outlines and rococo ornamentation, with a striking carved cartouche on the headboard. The canopy was rich scarlet velvet, a color picked up in the print of the wallpaper and the pattern of the tapestry rug that stretched nearly wall to wall. A loveseat designed in the same restrained rococo style as the bed stood near the front window.

Amanda might not have known much about architecture, Southern or otherwise, but she knew a little about antiques. This furniture was as valuable as it was beautiful.

She liked this room. Even with the elaborate furnishings and rich colors, it was more a comfortable room than an opulent one, and Amanda felt comfortable in it. She opened the front window to take advantage of a slight breeze, pausing to breathe in the faint scent of honeysuckle and absently noting that Kate had apparently come back inside the house since she was no longer visible, then went to a set of gauze-curtained French doors that opened out onto a cast-iron balcony at the west side of the house. Stepping out, she discovered that it was a small balcony for this room only, with its own spiral staircase providing a private entrance.

No doubt intended for guests to be able to take a moonlight stroll through the woods or rolling pastures and return to their room without disturbing the rest of the house, the balcony and spiral staircase were designed with a Louisiana flavor, the fine metalwork done with intricate vines and honeysuckle, and the balcony supported by slender Gothic columns. It wouldn't have looked out of place in the French Quarter in New Orleans, and it was lovely.

Amanda liked the fact that her room had a private entrance, but when she went back inside, she checked the French doors carefully to make certain they had a sturdy lock. Then, leaving the doors open, she began unpacking.

She worked briskly, trying not to think too much. Already, she could feel the strain of being forced to weigh every word before she spoke it, and she had been in this house no more than a couple of hours. What would it be like in a week? Two weeks? A month? With so many people watching her, waiting for her to make a mistake, how long would it be before, inevitably, she betrayed herself?

Amanda carried her toiletries bag into the bathroom, hung blouses, slacks, and her few summer dresses and skirts in the roomy closet, and put several pairs of shoes neatly on the closet floor. Then she began filling the dresser drawers with piles of tee shirts and other cotton and knit tops, as well as jeans, shorts, and underwear. She ignored the two tall chests since she didn't need them; unpacked, she was ruefully aware that all her belongings occupied a very small amount of the available space.

She went to the bedroom door, hesitated for a moment listening, then gently turned the old-fashioned brass key in the lock. She was a little amused at herself for taking that precaution while leaving the balcony doors wide open, but told herself that none of the large people in this house could possibly climb the iron staircase outside in silence. So she'd have warning before an unfortunate interruption. Probably.

She went back and sat down on the bed beside her biggest suitcase, now emptied of clothes. Carefully, she opened the concealed false bottom. Handy for keeping papers neat, the salesman had offered without a blink. The two manila folders Amanda had placed there were certainly uncreased, as were the three small hardbound books.

Amanda smoothed her fingers over the books slowly, then set them aside and opened one of the manila folders. It was filled with photocopies of magazine articles and photographs. There were quite a few, because Glory was probably the most-photographed and most-written-about house in the entire South. She flipped through the pages, studying the pictures she'd gone over so many times and skimming the articles where, with a yellow marker, she had highlighted entire paragraphs.

Glory. By now, it was equal parts strange and familiar to her. Blindfolded, she might have been able to find her way through the house, but its sheer size—in the flesh, so to speak—had surprised her. The master bedroom, Jesse's bedroom, had been identified and photographed in exhaustive detail—but Amanda wasn't sure where the other occupants of the house slept.

Would Sully be in the rear wing rather than this main section, as far away from Jesse as possible? What about Reece? And Maggie, obviously much more than a housekeeper—where was her room?

So many questions.

Frowning, Amanda closed that folder and set it aside, then opened the second one. This one also held numerous clippings, mostly from newspapers, as well as photocopies of very old articles from myriad newspapers, books, and magazines. From their earliest days in America, around the time of the Revolution, to the present, these pages contained the varied and colorful history of the Daulton family.

Important even before old Rufus Daulton had acquired thousands of acres of Carolina land in speculation deals in the 1700s, the Daultons had made a name for themselves during the Revolution when twin brothers George and Charles Daulton had become heroes of that war. Only one had survived, George having been betrayed by a woman whom Charles later strangled with his own hands. He had been tried as a matter of form, acquitted promptly, and gone on to marry the dead woman's sister and sire seven children.

Amanda shook her head over that, as she had the first time she'd read the story and every time since, bemused and wishing the sister had left a journal or letters to explain her thoughts and feelings about such a bizarre situation—and its outcome. But history kept that woman silent, just as most of the Daulton women were. The men, with larger-than-life personalities and actions, seemed to delight in making themselves heard in every generation, but the women were, at least to history's eyes, mere footnotes.

It must have been difficult, Amanda thought, for any woman to hold her own with those big, darkly handsome, and fiery-tempered Daulton men, especially given the times. Yet women had married them, borne them, nursed them when they were sick, and buried them when their uncommon strength failed them.

Amanda flipped through the pages slowly, studying the photographs and scanning the sections of text she'd highlighted. An interesting family, to say the least, with plenty of stories at least as curious as the one concerning the twins. Hard-drinking, like most mountain Southerners, the Daultons had fought for their country, brawled with their relatives, and feuded with their neighbors generation after generation.

Lucky enough to plant Burley, a popular tobacco that grew well in the sandy soil of the Carolina mountains, they were also shrewd enough to begin branching out even before the Civil War brought about changes in their way of life. While continuing to grow tobacco, they established a sound program of breeding and training Thoroughbred horses, mined gold and other precious metals in the mountains, and, later, got into textiles and the manufacture of furniture as well.

The Daultons, always lucky in finance, made money hand over fist while other great families floundered in the ever-changing rush of progress. Yet, in every generation, the reins of control for the family were held in one pair of hands—usually that of the oldest male—who, rather like the masters of the old British and Dutch trading houses of Hong Kong, enjoyed a position of ultimate power and authority. He wasn't called a *tai-pan,* and his authority wasn't spelled out in ancient documents, but the leader of the Daulton clan was very much in charge.

Amanda continued through the clippings until she reached more recent times. Separating this group of articles from the earlier ones was a sheet of white paper on which was hand-drawn a simple, three-generation family tree.

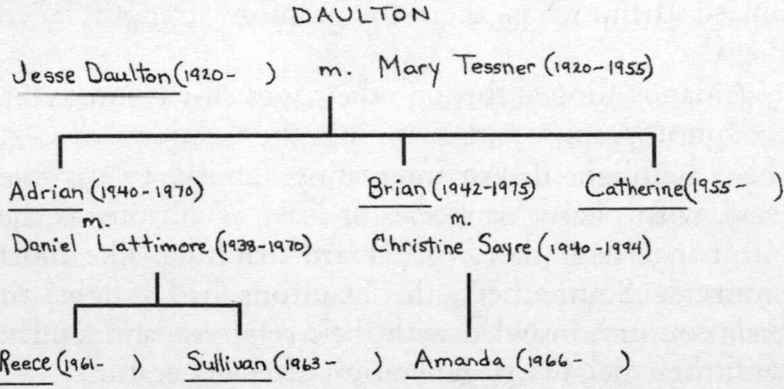

Amanda studied the tree, one finger tracing the lines from parent to child. She let her thoughts drift. Their thirties seemed an especially arduous time for the Daultons. Adrian had been killed at thirty, Brian at thirty-three, and their mother had died in childbirth at thirty-five. Reece and Sully were in their thirties now with Kate barely past hers—definitely a stressful period, what with the abrupt arrival of long-lost Amanda.

Shaking those thoughts off, Amanda considered for a moment and then returned the folders to the suitcase. It was not an obvious hiding place, since few people would think to keep searching a conspicuously empty bag, so it seemed to her the most secure place in the bedroom.

She looked at the three small books, then opened the topmost one. On the first page, handwritten in neat but flowing letters, was the word *Journal*. Farther down the page, in the same writing, was *Christine Daulton*. And at the very bottom was the notation *1962–1968*.

The second journal was dated *1969–1975*. Both journals covered her life from the date Christine married Brian Daulton until the year of his death. The third and final journal covered the same period, but in a much more specific way. It was labeled *Glory,* and the notation of dates read *Summers 1962–1975*.

Amanda found herself lightly touching the first page of the third journal, her index finger tracing the letters forming the name of this house. Interesting, how Christine had set apart the time spent here. They had spent every summer here after their marriage, from late May to early September. As a world-class horseman, Brian had enjoyed riding in the shows and hunts common in this area, and it was clear from her writings that Christine had loved this place.

Amanda had read the journals. What she hoped was that, now that she was here at Glory, some of the enigmatic and ambiguous entries might make more sense. Probably because these were journals rather than diaries, with no locks meant to keep the contents secret, Christine's entries were sometimes vague or oblique. She often wrote, Amanda thought, as if guardedly aware that other eyes would read what she wrote.

Whose eyes? Her husband's? Had Brian Daulton been the kind of man who believed there should be no privacy between husband and wife?

Amanda found that speculation unsettling. As adults, children often found their parents to be relative strangers with unsuspected secrets and undisclosed pasts, but Amanda felt herself even further removed than that. Brian Daulton had been dead for twenty years, and Christine Daulton's journals revealed only snippets of feelings and the occasional noting of a problem or argument between them; there was no journal for the years after Brian's death, and not so much as a hint in any of the personal papers she'd left behind of her thoughts and feelings about him.

What, if anything, did it mean?

Amanda shook off the thoughts and looked around her room. There was a shelf holding a number of books near the door, and she contemplated it for a few moments before electing to return the journals to the suitcase's hidden compartment. The journals might have fit in anonymously with the several hardback and paperback novels provided for a guest's bedtime reading, but Amanda preferred not to chance it.

She closed the bag and set both her cases inside the closet. Her makeup case was on the dresser; she opened it and lifted out the tray holding various brushes and compacts to reveal the small niche designed to hold jewelry. Amanda had very little good jewelry: a small diamond cluster ring and one emerald band with very small stones, a couple of bracelets and chains of fine gold, some delicate earrings.

She ignored those pieces, drawing out a small velvet pouch, which contained a small pendant on a delicate chain. The pendant, hardly more than an inch from top to bottom, was the outline of a heart done in tiny diamonds. It was not an expensive piece or an impressive one, but when she put it on and looked in the mirror above the dresser to study the heart as it lay in the V opening of her blouse, it felt to Amanda as if she had fastened something very heavy around her neck.

Pushing her luck, there was no question about it. The smart thing would be to say very little and listen to everything during these first days, especially while she was trying to get the feel of this place and these people. Why ask for trouble so soon? She touched the little heart with a fingertip, hesitating, then sighed and left it.

She fingered a few other items in the jewelry niche thoughtfully. A man's gold seal ring, a pair of very old pearl earrings, an ivory bracelet—all pieces much older than the others in the niche.

Tucked into a corner and wrapped in tissue was a small crystal trinket box, which Amanda carefully unwrapped and placed upon the dresser. She took off the lid and removed another bit of tissue paper, this wrapped around an opaque dark green stone.

There was nothing particularly memorable about the stone. It was hardly more than a couple of inches from end to end, a roughly oval shape with several jutting facets common to quartz. Amanda held it for a moment, her fingers examining the shape and hardness of the stone, rubbing the smooth facets. Then she returned it to the trinket box, adding the two delicate rings and several pairs of earrings from the jewelry niche. Satisfied with the resulting jumble, in which the green stone seemed merely a bit peculiar, she replaced the lid on the box.

After a moment's thought, she deliberately cluttered the dresser's polished surface, putting out her hairbrush and comb, a bottle of perfume, and several items of makeup. She left the case open.

A glance at her watch told her it was only three-thirty, which meant she had some time to kill. Supper at six, Jesse had told her, and she might want to wander around and explore this afternoon. Obviously eager to spend time with her, he had nevertheless made a conspicuous effort to avoid overwhelming her, to give her room and time to herself. There would be a car and driver at her disposal if she wanted to go into town, he had said, and if there was anything she needed—anything at all—she should tell either him or Maggie.

Amanda felt a brief craven impulse to remain here in her room until suppertime, but shook it off. She'd come this far, and so going on was inevitable.

She left the window open since it was screened, but closed the balcony doors; summer wouldn't officially begin for another month, but until Amanda found out how bad the flies and mosquitoes were around here—according to what she'd read, it varied from year to year—she had no intention of issuing a blatant invitation to the insects to enter her bedroom. She went to the hall door and unlocked it, and went out into the hall.

She turned left to head toward the stairs, moving slowly as she studied several landscapes and the occasional furnishings lining the wide, carpeted hallway. She had stopped to examine a beautiful gilt mirror and was still a good twenty feet from the head of the stairs when she heard a low, guttural sound that caused the fine hairs on the nape of her neck to rise, quivering.

Very slowly, she turned her head. Back toward her room and not six feet away stood two black-and-tan dogs. Like so much else about Glory, they were big, heavily muscled, and wickedly powerful. They were Doberman pinschers, and they were not happy to find her here.

Amanda considered her options rapidly and decided that one thing she couldn't do was stand here and scream for help. Even if the dogs didn't get more pissed off just because of the noise, she didn't want any of the large—and undoubtedly courageous—people in this house to find her frozen with fear and yelling her head off.

So, forcing herself to relax, she turned to face the dogs and dropped to her knees in the same motion. "Hi, guys," she said to them, her voice calm. "Want to be friends?"

It took nearly ten minutes and all the patient tranquility Amanda could muster, but she liked dogs and that helped her to get on the right side of these two. Whether it was her voice, her scent, or her attitude, the dogs decided to accept her.

They were extremely friendly once that decision was made, and she ended up having to (gently) push one of them off her lap before she could get to her feet. Both the dogs were wearing silver chain collars, and she paused to examine the engraved tags announcing their names.

"Hope you guys haven't heard the stories," she murmured with a wince, wondering if she had just been granted a glimpse into the darker—or, at least, darkly mischievous—side of someone's nature. To whom did the dogs belong, and who had named them?

Filing the question away to be answered later,

Amanda continued on her way downstairs, a dog on either side of her. She paused only once, reaching out to gently touch the ancient grandfather clock on the landing, then shook her head a little and went on.

She had just reached the polished floor of the entrance hall when Maggie appeared in the hallway leading to the rear of the house and looked at the threesome in surprise.

"I'll be damned," she said. "You made friends with those hellions?"

"I didn't have much choice," Amanda replied with some feeling. "They were just *there* in the hall upstairs when I came out of my bedroom."

Maggie frowned. "They were supposed to be shut up in Jesse's bedroom until he could introduce you."

Which answered the question of the dogs' ownership.

"Maybe he let them out," Amanda offered.

"No, he wouldn't have. Besides which, he's down at the stables looking over a couple of new horses." Maggie studied the two dogs, which stood on either side of Amanda so that her fingertips brushed their glossy black coats, and shook her head slowly. "I've never seen them take to anybody but Jesse; they just tolerate the rest of us."

"I like dogs."

"A good thing, I'd say. Are you exploring?"

"I thought I would. If it's okay."

With a lifted brow, Maggie said, "I thought Jesse had made it pretty clear. You can do just about anything you please here, Amanda." Then, briskly, she added, "The garden is beautiful this time of year. Just go straight down that hall and out through the sunroom—exploring along the way, of course."

"Thanks, I will."

They passed each other in the entrance hall, since

Maggie was going upstairs. But with one foot on the bottom tread, the housekeeper called Amanda's name.

"Yes?"

"That necklace you're wearing. Christine had one just like it."

"Yes." Amanda's voice was deliberate. "She did."

Maggie looked at her for a long moment. "Keep the dogs with you. They'll protect you."

Amanda felt a chill. "Protect me? What do I have to be afraid of here?" she asked.

"Snakes." Maggie smiled. "Watch out for snakes. The black snakes won't hurt you, but copperheads are poisonous." Then she continued on up the stairs.

Alone once more but for her canine companions, Amanda drew a breath and looked down at them. "Come on, guys. Let's take a look at Glory."

The mountain trail was narrow and winding, crossed here and there with fallen trees and rusting barrels and moldy bales of hay that made up crude but effective jumps. Only an expert rider with a highly trained—or suicidally obedient—horse would have attempted the rugged course, and then only at a carefully balanced canter.

Not a flat-out gallop.

But the big Roman-nosed black climbed the trail like a mountain goat, taking the jumps in stride, his ears flat to his head and his gait so smooth that the man on his back hardly felt the unevenness of the trail.

It took an unusually large and powerful horse to carry Sully for any length of time, particularly at top speed over rough terrain. That was the major reason he'd stopped competing in his late teens, because he was simply too big and too heavy to give most horses a fighting chance over jumps, and that was the only kind of riding he really loved. This kind of riding. And this horse, the only one he currently owned that was capable of taking him up this trail.

Beau soared over the last jump, a stack of hay bales sprouting oat seedlings, and shook his head fiercely when Sully eased back on the reins. But he gradually obeyed the skilled and patient touch of his rider, and by the time the trail began meandering back down the mountain toward Glory, the stallion was moving at a shambling walk.

Sully wished his own edgy temperament could be as easily calmed. Not, of course, that the hand on *his* reins was overly patient—but Jesse was certainly skilled at forcing obedience from those around him. Give the old man his due: even on his last legs he was still firmly in charge.

Automatically, Sully guided his horse off the main trail, stopping a moment later on an overlook formed by a small granite outcropping. From here there was an exceptional view of the valley below. An exceptional view of Glory.

Back in college, Sully could remember when one of his friends had been dumped by the girl he'd dated since puberty. "She broke my heart," he had said numbly. Some of the guys had laughed, but Sully hadn't. Because he knew how it felt to love something so much it was terrifying, the loss or threatened loss of it crippling. He knew.

Sprawling out across the valley, Glory was so beautiful it made his chest ache almost unbearably. The house and garden, the rolling pastures dotted with glossy horses, the neat stables fanning out on a hill on the other side of the house and, beyond them, the training ring he had designed and built almost entirely with his own hands. It was more than home, it was his soul, his lifeblood. The years away at college had been agony, and he literally couldn't imagine living anywhere else.

Sully saw Beau's ear flick back, felt the animal shift uneasily, and realized only then that some curse had escaped his lips with a viciousness the horse responded to instinctively. He made a conscious effort to relax, reaching up a hand to stroke the shining black neck.

"Easy, boy. Easy." The high-strung stallion was perfectly capable of launching himself off this overlook if he took a mind to, and then they'd both end up at the base of the mountain with maybe two unbroken bones left between them. That would solve his problems once and for all. Yes, sir. He'd be gone, and when Jesse finally met his Maker, Reece and Kate could join forces and fight the will the old man would undoubtedly make in favor of his long-lost Amanda.

Sully stroked his horse with a gentle hand and scowled out over the peaceful beauty of Glory. Amanda. But was she Amanda? Walker McLellan didn't think so, and though he tended to be a cautious bastard even for a lawyer, he was no fool when it came to people. She *looked* sort of right, even if she was about half the size of most Daultons, but Sully had been so furious when he'd stared at her that he couldn't remember much beyond black hair and grayish eyes.

Not that any of that mattered. All that mattered was whether Jesse accepted this woman as Amanda, and he'd made it pretty damned plain even before she'd arrived that he believed—even in the face of vague holes in her story and Walker's repeated warnings to be skeptical—that she was his granddaughter.

He wanted his precious Amanda back before he turned up his toes, and by God he meant to *have* her back.

This time when Sully spoke, it was softly so as not to disturb his nervous horse, but the words were no less fierce.

"You won't take Glory away from me. I'll see you in hell first."

Three

THE DOGS SHOWED NO SIGNS OF WANTing to stray from her side. While Amanda wandered toward the rear of the house, looking into rooms as she slowly got her bearings, they matched their pace to hers. She stroked them from time to time or scratched idly behind a pointed ear, but she was paying more attention to her surroundings than to the dogs.

The large front parlor where she had met Jesse and the others took up most of one side of the long hallway, but on the other side was a room with a locked door (Jesse's study, she was willing to bet, and interesting that he apparently felt the need to lock doors in his own house); another parlor or den boasting an extensive audio and video entertainment system—top of the line, naturally; a small, neat half bath (or powder room); and a spacious formal dining room.

Across from the dining room was the kitchen, where Amanda hesitantly introduced herself to the tall, bone-thin cook for Glory, a middle-aged woman named Earlene. She was peeling potatoes, and when Amanda asked—again diffidently—she explained that there were three maids who did the housework, coming in daily and always finished by noon.

"Always?" Amanda asked, surprised.

"Of course. Mr. Jesse can't abide tripping over people every time he turns around, so the household staff, gardeners, and groundskeepers come early and get their work done by noon. 'Cept me, naturally. But the cooking's no problem, and I'd just as soon have the kitchen to myself. Maggie helps serve and clean up after meals, and that's all the help I need most days." She handed Amanda a slice of raw potato with the reflex action of someone born to feed others.

Absently munching on the starchy treat, Amanda said, "Then I should be out of my room early every morning?"

"Lord, no, child, you get up whenever you please. The girls will do the downstairs first, and any unoccupied rooms on the second floor, but they won't disturb you. Maggie has them trained right. They aren't even allowed to run a vacuum until Mr. Jesse's up and has his breakfast—usually by about ten. Just leave your bedroom door open when you leave the room, and they'll take care of it."

"Mmm. And the groundskeepers do their work in the morning?"

"Yes—the mowing last thing, of course, after everybody's up. Sherman—he's the head gardener—always asks me or Maggie, just to make sure. Mr. Jesse would not be happy if one of those godawful machines woke him up."

"I guess not. Are there many gardeners?"

"Four. Well, Luke is really the pool man, but he helps out with the rest once his work is done."

"There's a pool?"

Earlene seemed a little amused by all the questions, but not especially surprised by them. "Mr. Jesse put it in about ten years ago, just before I came to work at Glory. It's out past the sunroom."

Amanda accepted another slice of potato, then looked down guiltily when one of the dogs leaned against her leg and whined softly. "I guess I should have kept them from coming in here," she said to the cook.

"They have the run of the house." Earlene was concentrating on her work again. "Looks like they've taken a shine to you. Mr. Jesse'll be pleased by that, I expect."

"Are they—attack dogs?" Amanda asked.

"Guard dogs, supposedly, whatever the difference is. Either one will tear an arm off a stranger if he invades their territory, is what I hear. Nice names he gave them, don't you think?"

There was no sarcasm in that calm voice, but Amanda's response was wry. "Just dandy. Was he trying to make a point, or was the aim to scare the pants off unwary visitors?"

"You'll have to ask Mr. Jesse that." Earlene paused, then added deliberately, "He's not an easy man to understand. Hard, some say, but I've always found him fair." She turned her head suddenly and smiled. "Of course, I know how to make all his favorites just the way he likes them, so I generally see his good side."

Amanda smiled in return. "Well, I'll get out of your

way. Thanks, Earlene. Come on, guys—let's go see the sunroom and the pool."

It was only a few more steps down the hall and around an unexpected corner to the sunroom, a large addition built onto the house sometime during the past fifteen or twenty years from what had been a tiled patio. The ceiling was half glass to let in a maximum amount of light, the walls were made up almost entirely of French-style windows, most of which could be opened like doors, and the combination of white wicker and black wrought-iron furniture with floral cushions was set off beautifully by a stunning profusion of healthy plants and flowers growing in decorative clay pots and wicker baskets.

Set at the north end of the main house and half shaded on its western side by the rear wing, which gave Glory its L shape, the sunroom was clearly designed to be a pleasant place from morning to afternoon. And, judging by the wrought-iron, glass-topped table that could easily seat six or eight people, any number of meals were probably taken out here.

At least Amanda hoped that was so. This was much nicer and considerably less daunting than the formal dining room down the hall.

One set of French doors was standing open, and she walked outside into the bright sunlight and down several wide steps to find the promised pool. It was there, a neat oval on the same large scale as everything else here, surrounded by ceramic tiles that formed a wide patio all the way to the house on two sides and beautifully lush landscaping that included a truly exquisite waterfall spilling into the pool.

With her canine escorts still pacing dutifully at her sides, Amanda walked to the ribbon of tile along the side of the pool nearest the garden and stood looking around. Since the house was on a slight rise, the land fell away gently and gradually just past the pool, and she could see over the casually laid-out garden all the way to the stables, about a mile away to the northeast. She could also see, beyond the garden and directly north between mountains that shouldered each other as if for room, the rolling green pastures that spread out for the length of the huge valley, seemingly forever.

Daulton land. As far as she could see, farther, was Daulton land. The mountains that looked down on this valley were Daulton, and the next valley over was Daulton and probably the one beyond that. Even the small town ten miles away was named Daulton for the family that had helped found it and sustain it. . . .

Amanda fought the sudden panic, telling herself fiercely that she would *not* let herself be overwhelmed by these enormous people with their forceful personalities and effortless power. *She would not.*

The panic subsided, if slowly, and Amanda flexed her stiff shoulders methodically in an effort to relax. She patted the whimpering dogs, then murmured, "Onward, guys," and followed a neat gravelled path down into the garden. It was, as Maggie had said, lovely, with any number of flowers and blooming plants offering their colors. There were stone benches scattered here and there, a massive oak tree at the northwest corner of the garden provided plentiful shade for those plants and people preferring it, and the meandering paths invited lazy strolls.

She hadn't intended to go beyond the garden, at least not today, but her escort had other ideas. When she would have turned away from a path that clearly led out of the garden and toward the distant stables, the dogs rather insistently objected, whining as they stood on the path.

They were no doubt anxious to be reunited with

their master, and inexplicably wanted her company, and though she didn't feel ready to face the stables yet, she felt even less inclined to protest. Like Earlene, Amanda wasn't entirely sure of the distinction between an attack dog and one trained to guard, and she was reluctant to upset her new chums just to find out how they would react.

"All right, all right, we'll do it your way. But if you two intend to get anywhere near a horse—you're on your own," she told them uneasily.

It wasn't an overly long or unpleasant walk out to the stables, and since Amanda habitually wore comfortable shoes she wasn't worried about her heels sinking into the ground or grass stains on her loafers. Instead, she occupied her time in erecting the calmest facade of which she was capable, knowing that she would very likely need it. Even before she reached the stables, the breeze brought her the scent of horses, and her stomach tied itself into queasy knots.

Horses. Why did there have to be *horses*?

The path led toward the center two of four separate buildings arranged in a fan shape, and she was relieved to immediately see Jesse leaning against the fence surrounding a small training ring between the two center barns; she wouldn't have to actually go inside one of the stables, then, thank God. Jesse was watching a chestnut horse on a long longe line trotting in a circle around yet another tall man—this one blond and ruggedly handsome—with Kate standing nearby holding another horse.

"Reverse him, Ben," Jesse called, then caught sight of Amanda approaching. An immediate smile lit his face, but it faded a bit when he noticed the dogs still at her side, and his voice was a rather incongruous blend of gentleness and censure. "I'm glad you've made friends with them, honey, but you should have waited for me to introduce you. It's dangerous to approach trained guard dogs when they don't know you."

Amanda hesitated, then shrugged as she stopped a couple of feet away from him. "I didn't have a choice, I'm afraid. Somebody must have accidentally let them loose."

Jesse frowned. "Nobody in my house would do such a stupid thing, Amanda."

She shrugged again, unwilling to make an issue out of it. "Well, it worked out all right. They wanted to come down here, so I came along." The dogs were frisking around Jesse now, obviously happy to be with him—an interesting reaction, since he didn't pet or speak to them. Amanda glanced past him at Kate and nodded a greeting, tentative because the older woman was so preternaturally serene.

Kate nodded in return, but all she said was, "You don't like horses, do you?"

"Nonsense, of course she does," Jesse snapped without looking at his daughter.

Amanda, who had hoped her wary glances toward the horse trotting in a circle only a few feet away had passed unnoticed, managed a faint smile. "Actually, Jesse, I'm afraid I don't. Sorry to disappoint you."

A shadow crossed his face. "You loved horses when you were a child. And you were fearless—you'd climb up on any horse, no matter how wild, and go anywhere. We could hardly keep you out of the stables."

"People change." She knew it was a lame comment, but it was the best she could do.

"I'm sure it'll come back to you if you'll just—"

"No." Amanda took a step backward before she could stop herself, then went still as she realized he wasn't going to grab her and throw her up on the nearest horse willy-nilly. "No, I—I don't like them, Jesse. Really. In fact, I think I'll go back to the house."

"Wait a minute, and we'll walk up together." Jesse was clearly disappointed by her feelings, but showed none of the scorn he had demonstrated when Reece had indicated his lack of passion for horses. He watched the horse in the ring a minute or so longer, his gaze intent, then nodded and called out, "Okay, Ben, that's enough."

"I think he might be up to Sully's weight," the blond man called back as he stopped the horse and gathered up the long longe line.

Jesse grunted. "Maybe." He waited until the man led the chestnut up to the fence, then said, "Honey, this is Ben Prescott, one of our trainers. Ben—my granddaughter, Amanda." His voice was filled with pride on the last three words, and his smile was exultant.

Made uncomfortable by the repeated endearment and peculiarly conscious of Kate's silent attention, Amanda forced herself to smile at the blond man. "Hi, Ben."

"Nice to meet you, Amanda," he returned politely. He was about her own age, maybe a year or two older, she thought, and she liked the steady way he met her gaze. She also liked the fact that he didn't show a sign of scorn or even awareness when she eased back away from the fence—and the horse.

"Put him in with Sully's string for the time being," Jesse told Ben. "The bay needs to go to Kathy; she has the lightest touch."

"Right. I'll see to it." Ben led the chestnut toward the gate on the far side of the ring. He nodded at Kate as he passed her, saying, "I'll take the bay over to barn four as soon as this one's stabled."

"Don't bother," she replied. "I'll take him."

Amanda looked at Jesse, then at Kate. "You aren't coming to the house?"

"Not just yet." Kate smiled suddenly. "I have something to take care of first."

Amanda hesitated a moment longer, then turned away from the older woman and joined Jesse on the path that would take them back to Glory. Them—and the guard dogs he had named Bundy and Gacy after two of the most vicious killers ever known.

Each of the four barns had a small apartment taking up about a quarter of the loft space. The apartments could be reached either by an exterior stair or a second stair inside each barn; each apartment had water and power and all the other modern conveniences—except air conditioning. Jesse claimed it would bother the horses.

The apartments were occupied according to seniority and choice; most of the trainers and riders preferred to live nearer to town, but several found it more comfortable or convenient to remain here even during most of their off hours.

It was to the apartment above barn number four that Kate went after she'd taken the bay horse to his stall in the building. She didn't sneak, but she did take care that no one observed her climb the outer stairs and let herself into the quiet, neat little apartment. There were a few sounds from the barn below, the snorts and nickers of the horses, an occasional laugh or shout from one of the trainers or young riders, the clank of a chain and the thud of something heavy falling to the ground.

She didn't have long to wait. It was midafternoon, hardly the best time to expect privacy, but Kate didn't care. As soon as he came into the apartment, she pushed the door shut and went into his arms. He smelled of leather and horses and sunlight, strong, earthy scents that made her blood run hot and her heart thud wildly against her ribs.

His mouth ground into hers and she moaned, her fingers lifting quickly to her blouse and coping with the buttons in feverish haste. She could feel him struggling with his own clothing, but the heat between them built quickly to such a frenzied pitch that neither of them managed to get completely naked. Her bra, unfastened between the cups, dangled from her shoulders, and though she managed to get her panties off, the buttons of her skirt were stubborn and the garment was rucked up around her waist when he pushed her back against the wall and kneed her legs apart. And though he managed to get rid of his shirt, his jeans and shorts were shoved down only as far as necessary.

Even in the grip of lust, however, he automatically put on a condom; she had made her wishes on that subject very, very clear, and by now the habit was ingrained. Upon getting dressed every morning, sliding a couple of condoms into his pocket on the chance of a meeting with Kate was as routine a practice as putting on his socks.

"Yes," she whispered when he slid his hands around to grasp her buttocks and begin lifting her. "Yes, Ben." Her legs closed around him, gripping him, and he groaned when her hot, slippery sheath enveloped his aching flesh.

With her back braced against the wall and her legs wrapped around his waist, he was supporting most of her weight, and she was not a small woman. But he was strong, and so caught up in lust he never noticed the effort as he heaved and thrust. She was urging him on frantically, her low voice strained and throaty as she moaned and whimpered her pleasure, and they knew each other's responses so well that their climb toward orgasm was swift and perfectly in sync.

When they climaxed, almost in the same second, it was with the slightly muffled cries of two people always conscious of the need to keep their activity as quiet as possible.

For a few moments they remained locked together, breath rasping and bodies trembling, the wall and willpower holding them upright. But, finally, she loosened her legs and allowed them to slide down over his, and he steadied her as their bodies disconnected and her feet—still wearing neat and ladylike espadrilles—found the floor.

Ben looked at her as he eased back away from her. Her hair was still tidy in its customary French twist, her face serene as always, but there was a sensual flush over her excellent cheekbones, a heavy, languid expression in her eyes, and her mouth was softened and redder than normal.

He kissed her slowly, wanting her even more now, which was also a customary thing; having Kate, though it was, God knew, wildly exciting and always satisfying, seemed to only intensify rather than satiate his desire for her. But he could tell by the relaxed way she returned his kiss that it would only be once today and, wary of pressing her, he drew away.

He pulled his jeans partway back up, then went into the bathroom to take care of himself. When he came back out a couple of minutes later, his jeans fastened and a damp washcloth in his hand, she had her bra in place and was working on the blouse, hiding her magnificent breasts from him. He sighed with more than a pang of regret.

"You needed it bad," he noted, bending to pick up her discarded panties.

"And you didn't?" Her voice was dry rather than defensive, and he grinned.

"Always. We both know I can't get enough. As a matter of fact, if you stand there much longer with your skirt hiked up like that—"

"No, I have to get back to the house." She took the damp cloth from his hand and cleaned herself with the fastidious deftness of a cat, then handed him the cloth, took her panties, and finished dressing.

He watched her, admiring her beauty but even more fascinated by her self-possession. She had been completely natural from the first with him, utterly comfortable in her own skin and lustily interested in his, and Ben found that a refreshing change. All the other women he'd known always seemed either self-conscious or anxious after sex, worried about how they looked naked and about how they felt or were supposed to feel—and how *he* felt or was supposed to feel.

But not Kate. She came to him to get laid—pure and simple. He hadn't been the first, and he knew damned well he wouldn't be the last, and once he'd gotten past the natural worry that it might cost him his job, he'd enjoyed their frequent couplings just as any healthy thirty-year-old male would have. It had been more than six months now, and if she was getting bored with him he hadn't seen a sign of it.

"It's Amanda, isn't it?" he probed as she smoothed her skirt down over the long, sleek legs he loved. "Her coming back here got you tied in a knot."

"You think I only come to you when I'm tense?" Her voice remained calm, a long way from the husky moan that passion roused from her.

"I think you *usually* come to me when you're tense. I'm a glass of warm milk, Kate. I'm a pleasant way of unwinding after a rough day."

She looked at him oddly. "And that doesn't bother you?"

Ben shrugged. "Why should it? I sleep a lot better myself after a visit from you. Hey, if you just wanted something presentable to wear on your arm in public, you bet your ass I'd be bothered. In fact, I'd be gone. I'm no toy. And I'm no gigolo to be pampered and paid and turned into a rich woman's pet. But as long as you want to have fun between the sheets—or against a wall—I'd be out of my mind if I objected."

Her gaze was still thoughtful, considering. Automatically, her slender fingers checked to make sure her blouse was buttoned correctly and tucked into her skirt, that the skirt hung as it was supposed to. A quick touch reassured her that her hair was still neat, caught up in a twist.

Every inch the lady, Ben thought. There was just something *about* her, something beyond the way she dressed and moved, beyond the tranquil beauty of her face and the cool intelligence of her voice. Catherine Daulton was the kind of lady that a man instinctively respected—even when he watched her dress after a bout of hot sex.

"God, you're gorgeous," he said, shaking his head.

She was momentarily surprised, and a faint smile flitted across her lips. "For an old bag, you mean?"

Honestly surprised himself, Ben said, "Somebody been calling you old? It sure as hell wasn't me. If it comes to that, I don't even know how old you are. What the hell difference does it make, as long as we're both past the age of consent?"

"No difference at all," she said after a moment. "Give me a few minutes before you leave; we don't have to go out of our way to stir up any more gossip."

"About us? There isn't any, Kate, at least not for

public consumption. In case you didn't realize it, most of the people around here like you."

She didn't say anything to that, but Ben thought he had startled her yet again. It didn't surprise him this time. He was no psychologist, but it didn't take one to figure out why Kate would be surprised that people cared about her.

After all, her own father didn't give a shit about her and didn't care who knew it.

At the door, she turned suddenly to look at him. "Come to the house tonight."

Ben knew very well he wasn't being invited to supper. "I told you how I feel about that, Katie."

"Don't call me that," she interrupted. "I've told you."

She had indeed told him; she was as adamant about her name as she was about using protection. Maybe, Ben thought, she believed the diminutive lessened her in some way. He didn't know, and hadn't asked her about it.

He half nodded in acknowledgement, then continued on the subject of his visiting the house. "Aside from the danger of running into those bloodthirsty mutts of Jesse's, I'd rather not creep in and out of your bedroom like a damned thief."

"It wouldn't excite you?"

"I don't need to sneak anywhere to find you exciting. That's hardly the point."

"Oh? And what is the point?"

Ben realized he was still holding the washcloth, and tossed it toward the bathroom. "We both know what it is," he told her wryly. "You aren't quite brave enough to tell Jesse about us, but you'd love it if he caught us. It might even get a reaction out of him, huh?"

"Shut up." Her eyes were glittering.

Without pursuing that, Ben merely shrugged. "Kate, I work for Jesse, and I like my job. If you think I'm going to crawl all the way out to the end of that limb you've got me on, you're crazy. I'm out far enough as it is."

She was silent for a moment, then murmured, "You're a real son of a bitch, Ben."

"Yeah." He grinned. "But a horny son of a bitch, we both know that. I need to try out one of the new horses tomorrow, so I thought I'd ride up along the north trail during the afternoon, toward the waterfall. No training rides tomorrow, so it ought to be deserted up there. Quiet. Private. About three-thirty or so, I was thinking. If you happen to be exercising Sebastian around that time . . ."

"Maybe." She drew a breath. "Maybe I will." Then she slipped out of the apartment.

Ben's smile died, and he stood there unmoving for a long time. It might have been kinder to tell her the truth, but so far he hadn't been able to. He wasn't really averse to sneaking into her bedroom, and he wasn't afraid of losing his job if Jesse found out about them.

Because Jesse knew. He had always known about Kate's men. And he didn't give a shit.

A telephone call sent Jesse to his study to cope with paperwork just after they returned to the house (she'd been right about its being behind the locked door, and Jesse had the key in his pocket), so Amanda found herself alone with the dogs once again. She was a little surprised that they remained with her, but decided to view it as a good thing; being on the right side of guard dogs seemed infinitely preferable to the alternative. In any case, they were merely companionable, staying close without getting in her way, and seemed content to be patted or talked to occasionally.

Neither seemed to take it personally that she chose to address them as “guys” rather than by name.

Still trying to get her bearings, Amanda found the correct hallway to take her into Glory’s rear wing, and continued exploring. Constructed more recently than the main house, it was nonetheless more than a hundred years old—though modernized like the rest.

The ground floor held a parlor—or sitting room or den, whatever it was called—along with a very large game room that boasted pool and Ping-Pong tables, and several pinball machines that seemed quaintly old-fashioned and would probably be worth a fortune one day. The game room opened out onto a patio by the swimming pool. The wing also contained a couple of guest suites, each composed of a sitting room, bedroom, and bathroom, very private and very nice.

Amanda hesitated when she reached the far end of the wing, where an exterior door provided access to the garden and a narrow but lovely staircase led up to the second floor. She assumed more bedrooms were upstairs, but until she knew if they were occupied, if family members or Maggie slept up there, she felt uneasy about exploring further.

Almost idly, she rested a hand on the newel post that was thick and heavily carved, her thumb rubbing over the time-worn ridges of a swirling abstract design. The entire house was impressive, so much so that it was overwhelming . . . something larger than life. People didn’t live this way anymore, at least not many of them.

She was about to turn and make her way back to the main house when the thuds of heavy footsteps descending the stairs froze her. A quick glance showed her that the dogs were calm, gazing upward with only cursory interest, which told her they didn't regard whoever was approaching as a threat.

Amanda wished she could have said the same.

He stopped on the landing when he saw her, his face going a little hard but not expressing nearly as much emotion as it had earlier. His black hair still damp from a recent shower, he was dressed more neatly than the last time she'd seen him, in dark slacks and a white shirt. He was rolling the sleeves of the shirt up over tanned and powerful forearms, and paused there on the landing to complete the task while he frowned down at her.

Then he continued down the stairs, not speaking until he stood on the polished wood floor a couple of feet away from her. He totally ignored the dogs, and they regarded him with acute detachment. "So, you're Amanda." His voice was deep, a touch impatient but not nearly as innately harsh as Jesse's voice seemed to be.

She nodded just a little. "And you're Sully."

Without trying to be subtle, he looked her up and down quickly but thoroughly. "Well, you have the coloring, if not the size of most of us," he observed somewhat mockingly. "But that hardly makes you Amanda Daulton. I'm sure you'll forgive me a few lingering doubts."

Amanda was too relieved by his obviously improved temper to let his suspicion bother her. "No, I expected as much," she told him.

"Did you?" Sully's smile was humorless. "But I'm one of the few voicing any doubts, right? Just me—and Walker, since it's his job to be suspicious. Kate's being her usual placid self, Maggie's neutral, and Jesse's already convinced you're his beloved Amanda. And I'll bet my brother's already calling you cousin, since he wouldn't dare oppose Jesse."

She decided not to respond to that. Instead, she said, "Look, I want you to know that I didn't . . . come back here to—to displace anybody."

He shrugged, in open skepticism rather than unconcern, his gray eyes suddenly very hard. "Yeah, right. So why did you come here?"

It was, oddly enough, a question only Walker McLellan had asked her, and she gave Sully the same response. "Because after my mother died, I found out my real name, and I wanted to know the rest. Who I am, where I came from, what my family's like. And why my mother chose to leave her husband and this place in the middle of the night—and never come back."

Sully frowned down at her. "What makes you so sure you'll find that last answer here? She's gone, Brian's gone, it's been twenty years. We never knew what happened between Christine and Brian, and since he was killed just a few weeks later, we'll probably never know."

"You weren't much older than I was then, so how can you remember what you may have seen or heard?"

"I was twelve—and I remember enough. But I spent most of my time with the horses even then, and I was away a lot showing. I didn't know or care very much what the adults were up to, but I don't recall anything unusual about that summer or that day. Like I said—we'll probably never know what really happened."

"Maybe that's true." Amanda managed a shrug, wondering why she didn't quite believe Sully was as disinterested in that summer twenty years ago as he claimed. Something in his tone, maybe, or the guarded look in his expressive face. "But I can still find out more than I knew about my family by being here. Do you begrudge me that?"

Sully smiled another humorless smile. "I don't begrudge you anything—Amanda. So far, anyway. In fact, if you can keep the old man happy and off my back for the time he's got left, I'll owe you one."

"The time he's got left?" She felt peculiar all of a sudden. "What do you mean by that? Maybe he's old, but he looks fine."

"Some people look healthy right up till the end, I'm told," Sully said, his narrowed eyes intent on her face. "Oh, come on, don't ask me to believe you didn't know. According to Walker, the last woman claiming to be you certainly knew all about it. We've been able to keep it out of the papers, but it's common knowledge around here—and easy enough for anyone investigating the family to find out."

"Find out what?"

"That Jesse has cancer. His doctors say he'll be dead by Christmas."

Amanda was glad she still had a hand on the newel post. She knew she was staring at Sully, but she didn't really see him.

"Very good, the perfect reaction of a loving granddaughter," Sully observed in a sardonic tone. Then, a moment later and in quite a different voice, he said, "Hey, are you all right?"

She blinked, seeing his sudden concern even as she became conscious of his large hand gripping her arm. Had she swayed on her feet? But the sudden and unexpected dizziness was passing now, and with an effort she was able to meet his eyes steadily. "Yes, thank you. I'm fine."

Sully released her arm and stepped back, still watching her critically. "You really didn't know, did you?"

"No." She cleared her throat. "No, I really didn't know."

"Well . . . sorry to break it to you like that, then." Sully was abrupt, but seemed sincere. He hesitated, then said, "Jesse doesn't like to talk about it, but it's pretty clear he believes the doctors—this time. He's been fighting this thing for more than two years now, and at first he thought he'd beat it. But not anymore."

"And the doctors say—?"

"Six months, if he's lucky. He might make it to Christmas, but nobody's counting on that."

"I see." She wanted to think about this, because it meant things were different, that time had become even more important than she'd realized, but her thoughts were confused and she couldn't seem to make them come straight.

Sully gazed at her for a moment, then looked briefly at his watch. "It's after five. In case nobody told you, we usually gather in the front parlor before supper."

She had been told. And she wanted to change clothes first, to put on a dress or at least something less casual. *Armor, I wish it could be armor.*

Nodding, she turned back toward the hallway that led to the main house, with Sully on her left and both dogs pacing along silently on her right. And even though she didn't see or sense the same fury in Sully that he'd exhibited earlier today, she had a hunch he was both more dangerous and a lot more complicated than the dogs could ever be.

"What are you doing in here?"

Amanda looked quickly toward the door of Jesse's study to find Walker McLellan observing her narrowly. Caught by surprise, she said, "I came down the back stairs from my room and passed by . . . I hadn't been in here yet." *I sound guilty. Damn the man.*

"Jesse usually keeps this room locked," Walker told her, his lazy voice still not overly warm. He came into the big, book-lined study and joined her before a marble-faced fireplace, where a large oil painting hung above the mantel.

She was disturbingly aware of his nearness, and told herself firmly that it was only because he was less formal than she'd yet seen him, in an open-necked white shirt with the sleeves turned back casually, and dark slacks. No tie, no jacket. But the same unrevealing face and sharp green eyes, she reminded herself. The same suspicious lawyer.

"I don't think he'd mind me being in here," she said, trying not to sound defensive.

"No, probably not."

Avoiding his gaze, she turned her own back to the painting. Beautifully done and amazingly lifelike, it was a much-photographed portrait of Brian Daulton, his wife, Christine—and a wide-eyed and sweet-smiled three-year-old Amanda. The little brass plate on the bottom of the frame proclaimed that it had been painted in 1969.

"I don't look much like my mother," Amanda said, determined to say it before he did.

The woman in the portrait, dark-haired like Amanda, was obviously much taller—though she was very slender and delicate, almost fragile. Her flawless skin was tanned gold, which made her black-lashed, pale blue eyes appear even lighter and more striking, and her faintly smiling mouth was unusually lush, explicitly erotic.

Christine Daulton was . . . *more* than Amanda knew herself to be. Of the three in the painting, as lifelike as all of them were, she stood out, captured more completely than her husband or child. If the artist had not been completely captivated by her, he had certainly been fascinated.

He had painted her soul.

Spirited, vibrant, the intensity almost radiating from her, she seemed about to move or laugh aloud or beckon with a slender finger. She was a coquette; in the arch of her eyebrows there was provocative humor, and in the curve of her lips there was playful seduction.

She didn't look like a mother. Like anybody's mother.

Like Glory, the woman in the painting was magnificent and curiously overwhelming to the senses, and though she was not at all voluptuous, there was about her a physical carnality that was conspicuous, a blatant sexuality neither she nor the artist made any effort to hide.

A woman who would never be forgotten, particularly by any man who had ever known her.

"She was very beautiful then," Walker said dispassionately. "I'm told Brian took one look at her and proposed—and he was barely twenty, still in college."

"That couldn't have made Jesse very happy," Amanda ventured, deciding not to comment on whether his statement had been intended as a tacit agreement with her own. "I mean, his only son eloping with a waitress two years older and hardly . . . from the same background."

Walker shrugged. "I suppose you read that in one of the newspaper or magazine articles about the family; there were plenty of them, easily available. So you must know that however mad Jesse was, all was forgiven when Brian brought Christine home. I don't remember myself, but they say she charmed men completely and with no apparent effort. And nobody ever claimed Jesse was immune to feminine charm. As for her background, she seemed to fit in here well enough."

His tone was the lazy, dispassionate one that had become familiar to her, but Amanda found it abruptly irritating. Thinking, the man was always *thinking*. That cool, rational mind of his probed her every word and distrusted most of them even while he held himself aloof, observing her with detached interest, and it was really beginning to bother her.

Amanda looked at Walker just in time to intercept a glance, and realized he had looked at her diamond heart necklace—which matched the one Christine Daulton wore in the portrait.

"Yes, it's the same one," she said, lifting one hand to briefly touch the little heart. "Of course, I can't prove it. After all, I could have seen this painting reproduced in some of those magazine and newspaper articles I read, and then had a matching necklace made easily enough."

"Yes," he agreed, undisturbed by her mockery, "you could have."

She made herself look away from his shuttered eyes and back at the painting, this time fixing her gaze on Brian Daulton. She concentrated on him. He'd been twenty-seven when the painting was done, but looked considerably older. Dark and gray-eyed like virtually all of the Daultons, he had been inches shorter than most at barely six feet, and wiry rather than massive. But he'd had his father's face, without doubt, a dramatic handsomeness that already, even then when he was so young, showed the first signs of dissipation.

"Did he drink?" Amanda asked suddenly.

"Brian? No more than on social occasions, I believe. If it's all those lines on his face you're looking at, chalk it up to about eighty percent heredity and twenty percent a life spent outdoors in the sun. And his temper probably contributed."

Amanda hesitated, then said, "Before I came here, I did read some things about the family." She glanced warily at Walker to find him looking at her, and rushed on before he could pounce on this admission of deliberate study. "All the Daulton men tend to have bad tempers, don't they? Going back hundreds of years."

"So they say."

"I don't remember my father having a temper."

"Don't you?" Walker apparently considered and rejected an urge to remark—no doubt suspiciously—on the point of what she should and shouldn't remember, then shrugged and added, "I don't think his temper was too bad."

Amanda wanted to ask him to elaborate on that a bit, but decided to let the subject drop. Instead, she looked at the little girl in the painting, with her short black hair done up in careful curls embellished with a pink ribbon and her wide gray eyes filled with innocence and that sweet smile.

As surely as if she turned her head and saw him, Amanda knew that the tall man beside her was also looking at the little girl in the painting and, as surely as if he spoke aloud, she knew what he was thinking. She wasn't very surprised to hear herself respond to the doubts that lay heavily between them.

"People change so much from toddler to adult. But, still, you're convinced I was never that little girl. My hair is straight, not curly like hers. My mouth isn't bow-shaped. And look—aren't her ears set just a fraction higher than mine? That's what you're thinking, isn't it, Walker?"

After a long moment, he said, "More or less."

She looked at him then, turning so that she faced him squarely. His face was hard, and she wondered if she had imagined, earlier today, that he might feel a twinge of sympathy or compassion for her. If she hadn't imagined it, it had certainly been a fleeting thing.

Quite deliberately, she made no attempt to assuage his disbelief. Instead, in a mild tone, she merely said, "Aren't we supposed to meet in the front parlor before supper?"

"That's the custom," he said, as matter-of-fact as she had been.

But when he stepped back and gestured for her to precede him, she was virtually certain she caught a spark of anger in his eyes. It was, she decided, the first crack in his armor of imperturbability.

Now all she had to figure out was whether it would be a good thing or a bad one to annoy, needle, and otherwise provoke Walker McLellan until he felt about her instead of merely thinking about her.

"A PARTY IS WHAT WE NEED," JESSE SAID decisively, after the salad and before the entree. "Reintroduce Amanda to our friends and neighbors. Maggie, Kate, you see to the arrangements. Make it a week from this Saturday night."

"All right, Jesse," Kate said.

"It's getting hotter," Maggie said practically as she helped Earlene serve the main course around the formal dining table. "Why not something casual like a cookout?"

"Japanese lanterns by the pool?" Reece suggested.

"I have a show," Sully said.

Walker was watching Amanda, who sat across from him on Jesse's right. The idea of a party to meet the neighbors, he decided, didn't suit her at all. Not that she was frowning or clearly upset, but there was definite wariness in her eyes and a tinge of uneasiness in her expression.

"Jesse, maybe—" she began, but her soft voice was unintentionally drowned out when Jesse snapped at his younger grandson.

"There's no reason why you have to go to that show—or any other, for that matter. It isn't like you're riding."

Sully's already militant expression darkened even more, and he shot a flinty look at his grandfather. "I trained those horses and I'll damned well be there when they're shown. It's a three-day event, for God's sake—and two of my riders have never been over the course."

"So? The others have. And stop making noises like it's an Olympic trial. It's sponsored by a *barbecue* house." Jesse laughed derisively. "The prize money stinks, and—"

"And it's experience for the horses and riders," Sully reminded him harshly. "I have to be there."

"No, you don't. You have to be here. Understand?" Jesse waited a moment, then repeated very deliberately, "Understand, Sully?"

A dull flush crept up Sully's face and his gray eyes were stormy. But he gave in. "Yeah," he muttered. "Yeah, I understand."

Nobody at the table spoke until Maggie slid into her place after the serving was done and remarked, "With a dozen new young horses to start training this summer, Sully, I'm surprised you even want to leave."

Her casual tone was just right, easing the tension around the table and providing Sully with an easy out. With a smile—however faint and brief—in her direction, Sully said, "That's true enough."

"About the party," Kate said. "The usual people, Jesse?"

Jesse nodded. "We'll have steaks. And that band from Nashville, the one we got last time."

"Two weeks isn't much notice," Walker commented, "and the band's probably already booked for that weekend. It'll cost you, Jesse."

"That doesn't matter," said the man who had just disparaged a small equestrian event for having modest prize money. Sublimely unconscious of inconsistency, Jesse smiled at Amanda. "You'll like our friends and neighbors, honey."

"I'm sure I will," she murmured.

Walker wondered if she had abandoned the idea of protesting because she'd thought better of it or simply because Sully's attempt had quickly taught her the futility of arguing with Jesse. He didn't know, and her face gave nothing away.

It was a lovely face, no argument there. Even sitting at the same table with Kate, Amanda more than held her own. The finely drawn and delicate features might not be recognizably Daulton, but they were certainly attractive.

No. Beautiful. And surrounded by all these large, sun-bronzed, and robust people, she seemed doll-like in her pale, exquisite beauty. Even the casual spring dress she wore was a soft thing, touching her body lovingly.

Couldn't fault her taste, so far anyway.

Looking at her across the table during the remainder of thc meal, Walker watched her sip the red wine Jesse had chosen—to celebrate her return, he'd said—and listened with half his attention to Reece telling her that Glory's summer parties were famous, there were usually four or five every year, and that the band from Nashville was really a good one. Reece seemed intent on making up for Sully's churlish taciturnity; he was as polite and friendly to his "cousin" as Jesse could have wished.

"Do you still ride, Amanda?" he asked her about the time everyone was finished eating.

"No, I'm afraid not." She smiled and didn't elaborate.

"Pity. The only real way to see some of the prettiest parts of Glory is on horseback. There's a mountain trail, for instance, with a gorgeous waterfall."

"I'll make a point of seeing it," she promised him, "on foot. I like to take walks."

She had very delicate hands, Walker thought. They were small, with long, slender fingers tipped with neat oval nails, and, though graceful, seemed without force. If she'd inherited the rather fierce Daulton strength as well as gray eyes, it certainly wasn't apparent, Walker decided—and then realized where his unguarded thoughts had led him.

What on earth was wrong with him? He had no more reason tonight to believe she was the real Amanda than he'd had at any point today or in weeks past. Less, in fact, after she herself had blandly pointed out the lack of resemblance between her and Christine Daulton—and between her and the little girl she had once supposedly been.

And the fact that, after pointing out the lack of any resemblance, she had not made the slightest attempt to offer any explanation for those differences made it worse. She didn't give a damn whether *he* believed her, Walker reflected grimly, because after her welcome to Glory, she could now be fairly confident that Jesse did.

And Jesse's belief was all that really mattered.

"The path to King High is a nice walk," Kate told Amanda in her usual tranquil voice. "There's a creek with a footbridge and a little gazebo. And straight through the valley is lovely if you don't mind going through the pasture."

Even Kate accepts her.

Walker heard himself say, "She minds. She's afraid of horses." And he was only a little startled to realize he sounded as morose as Sully on a bad day.

Amanda seemed surprised as she looked at him, but all she said, and with a quiet dignity that turned his assertion into an unjust accusation, was, "I know I used to love horses, but I had a fall when I was about twelve. A bad fall. And, no, I don't like horses anymore. I'm sorry if that disappoints everyone."

Walker felt like a total bastard, despite all his furious silent reminders to himself that she was probably lying through her teeth. Naturally she'd had to think up some excuse for being afraid of horses when the real Amanda had loved them.

Jesse reached over to pat her hand. "Everybody understands that, honey," he said, sounding relieved that her un-Daultonlike trepidation had a reasonable cause. "A bad fall can shake anybody's nerve. And who knows? Now that you're home and around horses, you'll probably be riding again before you know it."

She looked doubtful, but smiled at him. "Maybe. Anyway, I'll . . . probably avoid the pastures for a while."

"Still plenty of trails," Reece told her cheerfully.

"And I have a map with them all marked out," Jesse said, giving her hand a last pat. "Remind me later to get it for you, honey—it's in my study."

"Is everybody ready for dessert?" Maggie wanted to know.

Amanda excused herself at just after eight o'clock, pleading tiredness after a rather full day, and left the others in the parlor—all the others except Sully, who had vanished after supper without explaining where he meant to go. Instead of going directly up to her room, she slipped out the front door and walked across the porch to lean against a white column and gaze over the neat front lawn of Glory.

In late May it was still fairly cool in the evenings, and though Daylight Savings Time was supposed to delay the sun setting, it appeared to sink early here in the shadow of the mountains; twilight had arrived. The air was crisp, the light plentiful without being bright, and a full moon was rising.

Her mind was full of thoughts and questions and speculations, all of them churning, and one of those thoughts was that she might be simply too tired to sort out everything right now. *Let everything soak in for tonight,* she thought. *Tomorrow I'll be able to start figuring this out.*

But, even weary, she was too restless to go up to her room just yet, and the thoughts wouldn't just lie there obediently and seep into her tired mind, content to be explored tomorrow.

Hard to believe she'd been at Glory only a matter of hours. It seemed much longer. Yet, at the same time, she felt very much a stranger here, very wary of saying the wrong word or doing the wrong thing. And they watched her so much, all of them, with expressions that ran the gamut from Maggie's neutrality to Sully's hostility.

The biggest hurdle was behind her: Jesse. He all but danced with delight whenever he saw her, and if, as she shrewdly suspected, his belief that she was his Amanda had more to do with hopes inspired by his failing health than any evidence she had offered—well, the end result was nevertheless what she cared about.

Unless something pretty serious happened to shake

his faith in her—such as an absolutely conclusive negative finding by the private lab doing the DNA tests—Jesse was unlikely to be swayed by anyone else's doubts about her.

Walker McLellan's, for instance.

He had assigned to himself the role of observer in their little drama, and it was clear he intended to remain detached and alert while the situation evolved. The dispassionate lawyer, far removed from a tangled situation and untidy emotions. But whoever had said that bit about the best-laid plans of mice and men had known what he was talking about; Walker, it seemed, was having trouble sticking to his plan.

He had watched her most of all, often with contained but discernible irritation, and if she had the satisfaction of knowing she had disturbed his emotions as well as his logical and analytical mind, that satisfaction was somewhat marred by his definite suspicion of her.

The opening of the door behind her caught Amanda's attention, but she only looked back over her shoulder to watch Walker cross the porch and join her.

"I don't see your car," she said, for something to say, as she returned her attention to Glory's front lawn.

"I walked over." He nodded toward the west, and when she looked she thought she could make out the beginning of a path that started at the edge of the lawn and disappeared into the woods.

"Handy," she noted.

"And good exercise." His voice was cool once more.

Since he didn't seem to be leaving yet, Amanda cast about in her mind for a safe subject. "Why doesn't Sully ride in the shows? Isn't he good enough?"

"He's probably the best rider in the Southeast,"

Walker told her, still dispassionate. "But he's too big and heavy to give most horses a decent chance over jumps. So—he trains them. And other people show them."

"How . . . galling," she said slowly. "Not to be able to do fully what you love most."

"Sympathy? He'd hate that, and it's wasted. What Sully loves most is Glory. As long as he has this place, he'll be fine."

"But he doesn't have it, does he? I mean—" *Damn, why did I have to say that?*

"I know what you mean." His impersonal voice took on a sardonic edge. "No, Glory belongs to Jesse, to give or bequeath as he chooses, and everyone here knows it. Kate, Sully, Reece, all of them raised here and all of them with their lives invested in this place, could find themselves out in the cold without so much as a by-your-leave. *If* Jesse so decrees. And once he makes his wishes known, there isn't a judge in the state who'd set aside his will. Is that what you wanted to know?"

Amanda looked at him for a moment before responding, and she was a little startled at how unsteady her voice was. "I know you don't believe it, but I don't want Glory. I don't want the money or—or any of it. All I want is my past—and my name. Is that too much to ask?"

Walker smiled without amusement. "You're right. I don't believe it."

She wasn't surprised, except that his flat statement caused her an unexpected twinge of—of what? Of pain? "Why can't you believe it?" she heard herself ask. "Why do all my motives have to be greedy ones?"

"The least improbable explanation generally turns out to be the truth," he replied dryly. "And avarice is very probable. I can't begin to tell you how many normally rational and devoted relatives I've seen squabble over the wills of the dearly departed. To hear no objection during the reading of a will is the exception, not the rule."

"Even so, can't you accept that there might be something more important to me than money?" Disturbed, Amanda realized that this wary lawyer's opinion of her meant far too much for her peace of mind—and when had it happened?

"I could accept it," he told her, still as dry and unfeeling as dust, "if you had told the truth about everything else. But you haven't—Amanda. The background you offer is full of holes, you're vague and evasive about what you supposedly remember, and how you spent the past twenty years is anybody's guess. You reappear suddenly and without much explanation, claiming virtual amnesia—and there's a fortune at stake. Shall I go on?"

"No." She turned her gaze to the peaceful scene spread out before them, and wished she could be as tranquil. "I think you've made your opinion quite clear."

"Then we understand each other. I don't believe you're Amanda Daulton, and I won't change my mind without a hell of a lot more proof than you've offered so far."

"Then," she said, "I'd call it a good thing that Jesse's in charge here instead of you. A very good thing."

"Don't be too confident," he warned her with a very faint bite in his lazy voice. "If you think Sully and Reece are going to stand by and do nothing while you get your hooks into Glory, your research into the Daulton family was seriously deficient."

He left without another word, striding across the

lawn and vanishing from her sight as he took the path home.

Amanda didn't move for a long time, and she didn't try to figure anything out. But her weary mind did offer up one fairly reliable conviction for her to ponder. Walker McLellan was definitely feeling about her now.

And she didn't think he liked her very much.

"Be careful you don't burn," Maggie advised, pausing as she took a shortcut across the patio from the rear wing to the main house.

"I'm wearing three layers of sunscreen, two of them waterproof," Amanda promised, setting her tote bag down beside a lounge chair at the pool. "It's as automatic as putting on my clothes, believe me; I practically burn with a roof over my head and on a cloudy day. But I've been looking at this beautiful pool for three days now, and I couldn't stand it anymore."

Maggie smiled. "Better to start now than in July; maybe you can build up some resistance."

"Maybe. Anyway, Jesse said he needed to work in his study after breakfast, so I thought I'd swim a little. Is swimming at night allowed, by the way?"

"Allowed—but don't come out here alone. The house is so big that if you got in trouble we might not hear you."

"That sounds like a sensible precaution," Amanda agreed. "And do the dogs go in?"

The housekeeper glanced at the two big Dobermans, who had become Amanda's near-constant companions since she'd arrived and now sat on the other side of the lounge with an air of waiting interestedly to find out what she was going to do next.

"They might well go in today," Maggie told

Amanda. "It isn't their normal habit, but they seem reluctant to get too far away from you. They sleep at your door now, don't they?"

Amanda looked down at her canine chums with faint vexation. "They'd sleep in my bedroom if I'd let them, probably on the bed. But I don't think that's what Jesse had in mind when he got them."

"No, they're supposed to run loose in the house at night."

"So I figured."

"Not that Jesse would say anything if you did let them into your room."

Amanda smiled. "I don't know about that. He's exasperated with me; I can't seem to master his beloved chess."

"Don't feel bad about that. Walker's the only one around here who can give him a decent game, even though he made all of us learn to play years ago. I'm too predictable, he says. Sully is too reckless, Reece too cautious—and my poor Kate has an unfortunate tendency to simply play badly."

Poor Kate indeed. Amanda hadn't been here twenty-four hours before she'd realized that Jesse viewed his daughter with an indifference that seemed to her more dreadful than hate, and that Kate, tragically, knew it as well as the rest of them did.

"Well," Amanda said, "at least I can play bridge *and* poker, so I'm not completely hopeless."

"If you could play the piano," Maggie said, "you'd be perfect."

Amanda untied the belt of her terry-cloth robe and shrugged out of it, dropping it on the lounge. She stepped out of her thongs, responding casually, "That's something Mother never taught me, I'm afraid."

She wore a simple black two-piece swimsuit that

was fairly modest by current standards but nevertheless left most of her slender body bared, and as she looked down at herself Amanda couldn't help wishing, as she wished every summer, that tans were not only safe and nonaging but also possible for her. She'd tried the bottled no-sun tanning stuff, but it reacted oddly with her skin to produce a jaundiced hue that was hardly flattering, and a genuine tan was simply out of the question.

It didn't help one bit for her to be fairly certain that her skin would look much better in the coming years because she *hadn't* tanned; golden skin was just lovely and Amanda hated looking so fair and . . . *fragile.*

And she bruised easily.

Realizing suddenly that the silence from Maggie had gone on at least a couple of minutes too long, Amanda looked up at the older woman and knew instantly that she'd said something wrong. *Oh, lord, what?* Christine Daulton *had* played the piano, so—

Maggie smiled. "It's probably just as well," she said. "Perfection would be boring, I should think. Don't stay out here too long on your first day sunning, Amanda."

"No, I won't."

The housekeeper continued on her way across the patio, passing through the open doors of the sunroom and into the house.

After a minute or so, Amanda turned and went down the wide steps leading into the pool. The dogs, though momentarily undecided and obviously tempted, remained on the side and watched her intently rather than join her in the cool water, which was fine with Amanda. She went under briefly, then struck out with lazy ease.

The pool was certainly long enough for laps, and Amanda went back and forth methodically, working faster and harder once her muscles warmed up. She loved to swim and was good at it, so the exercise was a definite pleasure.

She cooled down the way she had warmed up, swimming a few lazy laps, then let herself drift, face turned up to the sun and eyes closed against the brightness. And brooded.

Damn. What did I say to upset Maggie? And just when things were going so well, too!

"Things" had gone exceptionally well the past three days. She'd arrived here on Tuesday, this was Saturday, and the interim had been much less tense than she'd dared to hope for. Jesse had been eager to spend time with her, and during their interludes together she had encouraged him to talk about this place, the Daulton family, and the long history of this area—which he knew well and related colorfully.

They had spent hours looking through photo albums filled with decades of the Daulton family, and scrapbooks stuffed with newspaper and magazine clippings detailing their milestones and accomplishments, while Jesse had talked about the rich Daulton heritage.

Not only had Amanda learned more than she'd known about this place and its people, she had also managed to avoid more touchy subjects.

As for the others, the first night had revealed attitudes that had not changed very much in the days since. Maggie was friendly but neutral; Kate was rather withdrawn but certainly pleasant enough when they encountered each other—which was, either by chance or by design, rarely; Sully spent as much time as possible at the stables with his horses, appearing only for meals, and his attitude toward Amanda could best be described as truculent; and Reece was so puppy-dog friendly that Amanda distrusted him just on principle.

And then there was Walker. So far, he'd appeared every evening for supper, presumably by invitation although she had yet to hear one issued. He hadn't stopped watching her and, she assumed, waiting for her to betray herself, but though she was reasonably sure she'd seen anger flickering in his eyes more than once, there hadn't been any further hostilities between them.

She supposed that was something to be grateful for.

In any case, she was now familiar with the layout of Glory, was beginning to get a feel for the people here, and thought the time was probably right to begin looking for the answers she'd come here to find. After all, next week would see the beginning of June and her second week here—and the days were already hurrying, blowing past on increasingly hot Southern mountain breezes.

Forcing herself to abandon the peaceful cradle of the pool, Amanda drifted to the steps and got her feet under her. She came up the steps to the sun-warmed tile, pausing to sleek water from her hair, and reached for her towel. Her fingers had barely touched it when both dogs growled briefly and a low wolf whistle caused her to start in surprise. She jerked the towel up before turning quickly to face her admirer.

Though her swimsuit was relatively modest, she felt disconcertingly unclothed and vulnerable—even more so when she faced the man watching her a few feet away. She had thought all the gardeners and groundskeepers had finished in back and were working on Glory's front yard, but it seemed she had been wrong about that.

But then she realized that this man was no gardener. He was about forty, lean and quite handsome, and though casually dressed in jeans and a short-sleeved blue denim shirt, he also wore riding boots. One of the trainers or riders, then?

"You," he said in a low, husky voice, "must be Amanda."

She felt heat rise in her face, and it had nothing to do with the warm morning sunshine. His blue eyes had brushed aside the towel and removed her suit, stripping her with a single sweeping glance, and his voice expressed lustful appreciation so obviously he might just as well have invited her to his bed with words of one syllable and a leering pat on her behind. Amanda had never before in her life encountered such a blatantly sexual man, and she was dismayed to realize that even as her mind and emotions recoiled from him, her body reacted as if to some primitive carnal signal it was programmed to obey.

"Yes, I'm Amanda." She dropped the towel for a naked moment and shrugged into her terry-cloth robe, wishing it was longer and covered more territory. "And you are?"

"Victor. Victor Moore." His voice was still husky, suggestive. "I manage the breeding program here at Glory."

He meant, she realized, the *horse* breeding program. Or maybe not. "I see." She'd gotten her physical reaction to him under control with, happily, little effort; it had been an instant, instinctive thing, she thought, somewhat like the gut reaction to a snake or a spider.

"I came up here to talk to Jesse," he said as if she'd asked, walking along the ribbon of tile toward her. "I've been getting ready to go out of state on a buying trip; that's why I haven't been around to salute the return of the prodigal granddaughter. If you were wondering."

Amanda occupied herself in sitting on the lounge and digging into her tote bag for sunglasses. "I suppose I thought Sully bought the horses," she said, more for something to say than out of any real interest.

"The show horses, he does. And he's responsible for the training program, of course. But I'm in charge of breeding stock. Jesse likes to . . . spread authority around, if you know what I mean."

She did know. It had already occurred to her that Jesse Daulton made sure nobody except he had much power here at Glory. Doubtless Sully could have managed every aspect of the Daulton stables, and doubtless Reece was more capable than his junior vice presidency of Daulton Industries indicated, but Jesse was clearly reluctant to grant either of his grandsons the authority to substantially affect the family's fortunes. Not, at least, while he was still aboveground.

"I must say, you're a fine addition to the family," Victor observed, sitting down in a chair very near her lounge and smiling at her.

The dogs, after those first rumbling growls, viewed him fixedly but seemingly without malice.

"You're too kind." Amanda was glad of the shield of her sunglasses, which helped to keep her expression neutral. Maybe the dogs reserved judgment, but her mind was made up. Victor had a tattoo on his left forearm—of a stallion mounting a mare. Artistically speaking, it was impressively detailed. It was also disturbingly crude.

Clearly unaware of—or unwilling to accept—irony, Victor merely nodded. "Definitely. And it's nice to see a petite Daulton woman, for a change."

Amanda wondered if he was convinced she was really who she claimed to be, or if he simply considered it politic to accept Jesse's decree on that point. But she was less interested in that than in what had sounded like a verbal slap at Kate.

"I don't know why anyone would prefer short over tall," she said dryly. "At least, not when tall looks like Kate."

Victor smiled and, very gently, said, "Different strokes for different folks—and I like my ladies delicate."

So much for my fishing expedition. Victor, she thought, would nibble at bait dangled before him and would even dangle some of his own, but it seemed to her that he was too smart to sabotage his position here by openly insulting one of the Daultons, whatever his opinion of them might be. Amanda didn't know why she was so sure of that, but accepted instincts that had more than once proven themselves reliable.

She was also reasonably sure that while Victor clearly relished suggestive remarks and no doubt enjoyed an active sex life, he would probably be cautious about going beyond words with her, since that too could be a quick way of derailing his career. So his sensual way of speaking and the deliberate leer in his stare didn't disturb her as much as they might otherwise have done. In fact, she was able to smoothly change the subject without a blink and without responding to his declaration of his preferences.

There was, after all, no time like the present to start looking for her answers.

"Have you been here long?"

"More than twenty years. I started out working for Jesse as a stablehand and exercise boy while I was still in high school. Don't you remember me, Amanda? I remember you. You were a skinny little thing with tangled hair and skinned knees, and you always seemed to be missing a tooth. You spent most of your time here underfoot down at the barns, and if I wanted to run you off, I just called you Mandy. You hated that."

"I still do." She spoke absently, but he had her full attention now. "Were you here that summer? That night?"

"You don't remember?"

She shook her head. "Nothing specific, just bits and pieces. Were you here?"

"I was here." He shook his head a bit and frowned, then said suddenly, "You remember Matt, of course."

"Matt?"

"Matt Darnell. At the time, he was the senior trainer."

It was Amanda's turn to frown, though she hoped the sunglasses hid the depth of her puzzlement. "I guess kids don't pay too much attention to the adults around them," she offered.

"Now, I find that definitely odd." His smile was different now, almost mocking. "Because you should remember him, you know. If you're really Amanda Daulton, that is."

She kept her body relaxed with an effort, even though tension was seeping into every muscle. "Oh? Tell me, Victor, do you remember every person in your life when you were nine years old? Even the people you hardly knew?"

"No. But I think I'd remember a stepdaddy. Or didn't Christine make an honest man of him after Brian was killed?"

The sunlight shimmering off the pool seemed to dance before Amanda's shaded eyes, so sharp and bright it made her dizzy. She heard her voice, steady beyond belief, and it seemed to come from someplace far, far away. "What are you talking about?"

"I'm talking about the affair your mother was having with Matt Darnell, Amanda. The affair that must have continued after she left here—because he left with her."

The light was so *bright*. It hurt her eyes. It hurt her head and made thinking so difficult. "You're wrong," she heard herself say. "She—we left alone that night. Just the two of us."

"Sure you did. And Matt packing all his things and leaving that same night was a coincidence. Look, I *know* Matt was in love with Christine, because it was painfully obvious and because more than once I heard him begging her to run away with him. And I know they were screwing because they did it down at the barns. Hell, I'd seen them at it not two days before, in a tack room on top of a pile of horse blankets. And that wasn't the first time, believe me. They'd been going at it for weeks."

The man with the raw image of mating horses on his arm was letting his inherent crudeness show plainly; it was obvious to Amanda even in her confusion that he enjoyed painting that stark image of adultery for her.

"If he didn't leave with her," Victor said, "then he sure as hell followed her."

"I don't believe you," she said.

"Suit yourself . . . Amanda. But they had an affair. If you want proof—"

"Victor?"

They both turned their heads at the interruption, and saw Maggie standing in the open doorway of the sunroom. It wasn't clear if she had overheard at least part of the conversation at the pool; her weathered face was calm, her voice revealing nothing.

"Jesse's waiting for you," she told Victor.

Victor got to his feet and looked down at Amanda briefly. "Nice meeting you, Amanda," he said in a polite, pleasant tone.

Amanda didn't say likewise. She didn't say anything. She just watched him walk across the tile to

Maggie, and watched them both disappear into the house. She didn't move for a long time, but when she did move it was very quickly. She picked up her tote bag as she rose, slid her feet into her thongs, and went into the house.

She took the rear staircase up to the second floor and went to her bedroom, vaguely grateful that she met no one along the way. The housemaids must have been working in another part of the house, but they'd already done Amanda's room; the lemon scent of furniture polish was in the air.

Amanda paused only to close and lock the door to the hallway, then dropped her tote bag and went to get her luggage from the closet. In less than a minute, the bag was open on her bed, and she had one of Christine Daulton's journals in her hand.

She remembered, dimly, the passage; it was in the Glory journal and had been written near the beginning of that last summer, but it took her several minutes to find it. Finally, she did. It was dated June third, and it was brief.

> *Last night I dreamed I was caught up in a storm. There was thunder so loud it deafened me and lightning so bright it blinded me, and I hardly knew what to do . . . except to take shelter and wait it out. I wonder if I'm trapped by the storm, or escaping into it.*

There was nothing particularly memorable about the passage, and Amanda had thought it odd only after her third or fourth time reading the journals. It was odd because, until that date, Christine Daulton had never mentioned her dreams in any of the journals; after that date, during what would be her final weeks at Glory, she mentioned the storm dream frequently.

A dream of a storm . . . a metaphor for an affair?

Amanda turned the pages slowly, scanning the entries from June third on, halting to read only when key words caught her attention. *The wind lashed me until I could hardly bear it . . . the driving rain touched my skin like needles of fire . . . the thunder seemed to echo all through my body like a heartbeat . . . I was carried away by the storm . . . swept away by the wind . . . caught up in its fury, helpless . . . I could only bend, submit, give in to a force greater than any strength I possessed to fight it . . .*

Underneath the vivid descriptions that were in themselves a bit unusual for Christine's entries lurked a distinct and striking sensuality. The images she evoked were filled with the senses and with a kind of primitive fury that certainly depicted a storm—or possibly the stormy intensity of an affair.

Amanda closed the journal and sat there on her bed gazing down at the small book. She thought, as she had before, that secrecy was not an issue. None of the journals had locks, and they'd probably been kept in a desk or nightstand drawer where anyone might have seen them. Perhaps read them.

If she had kept a journal anyone might have read, Amanda thought, she would have been careful what she wrote—and how she wrote it.

Had Christine Daulton, wishing to record the overwhelming emotion of a secret affair but hide it from curious eyes, created her own private code for the journals? The recurring "dream" of a violent storm as a metaphor for passionate encounters? And, if so, were all the other cryptic entries on those lined pages also metaphors for sensitive subjects and events Christine had cannily hidden from prying eyes?

In some things, she had been blunt, and Amanda had come here already aware that Christine had not been a particularly happy woman during those years. She had not tried to conceal her general dissatisfaction with her life, commenting in the journals more than once—particularly early in her marriage and again that last year—that she felt "totally useless" as a person and wished she had not dropped out of college. And she had recorded her opinions of the people she knew, usually candid and frequently—Amanda realized now, having met some of those people—shrewdly intuitive.

But sprinkled in amongst the frank entries were whole sections seemingly filled with a kind of vague stream-of-consciousness outpouring that made little sense—*unless* Christine Daulton had indeed hidden her most intimate feelings, thoughts, and experiences behind a veil of obscure references and metaphors.

Which was going to make sifting the vital from the unimportant a bit difficult.

Amanda opened the Glory journal again and turned to the last entry, which was dated two days after Christine had left.

Amanda slept most of the way, poor baby, she had written. *I think she's still in shock. But at least she's safely away from Glory. At least we both are. And we can never go back. Neither of us can ever go back.*

"Damn," Amanda said quietly in the silence of her bedroom. "Now what?"

There was no one to answer her. She put the journal away and returned the suitcase to her closet. She took a shower to wash away the pool's chlorine, dried her hair and tied it casually back with a silk scarf, and dressed in jeans, a short-sleeved cream blouse, and a loose denim vest.

All the time she was getting dressed, she brooded over what Victor had told her. Could she believe him? Or, perhaps more accurately, could she *dis*believe him? What, after all, did he have to gain by lying about something that supposedly happened twenty years ago, especially when the principals involved were either gone or dead? Nothing, as far as she could see. And the journal entries seemed to provide, if not actual confirmation, then certainly at least the possibility of an affair.

And why not, after all? In 1975, Christine Daulton had been in her thirties, very much a sexual creature no matter what a little girl might have thought. Her marriage had not, Amanda knew from the journals, been without its problems, and Brian Daulton had more often than not left his wife here at Glory for long stretches during the summer while he'd followed the show circuit through the Southeast.

Christine had tolerated rather than liked horses and though she had been able to ride, she had not, apparently, done so often; it would be ironic if she had conducted her affair in the "smelly" stables she had so often deplored.

"If you want proof—"

Amanda wondered what proof Victor had meant. Surely he hadn't hidden in the stables and secretly photographed the affair? Then again, perhaps he had. For his own titillation, maybe, or because he'd wanted a raise in pay and thought a spot of blackmail might be more effective than anything else.

Or maybe she was wronging Victor.

In any case, she had to talk to him. He knew something, or thought he did, about the goings-on that summer—and may have seen something helpful that last night. It was probably a long shot, but Amanda had to ask him. She had to find out what had happened that night; it was one of the reasons she had come here, after all.

Amanda went downstairs, encountering Maggie in the entrance hall, where the housekeeper was sorting mail at a marble-topped table, and asked her if Victor was still here.

"No, he's gone," Maggie replied. "Kentucky, for a broodmare sale."

"When will he be back?"

Maggie shrugged. "Not for at least a week, and probably longer. But there's a phone in the van if you need—"

"No." Amanda conjured a smile. "It's just . . . well, he was here twenty years ago, and I thought he might be able to help me fill in a few blanks."

"That's what you two were talking about out at the pool? I thought he was just hitting on you."

"That too," Amanda said. "I got the feeling it was sort of automatic for him."

"I wouldn't go that far. He doesn't hit on every woman—just the ones under sixty-five. But he values his job too much to do anything stupid, so you shouldn't have any problems with him."

Amanda nodded, then said hesitantly, "Maggie? Is there anything you can tell me about that summer? You were here."

Maggie had turned her attention back to the mail she was sorting and didn't look up. "I was here. But if you're asking me if I know why Christine left, the answer is no. She seemed the same as always that summer."

After waiting a moment, Amanda said, "She and—and my father hadn't fought?"

"No more than usual."

"I don't remember them fighting."

Maggie looked at her then. "No, you wouldn't. Whatever else they were, Brian and Christine were good parents. They never argued around you. As a matter of fact, they never argued around any of us."

"But you know they did argue," Amanda said slowly.

Maggie looked at her then, her mouth curved in a small smile. "This is a big house, and the walls are thick. But if you spend enough time in the same house, you learn a lot about the people you share it with. And I've been here forty years. Daulton men are possessive about their women and always have been—sometimes to the point of obsession. Brian was obsessed with her, I'd say. Unfortunately, Christine was . . . a bit of a flirt. She liked men, and she liked being noticed by men. And sometimes she made sure Brian saw other men watching her. Or so it seemed to me."

"Why would she have done that?"

"To make him jealous, to get his attention—I really don't know. It was a long time ago, and I didn't think much about it at the time. It wasn't my business. Christine and I weren't close, so she didn't confide in me. I was busy with my own life, and I just . . . didn't notice much else. No one knew that summer would be important, Amanda. I suppose if we had known, we would have paid more attention. But we didn't." She shrugged. "I'm sorry I can't help you."

"So am I." Amanda smiled. "But I really didn't expect this to be easy. Finding out what happened, I mean. As you said that first day, twenty years is a long time."

Maggie nodded, then handed Amanda a stack of mail. "Why don't you take this to Jesse in his study?"

"And offer myself up for another chess lesson?"

"It would be," Maggie said, "the dutiful thing to do."

AMANDA SPENT THE HOUR OR SO UNTIL lunch having another chess lesson, and did well enough to earn a smile from Jesse. She couldn't help wondering why he was bothering to teach her—or, indeed, even to play at all—when he had so little time left, but assumed he was giving her lessons because it gave them time together and the latter was true because he was determined to lead as normal a life as possible.

She hadn't decided how she felt about Jesse's illness (which he had yet to tell her about). He was still very much a stranger, and because of that she was generally able to view him with more detachment than emotion; grief had not come into it, at least not yet. She wasn't sure it ever would.

Jesse was not a particularly likable man, as far as she

could see. He ignored his daughter and treated one of his grandsons with an edge of contempt and the other with heavy-handed domination; though his employees clearly respected him and gave him their loyalty, it was also clear to Amanda that they felt little if any affection. Not that he cared, apparently, since he made no effort to endear himself to those around him.

With Amanda, however, Jesse seemed to put his best foot forward—though how much effort that required was difficult to gauge. Still, it made their time together pleasant, especially since he so clearly accepted her as his granddaughter.

After lunch, Jesse casually told her he had to drive to Asheville—the only city of any size in this part of the state—on business, and wouldn't return until early evening. He didn't ask her to come with him, and it wasn't until Maggie explained while they saw him off that Amanda found out the "business" was actually the weekly treatment for Jesse's illness and that he always went alone.

"He hates to have anybody with him," the housekeeper explained after the big Cadillac, with Jesse seated regally in the back, was out of sight.

"I guess the treatments leave him feeling . . . pretty bad," Amanda said, remembering some of the horror stories she had heard. Standing beside Maggie on the front porch, she gazed after the now-vanished car and felt a pang of compassion.

"Bad enough," Maggie said. "The doctors have to throw everything they've got at the cancer, of course. It's the only way to beat the thing."

Amanda looked at the older woman in surprise. "Beat it? But I understood—that is, Sully told me it was incurable."

It was Maggie's turn to look surprised—even annoyed. "Nonsense. It would take more than a few tumors to get the best of Jesse. He's going to be fine. Just fine."

"I hope so, of course," Amanda said slowly.

Maggie smiled at her. "Oh, he will. Did you say you were going for a walk, Amanda?"

"I thought I would. Explore a bit away from the house."

"Do you have the map?"

Amanda patted the back pocket of her jeans. "Jesse made me a copy. Don't worry, I won't get lost."

"Well, stay on the trails and paths, and watch out for snakes."

Amanda smiled an acknowledgement, and waited until Maggie had gone into the house before she went down the broad steps to the sidewalk. The dogs, as usual, were with her, and as usual she talked to them as she walked.

"Which way should we go, fellas?" Both Dobermans merely looked up at her, responsive but not particularly helpful. They were quiet creatures; she had yet to hear either one of them bark. Amanda sighed and looked across the neat lawn toward the beginning of the path that led to King High, and unconsciously shook her head. No. Not that way.

According to the map, trails and paths abounded all over Glory, most used for working the horses being trained for cross-country events. That fact made her just a bit wary, but since horses were hardly known for sneaking up on people, she knew she'd have time to get off a trail should they gallop through. Surely.

"Northwest," she decided arbitrarily after examining the map. "Lots of trails on that mountain. Okay, guys?"

Since the guys replied only with intent looks, she set out briskly, breathing in honeysuckle-scented afternoon air that was not *quite* hot yet here at the end of May, but showed definite promise of heat to come. There was a nice breeze, just enough to stir the air, and the sunshine was very bright. Amanda had opted not to wear sunglasses, primarily because she knew most of her walk would take place in the woods, so she squinted a bit until reaching the shade of the towering hardwood trees that climbed the northwest mountain.

She found the trail easily since it was heavily marked by the passage of many hooves over years. It wound among the trees, now and then crossed by some kind of barrier Amanda had to go around, such as a tangle of fallen trees or other manmade jumps. She went on, amused to find that the dogs had apparently divided the duty; while one remained always no more than a couple of feet away from her, the other would dash off in a burst of energy, vanishing from sight only to reappear a few minutes later and take his place as escort.

Amanda wondered what they thought they were protecting her from, but shrugged off the thought.

The ascent was gradual, so much so that she was surprised upon reaching a rocky overlook to find out how high she'd climbed. Through a gap in the trees, she could look down on the very end of the rear wing of the house and a bit of the garden, and on a slice of green pasture dotted with grazing horses and, beyond that, the first of the four barns in the distance.

She could also see . . .

Amanda blinked, then narrowed her gaze and looked harder. She could, more clearly now, make out two people down in the garden. From any other angle they probably would have been hidden from prying eyes, since they were in a small but lush bower formed by tall hedges and a long trellis covered with red and white roses. The grass was probably soft there.

At least Amanda hoped so, for their sake, because it was fairly obvious even from this distance what they were doing.

"My, my," she said to one of the dogs conversationally. "I guess when the cat's away, the mice *do* play. I have a feeling Jesse would frown on that being done in his garden. Especially in broad daylight."

And who would have thought it of Kate? It had to be her; that gleaming black hair, though tumbled about her shoulders in a *most* uncharacteristic disarray, looked somehow regal even from here. Besides, other than herself, Amanda had seen no other woman on the place with coal-black hair.

"Still waters," Amanda confided to her canine companion. "You just never know about people." She felt a little amused and inexplicably cheerful.

Feeling only mildly guilty for not instantly turning away (she couldn't, after all, see anything of real importance, she assured herself), Amanda considered the man with Kate. The man who was neither dark nor hawklike, she was sure. He was, in fact, quite obviously blond. And since his broad shoulders were not currently covered by a shirt, it was easy to see he was nicely tanned.

Granted, Amanda certainly hadn't seen everyone at Glory yet, but still . . .

"Five will get you ten," she told the dog, "I know who that is. And aren't they the sly ones; there wasn't a sign of it the other day. Now why do you suppose Kate's carrying on secretly with one of the trainers? She's old enough to do what she wants, and I doubt very much Jesse would care who she slept with. Is she protecting her reputation, do you suppose?"

The dog—Gacy; she could tell them apart now—appeared to hang upon her every word with flattering interest, but offered no speculation of his own. A moment later, Bundy returned and they switched off, with Gacy dashing away to explore a briar thicket farther up the trail. Bundy sat down near Amanda and looked at her quizzically.

"If you come late," Amanda told him severely, "you just have to miss things." She laughed at herself a little and turned away from the vantage point, leaving Kate and her lover once more unobserved in their garden hideaway.

A higher overlook would no doubt allow her to see most of Glory spread out below; Amanda made up her mind to keep walking until she found such a place. Not that she wanted to spy on Kate and Ben—she just wanted to look at Glory from a more distant and possibly detached viewpoint.

She continued to climb a trail that was growing gradually steeper, pausing occasionally to catch her breath and reflect wryly on city living that dulled the senses and left legs overly dependent on wheels in order to get around.

That thought had barely crossed her mind when Amanda realized she and the dogs were no longer alone on the trail. She heard the sound of approaching hooves and felt the vibration under her feet long before she saw the horses, and that gave her ample time to get well off the trail. She was a good twenty-five or thirty feet away, uphill since she'd climbed, when three horses galloped past. The riders, vulnerable human heads protected by crash helmets, crouched in the stirrups, leaning forward as the horses scaled the steep trail.

Watching them unnoticed from her place above, Amanda felt only a mild, dispassionate interest. The riders were obviously expert; two young women and a young man, one of the women leading on a gray horse while the other two followed on bay horses. Absorbed human faces, and powerful muscles moving under glossy equine coats. The thuds of hooves and snorts of effort and the faint jingle of metal and the creak of leather.

Then, just as the horses disappeared around a bend in the trail, the breeze shifted and Amanda caught the warm, faintly musty scents of horses and sweat and leather. Her stomach knotted painfully and dizziness swept over her so swiftly that she swayed on her feet and had to clutch a sapling to maintain her balance. She lifted a shaking hand to wipe cold perspiration from her upper lip, and her breathing seemed very loud in her ears.

"It's getting worse," she murmured, finding the realization both bewildering and threatening.

It hadn't been so bad at first, but by her third day at Glory, even a brief wayward breeze from the stables or pastures was enough to leave her feeling sick and shaken. And last night she'd awakened from a nightmare she couldn't remember except to know that everything had smelled of horses and she had been terrified.

She didn't know what it meant, only that these odd experiences—her reaction to horses and the nightmare—both left upsetting feelings of panic and nausea lingering in her, and sometimes for hours afterward she felt an almost uncontrollable urge to run, to get away before . . .

Before what? Amanda didn't know, any more than she knew where the awful fear of horses came from. If she had ever fallen from a horse or been otherwise hurt because of one, she didn't remember it—despite the lie she had told Jesse and the others. But as far back as she could clearly remember, there was in her a fear of the animals not aroused by the sight or nearness of them—but by their scent.

She tried to shake off the sensations now, but that proved impossible. The breeze had carried the smell of horse away once more, yet she was still shivering.

"Never mind looking down on Glory," she told both dogs, hearing the tremor in her voice. Finding a nice vantage point could be left for another day. She fumbled for the map and studied it, searching for a path—any path—that would take her away from the riding trails and eventually back to the house. Not a minute later, with both clearly anxious dogs sticking close to her now, Amanda changed direction and began heading downhill once again.

"We're crazy," Kate said. "Down in the grass like a couple of teenagers . . . Anyone could find us here, you know that, don't you?"

"No one's going to find us here," Ben said. "The gardeners are finished for the day, Maggie's in the house, and you said Amanda went for a walk. All the riders and other trainers'll be out for at least another hour, Sully's with the blacksmith in barn one, and Jesse's gone until evening. Besides—we're safer here than we've been some other places."

"It's indecent. And I'll never get the grass stains out of this blouse," Kate said, but not as if either point troubled her much. She stretched languidly, her naked breasts lifting and her stomach hollowing below her ribs, and Ben watched her with pure enjoyment.

"You're beautiful, Katie."

"Don't call me that," she said instantly.

"I like it," he said.

"I don't."

As usual, they'd only partially undressed. Ben was still wearing his boots and though he'd pulled his jeans back up, they remained unfastened. His shirt, at least two of its buttons now missing, was flung across an ornamental stone bench a few feet away from them. As for Kate, she had pushed her skirt back down over her thighs but her blouse was still open.

She wasn't wearing panties or a bra, and when Ben had realized that, he hadn't been able to find a secluded corner of the garden fast enough. He hadn't even thought about how close to the house they were —closer than ever before—and he didn't give a damn now that he did think about it.

This little arbor was mostly shaded in the afternoon, but there was just enough sunlight to dapple the ground and paint Kate's golden flesh with enticing shadows. He loved to look at her. He only wished that they had the time and a place where he could see her completely naked and look his fill.

A bed would be nice. All night in a bed would be nicer. Waking up to Kate, Ben thought, would be nicest of all. He wondered how she would respond to him then, drowsy, her lithe body quiet with sleep. And, wondering, he was suddenly possessed by the desire to make it happen.

But how? How, when Kate rationed their time together in minutes?

"Why can't we sleep together?" he heard himself ask.

"I asked you to come to the house," she reminded him. "You refused."

"You wouldn't have let me stay all night."

Her silence gave assent.

"I have a bed, you know," Ben stated. "A perfectly good bed in a nice, quiet apartment. Why haven't we ever spent the night there?"

"I'm too old to be sneaking back home at dawn," Kate told him with a touch of asperity. She drew her blouse closed, then reached up a hand to her hair and instantly frowned. "What in the world—"

Ben chuckled and leaned over to kiss her. "Sorry about that, but I love your hair down. I took the pins out because I wanted to watch it move while you were on top."

Her hair had probably moved a lot while she'd been on top, Kate reflected, since she had been extremely . . . active. To her astonishment, she felt her cheeks warm; she had thought herself long past the age of embarrassment, especially with any man, and she had certainly never been fazed by anything she had said or done with Ben—but lately he seemed to have acquired the knack of making her feel self-conscious.

"Dammit," she murmured, sitting up as she tried to finger-comb her hair into some semblance of order. "You know I don't have a brush with me. And what Maggie will think—"

"She isn't your nurse anymore, Kate, and hasn't been for years." Ben pulled her gently back down beside him and slid long fingers into her loosened hair with obvious pleasure.

She told herself she should protest again, or move. That was it—she had to move, to get up and straighten her clothing and leave briskly with a casual farewell because that was the way it was between them.

But she didn't want to move. Not now. Not yet. It felt marvelous, his hands on her, that soothing yet peculiarly arousing touch against her scalp, and Kate wished she could lie here all day. He bared her breasts again, brushing the material of her blouse aside and using that hand to slowly stroke and fondle while his mouth took hers again and again in kisses so deep she felt consumed by them.

There was always a moment, when desire for him first surged inside her, that Kate felt strangely uncertain. It had never happened to her with other men, this sense of vulnerability that was a kind of ghostly panic, and with Ben it never lasted long enough for her to try to understand it. But every time she became aware of it, she was unnerved enough to think, *This is the last time.*

Until the next time.

"My turn," he murmured against her lips, "to do all the work." He guided her arms so that they lay stretched out on the grass above her head. "Don't move. Just feel."

Kate felt, and vulnerability vanished as if it had never been. Desire, sharp and hungry, coursed inside her, carrying all else before it.

She moaned when he began to rub his face slowly back and forth against her breasts, the contrasting sensations of his soft lips and the very faint stubble of his afternoon beard driving her mad. Eyes closed, stretched out half naked on the grass like some mindlessly willing pagan sacrifice, Kate gave herself over to him completely.

He knew her well. Skillful fingers probed and stroked, unerringly finding her body's most rawly sensual places—particularly the ones only a lover generous enough to pay attention would ever discover. He knew that if he brushed his lips just under her left ear, her whole body would shiver in pleasure. He knew that the silky flesh on the insides of her elbows was exquisitely sensitive, like the lower curve of each breast, and all around her navel.

He knew that if he caught her lower lip gently between his teeth she would make a throaty little sound of need, and if he touched his tongue to the tiny birthmark just beneath her left breast she would gasp, and if he glided fingertips down her spine to its base she would moan and arch her back.

Ben knew all those things, and he used all the knowledge to arouse Kate until she was frantic for him. Then he went further, teasing in a way he'd never done before, prolonging each caress until she was writhing in need.

When he finally gave in to her husky pleas and settled himself between her trembling thighs, Ben had held himself on the fine edge for so long that his own need made him wild and a little rough. Their passion was always explosive, but this time it was something fierce and primitive.

Kate recognized the difference, even though she didn't think lucidly about it; her body was utterly caught up in sensation and her mind was buffeted as if from the force of a gale. The scent of roses was heavy in the air and she could hear birds chirping, and when her release finally came she cried out incoherently, forgetting to mute the sound. Ben cried out as well, his powerful body shuddering in pleasure, and Kate clung to him with a sudden alarmed sense of having lost all control of the situation—and of herself.

Ben was first to move eventually, easing away and lifting himself off her. He didn't kiss her, as he normally did at that moment, and his expression was unusually intent. He remained between her legs on his knees, pulling up his jeans and fastening them as he looked down at her in silence.

For no reason she could have explained, Kate felt an abrupt wave of anxiety. The pleasantly limp aftermath of orgasm was all too brief; she had to force spent muscles to obey her commands. She sat up quickly, pushing herself a little back on the grass so that she put some distance between them and was able to close her legs—and also allowed the friction of the movement to work her skirt back down over her hips and thighs. She drew her blouse closed over her breasts and buttoned it, focusing all her concentration on the task.

"Kate."

He had scattered her hairpins, she realized, and they were no doubt lost in the grass. Now, how was she supposed to put her hair back up? Anyone looking at her would *know*—

"Kate, look at me."

She did, but spoke before he could. "We're not going to be able to meet again for a while," she said as if it didn't matter. "I'm going to be very busy."

Ben didn't look surprised. "I've gotten too close, haven't I, Kate?"

"I don't know what you're talking about." But her denial was too swift, too adamant, and Kate knew it.

"Is this how you've always handled it before?" Ben's voice remained curiously flat. "A lover gets too close, maybe begins to look at you in a different way or asks why he can't spend the night with you, and you break it off?"

"I didn't say I was breaking it off. I just—"

"You won't be any busier this summer than usual."

"I'm volunteering at the clinic," she said. "Three afternoons a week. And I'm helping raise money for the new park, and—"

"Kate, I didn't say you weren't busy, so don't sound so defensive. Between the charity work and doing the books for Glory, you're plenty busy. I know that. But you've found time to meet me for more than six months now."

"I want to spend time with Jesse. He—"

"He," Ben told her stonily, "wants to spend time with Amanda."

She drew in a quick breath as that blow landed. "I said you were a son of a bitch, and I was right."

"Because I tell the truth? Kate, when are you going

to accept the fact—the *fact*—that nothing is going to change between you and Jesse no matter what you do? He'll go to his grave feeling nothing for you except indifference, and the sooner you realize that the sooner you can make some kind of life for yourself."

"I have a life!"

"You have Jesse's life. Ever the dutiful daughter, you follow along behind him, eager to be helpful, to do anything he asks, pleasant and low-key and a willing target for abuse if he feels like yelling at someone. You stand in his shadow hoping against hope that he'll throw a smile or maybe a kind word your way—and it isn't going to happen."

Kate managed a laugh, but it hurt her throat. "Who gave you a license to practice psychology?"

"I don't have a license. But I minored in psychology. Horses aren't my entire life, you know—or would know, if you cared enough to ask." He looked at her, suddenly, as if he were a psychologist and she were on his couch. "You're Daddy's girl, and Daddy doesn't care, Kate. And if it weren't for one small but vital difference, you'd end up like those stereotypical Southern virgin spinsters we've all read about, worshipping Daddy long after he's gone and living in a mausoleum devoted to his memory."

Through lips so tight they felt numb, she asked, "What difference?"

He smiled, without amusement. "You're about as far from being virginal as a woman can get."

Ben caught her wrist easily when she would have hit him, and held her glittering silvery eyes with the same inescapable force. "Insulted, Kate? Don't be. It doesn't make a damn bit of difference to me how many men you've had. I don't even mind being used as a stress-buster, if that's what you need. But I'll be damned if I'll meekly let you break it off with me just because I might want more than you're willing to give. I warned you more than once—I'm not a toy, Kate, I'm a man."

She laughed with a brittle sound. "You got what you wanted out of this, and don't pretend otherwise."

"Sure I did, in the beginning. Now I want more."

"Oh, I see." Kate's smile was bitter. "You won't be a rich woman's pet, but you wouldn't mind a bit of compensation for all your extra . . . work. How much?"

Ben flung her wrist away from him in a gesture of disgust, his expression suddenly furious. "If you can think that, then the hell with you, *Miss* Daulton." He got up and got his shirt, shrugging into it angrily. "Find yourself another stud."

"Maybe I'll do just that," she snapped.

"Be my guest. But if it's Jesse you're trying to punish by jumping from man to man, you can save yourself the trouble. He doesn't give a shit, Kate."

"I don't know what you're talking about," she told him in a voice shedding icicles.

"Don't you? Then I'll explain it so you do. Jesse knows about us. He's known about all your men."

She blinked in shock, her righteous fury draining away as though through a gaping hole in her defenses. "No—he's never said—"

"Get it through your head. He doesn't care." Ben's voice remained hard, precise. He tucked his shirt into his jeans with jerky movements.

Kate was shaking her head. "He'd care. At least for —for our good name," she all but whispered.

Ben shook his head, pityingly. "Jesse's good name is invulnerable no matter what the rest of you do, and he knows it. Besides, Daultons have always been known for—taking lovers. He told me that himself, Kate. He wished me luck with you. He said nobody ever lasted long. He even said he was thinking about formally adding it to the expected duties of Glory's trainers. Must oversee a dozen horses and riders at any one time. Must prepare both for shows. Must get results. Must fuck Kate."

"No."

"That's what he said. And that's a direct quote."

"I don't believe you," she said numbly.

"Oh, yes, you do. Because when you take off your rose-colored glasses, you can see him as well as the rest of us can—and you know he's capable of it."

Kate looked at Ben with hatred. "Get away from me. Do you hear? Get away and stay away!"

"Gladly." He walked past the trellis of roses, turned a corner formed by shrubbery, and disappeared, leaving her sitting on the shady grass.

She sat there on the ground, long legs curled to one side, skirt smoothed down and blouse neatly buttoned and tucked in, and when she heard a little whimpering sound, Kate was shocked to realize it came from her. She pressed her fingers hard to her lips, trying to contain the pain and stop the trembling and summon enough control to enable her to get up and seek the more secure refuge of her bedroom.

God, it hurt. It hurt because she believed every awful word Ben had flung at her, because she knew it was the truth. It hurt because what he'd told her about Jesse—what Jesse had said to him—was the ultimate betrayal, an unthinkably callous reaction from a father to a daughter's sexuality. It hurt because it shattered the last fragile hope she'd had that Jesse loved her despite all evidence to the contrary.

She was nothing to him. Worse than nothing.

Her whole body hurt.

Kate forced herself to get to her feet, and it was only when she stood on shaky legs that another shock distracted her from her anguish. For the first time in her life, she felt the warm wetness of a man's seed trickling down her inner thighs, and she realized that during that second frantic coupling with Ben, he hadn't worn a condom.

She should have made sure, since it was her responsibility as well as his—why hadn't she? In twenty years, she had not *once* so lost control of herself with any man that she hadn't made very sure protection was used; she'd had no intention of being forced to deal with an unexpected pregnancy.

And even though she wasn't much worried now about getting pregnant—she'd been on the pill for nearly a year to correct a hormonal imbalance—she was more than a little unsettled by such an unprecedented lack of caution. Why hadn't she reminded Ben? Why hadn't she even *noticed*?

And why had Ben, always before so observant of her wishes, forgotten this time?

Kate rubbed her forehead fretfully, then made a halfhearted attempt to smooth her hair and looked down at herself. The back of her blouse was probably one big grass stain, and the stuff was probably all in her hair. She knew her lips were swollen because they were hot and tender, and her breasts felt heavy, aching, and sensitized. She knew she looked as if she'd just left a lover.

"You're about as far from being virginal as a woman can get."

Cheap, he'd meant. She was cheap. She had given herself to too many men, mostly for the wrong reasons, and what she had to show for the various brief relationships was . . . nothing.

Her life was going by with shocking speed, and what did she have? She had no career, no absorbing interest to fill her time, no skill to refine. She had no husband, no child, no home of her own—because Jesse would certainly leave Glory to Amanda or, failing that, one of the boys, Sully probably. But Amanda was more likely, of course, and even if she wanted Kate to stay, it would be impossible.

She could have a house of her own, Kate thought vaguely. She had a trust fund that had come from the mother she'd never known, more than enough for a house . . . and a life.

But the house wouldn't be Glory, and the life . . . What would the life be? Ben had been right about that, too. She didn't have a life. And when Jesse was gone, even whatever she had now would be in the grave with him.

She had tried all her life to get her father to look at her and *see* her—if not as a loved daughter, then at least as a person who counted—and no matter what she did, no matter how hard she tried, it had never been enough.

It would never be enough.

Kate felt very much alone right now, and the anguish was terrible.

Walker saw the dog first, and stood waiting until the big black and tan animal bounded up to him. "Hello, Bundy. What are you doing so far from home?" The Dobermans, trained to guard, tended to stick close to Glory; he couldn't remember ever finding them out here.

Bundy paused to have his small, pointed ears briefly rubbed, then whirled away and went a few yards before halting to stare back at Walker, his stump of a tail wagging.

"Okay, Lassie," Walker said, amused at himself for

reading human intelligence—or, at least, deliberation—into canine behavior, "I'll follow."

He did, and it wasn't until he topped a rise and stood looking down on a clearing that Walker realized he had unconsciously expected to find Amanda with the other dog. He had noticed, during the past few evenings, that they seemed to have adopted her, and Jesse had told him, proudly, that Amanda had won them over.

After a momentary hesitation, Walker began making his way down the slight incline toward her. She hadn't seen him. Hands on her hips, she was studying the clearing with a faint frown of puzzlement.

"It's called a bald," Walker said.

She jumped and glared at him. "Dammit, don't sneak up on a person."

It was the first time since they had met that she'd looked at him without wariness in her eyes, and Walker was surprised by how different she seemed. More vivid and alive. Younger somehow—or maybe that was due to her jeans and the way she'd tied her hair back with a colorful silk scarf.

"I didn't sneak," Walker told her, "you just didn't hear me."

Amanda eyed him when he stopped a couple of feet away from her. "Next time wear a bell," she told him.

He ignored the suggestion. "These clearings," he said with a slight gesture, "are called balds."

She accepted the change of subject with a shrug. "This is the second one I've seen today. Did somebody cut all the trees?" she asked.

"No, trees won't grow here. Nobody knows why. There are balds scattered all through the mountains. Ones like this—where there's only grass, weeds, and wildflowers—are called grass balds. Heath balds support some shrubbery. But never trees."

"A little eerie," she commented, her tone thoughtful.

Walker shrugged. "Superstition has it that the balds were created when the devil walked through the mountains; each footfall resulted in a bald. And, of course, nothing of any consequence would dare grow in the devil's footprints."

"Definitely eerie." She lifted her gaze to the spectacular scenery all around them and added, "And . . . almost . . . believable. I wonder why."

"Probably because these are old mountains, and the age shows. They were here when the world was young. When uncanny things might have been possible. When giants might have roamed the earth." He paused, then added, "Dinosaurs, maybe."

Amanda smiled slightly. "I thought you were getting a little whimsical there for a minute. Very unlike you, Walker. Dinosaurs, huh?"

"They were everywhere else."

She gave a little laugh and shook her head, but whether at his comment or his reliance on science over less tangible faiths, he couldn't tell.

"What are you doing out here?" she asked, then looked around them with a frown. "I am still on Daulton land?"

"This is Daulton land. And I'm out here because I sometimes am on Saturdays. I enjoy hiking. As you obviously do." He shrugged. "I sometimes ride, but my horse cast a shoe the other day and . . ."

Even as his voice trailed off, the wariness returned to shadow her eyes. She slid her hands into the front pockets of her jeans and looked at him with a faint smile holding far less humor and acceptance than only moments before.

"I suppose I hadn't thought about you on a horse,

but everyone else around here seems to ride. Do you show horses?"

"No, I'm a Sunday rider," he told her, surprised at the pang of regret he felt. "Barely good enough to know what I'm doing in the saddle, and for pleasure only. I have an old retired show horse that gives me a quiet, calm ride when I feel the urge—which is less and less frequently these days. I probably would have sold him years ago, but since he's pastured with the broodmares, he has company and exercise even if I don't take him out for months."

"The broodmares?"

"Glory's. Expectant mothers seem to do better in quiet surroundings while they're waiting to foal, and all the barns and paddocks at Glory tend to be on the noisy side with so much activity going on. So Jesse and my father made a deal years ago, before I was born. Jesse provided the money to rebuild and keep up the old stables at King High—which hadn't been used for anything except hacks in years—and put up new fencing. In return, he has pasture and stable rights for his broodmares. I have the pleasant sights and sounds of horses at my place without the responsibilities or expense, and my pastureland is kept in good shape."

"And the horses have a quiet place to foal."

"Right. The vet visits regularly, and a couple of stablehands keep the place neat and keep an eye on the mares. One of Jesse's people usually rides over every other day or so to check on them."

"Victor?" she guessed.

"Sometimes. So you've met him?"

"Yes." She didn't elaborate.

Walker looked at her thoughtfully. "He's excellent with horses. A bit rough-edged with people."

Amanda nodded responsively, but her eyes were

even more wary than before. Before he could comment, however, both dogs whined rather insistently, demanding attention.

"It's later than I thought," Amanda said, looking at her watch. "Almost their suppertime. All right, guys, we'll go back to the house."

She glanced at Walker, but didn't offer a farewell, and he told himself that was why he fell into step beside her as she turned away from the bald and toward a path that would lead them to the house.

"Jesse made a copy of that map for me," she said.

"Did he?"

"Yes. So—I can find my way back. If you were wondering."

"I wasn't." Walker didn't offer her an excuse for accompanying her back to Glory, mostly because he didn't have one.

She sent him another quick glance, which he met calmly, then said a bit hastily, "Maggie keeps warning me about snakes, but I haven't seen any so far."

He wondered why that particular topic had suggested itself to her, but decided not to question. "Copperheads can be deadly, but you're more likely to see black snakes and they're harmless. Just keep your eyes open and watch where you step. This time of year, with everything green, copperheads are fairly easy to see since they're marked with bands of reddish colors."

Amanda nodded gravely. "Thanks for telling me. I guess I should probably wear hiking boots when I'm out like this."

Walker, who was wearing boots, looked down at her running shoes and agreed. "Safer—and probably better for your feet. Running shoes are designed for smooth surfaces."

They walked in silence for several minutes, the path

they followed winding among tall trees in a steady but slight downhill grade, and then she spoke abruptly.

"I know Jesse has cancer."

He wasn't especially surprised, either by the statement or by his inability to determine from her composed expression how she felt—or if she felt anything at all—about the matter. "Maggie tell you?"

"Sully."

"One of them was bound to. I had a feeling Jesse wouldn't."

"Why not?"

"Because he doesn't want pity. Especially from you."

She digested that in silence for a moment, then said, "Sully told me—he probably wouldn't last until Christmas."

Evenly, Walker said, "That's what the doctors say."

"Does Maggie know that?"

"Of course she does. Why?"

Amanda shook her head. "I just—I don't think she wants to believe it, that's all."

Walker shrugged. "Probably not. She's been at Glory a long time, since Kate was born. She's the only one of us even close to being Jesse's contemporary, and they understand each other."

"You understand him too, don't you?"

He looked ahead of them to watch the dogs crisscrossing the path, always within sight of Amanda, then looked at her briefly. "Well enough. Why?"

"It was a fairly unimportant question," she said after a moment, her tone now as guarded as her eyes. "You don't have to pounce on it as if I were trying to pry a secret out of you."

"Did I do that? Sorry. Call it an occupational hazard."

"I wish I could call it that. But I think we both

know it's something else. I'm not trying to pump you for information, Walker, I was just curious."

"I said I was sorry." He was conscious of tension, of an abruptly heightened awareness between them that their mutual distrust seemed to intensify. He was, suddenly, so conscious of her that he could almost hear her breathing.

"So you did." Her voice was very noncommittal.

Silence again, thick this time. Walker didn't like it, but said nothing as they walked on. Eventually they came to a fairly narrow stream, and she paused on the bank, frowning. Since there were large, flat stones arranged by nature or human hands to provide an easy and sturdy crossing, he assumed something else was bothering her.

"What?" he asked, keeping his tone neutral.

"This looks like a new stream—it's hardly cut into the ground at all. Didn't we pass through an older dry streambed back there?" she asked, her own voice carefully prosaic.

He nodded.

"Did beavers change the course of the stream, or—"

"They do from time to time, but this was from a flash flood last year. They're fairly common in the spring and early summer. The force of the floodwaters caused broken branches and brush to dam up the stream and reroute it. The next flood may change it again—or put it back the way it was."

"Oh." She stepped on the flat stones to cross over.

"You're very observant," he noted, following her.

"Just curious by nature." She paused, then added deliberately, "About most everything. I tend to ask a lot of questions."

"I'll remember that."

Her smile was brief. "Sure you will."

Her disbelief bothered him a lot more than it should have. "You could meet me halfway, you know," he suggested. "Supply a few answers instead of just questions."

She paused as the path they were following ended at the edge of the woods on the northwest side of the lawn, and watched the dogs race off toward the end of the rear wing of the house. As if she hadn't heard him, she said, "I guess they mean to get to the house by going through the garden. It's closer from this point, anyway."

Walker caught her arm when she would have followed the dogs. "Discussion over?" he demanded cynically.

She looked up at him, for a moment expressionless, and pulled her arm from his grasp. Then she said, "I thought it was. Meet you halfway? When you're still pretty much avoiding the bare courtesy of using my name? Why on earth would I want to tell you anything at all?"

He watched her walk away from him, telling himself her words were no more than a facile justification for her secrecy, her evasiveness, and her refusal to come clean about her past. He told himself that several times, emphatically. *He* was not in the wrong, *she* was.

So why in hell did he feel so defensive?

"Dammit," he muttered, and followed her.

Six

AMANDA HADN'T EXPECTED HIM TO come after her, and when he caught up to her at the edge of the garden, she had no idea how she would react.

"Amanda, wait."

"So you do know the name," she marvelled, more sharply than she intended.

He didn't try to stop her, but walked beside her on the wide main path that wound through the garden and led toward the house.

"I haven't avoided using it," he told her. "Not deliberately, anyway."

"That makes it worse."

"Don't hold me accountable for my subconscious. We both know I'm not convinced you're Amanda Daulton."

She stopped and stared at him, wishing this didn't bother her so much but unable to pretend it didn't. "And I can't prove to you that I was born Amanda any more than I can prove I was born a Daulton. But, dammit, Amanda *is my name*. I've never been called anything else. At least give me that much."

He looked at her for a moment, then nodded. "All right. You're Amanda."

"Thank you."

She wondered if he really accepted it this time, but managed to keep most of the sarcasm out of her tone. She continued along the path, following the impatient dogs, who never got out of sight of her and so couldn't get far ahead in the maze of the garden. She was too aware of Walker beside her, and it worried her to know how easily he could shake her off balance.

Maggie greeted them at the door of the sunroom and told Amanda she would take the dogs to be fed. Though the Dobermans accepted Amanda completely, they had been very carefully trained with security in mind and would accept food from only two people: Jesse and Maggie.

"Are you coming to supper, Walker?" she asked.

"Am I invited?" He was looking at Amanda.

Amanda sat down on the foot of a rattan lounge and pulled the scarf from her hair, wondering even as she did it if she wanted to hide behind a protective veil of hair. Mildly, she said, "Kate's the hostess of Glory, not me."

Maggie looked from Amanda to Walker, seemingly amused, then told the lawyer, "We're eating at seven tonight since Jesse won't be back until late. You're welcome."

"Thanks," he said dryly.

When the housekeeper had called the dogs to heel

and left the sunroom, Walker sat down in a wrought-iron chair near Amanda's lounge and looked at her.

Interpreting that look, she said in a dry tone of her own, "Since I don't belong here, how could I issue any kind of an invitation?"

"Was that your reason?" he asked.

Amanda fixed her attention on the scarf for a moment, smoothing the silk and loosely folding it. But he was waiting for a response with characteristic patience, and she finally dropped the scarf beside her on the lounge's floral cushions and met his steady gaze.

"Believe it or not, that is more or less the reason. Jesse accepts me, but the others haven't yet, and I don't want to presume."

Walker didn't react with either belief or disbelief; he merely said, "Jesse won't be here tonight to . . . keep a tight rein on the situation."

Amanda had thought of that, and she wasn't particularly looking forward to the evening. She managed a shrug. "And you think the results might be entertaining? Fine. Come watch. But I don't plan to provoke anybody."

Walker stood up when she did, but he didn't follow when she headed toward the hallway, and he spoke only when she reached the door. "Amanda?"

She paused to look back at him.

"If you brought along any armor, you'd better wear it tonight." His voice was mocking.

"Thanks for the suggestion." She went out of the sunroom, catching a glimpse of her tense face in the mirror that hung on the wall as she turned the sharp corner into the hallway, and told herself to stop letting the man *get* to her. Why did she always feel so . . . so prickly when he was near?

What she needed to do, and quickly, was cultivate an attitude of complete indifference toward the lawyer. It shouldn't be that hard, Amanda reassured herself. All she had to do was remember why she was here. That should be enough.

She had gone only a few steps when she realized that she'd left her scarf behind, and because it was one of her favorites she didn't want to leave it lying about. Sighing, hoping Walker had gone, she turned back.

Wary of facing him again, she looked into the mirror before she turned the corner into the sunroom; she had already realized that from that specific angle, it was possible to see a large portion of the sunroom reflected in the mirror.

Walker was still in the room.

Amanda stopped, watching him without his awareness, feeling like an idiot for being reluctant to face him, but nevertheless unwilling to, at least until she'd spent some time practicing her indifferent attitude. He was standing by the rattan lounge where she'd been sitting, his brooding gaze directed downward.

He didn't look very happy, she thought. In fact, he looked a bit grim. While she watched, he bent down and then straightened with her scarf trailing from his long fingers.

He folded the narrow oblong of silk a couple of times with slightly jerky movements, his fingers examining the texture of the soft fabric. Then he lifted his hand to his mouth and brushed the silky material back and forth across his lips. Paused. Inhaled slowly. His eyelids grew heavy, sensuous. A muscle flexed in his jaw.

Then he swore softly, dropped the scarf onto the lounge, turned, and left the room.

Amanda leaned her shoulder against the wall, staring at the bright reflection of a sunroom now empty of troublesome—and troubling—lawyers. She could hear herself breathing unevenly. Her legs felt unsteady and her heart seemed to be beating all through her body. When she lifted a hand to her cheek, her skin felt hot. And her hand was trembling.

Indifference.

"Now what?" she whispered.

At first it seemed that both Amanda's misgivings and Walker's warning about the evening would prove to be groundless. Everyone met in the parlor before supper, that habit being ingrained, and if nobody had very much to say, at least the occasional silences held little noticeable tension.

Walker sat beside Kate on one of the sofas and talked to her; she seemed more animated than usual—or else he was particularly entertaining this evening, Amanda decided. They certainly seemed pleased with each other's company. However, since the lawyer talked in a low voice, she had no idea what the conversation was about.

As for herself, she listened to Reece painstakingly explain the duties and responsibilities of a vice president of a large and sprawling company, trying to look interested and aware that Sully watched them sardonically.

By the time Maggie came to tell them that supper was ready, Amanda was tempted to plead tiredness and escape to her room. But she couldn't do that. It would have been cowardly. And she refused to give Walker the satisfaction.

Jesse's place at the head of the formal dining table of course remained empty; the idea of somebody else sitting there, Amanda thought, hadn't even occurred to the others. No one ever sat at the foot of the table, that place apparently being reserved for Jesse's long-dead wife, Mary. So tonight, those present were ranged on either side of the long table—Amanda, Reece, and Maggie on one side while Walker, Kate, and Sully took up the other.

Amanda listened to a continuation of corporate tales from Reece through the soup and most of the entree, conscious of more mocking glances directed at her—this time from Walker. Sully and Maggie were talking about horses; Kate and Walker seemed to have run out of things to say to each other, and her earlier animation had vanished, leaving her with a faint look of strain in her lovely face.

When the dogs jumped up from their places behind Amanda's chair and dashed toward the front of the house, their claws clicking on polished wood, nobody had to guess where they were going and why.

"Jesse's home," Maggie said. She leaned forward to look past Reece at Amanda, and added rapidly, "If he feels well enough, he'll come in here—otherwise we're to leave him alone. And don't mention where he's been."

"Right." Amanda was grateful for the explanation, and not terribly surprised by another of Jesse's directives. At least twice a day, she seemed to hear "Jesse says" or "that's the way Jesse wants it" about one thing or another. She wondered suddenly if the next master—or mistress—of Glory would exert such sweeping control over so many aspects of the family.

Jesse came into the room a moment later. He looked very tired and a bit pale, and seemed to move stiffly—but that was probably due as much to the long trip in the car as it was to his treatment. He went to the head of the table, touching Amanda's shoulder and smiling a greeting at her, and nodding at the others. He didn't sit down, but merely rested his hands on the back of his chair.

"I'll have Earlene fix you a plate," Maggie said, beginning to rise from her chair.

Jesse waved her back. "No, I'm not hungry." He looked around the table, his tarnished-silver eyes unreadable. "I have something to tell all of you, and tonight's as good a time as any."

Amanda put her fork down and clasped her fingers together in her lap. She had never really believed in ESP, but in that moment she was absolutely positive she knew what Jesse was going to say. And she doubted she was the only one in the room gifted with clairvoyance, because the level of tension was suddenly so high the very air seemed to vibrate with it.

"Jesse—" Walker began.

"I'm glad you're here, Walker. When you've finished, come into my study."

"All right, but—"

"I want to get all the details worked out tonight." He looked around the table with a little smile on his thin lips. "No reason to put it off now that Amanda's come home. I've decided to change my will."

Amanda closed her eyes briefly, and when she opened them she fixed her gaze on her plate. She dared not look at the others. She wondered if any of them were breathing.

"Jesse," Walker said slowly, "I wouldn't be doing my job if I didn't advise you to consider this carefully."

"I have. I know what I'm doing, Walker, believe me." He looked around the table again, and his smile turned satirical. "I know exactly what I'm doing."

Sully ground out a vicious curse, shoved his chair back from the table, and stormed from the room. Jesse didn't attempt to call him back; he merely laughed shortly, said again to Walker, "When you're finished," and left the room himself.

There was a long silence. Then Walker quietly said, "If you'll all excuse me," and left the table to follow Jesse to his study.

Kate was the next to leave. She said, "Excuse me," very politely in her usual tranquil voice, and folded her napkin, and she didn't hurry.

Reece, having said nothing, but white-faced and rigid, was right behind her.

Amanda looked up at last, and turned her head to look down the table at Maggie. She couldn't read anything in the housekeeper's undisturbed expression, but she couldn't help feeling a pang of hurt when Maggie pushed back her chair and left the dining room without a word.

"Damn." Amanda pushed away her plate and propped her elbow on the table.

Earlene came in from the kitchen and looked around the almost-empty room in surprise. "I fixed peach cobbler for dessert," she said a bit aggrievedly. "What happened?"

Amanda looked at her and, bitterly, said, "Hurricane Jesse happened."

Walker looked down at the legal pad filled with notes, then raised his eyes to watch Jesse pace the room restlessly.

"Have you got that?" Jesse demanded.

"I've got it." Walker leaned back in the big leather chair behind Jesse's desk and sighed. "But I have to say again, it's a bad idea, Jesse. Can't you at least wait for the DNA test results before you do this?"

"No. I don't need some stranger peering into a goddamned test tube to tell me Amanda's my granddaughter."

"If you'd just wait—"

Quite suddenly, Jesse put his hands on the desk and leaned forward, glaring down at Walker. "Wait? Until when, boy? Until hell freezes over? Until *you* have every *i* dotted and every *t* crossed and feel sure you've satisfied a thousand conditions in all those moldy law books of yours?"

"Until we know," Walker snapped.

"I know now!" Jesse all but roared it, then winced and caught his breath at an obvious stab of pain. In a quieter voice, he said, "Walker, I don't have much time left. The doctors say . . . Christmas is the outside limit. Do you understand what that means? I'm marking off the days of my life in red ink, and there aren't many left."

Walker nodded slightly, and his own voice was calm again when he spoke. "I realize that. But I can't help being concerned, Jesse—and not only because you've accepted Amanda so completely without enough evidence. It's the rest of this, too." He waved a hand over the legal pad of notes.

"Questioning my business judgment? You've never done that before. My mind's still sound, I promise you."

Walker watched Jesse sit down in one of the chairs in front of the desk. "I know your mind's as good as ever. But I don't believe you've thought this through. You haven't changed the bequest to Maggie, but . . . Sully, Reece, Kate—what are they going to think? How are they going to feel?"

"They're taken care of," Jesse said flatly.

"They lose what matters to them most. You've left them with *jobs,* Jesse. With some money and a little land and a few shares of stock each. Sully gets to go on working with the horses, but he won't own them; Reece can keep his job, but he has no real authority in the company and you've made sure he never will have; and Kate—"

"She has money from her mother," Jesse said in a harsh voice. "Plenty of it. She can go someplace else if she wants. Or maybe Amanda will ask her to stay on here."

"Listen to yourself," Walker suggested, keeping his voice quiet with an effort. "Do you hear what you're saying? Kate is your daughter. My God, she was born here in this house; even if Amanda is who she claims, she wasn't. She spent summers here as a child, not her life. She's afraid of horses, and I'm willing to bet that what she knows about furniture, textiles, or business of any kind would fit in a teacup."

"It's her birthright," Jesse said.

Walker nearly swore aloud, frustrated by the old man's inability to see beyond his precious Amanda. Then he said, "Okay, then consider this. Everybody in that dining room understood what you intended doing when you made your little announcement. They know you mean to leave virtually everything to Amanda."

"So? Everything is mine to leave where I choose."

"No argument. But you're leaving Amanda to cope with a hell of a lot of resentment and bitterness, Jesse. Maybe you'll be able to keep Sully and Reece in line, and God knows Kate's never tried to fight you, but what about after you're gone? Do you honestly think Amanda will thank you when she has to go to court to defend a very inequitable will?"

Jesse snorted. "There isn't a judge in the state who'd set aside—"

Walker remembered that he had, in fact, told Amanda virtually the same thing. "If this division of property was anywhere near fair, I'd agree with you. But let's suppose for a moment that the DNA tests come back either inconclusive or else support the likelihood of a false claim."

"They won't."

"It's entirely possible that the results will be inconclusive even if she *is* Amanda and you know it. What if they are? Kate, Reece, and Sully would have at least a decent claim against the estate, arguing the possibility of misrepresentation and fraud. Hell, I'd advise them to."

"You—"

"I'm the Daulton *family* lawyer," Walker said evenly. "And I'd look out for the interests of my clients. If Amanda isn't who she claims to be, then she has absolutely no legal right to any part of your estate, and certainly not to the bulk of it. I'd take it to court. The judge might wonder if maybe you were sicker than you thought, Jesse, sick enough to have seen what wasn't there. If maybe you just wanted to believe she was Amanda because you were running out of time."

The old man was pale, but his tarnished-silver eyes were fierce. "You listen to me, Walker, and listen good. I want my will rewritten just the way I've told you, and I don't expect it to take weeks to be ready for my signature. And I want to advise you that I'm going to write several letters of intent, which I will send to a few influential people in this state, outlining my reasons for disposing of my property as I have done, and warning them that some of my greedy relatives may intend to challenge my will—which upsets me greatly. And I'll follow those letters with personal calls, just so everyone understands—and can swear in court—that I know what I'm doing. I also mean to talk to Judge Ferris and the sheriff at Amanda's party next Saturday, along with as many friends and neighbors as possible, then and every other chance I get.

"The mayor, the city council, the doctors and nurses at the clinic in town—hell, even the librarian." Jesse drew a harsh breath. "And I'll tell them all the same thing, Walker. I'll tell them that Amanda is my granddaughter because I *say she is.* I'll tell them that I don't give a damn if the blood in her veins turns out to be genetically ambiguous. She's my granddaughter. And I intend to leave *my* property to her."

"Jesse—"

"I'll also be sure to tell them that there's been no fraud or misrepresentation on Amanda's part. She hasn't asked me for a dime, Walker, and I don't expect her to. She wouldn't let me order a new car for her the way I wanted to—even when I told her I'd get her a temporary license until she got a chance to take the test, she said she didn't need a car. She said she didn't need charge accounts at any of the stores in town, or a checking account or charge card from the bank. Does that sound like a greedy bitch to you?"

"I never said that."

Jesse ignored the statement. "So you just go ahead and advise the rest of them to fight the will. Good luck. In the meantime, I'll expect it to be ready for my signature as soon as possible." It was a dismissal, and it was final.

Walker was only too aware of the fact that the old man was tired and probably in pain, and that he simply would not listen to reason, at least not tonight. Maybe later he could be brought to see the unfairness—and the danger—of what he was doing.

Maybe.

Carrying the notes from the legal pad folded in his hand, Walker left the study and headed for the front door. He didn't especially want to see or talk to anybody at the moment—and, naturally, the very last person he wanted to see was in the foyer, about to go upstairs.

"Walker?" Amanda's voice was tentative.

He halted in the center of the room and stared at her, wondering if his face looked as stiff as it felt. "If you're planning to celebrate," he said coldly, "don't. You're still a long way from inheriting."

"I didn't want Jesse to change his will," she said.

"Yeah, right."

She took a hesitant step toward him, those haunting eyes of hers darkened, seemingly troubled, and Walker felt an unaccustomed flicker of fury. Christ, she looked so anxious, so damned distressed, and *why did he believe it was genuine?*

"He hasn't changed it yet, has he?" she said. "I mean—it'll take time to—"

"I'll get started on it first thing Monday. It's a complex document, with or without changes, so it will take at least a few days and probably a week to draw up," Walker told her, his voice so harsh it hurt his throat. "And I intend to do everything I can to bring Jesse to his senses in the meantime. So don't start counting the money just yet."

He didn't wait for a response, just went on through the foyer and out the front door. He didn't slam it, but only because he controlled himself at the very last instant.

The Daulton family belonged to one of the local Baptist churches, but Kate, Amanda discovered, was the only family member who regularly attended services on Sunday. Jesse was generous financially, being the first to contribute when there was a need for a new roof or a new bus, but he strongly disliked "being preached at" and so avoided services; Reece attended at Christmas and Easter, which he apparently considered sufficient to maintain his place in heaven; Sully never went and made no excuses about it; and Maggie was, rather surprisingly to Amanda, cynical on the subject of religion.

Amanda discovered all this from Maggie at breakfast Sunday morning, a meal only the two of them appeared for in the bright sunroom. And though Amanda hadn't felt quite at ease with the housekeeper since their talk by the pool and had no idea how Maggie felt about Jesse's announcement the night before, she kept her own manner as casually low-key as before.

"Jesse's still asleep," the housekeeper explained when Amanda asked. "Kate's already gone; she's helping in the church nursery before services. Sully's working with one of his young horses, and Reece usually sleeps in on Sunday. But if you want to go to church, Amanda, Austin can drive you."

"No, I don't think so." Amanda sipped her coffee and shrugged. "I'd feel odd walking in alone."

Maggie nodded in understanding, but said, "I'm a bit surprised that Preacher Bliss hasn't dropped in on one of his visits to get a look at you."

"Bliss?"

"It's a severe trial to him, but most people ran out of jokes years ago."

Amanda couldn't help but smile. "I imagine it would be difficult. Is he a good preacher?"

"He preaches good at parties and when he visits," Maggie said. "I've never heard him in the pulpit. I've never had much patience with religion. Too many easy and asinine explanations for the whims of fate."

"For instance?" Amanda asked curiously.

"Oh . . . that bad things happen for some ultimately good reason. When innocent people die or children are abused, there's no ultimate good. I could never believe there was, so I could never believe in religion." Maggie smiled suddenly. "However, I was saved and baptized as a girl."

"Just in case?"

"Hard to be a complete atheist, I guess. Were you baptized, Amanda?"

Amanda set her cup down and smiled faintly. "Mother wanted me to make up my own mind. When I was sixteen, I did."

Maggie didn't ask what that decision had been; she merely nodded and changed the subject, talking idly while they finished eating breakfast about the guest list for the party the following Saturday. Apparently, everyone of importance in the entire county would attend, all no doubt eager to get a look at Amanda and decide whether she was an impostor.

Not that Maggie put it quite like that, of course. The way she put it was, "You're the juiciest topic of gossip around here since our former minister was caught in bed with one of the deacons' wives."

"I'll try not to disappoint," Amanda said, wincing slightly.

"You won't. Of course, quite a few people got a look at you in town before Walker brought you out here, so most have that curiosity satisfied. They'll be watching us as well as you, naturally, and you'll be asked a lot of questions, few of them subtle."

Amanda nodded. "I expected as much."

"It should be a good party, though," Maggie said reassuringly. "The people around here tend to be friendly. About half the women will bring desserts, mostly pies; we don't have a big county fair, so the best cooks in the area have no place to compete with each other except for parties. It's been an unspoken tradition for years now."

Amanda couldn't help but smile. "Will Jesse award a blue ribbon?"

"Not quite that, but there'll be a lot of discussion about whose pie was best, believe me. The discussions have been known to end with hostilities. Very entertaining. By the way—if you don't want to hurt anybody's feelings, sample everything. Everyone else will, and what you eat will definitely be noticed."

"And I'm not a dessert person," Amanda said with a sigh. "I love most berry pies and peach pie, but everything else pretty much leaves me cold."

"Well, you're in luck—Sharon Melton always fixes a blueberry pie that'll bring tears to your eyes, and Earlene's peach pie is wonderful. As for the rest, just sample and look impressed. You're such a little thing that nobody'll expect you to eat a lot anyway."

"Thank God for small favors—if you'll forgive the pun."

Maggie smiled. "Things could be worse. If Jesse had decided on a country supper–type party, everyone would bring at least two dishes—and you'd be up to your ears in odd casseroles."

"Lovely."

"You may well look horrified. Last summer, the competition seemed to be who could create the most impressive broccoli dish. We had a very *green* summer."

"Oh, shoot—sorry I missed it."

Maggie laughed, and went on casually talking about the people who would attend the party. Amanda listened with only a portion of her mind now, feeling a growing and uncomfortable certainty that Maggie was no longer as neutral about her as she had been at first. In spite of her easy conversation and apparent acceptance, the housekeeper looked at her differently,

Amanda was convinced; her gaze was more intent—suspicious?—and she seemed subtly more guarded.

But why? Because Jesse had announced his intention to change his will? No; Amanda had half-consciously noticed the housekeeper's subtle change toward her earlier. Because when they had spoken briefly by the pool, Amanda had casually confessed her mother hadn't taught her to play the piano? *What is it about the piano, dammit?*

Amanda didn't know, and dared not ask. Bothered, but unable to do anything about the problem at the moment, she forced herself to listen and respond calmly to Maggie. Still, it wasn't until they had finished eating that her full attention was caught.

"Jesse told me last night that he hoped you'd spend the afternoon with him today," Maggie said. "I think he wants to start familiarizing you with the family businesses."

Amanda half nodded, but said, "I didn't want him to change his will, Maggie. That's not why I came back here."

"It was bound to happen." Maggie's voice was dispassionate. "It's no secret he hasn't been happy with Reece's head for business, and Sully's not interested in anything beyond his horses."

"What about Kate? She's his daughter."

Her face wiped of expression, Maggie said, "As far as Jesse's concerned, Kate killed Mary."

"And he had nothing to do with getting his wife pregnant?" Amanda demanded, struck by the unfairness of that.

"You'd think." Maggie shrugged. "He had to blame somebody when he lost her, and he's not a man to blame himself. Even if it wasn't her fault, Kate was the cause. It's been forty years, and his attitude is set in cement. At least he tolerates Kate now; when she was a child, he couldn't bear her anywhere near him. I came here as her nurse, you know."

"Yes."

"It was a lonely job at first. Jesse was half crazy with grief and wouldn't have anything to do with the child. Adrian was fifteen, Brian barely thirteen. With Mary gone, there was no one to run the house, so I did what I could. By the time Kate was in school, this place was home to me. Jesse liked the way I ran things, and asked me to stay on."

"You must have been very young when you came here," Amanda said.

"I'd just turned twenty-one." Maggie smiled. "Things were different in those days; infant nurses weren't expected to have degrees in child care—just to know what they were doing. I came from a large family, most of my siblings younger, and that was enough. Duncan McLellan—Walker's father—was the one who hired me; Jesse was in no state to judge."

Amanda hesitated, then said, "So you're the only mother Kate's ever known."

"I raised her, but she never looked on me as a mother once she was old enough to understand her own mother had died. I suppose," Maggie added with detachment, "if she felt that way for anyone it was Christine. Kate was only seven or eight when Brian brought Christine here that first summer—and you didn't come along for another four years. Christine liked kids. I guess it was natural for Kate to take to her."

Amanda shook her head a little. "I . . . don't have many memories of Kate."

Again, Maggie spoke with detachment. "Jesse insisted she spend a few weeks each summer away at camp, so you didn't see very much of her. He would have sent her away to boarding school, but I talked him out of it. As I said—she was nearly grown before he could stand having her around him."

"That's . . . cruel," Amanda said quietly. "And so unfair."

"Jesse gave Kate as much as he could," Maggie said, defending him staunchly. "She's never wanted for anything—and he's never lifted a hand to her."

Amanda wanted to say that emotional neglect was also abuse, but she said nothing more on the subject. Instead, she said, "I haven't seen a painting of Mary. Is there one?"

"Yes. In his bedroom." Excusing herself, Maggie got up and, carrying her plate, headed for the kitchen.

Gazing after her, it occurred to Amanda quite suddenly that Maggie was in love with Jesse and probably had been for a long, long time.

His treatment had left Jesse visibly tired, and Amanda managed to postpone their afternoon in his study by saying she was too restless to remain cooped up inside on such a pretty day. She hardened her will to his obvious disappointment, and was rewarded by finding out later that he had gone to his room after lunch, at Maggie's urging, to take a little nap.

It was a reprieve, Amanda knew—not a pardon. She would still have to face Jesse, and she was not looking forward to it. He wouldn't understand, and he wouldn't be happy with her when she told him how she felt.

Worst of all, she wasn't sure she'd be able to convince him no matter what she said. Which meant she'd have to resort to threats—and Jesse was not a man to be backed into a corner without prudent consideration and great care.

Wandering through the garden after lunch with her

canine companions, Amanda worried the problem in her mind. Jesse's announcement had been so premature she hadn't been at all prepared for it; she had been fairly certain he meant to change his will, but not so soon, and the very public declaration had put her in an impossible position.

Not that he would have considered that, of course. Just as no one in *his* house would have been stupid enough to let the dogs out—even though someone indisputably had—that first day, so no one in his family would dare oppose his wishes. Even if he was bent on disinheriting them.

It was Jesse's blind spot, Amanda thought. He was so utterly convinced of his own invincibility that it simply did not occur to him that by announcing his intentions, he might possibly have drawn a neat target on Amanda's chest.

Amanda had no illusions. There was a hell of a lot of money at stake, besides the glory that was Glory, and people had been murdered for far less. A cheerful thought. She didn't know any of these people well enough to even begin to guess if any of them might be driven to kill—but it seemed to her that Jesse was certainly doing his best to motivate *somebody* along those lines.

And it wouldn't do a bit of good for her to make an announcement of her own that she had no interest in inheriting any of it, because nobody would believe her —particularly while Jesse was busily changing his will.

Time, always ticking briskly away, was definitely rushing now, and she was no closer to finding the answers she had come here to find. And now she couldn't afford to merely be watchful and wait for opportunities; Jesse had effectively removed that option for her.

A few days, Walker had said, maybe a week. She

could count on him to stall the process as long as he was able, but eventually Jesse's new will would be ready for his signature. And if Amanda wasn't able to make him listen to her—then what?

Her avowed restlessness hadn't been a lie, and the lazy stroll wasn't helping. Amanda decided to go for a swim, and headed for the house to change into her suit. When she got back down to the pool, Kate was there, and Amanda hesitated briefly before setting her tote bag beside a lounge a few feet away from the one on which Kate had left her robe and towel.

Kate was lithe and graceful in a black one-piece suit, and Amanda watched the older woman swim laps briskly while she shrugged out of her robe and applied another layer of sunscreen to deflect the afternoon sun. By the time she was finished, Kate was coming up the steps out of the water, and with genuine admiration, Amanda said, "You look wonderful."

Kate paused a moment. Her gaze swept over Amanda, and then she looked at the younger woman's face with an odd expression on her own. She seemed briefly surprised by what Amanda had said, but then her usual tranquility settled over her perfect features, and she crossed the tiles to her lounge and picked up her towel. "Thanks. Good genes."

"And an active life. Obviously, you swim. And you ride a lot, don't you?"

"A few times a week, usually." Kate sat down on the lounge, drying her golden arms as she looked at Amanda. Those tarnished-silver eyes she'd inherited from Jesse were unreadable.

Amanda smiled. "I wish I felt differently about horses. After exploring on foot yesterday, I realize how big this place really is. Riding, I could see more of it."

"I suppose."

Amanda put on her sunglasses and tried again. "This party Jesse wants for Saturday—it's bound to be a lot of extra work for you and Maggie."

"We always have parties in the summer."

"Still, if there's anything I can do to help—"

"I think," Kate said politely, "you've done quite enough."

There was a lengthy silence, and then Amanda sighed. "Kate, I realize you have no good reason to believe I am who I claim to be, but—"

"I know who you are." Kate's voice was suddenly flat. There was an odd little smile in her eyes. "And I know you came here to destroy this family."

"That isn't true. Kate, please—"

The older woman got to her feet and put on her robe, then slid her feet into a pair of thongs. Her expression was cold, though her eyes still gleamed. "Please what? Please understand? I don't think so. How can I, when I wish you hadn't come here? Things would have been better if you hadn't come, I know they would have."

"If it's Jesse's will you're upset about—" Amanda began, but was cut off by a short laugh from Kate.

"His will? I don't care about that. All I care about —all I wanted—" She broke off and fought visibly for control. Then, quietly, she said, "You have no idea what you've done." She picked up her towel and went into the house.

"We can't let him do it," Reece said.

Grooming a nervous young horse, Sully looked at his brother and said, "Lower your voice."

Reece made an impatient sound, but kept it low; the excitable filly had already tried to kick him when he'd merely walked past her, and the way she was looking at him now made him decidedly wary. He didn't have Sully's inborn knack of gentling horses—the opposite, if anything; he seemed to make them as jumpy as they made him.

"Just how do you propose we stop him?" Sully asked.

"There has to be a way we can do it. You know as well as I do that he means to cut us out, probably all the way." Reece moved restlessly, but kept his distance from the young horse. Standing in the doorway of the tack room, he fiddled with a bridle hanging on a hook, and absently drew a finger across a dusty shelf holding brushes.

Sully dropped the brush he was using into a carrying tray and looked at his older brother, one hand still stroking the horse. "He could leave everything to a home for aged cats and we couldn't do anything about it. Besides, if you're surprised he means Amanda to inherit, all I can say is I'm not."

"And it doesn't bother you? Come off it, Sully. This is me, remember? I know how badly you want Glory. Even if you think you could stand her running things around here, what happens if she decides to sell out? You couldn't afford to buy the house *or* stables any more than I could afford the rest. We could both be out on our asses watching strangers here."

"She wouldn't sell Glory. Nobody would."

Reece uttered a short laugh. "Just because you think Glory is the center of the universe doesn't mean everybody else believes that. Even if she is the real Amanda, she hasn't been anywhere near this place in twenty years—and I very much doubt that Christine offered any glowing recommendations. To our dear *cousin,* this place is no more than a cash cow."

Sully picked up another brush and continued grooming the horse, his gentle hands and low voice in stark contrast to the black scowl on his harsh face. "I don't believe that. Not if she has a drop of Daulton blood in her veins."

"Yeah, well, I say she doesn't."

"The DNA tests will tell us that."

Reece shrugged. "Maybe—and maybe not. If you'll remember, we were warned the test might not be conclusive no matter who she is. And in case you haven't noticed, the old man isn't waiting for the results. He's changing his will now."

"It isn't a done deal, not yet. Walker's bound to drag out the paperwork as long as he can; he's no happier about it than we are."

"And in the meantime—what? We wait for providence to step in and cause sweet Amanda to trip and fall down the stairs?"

"Very funny."

"Then what? Jesse hasn't changed his mind about anything since he initially took Nixon's part in Watergate, and he didn't change his mind about *him* until after the resignation. He won't change his mind about her, or his will, not without a hell of a lot of proof she's a phoney. And once he signs the will, we're out. I told you what I heard outside Jesse's study last night; breaking the will in court will be next to impossible if he writes all those damned letters and talks to everybody in the county."

"I've never known anybody to keep Jesse from talking," Sully said without much humor. "And it's a federal offense to intercept the mail."

"Be serious. We have to stop this."

Finished with the grooming, Sully stabled the young horse in silence, then went past Reece into the tack room to put away the tray of brushes.

"Well, say something," Reece ordered angrily.

"What the hell do you want me to say?" Sully was

no less angry. "I know damn well *I* can't persuade Jesse to change his mind, and I seriously doubt you can. So? If you have any bright ideas, I'd love to hear them."

"Maybe we should look at the problem from a different angle," Reece said. "If changing Jesse's mind won't work, then we concentrate on Amanda."

"And just politely ask her to give up Glory and the business when she inherits?"

"Don't be a fool. We have to find a way to prove she's a liar and a cheat."

"We don't know that she is," Sully pointed out dryly.

"Oh, come on—you don't really believe she's the real Amanda? Appearing out of nowhere after twenty years and conveniently just before the old man cashes in his chips? For God's sake, look at her. There isn't a Daulton on the entire family tree who was under five foot eight, male or female. She didn't get that pale skin from the Daultons, and Christine turned brown if you just *mentioned* sunlight."

"I don't remember," Sully said.

"Well, I do. Besides, it's obvious in the painting and in all those photos Jesse has. No, our little pretender is not who she claims to be."

"You can't know that, Reece."

"Can't I? Have you noticed that she's a southpaw?"

Sully frowned. "No, but so what?"

"Amanda was right-handed."

Sully's frown deepened. "Are you sure?"

"Positive."

"And nobody but you noticed?"

Reece shrugged. "Apparently nobody's thought of it—probably because everyone's attention's been on the so-called science of the DNA test. I only remember because there was a lot of rain that last summer, and Amanda was always off in a corner somewhere drawing horses. Right-handed."

"So tell Jesse that."

"And listen to him call me a liar? It's no proof, and with my luck nobody else will remember either way since it was so damned long ago. But *I* remember, and I know she's a phoney. If she slipped up on that point, there are bound to be others. All we have to do is find them."

"Even if we do, what makes you think Jesse will care?" Sully's voice was impatient. "He's running out of time, and he wants Amanda back so bad that she could probably explain away anything we came up with. And if you alienate Jesse, you'll be worse off than you are now. I say let it alone, Reece. Don't make Jesse choose, or you'll lose."

"I haven't busted my ass all these years trying to please Jesse to watch it slip away now," Reece said. "If you won't bother to try, I'll do it myself. I'll do whatever it takes to protect my interests."

Sully followed his brother from the tack room and to the end of the barn hall, and stood there for a moment watching Reece stride off toward the house. Then, swearing under his breath, he turned toward barn three and tried to turn his thoughts to the yearling that was next on his list to be handled today.

He didn't look back, and so he didn't see Ben Prescott come down the last few stairs from his apartment above and stand gazing after him.

Jesse was on the phone when Amanda came into his study late that afternoon. She responded to his immediate smile and beckoning fingers by closing the door behind her and wandering over to study the painting of Brian, Christine, and Amanda Daulton.

A lovely little family. But not, it seemed, a perfect one. Christine had been restless for most of her marriage and possibly adulterous that last summer; Brian was apparently by turns neglectful and obsessively jealous of his wife.

As for Amanda . . . what did a child know? That beds were soft and food was good and parents were always there. That lightning bugs glowed after death. That summer smelled a certain way, and thunder couldn't hurt you, and new shoes creaked when you walked. That there was no crayon to exactly match a clear summer sky. That butterflies would poise on your finger if you were very, very still, and that newborn foals wobbled comically. That crayfish could be caught by tricking them into scooting backward into a jelly jar. That nightmares weren't real, even if they felt that way.

"She was a strong-willed woman, your mother," Jesse said.

Amanda turned to look at him. "Then I come by it naturally, I guess. I'm stubborn, too."

"I'd be very surprised if you weren't, honey."

She went across the room and sat down in a chair before his desk, her face grave. "We have to talk, Jesse."

"About what?"

"About your will."

Seven

"SHE HASN'T," SULLY SAID, "PUT A FOOT wrong all night."

"I've noticed." Walker gazed across the tiled patio at where Amanda stood talking to the Reverend Bliss. The good reverend was, as usual, intent on saving a soul—whether or not it needed saving—and she was polite, gravely receptive, an abstemious soft drink in her hand and her simple summer dress not only flattering but also demure.

Her gleaming black hair was arranged in loose curls held off her face by one of the silk scarves she favored. The simple change in her appearance made her look eerily like the little girl in the portrait—but, of course, that had been her intention, Walker thought.

"Yeah, I've noticed you notice."

Walker shifted his gaze to Sully's face, met slightly

mocking gray eyes for a moment, but all he said was, "Is it my imagination, or is there some tension between her and Jesse?"

Sully accepted the deflection with a shrug. "That's right, you haven't been around this past week."

"Jesse kept me buried under paperwork for that development deal." Not for the first time, Walker wondered if he had been kept busy and out of the way just so Jesse didn't have to argue with him about the new will. "What's going on?"

"Hard to say." Sully took a swallow of his drink and watched broodingly as Amanda was rescued from Preacher Bliss by Maggie and taken to meet the newly arrived mayor and his wife. "Neither of them has said anything that I've heard, and there's been no open argument. *Very* unlike Jesse."

"I'll say."

Sully shrugged again. "At a guess, our little Amanda has somehow backed Jesse into a corner. I don't know what it's about, but he's so frustrated he can hardly see straight."

Walker frowned. "That doesn't sound likely."

"Agreed, but it's my guess. From what I can tell, he keeps trying to . . . persuade her in some way, and she's refusing to do whatever it is he wants. All week long, he's been stomping around the house glaring at everyone else while she's kept to herself and out of his way. Out of everyone's way, as a matter of fact."

"What do you mean by that?"

"Just what I said. It's been a fairly tense week for Amanda, I'd say. Not only is Jesse pissed off at her, but Kate gets a frozen look on her face whenever Amanda comes near and Maggie hasn't gone out of her way to be friendly."

"I see," Walker commented, "that you've noticed quite a bit yourself."

Sully's smile was sardonic. "I've been running back and forth from the stables to the house all week. Who do you think the old man's been taking out his temper on? Yesterday he called me up to the house just to spend half an hour roaring about why the training ring fence hadn't been painted this year. And when Victor called to say he'd be delayed, guess who took the flak for it."

Walker looked at him thoughtfully. The two men were standing near a long table at the edge of the patio where a dessert buffet had been set up, and no one else was near them. It had been Sully who approached Walker, evidently because he'd had things to say, but it was uncharacteristic of him to complain about his grandfather's treatment of him, and Walker suspected Sully had something else on his mind—which he would get to when he was ready and not a minute before.

The party had been going on for more than two hours now; torches placed here and there brightened the twilight as well as warded off pesky insects, and the guests had spilled over onto the lawn and into the garden, many trying to make room for dessert by lazily walking off the thick steaks and roasted vegetables consumed earlier. The faint smoke and hickory aroma of grilled food continued to hang in the still air, along with the appetizing scents of fresh-baked pies, cakes, and cobblers.

There were still guests sitting at the tables scattered around the patio, talking in small groups or else just listening to the pleasantly muted sounds of the band from Nashville. Muted because Jesse disliked loud music, and so had placed the band on a platform off to the side and forbidden amplifiers. This was not a concert, he'd told them; they were not to drown out the conversations of his guests or to wait expectantly for applause.

The band, extravagantly paid as well as lavishly housed and fed, hadn't complained, and the guests obviously appreciated being able to talk without shouting. Some even danced to the slower tunes, turning the tiled area around the pool into a dance floor.

As for the guest of honor, she had indeed played her part to perfection. Greeting the guests at Jesse's side, she had been friendly without gushing, deferring to Jesse in a pretty way not a whit overdone, and Walker had heard several people remark on how very much she (still) resembled the little girl in the famous painting and how wonderful it was for Jesse to have found his beloved granddaughter.

As far as the townspeople of Daulton were concerned, Amanda Daulton had come home.

And Amanda seemed completely comfortable in her surroundings. She was courteous and gracious to everyone, seemed flatteringly interested in whatever anyone had to say to her, and displayed a sweet, soft-spoken temperament that pleased everyone who spoke to her. She was even beginning to sound distinctly Southern.

Walker thought she was a fine actress.

It was only, he thought, because he watched them so closely that he had picked up on the slight tension between her and Jesse. It wasn't obvious, but it was there. And at least twice he had seen Jesse say something to Amanda that met with a slow shake of her head, a reaction that clearly displeased Jesse.

Walker didn't know what it was about, but it made him acutely uneasy.

Kate came by the dessert table just then to make sure plates, forks, and napkins were laid out and ready, as usual performing the many small and large duties with an attention to detail that made her such an excellent hostess. If she resented Amanda's presence and her place in the spotlight, it wasn't apparent, and the coldness Sully had alluded to was not visible.

"Nobody's eating dessert," she said to Walker, a good hostess worried that her guests were not satisfied.

"They will. We will. It's just that the steaks were huge."

She made a little grimace. "Well, for heaven's sake tell Sharon her blueberry pie is wonderful; she's testing a new recipe, and *I* can't try it because of my allergy."

"I hate blueberry pie," Walker reminded her.

"Do you? Yes, of course you do. I wonder why I'd forgotten that. Sully, you can—"

"I," Sully said, "hate pie. Period."

"Do you have to be so hard to get along with?" she asked him a bit plaintively. "Go ask Niki Rush to dance, why don't you? She's been eyeing you all night."

Unmoving and unmoved, Sully said, "I also hate to dance. Particularly with grown women who spell their names in cute ways."

Kate rolled her eyes at Walker, then headed off, apparently to herd stuffed guests toward the dessert table.

"Has she lost weight?" Walker asked Sully.

"Probably. Like I said—the past two weeks haven't exactly been fun for any of us, and this last week has been worse. Jesse's new will ready?"

Walker looked at him. "Not quite. The computer blew a hard disk, causing a delay."

"Handy things, computers."

"When they work."

"And sometimes when they don't." Sully shrugged, then added abruptly, "He's cut me out, hasn't he?"

"You know I can't answer that."

Sully's mouth twisted. "You're a discreet bastard, aren't you?"

"It's my job, Sully."

"Yeah." Sully set his glass on the dessert table and muttered, "I've been here long enough to satisfy the old man, I think." He took a couple of steps toward the house, then paused and looked at Walker. "By the way," he said, "according to Reece, twenty years ago, Amanda was right-handed."

Walker stared at him.

Sully smiled. "Interesting, huh? See you around, Walker."

"We didn't have the clinic then; Jesse put up the money for it about fifteen years ago—before that the doctor worked out of a house on Main Street," Dr. Helen Chantry explained. "And I was hardly dry behind the ears, so to speak. Educated and willing, but inexperienced. In 1974, old Doc Sumner had just retired and I'd taken over his practice late in January."

Amanda nodded. "Then you were—when my father was killed, you were called?"

"Well—yes." Shrewd dark eyes studied Amanda for a moment, and then Dr. Chantry said impersonally, "There was nothing I could do for him. The fall broke his neck."

"He was such a good rider," Amanda murmured.

"Even Olympic-class riders come off their horses sometimes; Brian Daulton came off his. Unfortunately, he hit the fence at the precise angle and speed to turn what should have been merely a bruising fall into a deadly one. He died instantly."

Amanda was silent for a moment, listening with half an ear to the band and gazing around at the small tables on the patio, most occupied by guests sampling desserts. A couple of uniformed maids moved about emptying ashtrays and refilling glasses, and three couples danced languidly near the pool.

"I'm sorry," Dr. Chantry said.

Amanda looked at her and smiled. "No, I asked. Besides—it's been twenty years and I barely remember him. I was just curious because . . . well, because in the newspaper clippings about the accident, it said he was killed attempting to take a young horse over an impossible jump. That doesn't sound like an Olympic-class rider, does it?"

"No, but people sometimes do stupid things—especially when they're upset."

The doctor didn't say that Christine's abrupt departure scant weeks before that day might well have caused Brian Daulton to do something stupid. She didn't have to say it.

"I suppose." Amanda hesitated, then asked, "Do you remember my mother?"

Helen Chantry, who was about the same age Christine Daulton would have been, nodded. "Socially, though—not professionally. She never came to me with a medical problem."

Amanda hesitated again, then said, "Doctor—"

"Helen."

"Helen, then. Thank you. Do you . . . have any idea why my mother left so abruptly?"

"Jesse said there were things you didn't remember, but—didn't she tell you later?"

"No."

"Odd." Helen looked at her thoughtfully. "I wish I could help, Amanda, but I honestly don't know that answer. As I said, I only knew her socially. We weren't friends. I don't think she had any female friends. She wasn't a woman's kind of woman, if you know what I mean."

Slowly, Amanda said, "She was beautiful. She attracted men. Is that what you mean?"

Helen smiled. "More or less. She didn't just attract men, though, Amanda, she fascinated them. Maybe even . . . enthralled them. Whatever she had packed quite a wallop, and I don't believe it was really deliberate, that she controlled it. I can recall more than one happily married and perfectly level-headed man looking at her with glazed eyes when she walked by on a public street. It was actually sort of eerie."

"She wasn't like that later." Amanda distractedly pushed a small plate containing a couple of leftover spoonfuls of peach cobbler and apple pie away from her. There were still half a dozen desserts left to sample, but she wanted to wait a few minutes before making the attempt.

"What do you mean?" Helen asked.

Amanda recalled her wandering thoughts. "Oh . . . she was restrained, I guess. Not at all provocative in any way. Self-contained. Very quiet."

Curiously, Helen said, "Tell me it's none of my business if you like, but—she never remarried?"

"As far as I know, she was never even involved with a man after we left here." *Or was she? What about Matt Darnell?* "Of course, I might not have known those first years, since children often don't notice such things, but I think I would have when I got older. Surely I would have."

Whatever Helen might have said to that was lost for the moment as Jesse called to her from a neighboring table to come and settle some bit of medical dispute.

"Our master's voice," she said to Amanda with a smile.

Amanda rose along with the older woman. "Well, I have to go back to the dessert table anyway. There's still strawberry, blueberry, and about four other berries to sample."

Helen chuckled. "I see you've been warned."

"In spades. I played a careful game of word association with myself just to make sure I'd know and remember who made which dessert. I don't want to offend anybody."

"If you get it right, in the next election we'll put your name on the ballot for mayor."

Amanda was still smiling as she went to the dessert table. She had rather hoped to find most of the remaining pies all sampled out, but there was still enough left of each to provide one more generous serving or several test-size ones. Sighing, she got a clean plate and began cutting tiny wedges to sample.

Strawberry belonged to Mavis Sisk, who had red hair. Blueberry belonged to Sharon Melton, who was wearing a pair of blue topaz earrings and a blue ribbon in her hair. Amy Bliss, the preacher's wife, had contributed raspberry (for some reason, Amanda had no trouble connecting those two without benefit of further association). And a fine gooseberry pie belonged to a very sweet older lady with snow-white hair named Betty Lamb. Goose—lamb; it wasn't perfect, but it worked for Amanda.

"You going to eat all that?"

Amanda looked up at Walker McLellan and felt her rueful good humor evaporate. She also felt her pulse skip a beat. She'd been aware of him all evening, aware of being watched by him. She had known that sooner or later, he would come to her—with, no doubt, some new accusation or variation on an old one.

Her memory of their last encounter, of his cold face and harsh voice, helped stiffen her spine and raise her chin—which was all to the good. She felt disturbingly vulnerable, and needed all the help she could get. He was angry; she couldn't see it, but she could feel it.

"I have to sample," she said, trying for a light note. "Wouldn't want to hurt the ladies' feelings."

"Your accent's getting thicker," he said.

"You just haven't heard it in a while." Amanda wished she could take back the remark, annoyed at herself for letting him know she'd noticed his absence these last days.

"I've been busy," he said. "Why don't you ask me about the will?"

"Maybe I'm not interested in the will."

"Or maybe you're just content to wait—knowing it's only a matter of time now until you have it all."

Amanda began to turn away, but stopped when she felt his hand grip her arm. "Let go of me, Walker," she told him evenly.

"I have a question."

"Let go of me." She was glad the music from the band kept them from being overheard, but she was all too aware that more than one pair of eyes watched them curiously. *That* would be all she needed—to make a scene with the Daulton family lawyer.

He held her arm and her gaze for a deliberately long moment, then released her arm. "It's a simple question. You're left-handed, aren't you?"

"Yes."

"Amanda Daulton," he said, "was right-handed."

She smiled. "I'm surprised it's taken you this long to bring up the subject. Wasn't it on your list of verifying traits? Black hair, gray eyes, AB positive blood —right-handedness."

"No. It wasn't on my list." His voice was tight.

"Maybe you're slipping, counselor." Amanda went back to her table, now deserted with the doctor gone, and tried to keep a pleasant expression on her face for the benefit of onlookers. Of which there were many. She put her plate down, but before she could sit, Walker was there and had her hand.

"Dance with me," he said curtly.

It was the last thing Amanda wanted to do, but she couldn't jerk away or protest with so many people watching—and he knew it, damn him. He led her toward the tiled area around the pool, where several couples were dancing to a slow, rather erotic beat, and pulled her firmly into his arms.

She had never been so close to him, and Amanda was overwhelmingly aware of the fact. His body was harder than she would have expected, his arms stronger and, curiously, more possessive. He smelled of something sharp and tangy, a woodsy aftershave and pipe smoke, she thought, even though she'd never seen him smoke a pipe. The combination was pleasant.

Too pleasant.

He moved easily to the music, guided her easily. He was looking down at her; as always, she could feel it. She lifted her own gaze reluctantly and only when she thought she would be able to hide her thoughts from him.

"You've had time to think about it," he told her, his voice still abrupt. "So let's have it. How did a right-handed girl become a left-handed woman?"

"You're so sure I have an answer?"

"I'm counting on it."

Amanda wondered at that reply, offered with every word bitten off, but gave him the answer anyway. "I broke my right arm a couple of years after we left here. It was a long time healing, and there was nerve damage. I had to learn to be left-handed. Even now, my right arm's weaker."

"Was this the same accident that caused your fear of horses?" Walker asked mockingly.

She ignored the derision. "No. The truth is, I fell out of a tree."

"That was careless of you."

Amanda held on to her temper with difficulty. "Wasn't it? And all because I wanted to see inside a bird's nest. Which turned out to be empty, wouldn't you know. So I ended up with a broken arm and a concussion."

He nodded, but it was the gesture of a man who had been given something expected and was, therefore, unsurprised. "Very good. Simple, but filled with creative details. Believable. And I'll bet if I had a talk with Helen, she'd tell me it was medically quite possible."

The beat of the music slowed even more, and Amanda had to fight a sudden urge to break away from him. She hated this, hated being held by him when he looked at her this way, when his voice bit and his eyes scorned. She hated it.

"It's the truth," she said.

"You wouldn't know the truth if you fell over it," Walker told her.

Amanda felt a hot throbbing begin behind her eyes. *Oh, God, not a migraine.* But, of course, with her luck that's what it would be. She'd had only a few in her life, but those had been memorable. They tended to be triggered by stress. She felt very stressed at the moment.

The music stopped with a flourish just then, and Amanda pulled away from Walker with more haste than grace, not caring now how it would look to those watching. She returned to her table, where pieces of pie waited to be sampled, and she thought that if he followed her and kept hammering away at her, she'd dump the pie in his lap.

He didn't follow immediately, but came soon and brought drinks with him. Wine.

"No, thank you," she said politely, trying the strawberry. It was good, very good. "I'm not drinking." The blueberry had been even better, and the gooseberry was remarkable.

"To keep a clear head?" he asked mockingly, sitting in the chair beside hers with the air of a man who wasn't going anywhere anytime soon.

"If you say so."

Amy Bliss, Amanda decided, had better have talents other than pie baking, because her raspberry pie was lousy. Naturally, Amanda wouldn't *tell* her that—so what could she say? That the crust was crusty?

"Amanda, stop picking at that pie and look at me."

"I'm not picking, I'm sampling." *At least he said my name.* It was so hard to get the man to say her name. You would have thought he expected to be drawn and quartered for it.

The throbbing was still there, behind her eyes, and now she was aware of a burning, tingling sensation spreading all through her body. Her tongue felt strange, almost . . . numb. And she was getting queasy.

Oh, God, what if Amy Bliss's terrible raspberry pie was making her sick? That would be just dandy, that would. Couldn't turn *that* reaction into something complimentary.

"Amanda—"

She got up abruptly and carried her plate to the dessert table. Halfway there, the queasiness increased, and dizziness swept over her. She managed the last few steps, putting her plate down with a thud, then went a little beyond the table, where a clump of azalea bushes bordered the outer edge of the patio.

She had to get away from all these people. And something to hold on to would be helpful, because her legs felt damnably shaky. Too shaky to keep moving as they were ordered to do.

"Amanda."

Everything was getting blurry, and a chill presentiment of dread touched Amanda. This wasn't normal, was it? Her mouth and throat felt numb and the nausea clawed at her. With a helpless little moan, she bent forward and was violently sick into the azaleas.

Strong hands held her shoulders while she retched and heaved, and when she was finally emptied of everything she had ever eaten in her entire life, he eased her upright and held her so that she was leaning back against him. She felt his hand on her brow, gentle and blessedly cool.

It was, she realized dimly, very quiet. The band no longer played. Somewhere behind her, the guests were apparently staring at her in horrified disbelief. Even the crickets had fallen silent.

People of Daulton—meet Amanda.

"Oh, God," she whispered.

"It's all right." Walker's voice was low, calm. "A little too much of everything, that's all. Including me." His hand moved to touch her cheek.

Amanda felt a flare of panic rout embarrassment—because it was as if his fingers touched someone else's cheek rather than hers. Her face was numb. Everything was still blurry, and she thought—she was sure—it was getting harder to breathe.

"Walker, I—" A sudden pain knifed through her middle, and she cried out.

"Amanda?"

She couldn't answer him. It was terrifying, what

was happening to her, and she couldn't control it. She thought that her legs were no longer under her, thought that, for an instant, she was looking into Walker's alarmed eyes and was trying to tell him something dreadfully important.

But then everything was going dim and she felt as if all the strength had rushed out of her. There was an awful, crushing weight on her chest, punishing her for every precious breath she drew. And then a wave of blackness swamped her, and coldness flowed through her as though her veins had filled with ice water.

She was so cold.

"What's wrong?"

"I don't know, dammit. Helen—"

"She's having trouble breathing. Keep her propped up like that. Maggie, my bag—oh, thanks. Her pulse is weak, way too slow. Wait, while I . . . Jesus, her pressure's falling like a rock."

"Do something!"

"Let's get her inside. Hurry."

Amanda was, on some level of her consciousness, aware of things around her. People. Movement. Sounds. She heard the muted thunder of Jesse's voice, harsh and demanding as usual. She heard the unfamiliar sound of Walker's lazy drawl sharpened and imperative. She heard the newly recognized voice of Helen, brisk and capable.

She kept drifting away. She was cold, so cold she thought she'd never be warm again, and for a long time it hurt to breathe. Unpleasant things were done to her, and she couldn't summon the will or the voice to stop them. Needles pricked her, and foul liquid was forced down her throat, and then there was another miserable bout of vomiting and she cried weakly, hating the helplessness, while voices soothed her.

Maggie's voice. Kate's. Jesse's voice, always Jesse's. And Walker's voice, she thought, even though it sounded different. Helen telling her she was going to be fine. Now and then a strange voice.

Why wouldn't they all leave her alone, just go away and let her die in peace?

"We'd better let them out of my room and in here before they tear the doors down."

"The doctor—"

"I'll take the responsibility. They know something's wrong, and they won't settle down until they're with her."

Finally, she was getting a little warmer, and the crushing weight on her chest had eased. Things were getting better. She didn't feel quite so panicky now, so frightened by her body being out of control. Her heart had stopped jumping around inside her, and the pain faded. Whatever she was lying on was no longer twirling about the room.

She just felt very weak, very tired, and wanted to sleep.

"At least a dozen more, Helen says. Varying degrees, but none as severe as Amanda's. The party's going to be remembered for quite a while, Jesse."

"What the hell did it? Was the meat bad?"

"J.T.'s sent samples of practically everything off to be analyzed, just in case we have a bigger problem, but Helen thinks it was baneberry."

"What?"

"Yeah. Sharon Melton bought her blueberries at a roadside stand, and now it looks as if there were baneberries mixed in. It's hard to tell . . .

". . . the difference unless you look closely. Sharon didn't. She's horrified, naturally." Walker kept his voice low, because Amanda's bedroom door was open and even though she appeared to be sleeping deeply, he didn't want to disturb her.

Jesse leaned against the doorjamb, his gaze fixed on the still figure in the big antique bed. He hadn't ventured far from Amanda's room in more than twelve hours; it was nearly noon and he hadn't slept at all the night before.

"She'll be all right, Jesse."

The older man looked at Walker, his eyes burning silver. "You heard Helen. If Amanda hadn't gotten sick so fast and thrown up the stuff, she could have died."

"But she isn't going to die. She'll probably wake up in the next hour or so, and by tomorrow morning she'll be up and about with no harm done."

"No harm done." Jesse returned his gaze to the bed where, on either side of Amanda's legs, a Doberman guard dog lay quietly. An IV bag hung on a metal stand by the bed, dripping fluids into her body to replace what had been lost and restore the balance of electrolytes.

"And there's nothing you could have done to prevent it," Walker reminded him, as he had before now. "It was a stupid accident, Jesse. Baneberries have been mistaken for blueberries before now, and probably will be again."

Jesse nodded, but his thoughts seemed far away. "If I had lost her again . . . I was angry with her, Walker, did you know that?"

"I knew there was some tension."

"Did you know why?"

"No."

Jesse looked at him with a twisted smile. "I told you she hadn't asked anything of me, didn't I?"

Walker nodded. "You mean she—"

"She doesn't want anything. *Anything.* She doesn't want Glory. Can you beat that?"

"What do you mean, she doesn't want it?"

"I mean she sat down in a chair in front of my desk and told me that if I signed a new will leaving this place or the businesses to her she would walk away from Glory and never come back. She said that if I thought I could get away with signing a new will on the sly, after I was gone she'd have a deed of gift drawn up, turning the entire estate over to Kate, Reece, and Sully."

"And you believed her?"

"She meant every word. I've been trying all week to make her back down, but she wouldn't give an inch. She said she hoped Glory would always be a place she could visit, but that it could never be home to her, not the way it is to the rest of us."

Walker looked at Jesse, knowing very well that anger had hidden hurt; the old man would never understand how anyone—far less a blood Daulton—could not find Glory the most wonderful place on earth. But he also respected strength, and it was clear Amanda had won his respect with her resolve.

As for Walker, he was baffled. "I don't get it," he said slowly. "What's her game?"

"Has it ever occurred to you that maybe, just maybe, she isn't playing a game? You're far too cynical for a young man, Walker. Hell, you're too cynical even for a lawyer." Looking suddenly exhausted, Jesse sighed and said, "I think I'll go lie down for a while. But—"

"The nurse will come get you when Amanda wakes up," Walker said, glancing into the bedroom to receive a nod from the uniformed nurse who sat near the bed (unnecessary, Helen had said, but Jesse had insisted).

Jesse started to turn away, then paused. "Do me a favor, Walker. Tell the others that—for now, at least—my old will stands."

"All right." Alone at the doorway of Amanda's room, Walker looked at the silent, still shape, so small in the big bed, and the unaccustomed bewilderment he felt intensified. Questions and conjecture swirled about in his mind.

So many things were wrong. She was too small and too delicate, left-handed instead of right-handed, and far too wary and secretive for a woman who had come home. There were things she should remember and didn't. There were secrets in her eyes, and too much of her story left untold, and too many questions left unanswered.

Yet . . . so many things were also right, or could be. Her coloring and blood type, some of her knowledge, an occasional "memory." Broken arms *could* cause nerve damage, Walker supposed, and handedness *could* therefore, out of necessity, be changed. A gene pool rich with many tall and massive Daultons could produce at least one small and delicate one.

And maybe . . . just maybe . . . greed played no part in her motives for being here.

Walker hesitated for a moment longer in the doorway, remembering that first terrifying moment last night when he had realized that much more was wrong with her than simple nerves. When she had gone limp against him and he had lifted her, when she had looked at him for an instant with the utterly defenseless gaze of a frightened child.

Other terrifying moments had followed in rapid succession. The cold pallor of her shock. Her laborious struggle to breathe and her tumbling blood pressure. Her erratic heartbeat and the low moans that had spoken of pain, and a very, very bad few minutes when she had convulsed.

Like Jesse, Walker had not slept, and like Jesse, he had not ventured far from Amanda's quiet bedroom.

It had been a hectic, anxious night, and he was too tired to think this out, he knew. Too tired to think at all. That had to be it, had to be what was wrong with him, because why else did his chest hurt whenever he looked at her? Why else was he so reluctant to leave her even to go downstairs? He wanted to sit on the edge of her bed and wait until she opened her eyes, until she spoke to him.

He wanted to be reassured.

Absurd, of course. Helen had said that Amanda would be fine, and Helen was a fine doctor who knew what she was talking about. So Amanda would be fine. And there was absolutely no reason and no need for him to stand here under the mild gaze of the nurse and stare at Amanda while she slept.

"I'll be downstairs," he told the nurse.

Mrs. Styles nodded placidly. "Yes, sir. She'll be just fine, sir."

With the uncomfortable feeling that the nurse was about to tell him *he'd* be fine as well, Walker abandoned the doorway at last and went downstairs to make a baffling announcement.

Amanda opened her eyes with a start. She was looking up at the canopy of her bed, red velvet trimmed with a fringe. The fringe appeared to dance for a moment, but only a moment.

"So, you're awake."

Turning her head quickly was a mistake; it felt as if a dozen hammers slammed down at once. Amanda closed her eyes, then opened them to see a middle-aged woman—apparently a nurse—rise from a chair and come toward her.

Two deep growls greeted the nurse's approach, and Amanda turned her aching head again, bewildered, then lifted it a bit to see Bundy and Gacy stretched out on the bed on either side of her legs.

"Now, we've been through this," the nurse told the dogs severely. "I'm here to help, not hurt her. Be quiet, the both of you."

Amanda fumbled her left arm from the covers and reached her hand down to pet the dogs. "It's all right, guys." Was that her voice? So . . . so weak?

"We'll just raise you a bit," the nurse said, slipping her hands behind Amanda and lifting with expert care, and then deftly placing another pillow behind her head and shoulders. "You'll be a bit dizzy for a moment, but that'll pass."

She was, and it did. When the room had stopped spinning, Amanda opened her eyes again cautiously. So far, so good. She looked down at her right arm, into which was stuck an IV needle. What on earth?

Then it all began to come back to her. The party. A sea of mostly friendly faces. Some probing questions, but nothing she hadn't been able to handle. Feeling herself relax—too soon, as it had turned out. The edgy clash with Walker. The sudden wave of sickness that had been—obviously had been—more than just a lousy piece of pie.

"The IV can come out a little later, Miss Daulton. I'm Mrs. Styles; I work in Dr. Chantry's clinic in town."

Amanda looked at her. "I—I see. I don't quite remember . . . that is, what happened to me?"

"A stupid mistake." The nurse shook her head. "Baneberries mistaken for blueberries and baked in a pie. They're terribly poisonous, you see, and it's difficult to tell the two apart; both grow wild in these parts during the summer, and both ripened early this year. A dozen people besides you got sick from that pie." She smiled suddenly. "You wouldn't think a single pie could feed more than a dozen people, would you?"

"Sampling." Amanda conjured a rueful smile of her own. "We were all sampling the desserts. So—nobody had a regular-size serving of anything."

"Ah, I see. That would explain it, of course."

Amanda shifted a bit, wishing her headache would go away. An aftereffect of the poisonous berries, she supposed. Or of the sheer violence of her body's reaction to the poison.

"You'll be feeling better soon," Mrs. Styles assured her. "Dr. Chantry will be by to check on you in an hour or so, and after that I'm sure she'll say you're ready for a light meal."

Since her stomach barely flinched at the idea of food, Amanda thought she might be brave enough to try it; she was unexpectedly hungry. Sighing, she said, "I guess I made quite an impression on the neighbors."

Mrs. Styles clearly understood the mortification behind that statement, because she patted Amanda's arm and said comfortingly, "I wouldn't let myself get upset about that if I were you, Miss Daulton. Everybody was just vexed that it happened at all. Why, Dr. Chantry told me that when Mr. McLellan carried you into the house, the rest of them were so worried that not one guest left until after midnight, when it was certain you'd be all right."

"That was . . . kind of everyone."

The nurse smiled at her. "Do you feel up to having visitors? Mr. Jesse's been frantic; he wanted to be called as soon as you woke."

Amanda nodded and watched Mrs. Styles bustle from the room. When she was alone in the bedroom except for the watchful dogs, she looked at them, her free hand still petting glossy black fur and velvety muzzles. Two pairs of liquid brown eyes gazed back at her.

"Carried me," she murmured.

"Well, I'd say you were pretty lucky," Helen Chantry said, closing her little black doctor's bag and sitting on the edge of Amanda's bed. "You got most of the stuff out of your system on your own."

"Please," Amanda said, "don't remind me." The two women were alone in the bedroom; Jesse had taken the dogs with him at Helen's request, and Mrs. Styles was downstairs supervising the preparation of a bland meal for Amanda.

Helen smiled. "Embarrassing, I suppose, but it's the best thing that could have happened, Amanda. The poison didn't remain in your stomach long enough for much to be absorbed. Actually, your reaction was the fastest and most violent I've ever seen—and I've seen numerous cases of baneberry poisoning over the years."

Amanda rubbed her right arm, which now bore only a discreet Band-Aid where the IV needle had been. "The nurse said . . . other people got sick?"

"Yes, but it was hours later, after we'd stabilized you. I had my hands full last night, let me tell you. But most of the other reactions were fairly mild; we were extremely lucky that no one got enough poison for it to be fatal." Helen smiled suddenly. "By the way—it may comfort you to know that everyone who had a piece of that pie was forced to upchuck. I wasn't about to take any chances."

"I hope Jesse didn't have to—"

"No, he didn't have any of the pie. As a matter of fact, you and Maggie were the only ones here at Glory who did. Most of the other unlucky victims were guests." Helen chuckled. "And once they realized what I meant to do, several of them tried to deny eating the pie. Amy Bliss held to it tooth and nail that she hadn't eaten a morsel—right up until she got sick with absolutely no help from me."

"It sounds like *you* were popular last night."

"Oh, definitely."

Amanda couldn't help but smile. "I thought it was Amy's awful raspberry pie making me sick."

"You weren't alone in thinking that. Several even expressed the hope that it would cure her of this misguided urge to bake. However . . ."

Amanda said slowly, "You know . . . I sort of remember it all, now that I've had time to think about it. I mean, my eyes were closed, and I couldn't say anything, but I heard most of what was going on around me. I think I could even repeat some of the conversations verbatim."

"That's interesting." Helen frowned slightly.

"Why?"

"Well . . . it isn't the usual reaction to the stage of baneberry poisoning you'd reached; by then, unconsciousness tends to be total. Your pulse was slow, too."

"I don't understand."

Helen hesitated, then said, "The characteristics of baneberry poisoning are similar to those of digitalis poisoning. You had most of the symptoms. Nausea, vomiting, convulsions, shock. But your blood pressure dropping like that . . . When it first started, you were dizzy?"

"Yes."

"Sharp pains in your head?"

"I noticed a headache just before I got sick. But it was more a dull throbbing. I thought I was getting a migraine. Then there was a . . . a burning, tingling sensation spreading through me. My tongue felt funny, numb." Amanda frowned, concentrating. "Then the dizziness and nausea, blurred vision. After that I got sick, very sick. The numbness in my mouth spread over my face; that's what really scared me. And then my vision was getting worse, dimming, and I knew it was more than just bad pie."

"You also had trouble breathing."

Amanda nodded. "It was awful."

"Chest pain?"

"I think . . . there was some, yeah. As a matter of fact, I hurt all over. My stomach was cramping even after I was sick, and then later . . ."

"What?"

"I was cold. Terribly cold." Amanda looked at the doctor's grave face and felt a different kind of chill. "So—what does it mean?"

Helen was silent for a moment, frowning, then said carefully, "The treatment for most poisons is fairly consistent; get the stuff out of the body if at all possible, neutralize it otherwise, and then treat symptoms. That's what I did with you. There wasn't really time to think about it. But now that I can, now that you can tell me what you were experiencing . . . most of those symptoms aren't consistent with baneberry poisoning, Amanda."

"Then what *are* they consistent with?"

Again, Helen hesitated. "If I hadn't just completed a toxicology course not six weeks ago, I probably wouldn't have that answer; there are so many kinds of poison."

"But you suspect a particular kind?"

"It could be almost anything. But . . . the numbness and loss of vision, the low blood pressure and slow pulse, the difficulty breathing, and especially the chills . . . It could have been monkshood. Offhand, I can't think of anything else that would have produced just those symptoms. And if it was monkshood . . . it shouldn't have been put into a pie by mistake."

Amanda didn't respond for a long minute, and when she did, her voice was calm. "We're speculating, when we can't possibly *know* anything. There were samples sent off to be analyzed, weren't there?"

"Standard procedure, in case we have to deal with botulism or some other kind of food poisoning." Helen shook her head. "But all the labs are snowed under; that's why your DNA test is taking so long. It could be weeks before we get results." She paused, then added neutrally, "Unless, of course, I tell J.T. that I suspect deliberate poisoning. As sheriff, he could request the lab work be expedited."

Amanda shook her head immediately, even before Helen finished speaking. "I just had an unusual reaction to the baneberries. That's possible, isn't it? Likely, even?"

"Possible, I'll give you. Likely? I don't think so."

"You said nobody else got as sick as I did, and more than a dozen of us ate the pie. So—"

Helen shook her head. "The symptoms of the others were definitely consistent with baneberry poisoning. And I can't explain that—unless you got something extra. Unless something was added to your piece of pie after you cut it, and before you ate it. Is that possible? I mean, was there an opportunity for someone to slip something onto your plate when you weren't looking?"

Amanda remembered putting her plate down on the table, and then moving away to dance with

Walker. She couldn't recall having even glanced back at the table during the dance, and had no idea who might have wandered past bearing a pinch of—what had Helen said? Monkshood? Almost anyone could have done it. Walker was, actually, the only person she could rule out—if, of course, someone *had* deliberately tried to poison her that way.

"Amanda—"

"Helen, it was an accident, that's all. Just an accident." Amanda held the older woman's skeptical gaze with her own. "Until we know differently, that's all it was."

"And I suppose," Helen said, "you'd rather I didn't mention any of this to anyone else?"

"I'd rather you didn't. It would only upset everyone—especially Jesse."

"I don't like it."

Amanda hesitated, then said, "Helen, yesterday there might have been a reason for someone to want to . . . get rid of me. Today there isn't. I had told Jesse I didn't want to inherit any of this, and today he told me he'd do as I asked and wouldn't change his will in my favor. The others know it now."

"I still don't like it," Helen said. "If we do nothing, somebody could think they'd gotten away with an attempt against you."

"What if we *did* do something—make a big deal out of this and claim I'd been deliberately poisoned—and it turned out we were wrong? The family's under enough strain."

"You could go away for a few weeks," Helen suggested. "Until we know for sure. Remove temptation, so to speak."

Amanda shook her head. "No, I can't do that."

Helen looked at her impassively. "Because the

DNA test results would make it impossible for you to come back?"

Amanda managed a smile, though it felt a bit strained. "Wasn't it you who first told me that I could have pints of Daulton blood and the test might still come back inconclusive?"

"Yes. I also told you that if you had no Daulton blood, the test would almost surely tell us that."

"I thought you believed I was a Daulton."

"I do. In fact—I'm fairly sure you are."

Amanda gazed somewhat warily into Helen's grave face. "How come that sounds like a qualified answer in spite of all the positive words?"

Helen smiled slightly. "My opinion doesn't really mean much, does it? The point is, Jesse accepts you, and that makes you a threat to anyone else who might covet any part of his estate—especially Glory. Why won't you go away for a few weeks, Amanda?"

"I can't. Jesse doesn't have much time left. And . . . I think if I miss this chance to find out what happened twenty years ago, it'll never come again."

"Why not?"

"I don't know—it's just what I feel. I have to stay here, have to be here now." She shook her head. "Besides, we're both jumping to conclusions. It was probably just a simple accident, and I had an unusual reaction. That's all."

"If I've learned anything in my life, Amanda, I've learned that nothing is ever as simple as it seems. As long as Jesse is alive, he *can* change his will in your favor. We all know he wants to. We all know he has a tendency to get what he wants."

"I have the same tendency," Amanda told her.

After a moment, Helen said, "When Walker brought you into the clinic for your blood test, I knew you were an intelligent woman. Don't disappoint me, Amanda. Be careful."

Amanda could only nod in response to that. But when she was alone in the bedroom, her head still aching, she had to ask herself if she was intelligent at all.

Eight

THE THUNDER WOKE HER LATE THAT night, the noise crashing and rolling as if the world were being torn apart. After a moment of disorientation, Amanda lay watching the room being lit with flashes of stark light and listened to the rain and the thunder and petted the dogs—who were sleeping on her bed for, Amanda had told herself, this one night.

It was the first storm since she had arrived here almost two weeks ago. It had been a quiet spring, everybody said, and so the summer would no doubt be a rough one.

Amanda wasn't afraid of storms, but they had always made her feel restless and jumpy. And she had been in bed all day, which was not something she was used to, so the restlessness was even stronger than usual. The clock on her nightstand told her it was after midnight, and nothing had to tell her she wouldn't sleep for quite a while.

She sat up and pushed back the covers, moving carefully just to make sure there was no lingering dizziness. But when she was on her feet beside the bed, it was to find herself clear-headed and steady, which was a relief. She slid her feet into a pair of fuzzy bedroom slippers, got her robe from the chair near the bed, and, accompanied by the dogs, left her bedroom.

The upstairs hall was dim but not dark, lit by several lamps turned down low. Amanda moved quietly; she wasn't especially worried about waking anyone, since there were no occupied bedrooms between her room and the main stairs, but after the previous night's commotion, she certainly didn't want to even take the chance of disturbing anyone.

She paused at the top of the stairs, watching the dogs start down the carpeted treads, then turned her head as a hint of motion caught her eye.

At the other end of the hall, where the master bedroom was located and where the rear staircase led down to the back of the main house, a faint light could be seen underneath Jesse's door. There was no lamp nearby, but it was easy to see Maggie because she wore a filmy white nightgown. She reached Jesse's door, opened it, and slipped inside. A few moments later, the faint light inside the room went out.

After an instant of surprise, Amanda said to herself, *Well, why not?* Maybe it was sex, or maybe just comfort. If it was comfort the two shared, who could wonder at it? For all his strength and autocratic ways, Jesse was a man facing his own mortality, and at such times even the strong might need to lean on someone else, however briefly or secretly. And if it was sex . . . well, why not?

Jesse had been a widower for forty years, and if he

was the typical Daulton male, sex was an important—not to say vital—part of his life. Judging by what Amanda had read, Daulton men were sexually active right up until burial—several had fathered children into their eighties—and given his potent energy even in these last months of his life, it was likely Jesse enjoyed sex as well as he enjoyed all of life's other pleasures.

Maggie had come into this house an unattached young woman, undoubtedly attractive, and had probably fallen in love with Jesse—who'd been only thirty-five then and no doubt at the peak of his vitality—early on; he had just lost a beloved wife, and might well have reached out to her at some point because he needed comfort—or only sex.

Frowning a little, Amanda followed the dogs down the dim stairs. She couldn't help wondering if Maggie had ever hoped Jesse might marry her. Surely she had; a woman of her generation must have found the prospect of being a lifelong mistress impossible to envision, particularly at a time and in a part of the country where such a thing, if publicly known, would have been viewed with harsh disapproval.

But in all probability, Amanda thought, Maggie had never imagined that relationship would go on for so many years. Probably, she had expected marriage all along and had, finally and perhaps only recently, looked back at the decades with a shock of realization.

Jesse was dying . . . and Maggie would never be his wife.

I'm being fanciful. I don't know any of this.

But if she was right, Amanda thought, it was, at least on the face of it, yet another black mark against Jesse. To keep a woman in his house for so many years, first as a nurse to his child and then as his housekeeper, paying her for those duties, and all the time to receive her into his bed completely on his own selfish terms was . . . it was positively medieval.

Amanda paused on the landing as a flash of lightning illuminated the old grandfather clock there. She looked at the clock without really seeing it, then shook her head and went on.

It was none of her business, of course. Maggie was certainly a grown woman and able to leave; she wasn't a slave or an indentured servant, after all. And, anyway, Amanda didn't *know* she was right about any of this. For all she knew, it was Maggie who disdained marriage, preferring no legal tie, and Jesse who wanted one.

Except that Jesse *did* tend to get what he wanted.

Those thoughts and speculations fled when Amanda reached the kitchen. There was a light on, but she was still a little surprised when she saw Kate sitting at the small wooden table with a mug before her. The older woman wore a silk robe over her nightgown and her hair flowed loosely over her shoulders. She looked younger, and peculiarly vulnerable.

"I'm sorry," Amanda said as she and the dogs paused just inside the room. "I didn't know anyone else was up."

Kate shook her head a little. "I hate storms," she said. "I thought some herbal tea might help me relax." She smiled briefly. "It isn't working."

Amanda waited for booming thunder to diminish, then said, "I don't like them much myself." She got a glass from the cabinet and went to the refrigerator to pour milk; Helen had instructed her to stick to bland food and drink for a day or two and, anyway, she thought it might help her sleep.

She hesitated, wondering if Kate wanted to be alone, but when the other woman gestured slightly, she sat down on the other side of the table. Interesting, she thought. Kate had been freezing her out for days.

"You're obviously feeling better," Kate said.

Amanda nodded. "Much." She sipped her milk and waited somewhat warily.

Kate looked at the mug her long fingers held, then said, "I'm sorry about what happened at the party."

"It wasn't your fault," Amanda said neutrally.

"Still, I'm sorry." Kate was silent for a moment. Then, awkwardly, she said, "I'm sorry about all of it, Amanda. The way I've been acting, I mean."

So you did care about Jesse's will, after all. Either that, or . . . Or had she been shocked, perhaps, by the reality of what a pinch of poison could do? Either way, it appeared that Kate wanted to make peace.

Amanda conjured a disarming smile. "Kate, I'm a stranger to you. Even more, I'm a stranger who—unintentionally, please believe that—stepped between you and your father. If you want the truth, I'm surprised you've been as polite as you have been."

Kate looked at her for a moment and then, with obvious difficulty, said, "You didn't come between us. I wanted to believe you had. Tried to believe it. But . . ." She shook her head. "Nothing would have been different if you hadn't been here, not for me. And maybe it's time I accepted that."

Amanda didn't know what to say, but she made a hesitant attempt. "I have a friend who grew up in a very bad situation. Her father . . . never should have been a parent. He wasn't physically abusive, but nothing she ever did, in her entire life, was good enough for him. She grew up believing she was worthless. It was only after he died and she no longer looked at herself through his eyes that she began to see herself as she really was. It took a long time for her to heal from what he'd done to her, but she did heal."

Kate ventured a small smile. "We're all so . . . bound to our fathers, aren't we?"

"Whether we like it or not." Amanda smiled responsively. She listened to a roll of thunder, then said, "I have no clear memories of my father, not really."

"Brian was very much like Jesse," Kate said of her brother.

"Was he?"

"Oh, yes."

Amanda waited, a little tense, and her patience was rewarded when Kate went on in a musing tone.

"I suppose it would have been remarkable if he hadn't grown up very like Jesse; he was encouraged by Jesse to believe that what he thought and wanted was more important than the thoughts and opinions and needs of anyone else. And he had the Daulton temper and pride, so of course that made it even worse, made him more . . . arrogant.

"He was thirteen years older than I was, and already an Olympic-class rider by the time I reached school age, already famous in his sport. He rode a lot in those days, year-round, so he wasn't home much. But when he was home he . . . made his presence felt. He'd been spoiled, as I said. Jesse gave him anything he wanted, and he never had to work for a living. But he was kind to me, in his way. Maybe he felt sorry for me."

"Or maybe," Amanda suggested, "he liked you."

Kate smiled. "Maybe."

"You were only—what?—seven or eight when he brought my mother here to Glory?"

"Seven. I remember thinking that Christine was the prettiest lady in the whole world."

Amanda waited a moment, then said, "They—we—had a place in Kentucky, I remember vaguely. It's where I went to school most of the year."

"That was Christine's idea," Kate said. "Maybe she even insisted on it just so they'd have privacy and she could get Brian away from showing for at least part of the year—I don't know. But I know Jesse bought the house for Brian *and* set him up in those equipment stores only because Christine wanted them to have a place of their own. But Jesse insisted they come back here from spring to fall, and since Brian wanted to ride and enjoyed the cachet of riding for Glory, he was more than willing. Christine was . . . less enthusiastic."

"I know she usually didn't go with him when he was following the show circuit."

"No, she stayed here. Looking back now, I guess she was pretty bored most of the time, but then it seemed she had things to do. She loved the garden. She read a lot. And she rode some, even though it wasn't her favorite pastime. She also spent a lot of time with me."

"Maggie said something like that."

"Christine was very kind to me, especially in those first few years." Kate hesitated, then said, "Once, during her second summer here, I even heard her fighting with Jesse over me. She called him a monster for ignoring me."

"What happened after that?" Amanda asked curiously.

Kate's smile was brief. "Every summer after that, until I was eighteen, I went to camp for several weeks. Sometimes two or three separate summer camps."

Amanda winced. Jesse's methods of handling criticism were, to say the least, telling. "I'm sure Mother didn't intend—"

"I know she didn't. I never blamed her."

There was a short silence, both women listening to the diminishing sounds of the storm and sipping their drinks. Amanda hesitated to probe too deeply, especially since this was the first time Kate had opened up with her, but she was too conscious of time passing not to take advantage of the opportunity.

"Kate . . . you were here that summer. And the night my mother left."

"I was here." Kate frowned a little as she looked down at her mug of tea.

"Do you know why she left?"

Thunder grumbled outside, a storm exhausted by its own violence. Kate lifted her gaze and looked gravely at Amanda. "No," she said. "I have no idea why she left."

Just as she had with Sully, Amanda got the distinct impression that Kate was lying. But before she could even decide if it would be wise to push, Kate was going on quietly.

"Is it really so important to answer that question, Amanda? It was a long time ago, after all. Brian and Christine are gone, and knowing what—oh, final blow, I suppose—ended their marriage can't really matter now. Can it?"

"It does to me."

"Why?" Kate shook her head. "You were a little girl; whatever happened obviously had nothing to do with you. If you were blaming yourself, I mean."

Amanda frowned. "You know, it's funny . . . I never did. Blame myself, I mean. I know kids often do, but I never did. It's just that I have to know what happened. It was all so . . . abrupt, her leaving."

Kate hesitated, then sighed. "Not really. She wasn't happy, Amanda, we all knew that. Jesse was at least partly to blame, something he'd never admit. But he insisted they come home for nearly half of every year, and he thought it was fine for Christine to be stuck here while her husband was off participating in a sport she had no love of. It put enormous strain on a marriage that was never strong to begin with."

"Couldn't Jesse see what was happening then?" Amanda asked. "Couldn't my father?"

Kate smiled a bit thinly. "I said they were very much alike. Neither of them believed she'd leave, no matter what. She loved Glory, they both knew that. You were happy here, and your happiness was important to her. And, once married to Brian, Christine was a Daulton. She was expected to adapt herself to her husband's life and his wishes."

Amanda scowled. "That's . . . absurd."

"Oh, I agree," Kate said, obviously realizing that *absurd* had been chosen over a less polite word. "But remember how much the world has changed in thirty years. They were married in sixty-two; the sexual revolution was just getting under way, and as far as most people were concerned, women's lib was hardly more than a gleam in a few hopeful eyes. The Daulton men were worse than most, but they weren't so different in what they expected of their wives."

"Still."

"Yes—still." Kate shook her head wonderingly. "They really didn't have a good excuse, did they? You'd think that educated and supposedly worldly men—even then—would have seen what was coming, would have recognized that women were changing. But . . . This is an isolated place in a lot of ways, and people tend to cling to what they know. The younger generations are changing, of course, but the older ones are still stuck in the general vicinity of 1950."

Amanda finished her milk and sat there turning the glass slowly, absently. "So you're convinced that it was only a matter of time until my mother left here?"

"I'm afraid so. I know she tried to tell Brian she

was unhappy, but either he didn't hear her or else he believed it was something she'd get over."

Thinking of the possible affair conducted in the weeks before Christine had run away from Glory, Amanda said cautiously, "But she was happier that last summer. I think . . . I remember she was happier. Wasn't she?"

Kate looked at her for a moment. "I don't think so. If anything, she was more strained than ever before. I think she was trying. She rode more than usual that summer, and she talked about enrolling at the community college for summer courses. But she was very restless. Almost brittle."

Amanda managed a smile. "Well, my memory's been playing tricks all along. And I was only nine."

"It's natural that summer would be so important to you," Kate said, "but it *was* a long time ago, Amanda. Maybe the best thing you could do would be to just let it go." She got up and took her mug over to the sink, adding, "Now that the storm's passed, I think I'll go back to bed. Good night."

"Good night, Kate." Amanda sat there at the table for some time after the older woman had gone. She didn't believe Kate had told all she knew of that last summer, but at least she had offered a bit more information about Brian and Christine Daulton. And at least there was, clearly, a thawing of Kate's frozen attitude.

But Amanda would have been a lot happier if that thaw had begun *before* she had eaten a piece of blueberry pie.

Kate eased back on the reins and Sebastian, well trained as well as familiar with her cues since she had ridden him for more than ten years, obediently slowed his gait to an easy walk. It was pleasant on the trail, the air so early this Monday morning still holding the damp cool of dawn, and the storm the night before had left behind it a freshness that made all the noise and fury seem almost worthwhile.

This is ridiculous. I should not be doing this.

He probably wouldn't be at the waterfall anyway. Just because he'd ridden up this way . . . And if he *was* there, what kind of reception did she really expect from him?

The harsh words Ben had flung at her more than a week before still ached in her. For hours after he had left her in the garden, she had been sure she hated him. But then that night, Jesse had talked of changing his will, and it seemed to Kate that her whole world was built on unsteady ground.

It hadn't gotten better.

The only thing in her life that had never been complicated was sex. That was why she felt this longing for Ben, of course. He could make her forget everything else. He could make her feel like a woman worth something, a woman who meant something to a man—if only as a bedmate.

Or, at least, he could if he would.

Kate was more than a little puzzled at herself for this urge to repair her relationship with Ben. There were, after all, other men available who would welcome sex for its own sake. Why not find herself another lover? Kate was not vain, but finding willing lovers had never been difficult, and she didn't expect it would be this time. So, why didn't she?

She had never let herself get close enough to any man for the loss of him to hurt her—or even disturb her. In fact, she seldom knew much about her lovers beyond their skill and the way their bodies felt against hers. She had never needed to know more. They had been names connected to faces and adept hands and male bodies. They had not, really, been people to her. She had never been interested in their thoughts or feelings, only in the physical sensations she could rouse in their bodies and they could rouse in hers.

She had never let herself . . . *personalize* sex.

But Ben . . . Something had happened with Ben. Something that frightened her, and yet drew her irresistibly. Ben had the power to hurt her as easily as he pleased her. Ben had discovered where she was most vulnerable, and had not hesitated to strike her there when she had insulted—when she had *hurt* him.

It hadn't been an easy thing to accept, this longing for Ben. Not for a male body or a pair of skilled hands or the simple relief and release of orgasm. For *Ben*. For the feeling of his muscles moving under her hands, and his silky hair trickling through her fingers, and his hard hips between her thighs. For the sound of his voice husky in desire, and the way he whispered her name, and his guttural groan of satisfaction. For his eyes gleaming down at her in a smile of understanding that made her ache . . .

It had gone beyond desire, what she felt. It had become, now, a kind of force, a thing with a strength and will all its own, tormenting her body and filling her thoughts until nothing else seemed real. She had tried to withstand it, telling herself it was only a momentary insanity. For days, she had stayed away from the stables and avoided any possibility of encountering Ben, and assured herself that she didn't miss him.

Not at all.

So . . . here she was not long after dawn on Monday morning riding along the north trail toward the waterfall. Because Ben had ridden one of his young horses up this way a bit earlier. Here she was following him, tense and scratchy-eyed after a virtually sleepless night and the lonely, storm-prompted establishment of a tentative peace with Amanda—something she was still very unsure of.

With precious few defenses left to her, here she was.

Kate almost turned back when she faced that terrifying fact; her horse, attuned to her, actually stopped on the trail. But she lifted the reins and murmured, "No. Go on." And Sebastian went on obediently.

A long curve in the trail brought them to a clearing where one of several streams on Glory's land tumbled down the steep mountainside and threw itself over a granite precipice to splash into a rocky pool some fifteen feet below. The rush of water was resonant in the morning quiet, but peaceful as well.

Kate didn't really hear it, and she didn't really see it. All she saw was Ben.

He had dismounted from his young horse, and had tethered it to a sapling and loosened the girth, obviously resting the animal after the long climb up the north trail. Then he had seated himself on a broad, flattened boulder at the pool's edge, and was gazing broodingly at the waterfall.

Kate looked at him hungrily. He wore his usual jeans rather than jodhpurs, and scuffed black knee-high riding boots. His white shirt was unbuttoned at his throat, the long sleeves rolled back over tanned forearms. His blond hair fell over his brow, thick and a little shaggy. She loved his hair. It was like silk.

She might have sat there on her still horse for God knows how much longer just staring at him, but Ben's young horse greeted Sebastian eagerly then, and the piercing sound brought Ben's head around swiftly.

He looked at her, not surprised. Not, she thought, anything at all, at least that she could tell. His expression was closed, giving away nothing. His eyes were flat, reflecting only the light of the morning.

Kate hesitated a moment, unsure, damnably unsure. What if she dismounted and tied her horse and walked over to him—and he got on his horse and rode away? What if he ignored her? That would be worse, if he ignored her, because he knew too well how deeply it hurt her to be ignored. She would much rather he said something cruel to her, or laughed at her for her desperate, pathetic need for him. Much rather.

Coming to him like this. *Following* him, for God's sake.

She hated this. She *hated* it.

Stiffening her resolve but conscious of an inner tremor, Kate dismounted and tied Sebastian near Ben's horse. She walked slowly across the clearing, dressed much as he was but in riding breeches rather than jeans and wearing a pale blue blouse. Her hair was, very atypically, loose about her shoulders and held back away from her face with a casual barrette.

Ben watched her approach, and said nothing.

She had tried to think of something nonchalant and meaningless to say. That was what she should have done, of course, just pretending that their last meeting in the garden had not ended as it had—or pretending that she didn't care how it had ended. That was what she wanted to do. Because it was only sex between them, it *was*, and therefore feelings didn't enter into it.

"Did you want something, Kate?"

She wanted to hit him.

"You aren't going to make this easy for me, are you?" she demanded with sudden resentment.

"Make what easy for you?"

"This. Coming to you like this."

Ben turned a little more toward her and wrapped his arms loosely around upraised knees. His expression was still unrevealing. "Is that what you're doing?

Coming to me? Why would you want to do that? I was under the impression that we were finished."

"We are!" But she didn't move, didn't turn away.

Ben looked at her and waited. Patiently.

"You're a son of a bitch, Ben."

He smiled slightly. "And you're repeating yourself, Kate."

"I hate you."

"Still repeating yourself."

"You had no right to—to say what you did."

"Which part? When I asked why I couldn't spend the night with you? When I said I wanted more? Or when I told you Jesse didn't care how many men you slept with?"

"All of it. You—you had no right."

"Then we're definitely finished." His eyes hardened. "I'll say it one last time, Kate. I'm not a toy. I have been, for more than six months, your lover. *That* gives me rights. It gives me the right to sleep in your bed from time to time, and to expect you to sleep in mine. It gives me the right to walk beside you in public. It gives me the right to expect to be treated like a human being. And it gives me the right to tell you the truth even if you don't want to hear it."

She shook her head a little blindly. "You're asking too much."

"I'm not asking, Kate. I'm demanding. From now on, we're public all the way—or we're nothing."

Kate braced her shoulders. "And then? If—if I say yes?"

"Then we have a normal, healthy relationship. We get to know each other. We spend time together with our clothes on. Maybe even go out to dinner and a movie. But it won't be *just* sex anymore. Not ever again."

"I can't," she told him raggedly.

"Then leave." His eyes remained hard, his face impassive. "Get on your horse and get out of here. Go find yourself a toy."

She intended to turn away. Wanted to.

Couldn't.

Her shoulders slumped, and Kate felt hot tears burn her eyes. "Damn you," she said. "Damn you, Ben."

She didn't see him move, but suddenly he was there, his arms around her, and she heard a little moan of incredible relief escape her. She was beyond being embarrassed by it.

"God, you're stubborn," he muttered, kissing her fiercely. "I've been waiting for days."

She felt his fingers tangle in her hair, and nearly purred. "You could have come to me."

"No. You had to come to me. It was your call." He kissed her again, then framed her face in his hands and looked at her with eyes that weren't flat anymore, eyes that were alive. "Katie, I'm sorry I told you about Jesse like that. You needed to know—but not like that."

"Maybe that's exactly how I needed to hear it." She glided a finger across his bottom lip, fascinated by the texture. Something so soft on such a hard man; it was remarkable. It was enthralling. "What you said was so—so naked I couldn't pretend anymore. I had to face it. I didn't have Jesse. I never had him."

"You're fine without Jesse," Ben assured her huskily. "Perfect without him."

She kissed him suddenly. "I'm sorry I hurt you. I never really believed you wanted money."

"I only want you," he said. "God help me. Just my luck to fall for a woman more maddening than a Chinese puzzle. I must be out of my mind."

"I'm too old for you," she whispered.

"Shut up. Idiot. I love you."

Kate didn't know what she would have said to that astonishing revelation if he'd given her a chance to say anything. But he didn't. She was swept up into arms strong enough to carry even a big woman with effortless ease, and a moment later she found herself on a reasonably comfortable grassy bed in a patch of sunlight near the pool.

Even though it was not a particularly private spot (riders tended to use this trail once or twice a day) and they would have little warning if anyone approached, it wasn't enough for either of them to simply remove what was necessary in order to have each other. It wasn't something they said aloud, it was something both of them knew.

For the first time, their hunger was tempered by humor and a kind of playfulness that was new to them. And they took their time, as if they had all they'd ever need. Every kiss and touch was lingering, intense with desire and yet lazy, sweet. Stubborn buttons and zippers roused chuckles, and the awkward removal of close-fitting riding boots provoked outright laughter.

When they finally lay naked together in the morning sunlight, humor and playfulness alike fled. As it always did between them, desire exploded, too powerful to control. In this, they knew each other very, very well. There was no hesitation, no questioning, no awkwardness. There was only passion that spiraled higher and higher until it carried them far beyond themselves.

"We'll get burned," Kate said idly.

"Neither of us ever burns," Ben replied. He swept one hand down over her hip and rubbed her upper thigh gently. It lay across his thigh and she cuddled close to his side. "But we might end up embarrassed," he added dryly. "There's a training run scheduled for this trail sometime this morning."

She lifted her head and looked down at him. "Oh, lovely."

He smiled when she made no effort to move, but then said, "I forgot again."

He meant he'd forgotten to put on a condom, she knew. Kate was grave. "Did you forget before? In the garden? I wondered."

Ben hesitated, then shook his head. "I don't know. Maybe. Maybe I let myself forget because you were always so adamant about it. Maybe I wanted it to be different with us, at least that one time."

She touched his face. "Maybe that's why I forgot, too."

"Still—it was careless of us."

"I know. But I'm on the pill, so we don't have to worry about that. And we're both healthy."

His arm tightened around her reassuringly. "Perfectly healthy. Do you want kids, Katie?"

She was a little startled by the abrupt question, but answered seriously. "I don't know. It's . . . it's a little late for me anyway. I'm forty, Ben."

"Idiot," he said, as he'd said before. "Women have babies in their fifties these days. What does it matter as long as you're ready to be a parent?"

"I don't know if I am."

He smiled and pulled her head down so that he could kiss her briefly. "I don't know if I am either. But it's something to think about."

Cautiously, she said, "Are we . . . going in that direction?"

"It's something to think about," he repeated.

She was silent for a moment, just looking at him,

then said uncertainly, "This is going to take some getting used to."

Ben was amused. "Having a serious lover?"

"Yes."

"Don't worry—I'll give you time to get used to it. I won't insist we sleep in your bed tonight, or that you invite me to supper tomorrow night." He brushed a strand of glossy black hair away from her face and turned very serious. "It's your call, just like coming to me had to be your call. This is your home, Katie, your family. If you want to start slow, fine. We'll ride back together. We'll groom the horses together and talk, and not pretend we're virtual strangers if anyone is watching. And tomorrow, if you feel like it, we'll ride out together. Maybe we'll take a picnic lunch. Maybe, by the weekend, we'll even go out to a movie."

"Are you really going to be that patient?" she asked.

"Well, for a while." Ben smiled at her. "As long as we know—you and I—that we're together, I can wait for everyone else to realize it."

Kate leaned down to kiss him lingeringly. She was smiling a little, more content than she could remember ever being and yet still uneasy. He was so close, leaving her no defenses at all, and that was a frightening thing.

He'd said he loved her.

"Ben—"

"Don't panic on me, now."

"No. No, I won't. But I have to say—I don't know how I feel, not really. About you."

"That's all right. *I* know."

"You do? You know how I feel about you?"

"Yes."

Kate eyed him, suddenly wary. "Well?"

"You love me."

She began to feel annoyed. "Is that so?"

"Of course." Ben's smile widened. "I've been calling you Katie and you haven't objected once. If that isn't love, it's something damned close."

After a moment, Kate felt herself smiling.

Casually, Ben said, "And now I think we'd better get dressed. Because from the faint vibrations I can feel in the ground, I'd say we're about to have company."

"Oh, *lovely* . . ."

They were—almost—dressed by the time four riders trotted their horses briskly past the waterfall. The riders didn't pause, merely holding up hands in quick greeting as they passed, and if they saw Ben putting on his boot, it seemed plain from their detached expressions that they thought he'd merely removed it to shake out a pebble or some such thing. And if any of them noticed a sprig or two of grass in Kate's tumbled hair, that was apparently not worth commenting on either.

"Tactful souls," Ben noted, wrestling with his boot.

"God, I think I'm blushing," Kate said in wonder.

He grinned at her.

A few minutes later, Ben and Kate were riding back down the trail toward the stables. The trail was just wide enough for them to ride abreast, and they talked companionably about nothing in particular—also a new thing for them. It wasn't until they had nearly reached the valley that Ben asked a sober question.

"How're things between you and Amanda?"

"Neutral. I think." She sighed. "You know about what happened at the party?"

"Oh, yeah." Ben looked at her thoughtfully. "Are the two things connected?"

"In a way. She was so sick. She could have died. All those hours when we weren't sure she was going to make it, all I could think was how unfair I'd been to her. I mean . . . it isn't her fault that Jesse . . . well, that he treats me the way he does. He did that before she got here, after all. Her being here didn't change that. And I couldn't keep blaming her for it."

"So you made peace?"

"I tried. We'll see."

"She was amenable?"

Kate nodded. "I think so. Wary—but that's hardly surprising."

After a moment of silence Ben said slowly, "Katie, do you believe she's the real Amanda Daulton?"

Kate didn't answer immediately, but when she did, her voice was certain. "Yes. I do."

"Why so sure?" he asked curiously.

Why, indeed. Kate hesitated, unaccustomed to even considering revealing things about herself and her family to outsiders. But then she realized that Ben was no outsider. Not now. Not anymore. She looked at him, met the warmth and shrewd understanding in his eyes, and felt as if a weight she had carried for a long, long time slipped easily from her shoulders.

While their horses walked slowly, following the fence line across the valley floor toward the stables, she told Ben why she was so sure Amanda had come home.

During the days after the party, Amanda could hardly help but feel uneasy. Despite her confident words to Helen, she knew it *was* possible that someone at Glory had tried to get rid of her, and even though Jesse's announced change of mind about the will might have put that person's plans on hold, it did not necessarily guarantee Amanda's safety.

As Helen had so shrewdly pointed out, as long as

Jesse was alive, it was at least possible that he would change his mind yet again and designate Amanda as his principal heir. And it was also possible that someone in the house might not want to take the chance of waiting around and letting that happen.

For the first week after the party, Amanda felt almost paralyzed by the possibility. In her more panicky moments, she was tempted to leave, but each time she reminded herself of what was at stake. Once Jesse was gone, she was convinced that everything at Glory would change and that her chances of finding out what had happened twenty years ago would drop off sharply.

No, she had to stay. And that meant she had no choice except to be extremely cautious. Judging by the possibly poisoned pie, it seemed clear that an accident rather than wanton murder had been planned—if anything had been planned, of course—and that argued the unlikelihood of an open attack against her. She couldn't believe that anyone was desperate enough to risk that, not yet anyway.

So all she had to be wary of, she convinced herself, was some sort of accident.

But as the days passed even Amanda's uneasiness, with her for so long, began to fade. Life at Glory went on normally, and as far as she could tell, nobody betrayed the slightest desire to do away with her. Maggie was pleasant and seemed once more neutral about Amanda; Kate, thawed, was actually friendly; Reece was so obviously relieved about Jesse's change of mind about the will that he beamed at everyone; and even Sully seemed in a better mood.

Walker had resumed his habit of dining at Glory virtually every evening. He said nothing except the most casual and meaningless things to Amanda, but he watched her. He watched her a great deal.

He made no reference to the night of the party; he might never have held her while she was violently sick or touched her face with gentleness, and he certainly seemed far removed from the man who had carried her in his arms. The closest he came to mentioning the party was when he said, with no particular expression in his voice, that he had asked Helen about an injury to the arm changing handedness.

"And what did she say?" Amanda asked. They had paused in the doorway of the dining room, the last to enter on this particular evening, and both kept their voices low.

"She said it was possible."

"Disappointed, Walker?" Amanda drawled.

His jaw tensed, and something hot stirred in his green eyes. "One of these times," he said, "I'll ask a question you won't have a ready answer for."

Amanda had felt Jesse's gaze on them, but she paused a moment longer there in the doorway to smile easily up at Walker. "I wouldn't bet on it," she advised him sweetly, and went to her place at the table.

"Something wrong?"

"Not a thing, Jesse. Not a thing."

After that, Walker had kept his comments fairly neutral. But he watched her. He did watch her.

Jesse, of course, was very much himself. Once he'd recovered from the fright of nearly losing her, he had tried at least twice to persuade her to change her mind about inheriting Glory.

"It's your birthright, Amanda!"

"My only birthright is my name; everything else I have to earn. And I haven't done a single, solitary thing to earn any part of Glory."

"But—"

"Checkmate."

Jesse stared down at the board on which they were

playing his favorite game, and scowled. "I didn't teach you that move."

"Yes, you did," she murmured, and smiled at him.

He had given in then, with a short laugh, but he hadn't abandoned his intention of persuading her. The only good thing about it, Amanda thought, was that Jesse never brought up the subject except when they were alone together. It was entirely in character for him that he disliked an audience when he was uncertain of winning an argument.

So the others were, she hoped, unaware that Jesse was still bent on leaving most of his estate to her. Although, if they knew the old man at all, nobody in the house could possibly believe the fight was over.

But things were peaceful in the meantime, and Amanda gradually began to wonder if she had frightened herself for no good reason. Deliberately poisoned? Probably not. Probably, she had just experienced an unusually severe reaction to baneberries accidentally baked into a blueberry pie.

Probably.

June, which had come in with a lamb's softness, toughened considerably by midmonth. It got hot. It got very hot. Thunder rumbled almost every afternoon and evening, and though the mostly dry storms muttered angrily in the mountains and laced the night sky with iridescent patterns of vivid lightning, none of the violence touched Glory.

Only the heat.

Amanda had been here for slightly more than three weeks when the serious heat came, and it quickly reminded her that though Glory sprawled in the mountains and foothills, this was still very much the South. A South in which the long days were very hot and very intense, and peculiarly still. A South in which nighttime temperatures hovered around eighty and there was hardly a hint of a breeze.

The house, though comparatively cool in the mornings, warmed rapidly throughout the day, and by nightfall the upstairs particularly was uncomfortably stuffy.

Amanda adapted fairly well to the heat and lack of air conditioning at Glory, but she found it difficult to sleep and woke often through the muggy nights. She sometimes left the French doors of her private balcony standing open, preferring the occasional mosquito (they weren't numerous, due to the hard work of gardeners and maintenance people) to the stuffiness of a closed room.

She didn't sleep, of course, with those doors left open—aside from her uncertainty whether enemies might be about, years of city living had left her too wary for such open trust—but at least the miserable wakefulness was a bit more bearable. And there were a few nights when she pulled on shorts and a tee shirt and slipped outside, walking on the lawn or in the garden until she felt able to sleep.

The dogs were never happy with her leaving the house, she quickly discovered. They had been exiled outside her bedroom door once again in order to do their guarding jobs, and tended to begin whining immediately if they heard (and they always did) Amanda venturing toward her balcony—so she got in the habit of frequently letting them in and taking them outside with her rather than risk their disturbing anyone else. She felt better having them with her, anyway, and knew the brief strolls outside wouldn't interfere with the dogs' guarding.

The strolls didn't do much to curb her growing restlessness, however.

It was a sweltering Thursday night—Friday morning, actually, since it was after midnight—when Amanda finally gave in to the urge she'd been conscious of and fighting against for days.

In the darkness of her bedroom, she peeled her nightgown off and quickly dressed in a thin blouse and shorts, and slid her feet into canvas shoes.

"Quiet," she told the dogs, who had begun whimpering outside her door. "Tonight, you stay. Hear me? Stay."

The whimpering became silence.

Reasonably sure they had adjusted to her occasional solitary strolls, Amanda went out onto her balcony, leaving the doors open behind her, and then down to the lawn.

Without hesitation, she started toward the path that led to King High.

I'LL PROBABLY STEP ON A SNAKE.

The thought, though slightly unnerving, wasn't enough to stop Amanda. She went on, following the path that led through the woods toward the west.

It was a narrow path, an obvious footpath rather than a trail horses used. It meandered, going left around one tree and right around another, past azalea bushes no longer in bloom and honeysuckle thickets that smelled sweet. One bend in the path nearly wrapped itself around a huge granite boulder before straightening out to climb a rocky slope.

Just a restful evening stroll to cool off.

It was certainly cooler in the woods, but . . . Amanda paused at the top of the slope to catch her breath, resentfully considering country-bred people who apparently thought any walk of less than ten miles should be effortless. No wonder Walker was in such good shape; this little stroll could condition a marathon runner.

She reached up to lift her hair off her neck and sighed.

Why am I doing this? It's ridiculous.

It was ridiculous, she told herself as she went on. If she wanted to see King High, why didn't she walk over when there was daylight by which to see? And if she wanted to see . . . anything else, well, same point.

"Amanda, you're an idiot," she remarked to a wild rosebush climbing a maple tree.

Yes, she was.

A bend in the path brought her suddenly to a languid stream, over which had been built a narrow bridge. She walked to the middle and stood for a moment looking down at the water. Here in the woods, little moonlight could penetrate, and so the water was a dark mass moving sluggishly.

Amanda shivered without knowing why, and went the rest of the way across the bridge a bit hastily.

Only a few yards beyond, just off the path to one side and balanced over several of the flung-out roots of a giant oak tree, the solid octagonal shape of a gazebo was visible. Amanda didn't get off the path to investigate; she merely stood looking for a few moments at the small wooden structure. It appeared to have built-in seats on the inside of two of its latticework half walls; there were four distinct half walls, the spaces between them open doorways, and the flooring of the structure was, like the rest of it, wood.

There was a clearing here, so a little moonlight drifted down to give the gazebo its shape and paint latticework shadows.

Turning her head to gaze farther along the path,

Amanda could just faintly see a hint of white through the trees. She knew she was close to King High—but it seemed an odd place to put a gazebo, so far from the house.

Odd—but nice. It made her smile.

She went on, following the final yards of the trail until the woods ended abruptly at the edge of a neat lawn.

King High. Bathed in moonlight. It was, in its way, every bit as perfect in its setting as Glory was. It didn't overwhelm the senses, but rather soothed somehow; it didn't step out boldly to meet visitors, but beckoned graciously; it didn't rear commandingly in a shout for attention, but waited quietly to be noticed.

Amanda was conscious of the oddest sensation as she stood there staring at it, a kind of empathy she had yet to feel at Glory.

The big, two-and-a-half-story house was designed like many found farther south, with wide galleries running across the front and back on the second floor and brick-paved loggias on the ground floor; the galleries had exterior staircases at each end. Each of the second-floor bedrooms opened out onto the galleries, where white ceiling fans turned lazily to keep the air stirring and white wicker furniture provided comfortable seats.

It was no longer a common layout, and galleries had grown scarcer than hen's teeth in this modern age of air conditioning, but the design suited both the massive, century-old oaks surrounding the house and the humid heat of Carolina summers.

Amanda hadn't intended to go closer once she reached the edge of the woods, but she found herself walking steadily onward, across the damp, soft grass of the neat lawn and underneath the huge oak between the woods and house. She could smell more of the heavy sweetness of honeysuckle somewhere near, and lightning bugs flickered here and there, but her attention was fixed on the house that had been named King High for the poker hand that had won Daulton land for the McLellan family.

It was a big house, far too large for one laconic lawyer. A white elephant, Walker had termed it—but it seemed clear he had no intention of unburdening himself of it. And either he cared more deeply than he let on, or else his sense of responsibility to his heritage was strong, because the house and grounds looked to be in excellent repair, and that would demand an inordinate amount of both time and money.

She stopped suddenly, her gaze fixed on the second-floor gallery at the end nearest her. A match flared, illuminating his hard face as he stepped out of the shadows and toward the railing. He was lighting a pipe, but his eyes were directed beyond that action. Even at this distance, she knew what he was looking at. He was looking at her.

He saw her, knew she was there. And he wanted her to know that he was watching, waiting. Her instincts told her that he was giving her the opportunity to retreat, to maintain the careful distance between them, and that if she did go away he wouldn't say a word about having seen her.

Just as he had not said a word about having held her comfortingly when she had been sick and in pain. Not a word about having carried her.

Things would go on as they had.

Amanda stood there for a long moment, watching until his pipe was lit, until the match died. Then she drew a breath and walked on.

When she reached the stairs, she climbed them steadily, and in the strong light of the moon she could see him clearly as she reached the top and walked across the solid flooring of the gallery toward him. He was shirtless and barefoot, wearing only a pair of jeans, leaning a shoulder against one of the columns and smoking his pipe methodically as he watched her approach.

Waiting.

As always, he was calm, handsome features expressionless because he'd trained them to be. She knew that if there had been more light, she would be able to see that his eyes were veiled as usual, hiding his thoughts and not even hinting at whatever he might be feeling. Unless she annoyed him, of course. Then the green eyes would burn.

He didn't believe she was Amanda Daulton, and she doubted he would be convinced without absolute scientific proof. But that didn't concern her tonight. Tonight, she didn't want it to matter who she was or wasn't.

Didn't want it to matter to her.

And, most especially, didn't want it to matter to him.

She made herself look beyond him, and near open French doors probably leading to his bedroom, a mattress from a single bed or daybed had been placed on the gallery floor, covered simply with a white sheet. As many people used to do, he apparently spent the hottest nights out on the gallery, where the fans stirred the night air and made it at least bearable.

No wonder he was comfortable with Jesse's forbiddance of air conditioning, she thought; he must have gotten used to doing without it in his own home. But she asked anyway. It seemed as good a way as any to begin a conversation that she had a feeling was going to get complicated.

"No air conditioning?"

He shook his head, one hand cradling the bowl of

the pipe and the other resting on the railing beside him. Between lazy puffs, he said with his usual calm, "No air conditioning. How can anyone enjoy the seasons' change if they're constantly shut up in a temperature-controlled environment? I like summer. I like the sights and sounds and smells and feeling of it. And I don't mind sweat."

His pipe smoke wafted toward her, the scent of it rich and sweet, and Amanda breathed it in unconsciously. She could smell him as well, spicy soap from a recent shower and the underlying musk of a man. She liked it. "In the city, you get used to being shut up most of the time. It's really the only way to live because of the dirty air and noise. But out here . . . it's like another world."

"A new world? Or one you've come back to?"

She felt herself smiling, unsurprised. "You never stop, do you? Always questioning, probing, weighing. Why do you bother, Walker? You don't believe anything I say anyway."

"Maybe I keep hoping that you'll say something to convince me you are who you say you are." He took the pipe from his mouth and studied it for a moment, then set it carefully on the railing.

Amanda waited until he met her gaze once more, then said deliberately, "Does it really matter who I am?"

"You know damned well it does. The estate aside, Jesse deserves his real granddaughter—"

"No, that isn't what I mean. I'm not talking about the others and what they think or believe. I mean, does it matter between us? Right now, with no one else around. No one else watching or listening. When you look at me, right now, do you really care whether I'm Amanda Daulton? Do you, Walker?"

"Does it matter whether I care?"

"Never answer a question with another question."

He shrugged. "Okay. It's after midnight, and a beautiful woman just walked into my bedroom—so to speak. And in a certain frame of mind, who she is probably wouldn't matter."

"So guarded," Amanda murmured. "Do you ever give an inch, Walker?"

Instead of answering that, Walker said, "It's hot as hell, and I'm in no mood to play games."

"Did I say anything about playing games?"

"You're here. Why are you here, Amanda?"

"I couldn't sleep. I thought a little walk might help."

"A little walk of a country mile? Through the woods?" He made his voice mocking. "Bored, Amanda? Looking for a little action? After Boston, this place must seem like the ass end of the world to you, and I imagine playing sweet Amanda for Jesse gets pretty tiresome. And with most of the men around supposedly related to you, finding a nonincestuous bedmate must be a matter of prime concern to you."

It wasn't like him to be cruel, and for a moment the attack left her unable to say anything at all. But finally she drew a short breath, holding on to composure, to a smooth mockery of her own. "You really are a bastard, aren't you? I can't decide whether you hate my guts or just want me to think you do."

"I don't play games."

"Bull. We all play games. And you and I have been playing this one since the day I walked into your office."

"I'm not playing a game. I want the truth."

"The truth?" She managed to laugh, and the sound was even amused. "What's the truth got to do with this?"

"Everything."

She shook her head. "Maybe you'd like to think so, but you know better, Walker. I asked you a question before, and I'd like a—truthful—answer. Does it really matter, right now, at this minute, whether I'm Amanda Daulton?"

"No." The word was almost forced out of him, and Walker felt the tension inside him wind tighter and tighter.

Damn her. *Damn* her.

Amanda didn't laugh or even smile; she merely said, quietly, "Maybe you'd sooner trust a cobra reared up in front of you, but that doesn't change anything, does it? You want me, Walker. And we both know it."

"Whatever I may or may not want, I'm old enough to keep my head about it." His voice was harsh, and hurt his throat. She had pulled his desire out of hiding, laid it bare and naked between them, and even though he knew he had goaded her, the knowledge did nothing to help him.

"Are you? But what if I'm not?"

He didn't move. Very carefully, he didn't move. "What are you saying, Amanda?"

"So like a lawyer," she murmured. "Needing everything spelled out in detail. But I thought you already knew why I'm here. Didn't you say so? Didn't you say I must be bored and looking to get laid? Or words to that effect."

"Amanda—"

She cut him off, her voice no longer quiet, but flat and sarcastic. "I'm mostly surrounded by relatives, and this summer's already turning into a . . . sultry one. The nights are so long. And so hot. What's a girl to do? Oh, I suppose I could wait for Victor to come back, since he's indicated his interest, but I'd really rather not pander to his inflated ego, and besides, men who believe they're the world's greatest lovers never are."

He could feel something moving inside him, slow and massive and unstoppable, and wondered dimly if she had any idea what this night would unleash. "A waste of your time, in fact."

"Worse. I've a notion Victor has a few nasty habits when it comes to sex, so I'd just as soon avoid his idea of fun."

"Which leaves me."

She smiled. "Naturally. So why don't we just complete this little scene, shall we? Then we can ring down the curtain in style."

Even in the grip of his own tumultuous emotions, Walker had the sudden realization that he had unquestionably succeeded in shattering her calm facade. She was wildly furious, definitely offended and possibly hurt. Her smile was bright and false, her voice so sweetly mocking it was unsteady, and she was shaking visibly. Before he could say anything, she was going on in that dulcet, taunting tone.

"Why don't I make it easier for you? I'll say to you that since you're the only interesting and available stud in the immediate neighborhood, I did stroll over here tonight to get laid. And then, while I wait expectantly, you can tear me to shreds by voicing your scorn and loathing and telling me what a whore I am. And if that doesn't make you feel a nice sense of superiority, you can add a few choice insults regarding my utter lack of attractiveness and desirability as far as you're concerned."

"Amanda—"

"Oh, go ahead, Walker. Isn't that what you've been trained to do—decimate an adversary by whatever means are required? Isn't that what you've been doing? If you can't gain control of the situation any other way, then just fall back on the tried and true, and humiliate and degrade me. That'll teach me a lesson. And I sure as hell won't stroll over here again looking to get laid—no matter how hot the nights get."

"Amanda, wait." He stepped forward and caught her arm as she was turning away. She froze, and eyes as intense as a cat's in the dark glittered at him.

"Go to hell." She jerked her arm from his grasp and hurried toward the stairs.

Walker hesitated only an instant, then swore and went after her. He caught up with her under the big oak tree between the house and the woods, and was hardly aware of the soft, damp grass under his bare feet. When he grabbed her arm this time, she made a wild sound and tried to claw at him with her other hand, but he caught her wrist before her nails touched his face.

"Amanda, I'm sorry," he said roughly. Her wrist was shockingly small in his grasp, and he was abruptly, overwhelmingly conscious of how defenseless she was in the grip of any man.

She went still, but her voice dripped scorn. "No, you aren't. And I'm not either. It's a relief to know where I stand with you. I knew you thought I was a liar—now I know what else you think of me."

"You know I want you." His hands shifted to her shoulders, and he shook her a little, aware of his control splintering and unable to do a thing about it. Between the two of them, they had torn down the barriers, all the barriers, and the only thing that was left was the truth. This truth. "You were right about that, and we both know it. Right that it doesn't matter who you are."

She pushed at his hands. "Let go of me—"

"No, not until you listen to me. I'm *not* in control

of this situation, and it *is* driving me crazy—and that's why I tried to hurt you. Why I'll probably try to hurt you again." His fingers tightened, biting into her shoulders. He didn't want to say this, but the naked words spilled out of him, quick and sharp with urgency.

Jesus, why couldn't he stop this?

"I think about you all the time, every day and every night, at the office and in court and here and at Glory, until I'm half crazy with it. Christ, I am crazy. I can't sleep because I dream of having you and wake up so frustrated I have to pace the floor like some caged animal."

He shook her again, and his furious voice was like a lash. "Do you understand now? *Want* is a feeble word to describe how I feel about you, and *desire* doesn't begin to cover it. I'm obsessed, damn you, so filled with you there's no room for anything else."

She was staring up at him, still for an instant but then moving again, trying to jerk away from him. "Stop it—let go of me, Walker!"

He laughed harshly. "Not what you had in mind, is it? Too intense, too unromantic, too abrupt—too much. But that doesn't matter either, does it? Because you want me too, Amanda. That's why you came over here tonight."

She was still again, wide darkened eyes fixed on his face. She wet her lips in a gesture that was nervous rather than provocative. "I—I don't know. . . . I didn't mean to come over here tonight, not all the way to the house, I just started walking, following the path, and when I saw you, I . . ."

"You expected a civilized conversation followed by a little genteel necking?"

This time, his harsh mockery didn't disturb her, because she was so absorbed by the startling change in him. It astonished her that the sleek, cool, and rather dispassionate man of the past weeks had hidden within him such fierce, dark, turbulent emotion, and she didn't know quite what to make of him. He was right —she had thought no further than likely kisses and possibly an affair of sorts—hadn't let herself think further than that—and it was utterly tame compared to the obsessive desire he described so vehemently.

He was also right in believing it wasn't what she wanted. Not now. With the overwhelming complications in her life right now, the various strains and tensions and undercurrents and puzzles, the last thing she would have gone looking for was anything—*anything* —demanding more of herself than she wanted to give.

"It doesn't matter what I expected," she managed to say calmly, very conscious of his nearness, his unexpectedly powerful chest and arms, and the way his fingers kneaded her shoulders with strong, restless movements he probably wasn't even aware of. "You don't like what you feel, and I don't have the emotional energy to cope with—" She conjured a twisted smile. "—with anything more complicated than getting laid."

"Then I'll have to settle for that, won't I?"

Even in the dimness, his expression was almost frightening in its intensity, and Amanda felt a queer inner jolt, as if all her senses had received a profound, almost primitive shock. She wanted to back away— no, to *run* away—but she couldn't move at all. Her heart was pounding, and suddenly it was difficult to breathe and deep inside her was a heat she had never felt before.

"No." She swallowed hard, unable to even look away from him. "I can't. You want too much. You—"

He bent his head in an abrupt movement, his mouth covering hers hungrily, and Amanda forgot whatever she'd been about to say. Her hands were on his naked chest, fingertips probing thick, soft hair and hardness beneath. He didn't feel like a man who spent his days in a suit behind a desk. He felt like a construction worker or a rancher, like a man who used his muscles in the vigorous daily struggles of life.

And he was hot, hotter than the night, his skin burning as if it could hardly contain the fever raging inside him. Her lower body molded itself to his of its own volition, and the shock of his arousal sent another wave of heat through her. She knew she was kissing him back, her mouth as fierce and blindly compulsive as his, and that almost-brutal desire was so powerful and so unexpected it made her dizzy.

Then Walker jerked his head up, leaving her lips feeling swollen and throbbing, almost bruised from the force of him, and he drew a breath that sounded more like a growl. "I need you." His voice grated. "*Need* you. I thought it would go away, but it hasn't, it's only gotten worse."

Amanda stared up at him, mesmerized. She had the hazy understanding that she would have been able to pull away if he had offered only the lustful but in-control desire she had seen and felt before, and understood. A passion of the flesh only, touching the emotions but lightly and the soul not at all. She could have walked away from that, or stayed without anxiety, accepting what he offered in the mutual understanding of pleasure for its own sake. That would have been . . . civilized.

There was nothing civilized about this. His desire had burst forth like floodwaters over a dam, sweeping her into a burning current she was unable to control, and even as she was carried along wildly, the sure knowledge that he was every bit as overwhelmed was incredibly seductive. She had never in her life felt so *necessary* to a man.

"Goddammit, Amanda." He surrounded her face with hands that shook and kissed her again, his mouth as hard and fierce as his voice. "Either say yes or else tell me to go to hell again, but don't make me wait another minute for some kind of answer."

Somewhere in her mind was the whisper of a sane warning to slow down and think about this, to estimate the cost of allowing him to see her vulnerable, but rational thought was swamped by wild emotion. Shaken, she heard an unnervingly sensual little whimper escape her, a response to him and to her own burning desire, and her hands slid slowly around him until her nails dug into the shifting muscles of his back. The tips of her breasts, already visibly aroused beneath the fine cotton of her blouse, touched his chest.

Walker caught his breath. "Yes?" he demanded thickly.

"Yes." She wasn't even sure she would say it until the word emerged, but uncertainty dissolved in a flood of sensations when he kissed her again with that intense, overwhelming hunger.

His fingers slid down her throat and followed the thin lapels of her blouse until he reached the first button. Before Amanda could move to help him, the blouse was swiftly opened and jerked down her arms, making her back arch and her naked breasts rake hard against his chest.

He made a rough sound, his teeth and tongue playing with her lips in carnal bites and enticing touches more wildly arousing than simple kisses could ever be, and his hands slid down her back to pull her close to him. He was moving, rubbing himself against her swelling breasts.

Amanda heard herself whimper, felt her breasts ache and her nipples burn, the urgent desire rising in her so quickly it was like some kind of madness taking hold of her. Wild and rapt, she caught his bottom lip between her teeth, and the low sound he made in response was a growl, their breath mingling. His hands were at the elastic waistband of her shorts, pushing them down over her hips, and only when she felt the damp grass beneath her bare feet did she realize she had gotten rid of her shoes.

She fumbled for the snap of his jeans, her fingers awkward in her impatience but still able to open the snap and slide the zipper down. He caught her hand when she would have reached for him, and his voice was hoarse.

"No. If you touch me, I'll—"

"Hurry," she whispered, no longer surprised by her own compulsion to have him.

Walker shuddered and made another low sound, but then he was shoving his jeans and shorts down, kicking them to one side as Amanda kicked her shorts out of the way. He pulled her down to the ground and pressed her back into the dew-wet grass, and she moaned when she felt him dispense with her panties by simply tearing them off her.

"I can't wait," he muttered, one heavy hand rubbing over her breasts and stomach and then sliding down to ease between her shaking thighs and cup her mound.

Amanda whimpered, her hips lifting needfully when his long fingers probed and stroked. She was burning, aching, empty in a way she'd never felt before. Nothing else was important, nothing mattered except feeling him inside her. "Don't wait," she told him, her husky voice curiously broken.

"I have to. I have to slow down. Christ, it's like I'm starving for you . . ."

His mouth was at her breast, and he let her feel his teeth as well as his tongue tease her nipple as he sucked strongly. His hunger was so powerful it made his caresses ferocious, primitive, and he almost hurt her. But his very lack of control was arousing in itself, evidence of the depth of his need, and Amanda felt freer to let herself go, to enjoy her own passion without holding anything back.

She pulled at his shoulders frantically, her body arching up off the wet ground as his mouth and fingers drove her higher and higher, so high it was frightening. Then his mouth was sliding hotly down over her quivering stomach, lower, and she let out a low, wordless cry of pleasure when his tongue stroked the most exquisitely sensitive spot her body possessed.

She fought to catch her breath, to be still, but there was no control left to her. At first dizzily aware of the scents of grass and honeysuckle and the soap he'd used, aware of the humid heat of the night and the sounds of crickets and the faint rumbles of thunder off in the mountains and their breathing, all her senses began to focus until she was aware of nothing but him and the raging needs of her own body.

"Walker . . . I can't stand it . . . please . . ."

He moved back up her shaking body with painstaking slowness, his mouth caressing the silky flesh over her belly and rib cage, her breasts, her throat. His hips spread her thighs wider, his hardness rubbing against her, and Amanda moaned.

"*Damn* you. . . ."

"Easy," he muttered, but he seemed to be ordering himself because his every movement, every caress, lingered achingly. When he raised his head, his face was taut, his eyes glittering down at her with the almost-blind look of frantic lust. "I wanted to . . . make it last . . . but—"

Amanda felt him, hard and insistent, and she made a choked little sound as her body began to admit him. It had been a long time for her, and his slow penetration stole what was left of her breath. She opened for him, stretched almost painfully, gripped him tightly. She was full of him, so full, and then he abruptly withdrew and thrust hard just once, and she writhed with a sob because she had never felt anything so wildly perfect.

"Jesus—" He groaned gutturally and bore down as if he needed to go deeper inside her, then uttered another harsh, primitive sound when she moaned and raked his back with her nails. "I have to—"

"Yes, Walker, please," she pleaded, her legs lifting and gripping his hips desperately.

His forearms slid under her back, his hands gripping her shoulders, and the heavy thrusts, deep and hard, quickened until he was like some untamed creature obeying ancient drives to possess its mate. Amanda felt possessed, taken in a primal way unlike anything she'd ever experienced, and her body gloried in it. Her hips lifted eagerly to receive him, her hands roamed over the rippling muscles of his back in the frenzied need to touch and seek and hold, and her body shivered beneath the onslaught of his possession.

Without warning, the coiling tension inside her snapped, and Amanda cried out as waves and waves of throbbing pleasure swept through her and over her. He groaned and kcpt driving into her, holding her pinned beneath him and refusing to allow her to drift away from him. Dazed, all her senses buffeted, she felt her body obey his insistence as fresh tension wound swiftly and sharply inside her, and when it peaked this time the release was so devastating that her scream of pleasure was utterly silent.

Still shuddering, she felt him jerk and heard the hoarse cry that seemed ripped from deep in his chest. Then he was pouring his seed into her, his weight heavy on her as he bore her back into the ground.

Amanda didn't know how much time passed, but gradually she became aware of her surroundings. Beneath her, the grass was thick enough to provide a marginally comfortable bed and she no longer felt the dampness of dew—probably because both her body and his were slick with sweat. Not that she cared. The air was hot and still, humid, and when she opened her eyes she saw lightning bugs flickering high up in the spreading branches of the old oak tree. She could hear crickets and, faintly, thunder. She could hear her still uneven breathing, and his.

Walker lifted his head, easing himself up onto his elbows. There was an indefinably male look of satisfaction stamped into his handsome features but no triumph, as if he realized that this had been more a respite than a resolution. He kissed her, slowly and thoroughly, then lifted his head again.

"That was . . . remarkable," he said, his voice low but matter-of-fact.

Knowing it would be useless to try hiding how completely overwhelmed she had been, she merely said, "I think I'd choose another word. Maybe . . . frantic."

"Did I hurt you?"

"No." She glided her palms over his back slowly and remembered digging her nails in more than once. "But I think I drew blood."

He chuckled, a lazy sound of amusement. "I don't think you broke the skin."

Amanda didn't protest when he lifted himself off

her and relaxed by her side, but when he kept one hand on her just beneath her breasts, she was obscurely glad he didn't withdraw completely from her. She should have been uncomfortable lying there naked, she thought, but though she was mildly astonished at herself for having sex right out in the open under a tree on a brightly moonlit night, she wasn't embarrassed.

A slight breeze stirred then, rustling in the tree above them and wafting over her moist body, cooling and drying her feverish skin. It felt wonderful. She didn't want to move.

Rising on his elbow beside her, Walker looked down at her for a moment, then began to fondle her breasts with indolent interest, kneading, lifting, and shaping them. It was as if he had to touch her, as if his desire had been only temporarily appeased rather than sated.

"I think you have a perfect body," he told her, still casual.

She gazed at his absorbed expression, feeling her pulse begin to quicken and her flesh respond to the caresses, and she tried to hold her voice steady when she murmured, "Thank you. Good genes, I suppose." His hand paused, and Amanda silently swore at herself for reminding him. For reminding them both.

Then he was stroking again, his fingers tracing curves and examining her tightening nipples. "You're surprisingly voluptuous for such a little thing," he murmured. "Judging by the painting, your mother wasn't."

If she was your mother, of course.

He didn't have to say it, and Amanda felt herself tense. With an effort, she kept that out of her voice. "No, she always bemoaned having the figure of a child. Whenever she bought my bras, she said it depressed her no end that mine were a cup size larger than hers."

Walker pulled gently at a stiff nipple, then leaned over and flicked it with his tongue in a brief but wildly arousing caress. When he raised his head, he was smiling. "Nice detail."

Knowing damned well he wasn't referring to her breasts, she pushed his hand away and sat up, reaching for her clothing.

He sat up as well, catching her shoulders to hold her still. "All right, I'm sorry."

Now Amanda felt uncomfortable naked, and she didn't like the feeling. Shifting her shoulders jerkily to escape his grip, she drew her knees up and hugged them to her breasts. "We both know you're not, so skip it," she said tensely. "It doesn't matter anyway."

"It matters to me, even if it doesn't to you," he told her flatly. "I *am* sorry, Amanda. I don't want my . . . suspicion to ruin what we have together."

That didn't really surprise her, and there was irony in her voice when she laughed. "What we have together? You mean the sex? God, you men will suppress every doubt and ignore every rational thought in your heads if it means getting laid."

"Don't lump me into a group." He was smiling slightly, more amused than insulted. "I'm neither suppressing nor ignoring anything, and I certainly don't expect you to sleep with me just to keep my mind off my questions; since Jesse's already satisfied, my opinion hardly matters. Am I convinced you're Amanda Daulton? No. But that, as you pointed out earlier, hardly matters either. I want *you,* whoever or whatever you are, and if you don't believe that after the last hour or so, then there's something wrong with one of us."

Amanda didn't say anything for a moment, wrestling silently with the choice she knew she was making. She could gather up her clothing and leave with what dignity she could muster, refusing to have a sexual relationship with him in the face of his suspicion, or else she could accept his distrust as a thing apart from the explosive passion between them and not let it end what promised to be the affair of a lifetime.

"Amanda?"

She drew a breath. "I want your word on something."

With a lawyer's natural wariness, he said, "What?"

"I want you to promise me that when we're together like this, whether or not I'm Amanda Daulton is a taboo subject. Off-limits. No sly little questions or subtle probes. No hints or digs designed to catch me off guard. No exceptions."

He nodded promptly. "All right, you have my word—when we're like this. But I can't make the same promise for any other time."

"I don't expect you to." She eyed him somewhat warily. "Well, this should be interesting."

"On that, we definitely agree." He leaned over and kissed her, his hands gently pushing her legs down so that he could begin fondling her breasts again.

Amanda didn't know whether to be upset at herself or at him for being able to change the tension of anger into an entirely different tension so swiftly and completely. For the second time tonight, he had first enraged her and was now seducing her.

"You're maddening," she told him as he pushed her back to the ground.

"But you want me as much as I want you." His lips trailed down her throat toward her breasts. "Don't you?"

"Yes, damn you." She gasped, her eyes closing because waves of pleasure were making her dizzy. The feelings he evoked were so overwhelming and escalated so swiftly that they would have frightened her if he had given her a chance to think. But he didn't. However satisfied their earlier joining had left him, it was clear his desire for her was every bit as potent as it had been the first time.

So was hers.

"I'm glad," he muttered against her flesh. Then he made a little sound, and there was a thread of rueful humor in his hoarse voice when he added, "If this were one-sided, I think I'd kill myself."

She slid her fingers into his thick hair, her eyes still closed as she absorbed the blissful sensations of his mouth at her breast. Huskily, she said, "Stop talking, Walker."

He did.

The panties were hardly more than torn scraps of material. Amanda shook her head over them and then stuffed them into the pocket of her shorts. She pulled the shorts on, lifting her bottom off the ground without getting up. She shook out her blouse and shrugged into it, discovering two buttons gone.

"Are you going to be this rough on my clothes in the future?" she asked him.

Walker, who had climbed reluctantly to his feet and reclaimed his jeans, chuckled as he reached down for her hands and pulled her up. "Probably. Not intentionally, you understand, it's just that they get in my way."

"Mmm." Amanda looked down at her blouse for a moment, then sighed and tied the tails in a loose knot beneath her breasts. She didn't expect to meet anyone on the walk back to Glory, but if by chance someone else was wandering the night in search of coolness, at least she'd be decently covered and the missing buttons wouldn't be noticed.

"You could stay here," Walker suggested.

She looked up at him, wondering if it would have been any easier to read his expression in the daylight. The fierce, intense lover of only minutes ago was back in his deceptive skin, calm and lazy once again.

"No," she said, "I should get back. It'll be dawn in a few hours."

"And you have to be safely in your own bed when the sun comes up?"

Amanda hesitated only an instant before saying deliberately, "Of course. After all, it would certainly ruin my sweet-Amanda act to have it known I'd spent a night fornicating underneath an oak tree in your yard."

"What makes you think I won't spread the word?" he asked her with equal deliberation.

She wondered why she was so sure he wouldn't. "Oh, I don't know. Because you want more than one night?"

A reluctant laugh was forced out of him. "I suppose that's as good an answer as any. You don't have any illusions, do you, Amanda?"

"Not many." She found and put on her shoes, then looked up at him again when he stepped closer. "In case you're wondering, I hadn't planned to be especially secretive about this. I just don't think it would be a good idea to be blatant. I'm still a curiosity in these parts, definitely on probation while everyone makes up their mind about me, and I'd rather not give them even more to consider just now. Besides—as I remember, small towns tend to be unforgiving of certain . . . sins."

"They are that," he agreed after a slight hesitation. "So we let them wonder without providing proof?"

"I think so."

"What about the family? Jesse?"

It was Amanda's turn to hesitate. "Why don't we play it by ear?"

He half nodded, then reached out and combed his fingers through her hair slowly several times. "You have grass in your hair."

Amanda was reasonably sure she had grass in other places as well, and no one getting a good look at her would doubt she had spent the past couple of hours in sensual pursuits. Her lips felt hot and swollen, her clothing was decidedly wrinkled (not to mention the missing buttons), and she had the uneasy suspicion that his passion had left at least a couple of faint bruises on her neck. But she remained silent and still under what felt more like a caress than anything else.

"We were careless," he murmured, his fingers moving slowly against her scalp.

Again, she would have chosen a stronger word. *Insane* sprang to mind. But she replied to him mildly and straightforwardly. "I've been on the pill the last few years for an irregular cycle. As for any other . . . dangers . . . you of all people should be sure I have a clean bill of health. As I remember, that first blood sample you demanded was weighed, measured, and analyzed about six ways from Sunday."

Walker nodded slowly. The blood testing had been at his insistence, required as a first step in establishing proof of a claim to the Daulton estate, and it had swiftly discredited at least one woman more than a year before simply because she'd had the wrong blood type.

This woman, however, had the right one.

Walker said, "The sample was screened, just as a matter of course. Screened for known infectious diseases, none found. Screened for venereal diseases, none found. Screened for HIV—results negative." He paused, but when she said nothing, he added, "I had a routine physical a few months ago. You don't have to worry."

"I know."

He looked at her curiously. "How can you?"

Amanda smiled. "If I know anything about you, Walker, it's that you're a careful man. A very careful man."

He glanced aside at the flattened grass of their outdoor bed, tempted to disagree with her judgment. A careful man, he wanted to say, would hardly have mated lustfully under an oak tree with a woman for whom he felt uneasy suspicion at best and outright distrust at worst. And if he was unwise enough to do that, he wouldn't make the situation worse by anticipating—with undiminished hunger—a repeat performance in the very near future.

Pushing that knowledge away, Walker bent his head and kissed her, making no effort to hide the hunger from her. It was useless anyway, because her response was instant and that was like throwing kerosene on a fire. He wanted to pull her down to the ground again and lose himself in her. His desire for her was so intense and compelling it was like something with a life all its own and only marginally under his control.

Her mouth was incredibly erotic, soft and warm and sweet. . . .

He couldn't seem to let her go, to take his hands off her and watch her walk away from him. *Jesus, stop making a fool of yourself and let her go!* With an effort, he managed to raise his head and let go of her, but when he heard his voice, he wasn't a bit surprised at the raspy sound of it.

"Have supper with me tomorrow. I mean today."

Amanda hesitated, then nodded. "All right. Jesse's going into Asheville before lunch, for a business meeting and then to get his treatment, and he won't let me go with him."

Walker heard something in her husky voice he couldn't quite pin down, and it made him uneasy. "Then you'll be at loose ends all day? Come into town and have lunch with me."

"You're going to work today?"

Understanding her surprise, he said, "I never get much sleep on summer nights, and it doesn't seem to bother me much. I don't have to be in court, but there's paperwork to take care of. I'm free for lunch—how about it?"

Evasive, she murmured, "We'll see. I have some shopping I need to do in town, but . . . Don't worry; I'll call before I show up at your office."

He was positive she didn't mean to show up for lunch, but he was wary of pressing her. "Good enough. As for supper, why don't you meet me halfway down the path around seven?"

She was surprised. "The path? Have you got a burger joint stashed away in the woods?"

"No, but I have a wicker basket and my housekeeper and cook fixes a mean bowl of potato salad."

A picnic. Amanda nodded her acceptance. "All right. Should I bring anything?"

"No, I'll take care of it."

"Okay." She seemed a bit hesitant for an instant, then turned and started toward the path through the woods.

Walker knew he should say something else, though he wasn't sure what. He was reasonably certain she'd throw something at him if he thanked her for the evening, and calling out a "good night" seemed oddly inappropriate.

Besides, he had a feeling that if he opened his mouth at all he'd end up babbling like an idiot, begging her not to leave him tonight. And that was a hell of a note.

That was really a hell of a note.

Ten

AMANDA WAS UP UNUSUALLY EARLY for breakfast on Friday morning. Truth to tell, she hadn't slept much at all after returning to Glory; this new relationship with Walker struck her as being rather like walking a high wire without a net—in more ways than one. He was still suspicious and hardly trusted her, and yet the desire between them made clear thinking virtually impossible.

The combination of distrust and desire, she thought, was probably as explosive as any mixture could possibly be, virtually guaranteed to blow up in somebody's face. And Amanda was very much afraid it would be in hers.

By the time the sun rose, she had been more than ready to leave her bed. She didn't feel particularly tired, which surprised her a bit considering how active her night had been, but chalked it up to having been rested from the peaceful days of the last week or so.

She discovered while dressing that her sensitive skin bore several faint marks of Walker's ardor, which didn't surprise her considering how easily she bruised. Luckily, the collar of her blouse hid two of the small, pale bruises and the blouse itself hid one more. But the one on her left wrist . . .

That had been before the lovemaking, she remembered. When he had caught up to her under the big oak tree, and she had wildly tried to scratch him.

Amanda shook her head a little as she looked at the faint violet marks of his fingers. Odd—she hadn't been conscious of pain or even discomfort when he grabbed her wrist. But, then, she had been so mad she probably wouldn't have felt the jab of a knife.

Her watch, which she normally wore on her left wrist anyway, hid most of the marks, and Amanda shrugged as she left her room. It would have to do. If anyone noticed, and drew their own conclusions about what they saw, well, so be it. The change in her relationship with Walker probably wouldn't pass unnoticed for long anyway.

When it came to sex, there seemed to be precious few secrets at Glory.

The dogs weren't waiting outside her door, which was unusual, but Amanda didn't think much about it. She went downstairs and into the kitchen, finding Earlene preparing some of the fresh-baked bread Jesse enjoyed so much.

"Morning. You look bright-eyed today."

"Morning. Do I?" Amanda fixed herself a cup of tea; she preferred it to coffee, and Earlene always kept a steaming kettle ready in the mornings. "I . . . had a good night."

"You must be getting used to the heat," Earlene remarked.

"Mmm." Amanda fought a sudden and ridiculous impulse to giggle.

"Want your usual breakfast?"

"Yes, just fruit, I think." The blueberry-baneberry-whatever pie hadn't spoiled her taste for fruit, though she doubted she'd ever be able to look at a pie in the same way again. "Is it on the table?"

Earlene nodded. "You should eat more," she said in what was becoming a litany. "Eggs, bacon, pancakes—you know I'll fix whatever you'd like—"

Amanda patted her arm. "I'm fine, Earlene, really. I'll just have fruit." And, to avoid further conversation on the subject, added, "Who else is up?"

"Everyone, for once. Even Reece. And Jesse, because he has to go to Asheville this morning."

It was rare that everyone sat down to breakfast together, and Amanda couldn't help hoping the meal would be more peaceful than suppers tended to be.

She got as far as the doorway, then paused and looked back. "Earlene, have you seen the dogs?"

"No, not this morning. I usually let them out for their morning run when I come in, but not today," the cook replied. Earlene lived in; she had her own suite of rooms in the rear wing, where Sully, Kate, and Maggie also had bedrooms.

"Somebody else probably let them out then."

"Probably."

Amanda looked at her watch as she went toward the sunroom; it was a little before seven, early for her. That was probably why she felt vaguely uneasy, she decided, because she was normally still asleep at this ungodly hour. That, and her active night.

Jesse was in the sunroom. So were Maggie, Kate,

Sully, and Reece. The doors to the patio were open. But the dogs were nowhere to be seen.

Amanda greeted the others politely and went to her place at the glass-topped table. She was relieved to see that everyone appeared to be in a good mood; even Sully nodded courteously in response to her good morning, before concentrating once more on his breakfast.

"Sleep well, honey?" Jesse asked as she sat down.

"Fine. Are you sure I can't go with you today?"

"The meeting'll probably drag on until after lunch, Amanda; you'd just be bored."

"Maybe, but I could sit with you at the hospital later."

Unlike the others, who seemed to tread carefully regarding Jesse's medical treatments, Amanda had been blunt with him since their conflict over the will had begun. She knew how sick he was, she had told him forthrightly—believing, as Walker did, that the old man definitely did not want pity—and she had no intention of pussyfooting around the subject.

Jesse had seemed rather pleased about that.

His harsh face softened now as he looked at her, and Amanda thought, as she had before, that no one in this house could mistake that look. She had power. As long as Jesse was alive, she had great power.

"I don't think so, honey, but thanks."

Amanda rolled her eyes a bit, but accepted his refusal and began serving herself some fruit. "All right. Has anyone seen the dogs?"

Everyone shook their heads, with Jesse replying, "Not this morning. Earlene probably let them out for their run, and they haven't come back yet."

Amanda started to say that the cook had denied this, but decided it didn't really matter. With the patio doors open—as they were every morning before breakfast—the dogs had undoubtedly gone out on their own some time earlier.

The old man turned his attention to his younger grandson, and for once his voice was relatively pleasant. "Sully, when Victor finally gets back—"

"He did, sometime last night," Sully reported. "Or, at least, the van did. I saw it parked outside barn two when I looked out my window this morning."

"It's about time," Jesse said, but mildly and not as though he blamed Sully personally for the delay. "Tell him I'll want to see the paperwork on the new horses tomorrow afternoon."

"All right, I'll tell him." Sully sent his grandfather a slightly wary glance and, apparently encouraged by Jesse's exceptional calm this morning, added, "I've been meaning to tell you, that new rider I hired last week is working out fine. In fact, she's good enough to show."

"About time we found another decent rider." Jesse's voice was still mild. "She just turn up looking for a job?"

"Pretty much. Had all her stuff packed into a beat-up Jeep. But her boots are first-rate, and so's her tack; she's spent most of her life around horses, I'd say. I put her in the apartment over barn one, since it was empty and no one else wanted it."

"Who is she, Sully?" Maggie asked curiously.

He shrugged. "Name's Leslie Kidd. I'd never heard of her; she says she's ridden mostly on the West Coast. I had her up on a few of our worst horses to try her out, and she did great."

From Sully, that was extraordinarily high praise; he did not throw the word *great* around casually.

"Ben says she's very talented," Kate remarked.

"Is she riding for him too?" Amanda asked, thinking that Kate was apparently taking her relationship with the trainer public; they were beginning to spend time together openly, and this wasn't the first casual remark she'd made about him in the presence of the family.

"He said he stole her away from Sully for one of his horses," Kate replied with a smile, "because she has a way of reaching the difficult ones that's almost eerie."

"I think she's telepathic with them," Sully said with evident seriousness. "And if you see Ben before I do, Kate, tell him to keep his paws off my riders—he has half a dozen of his own." His tone was faintly amused rather than annoyed.

Sully and Ben, like the other two trainers at Glory, each had their own string of horses and their own riders, but they did occasionally require a particular skill from a rider working under another trainer. Since Sully oversaw all the training, he also more or less had his pick of riders; it was rare that anyone borrowed from *him*.

"I'll tell him," Kate replied. "But he might fight you for her, Sully. He's very impressed."

Sully grunted and returned his attention to his breakfast just as Reece pushed his chair back from the table. He seemed a bit preoccupied, and looked somewhat tired.

"I've got to go. Anybody need a ride into town?"

Kate said, "Maggie and I are going into town to do some shopping this morning, but we won't leave until a little later. Thanks anyway, Reece."

He lifted a hand in farewell and left the sunroom.

"Amanda, you're more than welcome, if you'd like to come," Kate offered.

"Thanks, but not today, I think." Amanda smiled at her.

"Sure?"

"I'm sure." Victor was back, and Amanda had every intention of talking to him as soon as possible—even if that meant braving the stables. It made her feel shaky just to *think* about going down there, but she had little choice. If she waited until Victor came to the house to talk to Jesse tomorrow, it might not be possible to speak to him alone, or unobserved—and since she didn't know what he would tell her, discretion seemed advisable.

In fact, it seemed essential.

Still without her usual canine escort, but deciding that putting off the ordeal would only make it worse, Amanda set off down the path toward the stables shortly after breakfast. Maggie and Kate were getting ready for their shopping trip, Jesse had left in his Cadillac for Asheville, and Sully had gone to the stables no more than ten minutes before Amanda headed in that direction.

So she was surprised to see him striding toward her when she had covered little more than half the distance. She stopped, waiting for him, and the closer he got, the more uneasy Amanda became.

"Sully? What's wrong?"

His harsh face was very grim, and when he spoke his voice was the same. "Has Jesse left?"

"A few minutes ago."

"Damn. Where are you going, Amanda?"

She gestured slightly past him toward the stables. "Down there. I don't *like* being afraid of horses, you know. I thought I'd try again."

"Better make it another day."

"But why? If you think I'll get in the way—"

Sully hesitated, then said, "No, but— Look, just

stay away from barn two, will you? That's the second one from the right."

"Why?"

"Because there's been an accident, and I'm afraid it isn't very pretty. I've called the sheriff, and I was hoping Jesse was still here. . . ."

Amanda felt very cold. She was afraid to think, afraid even to guess. "An accident? You mean . . . a horse?"

"No. Victor. He's dead."

It had, obviously, been a stupid accident. The big horse van was old, and the hydraulic ramp had been giving trouble and should have been fixed or replaced long since; that was undeniable. Victor should have had it fixed, because that particular vehicle had been his responsibility. And Victor should, certainly, have awakened someone to help him unload the stock when he arrived back at Glory sometime during the night, rather than do it all himself.

He had parked the big van beside barn number two, where it belonged when it was not in use. The horses had been safely unloaded; all six had been released into the big training ring in order to stretch their legs after the long trip, as was customary. And then Victor must have returned to the van and begun raising the hydraulic ramp.

At some point, he had, apparently, stood underneath the rising ramp, breaking the first rule of good sense around such mechanical devices. And at some point this particular mechanical device had failed, dropping straight down onto Victor. It was a very heavy ramp, and it had fallen hard.

There wasn't a great deal left of Victor's skull.

Amanda hadn't seen that, and didn't intend to. She

had not returned to the house, however, despite Sully's warning. Instead, she stood leaning back against the white board fence of what was called the front pasture, which lay between the barns and the main road and from where she could watch the activities in the area between barns one and two without getting in the way or seeing anything she preferred not to see.

The only reason she was able to get this close was because there were no horses near her and because a strong and steady breeze blew past her shoulder and toward the barns, keeping the scent of horses away from her. But winds had been known to shift, and Amanda was ready to bolt toward the house at the first hint of a change in direction.

That was why she was so tense, of course. Why she was shaking.

The sheriff had arrived. So had Helen, who acted as medical examiner for the county. Maggie and Kate had postponed their trip into town and were also here—as was practically every soul who had anything at all to do with the stables, and a couple of the gardeners as well.

The arrival of yet another car on the stables' private blacktop drive caught Amanda's attention, and she watched as Walker got out of his shiny Lincoln, glanced around swiftly, and came directly to her.

"What are you doing here?" she asked when he reached her.

"I'm always called if anything happens at Glory." He put a hand on her shoulder. "Are you all right?"

Amanda was aware that eyes were on them, but she didn't much care. "Why wouldn't I be? I didn't find the—the body. Sully did."

Walker frowned, but didn't respond to her somewhat belligerent tone. Instead, he said, "You're shaking."

"Am I?" She managed a smile, and hoped it didn't look as strained as it felt.

He pulled her into his arms.

Amanda sighed and briefly closed her eyes as she relaxed against him, her arms slipping inside his suit jacket and around his lean waist. For just a moment, she told herself, she would lean on him and take the comfort he offered. For just a moment. She was entitled, wasn't she?

"So much for our little secret," she murmured.

"Was it going to be a secret?" He rubbed his chin in her hair.

"Well, for a while. At least a day or two." She lifted her head—with rather terrifying reluctance—from his chest and looked up at him. "I'm all right, really."

Walker kissed her, taking his time about it and resolving any doubts the watchers might have had as to their interpretation of the hug.

"You did that deliberately," Amanda told him when she could, bemused to see that she was clutching at his shirt. She smoothed the fine linen absently.

"Of course." He was smiling, and the green eyes were alight. "A kiss should always be deliberate."

"You know what I mean."

"I don't like secrets," he said, and released her. "I have to go talk to the sheriff. Wait here for me, all right?"

"Unless the wind changes."

"Excuse me?"

She heard a brief laugh escape her. "I'm only afraid of horses when I can smell them. So—if the wind changes, I'll have to get out of here."

Walker looked at her for a moment, then shook his

head and went off toward Sheriff J. T. Hamilton's tall, skinny form.

Amanda leaned back against the fence again and shoved her trembling hands into the pockets of her jeans. He didn't like secrets. Wonderful. Not that she hadn't already known that, of course, but the reminder was unnerving.

The entire morning had been unnerving—beginning just after midnight.

She brooded for a few minutes, not really paying attention to the people milling about. But then she realized that Sully was coming toward her, accompanied by a slender woman of medium height with bright red hair cut short on her well-shaped head.

"Leslie wanted to meet you," Sully told her in his usual abrupt way. "Leslie Kidd, Amanda Daulton."

Amanda met Sully's steady gaze for just a moment, surprised, then looked at Glory's newest rider and smiled. "Hello, Leslie."

"My friends call me Les." Her eyes were a melting brown, lovely and oddly gentle in her face; she wasn't beautiful or even especially pretty, but there was something curiously compelling about those eyes. And her voice was soft and sweet without being at all childlike. "What about you? Does anyone ever shorten it to Mandy?"

"Not more than once."

"I'll remember that—Amanda." Then Leslie's smile faded and she added, "This is an awful thing."

"Yeah." Amanda looked at Sully. "What's going on over there?"

"Helen's examining the body, and J.T.'s examining the ramp," Sully replied. "Who called Walker?"

"He said he was always called when anything happened at Glory. I didn't ask by who."

Sully grunted. "J.T., probably." Then he eyed

Amanda with a certain sardonic amusement. "Nice going, by the way. I've heard of being in bed with the opposition, but you're the first I've seen take that literally."

Clearly, he had not missed the embrace and kiss from Walker. Conscious of Leslie's silent attention, Amanda merely said, "I believe in covering all my bases."

"Apparently, that's not all you've covered." Sully waited a moment to see if she had a response, then turned around and headed back toward the others.

Amanda let out a little sound of frustration that was almost a growl, and muttered, "I knew it was too good to last."

"What was?" Leslie asked curiously.

"He was being nice to me. It must have been too great a strain on his temper."

"Well," Leslie said fairly, "when you and this—Walker, is it?—greeted each other, we could feel the heat way over there. Being Sully, he could hardly resist a remark or two."

Amanda eyed her. "You seem to have gotten to know him rather quickly."

"Sully?" Leslie's brown eyes were innocent. "Well, he's really not very complicated, you know."

"He's not?"

"Oh, no. It's just that he'd die for this place, and he's afraid he's going to lose it."

"He won't. Not if I have anything to say about it."

Leslie nodded slowly, then said, "He surprised you when we first came up. Why?"

"Because he said I was Amanda Daulton as if he really believed that's who I am."

"Maybe he does."

"Maybe." Amanda turned her gaze back toward the barns, just in time to see a black body bag on a stretcher being wheeled toward a waiting ambulance. The sight made her feel a little queasy, and in her mind was the question she'd been asking herself ever since Sully had told her what had happened.

What if it hadn't been an accident?

As if she were indeed telepathic and not only with horses, Leslie Kidd said softly, "I didn't hear a thing. Didn't see a thing. And my apartment's right above where it happened."

Amanda looked at her, but before she could say anything, another woman was approaching and Leslie murmured, "I'd better go. Dr. Chantry'll probably want to talk to you alone." Then she paused, adding flatly, "Be careful, Amanda."

"I will." Watching Leslie Kidd walk away and Helen approach, Amanda found herself uneasily preoccupied with the breeze that was beginning to die down—and change direction. "Why would I be afraid when I smell horses?" she demanded of Helen when the doctor reached her.

"Afraid?" From her imperturbable reaction, it seemed Helen was used to having things come at her quickly.

"Yeah. But only when I smell them. Why?"

"Probably some kind of trauma. You've associated the smell of horses with a frightening or painful experience, probably when you were a child, and so the smell of them triggers fear."

"I don't remember anything like that."

Helen looked at her thoughtfully. "Is the reaction getting stronger?"

Amanda nodded. "Since I came to Glory, yes. Much stronger. Especially in the last week or two. And . . . sometimes I wake up scared to death, and all I can remember is that everything smelled of horses."

"Then you might be as close as one dream away from remembering why you're afraid. It sounds like your mind is preparing you for some kind of shock, for some . . . revelation you've avoided remembering."

"Is that possible?"

"Of course. The mind is a responsible guardian, Amanda; it often protects us, for as long as necessary, from shocks we aren't capable of surviving or which would devastate us. We remember when we're ready to, when we're strong enough to take the shock. And as for the smell of horses triggering your fear—smell is one of the strongest memory triggers we humans have."

"I don't like the sound of any of that." Amanda felt profoundly uneasy.

Helen smiled at her. "Don't worry too much about it. When you're ready to remember, you will. It won't do any good to try forcing it—or escaping it."

Amanda nodded, though she was not at all reassured. Changing the subject, she said, "About Victor. It was an accident, wasn't it? A careless mistake?"

"So it seems." Helen shrugged. "There's no evidence of anything else, not that I can find. The hydraulics could have failed, dropping the ramp when Victor was under it. On the other hand," she added deliberately, "someone could have hit the release button—it's there for emergencies, in case the ramp has to be lowered very quickly—and intentionally used it to kill him."

"Why would anyone have wanted to kill him?" Amanda asked quickly.

"I don't know. Do you?"

Amanda hesitated a moment, then shook her head. After all, she told herself, as she had before, no one else could possibly have known that Victor had told her about something that had happened here at Glory twenty years ago—and even if someone *had* known, or if Victor himself had told someone else about it, so what? Christine was dead, Matt Darnell long gone; who would care about their affair even if it had taken place?

"He didn't strike me as a very likable man," she told Helen. "But he'd been at Glory for more than twenty years, and I assume if someone here had wanted to kill him they would have done it before now."

"That's the way I saw it."

Amanda changed the subject again. "I guess there's no news on what made me so sick the night of the party?"

"Not yet." Helen sighed. "Damned labs don't seem to be making any headway. But the test results should come directly to me, so I'll let you know."

"My DNA test too?"

Helen was surprised. "No, those results will go directly to Jesse. He insisted, and since he's footing the bill, he gets what he wants."

It was Amanda's turn to be surprised, but only for a moment. Then she realized why Jesse would have arranged things that way. A master manipulator, he was perfectly capable of looking at an inconclusive DNA test result and announcing to the family that it had, in fact, been conclusive. He might even be capable, she thought, of claiming absolutely negative results to be positive; Jesse hated to be proven wrong.

"I didn't know," Amanda said. Before she could say anything else, the breeze began to shift, and the warm scent of horses wafted past them.

"Amanda?"

She swallowed hard, trying to control the panic. "I

—I have to go, Helen. Um . . . tell Walker I couldn't wait, all right? I'll—I'll talk to you later."

Without waiting for a response, and hardly caring what any watchers might think of her sudden retreat, Amanda bolted for the house.

"Seems clear to me," Sheriff Hamilton said in his habitually weary voice. "The ramp dropped and Vic had the misfortune to be under it when it did."

Walker nodded. "I'd say so. But neither one of us knows anything about hydraulics, J.T. If I know Jesse, he'll want this van checked out stem to stern, and pronto. You want to arrange to have it towed to town, or you want me to?"

"Why towed?" The sheriff sounded a bit plaintive. "Jesus, Walker, it was the ramp failed, not the engine."

"It's an old van, remember? The brakes are hydraulic too. *You* want to drive it ten miles on mountain roads?"

Hamilton pushed his trademark fedora onto the back of his head and sighed. "Guess not. I'll have it towed."

Walker nodded, but somewhat abstractedly. He studied the ramp of the van—raised now and carefully locked into place, its black-painted surface showing no stains of violence—and then looked at the now churned-up sand that had cradled Victor's body for at least several hours before he'd been discovered.

"What's eating at you?" the sheriff asked, his voice still drawling but his faded blue eyes sharp.

"I'm not sure. Something about this just doesn't feel right." Walker frowned, then said, "Lower the ramp again, will you? I want to have a look inside."

J.T. motioned to his deputy, and they went to either side of the rear of the van so that they could slowly and carefully—with a manual crank—lower the ramp to the ground.

Sully stepped up to Walker. "What's going on?" he asked.

Positioned so that he could look directly into the van when the ramp was down, Walker studied the interior of the vehicle for a long moment without answering. Then, slowly, he said, "Why was he raising the ramp, Sully?"

"What do you mean?"

"I mean, what was the point? Why close it up after he unloaded the horses? I've seen this van parked here whenever it wasn't in use, and the ramp was always down."

The sheriff, stepping closer to listen, asked Sully, "Is that right?"

"Yeah, I guess it is." Sully frowned. "It's here between the barns, out of the way, and there's never a real reason to close it up. Open, it stays aired."

"Speaking of airing," Walker said, "there's another reason Victor wouldn't have closed up the van. After a long trip with six horses, it's pretty ripe in there. Look around you—no shovel or pitchfork, no wheelbarrow; he obviously didn't intend to clean out all that manure, at least not until he'd got some sleep."

"He wouldn't have anyway," Sully said. "He'd have got one of the maintenance people to do it. But . . . you're right, Walker. There's no good reason why he would have raised the ramp."

The three men looked at each other, and then the sheriff said unhappily, "Well, shit."

"Not a chance in hell of finding anything useful now," Walker said. "Dozens of people have been all over this area this morning. If there was any evidence it was deliberate, it's gone now."

"Who would have wanted to kill him?" Sully demanded, keeping his voice low. "I mean, sure, Victor could be a jerk, especially where women were concerned, but you could say the same of half the men in this county. He didn't get along with everybody, and he was a sarcastic son of a bitch; so what? You don't cave in a man's skull just because he pissed you off."

"And who'd a thought up such a thing?" the sheriff offered, still acutely unhappy. "Gun or knife, sure. Hell, even a stick. But a ramp? How'd whoever it is know he'd obligingly walk under the thing?"

"It does seem an awkward way to murder someone," Walker said slowly. "At the same time, it might have been the easiest way. Somebody could have raised the ramp while Victor was leading the sixth horse to the training ring, and the way the van's parked, he might not have realized anyone was here. He would have walked beside the van from the front . . . wouldn't have seen the ramp up until he got back here . . . and probably would have headed for the controls on the other side without even thinking how wrong it was . . . and when he got under the ramp, whoever was hiding there could have hit the emergency release button."

Sully was shaking his head, still resisting the idea. "But why? It just doesn't make sense."

"Murder never does," Walker said absently, then added, "You know, it could have been a lot simpler. Somebody *could* have hit him over the head with a stick or rock—and then arranged for the ramp to drop on him to make it look like an accident."

"Why?" Sully repeated.

"I don't know why. I didn't care for Victor very much myself, but I was never tempted to kill him. Apparently, someone was very tempted."

"Nobody saw anything, nobody heard anything," Sheriff Hamilton reported wearily. "And unless Helen finds something in the postmortem, we've got nothing. All your theories aside, Walker, this'll likely end up stamped accident."

"Yeah." Sully's voice was morose. "But what if he's right, J.T.? What if we've got a murderer on Glory?"

To that, the sheriff had no reply.

Walker found her just inside the garden almost half an hour later. She was sitting on a stone bench in the shade, staring somewhat blindly, he thought, at a trellis where only one lone red rose still bloomed.

"Amanda?"

She jumped a bit, but at least there was no fear in her eyes when she looked up at him. Helen had said she'd run away from the stables with fear in her eyes. Terrible fear.

He sat down beside her. "The wind changed, huh?"

Amanda grimaced slightly and nodded. "Did Helen tell you I got spooked and ran?"

"She told me you were afraid." Walker turned a bit so that he could study her intently. "From the sound of it, more afraid than I realized. Why, Amanda?"

"I don't know. Helen says something must have happened to me, something I associate with the smell of horses, but if it did, I don't remember what it was."

"You said you had a bad fall," he recalled slowly.

Amanda shook her head. "I said that to offer Jesse some kind of concrete reason for being afraid of horses, but the truth is, I can't remember why they scare me." She glanced at him, a humorless smile twisting her lips. "Aren't you going to pounce, Walker? I'm admitting to a lie."

She was brittle, Walker realized as he listened to the tension in her voice. Wound so tight she was in danger of snapping. Because of this apparently escalating fear of horses? Or because of Victor's death?

"No," he said, "I won't pounce. The fear is obviously real, whatever caused it."

"And my lying about it doesn't bother you?"

Dryly, he said, "What's one among so many?"

With another sideways glance and brief smile, this one holding a touch of genuine humor, she said, "Bastard."

"You asked," he reminded her with a smile. "And —whatever happened to you, you'll remember it when you're ready," he said.

"That's what Helen said."

Walker looked at her for a moment, then reached for her hand. "Listen, why don't you go back to town with me, and we can have lunch together? It would probably do you good to get away from here for a few hours."

"I have to look for the dogs."

He frowned. "I assumed they were in the house, or—"

"No. They've been gone all morning. I've called them, but they haven't come." She shrugged jerkily. "So I have to look for them."

"They're probably out chasing rabbits."

"I don't think so."

With everything else that had happened, Walker wasn't particularly concerned by the dogs having been AWOL for a few hours, but Amanda's tension was definitely making him uneasy. He had the idea that she was holding herself still only with a great effort, that she was a breath away from jumping up and running—and a lot farther than just to the house.

"Amanda, look at me."

After a moment, she did, her eyes darkened with strain.

He touched her cheek with his free hand, and asked quietly, "What is it? What are you feeling?"

Her smile was as strained as her eyes. "It's been a rough morning. You may have noticed."

"You're being evasive, dammit."

She sighed. "And you're being a lawyer. The only thing I'm feeling right now is a bit of leftover panic. It's what I feel when I smell horses. I just . . . I want to run, that's all. I want to get away. It'll pass."

"Amanda—"

"Who's going to tell Jesse about Victor?" she asked quickly.

"I'll call him when I get back to the office. Probably catch him before he leaves his meeting." Walker frowned down at her. "Come into town with me. I'll bring you back after lunch, and if the dogs still aren't here, you can look for them then. A couple more hours won't make much difference."

She hesitated, but finally nodded. "All right. I need to go change first."

"And I need to go get my car." He smiled at her. "No reason to make you face the stables again."

"I hate being a coward," she confessed as they walked out to the garden's main path.

"Sounds to me like you can't help being afraid of horses," Walker told her.

"Maybe, but I hate it. It's bad enough to be afraid of something; being afraid and not knowing why you *are* is enough to drive anyone crazy."

Walker thought that would indeed make it worse, but all he said was, "Give yourself a break. And time." He thought she was a bit less tense now, and her hand was no longer rigid in his.

"I'll meet you out front in—fifteen minutes?" she suggested when they stood on the main path.

"Done." Walker released her hand and watched her

walk toward the house, then turned himself and began to retrace his way to the stables.

It was almost two o'clock when they stepped out onto the sidewalk, both blinking at the shock of bright summer light and intense heat after the dim coolness of the Golden Dragon Chinese restaurant, and Amanda shook her head bemusedly as she looked at the two enormous dragons—seemingly stone, but surely something less weighty—flanking the front door.

"I can't get used to them. And why does it strike me as peculiar for Daulton to have a Chinese restaurant?" she asked Walker.

"Probably because dragons look strange on Main Street, USA," Walker replied with a slight gesture at downtown Daulton.

It was a postcard-perfect scene, Amanda agreed silently. A grassy town square, complete with two magnolia trees and a fountain. A town hall with a clock. A barbershop with a striped pole outside. Several clothing stores that would never call themselves boutiques but nonetheless boasted higher prices than the mall out on the highway.

There was a church with bells at one end of Main Street and a Ford dealership at the other, two banks, a post office, the sheriff's department, and a fire station —and a drugstore that still had a soda fountain.

While they stood under the shade of the Golden Dragon's awning, Amanda looked at Daulton and smiled.

"I think you like this town," Walker told her, taking her hand.

"I think you're right." She tucked her purse underneath her free arm and added, "You don't have to take me back to Glory. I'm meeting Kate and Maggie at Conner's for some shopping, so I can ride back with them."

"I don't mind taking you back, Amanda."

She smiled at him. "I have some shopping I need to do, really. But you can walk me to Conner's, since it's on the way to your office."

She was much more relaxed, Walker thought as they began strolling down the sidewalk. She had even laughed once or twice. They hadn't talked about anything serious, by tacit consent avoiding all the touchy subjects between them.

Walker had found himself reluctant to tell her of his suspicions about Victor's death, though he couldn't have said exactly why. Perhaps because he had only suspicions without proof, or perhaps because she had been clearly shaken by the trainer's death—if only the violence of it.

Not, of course, personally shaken. Judging by what she had said last night—admittedly in anger—she had known Victor well enough to have received a blunt or at least obvious proposition from him. Which was to say that they had met. However, since Victor had left Glory only a few days after Amanda had arrived, Walker doubted they had had more than one or two encounters.

"Am I boring you?" Amanda asked politely.

Without hesitation, Walker replied, "You've made me mad as hell and driven me half out of my mind, to say nothing of giving me sleepless nights, but you've never bored me."

"Just wondering," she murmured.

He smiled down at her as they paused on the corner, waiting for the light to change before they crossed. "Proud of yourself?" he wanted to know.

"Well, a woman likes to know she's had some effect on a man." Amanda was smiling just a little.

"Rest assured—you have. I may never be the same again." He lifted the hand he was holding, her left, and added more seriously, "By the way—did I do this?"

Amanda didn't have to look to know he meant the faint bruises on her wrist—which had darkened a bit since morning. "I just bruise easily," she told him. "Besides, as I remember, I was on the point of scratching your eyes out at the time."

"I didn't hurt you? Tell me the truth."

"You didn't hurt me." She looked up at him steadily. "I know I look like a frail flower, Walker, but I'm not made of glass. I won't break."

"Promise?" he asked a bit whimsically.

"I promise."

He nodded, then lifted her hand and pressed his lips to her wrist.

Amanda cleared her throat. "You shouldn't do that on a public street," she murmured.

"Why not?" His green eyes were burning.

Because I'll look undignified melting into a puddle at your feet, dammit!

"Because . . . Oh, dammit, Walker—there's Preacher Bliss. Maybe we can—"

But they couldn't, of course. And since Walker refused to let go of her hand, Amanda had the bemusing experience of watching a slightly worried preacher trying to find out—without actually asking the question—if she had done anything to jeopardize her immortal soul.

Walker, not a particularly religious man, watched and listened with a tolerant smile.

"You were no help at all," Amanda accused when the preacher had finally gone on his way.

"I didn't want to interrupt." Walker's tone was innocent. "Besides, you did just fine alone. Especially since he wasn't quite brave enough to ask outright about the state of your virtue."

Amanda chuckled. "Lucky for me." Then she sobered suddenly. "He obviously hadn't heard about Victor."

"No, word hasn't got around yet."

As they approached the store where Amanda would meet Kate and Maggie, she said, "Kate told Maggie she felt a bit odd going shopping today, but Maggie told her not to be absurd."

"Maggie's right," Walker said.

"I suppose."

"We're all sorry it happened, but I've yet to meet anyone who actually *liked* Victor. So—we're sorry and we go on."

Amanda glanced up at him. "You sound like a slightly impatient philosophy professor I had in college."

"Did he give you a hard time?"

"Well, he couldn't figure out what a business major was doing in his class—especially when her minor was computer science."

"What *were* you doing in his class?"

"Trying to get a handle on life, I guess. And, before you ask, I'm as baffled as anyone else, so I assume the class didn't do much for me."

Halting beneath the awning that shaded the doorway of Conner's clothing store, Walker smiled down at her. "Remember what your fortune cookie said? 'Today, you will discover a great truth.' I'd say you just did."

"That life is baffling?"

"It works for me." He leaned down and kissed her, briefly but not lightly, and then said, "Remember, you're meeting me on the path about seven."

Amanda nodded. "I remember. Thank you for lunch, Walker."

"Don't mention it." He watched her go into the coolness of the store and then went on toward his office.

He hadn't taken three steps before his smile was gone. Just outside his office building, he never saw or heard the acquaintance who cheerfully greeted him, just as he didn't notice the mailman who had to hastily sidestep to avoid running into him on the stairs. And when he passed by his secretary's desk, she took one look at his face and didn't venture a greeting.

Walker went into his quiet office and locked the door behind him. He went to the big oak desk that had served three generations of McLellan lawyers, and sat down in the big leather chair that was usually so comfortable.

Then he unlocked the center drawer, drew out a file folder, and opened it on the neat blotter.

It didn't take him long to find it. A neat and complete list of the college courses Amanda Grant had taken. There was no philosophy course. There were no business courses, no courses in computer science. Amanda Grant had majored in design, with a minor in architecture.

Walker leaned back in his usually comfortable chair and stared at the file without seeing it. And his own voice startled him, low and harsh in the silence of the room.

"Goddammit, Amanda . . . what're you trying to do to me?"

Eleven

BY THE TIME AMANDA MADE HER WAY along the path to King High just before seven that evening, the unusually long day following a virtually sleepless night was beginning to catch up with her. She didn't feel tired so much as peculiarly *raw*, and uneasily aware that her ability to hide her thoughts and feelings was becoming uncertain.

Especially where Walker was concerned.

He was waiting for her at a point less than halfway to King High, leaning back against the huge granite boulder that the path wrapped itself around. The sun had not yet set, and the dappled light of the forest painted his white shirt and his face with shifting shadows.

When she first saw him, Amanda thought that his expression was a somewhat grim reminder of the way he had looked at her during her first days at Glory, but then he smiled and the impression of bleakness faded.

"Hi," she said casually as she reached him.

"Hi," he returned, equally casual. But then he put his hands on her shoulders and pulled her against him, and kissed her with an intensity that was a long way from casual.

Amanda told herself it was her fatigued condition that made the kiss so overwhelming, but she knew better. Her body reacted as if to a shot of pure energy, coming alive and throbbing with sudden desire, and her mind was filled only with the awareness of him and her hunger for him. It was as if they had built a bonfire the night before and it was still burning, hotter than ever.

She knew she was shaking when he at last lifted his head, and she knew he felt it.

"I've wanted to do that," he said huskily, "all day long."

All Amanda could think of to say was, "Good thing Preacher Bliss didn't see *that.* He wouldn't have had to wonder about the state of my virtue."

Walker kissed her again, briefly this time, and said, "Let him wonder. None of his business anyway." He kept an arm around her as they turned and continued along the path to King High.

Still trying to master the riot of emotions and sensations he, seemingly by magic, roused in her, Amanda said vaguely, "There's a storm coming, you know. Hear it thunder?"

"The thunder's in the mountains," Walker told her. "We'll just get rain, probably."

"I heard somebody—one of the gardeners, I think—say this morning that we need rain. But he said it . . . uneasily."

"We should have had quite a bit of rain by now," Walker explained. "That we haven't usually means one of two things. Either we're heading for a summer drought, with unrelenting heat and the danger of fires, or else July and August will be filled with very bad lightning storms."

"No wonder he sounded uneasy about it. Neither way sounds too good to me."

They walked for a moment in silence, and then Walker said, "The dogs turn up?"

"No." Amanda sighed, trying not to sound as worried as she felt. "This afternoon Maggie dug out the high-frequency whistles they were trained with, and we walked all over calling and looking for them. Even Kate skipped her volunteer work; she and Ben and a couple of his riders checked out some of the riding trails. No luck."

"They're valuable dogs," Walker noted slowly. "And valuable dogs are stolen every day. But I assume their training makes it unlikely they would have let themselves be carted off by strangers."

"Extremely unlikely. They're guard dogs; Maggie says Jesse had to formally introduce them to *all* the gardeners and maintenance people who'd be working around the house because the dogs were specifically trained to be very protective of the house and yard at all times. *Outside* the yard, they wouldn't attack a stranger, but they also wouldn't get near anyone they didn't know."

"They could have been lured into a trap," Walker said.

Amanda nodded, but said, "Who'd even try that? This is private land, *Daulton* land, miles of it; who would want the dogs so badly they'd risk Jesse coming down on them if they were caught stealing his property?"

"No one with more brains than a mushroom," Walker admitted. "Jesse is a bad enemy, and everyone in these parts knows it."

"Still . . . I'm afraid something's happened to them. They should have been back by now. They should have been back before breakfast."

The arm around her shoulders tightened, and Walker said, "One more bit of bad news for Jesse to hear today."

"He's not due back from Asheville until later tonight, so I wondered—how did he take the news about Victor?"

"Badly. Less because he liked Victor than because carelessness allowed a stupid accident to occur at Glory."

"Was it an accident?"

Walker looked down at her sharply. "Is there any reason you think it wasn't?"

Amanda was tempted for an instant—but only for an instant. She couldn't say yes, because if she did she would have to explain that Victor had had something to tell her about what had happened at Glory twenty years ago, and that she was afraid—not at all sure, but definitely afraid—that his "accident" had been arranged to keep her from hearing whatever he had to tell her.

She had no proof of that, of course. No evidence at all, in fact. But that wasn't why she found herself unwilling to offer the theory to Walker.

As long as Walker mistrusted her—which he most certainly still did—offering her own trust would be stupid and possibly dangerous. He was the Daulton family lawyer, Jesse's lawyer, and his first loyalty lay there; whether or not he believed her, if Amanda told him why she had come here, he was entirely capable of telling Jesse.

And then Amanda would have to do a lot more explaining than she was ready to do.

"No," she said after a brief hesitation, "there's no reason I think it wasn't an accident. It just seemed so bizarre. But I guess bizarre accidents happen when people aren't careful."

Walker continued to look at her for a moment, but then nodded, accepting her reply.

They reached the footbridge then, and as they walked across it Amanda looked down at the flowing water, bright and clear in the light of day. Nothing sinister, nothing to make her uneasy as she'd been the night before . . .

Bright light flashing off water . . . a stream—no, a gush of water where it hadn't been before, the drainage ditch swollen from the rain . . . small bare feet with muddy water squishing between the toes, and in the distance a light—

"Amanda?"

She blinked and looked up at him, realizing she had stopped dead in the middle of the footbridge. She didn't know what her face looked like, but from the way Walker was frowning at her, the expression she wore must have baffled him.

"I'm sorry." She put out a hand almost instinctively to touch his chest. "I must have been . . . daydreaming."

Walker shook his head. "Must have been some daydream. You look upset."

"Do I?" She attempted a little laugh and shrugged. "It was nothing, really."

"Are you sure?"

"Of course." She looked past him at the gazebo that was visible from here, and asked, "Is that where we're going to have our picnic?"

Walker hesitated for a moment, but then nodded

and, taking her hand this time, continued across the bridge toward the gazebo. "I thought so. If it's okay with you."

"It's fine." Amanda wished he hadn't spoken her name when he had, because she felt sure she'd been about to remember something very important. At least . . . she *had* been sure it was important. But even now, so quickly after, the flash of memory was fading from her, dreamlike.

Vanishing like smoke through her fingers. Damn, damn, *damn*.

"Watch your step," Walker advised as they left the path and made their way over several of a giant oak's sprawled-out roots to reach the gazebo.

Amanda glanced to one side and, noting what looked like the crumbling stone foundation of what had been a small building once upon a time, said, "Something else used to be here?"

"A gatehouse. Long time ago. This stream changed course when my father was a boy, and that changed the driveway to King High. The gatehouse gradually fell into ruins. I had the gazebo built a few years ago."

"So far from the house?"

"I like it here."

Inside the gazebo, a thick quilt was spread out on the solid wooden flooring, and a couple of oversize pillows promised comfort. An imposing wicker basket waited to be opened, and a large thermos jug held, Amanda assumed, something cold to drink.

"Tea," Walker replied when she asked. "I would have brought wine, but since you seldom drink . . ."

"Tea's better anyway, especially in this heat."

"The heat doesn't seem to bother you," Walker commented as they made themselves comfortable on the quilt and he opened the wicker basket in search of glasses. "You always look so cool and . . . unwrinkled."

Amanda laughed. "Unwrinkled?"

"A lawyer's literal mind—didn't you accuse me of that at some point? What I meant was that, even though other people look rumpled and wilted by the heat, you always look as though you just stepped out of a cool shower and put on fresh clothes."

Accepting a glass of iced tea from him, Amanda said lightly, "For anyone contemplating a life in the South, a necessary trait, I'd say."

"Are you? Contemplating a life here, I mean? You told Jesse you didn't want Glory."

"I don't. Glory is magnificent, but . . ."

"But?"

She shook her head, then smiled. "It overwhelms. Especially me. I don't think I was ever meant to end up there. The Daultons who live at Glory should always be big and tanned and bursting with life and temper. That isn't me. It's a beautiful place, but it'll never be home. Not to me."

Walker looked at her for a moment, then continued removing covered dishes from the basket. "But you like the South?"

"Very much—despite the heat of summer. But I haven't really thought much about the future." Unwilling to linger on that subject, she said, "What's for supper? I'm starving."

"Good," Walker said. "Because there's enough here for an army. . . ."

There was still plenty of daylight left when they finished eating and packed away the remains, though rain clouds had begun to hide the setting sun. It was very peaceful there in the little gazebo, and they leaned back on the pillows and talked casually, sipping iced tea and occasionally falling silent to listen to the birds and crickets.

"Didn't you say Reece almost married once?" she asked idly.

"Yeah."

"But not Sully?"

"I think somebody's going to have to get him pregnant first."

Amanda smiled, but then said in a musing tone, "I was engaged for a year during college."

On the point of asking her what had happened to end it, Walker was suddenly jolted by the realization that it was possible nothing *had.* She could, even now, be married. That hadn't been one of the questions he'd asked during the formal interviews in his office, since it was hardly germane to the question of her identity, and it hadn't occurred to him to ask since.

Christ, what if she was married? What if a husband waited patiently up North somewhere for her to contact him and report she'd been accepted by the Daultons? Walker was surprised and unsettled when he felt a rush of primitive emotions coil inside him so tightly it was actually difficult to breathe.

For the first time since this afternoon, something other than the lies he was sure she had told twisted his emotions into knots.

There can't be another man. Not husband, not lover—no other man. He couldn't believe she could have given herself to him so freely if there had been another man in her life. She couldn't have. Not even she could have.

"What happened?" He heard his voice, and knew it was too rough, too intense, even before she glanced at him in surprise.

"Nothing dramatic." She gave a little laugh. "Not

even anything specific, really. It just . . . didn't feel right to me. There was no big fight when I told him. In fact, I think he expected it." She shrugged and smiled.

Walker looked at her for a moment, then took her glass away and set it aside. He caught her shoulders and eased her back down against the pillows, following until he was raised on an elbow beside her.

"Was it something I said?" she murmured.

You said you grew up as Amanda Grant, and I don't think that's true. Why did you lie about it, Amanda? For God's sake, why?

Her eyes were growing sleepy with a sensual look he found utterly absorbing and so wildly arousing it made everything else, even lies, seem unimportant. What did it matter? What did anything matter except that he wanted her until he couldn't think straight? He knew her innocent question was more teasing than serious. But he answered anyway.

"If I remember correctly," he said, unfastening the bottom button of her blouse, "you said my name, very polite and guarded. Mr. McLellan. With a little nod."

"You mean . . . the day I came to your office," she remembered, watching him undo the next button.

"Yes. It was the first time I saw you. It was also when I began wanting you." He unfastened another button and slipped his fingers inside the white blouse to touch the warm, silky skin of her stomach. He felt her quiver, muscles and nerve endings reacting to his touch, and that instant response affected him with the suddenness and power of a punch to the gut. Heat rushed through him, and every muscle in his body seemed to contract in a spasm of raw need.

Jesus, how could she affect him like this?

Her eyes grew sleepier, the smoky gray darkening

to slate as they met his, and her voice was throaty. "Way back then? You waited an awfully long time to do anything about it. Even for a careful man."

"Christ, tell me about it." He heard the raspy sound of his own voice, and didn't give a damn that he was letting her see how wildly she affected him. Letting her? As if he had a choice. He finished unbuttoning her blouse, and opened it. She was wearing a bra, a delicate wisp of flesh-colored silk and lace that lovingly cupped her full, firm breasts and just barely covered her nipples. Under his enthralled, unblinking gaze, her breasts rose and fell in a quickening cadence and her nipples began to tighten, the tips thrusting against the material hiding them from him.

Breathless now, she said, "Walker, it's still broad daylight. Anyone could stroll along the path—"

"Nobody ever comes out here except me. Don't stop me, Amanda. I have to see you." He bent his head until his lips just grazed the upper curve of one breast. "The moon wasn't bright enough last night to let me see you the way I need to." His tongue probed the valley between her breasts, then glided along the bra's lacy edge toward a straining peak.

"You planned this," she accused him unsteadily.

"Guilty." He raised his head suddenly and looked at her while his hand slid up her stomach until his fingers touched the front clasp of the bra. He toyed with the clasp, acutely aware of her heart racing underneath his knuckles. "Do you want me to stop?"

Without so much as a glance toward the path, she shook her head mutely.

It began to rain about the time they lay naked together, and the steady rhythm of water dropping on the roof of the gazebo shut them off from the rest of the world as if by a curtain of sound. Cooled by the rain, the breeze wafted over them gently.

A part of Walker, the reserved man trained in logic and reason, wanted to demand that she tell him the truth about who she really was and why she had come to Glory, wanted to take advantage of the vulnerability of nakedness and blind passion to get his answers.

But he was blind, too.

The man of reason was overwhelmed by another man, a man of the senses and emotions, a man who desired with such primitive fury that all he cared about was the possession of his mate. And that man didn't give a damn about the truth.

He found the other marks of last night's passion on her pale flesh, but to his rough apology she replied only that he hadn't hurt her and then pulled his head down to end the discussion. And her response to his touch was so fervent, so immediate and guileless, that it was impossible for him to hold back in any way.

She fit him so perfectly it was as if they had been designed for each other.

He cupped her breasts, lifted them, closed his mouth over the hard tips. He could feel her heart beating, the rhythm of it as wild as his own, and her quick breathing matched his. He trailed his lips over her silky skin, pausing at the tiny birthmark shaped like an inverted heart that was placed high on her rib cage, and again just above her navel, where she was especially sensitive.

The little sound she made touched him like a caress, and her mouth was achingly sweet beneath his, and when their bodies joined—just the simple act of joining—it was so deeply satisfying that Walker went utterly still, conscious of the most incredible sense of *rightness*.

Amanda seemed to feel it, too; her gaze locked with his, gray eyes as mysteriously compelling as a mountain fog, and she whispered his name as if in answer to some question asked of her.

Then the power of sheer desire swept over him, over them both, demanding a more primitive satisfaction, and he was aware of nothing except the imperative necessity of finding a release of the spiraling, maddening tension inside him. He began moving, thrusting deeply, frantically, urged on by her throaty moans and the sensual undulations of her body.

Until she cried out wildly in elation, and the inner spasms of her pleasure pushed him over the edge and into a shattering, unbelievably powerful culmination.

"Stay with me tonight," he said.

"I can't," she answered after a moment.

Twilight had come, and the rain was ending, taking its time about going. And they had been lying together, in silence, for a long time.

Walker, a rational man, was conscious of the need to be careful, to not disturb the undefinable but undeniably powerful thing that had happened between them, and so he kept his voice low and matter-of-fact. "Why not?"

She lifted her head from his shoulder and looked at him gravely. "Unless you've told him, Jesse doesn't know about us yet. I'd rather he didn't find out by me not showing up for breakfast tomorrow morning."

"Somebody's bound to tell him," Walker said.

"I know. But I'd rather it was me."

He nodded finally, accepting.

"It's getting late." Amanda sat up with obvious reluctance, and reached for her clothing.

Walker followed suit, but said seriously, "Tell Jesse soon, will you?"

"I will."

After they were dressed, Walker said he intended to walk her back to Glory, and they set out together. The thirsty ground had soaked up the rain greedily, leaving only damp earth rather than mud, so they had no trouble on the path, and since the rain had dropped the temperature considerably, the stroll back was cool and pleasant.

The path ended in front of and to one side of the house at the edge of the yard, and when they reached that point they had a clear view of the garage. Jesse's Cadillac was home.

"I'll come in with you," Walker said.

She looked up at him, a little amused. "Why? To explain why my blouse is missing a button?"

He was momentarily distracted. "Is it? Did I do that again?"

"It is, and you did." She stood on tiptoe and kissed him. "And I can handle Jesse alone, thank you very much."

"Amanda—"

"Good night, Walker."

He watched her crossing the damp grass of the yard toward the house, and it took a surprising effort of will to keep from either calling her back or else going after her. He didn't know if it was because something remarkable had taken place between them in the gazebo or simply because odd things were happening at Glory and that made him apprehensive, but for whatever reason, he didn't like the idea of her going into that house without him.

Not a bit.

"Amanda?"

She went into his study to find Jesse working at his desk, despite the late hour and his extremely long and no doubt exhausting day. "Can't this wait until tomorrow?" she asked, gesturing to the paperwork he was engaged in. "It's after nine, Jesse."

"I know what time it is." He was looking at her, unusually grim. "I got home over an hour ago. Where have you been?"

"With Walker," Amanda replied without hesitation, certain that someone had already told him—since outrage was written all over his face—about Walker's very public display of passion this morning.

For a moment, Jesse didn't say anything at all. He just stared at Amanda, perhaps waiting for her to blink or stutter nervously or cower in guilty dismay. If so, he waited in vain. Amanda merely stood there, relaxed, meeting his gaze with a little smile.

Finally, Jesse said, "Am I to understand that you and Walker are . . ."

"The phrase," Amanda supplied helpfully, "is 'consenting adults.' And we are."

"How long has this been going on?"

"Not long."

"And I suppose you don't give two hoots about my opinion?"

Amanda shook her head. "I care very much about your opinion, Jesse. But I'm a grown woman, and when it comes to my sex life, I make my own decisions."

More irritable than outraged now, Jesse said, "You'll only threaten to leave again if I protest, won't you?"

Her smile widened. "It is a handy bit of leverage, I admit. But I don't know why you'd protest anyway. You trust Walker to handle all your legal affairs, and he's as welcome in this house as one of the family—so why not trust him with your granddaughter?"

"Are you going to marry him?"

"Jesse, I have trouble making up my mind what to wear every morning; big decisions generally take me a *long* time. Getting involved with Walker just sort of happened, and I'm not really thinking very much about it."

After a long moment, Jesse almost visibly turned from an affronted grandfather to a pathetic one. "I'd like to see you settled before I go," he said.

Unimpressed by that piteous declaration, Amanda put her hands on the desk and leaned toward him. "If," she said, "you say one word to Walker about him marrying me, or even hint at the subject, I *will* leave. So fast it'll make your head spin. Stay out of it, Jesse."

Frustrated, the old man snapped, "Hussy!"

She straightened again and smiled. "I'm a Daulton, remember? We manage our own affairs."

After scowling a moment longer, Jesse finally barked out a laugh. "All right, all right, I'll keep my nose out of it. What's this I hear about the dogs missing?"

Amanda wasn't surprised that he mentioned the dogs before Victor's death. Jesse's priorities, though peculiar, were at least consistent; his personal property was generally uppermost in his mind.

"Haven't seen a sign of them all day," she replied, sitting down in one of the chairs in front of the desk. "Maggie, Kate, and I looked, but couldn't find them. We tried the whistles, walked all over—nothing. Do you think someone could have stolen them?"

"Not likely. And they wouldn't have taken food from anyone, or eaten anything they found, so poison's out."

Amanda hadn't considered that lethal possibility, and it made her acutely unhappy to contemplate it now. "Then where could they be?"

"I don't know. We'll organize a more thorough search in the morning. For tonight—and just in case it was some lowlife's bright idea to get rid of the dogs to make the house vulnerable to a break-in—I've asked J.T. to send a couple of his boys over to keep an eye on the place."

Amanda nodded. She couldn't help feeling that theft had not been the point if the dogs had indeed been deliberately removed, but the only other reason that came to her mind was so unnerving she hadn't let herself think about it until now.

After the seemingly accidental poisoning at the party, she had believed that anyone who *might* have tried to poison her must have been dissuaded after Jesse announced he wouldn't, after all, change his will. But what if that someone had been unwilling to gamble on the chances of the old man again changing his mind? What if that someone had only waited a bit to avoid the suspicious circumstance of another misfortune striking Amanda so soon after the party?

Most everyone had remarked on the fact that the dogs seldom left her side, and no one could doubt that they would have protected her from any threat. So—the first step in arranging another "accident" to befall Amanda would have been to get the dogs out of the way.

"Amanda?"

She blinked and looked across the desk at Jesse. "Oh—sorry. I must be more tired than I thought. What did you say?"

"I asked if you got the chance to talk to Victor before he was killed."

Amanda blinked again. "Talk to him?"

A bit impatient, Jesse said, "After he'd gone on the buying trip, Maggie mentioned that you'd wanted to talk to him about the way things had been twenty years ago, since he was here then. I just wondered if you got the chance."

"No. No, I never did." She hesitated, but then asked as casually as possible, "Did Maggie tell anyone else I wanted to talk to Victor?"

Jesse had returned his attention to one of the papers spread out on his blotter, and replied abstractedly. "What? Oh, we were all there, honey. It was in the front parlor one night, after you'd excused yourself early."

Staring at his intent face, Amanda wondered for the first time if it was possible that the threat she posed to someone who wanted Glory might not be nearly as dangerous as the threat she posed to someone who wanted whatever had happened twenty years ago to remain locked in the past.

But what was it? *What had happened?*

And who could be threatened, now, by exposure? Reece and Sully had been boys, so it seemed unlikely they had been involved. Not impossible, Amanda supposed, but surely unlikely. Kate had been barely twenty—and what could a young woman have been involved in that required deaths twenty years later to keep the secret hidden?

Jesse? Maggie? Both were old enough; they'd been adults twenty years ago. But could Jesse possibly want to harm the granddaughter he so obviously—and genuinely, Amanda believed—adored? And could there possibly be such violence in Maggie's brisk and practical nature?

Or was it someone not a part of Glory at all, someone whose connection to the still-unknown events of that last night was so elusive Amanda had not yet discovered it? And might never now, since Victor had been killed.

Dammit, what happened that night?

"It was terrible about Victor," she heard herself say.

"He was careless, Amanda," Jesse responded in a hard tone. "No excuse for that."

She looked into those dynamic tarnished-silver eyes and felt an uneasy little chill. On the other hand . . . maybe Jesse was ruthless enough to destroy what he loved in order to protect something he valued more. But what? To a dying man, what could be so important?

"You do look tired, honey." He was smiling. "Why don't you go on up to bed?"

"You should too," she murmured.

"I will. In a little while. Good night, Amanda."

Amanda got up slowly. "Good night, Jesse." She left his study and made her way upstairs. She met no one along the way, so she didn't have to pretend. Didn't have to paste a smile on her face and act as if God was in his heaven and all was right with the world. Didn't have to make believe it wasn't true that for the first time since coming to Glory, she was deeply afraid.

Pulling up her horse, Leslie Kidd said to Sully, "We've covered miles with no sign of them. Do you really believe the dogs would have gone all the way out here?"

Halting his own horse, Sully passed a hand down Beau's glossy black neck and then shook his head. "No. Not unless somebody brought them this far."

"Somebody?" Relaxed in the saddle as only an expert rider could be, Leslie regarded him thoughtfully.

They were on one of the trails that crisscrossed Glory, this one at the extreme end of the valley to the north, and they were, in fact, some miles from the house and grounds. It was Saturday morning, and most everybody at Glory was engaged in the search for the missing dogs, either on foot or on horseback.

All the search teams on horseback were paired, and Sully had assigned Leslie to be his partner even though he usually rode alone. However, if Leslie had expected conversation from Sully during the outing, casual or otherwise, she had been disappointed. He'd hardly said a word.

Asked two direct questions, Sully looked at her, frowning. "What I said was clear enough, wasn't it? The dogs wouldn't be out this far unless somebody had brought them."

Leslie smiled. In her unusually gentle voice, she said, "Has anyone ever told you that you have an extremely short fuse?"

To his complete astonishment, Sully felt a tide of heat creep up his face. "Did I snap at you? Sorry."

"You snapped—not necessarily at me. The dogs being gone has you worried, doesn't it?"

Again, Sully felt surprise. He knew all too well that he had as much chance of hiding his emotions as the sun had of hiding in a clear afternoon sky, but it was rare that anyone could so exactly pinpoint the cause of his unease. He looked at her ordinary face with its remarkable eyes, and heard himself giving an answer he'd had no intention of giving.

"I don't like it, no. Guard dogs don't wander off to chase rabbits."

"Then somebody got them? Took them off somewhere, maybe to sell, because they're valuable?"

"Guard dogs don't let themselves be taken. It's part of their training. They're also registered and have their numbers tattooed inside their ears, so no reputable buyer would touch them without transfer-of-ownership papers."

After a moment, Leslie said, "You don't expect to find them alive, do you?"

"No."

When he urged his horse on after that flat denial, Leslie guided her own horse to follow. But her thoughtful gaze remained fixed for a long time on Sully's broad, powerful back.

The search for the dogs continued most of the day Saturday, but by afternoon it seemed obvious the animals had vanished without a trace. Jesse was more angry than upset about it, and talked about ordering another pair of dogs on Monday—as if they were a pair of shoes or some other inanimate objects to be sent for because the old ones had been mislaid.

That cavalier attitude disturbed Amanda, particularly since she had felt affection for the silent animals and since they had given her a sense of safety she had not fully appreciated until they were gone. But she said nothing about it.

Walker had come over late that morning, ostensibly to help with the search, although he told Amanda it was really curiosity that brought him; he'd wondered how Jesse would greet him.

"And how did he?" Amanda asked.

"Characteristically. He said if I hurt you he'd have me tarred and feathered, and then hanged."

Amanda smiled. "Well, at least now you know the potential price of sleeping with the boss's granddaughter."

"I knew that before he told me." Without explaining that abrupt statement, Walker added in a lighter tone, "I told him I intended to take you back to King High with me for supper—and the rest of the weekend."

She eyed him with amusement. "A little high-handed, aren't you?"

"Always." He put his hands on her shoulders and drew her against him, and kissed her.

They were standing together in the foyer near the foot of the stairs, having just left the front parlor, where a critical evaluation of their search methods was being offered by Jesse to the others, and Walker didn't seem to care that anyone might have walked out of the parlor and observed them.

Not, Amanda thought dimly, that she cared, either.

"Come with me, Amanda," he murmured, cupping her face in his hands now and looking down at her. "I want to wake up tomorrow morning and see you in my bed."

"Let me go change," she said, giving in without argument and barely stopping herself from inviting him up to her bedroom.

She told herself that she went with him only because she needed to get away from Glory, but even though that was partly true, she couldn't pretend even to herself that it was entirely true. The truth was that she wanted to be with Walker, especially now that there was so much to think about, so many things to consider.

She wanted to be with him because he made everything else seem unimportant—and she badly needed to forget, if only for a little while, all the questions and worries crowding her mind.

Since Walker had already announced his intentions to Jesse, they didn't bother to tell anyone else that Amanda would be spending the night at King High. As soon as she came downstairs they simply walked out the front door.

It was late afternoon, and hot, so the wooded path offered at least shade from the brilliant June sun. They walked slowly, lazily, not talking very much. When they crossed over the footbridge, Amanda glanced at the water warily, but there was no flash of an elusive memory, nothing to disturb her.

King High in the sunlight was every bit as gracious and welcoming as it had been in the moonlight, and Amanda felt the same sense of having found a peaceful place. She felt it even more strongly when they went in the front doors, and she stood in the cool quiet of the house, looking around her.

Unlike Jesse, Walker clearly did care for antiques; they were all around, arranged beautifully in the spacious rooms Amanda could see from the foyer, and the gleam of old, well-polished wood added to the feeling of cool peace.

Walker led her to the right and into a parlor or sitting room, and said, "I'll go get us something cold to drink, and then I'll give you the grand tour. How does that sound?"

"Fine."

"Good. Make yourself at home."

Instead of sitting down, Amanda wandered around the big room for a few minutes, looking at books on the shelves and pictures on the walls. She ended up standing before the fireplace and gazing at a painting of a lovely dark-haired woman with warm green eyes. There was a look of irrepressible humor hovering around her smiling mouth, and the resemblance to Walker was very strong. His mother, obviously.

"A-man-*da*."

The summons was high-pitched, eerily childlike, and swung her around in surprise. It took her a moment, but then she saw the perch standing at a nearby window and the large African gray parrot regarding her with bright eyes.

Amanda approached the bird slowly, various

thoughts flitting through her mind. In a soft voice, she said, "Has he talked to you about me, bird? Is that it?"

The parrot tilted his head to one side. "Aman*da*. Say hello."

She smiled and reached out a cautious hand, stroking the bird's glossy breast feathers. "Hello. What's your name?"

"Bailey says hello," the parrot responded brightly.

"Hello, Bailey." She hesitated for a moment, still petting the parrot, and then, hearing a step outside the room, raised her voice slightly and said, "Say my name. Say Amanda."

"Aman*da*. Pretty girl. Aman*da*."

"That bird's got more taste than I gave him credit for," Walker remarked as he came into the room and to her side. He handed her a tall glass of iced tea, smiling. "He drives me crazy most of the time, with a comment for everything."

"Hot today," the parrot announced with excellent timing. "Storm tonight? Hello, Walker."

"Hi, Bailey." Walker's voice was resigned. "No storm tonight. He hates storms," he added in an aside to Amanda.

"Did you teach him to talk?" Amanda wondered.

Walker seemed to hesitate, then shook his head. "No, he's older than I am. Mother raised him, and she was the one he picked up most of his vocabulary from. He learns fast, though. And he seems to be pretty good at remembering people even after meeting them only once."

Amanda looked at Walker for a moment, sipping her tea, then smiled. "I like the way he says my name —accent on the last syllable."

"Aman*da*," Bailey said promptly. "Pretty girl. Come see me. I love you."

Startled, Amanda laughed. "You feathered charmer, you."

"He's a born flirt," Walker warned her with a smile.

She smiled in return, but all she said was, "You promised me the grand tour."

"So I did. This way, ma'am . . ."

It was very late when Amanda woke up. She lay there for a few minutes, listening to the night noises, then very carefully eased from Walker's bed. Sleeping deeply, he didn't stir. Even though the room was a bit stuffy, they had ended up here rather than on the mattress on the gallery because it was a narrow mattress and Walker wanted more room than it provided.

She looked down at him, illuminated by the moonlight spilling into the room. Even in repose, his body was powerful, compelling. Without touching her, without even moving or being awake and aware of her, he made desire ignite deep in her belly, and Amanda had to force herself to turn away. She picked up their scattered clothing from the floor and tossed most of the things over a chair, then slipped into his white shirt. It smelled of him, a scent that was familiar to her now and yet still had the power to rouse hunger in her.

Amanda stood there, her head bent as she breathed in the spicy, musky scent of her lover. Finally, she fastened a couple of buttons and went to the French doors that opened onto the gallery. The doors stood open so that the bedroom could catch whatever breeze was forthcoming, but it was a hot, still night, and only the fans turning lazily out on the gallery stirred the air.

She walked out to the railing and stood there with

her hands on it, just looking around. Clouds, moving swiftly so high up where there was wind, hid the moon from time to time, casting King High into momentary darkness. Out here, the scents were cut grass and honeysuckle and, faintly, wild roses. Crickets and katydids filled the humid air with their harmony, now and then accompanied by a bullfrog and, once, by an owl.

I feel safe here.

How odd, she thought, that she should feel so at home here, so at peace, when Glory lay hardly more than a mile away. Then again, perhaps it wasn't so odd. Her emotions while at Glory tended to be negative ones, and even without those stresses Amanda doubted she would have felt all that different; Glory *was* overwhelming, and though she could genuinely admire it, she was not comfortable there.

She gazed out on King High, listened to the peaceful night sounds, and could almost feel what was left of her tension drain away from her. Behind her, somewhere in Walker's house, an old clock bonged the hour of two A.M. with sonorous precision. And it was in that moment, her body totally relaxed and her mind completely at peace, that Amanda felt herself again transported to another time.

There's the clock . . . sneak past the clock . . . ooh, it's after midnight, Mama won't like it . . . the wind's really blowing and—oh!—what lightning! But at least it isn't raining yet, and maybe I can get there and back before it does. I want to see Gypsy and her baby, maybe give them that piece of my apple I saved from supper . . .

Mud squishing between my toes . . . jump the drainage ditch—boy, is it ever full! Must be raining cats and dogs up in the mountains . . . There's the barn—but why's there a light inside? And that sound . . . that awful sound . . .

The rasping croak of a bullfrog brought Amanda back with a jolt. She blinked, staring around, conscious of her unsteady breathing, of her heart thudding wildly with a child's abrupt panic.

It was several minutes before the sensations began to fade, and when they did, the memory did as well. Vanishing like smoke through her fingers . . .

She remembered the *actions*—though the surroundings had been hazy and for the most part unidentifiable. But she remembered looking at a clock. Going downstairs and through a door. Across a field. Jumping over a ditch filled with muddy water. But now it was as if she had watched someone else do those things; there were no emotions connected, no thoughts or sensations such as those she had felt so briefly.

Amanda tried to recapture the elusive memory. She made herself relax, blanked her mind. She gazed out on King High and waited—but in vain. If she was indeed on the verge of remembering why she was afraid of horses or something else important, it seemed that Helen was right in saying it wouldn't be forced.

It would come at its own pace.

Dammit.

It was a long time later that Amanda became aware of a slight stirring behind her in the bedroom. She debated briefly, but in the end remained there by the railing and waited.

"Amanda?" His voice was quiet.

"Did I wake you? I'm sorry."

He put his arms around her and drew her gently back against him. "Couldn't you sleep?"

She leaned her head back against his shoulder. "I

came out here to listen to the night. It's so alive, isn't it? Yet so peaceful."

Walker's arms tightened around her. "If you were looking for peace," he murmured, "you shouldn't have come out here wearing nothing but my shirt."

Amanda smiled, very aware of the hard arousal of his body. "No?"

"No." His hand found several unfastened buttons, and slipped inside the shirt to touch her. "Definitely not. Come back to bed, Amanda."

She felt her legs go weak, her breathing quicken, and said a bit helplessly, "How can you *do* that . . . so quickly? How can you make me feel this way?"

"What way?" His mouth feathered a touch beneath her ear, down her neck. He pulled aside the collar of the shirt she wore so that he could press his lips to her shoulder.

"This way . . . You know. You have to know."

"Tell me."

"You have to know," she repeated, and then sucked in a breath when his hand closed over one of her breasts, a heat that owed nothing to the night flaring deep inside her. She wanted to turn and fling her arms around him, to press herself even closer and fit herself against him, but he was holding her still and she could only endure the shattering sensations.

"Look," he whispered. "Watch what I'm doing."

Amanda obeyed dazedly, looking down at herself to watch the wildly erotic sight of his hand moving inside the white shirt as he caressed her body. She felt his fingers tug at her nipple, roll it slowly back and forth, and the burning pleasure tore a shaken moan from her throat.

"Do you want me?" he asked her hoarsely.

"Yes."

His teeth toyed with her earlobe gently, and his free

hand found its way down over her hip, underneath the shirt there, and slid to touch her lower belly. Soft skin was stroked very slowly, then his fingers moved lower and found silky curls, tugged delicately. He rubbed, barely touching her until her hips rolled pleadingly, then stroked firmly, pressed harder.

"Tell me you want me."

"I want you. Walker . . ."

Amanda moaned again, trying and failing to catch her breath, to beg him not to torment her like this. She felt the most incredibly arousing sense of her own sexuality, an overwhelming awareness of the pleasure her body could experience. But, even more, what she felt was a hunger that went deeper than her bones, deeper than thought or reason, deeper even than instinct.

A hunger for him.

"Walker . . . please . . ."

Ending the torment abruptly, Walker groaned and lifted her into his arms. He carried her into his bedroom and lowered her to the middle of the big four-poster bed. Impatient as always with buttons, he merely ripped the shirt open to bare her to his intense gaze, and then lowered himself onto her.

Amanda cried out when he entered her, her legs closing around him strongly. The feelings were wild, sweeping over her with all the violence of a storm, and in the midst of that storm, tossed about and lashed by raw sensation and chaotic emotions she could no longer master, she heard herself cry out something else, releasing a captive truth because it had grown too vast to be held inside her.

Walker went still, his green eyes burning down at her, his face a moonlit primitive mask of hunger. No —more than hunger. A . . . craving. A brutal necessity. His breathing was harsh, labored, and his muscles quivered with strain.

"Say it again," he ordered thickly.

She didn't want to, didn't want to give it to him like this, when she couldn't think, but she was helpless to stop the now-whispered words.

"I love you."

He was still a moment longer, almost rigid, but then he was moving again, plunging deep within her again and again as if he sought to penetrate her very soul. Amanda forgot what she had told him, forgot everything except the burning pleasure he stroked into her body. She couldn't be still, couldn't breathe, couldn't do anything except feel.

When her climax came, it was shockingly intense, sweeping over her in waves and waves of hot, throbbing ecstasy. She was barely aware of whimpering, of holding Walker with all the strength left to her while he shuddered and cried out hoarsely.

It was almost dawn when it began raining. Amanda lay curled at Walker's side, feeling a damp but blessedly cool breeze blowing into the bedroom and across their naked bodies. He was asleep, she was sure, his breathing deep and even. But she was wide awake.

She hadn't expected him to say that he loved her too. No, not that. But he might, she thought wistfully, have said *something*. He might have said that he was glad—or that he wasn't glad. He might have told her not to be stupid, and didn't she know the difference between sex and love? He might even have smiled triumphantly, as males so often did with a conquest made.

Something.

Anything.

Anything to tell her it mattered at all to him that she loved him.

Twelve

AMANDA HUNG UP THE PHONE AND stared down at it, frowning. She had thought she knew every variant Walker's voice was capable of producing, but never had she heard him sound so . . . emotionless. As if all the feeling had been squeezed out of him.

"Amanda? Is anything wrong?" Kate came into the front parlor, where Amanda had taken Walker's call, and looked at her quizzically.

It was Monday afternoon, it was raining buckets outside, and the two women were alone in the house, since Maggie had gone with Jesse to the Daulton Industries office building, which was some miles outside Daulton.

"What? Oh—no, nothing's wrong. Walker wants me to come into town."

"Austin can drive you," Kate told her. "Just press

the button for the garage, and tell him when you want to leave."

"Thanks, I will." Amanda looked at the older woman for a moment, wishing she didn't feel so wary of everyone now. "It's a rotten day for a drive, though."

"I think we're getting our spring rains late. The ground's getting so saturated, we'll be lucky if we don't have flooding by the middle of the week." Kate's perfect features tightened suddenly in a spasm of pain.

"Are you all right?" Amanda asked quickly.

"Mmm." After a moment, Kate smiled. "Cramps. The pill doesn't do a damned thing about them, unfortunately."

"You too?" Amanda shook her head ruefully. "When my doctor put me on them to regulate my cycle, I thought I'd be home free. But the only difference is that now the cramps come like clockwork."

Kate sat down at the neat secretary near one of the windows, where she did the books for Glory. "It's the curse of being a Daulton woman," she said absently, opening a ledger and beginning to check a column of numbers against a stack of receipts. "Irregular cycles, hormonal imbalances, and the tendency to flirt with the idea of becoming an axe murderer one week out of most every month."

Amanda knew she should get ready and call Austin to drive her into town, but she hesitated, drawn by a rare feeling of sisterhood. "Have you tried B-complex vitamins? They work for me. Now I'm only tempted to maim every once in a while instead of every month, and I've actually stopped glaring murderously at total strangers in supermarket checkout lines."

Kate sent her a quick smile. "Helen suggested them —and they do work pretty well."

Amanda sat down on the arm of one of the sofas and said, "Is it a Daulton trait? I mean, the hormonal problems?"

"According to Helen it is. She has all the medical records for the townspeople, going back over a hundred and fifty years. And apparently, Daulton women have always been at the mercy of their hormones. Medical science can correct the problems nowadays, thank God; it must have been hell a hundred years ago. Can you imagine what it must have been like? Bursting hormones on a sweltering July day?"

Amanda shuddered. "Those poor women."

"I'll say." Kate nodded, and then looked thoughtful. "You know, it's no wonder so many people were convinced there was a strain of madness in this family. Between the wild mood swings of the women and the obsessiveness of the men—we probably *did* seem a little mad."

"The obsessiveness of the men?"

Kate looked at her for a long moment, then spoke slowly. "You won't find it written in all the magazine or newspaper articles, the history books—but there is a kind of madness in the Daulton men, Amanda. It usually happens only once in their lives, rarely twice—but it always happens. When they give their heart, whatever—or whoever—they love becomes their obsession. If it's a woman, she's loved with an intense, possessive jealousy—and in the past was often kept here at Glory, isolated and usually pregnant."

"The way my mother was isolated here?" Amanda said.

Again, Kate hesitated. But then she answered quietly. "Yes. Brian had two obsessive loves in his life, Amanda. Christine—and riding. He more or less gave up riding for six months every year to spend most of his time with her; for the other months, he had to ride.

Leaving her here was his way of making sure she didn't . . . get interested in anyone else."

"And if she had? What would he have done? How did this . . . madness show itself?"

With a detachment that made her words all the more dreadful, Kate said, "Daulton men have been killing other males over women for generations. It was usually hushed up, of course, or labeled self-defense—or something else, something to satisfy the curious and win the sheriff a few more sure votes in the next election."

"You're not serious."

Kate smiled. "Entirely. Like I said, Daulton men are obsessive when they love. It's in the genes, like black hair and gray eyes. A kind of berserk fury that takes hold of them when they face a threat to whatever they love. According to family folklore, a Daulton man quite literally loses his mind for whatever length of time it takes him to destroy his rival; he doesn't see or hear anything else, and often doesn't afterward remember what he did. But . . . it takes blood to sate his rage."

Is that what happened that night? Amanda wondered. *Is that why Christine Daulton left Glory—because she was terrified of her husband learning of her affair? Or because he* had *found out and she knew what he would do?*

"God, that's awful," Amanda said aloud.

Kate nodded, but then shrugged a little. "Ancient history, of course. Even Daulton men are more civilized in these modern times. Take Sully, for instance. He's very much a Daulton, but . . . his obsession is Glory; any woman he cares about won't have to worry about him losing his mind over her. He's free to love a woman with all his heart and none of his rage."

But what would he do to someone who tried to take Glory away from him? Amanda couldn't help but wonder.

"What about Reece?" is what she asked.

"Reece isn't a Daulton," Kate replied with unexpected flatness. "Oh—genetically. But not in any of the ways that count."

Since Amanda had felt that to be true, she couldn't argue. Still, it was a conversation she wanted to continue, and only a glance at her watch kept her from doing so.

"Damn—I've got to go change."

"I'll call Austin for you," Kate offered. "How soon do you want to leave?"

"Ten minutes. Thanks, Kate." Amanda hurried from the room, her thoughts turning once again to Walker and the odd tonelessness of his voice when he'd asked her to come to his office.

What was wrong?

All the way to town, Amanda worried over it. He had been fine when he'd brought her back to Glory Sunday evening—by car, since it had been raining still. They had spent most of the day in his bed, and if he hadn't said a single word about her declaration of love, he had at least left her in no doubt that he wanted her more than ever.

So what could have happened between yesterday evening and this afternoon to squeeze all the feeling out of his voice? And why had he asked her to come to his office rather than wait until this evening, when they would—surely would—see each other?

The town of Daulton, miserable in the rain, was practically deserted on this Monday afternoon. Amanda got out in front of Walker's office building, after telling Austin that he could return to Glory, and went quickly inside. She met no one in the lobby or on the stairs, and when she reached the outer office on the second floor, it was to find Walker's secretary away from her desk.

She hesitated, then went to the door to the inner office and knocked softly. She opened it and stuck her head in with a smile. "Hi," she said to Walker, who was behind his desk.

"Come in," he said. "Close the door behind you."

Amanda knew with the first word out of his mouth that whatever was wrong—it was bad. Very bad. His voice wasn't merely squeezed of feeling; it was deadened.

She came in slowly, pushing the door shut behind her, and crossed the spacious room to his desk. That old oak desk, which had always seemed so big to her, now seemed to spread out for acres. For miles. Behind it, he was very still.

"Walker, what's wrong?"

"Sit down."

After a moment, she did. And braced herself, pulling on a mask of calm. If he wanted it like this, strangers across a desk, then fine. She could do that. No matter how much it hurt, she could do it.

He opened a thick file on his blotter and removed a photograph. He closed the file, and pushed the photo across the desk toward her. "Look at that."

She leaned forward in her chair, picked up the photo, and studied it. A typical school yearbook–type picture, head and shoulders, hazy background. A fair young woman, with pale hair and dark eyes—unusual for a blonde. Pretty, with a smile full of teeth.

"Recognize her?" Walker asked.

Amanda looked across the daunting desk at him, noting the chilly light in his eyes. "Should I?"

"You tell me."

Amanda shrugged. "Sorry."

Walker drew a breath and spoke with the first sign of emotion in his voice. Anger. "That is a picture of Amanda Grant. You, supposedly. Senior year in college. According to the vital statistics I finally managed to get my hands on, seven years ago you were blond and brown-eyed, five inches taller, and more than thirty pounds heavier." He paused, then finished, "Amazing transformation."

After a moment, Amanda put the photograph on his desk, sat back in her chair, and conjured a faint smile with an effort she hoped didn't show. "I would have sworn I had covered that base. No pictures available. It was one of the reasons I picked her. Where did you dig it up?"

Walker's face seemed to be chiseled out of granite. Very cold granite. "I called a private investigator in Boston last Friday, and gave him what little I had. I told him to find me a picture of Amanda Grant. I was lucky; he turned out to be both fast and efficient. When he couldn't find a yearbook photo, he checked with the school. Amanda Grant had requested no photo be in the yearbook—students often do, for one reason or another—but she did have her picture taken along with everyone else. The school gave my investigator the photographer's name. I was lucky again; he was in today, and he still had the pictures from that year. The investigator transmitted the photograph to me a couple of hours ago."

Walker's smile was thin, hardly worth the effort. "Meet Amanda Grant."

Amanda shook her head, but kept her small smile. "Who looks nothing like me. Naturally, you find that . . . suspicious."

"Suspicious? I find it contemptible. You've been lying through your teeth, lady—and I can prove it now."

She didn't flinch away from his harsh tone. "All that picture proves is that I didn't grow up as Amanda Grant. It doesn't come close to proving I'm not Amanda Daulton."

"Why did you lie about it?"

"I have my reasons."

Walker shook his head once, hard. "Not good enough. You went to a lot of trouble to lead me down a blind alley—"

Coolly, she said, "It didn't suit me to have my background investigated. Am I a criminal? No. In fact, I'll give you my fingerprints if you like, and you can have the police check me out. The prints won't be on file, because I have no criminal record. But all that really proves, of course, is that I never got caught in a criminal act—right, Walker?"

"Right," he said flatly.

"So—stalemate. Oh, you can go ahead and tell Jesse what you've discovered. And now that you've warned me, I'll come up with some kind of cover story, something plausible enough to satisfy him that what you found out is meaningless. He'll believe me, Walker. We both know that."

Walker shook his head again. "Don't kid yourself—you have no idea how convincing *I* can be when all the proof's on my side. And I can certainly prove you lied. You lied to *Jesse*. He's not going to like that, trust me."

Amanda looked at him, at his chilly eyes and stony face, and felt a pang of hurt that was, she knew, completely irrational. He had more than enough reason to doubt her, after all. Even a passionate lover was likely to turn into a distrustful stranger when he discovered he'd been lied to.

Maybe *especially* a passionate lover.

For a long and very silent moment, Amanda weighed her options. And liked none of them. The only thing she was sure of was that she had to somehow convince Walker not to tell Jesse he'd discovered her lie. She couldn't afford to risk being asked to leave Glory, not now. Not when she felt so certain she was close to finding out the truth.

"All right," she said slowly. "I did lie about growing up with the name Grant. And I'd rather Jesse didn't know about that . . . just yet. I have my reasons. Can't you accept—"

"No way. Even if I wanted to—which I don't—it wouldn't be fair to Jesse if I kept something like this to myself. And we won't even talk about the fact that I could possibly be disbarred for it."

Amanda knew without even making the attempt that to appeal to Walker's softer feelings for her—assuming he had any—would be futile. The question of her identity had stood between them from the first moment she had walked into this office, and until Walker had that question answered to his satisfaction, he would not be able to trust anything she said.

"I have my reasons for keeping my background secret," she said, because she had to try.

"What reasons? For Christ's sake, you came here claiming to be Amanda Daulton—your past is the whole point of this."

"No, not my past. My identity. Where and how I spent the past twenty years has absolutely nothing to do with whether I'm Amanda Daulton. All that matters—all that should matter—is if I was born Amanda Daulton, the daughter of Brian and Christine Daulton. And I *was.*"

"Convince me," Walker invited, his voice hard.

"I can't, you know that." She didn't look away

from his cold eyes. "I have no papers you'd consider proof, nothing I couldn't have faked or just somehow gotten my hands on. No witness to call to the stand who would testify that he or she could swear to my identity. And I can't remember anything so specific that only Amanda Daulton would know it. It was *twenty years* ago, and it terrifies me to try to remember—"

A frown abruptly disturbed the wintry bleakness of his expression as she broke off, and Amanda felt a jolt as she realized she had said just one sentence too many. He was too intelligent and too alert to have missed it, and too curious not to want to know exactly what she meant by it.

Before he could speak, Amanda got up and went to the window at one side of his desk, gazing down on the mostly deserted, rain-drenched anachronism that was Main Street, town of Daulton.

"Suppose," she said in an idle tone, "I walked out of this office, and chose to disappear. Took a bus or train to Asheville, a plane from there. Suppose I didn't want to be found. Suppose I went back to being . . . whoever I've been for twenty years. Suppose I reclaimed that other life, and stopped being Amanda Daulton again." She leaned a shoulder against the window frame and looked at him. "Could you find me if I did that, Walker? Could anyone find me?"

He had turned his chair and sat watching her, one arm lying along the desk. The frown had remained on his handsome face, and if it was a dangerous expression on this particular man, at least it was less painful for her to see than the cold expression he had worn until now.

"No," he answered finally, his tone now considering rather than hard. "I suppose—knowing nothing about your life since that summer—that it would have been virtually impossible to find you."

She looked at him steadily, waiting.

"You're saying that's why you lied, because you might want to disappear? Why would you want that possible . . . escape?" he demanded. "To have someplace to run to in case you failed to convince the Daultons? That doesn't make sense. We both know that, if for no other reason than the publicity, Jesse wouldn't have you prosecuted for falsely claiming to be his granddaughter even if there was cast-iron proof. Why would you want to keep a back door handy?"

Amanda couldn't help but laugh a little, even though there was nothing of amusement in the quiet sound. "You know, from the very first, I found it . . . surprising . . . that none of you seemed to think what happened twenty years ago was particularly strange."

Walker's frown deepened. "Christine Daulton took her daughter and left Glory. So? She wasn't the first runaway wife, and she won't be the last. What has that got to do with your determination to keep your past a secret?"

She hesitated, then turned her gaze back out the window. "I suppose from that point of view, you're right. Maybe it isn't so surprising."

"But you believe it is. Why?"

She hesitated again, then abruptly lost her nerve. Lover or not—and, after this, probably not—Walker McLellan was legally and morally answerable to Jesse Daulton, not to her. She was not his client, was therefore not entitled to the privilege of having her confidences protected by law; anything she told him could be repeated by him. And, at least for now, she judged that to be the greater risk.

"Look, it doesn't matter." She kept her voice a bit

dry and offhand. "You don't believe anything I say anyway. You go ahead and do your job, Walker. Tell Jesse what you've found out. If he asks me to leave Glory, I'll leave."

There was a long silence before he spoke, and when he did his voice was hard again.

"Is it any wonder I have trouble believing you? You won't talk to me."

"You aren't my lawyer," she pointed out.

"Your *lawyer*? Jesus, Amanda, you spent most of yesterday in my bed."

She felt another pang, this one bittersweet. It was the first time he'd called her Amanda since she had arrived at his office. Not, of course, that it meant anything.

"So I did." She turned her head to offer him a small, ironic smile. "But today we're here. Today, you called me into your office, put an acre of desk and an arctic cold front between us, and offered me proof that I deliberately hid my past. Proof you went looking for *after* we became lovers. Today you are the attorney of Jesse Daulton and Daulton Industries."

They stared at each other in silence, and then Amanda nodded slightly.

"You can't have it both ways, Walker. Don't expect me to tell you things just because we're lovers—especially when I know only too well that you're just waiting for me to say or do something you can use against me."

"I wouldn't—"

"Oh, no? What about this little meeting?"

"I called *you*, Amanda—not Jesse," he reminded her tautly. "You. And, goddammit, don't try to put me on the defensive. I'm trying to give you a chance to explain yourself so I won't have to call Jesse."

She heard a faint sound escape her, maybe a laugh.

Or maybe not. "You sound so . . . betrayed, Walker. But maybe I'm the one who should be feeling that way. Because, you see—you fooled me completely. The past couple of days, I never guessed that your smiles and your passion were just . . . Walker biding his time. Until he could attack."

"You know that isn't true."

"Do I? How do I know that? Because you tell me so? You called Boston on Friday, Walker. Why?"

After a moment, he said flatly, "Because you told me you majored in business in college—and I knew Amanda Grant majored in design."

She uttered another of those faint sounds that mimicked amusement. "Like a cat at a mousehole, just waiting to pounce. Well, congratulations—you caught me in a lie."

Amanda turned away from the window and walked quickly across the office. She had to leave, now. Had to get away from him. She had to try to think, to decide what to do next.

But before she could reach the door, he was there, blocking the way out. He caught her, hard hands on her shoulders, and made her look at him.

"Amanda, tell me what this is all about!"

"I thought you knew." She gave him a bitter smile. "Didn't you tell me that greed motivated most people? Obviously, I'm a lying, scheming bitch just out for what I can get."

He shook her. "Stop it. I know damned well that isn't true. You could have had Glory, all of it, and you fought Jesse to make sure that didn't happen." He didn't shake her again, but his long fingers kneaded restlessly.

"Then what does it matter why I came here? You've done your job, Walker, you've protected the property and interests of the Daultons. And now you've exposed me for the liar I obviously am, so maybe you'll get a bonus—"

"Goddamn you." His hands lifted to her face, and he bent his head to cover her mouth with his in an almost bruising kiss. It was brief, but incredibly intense, and when he lifted his head, his breathing was uneven. "This isn't for Jesse or any of them, don't you understand that? This is for *me*." His voice was low, hoarse, angry. "Why won't you trust me?"

"Why should I?" Her voice was unsteady despite her best efforts, and she knew only too well that she had no hope of hiding from him how swiftly and easily he could affect her. "You've done nothing but doubt me from the first moment I walked into your office, so why should I trust you now?"

"Because *I'm* not hiding anything." His hands dropped to her shoulders again and tightened. "Look around you, Amanda. Most of the people in this town can tell you who I am. Want to meet the doctor who delivered me? I'll introduce you. Want to see *my* pictures in high-school and college annuals? I'll dig them out for you. My mother kept scrapbooks just crammed with pictures of my life, and the basement of King High still has shelves holding the rock collection I assembled as a boy."

"Walker—"

"Everything I *am* is right out in the open, in front of you. No lies. No deceptions or mysteries. Nothing hidden." He drew a rough breath. "So tell me, Amanda. Which of us has the right to ask for trust?"

She couldn't think of a word to say to that.

Walker let go of her shoulders and leaned back against the door. His face was set, his eyes burning. "I haven't been pretending for the past few days, not while we were together. I'm not that good an actor. When I touch you . . . when we make love . . .

nothing else matters. Nothing. Don't try to tell me you don't know that."

Amanda shook her head a little, but in bewilderment rather than negation. "I don't understand you, Walker. What do you want from me?"

"The truth. Just the truth. Finally . . . the truth." He waited a moment, then added huskily, "Trust me, Amanda, please."

She turned and moved away from him, back into the office. Almost aimless, she went to stand in front of the leather couch that was along one wall, gazing up at the painting of Duncan McLellan, Walker's father.

Hawklike good looks apparently ran in the family, she mused, studying the handsome face and shrewd greenish eyes of the man who, along with his wife, had died on a rain-slick, foggy mountain road nearly ten years before.

Walker's roots were here, sure enough. His life was here. And it was true that there was nothing of his life hidden from her, nothing deceptive. It was true that he had a better right than she to ask for trust.

She turned to find that Walker had remained at the door. He was still leaning back against it, watching her. Waiting. She really didn't know if she could trust him, didn't know if she would be making the biggest mistake of her life by confiding in him, but she did know that if she walked out of this office now, it would be over between them.

And that was it, of course. That was why anything would be better than walking out. She didn't want it to be over between them. Not now. Not yet.

Amanda sat down on the couch and, her choice made, felt the most wonderful sense of relief. "All right. The truth." She drew a breath. "The truth is, I *am* Amanda Daulton. And the truth is, I still can't prove it. But if you can't accept that—there's no point in my going on with the rest."

For a moment, Walker didn't say anything at all. But then, finally, he pushed himself away from the door and came across the room to her. He sat down on the couch, turned a little toward her, and reached for her hand. "All right."

The words were so simple, his tone so unquestioning, that Amanda was caught off guard. "You believe me?"

"Like you said—if I don't believe that much, there's no point in hearing the rest, is there?"

Amanda had a feeling she had just heard a lawyer's sly evasion, but she accepted it just the same. She had burned her bridges; there was no going back now.

"All right then. After my mother was killed last year in a car accident—"

"Where?" he interrupted.

So he wanted it all. Amanda shrugged again. "Outside Seattle. I grew up all over the country, but that's where we'd lived since I finished college."

"Long way from Boston," he noted.

She decided not to comment, and went on. "After the car accident, I had to go through my mother's papers. Including some she had in a safe-deposit box. I found her marriage license, newspaper clippings about Brian Daulton's death, three journals she'd kept during her marriage—and my birth certificate."

"The birth certificate you brought here," Walker noted, "was a photocopy dated just before your mother was killed."

Amanda nodded. "I think she had decided to tell me the truth. I even found the beginning of a letter to me in with some of her stationery—but she'd only gotten as far as saying there was a lot I had to forgive her for, and that she didn't know how to explain it all to me."

"What about the journals?"

"All they told me was that her marriage was troubled, and that although she loved Glory, she hated being isolated there. They were journals, Walker, not a diary. She described the things around her and . . . mused. Pondered her emotions in an abstract way. Like daydreaming written down. Anyone could have read the journals, and probably did; whether consciously or unconsciously, she didn't record anything too specific. There were entries in a kind of stream-of-consciousness style that was almost—maybe—like a private code. Anyway, they weren't much help."

"What did you do then?"

"You mean after I sat down and cried?"

Walker looked at her for a moment, then lifted the hand he held and rubbed it briefly against his cheek. "I'm sorry. It isn't just a recitation of events, is it? Not to you. The shock must have been overwhelming."

Amanda shook her head wonderingly. "My whole life had been a lie. She had told me our name was Reed, that my father had died in an accident when I was just a baby. I'd even had a birth certificate naming me Amanda Reed—but when I checked, I found out it was a fake.

"At first, I was too stunned to do anything. I didn't *remember* being anyone else. I tried to think back—and that was when I realized I didn't remember much of anything before my tenth birthday."

"You hadn't noticed that before?"

"No. And when I tried to remember then, to force myself, I got this sick feeling of fear. It was like . . . standing outside the closed door of a room, and knowing that what was inside was something terrible. I didn't want to open the door."

Amanda drew a breath. "For a few weeks after she was killed, I didn't do anything about the situation. I had a job—working for a publisher of specialty magazines—and that kept me busy. But when the numbness wore off, I knew I couldn't just pretend I didn't know and go on as if nothing had happened. Aside from everything else, I needed to know who I really was, for my own sake. But that fear . . . and realizing that my mother had been afraid, that the nervousness I'd gotten used to had actually been fear—"

"How could you know that?"

"I knew. It was as if her death and the shock of finding out my real name had—had ripped a veil away from me. I knew she'd been afraid. And I knew she had left Glory in fear." Before he could ask how she knew that, Amanda explained the final entry in Christine Daulton's journals, the one that mentioned Amanda being in shock and Christine's relief that they were "safely away" from Glory.

"But she didn't offer the reasons?"

"No. All I knew was that she had been afraid, and that I was afraid when I tried to remember." Amanda paused for a moment, then went on slowly. "I knew from the newspaper clippings and her journals that the Daultons were a powerful and wealthy family. I was . . . wary of just turning up here without warning, especially when I had no idea of what I'd find. So I found a private investigator I thought I could trust, and explained the situation. We put our heads together, and decided the best thing to do first would be to gather all the information we could find on the family."

"Sensible," Walker said. "And when you'd done that?"

"The first thing that struck me," Amanda said, "was that there was no public reference to anything having happened that night. Until the newspapers wrote up Brian Daulton's death, there wasn't even a mention of his wife having left him and taken their child with her."

"Jesse would have kept it quiet—probably, if I know him, thinking Christine would come back sooner or later."

"About her running away, that's what I thought. But I was convinced something else had happened, something that made her run away in fear—and if it happened, it happened without any public notice."

"Something you didn't remember—but feared."

Amanda didn't let the doubt in his voice discourage her. She kept her voice steady. "I knew something had happened. But I also knew, by then, that at least two other women had claimed to be Amanda Daulton, and it seemed likely I would be viewed with open distrust if I couldn't prove myself."

"Which you couldn't."

"No. But I didn't really have a choice; I needed to come here, to find out who I was, and to understand the family I'd come from. Even if . . . even if I never found out why my mother had run away from Glory, I thought I'd at least have a better understanding of who I was. But whenever I thought about coming here, I was always conscious of that locked room and the terrible thing inside it, the thing I was afraid of.

"My mother had gone to a great deal of trouble to hide us under a different name—and it seemed to me that it would be smart if I did the same thing. So, my investigator helped me to create a background for myself, just in case I had to . . . make a quick exit. I knew there were holes in it, but I didn't think it would have to hold up more than a couple of months. After that, either I'd know the truth about what had happened that last night, or it probably wouldn't matter."

"You'd be gone?"

Amanda leaned her head back against the couch and looked at him gravely. "I thought I probably would. From the moment I stood on that hill in the pasture and looked at Glory the day you took me out there, I knew I could never live in that house."

"Why? Because you were afraid?"

She managed a small smile. "Because I knew I didn't belong there. Oh—it was familiar. It's when I saw the house that I started remembering bits and pieces of my childhood."

He was silent for a moment, then asked, "What about that night? Have you remembered anything about what happened?"

"There have been a couple of flashes, very vivid but brief. I remember . . . going downstairs, past the clock. Out the front door and across the field. Jumping a ditch filled with muddy water, and getting near the stables. Seeing a light. Hearing . . . something. Something terrible."

"What?"

"I don't know. That's where the memories . . . and the nightmares . . . always stop."

After a silent moment, Walker said, "Does that night have anything to do with your fear of horses?"

"I think so. I loved horses before that night—but not after. So something must have happened, and whatever it was made me afraid of horses. I think . . . that night, I was sneaking out to see a mare who'd foaled a couple of weeks before. But I don't remember seeing her. It's . . . just a blank after that."

Walker shook his head. "Christine never told you *anything* about what might have happened that night?"

"Nothing. As far as I can remember, she never said a word to me about it. But I know she was afraid."

Amanda gazed steadily at Walker, willing him to believe her. "She was always afraid after we left here. And I don't know why."

Frowning, Walker said, "Have you asked any of the others what they remember?"

"Yes."

"And?"

"It was just another night to them. Maggie and Kate both said my mother had been unhappy, but neither noticed anything unusual about her. Neither did Jesse. But . . ."

"Someone did?"

"Victor."

"What?" Walker's eyes narrowed swiftly.

Amanda nodded. "Just before he went off on that stock-buying trip, we had a brief conversation by the pool. He said . . . my mother had been having an affair with a trainer named Matt Darnell that summer."

"Did you believe him?"

She hesitated, then nodded again. "He said he had proof. Before I could ask about that, he was called away, and we never spoke again. But I went back and checked her journals, and there are some passages that seem to hint at something . . . passionate happening that summer. And Victor said this Matt Darnell left with my mother and me. He seemed very sure of it."

"Then maybe that's your answer," Walker told her. "Maybe this frightening room you're afraid to look into was created when you were torn away from a place you loved in the middle of the night and taken from your father."

"What about the fear of horses?"

"It could have been a separate incident, something that happened before or after that night. You said yourself your memories have been flashes, too elusive to get hold of. Maybe it's all jumbled together in your mind."

"And my mother's fear?"

"She was a runaway wife, and the Daultons were powerful. She could have lost custody of you. She must have known Jesse wouldn't stop looking after Brian died, and if he'd found the two of you, you can bet he would have taken her to court."

"Maybe." The possible explanations he offered were plausible, certainly. But they didn't explain why Christine Daulton had continued to be afraid long after Amanda had come of age. They didn't explain why Amanda had absolutely no memory of Matt Darnell. And they didn't explain Amanda's growing certainty that her fear of horses *did* stem from something that had happened that night.

But for now, she was tired of thinking about it, tired of having all the questions and worries chasing their tails inside her head. Helen had said she would remember when the time was right, and Amanda had to believe that was true.

She was on the point of telling Walker that she might have been deliberately poisoned at the party, and that Victor might have been killed because of whatever he hadn't gotten the chance to tell her, and that maybe the dogs had been taken away so that someone could get to her—God, it was all so nebulous! Mights and maybes, whatevers and what-ifs. Walker would think she was paranoid, and she was beginning to think the same thing.

"So," she said instead, meeting his intent gaze, "now you know the truth. My story, with all the *i*'s dotted and the *t*'s crossed, just the way a lawyer likes them."

He smiled slightly. "Thank you."

She was a little surprised. "For what?"

"For trusting me."

Amanda looked down at his hand still holding hers, watched his thumb move gently to rub her skin. "Are you going to tell Jesse?" she asked almost idly.

"Not if you don't want me to."

"I'd rather tell him myself," she said. "Explain about the fake background, I mean. But . . . I'd rather wait awhile."

"Until you remember?" He smiled again when she gave him a startled look. "Yes, I know you don't buy my nice, logical theories about what may have happened twenty years ago. Well . . . I'm not so sure I do, either. In any case, giving you time to try to remember makes sense."

"And in the meantime?"

"In the meantime, we have this comfortable, private office all to ourselves. You may have noticed I gave my secretary the afternoon off, and forwarded all calls to my answering machine at home."

"I wondered why the phone hadn't rung," she murmured.

"That's why. Because I'm a man who plans ahead."

Amanda eyed him consideringly. "If you're thinking what I think you're thinking—how could you possibly know our little confrontation today would end on a positive note? I was going to leave, you know. I was going to walk out of here."

"No, you weren't."

"I wasn't?"

"No." His free hand began toying with the buttons on her blouse.

"You're very sure of yourself," she noted somewhat resentfully.

He leaned over and kissed her, taking his time about it, then smiled at her. "What I'm sure of is a whisper I heard in the night."

Amanda would have liked to have been able to stare him defiantly in the eye and ask what the hell he was talking about. Unfortunately, she knew her voice would betray her, just as her body was betraying her. She watched his nimble fingers cope with buttons, and caught her breath when they slid inside her blouse to touch her sensitive skin.

His green eyes were gleaming at her. Probably with male triumph.

"I did hear that whisper, didn't I, Amanda?" His lips feathered kisses over her cheek and down her throat.

"I don't remember any whisper," she managed.

"Don't you?" He unfastened the front clasp of her bra and pressed his lips to her breastbone.

"Well . . . maybe I do." She conjured a glare when he raised his head. "Are you going to seduce me right here under your father's picture?"

"I thought I would."

She blinked and lost the glare. "Oh."

"Tell me you love me, Amanda."

"You're not being fair."

"I know." He lowered his head again, and pushed aside the lacy cup of her bra so that his mouth could brush the straining tip of her breast. "But tell me anyway."

Amanda slid her fingers into his hair. "Bastard. I love you."

She caught the flash of a green glance and thought dazedly that there was definite male triumph there. So at least it mattered to him. . . .

It was nearly suppertime when Walker finally took her back to Glory, so of course he stayed for the meal. He might have stayed all night, except that Amanda gathered the scraps of her dignity about her and refused to ask him.

It rained all night.

It also rained all day Tuesday, and the weather forecasts were filled with warnings of the flash flooding possible in mountain streams. Walker called that evening to tell Amanda that the stream beside their gazebo was so swollen it was threatening to wash away the footbridge and that the path would be ankle-deep in mud for days if this kept up. He could always drive over, though, he said, if she felt like having company.

Still annoyed with him, Amanda retorted that it was a lousy night to go anywhere and she thought she'd curl up with a good book.

It rained all night.

Though Reece could get away to his office and Sully went to the stables rain or shine, Jesse, Amanda, Kate, and Maggie had more or less been stuck in the house, and all had been showing signs of cabin fever. By the time the sun made a tentative appearance on Wednesday morning, everyone was so delighted that they practically tumbled out of the house like children freed from the prison of school.

Kate bolted for the stables and Ben; Maggie coaxed Jesse out to walk in the garden; and Amanda briefly tried the path to King High before being forced to admit that Walker had been right—it was ankle-deep in mud. And he wasn't home anyway. So she contented herself with walking around the vast yard, breathing in the rain-washed air and stretching her legs.

The day teased them, sunlight disappearing from time to time behind angry clouds, and two brief showers driving them back inside the house, but by afternoon it seemed the worst was over.

"Afraid not," Kate said when Amanda offered that

hopeful statement. "I just heard the weather forecast; we're expecting a hell of a storm late tonight."

Amanda groaned. "Whatever happened to the *sunny* South? Much more of this and we'll have to build an ark."

"No kidding. And Sully says at least two of the streams nearby have changed course, so we've already got flooding problems on some of the trails. It's a mess."

It was indeed.

Amanda wandered the house restlessly during the second of the two brief showers, then finally broke down and called Walker about midafternoon. And at least he didn't crow—though he did chuckle—when he said he could cut his workday short around four and come over if she liked.

With time to kill and fair weather threatened, she decided to go for a walk, this time in the garden. Everyone seemed to have vanished from the house, but she found Jesse just coming out of his study when she passed by.

"Walker's coming over later," she told him.

"Is he?" Jesse looked at her oddly, then surprised her by lifting a big, weathered hand to touch her cheek very lightly. "I'm very glad you're here, honey. You know that, don't you?"

She nodded. "You've . . . made me feel very welcome here." It was a lie, but Amanda told it without flinching.

A smile softened his harsh face. "Good. That's good."

There was something almost fierce in his tarnished-silver eyes, and he made her a little uncomfortable because she didn't understand it. As smoothly as possible, she eased away from him and continued down the hallway, saying over her shoulder, "I want to catch some of this sunshine before it goes away again."

"Good idea," he called after her.

Amanda walked in the garden lazily, following the gravelled paths that were still neat despite pouring rain. Some of the June flowers were rather beaten down, their petals scattered over the grass, but all in all it seemed the garden was surviving nature's onslaught courageously.

She hadn't intended to go anywhere else, but Amanda could have sworn she heard a dog barking, and that drew her out one of the side paths to stand at the northwest corner of the garden. She stood listening intently, silently cursing a bird chirping merrily in a nearby tree. Had she been mistaken? Yes—

No. She heard it again, faint and distant but quite definitely a dog barking. Without even thinking about it, Amanda set off, hurrying across the lawn toward the northwest mountain.

If she had stopped and thought about it, Amanda probably would have waited for Walker; paranoid or not, she had stuck close to the house when she was alone—and she had caught herself being ridiculously careful on the stairs as well. But she didn't think about anything except the possibility of finding the dogs after all this time.

Amanda went some distance before pausing to get another navigational fix; she shouted the dogs' names, and listened until she heard the barks, still faint. She changed course slightly and went over a rise to find a creek where one hadn't been only days before. She picked her way across and climbed again, heading away from the noise of the water.

At the top of another rise, she shouted their names again, and this time frowned when she realized the responding sounds were still distant. Surely she'd closed at least some of the distance by now? But the barks were . . . oddly unexpressive, now that she thought about it. Flat, mechanical—not at all like two eager dogs hearing a human voice they were rather fond of. Not that she'd ever heard the Dobermans bark, but still . . .

A chill feathered up her spine, and Amanda looked around to realize she had gotten a long way from any recognizable path. *Don't panic! Turn around and retrace your footsteps—with all this mud you must be able to see them. . . .*

She found her footprints easily enough, but relief vanished when she became convinced someone was following her. She stopped twice, staring around her, but the trees in this part of the forest grew densely and little sunlight could penetrate even on bright days. Everything was dark and dripping, curiously alien, and Amanda thought she could hear her own heart pounding.

Beginning to panic, she slipped and slid down a slope, grabbing at saplings to keep her balance, and making so much noise that anyone following her must have known she was aware and trying to get away. The ground was impossibly muddy underfoot, slippery one minute and clinging thickly to her shoes the next, and Amanda was sure her breathing sounded as loud as the wind.

She might not have looked back that last time, except that her foot slipped and she was neatly spun around when she grabbed a supple little oak for balance. That was when she saw him. He was coming toward her, face grim . . . and he had a rifle in his hands.

It happened so fast that it was like a blur. Amanda heard a strangled sound that seemed to come from her own tight throat, and she tried desperately to use the sapling to propel herself forward, away from Sully. But she lost her balance and fell, slithering over last year's slimy leaves into some kind of a ditch that smelled foul.

A drainage ditch, she thought dimly, or what had been a creek. Then she looked down at the hard ring of rock surrounding her fingers—and screamed.

Half buried in oozing mud, a human skull grinned up at her.

Thirteen

"I'LL SAY IT ONE MORE TIME." SULLY'S voice was bleak. "I went into the woods because I thought I heard a dog barking, and I had my rifle because I'd planned to set up some targets out by the garden. I saw Amanda tearing through the woods like a bat out of hell, and I went after her. I didn't mean to scare her. Yes, I should have called out something, but I didn't think." His frown deepened. "You want to take a poke at me, Walker—go ahead. Take your best shot."

"Don't tempt me," Walker snapped.

"Who found the bones?" Sheriff Hamilton wanted to know, making notes.

"She did." Sully laughed shortly. "The hard way. That's why she fainted. Bit of a shock, I'd say, finding your fingers in what used to be somebody's mouth."

As if the remark triggered something, the sheriff licked the end of his pencil. "And you carried her into the house, Sully?"

"Yeah. She's upstairs with Kate now, getting cleaned up. That skeleton was stuck in about six inches of mud, and she had it all over her." He looked down at himself. "Which is why it's now all over me."

"Suits you," a new voice remarked.

All three men turned their heads to see a slender redhead watching them from a distance of about four feet. Hands in the back pockets of her jeans, she stood negligently and wore a little smile.

"In fact," she said to Sully, "you should always wear mud."

Nobody had the nerve to ask what she meant by that.

"What are you doing up here?" Sully asked instead.

Amused, Leslie Kidd said, "If you'd care to beat the bushes, you'll find most of the riders scattered about. It's not every day somebody finds a human skeleton in the woods; we're curious. I'm more curious than most, which is why I'm braver."

"Braver?" the sheriff asked confusedly.

"Standing out in the open rather than hiding in bushes," she explained solemnly. "Sticking out my neck and risking getting my head lopped off. Sully does that, you know. He's worse than the Red Queen."

Sheriff Hamilton did not appear to find this explanation at all helpful, and eyed her uneasily.

With a grunt that might have been a sound of amusement, Sully introduced her to the sheriff and Walker, neither of whom had met her formally. Then, barely giving them time to make polite noises, he said, "Who's riding?"

"Nobody." Her melting brown eyes widened at

him in an exaggerated expression of awe. "My idea. Aren't I brave?"

"You told the others they could quit for the day?"

"Yes, I did."

Sully, who had been known to raise hell and rain brimstone on anyone who usurped his authority in even a trivial way, said mildly, "You should have asked me first, Leslie."

She nodded gravely. "Next time, I will."

Before anything else could be said, Helen came out of the woods and crossed the lawn to where they were standing near one of the big magnolia trees that flanked the house. She wore thick rubber boots caked with mud and carried rubber gloves in one hand, and she looked a bit tired.

"Where's Jesse?" she asked.

"Inside," the sheriff told her. "But report to me first, if you don't mind, Doc."

"I was going to. You've got a skeleton uncovered by a flash flood, J.T.," Helen reported flatly. "There isn't much I can tell you as long as the bones are in the ground like that. When can I have them?"

Hamilton shook his head doubtfully. "I called up to Asheville and asked for a forensics team to be sent down, Doc; they don't want anything moved till they get here—probably tomorrow."

"Why the hell did you do that?" Sully demanded.

Aggrieved, the sheriff said, "Because I'm supposed to when unidentified bodies are found, dammit. With all these serial killers and whatnot around, you never know when some bone a dog dug up'll turn out to be Charlie Manson's third-grade teacher or Ted Bundy's left toe!"

Sully scowled at him for a moment, but then caught the glinting amusement in Leslie's eyes and found himself trying not to laugh. "All right, I just asked," he muttered.

Sheriff Hamilton straightened his fedora and settled his shoulders. "You were saying, Doc?"

Helen, who had waited patiently through this, said, "All I can tell you is that we've got the bones of a man, probably in his twenties or thirties when he died, and that it could have happened ten years ago—or forty. Your forensics specialists will be able to tell you a lot more."

"Was he murdered?" Walker asked abruptly.

Helen pursed her lips. "If I had to guess . . . I'd say he could have been. Lot of bones broken at the time of death, especially in the upper body, and I found a depression in the skull I doubt was postmortem."

"He could have fallen," the sheriff objected in the tone of a man cherishing hopes.

"Of course he could have. Could have buried himself, too. You'll have the paperwork from my so-called examination tomorrow, J.T." Helen nodded at them briskly, then headed off toward the house, presumably to report to Jesse.

"She doesn't think he fell," Hamilton said, more or less to himself. He sighed. "Well, I'd better go make sure my boys have that tarp rigged over the bones. Sully, I'm going to post a man up in the woods to watch it till that forensics team gets here. Tell Jesse, will you?"

"Yeah."

When the sheriff had trudged off, Walker said, "You heard a dog barking?"

"Thought I did." Sully met Walker's gaze.

"But you didn't see a dog?"

"No."

"Maybe you should look up there again, Sully."

"Maybe you should—" Sully began in a grim voice, only to be interrupted by Leslie's gentle one.

"Maybe a bunch of us should. I'll volunteer, Sully. We can form search teams again, this time concentrating on the area where you heard the barking."

For a moment, it seemed that Sully preferred to remain there and come to blows with Walker. He looked like a man who would have found a good fight to be a handy release valve. But, finally, he turned away from the lawyer and started toward the edge of the yard, slowing his customary headlong rush because Leslie Kidd habitually strolled.

Watching the turbulent Sully match his pace to hers as if by instinct, Walker had a sudden realization.

"I'll be damned," he muttered.

"I'm all right," Amanda said.

She wasn't, Walker thought, but she was better than she had been. Shock lingered in her haunting eyes, but her face was no longer colorless and her voice was steady.

Jesse said, "I know it was an awful thing for you to find, honey, but try to forget about it."

"I will."

She wouldn't, Walker knew, but before he could comment, Kate was asking a bewildered question.

"A body buried on Glory? Who could it be?"

"In the past forty years," Walker said, "how many people have passed through here? How many workers have quit or been fired, or just failed to show up one day? It must be hundreds."

"Any hope of identifying the body—I mean, the bones?" Reece asked of the room at large.

Walker shrugged. "Forensic science is incredibly sophisticated, but it all depends on whether there was a missing-persons report filed. If not, if he was somebody who just wasn't missed, then there probably won't be medical or dental records on file anywhere for comparison."

"We're upsetting Amanda," Jesse said.

"No," she said, "I'm fine."

She was sitting at one end of one of the sofas, looking curiously isolated even though Kate was sitting beside her. The mud of her fall had been showered away hours ago; as usual, she looked cool and neat, dressed now in white jeans and a pale blue polo shirt.

It was almost nine o'clock and not quite dark outside. A lone deputy sat miserably up in the woods by a tarp-covered patch of muddy ground, everyone else having been chased away by a brief thundershower an hour or so ago. The search teams had mostly given up and gone home, though Sully had not yet come in.

The other Daultons—plus Walker and Ben—were in the front parlor, where everyone had gravitated after a rather grim evening meal no one had done justice to. And though it was obvious curiosity about the skeleton was strong, it was also clear that everyone was choosing their words with care.

Amanda had been very quiet.

Walker hadn't had a moment alone with her since he'd got here; though he didn't give a damn about having an audience, and wanted to hold her in his arms so badly he ached, the first flickering glance she had sent him warned him to keep his distance. He had the feeling that Amanda had withdrawn from them all, that she was holding herself aloof out of necessity.

"You should have an early night, honey," Jesse said worriedly.

She looked at him for a moment and then smiled. "I don't think I want to go to sleep just yet. Not until I can close my eyes without seeing . . . that skull. Besides, when the big storm hits tonight, I'd just as soon be awake."

"I'll stay and keep you company," Walker said immediately.

"I was hoping you would." She sent him another brief glance, this one holding something other than warning, and then she looked at Jesse, brows slightly lifted. "It's all right with you if Walker stays—isn't it?"

The sound of the phone in his study ringing prevented Jesse from answering right away. He looked at Maggie, who slipped out to take the call, then Jesse gave Amanda a rather rueful smile.

"Of course it's all right." Then, to everyone's surprise, he looked at Ben and added calmly, "You too, Ben. It's up to Kate to invite you, of course, but I've no objection."

Ben, who was leaning on the back of the sofa behind Kate, said merely, "Thanks."

A slightly wry expression passed over Kate's beautiful features, and Walker understood it quite well. Jesse had at least noticed—and apparently accepted—his daughter's lover, but with entirely characteristic arrogance, he had voiced his acceptance to Ben rather than Kate.

Maggie came back into the parlor. "Amanda, it's for you; Helen wants to talk to you."

"Probably checking up on me," Amanda murmured as she got to her feet. "I keep telling everybody—I'm fine."

"Say it a few more times, cousin," Reece murmured, "and we might start to believe you."

Amanda smiled at him, then went out of the parlor and down the hall to Jesse's study. She went over to the desk, vaguely conscious of the faint scent of smoke in the room, but didn't think too much about it as she picked up the receiver.

"Helen?"

"Amanda, are you alone?" the doctor demanded without preamble.

"Right at this minute?" Amanda looked around. "Yes. I'm in Jesse's study. Why?"

"Listen. I just had a late delivery from the lab. The report on all the specimens from the party."

As she had been all evening, Amanda was peculiarly detached. "And?"

"The specimens from everyone else who got sick showed clear and definite baneberry poisoning. No question. But your stomach contents and blood analysis showed monkshood as well as baneberry. A very high concentration of monkshood. There's no way it could have been accidental. Someone tried to kill you, Amanda."

Someone tried to kill you, Amanda.

The words seemed to echo in her mind, and yet she didn't feel much of anything about them. She felt distant from everything, an observer only mildly interested in events.

"Amanda?"

"I heard you, Helen."

"Amanda, I have to report this to J.T. I don't have a choice, do you understand?"

"Yes. But can you wait until tomorrow?"

"Why? What difference will one night make?"

"Maybe . . . a big difference." Amanda paused for a moment, listening to thunder rumble distantly. "Helen . . . I think I can identify that skeleton. But I need some time."

"Amanda—"

"Please don't ask any questions, not now. There's

something I have to do, but I'll be all right. Walker's staying with me."

Obviously frustrated, Helen Chantry said, "I don't like any of this. Someone in that house tried to *kill* you, Amanda! And now you say you can identify the skeleton of a man dead and buried for years—"

"I don't think one has anything to do with the other." Amanda frowned to herself as she thought about it. "No, surely not. I was a threat to somebody because I might have inherited Jesse's estate, and that was why the poison. But the skeleton . . . that's something else. And everyone is gone now, so I'm the only one who could possibly care about what happened. Unless he had a family, of course."

"What are you talking about?"

"Never mind, Helen. Just please wait until tomorrow to call the sheriff. He wouldn't come out here again tonight anyway, would he?"

"No. No, I suppose not. But—"

"Then there's no problem. And I'll be fine, really."

There was a long silence, but finally the doctor sighed. "All right. It's against my better judgment, but all right. Just be careful, will you please?"

"I will. Good night, Helen."

"Good night."

Amanda cradled the receiver, and stood there for a moment gazing at nothing. But then her eyes focused, and she found herself looking at a big cut-glass ashtray on Jesse's desk. It was piled high with a fine white ash, and that was odd because Jesse didn't smoke.

Paper ash, Amanda realized. She reached out and stirred the ashes with one finger, and near the bottom she discovered the hard corner of an envelope. It was only scorched, and part of the return address was visible. Amanda recognized the address. It belonged to the private laboratory where her blood sample had been sent for the DNA test.

Clearly, Helen was not the only one who had received a delivery today.

"Results . . . inconclusive," Amanda heard herself murmur. Because surely if the results had been conclusive, Jesse would have immediately and happily shared them with the family. "Pints of Daulton blood . . . and still no proof." She heard herself make another sound, this one the ghost of a laugh.

She buried the envelope's corner beneath the ash once again, then left Jesse's study and went back to the parlor.

"Hi," Walker said. He was the only one in the room.

"Where is everyone?"

"Scattered. Jesse decided he needed an early night, Reece wanted to catch a ballgame on television, and Maggie said she had things to do in her room. Kate and Ben didn't explain where they were going, and I was too tactful to ask."

"And Sully?"

"Haven't seen him." Walker took two steps and pulled her into his arms. He held her tightly, and when she lifted her head from his chest, he kissed her.

"I thought you were going to do that in front of Jesse," she murmured when she could.

"I nearly did. Until you glared at me."

"I didn't glare."

"You didn't smile either."

She smiled now, looking up at him. "Sorry. Can my rough day be my excuse?"

He kissed her again, and in answer said, "You didn't tell Jesse and the others that it was Sully who scared you as much as finding that skeleton."

"I didn't tell you that," she said.

"No. Sully did." Walker related Sully's explanation of his presence in the woods, adding, "He said he didn't mean to scare you, but that he obviously did."

Amanda pulled away gently and went to sit on the arm of a chair. Thunder rumbled again, closer now, and she listened until it faded away. "I was just . . . startled."

"Amanda, what aren't you telling me?"

She didn't answer for a moment, and when she did her voice was tentative. "Something happened today when I looked down and saw that skull. I had another flash of memory, this one . . . horrible. Those sounds again. And—blood. Walker, I think I'm ready to remember what happened that last night here. But I need to . . . trigger the memory. Will you help me?"

"Of course I'll help you." His answer was immediate and calm. "What's the plan?"

Amanda drew a breath and, for the first time tonight, felt uneasiness stir inside her. "I have to go down to the stables."

"Tonight?"

She nodded. "It's . . . Tonight is like that night. It's hot, and it's been raining but it isn't now—and there's a bad storm on the way."

He frowned. "You think the similarities will be enough to trigger your memory?"

"I don't know, but I have to try."

Walker's frown remained. "Helen told you not to force it, remember?"

"I know."*But I'm out of time.*

"All right. Then let's give it a try."

It was obvious, she thought, that Walker didn't like the idea very much. But it was also clear he would go along with it because it was something she needed to do. She started to tell him about Helen's report of the poisoning, but decided that tomorrow would be soon enough for that. The most important thing was for her to remember what she needed to.

Amanda wanted to retrace the steps she remembered on that night, so they went out the front door instead of going through the house to the garden. They paused on the porch, and a hot breeze warned that the storm was on its way.

It took several moments for their eyes to adjust to the darkness. Walker took Amanda's hand in his, and looked down at her in quick concern. "Your hand's like ice."

"Is it?" She felt cold, and there was a queasy sensation in the pit of her stomach. She could smell the storm, hot and damp, and a tremor shook her.

"Amanda, maybe this isn't such a good idea—"

"No, I have to go down there. I have to try to remember."

"All right. But we need to go now. When this storm gets here, all hell will break loose."

He let her set the pace and pick the way, merely walking beside her as they crossed the yard and passed under the eastern magnolia tree. Then they were in the field, with the stables dark hulks in the distance. A drainage ditch gave Amanda pause for a moment, and he felt her hand quiver a bit as she stood looking at the fast-moving muddy water, but she accepted his help to half jump across the mini-river, and they went on.

"Which barn?" he asked quietly as they neared them.

"Two." Her voice was strained. "It was number two."

"Victor's apartment is—was—above barn two," Walker noted.

"It wasn't then. It was— Somebody else lived up there then." She stopped dead suddenly.

The wind had shifted. Walker could smell the

horses now. Thunder rumbled, ever closer, and lightning abruptly split the night sky with threads of white-hot energy. In the momentary brightness, he saw her face clearly, and something clenched inside his chest painfully.

"Sweetheart," he said, "let's go back. You don't have to do this—"

"There was a light." She began moving toward barn two with jerky steps. "It was . . . There was a light inside."

The barns were equipped with sliding doors at either end to close off the wide halls, though these doors were kept open in the summer; as they reached barn two, it was possible to see, dimly, the opening at the opposite end of the hall, more than three hundred feet away.

"Where was the light?" Walker asked, keeping his voice quiet, trying not to disturb the fragile wisp of memory she seemed to be following.

"It was . . . across from the tack room. Where the hay was stacked. I couldn't . . . I couldn't see anything at first. Just the hay."

They were inside the barn hall now, still yards away from the area across from the tack room. Walker hesitated, but the lawyer part of him was remorseless in its logic, insisting that a scene be re-created as closely as possible to the original if it was to have any real meaning.

"Amanda, stand still. Close your eyes."

"But why?" Her voice was childlike.

"Please, do as I ask. You trust me, don't you?"

"Yes."

"Then do it. Stand still, close your eyes, and don't open them until I tell you to."

"All right." But when he let go of her hand, thin panic soared in her voice. "Walker?"

"It's all right, sweetheart. I'm still here. Just stand still and wait for me."

Familiar enough with the barns to find his way in the near blackness, Walker went quickly to the area across from the tack room. Hay was still kept stacked in bales here, and feed was kept in barrels, and there were shovels, pitchforks, and rakes propped in a corner. It was, more than anything, a kind of maintenance area, boxed in by bales of hay stacked higher than a man's head. It was about twenty feet wide, and more than twenty feet deep.

Walker knew that while the light switches at the ends of the hall activated a row of shaded bulbs, there were also switches in the tack room and the maintenance area that activated single light fixtures. It didn't take him long to find the one for the maintenance area—and he had to admit that the light was welcome. Quickly, he went back to Amanda.

There were faint snuffling noises and snorts as some of the stabled horses reacted to their presence, but the main sounds in the barn were those from outside. The wind was blowing gustily, tossing the damp smell of rain into the barn hall, and thunder was rolling heavily down from the mountains.

"Amanda?" He took her tense hand in his and squeezed it reassuringly.

She let out a shuddering sigh. "You—you were gone a long time."

"I'm sorry, sweetheart, but there was something I had to do. Keep your eyes closed. Now—you came into the hall, right?"

"Yes. I went along the wall toward the hay." She suited her actions to her words, putting out her free hand to feel the wall because her eyes were closed. Still several feet from the hay area, she stopped.

"Is this where you saw something?" Walker asked.

"There was . . . I heard noises. Awful noises."

"How did they sound, Amanda? What did they make you think of?"

She shuddered. "Something . . . hurt. Something being hurt. And . . . and . . . and hit. Heavy, wet sounds. And . . . and the smell. Horses and . . . and blood."

Walker hesitated, wishing he could stop this now, before Amanda saw whatever had so terrified her that it had wiped out the first nine years of her life. But he couldn't.

"Open your eyes, Amanda. Tell me what you see."

From their position, all that was visible was the glow of the light spilling over yellow hay, and it seemed that was all she saw at first.

"The light. And somebody . . . I think there's somebody . . ." She walked forward slowly, her body rigid, one hand still gliding along the wall beside her.

They had to walk past a stack of hay bales before it was possible to see into the area. To see the light fixture hanging down and illuminating the roughly twenty-by-twenty-foot "room" made of hay. To see tools propped up in a corner, and an overturned wheelbarrow, and loops of baling twine hung on a peg.

Amanda let out a little moan, obviously seeing what she had seen twenty years ago, and fell to her knees as though all her strength had rushed away. "No. Oh . . . *no. . .*"

Walker knelt beside her, still holding a hand that felt as cold and rigid as ice. She was sucking in gasping breaths and shuddering uncontrollably, and he wasn't sure she would be able to speak at all. But he had to ask her to.

"What is it, Amanda? What's happening?"

"He's all bloody," she whispered, staring unblinkingly into an empty circle of light. "His eyes are wide open . . . looking at me . . . seeing me . . . and he's . . . all bloody . . ."

"Who, Amanda? Who do you see?"

"Matt. He's . . . *oh, nooo. . .*" There was horror in her voice, and agony. "Stop . . . don't hit him anymore . . . please, Daddy, don't hit him anymore . . ."

Walker felt a shock of his own, thoughts tumbling through his mind almost too fast to consider. Was she remembering the night Christine had taken her away from Glory? And if she was . . .

"Amanda." Walker held her shoulders and pulled her around to face him. "*Amanda.* Look at me."

At first her eyes were blind, but slowly they cleared, and she blinked at him. "Walker?"

"Do you remember what you saw, sweetheart?" he asked softly.

"I saw . . . Daddy—"

"Amanda, are you *sure* what you're remembering happened the night Christine took you away from here?"

She nodded jerkily, tears trickling down her white face. "She—must have seen too, because when I backed away, she was behind me. She took my hand and . . . and we ran."

"It was late that night?"

"After—after midnight. I saw the clock when I left the house."

Walker lifted his hands to cup her face. "Sweetheart, listen to me. It wasn't Brian. You didn't see Brian beating another man that night."

"It *was* him. I saw—"

"Whatever you saw, it couldn't have been Brian. Because he was at King High that night."

The rain just sort of *gushed* out of the sky, drenching Leslie before she could even think about taking shelter. Cursing under her breath, she wiped her face with one hand and tightened the fingers of her other hand around the grip of the gun.

Dammit, there's no place to hide in there!

Up the exterior stairs, that's where she needed to go. And then into Victor's apartment, and take the interior stairs down into the barn hall. That was her only chance to get close to the people inside without alerting them to her presence. The thunder was so loud, she wasn't afraid of making noise, but with lightning flashing like a strobe out here, there was no way she could creep inside the barn hall without being seen.

She backed cautiously away from the hall opening, planning to go around the corner to the exterior staircase.

He grabbed her just around the corner.

Leslie managed to bite back a cry of pain when he wrenched the gun from her hand, and she didn't struggle when Sully caught her other arm in a grip of iron and hauled her against his powerful body.

"What the hell are you doing?" he bit out.

Thank God for the thunder. She looked up into his harshly handsome face, streaming with water and lit intermittently by flashes of lightning, and she whispered fiercely, "You're breaking my arm, you big lug!"

"I'll break your neck if you don't tell me—"

"Shhhh! Do you want them to hear us?"

"Who?" Lightning turned his eyes to pure silver, and his furious voice was captured thunder.

"Them. Let go of me, Sully, I have to—"

Still holding the gun, he shifted his hands to grip both her shoulders, and then he shook her. Hard.

"You're not going anywhere until you explain who you are and what you're doing here," he said sharply. "I mean it, Leslie. I want the truth, and I want it now!"

Leslie had learned enough about this man in the past weeks to be utterly sure of one thing: it would be easier to uproot a century-old oak tree with her bare hands than to move Sully before he was good and ready to give way.

"In books, the heroine *always* confides in the wrong man," she told him severely.

If it was possible for a man to look both furious and bewildered, Sully managed it. He shook her again. "Goddammit, if you don't tell me—"

Leslie's inner clock signalled her that precious seconds were ticking away, so she abruptly abandoned humor. "All right, all right, I'll tell you who I am. But we've got to *move*."

So, as they moved, she told him.

"He was here," Amanda said. She pulled away from Walker and stumbled to her feet, moving a little distance from him and pointing into the hay area. "He was there. I saw him."

Walker rose as well, but didn't move toward her. "You couldn't have seen Brian any time after nine o'clock that night, Amanda. I didn't remember myself until a few minutes ago—but one of Brian's favorite mares was foaling that night over at our place, and she was having problems. My father called Brian, and he came to King High just before nine. The three of us and the vet stayed all night in the barn—Brian didn't leave until after the sun came up."

Amanda leaned back against a stack of hay bales and stared at him. "He wasn't here?"

"No. Not the night you and Christine left."

"Then—" She closed her eyes briefly, opened them to look at Walker uncertainly. "Then it must have been—"

"Jesse. You were in shock and the light was bad; you mistook Jesse for Brian."

"But why?" Amanda's voice was bewildered. "What reason would Jesse have had to beat Matt like that?"

"Because of your slut of a mother."

The new voice, harsh with emotion, jerked Amanda and Walker around, and they stared at Maggie as she stepped from the shadows of an empty stall. She had a gun in her hand, and it was pointed with the negligent ease of someone very familiar with firearms.

She was smiling.

Amanda felt cold clear through to her bones. "Maggie? I don't understand."

"No, I can see you don't. *Don't move,* Walker."

It had been instinctive; he was several steps away from Amanda, and the need to shield her from Maggie's gun and her hate was overwhelming. But he went still, certain that Maggie could and would kill them both if he provoked her.

"You hate me." Amanda was staring at Maggie. "Why?"

"I thought you would have figured it out by now, Amanda," Maggie said, still smiling that empty, chilling smile. "I mean, it's so obvious. Think about what you saw."

"That—that Jesse beat Matt Darnell?"

Maggie nodded. "And why do you suppose he would have done that? Victor told you about Christine's affair with Matt. And you saw Jesse beat Matt to death."

Amanda made a little sound. "The . . . the skeleton . . ."

"Matt. I buried him up there, you know. That night. Packed up all his stuff, too, and got rid of it. I had to protect Jesse. I couldn't let them take him away from me." Her mouth twisted bitterly. "Not that he ever—but I couldn't lose him."

"I don't—"

"Your slut of a mother, she tried to take him away from me. Oh, she pretended not. But she couldn't keep her sly eyes off him, I saw that. She knew he still hungered after her, she *knew* that. So she started sleeping with Matt, flaunting her shabby affair just to torment him. Just to punish him. She drove him to kill."

There was a dawning realization in Amanda's eyes. "You can't mean that he . . . that Jesse and my mother—"

"God, you're slow. Want it spelled out? You're not Brian's daughter, Amanda. You're Jesse's."

"*Maggie!*"

It was a cry of pain, and it made them all jump even though nobody moved when Jesse came into the half circle of light thrown out into the hall by the single light fixture. He was soaked from the rain and for the first time looked ill, his face peculiarly hollowed.

He looked at Amanda first, an imploring gaze she flinched away from, then turned anguished eyes to Maggie. "You can't do this," he told her.

Maggie laughed shrilly. "Did you think I wouldn't find out, Jesse? About you and Christine? I suspected, of course, the summer it must have happened. The summer before Amanda was born. You hardly touched me, so I knew there was someone. But I never dreamed . . . She was your son's *wife,* Jesse!"

"I know." His voice was low, wretched. "God, do you think I don't know? Do you think I didn't know then that I was damning my soul to hell for what I did?"

"Then why?" Maggie demanded. "What did you need from her that I couldn't give you?"

"Maggie, it wasn't a choice I made, don't you understand that?" Jesse sent Amanda another quick, tormented look, then fixed his gaze on the woman he had betrayed. "It wasn't something I *wanted.* It just happened. We were alone in the house together that day and . . . it just happened."

Maggie's mouth twisted. "In your bed?"

"No. Maggie—"

"In *hers*? In her marriage bed?"

"Does it matter?" Clearly, Jesse was reluctant to talk about it at all, far less to disclose intimate details, but he was just as clearly trying to placate Maggie and lessen the importance of his duplicity. "Maggie, it only happened once, I swear to you. Just once."

"And that once you managed to do what Brian couldn't in three years of marriage," she observed raggedly. "Your seed took root in her. God*damn* you!"

"I didn't know it was my child! I never even suspected until Amanda was older and—and then I knew."

Maggie's laugh was high, quavering, the sound of suffering rather than humor. "And then? Is that when you became obsessed with Christine again, Jesse? Is that when you took her back into your bed?"

"No! I swear to you, Maggie, I never slept with her again. She didn't— I didn't want to ruin Brian's marriage."

Maggie stared at him with incredulous eyes. "You

son of a bitch. Your son was calling his half sister his daughter, and you didn't want to ruin his marriage?"

"Maggie, please." Jesse flicked another glance at Amanda's white face.

"Please what? Please be generous enough to overlook the fact that you fathered a child on your daughter-in-law? Please forget that your obsession with Christine led you to beat a man to death not ten feet from where we're standing?"

Jesse made a little sound, harsh with pain. "No, he was still alive when I left him. He was breathing."

"He stopped breathing," Maggie told him starkly. "I suppose you thought he left that night with Christine? No, Jesse, Matt Darnell never left Glory. I covered up that mess for you, just the way I've covered up so many others. I protected you, and loved you, and all the time *she* was the one in your head, the one you could never forget."

"I'm sorry." Jesse took a small step toward her. "I've always loved you, Maggie, you know that."

She shook her head slowly, eyes still incredulous, agonized with knowledge. "No, you didn't. You just let me love you because it suited you to, because you wanted a woman in your bed."

"Maggie—"

"It's all her fault," Maggie murmured as if to herself. "She's still holding you with the child she gave you. But I can fix that. I can cut the tie. And then her hold on you will be gone. You'll love me then, I know you will."

Walker wanted to look away from her face, from the naked truth that this proud woman had loved Jesse so long and so absolutely that not even his terrible betrayal of her could destroy that love. But he couldn't look away.

The gun in her hand, held so steadily, lifted an inch to point squarely at Amanda's head.

"It isn't Amanda's fault, Maggie—you can't blame her for my sins! Please—give me the gun—" It was an indication of how shaken Jesse was that he was a supplicant, begging where he had always commanded.

"No, I have to get rid of her," Maggie said, abruptly reasonable. "I was going to kill her anyway because she's that whore's daughter, but now I see how important it is for Christine's hold on you to be gone. I have to cut the tie. I have to. Then we can be together forever."

He took a step toward her. "Maggie, listen to me." Another step. "I've been a bastard to you, I know, but give me the chance to make things right." Another step. "Don't ruin our last months together by hurting Amanda."

"Last months? No, we have years yet, Jesse, you know that. You won't leave me. After all I've done for you, you won't leave me."

"No, I won't leave you," he soothed.

"But I have to kill Amanda. You see that, don't you? You must see it." She was still being reasonable, trying to convince him.

"No, Maggie—" And then he leaped.

Walker, guessing what Jesse meant to do, was moving in the same instant to launch himself toward Amanda. He bore her backward into the maintenance area, hay cushioning their fall, and felt her jerk at the deafening report of Maggie's pistol.

Still shielding her, he twisted to look back, saw Jesse stagger and fall heavily. Saw Maggie's mouth wide open in a silent scream of torment, and saw her swing the gun around to take aim at Amanda once more.

Then there was a second report, and Maggie's pistol flew from her hand. She wailed, clutching her bleeding hand to her breast, then turned and ran, down the long barn hall and out into the violence of the storm.

Amanda was struggling, trying to get up. Walker relaxed his hold on her and then helped her up, turning his head to see Sully and Leslie Kidd, both wet and grim, coming toward them. Sully had a pistol in his hand.

"Amanda . . ." Jesse's voice was weak.

She dropped to her knees beside him, her hand grasping the big one held waveringly out to her. "Be still," she murmured. "We'll call Helen, and—and you'll be fine."

The bullet had caught him squarely in the middle of his chest, and it was obvious to everyone watching that Amanda was wrong. Jesse would not be fine. It was a miracle he was still breathing, let alone able to speak.

"Amanda . . . I never meant . . . you to be hurt. I loved your mother. I loved her very much. And I love you. Please . . . please don't forget that."

"I won't. I won't, Jesse." Her voice, beyond shock now, was numb.

His hand tightened even as the silver eyes began to dim. "I'm sorry," he whispered. "I'm so sorry . . . Amanda . . ."

It was Leslie who knelt on the other side of Jesse's still body and felt for a pulse. After a moment, she stood slowly and shook her head.

Amanda freed her hand from Jesse's loosened grip and placed his hand gently by his side. She pushed herself up, moving so slowly and stiffly it was as if her body was reluctant to move at all.

"Did you hear?" Walker asked Sully.

"Yeah." Sully stared down at Jesse's body. "We heard all of it."

Amanda turned, slid her arms around Walker's waist, and held on tight. He could feel her shaking, but she didn't make a sound.

"He'd been keeping an eye on you," Leslie Kidd told Amanda more than an hour later as they sat in the front parlor and awaited word from the sheriff and his deputy on the whereabouts of Maggie. She nodded toward Sully. "Doing my job."

Reece, bewildered by everything, said, "You're a private investigator? Amanda's private investigator? I thought you rode horses."

"I also ride horses. But I came here to keep an eye on Amanda, because both of us were fairly certain somebody was hell-bent to see her dead." The red-head shrugged. "It didn't take me long to realize that Sully had the same suspicion."

Walker looked at Sully. "Maybe I misjudged you."

"Until today, all I had was a suspicion. Maybe her being poisoned at the party was an accident, but I thought it was funny she was the only one to be seriously affected. But then the dogs disappeared, and that really bothered me." Sully shrugged. "There was only one reason to get rid of the dogs, the way I saw it. To get at Amanda. Obviously, somebody was after her. After she was lured out into the woods this afternoon with barking dogs, I was certain of it."

"Lured?" Amanda's voice still sounded numb, and her face was drained of color.

Sully looked at her, and his normally rough voice gentled. "Lured. A tape recorder or something is my guess. I found the dogs, Amanda. Dead, for days at least, probably poisoned—and in the bottom of an old abandoned well you were probably meant to be pushed into."

"She wanted Amanda's death to look like an accident," Leslie murmured. "At least—when she was thinking straight, that's what she wanted."

Amanda said, "How did she know I was—was his daughter? He burned the DNA test results."

"Maggie probably found out the same way I did," Kate said, her voice also sounding a bit numb. "She saw you in a bathing suit, Amanda."

Amanda shook her head blankly.

"You have a birthmark, on the left side of your rib cage just below your breast. An inverted heart."

"Yes. So?"

Kate, who had no doubt dressed hastily and was wearing a tee shirt over shorts, lifted the hem of her shirt up far enough to expose a tiny birthmark high on the left side of her rib cage. "Adrian and Brian both had one of these. So did Jesse's father and great-grandfather. It always skips a generation. So when Maggie saw it on you, she knew you were his daughter."

Bewildered, Amanda said, "But why didn't my— Why didn't Brian realize the truth?"

"He probably didn't know that you shouldn't have had his birthmark, Amanda," Kate replied. "He wasn't much interested in our family history, and the birthmark wasn't something Jesse told any of us about when we were kids. I found out by reading an old family journal—probably how Maggie found out as well."

"We often miss the obvious things," Leslie noted. "It's human nature."

"I guess so," Amanda murmured.

Nobody had very much to say after that. They merely sat and waited to find out about Maggie. It was a little after midnight when Sheriff Hamilton came into the house wearing a yellow rain slicker, to report that they'd found Maggie out in the valley under a big oak tree. Very peaceful.

And very dead.

Fourteen

THE MID--JULY MORNING WAS HOT EVEN at just after eight A.M., and it was already muggy. Walker felt both the heat and the humidity as he came out of his bedroom onto the gallery. He moved to the end, then leaned on the railing.

From this angle, he could see the beginning of the pasture fence in back, whitewashed boards gleaming in the strong sunlight. His placid, elderly saddle horse was standing with his head poked over the fence, eyes no doubt closed in blissful enjoyment as a gentle hand stroked his neck.

In another week or two, Walker thought, watching, Amanda would be ready to climb up into the saddle for the first time in twenty years.

It hadn't been easy for her, these last weeks. Jesse's violent death, Maggie's suicide—ironically with the same poison she'd used trying to kill Amanda—would have been difficult enough for both Amanda and everyone else to cope with, but the discovery of a twenty-year-old homicide and the virtual certainty that Victor's death had not been an accident had caused a great deal more than a nine days' wonder.

And not only locally. There had been national interest, with television crews and tabloid journalists seemingly behind every tree—and word had it there was already an unauthorized TV movie in the works.

The whole truth had had to come out—or, at least, as much of it as could when so many of the principals were no longer able to comment. At a family meeting to discuss the matter before they issued a public statement, Amanda had expressed her own feelings with no hesitation; she wanted no secrets hanging over her head. Secrets could be deadly. No matter how disturbing the revelation of her paternity turned out to be, her wish was to make everything public.

The others had agreed.

The town of Daulton, shaken by the revelations, seemed doubtful at first, but when Kate, Reece, and Sully all stood by Amanda—to say nothing of Walker—it was eventually conceded that another odd chapter in the Daulton family history had been written, and who could be surprised by it?

As for Amanda, the violent events of that last day had left scars that had been slow to heal. She slept long hours but not especially peaceful ones; that was normal, Helen said. And she was quieter than before, which was also to be expected. It was evident she felt guilty because her return to Glory had been the catalyst for so much tragedy, and that was something she was dealing with as well.

But she was a Daulton, and Walker was confident her inner strength would prevail. He had lost very little time in moving her to King High, a shift Amanda had accepted without question or protest and with definite relief; Glory would never be home to her.

It was, however, at least partly hers.

Jesse Daulton, characteristically, had pulled a fast one on all of them. His "business" trip into Asheville the Friday before his death had actually entailed a visit to a very expensive and efficient law firm, where he had, in the space of a few hours, gotten himself a new will drawn up.

And it was, Walker had to admit, a remarkable document. Named coexecutor along with Sully, he had himself read the will to the family, and although there had been a great deal of surprise, there would not be a legal battle over the estate.

Sully, who unquestionably loved Glory best, had inherited the Daulton stables outright as well as an equal share in the house and land. Reece, Kate, and Amanda were also left equal shares of that property. Reece had been granted outright control of the part of Daulton Industries he was best at, the manufacturing end—and Kate had been left in charge of the rest.

That was the real surprise, for although Kate certainly had a head for business, no one had realized that Jesse had noticed that ability in the daughter he—seemingly, at least—had virtually ignored.

Walker thought that Kate would probably be very good at running most of the family business, once she recovered from the shock.

As for Amanda, she had resisted the idea of inheriting anything at all at first, but Walker urged her not to make any decision for at least a few months. She was in no state of mind to consider the matter logically, he told her; she needed to give herself time to heal and then decide what she wanted to do. Glory was, after all, her heritage.

Walker doubted that his arguments had much effect, but the letter Jesse had left for Amanda certainly gave her food for thought. It had been delivered to her at the same time the new will had arrived, a sealed letter the law firm had been instructed to give her privately so that the remainder of the family would not know of its existence—unless Amanda chose to tell them about it.

He thought she probably would, one day. So far, however, only Walker had seen it. He hadn't asked to read it, but Amanda had offered it, saying she wanted him to know as much as she did herself about the past.

Walker had read the letter only once, but it remained vividly in his mind even now, and when he thought about it, it was Jesse's voice he heard.

My dear Amanda,

I wish there were some gentle way of telling you what I believe you need to know. I wish I had been strong enough to tell you before I had to leave you, but even though I wanted to, I could never find the courage. Please forgive me for that.

You understand love, don't you? You understand how it captures us without warning, giving us no choice to make except to fight what we feel—or endure it? I think you do understand, Amanda; I've seen the way you look at Walker.

I loved Christine. It was something beyond my control, not of my choosing. I fell in love with the wife of my son, and I can't begin to tell you what agony it was. The blame is mine for what happened, Amanda. I should have been strong enough to fight what I felt, or at least unselfish enough to stop insisting they spend so many months at Glory, so that Christine and Brian could attempt to work out their problems without interference.

But I was selfish. I wanted my son near, even though he was off riding so much of the time and Christine was too close. Too tempting.

It happened only once, Amanda. Christine was lonely, her marriage troubled because of Brian's selfishness—and mine. She was vulnerable. And by then I knew I loved her as much as I had loved my dear Mary. Perhaps even more.

I won't lie to you and claim I regretted what happened. I did not. I regretted only that she was my son's wife and so could never be mine. She said she loved me. Perhaps she did. She wanted to divorce Brian, but that I could never permit. The scandal of destroying my son's marriage and claiming his wife for myself was something I couldn't face.

But, in the end, what I did was worse, much worse.

I made her stay with him. Bribery, threats, whatever it took. Then she discovered that she was pregnant—and, for a time, Brian became a better husband. So she stayed with him.

I swear to you, Amanda, I had no idea you were mine. It wasn't until you were a toddler that I saw the birthmark, the mark only my child could have had, and by then Christine's love for me had turned to bitterness.

What could I do? The truth would have destroyed my son, ripped apart the family, and ruined your life. So I had to remain silent.

It was my punishment for what I'd done, being forced to watch you grow into a beautiful little girl and knowing I would never be able to tell you that you were my daughter. Being forced to watch Christine grow more unhappy year by year as Brian tormented her with his jealousy and his neglect.

What happened was, I suppose, inevitable. She fell in love with someone else.

I don't know how much you remember of that last night, Amanda. I don't know what you saw, or what your mother told you. I don't know how important it really is to you to know what happened. But I believe I owe you that much.

I had believed I no longer felt jealousy of Christine, but when I realized she loved another man . . . I went mad, I think. I don't remember everything, but I do know that I cornered her lover down in the stables and attacked him. I left him unconscious, and never saw him again after that night; I assume he ran from Glory.

As Christine did. She saw enough, I think, to frighten her badly. Perhaps she thought I would turn on her next, or that Brian would find out about her lover . . . I don't know. All I do know is that she took you and ran away.

I wish I could say that was the end of the story, the end of my insanity. But I can't. I did one more unforgivable thing, Amanda. In anger, I told Brian you were not his child. It was my fault he went wild that day, my fault he fell attempting a jump he would never have tried sane.

I killed my son.

You may never forgive me for any of this, I know. All I can offer in my defense is that I acted out of love, always. Love for Christine, for Brian, and for you.

As for the future, I leave it to you to decide if you will acknowledge your true paternity. Along with this letter, I have provided a signed and witnessed document attesting to the fact that you are my daughter. In addition, the private lab still has, in their files, the DNA test results proving your paternity.

There will never be legal questions, should you decide to go public.

Amanda, if you can't forgive me, at least please try to believe that I love you. You are the one good and precious thing to come out of an impossible situation, and neither I nor Christine ever regretted that.

Love,
Jesse

Walker was still, himself, coping with the shock of realizing how many lives Jesse had destroyed; he could only imagine how much more stunning Amanda had found the truth to be. It was surely no wonder she was so quiet even now. She had a great deal to absorb, to accept.

In the meantime, of course, she was with him, and that was all he had asked of her. He had been at some pains to make no demands, to wait patiently and give her the time she needed, and by this sweltering July morning he was reasonably sure the corner had been turned.

A rumble from the general vicinity of his knee made Walker look down. A big-boned black and tan creature with one ear flying was looking back at him.

"You can't have another of my shoes," Walker told the Doberman puppy sternly. "Go find your brother and help him dig up one of the flower beds if you feel bored."

The puppy Amanda had named Angel ("Because it's as far from serial killers as you can get") scratched behind his ear energetically and made the *woof* sound that was his idea of barking, then went looking for his brother, who was named Gabriel and who liked to dig up flower beds.

Walker turned his attention back to the sight of Amanda petting a horse. He watched for a few more minutes, then went down the steps and out into the hot sun.

"You'll burn to a crisp," he said when he reached her.

She gave the old horse a last pat and turned to him, smiling. "I'm wearing layers of sunscreen, as usual."

"That won't protect you from sunstroke." Walker bent his head to kiss her.

"True."

By mutual consent, they began to walk toward the path that led eventually to Glory. Most mornings they walked as far as the gazebo and back before having breakfast; it was a pleasant stroll and both enjoyed it.

"Les wants to meet for lunch one day this week," Amanda commented idly. "I think she's serious about staying."

Walker thought so too. Unlike Amanda, the slender, redheaded former private investigator clearly did not find Glory overwhelming. And she did indeed seem to communicate with animals with almost telepathic ease—and with large, intense, temperamental Daulton men as well.

"Speaking of staying," Walker said casually, "how do you feel about fall weddings?"

Amanda stopped and looked up at him. They had nearly reached the footbridge, and stood on the path near the gazebo. She was smiling just a little. "What did you have in mind?"

"A quiet ceremony and a long honeymoon. Beyond that, I haven't thought." He lifted a hand to her cheek and smoothed the sun-warmed skin over her cheekbone. Abruptly, no longer casual, he said, "I love you. God, I love you. Marry me, Amanda."

Her eyes searched his face very intently. Finally, after what felt like an eternity to him, she said huskily, "I already promised to do that."

Walker felt his heart skip a beat and then begin thudding heavily in his chest. Slowly, he said, "I . . . don't recall asking you in the last couple of months."

"No. You never did ask me. You just demanded my promise that I'd marry you. When I grew up."

He didn't move or say anything, even more conscious now of his heart pounding.

"You know," she said thoughtfully, "not once through all of this, not once in all these weeks, have you asked me if I remember you. Why didn't you ask?" She looked at him, smiling a little.

"At first . . . because I wanted to wait and see if you brought it up."

"You mean you wanted to wait and see if I realized that I *should* have remembered you?"

He smiled. "A pretender might have realized that belatedly after finding out that King High was so close—and that path so well-worn."

"Umm. But you eventually realized I was the real Amanda." Suddenly curious, she said, "When was that, by the way?"

"The day we made love in the gazebo," he replied without hesitation.

Amanda was surprised. "But . . . you called me to your office after that, to confront me about my not being Amanda Grant."

Walker nodded. "I knew you'd lied about that. But, as you said yourself, the name you grew up using had nothing to do with whether you were born Amanda Daulton."

Her gaze searched his face intently. "What made you so sure I was the real Amanda?"

He answered simply, his very conviction saying more than words ever could. "The way I felt about you. I could never have loved a pretender, and I realized that day I loved you so much it was terrifying."

After a moment, Amanda drew a breath. "Why didn't you ask then if I remembered you, Walker?"

"Maybe I didn't want to put it to the test." He shrugged slightly. "There was so much you didn't remember. I suppose I didn't want to hear you say I was part of those missing memories."

Amanda took his hand and led him toward the gazebo, her expression grave. "The first time you brought me out here," she murmured, "I wondered why you didn't say something about this place. Then I wondered if you were waiting for me to say something.

"Then it occurred to me that maybe it just wasn't important to you. I mean, you could have put a gazebo here only because it's a lovely place, or because you thought something ought to be built here near the ruins of the old gatehouse. That seemed . . . a reasonable sort of thing for you to do."

He waited, silent.

"I couldn't really ask you about it. I'd already made up my mind that it would be best if I offered no one absolute proof I was Amanda Daulton, that I'd be safer as long as there was still a doubt in most everyone's mind. So I was careful of what I revealed to anyone. I tried to stick to memories she *might* have told someone else, and made myself ignore the things she wouldn't have shared with another living soul. Like this place, and what it meant."

Releasing his hand at the gazebo, she walked to the old oak, stepping over the roots to get close to the trunk, and pushed aside the heavy branches of the azalea that hid so much with their thick summer foliage. Slowly, her index finger traced the awkwardly carved heart and the two sets of initials inside it. *WM* and *AD*.

"I suppose," she said, "even a fake Amanda might have found this. And drawn her own conclusions."

Walker cleared his throat and, hoarsely, said, "I suppose she could have."

She allowed the azalea branches to hide the heart again, then turned and came to him. Halting an arm's length away, she slid a hand into the front pocket of her jeans and drew out a small object. She held out her hand, palm up.

"But could she have found this?"

In her hand lay a green stone a couple of inches long and an inch or so wide. It was more opaque than translucent, the color deep and oddly mysterious. It might have been a chunk of green glass from a bottle, or a piece of the quartz so common to the Carolina mountains and streams. Or it might have been—

"You believed it was an emerald," Amanda said, looking up at him rather than the stone as he reached out slowly to lift it from her hand. "You had heard your grandfather talking about the night his father won King High, and how the winning pot held a number of raw emeralds, and when you found this here in the creek you were certain that's what it was. Even though your father told you it was only quartz, you believed it was an emerald. And so did I."

He raised his gaze to meet hers, finding her smoky gray eyes so tender it nearly stopped his heart.

"The night we left," she said, "I made Mama wait while I ran back to my room to get it. I knew we wouldn't be coming back, and I couldn't leave without it."

"Amanda . . ."

Softly, she said, "When a twelve-year-old boy gives his most precious possession to the little girl who adores him, it's something she'll remember—and keep—for the rest of her life."

With a rough sound, Walker pulled her into his arms, his mouth finding hers blindly, and Amanda melted against him with the deeply satisfied murmur of a woman who had, finally, come home.

Haunting Rachel

For my parents

PROLOGUE

May 24, 1988

"It won't take long," Thomas said reassuringly. "A week, maybe a bit more. Then I'll be back."

"But where are you going? And why does it have to be now?" Rachel's demand held all the natural impatience and indignation of a nineteen-year-old who was about to be deprived of the company of her fiancé at a somewhat inconvenient time. "Tom, you know Mercy's giving that shower for me on Thursday, and—"

"Honey, men are never welcome at those things. I'd just be in the way." He was still soothing, but also a little amused, and he smiled at her with the complete understanding of a man who had known her since her auburn hair had been worn in pigtails and at least two front teeth had been missing. He was ten years her senior, and at that moment every year showed.

Rachel didn't exactly pout, but when she sat down in a chair by the window, it was with a definite flounce, and her expressive face was alive with frustration and disappointment. "You promised. You said there wouldn't be any more of these mysterious trips of yours—"

"There's nothing mysterious about them, Rachel. I'm a pilot, and I deliver cargo. It's my job. You know that. All right, I know I said there wouldn't be any more trips out of the country, but Jake asked me to do him a favor, and he *is* my boss. So—just a quick run down to South America."

"You promised," Rachel repeated, not much interested in reasons.

Thomas put his hands on the arms of her chair and bent down, smiling at her with all the charm in his definitely charming nature. "Would it make you happier if I said that Jake's giving me an extra week off if I take this run? That's another week in Hawaii, honey. Think about it. Lazing around in the sun on Waikiki, breakfast on a balcony with a magnificent view—and shopping. Lots more time for shopping."

She couldn't help but smile. "You know that isn't my thing."

He chuckled. "Yeah, but you're no slouch at it. Come on now, say you're not mad anymore. I'll have a miserable few days if I fly off knowing you're mad at me."

It was virtually impossible for Rachel to resist his blandishments, a fact both were well aware of, and her sigh held resignation as well as a touch of resentment. "Oh, all right. But you'd better not hang around down in South America. Just remember what'll be waiting for you back home." She wreathed her arms around his neck and kissed him.

The passion between them had been nearly impossible for them to handle since the night of her sixteenth birthday and their first real kiss; familiarity had not bred anything except a better understanding of just how powerful desire could be, especially when it went unsatisfied. Though Rachel's willpower was shaky where he was concerned, Thomas, very conscious of the years between them and of her youth, had decided for both of them that sex would wait until marriage.

It wasn't a decision Rachel was happy with, and this wasn't the first time she had made an attempt to force his hand.

His voice was a little ragged when he pulled back slightly and muttered, "Stop that. I've got to go."

Rachel didn't want to let go of him. "You'll miss me. Say you'll miss me."

"Of course I'll miss you. I love you." He gave her a brief kiss and then firmly unlocked her arms from his neck and straightened. "Make my excuses to your parents about tonight, all right, honey?"

She sighed again. "Right. And I get to spend a boring Saturday night all by myself. Again."

"Just three more weeks, and that will no longer be a problem," Thomas reminded her with a grin. "I promise, honey, no more lonely nights for either one of us."

"I'll hold you to that."

Rachel walked with him to the front door of her parents' house, received another quick kiss, and stood there watching him stride down the walkway to his fast little car. He loved speed, Thomas Sheridan did, whether on the ground or in the air, and often teased her that she was the only love in his life that characteristically moved at a lazy pace.

He turned and waved before opening his car door, and Rachel admired the way the sunlight glinted off his pale silvery hair. He was a rare blond Sheridan on a mostly dark family tree, so different from his raven-haired sister Mercy that both had frequently maddened their mother by speculating humorously about blond-haired strangers in her past despite Thomas's undeniable resemblance to his dark father.

"See you in a week or so, honey," Thomas called out.

He slammed the car door before Rachel could respond in kind, so she merely waved with a smile. She watched the car until it vanished from her sight, then went back into the house to tell her parents that her fiancé would not be joining them for dinner that night.

Rachel woke with a start and sat up in her bed before she even knew what had awakened her. The room was filled with the somber light of dawn, and she was astonished to see him standing near the foot of the bed.

"Thomas? What're you doing back so soon? I—" Her voice broke off as though it had been cut by something sharp. It wasn't right, she realized. *He* wasn't right. Because she could almost see the curtains through him. A coldness more gray than the dawn seeped into her body, into her very bones, and she heard herself make an anguished little sound when Thomas seemed to reach out toward her, his handsome face tormented.

"No," Rachel whispered. "Oh, no . . ." She stretched her hand out toward him, but even as she did so, he was gone. And she was alone in the stark dawn.

Thomas Sheridan's plane never reached its destination, and no trace of it was ever found.

ONE

April 21, 1998

It was no more than a glimpse of movement on a street corner that caught Rachel's attention. She turned her head more or less automatically, drawn as always by the glint of sunlight off silvery blond hair. She expected to see, as she always had, a stranger. Just one more blond man who would, of course, not be who she wanted him to be.

Except that it was Thomas.

She stood frozen, with four lanes of cars filling the space between her corner and his, and when their eyes met, she almost cried out. Then the light changed, and traffic began moving briskly, and a noisy semi blocked her view of the corner. When the truck had passed, Thomas was gone.

Rachel stood there until the light changed again, but when she rushed across the street, there was no sign of him.

No. No, of course there wasn't.

Because it hadn't been him.

Realizing that her legs were actually shaking, she found a table at a nearby sidewalk café where she could keep an eye on that corner, and ordered a cup of hot tea.

It hadn't been him, of course.

It was never him.

"Are you all right, miss?" the waitress asked when she returned with the steaming cup. "You look sort of upset."

"I'm fine." Rachel managed a smile she doubted was very reassuring, but it was enough to satisfy the young waitress. Left alone again, she dumped sugar into the tea and fixed her gaze once more on the corner.

Of course it hadn't been Thomas. Her mind knew that. It had been only a stranger with a chance resemblance that had seemed stronger because distance had helped it seem that way. And perhaps a trick of the light had helped, as well as her own wishful thinking. But it couldn't have been Thomas. Thomas had been dead nearly ten years. No, they had never found a body, or even the wreckage of the plane, but Thomas's life had certainly ended somewhere in the impenetrable depths of a South American jungle.

Even though he had promised to come back to her.

Her knees were steady once more when Rachel finally got up nearly an hour later and left the café. And she didn't let herself stop or even pause when she passed the corner where a memory had so fleetingly stood. Knowing that she was late helped her to walk briskly, and common sense pushed the memory back into its quiet room in her heart.

It was after three o'clock on this warm and sunny Tuesday when she went into a building in downtown Richmond. She went up to the fourth floor, entered the law offices of Meredith and Becket, and was immediately shown in to see Graham Becket.

"Sorry I'm late," she said at once.

"Rachel, you didn't have to come down here at all," Graham reminded her as he moved around the desk to take her hand and kiss her lightly on the cheek. "I told you I'd come to the house."

"I needed to get out." She shrugged, then gently reclaimed her hand and sat down in his visitor's chair.

He stood looking down at her for a moment, a somewhat rueful expression on his face, then went back around the desk to his own chair. A tall, dark, good-looking man of thirty-eight, and a highly successful attorney, he was accustomed to female interest.

Except from Rachel. He knew Rachel fairly well. He had been her father's attorney for nearly ten years and one of the executors of the estate after Duncan Grant and his wife had been killed eight months ago. But knowledge didn't stop Graham from hoping that one day she would notice he was a man who was closer to being one of her contemporaries than her father's.

And a man, moreover, who had been half in love with her for years.

Today, she hadn't noticed.

"More papers to sign?" she asked, her slight smile transforming her serene and merely pretty face into something haunting.

Graham had tried to figure out what it was about that smile that made Rachel instantly unforgettable, but to date had been unable to. Her features, taken one by one, were agreeable but not spectacular. Her pale gray eyes were certainly lovely, but the dark lashes surrounding them were more adequate than dramatic, and her nose might have been a trifle large for her heart-shaped face.

Gleaming auburn hair framed that face nicely, but it was unlikely that fashion mavens would copy the simple shoulder-length style. Her mouth was well-shaped and her teeth even and white, but there was nothing especially memorable about either.

Despite all that, Rachel had only to smile that slow smile of hers to become a stunningly beautiful woman. It wasn't only Graham who saw the transformation; he had heard more than one man and a number of women comment on it over the years.

And even then, her smile was only a shadow of what it had once been. Before Thomas Sheridan's death. Until the loss of her fiancé had changed Rachel so fundamentally, she had smiled often, her face so alive that strangers had stared at her on the streets. Afterward . . .

"Graham?"

He recalled his wandering thoughts and opened a file folder on his desk. "Yes, more papers to sign. Sorry, Rachel. But I did warn you that Duncan's estate was complex."

"It's all right. I'm just wondering when it'll all be over."

He looked at her across the desk. "If you intend to keep a hand in the business, it'll never be over. But if you mean to accept Nicholas Ross's offer to buy you out . . ."

"I'm still thinking about that. Do you think Dad would have wanted me to sell out, Graham?"

"I think he expected you to. The past few years, your life hasn't been in Richmond except for holiday and vacation visits home, and those were brief. Ever since you moved to New York, I think he realized it wasn't likely you'd come back here to live."

"Yes—but I don't have to live here to keep the business. I could hire a manager to run my half, you know that. Between you, Nicholas, and a manager taking care of things day to day, I'd have to show up only periodically for board meetings."

He nodded. "True enough."

"I don't know beans about investment banking, so I could hardly be a hands-on boss anyway. And all those investments Dad had personally, they're so diverse, there's no way I could keep track of them on my own." She seemed to be arguing with herself, frowning a little. "At the same time, several of the companies Dad invested in aren't in a position to buy out his interest right now, so I'd have to find other investors if I wanted out—that, or take a loss. Either way, it means time and trouble."

Graham looked at her searchingly. "In a hurry to get back to New York? I thought you said you'd taken a leave of absence and didn't mean to go back until summer."

"That's what I said, and what I meant. But . . . I don't know, I'm getting restless, I guess." She shrugged. "I'm not used to being idle, Graham."

After a moment, he said, "But it's more than that, isn't it? It's memories. The house is getting to you."

Rachel got up and went to stand before a window that offered a view of the busy street below. Graham remained in his chair, but turned it to keep watching her, and when she remained silent, he went on quietly.

"After Thomas was killed, you couldn't wait to get out of that house. Went back to college first and then to New York. And your visits home even then were always brief, because you were always busy."

"Trying to make me feel guilty for neglecting my parents?" Her voice was a little tight.

"No. They didn't feel neglected, if that's been worrying you. They understood, Rachel."

"Understood what?"

"How much of your past was bound up in Thomas.

How old were you when you first knew you loved him? Twelve? Thirteen?"

Rachel drew a breath. "Ten, actually. He came to pick up Mercy from my birthday party, and he kissed me on the cheek. I knew then."

It required an effort, but Graham kept his voice dispassionate. "And since his sister was your best friend, you saw a lot of him. I imagine he was at the house quite often even before you two began dating. You were sixteen then, weren't you?"

She didn't seem surprised by his knowledge, probably attributing it to her father and casual conversation rather than any extraordinary interest in her. "Yes."

"So Thomas spent a lot of time at the house. Years, really. All the time you were growing up. Eating meals in the dining room, sitting with you in the den, listening to music in your bedroom, walking by the river. That place is filled with him, isn't it?"

She turned and leaned back against the window casing. She was smiling just a little, wistful, and it made her beautiful again. "Yes, the house is filled with him. And even now, after all these years, it hurts to remember him."

"Of course it does. You never really let him go, Rachel. You couldn't. There was no funeral where you could say good-bye, just a memorial service months later when his parents had finally given up hope. And, by then, you'd bolted off to college, where there weren't any memories of Thomas. For you, there was never any . . . closure."

She looked at him almost curiously. "You knew him, went to school with him. Was it so easy for you to accept his death?"

"Easier than for you, because I was never close to him. I wasn't . . . emotionally involved. His death was a tragedy and I was sorry, but no memories haunted me."

She hesitated, then let out an unsteady laugh. "Haunted. That's a good word. I thought I saw him today."

"What?"

"On a street corner while I was waiting for the light to change. I looked across—and there he was. I could have sworn it was Thomas."

"What happened?"

"A truck went past, and when I could see the corner again, he was gone. I ran across and looked, but . . . My imagination, I guess."

"You guess?"

"Well. My imagination of course."

"Or just a man with blond hair," Graham said steadily.

"Yes. I know."

"But this isn't the first time you thought you saw him."

Lightly, she said, "I'm going nuts, is that what you're saying?"

"What I'm saying is, don't let memories and wishful thinking become an obsession, Rachel. Thomas is dead. Don't you believe that if he were alive, he would have somehow gotten word to you, that he would have managed to come back to you?"

"Yes. Yes, I do believe that. Because he promised he'd come back to me." *And because he came back to me once, came back from death to say good-bye to me.*

But she didn't say that, of course. She had never told anyone about that, not even on that horrible dawn when she had awakened both her parents insisting her father try to get in touch with Thomas's boss because she was certain something terrible had happened.

"Then you know that what you saw was simply someone who looked a bit like Thomas." Graham's voice was still matter-of-fact.

Rachel felt a faint flicker of amusement as she left the window and returned to her chair. "I think you really are worried about my sanity, Graham. Well, don't be. I was shaken at first, but my common sense asserted itself pretty quickly. I know I didn't really see Thomas on a street corner."

Except for that first instant, when she had been *sure* . . .

"I'm glad. But, Rachel, if you need someone to talk to—"

"Thanks." She was grateful for his concern and the offer, and it showed in her affectionate smile. "But I think it's just as you said. I never got the chance to say good-bye to Thomas, and I've never faced up to all the memories at home. He's just very . . . alive to me right now. It's something I'll have to work my way through, that's all." She smiled at him. "Now—didn't you say something about papers to sign?"

The house where Rachel had grown up was an elegant Georgian mansion built on extensive acreage on the James River. The house was more than two hundred and fifty years old, and had been in the Grant family for much of that time. Remodeled from time to time by various Grants, it now contained such luxuries and conveniences as carpet, closets, and bathrooms, as well as modern wiring, central heating, and air-conditioning. Yet it had maintained its graceful air despite those changes, and was considered one of the most beautiful houses in Richmond.

Rachel got out of her mother's sedan at the front drive and stood for a moment, studying the house. Not for the first time she wondered if she was being hasty in even considering selling the place. Yes, the house was far too large for one young woman who didn't care for entertaining and didn't have to in her work—the only real excuse for a single person to own such a place. And, yes, there were too many memories here, many of them painful. And her uncle Cameron wanted it, would enjoy it, and would keep it in the family at least a while longer.

But . . . it was her home. She had actually been born in this house, with a doctor in attendance, since her parents had been determined to uphold that tradition. Until she had gone away to college and then moved to New York, Rachel had always lived here, just as her father and grandfather before her. Her roots were here.

Did she really want to give it up? And if she did, were her reasons the right ones? Or was she just being cowardly in wanting to run away once more to New York without facing the pain of loss?

Not questions that were easily or simply answered, she knew. Shrugging them off for the moment, Rachel went into the house. She was greeted just inside the door by the housekeeper, Fiona, who was as dour as usual. A part of the Grant family for more than twenty years, Fiona moved more slowly these days in late middle age, and her superstitious nature could be a trial at times, but she loved this house and took excellent care of it.

Which was why she resented any intrusion into her routine.

"That Darby Lloyd has been sending things down from the main attic all day. How'm I supposed to do my work with those men of hers tramping up and down the stairs, Miss Rachel?"

Rachel had known Fiona too long to be disturbed by the forbidding stare or acid complaint. Laying her purse on a side table in the large entrance hall, she shrugged and said, "You know it has to be done, Fiona. We have to have a complete inventory and appraisal of everything in the house—and that includes all three of the attics. Just be glad it's only Darby doing the appraisal. You'd really hate it if a bunch of strangers were constantly underfoot for the next few weeks. Wouldn't you?"

The housekeeper ignored the question. "But she has the second floor hallway filled wall to wall, and I can't even vacuum—"

"Fiona, you can vacuum later. I'm sure Darby's just moving the stuff out temporarily while everything's getting tagged, otherwise she wouldn't have room to work. Just be a little patient, all right? I'll go speak to her about blocking the hallway."

"If you can get through," Fiona sniffed.

Rachel was able to get through the upstairs hallway, though it required a bit of maneuvering. A family could fill large attics with an astonishing variety of furniture, especially over generations and many shifts in style and taste; items partially blocking the hall ranged from Revolutionary chests and Regency tables to—of all things—a sixties-style beanbag.

"My God," Rachel said when she finally managed to make her way up the fairly narrow staircase to the main attic. "Has this family kept every blessed stick of furniture ever to cross the threshold?"

"That would be my guess." Strands of her coppery hair escaping from the casual ponytail she wore and a smudge of what looked like soot on her otherwise creamy nose, Darby Lloyd came around a huge wardrobe with a clipboard in her hand. "Sorry for the stuff in the hall, but there was no other way to sort through everything."

Rachel waved a dismissive hand. "Don't worry about it."

"Well, I know Fiona's upset." Darby grimaced. "One

of my guys swore she put a hex on him when he asked if he could leave a Chippendale desk at the top of the stairs."

"She doesn't really hex people," Rachel said.

"Never underestimate the power of suggestion. Ten minutes later, Steve developed a migraine. Sam had to take him home. Which is why I'm up here alone and at my wit's end. Do you know, I think there's a fairly spectacular Queen Anne desk in that far corner, and I can't get to it. That's very frustrating, Rachel."

Rachel had to smile at Darby's intensity. A friend since elementary school, Darby had remained in Richmond after college, starting her own interior design company with a generous investment from Duncan Grant's bank. She was also an antiques dealer, which was why she was nearly drooling at what she was finding in the attic of this old house.

"You'll get to it eventually," Rachel reassured her soothingly. "Have you started the list of things you want to buy for your business and things you think you can sell for me?"

Darby rolled her eyes. "Have I ever. In case you don't know, there's a fortune in this attic alone. That first appraisal after your parents were killed was conservative, Rachel. Very conservative. I don't think that tax guy knew what he was doing, seriously. But you should send him flowers, because I'm willing to bet he saved you hundreds of thousands in inheritance taxes."

"I don't think he did more than open the door and glance in here," Rachel agreed. "All the antiques downstairs sort of dazzled him."

"They dazzled me too. But I've learned to roll up my sleeves and crawl into corners. And aside from all this glorious furniture—most of which is in fabulous condition, by the way—I've found three trunks so far, all filled to the brim with the kind of stuff to make an interior designer's mouth water. Vases, candle holders, figurines, picture frames. Jeez, Rachel, it's going to cost me a fortune to buy what I want just from in here."

"I told you we'd work something out. A consignment deal, maybe. I'm in no hurry for the money, you know that."

Darby's blue eyes brightened, but she shook her head even so. "You're being too damned trusting and way too generous."

Rachel laughed. "I don't think so. Look, Darby, financially, Dad left me in great shape. What I really want is for all these beautiful things to be seen and enjoyed by people. They've been locked away up here for far too long. And why shouldn't you benefit from that? You've worked your tail off to get your business established, and you've already developed a reputation for finding exquisite furniture for people who appreciate it. Clearly, you're the best woman for the job."

"Thanks, Rachel."

"Don't mention it. Now, why don't you knock off for the day? It's after four and, besides, you need your guys to move these big pieces for you. You can get a fresh start tomorrow." She smiled. "And I'll be sure and tell Fiona not to hex Steve again."

"I would appreciate that."

The two women left the attic together, and when they reached the second floor hallway, Darby said immediately, "I hadn't realized we'd moved so much out of the attic. God, Rachel, I'm sorry—"

"I told you not to worry about it."

Darby bit her lip, then said, "Tell you what. I'll make a list tonight of a few things I know I can sell quickly, and tomorrow I'll have the guys haul the pieces to my shop.

They'll be out of your way and mine, and we'll get the ball rolling. Okay?"

"That's fine."

"I'll check with you first, of course, before taking anything away. There might be a few things you want to keep for yourself, maybe transport to your apartment in New York."

Like most of the people around her, Darby assumed Rachel would be selling out and leaving Richmond, an assumption encouraged by Rachel's attitude and decisions so far. It wasn't something Rachel disputed, even though she was still uncertain about what she meant to do.

So she merely nodded in response and said, "Sounds good."

"Great. Then I'll see you tomorrow." Darby rushed down the stairs with an energy that belied her rather fragile appearance, and a moment later the front door closed behind her.

Rachel went to her second-floor bedroom in the east wing and stood at the doorway, looking down the hall toward her parents' bedrooms. Though she had gone through her father's desk here at the house as a business necessity, she hadn't yet been able to sort through his and her mother's personal belongings. It was something she knew she had to do, not a chore she could assign to anyone else. It would take time and require decisions as to what to do with clothing and so on, and so far Rachel had simply not been up to the task.

And still was not. She shied away from opening those doors just as she had shied away from any other chore that threatened her control. She wasn't ready yet. Not yet.

She went into her bedroom, a room she had been allowed to furnish for herself when she was sixteen. Since Rachel had inherited her mother's elegant taste in antiques, even as a teenager she had not been fond of the fads and often peculiar color combinations in vogue with her friends; her room was decorated in quiet tones of blue and gold, virtually all the furniture Louis XV pieces, delicate and lovely.

Rachel was comfortable in the room, and after so many years took the stunning antiques for granted. She went into the adjoining bathroom and turned on the faucets to fill the big oval tub, deciding that a hot bath might ease her tension and soothe the restlessness she couldn't seem to get rid of. It only half worked, but half was an improvement, and by the time she climbed from the tub thirty minutes later, Rachel definitely felt better.

She wandered back out into her bedroom wearing a silk robe, and went to stand at a window that looked out over the front drive and lawns. Plans for the evening were simple; dinner, probably with her uncle Cameron, who was currently staying in the house, and then television or a book. It had become her routine since she had come home two weeks ago.

"Jet-setting heiress, that's me," she murmured to herself wryly.

The irony, of course, was that she could have jetted off to wherever she wanted—and simply had no interest in doing so. Money was not one of the things Rachel had ever had to strive for, and so it was not something that represented success or achievement. Not to her.

Achievement, to Rachel, was bound up in whether the designs she had created would successfully adorn the fashion runways when next year's spring collections made their debut. She had apprenticed herself to one of the best New York designers, and after years of hard work had the satisfaction of knowing that her designs would be shown under her own name.

But that was months and months away, and in the meantime she had to decide just how much of her past she wanted to abandon.

Rachel sighed and began to turn away from the window, when a flicker of movement down by the front gate caught her attention. There was considerable distance between the house and the gate, but what Rachel saw was clear enough.

And definitely real.

A man with silvery blond hair was standing at the gate, looking up toward the house. He was very still for a moment, and then, with a hunching movement of his broad shoulders that might have been a shrug or some gesture of indecision, he turned and walked away, hidden immediately by the high brick wall and numerous tall trees.

Rachel lifted a hand as though to stop him, but her flesh touched nothing except the cold glass of her window.

TWO

I'm sorry, Rachel. I should have done this months ago." Mercy Sheridan, Duncan Grant's former assistant, had come to the house to bring Rachel a box of personal articles she had cleared from Duncan's office at the bank. She was still with the company at least through the process of settling the estate; she hadn't announced her decision about what to do beyond that time.

She grimaced slightly. "But it was hard enough to go through his files when I had to, never mind his personal things. I think this is everything not directly related to the business, though—unless I come across something misfiled."

Rachel had meant only to thank her, but heard herself say a bit dryly, "Does Nicholas want to move into Dad's office?"

Obviously surprised, Mercy replied, "Not that I know of." Her violet eyes softened, and she said gently, "He isn't trying to take your dad's place, if that's what you think. In fact, he's been pretty adamant about keeping Duncan's memory alive at the bank. He wants his office left just as it was, wants that portrait to hang in the lobby with a brass plaque saying that Duncan founded the company. And he doesn't mean to change the name after you sell out to him, Rache. It'll go on being known as Duncan and Ross Investments, Ltd."

Rachel hadn't known that, and it made her feel she had done Nicholas Ross an injustice. But all she said was "I'm glad. Dad would have liked that." He had chosen to use the name Duncan in his business because it was his mother's family name and because he'd liked the sound of it especially once Nicholas Ross's name had been added to the letterhead.

The two women were in the den, a comfortable room where Rachel spent much of her time. Mercy left the box she had brought on a side table, then joined Rachel on the Victorian settee near the fireplace.

"You are going to sell the business to Nicholas?"

"Probably. It makes sense to, after all." Rachel shrugged. "I guess I just have to get used to the idea first."

Mercy leaned back and crossed one long, elegant leg over the other. A beautiful, raven-haired woman with a voluptuous figure, she was still single at thirty despite the attentions of half the bachelors—and more than one married man—in Richmond. Rachel suspected she was involved with someone at the moment, but Mercy seldom offered details even to her best friend, and Rachel had been too preoccupied these last months to ask for them.

"Rache, are you thinking of staying in Richmond? I thought going back to New York was the plan."

"I'm just having second thoughts. Natural enough, I suppose."

"Sure. You've got a lot of history in this house." She paused a beat, then added quietly, "And a lot of memories."

"Yes." Rachel started to tell Mercy about the blond man she had seen twice, but bit back the words. Mercy had adored her brother, and Rachel couldn't bring herself to open up those old wounds. There was nothing to be gained by having Mercy as upset as she was herself, she thought.

"And maybe it's time you dealt with those memories," Mercy went on steadily. "You didn't go on with your life after Thomas was killed, you just started a whole new one."

"What's wrong with that?" Rachel frowned. "You know I'd always wanted to be a designer, and the best place to learn was in New York—"

"Yes, I know that. But, Rachel, you didn't *move* to New York, you *bolted* there. Virtually cut yourself off from everybody back here, including your parents and me. Put your emotions in a deep freeze—all of them, as far as I can see. And though you haven't brought up the subject, I'm willing to bet you haven't dated at all."

"I have dated," Rachel objected.

Unmoved, Mercy said, "Then you haven't gone out more than once or twice with the same guy. True?"

Instead of trying to deny that shrewd guess, Rachel said, "The fashion business is demanding and competitive, Mercy—I've been trying to build a career. That hasn't left me much time for a personal life."

"Which is just the way you wanted it."

"And I don't see anything wrong with that."

"I didn't say there was anything wrong with it." Mercy's voice was patient. "The problem is that you never came to terms with what you left behind."

Rachel wanted to dispute that but couldn't. "So?"

"So maybe it's time you did that. Maybe it's past time. Rachel, Thomas wouldn't have wanted you to bury your heart with him. And I think we both know you aren't the kind of woman who'll be happy to spend the rest of your life alone—in New York or here." Mercy smiled slightly. "Maybe your doubts about selling out and moving away for good are trying to tell you something. Maybe you need to face the past before you can decide whether to abandon it."

"Maybe." Although, Rachel could have added, not feeling very much had its benefits.

Mercy hesitated, then said, "You changed so much after Thomas was killed. Part of you died—or else got buried so deeply under grief that you lost it. Your laughter and enthusiasm. Your spirit. What Thomas loved most in you."

Shaken, Rachel murmured, "I just grew up, Mercy, that's all. I stopped being a child."

"You stopped being the Rachel we all knew and loved."

Rachel was silent.

In a gentler tone, Mercy said, "It's the first time you've been home long enough for us to really talk, so forgive me if I blurt out what I've been thinking all these years. But it's true, Rache. When you smile, there's just a shadow of what you used to be. Even your voice is quieter. And though you've always moved as if you had all the time in the world, there's a stillness in you that wasn't there ten years ago."

"I can't help how I've changed," Rachel said, uncomfortable under this dissection of her character.

"You can start living again. Let yourself feel again."

"I feel."

"Do you?" Mercy got to her feet, then added deliberately, "You haven't let yourself grieve for your parents any more than you let yourself grieve for Thomas. But sooner or later you'll have to. And if it all hits you at once . . . it'll be like a mountain falling on you."

It was an image that stayed in Rachel's mind throughout the afternoon, while she went over furniture lists with Darby and found other chores to keep herself occupied. She knew that she had indeed run away ten years ago, run away from pain and loss, and she knew she had not allowed herself to grieve as she should have. And when her parents had been killed, the same urge to flee had sent her running back to New York immediately after the funeral, where work had beckoned and there was no time to think. Or feel.

But now she was home. Surrounded by memories, and by people who would not let her keep running away from them. Feelings she didn't want were lurking too close now, just around the next corner, and it was a corner she knew she would have to turn. This time. That was probably why she felt so on edge, so restless.

And why she had twice seen the image of Thomas—nearby but out of reach.

The offices of Duncan and Ross Investments, Ltd., occupying a single building on a tree-lined side street near downtown Richmond, were elegant and rather formal, as financial institutions tended to be. Strictly speaking, this place was not a bank, or at least not the usual sort; clients of Duncan and Ross offered their deposits to be invested in whatever business ventures the firm saw fit to back. The rewards could be enormous.

So could the losses.

Duncan and Ross, however, had a solid reputation for backing winners, and their clients were, for the most part, happy. If they thought it odd that Duncan Grant had chosen to put his first name on the letterhead, and if they wondered why he had suddenly taken on a rather unusual and rather mysterious partner around five years before, both circumstances were, by now, accepted and hardly worth comment.

Mercy Sheridan strode briskly across the marble-floored lobby on this Wednesday afternoon, headed for her office. She wasn't sure just how much longer it would *be* her office, but for now she still had work to do. The paperwork involved when a partner died suddenly was incredible, and between that and the work she had been doing for Nicholas as a favor—he had never used a personal assistant, but found the need for one now that Duncan was gone—she had managed to keep herself busy.

Once Duncan's affairs were settled, however, she would have to start sending out her résumé.

"Mercy?" Leigh Williams came suddenly out of her side office, frowning. "Now that you're back, I need those balance sheets for the auditor. I hadn't realized you'd be gone so long. You *could* give me the combination to Duncan's safe, you know." A tall and sophisticated blonde, the office manager always made Mercy feel both underdressed and overly cautious, to say nothing of tardy and inefficient.

"Not without Rachel's permission," she said lightly, resisting an impulse to remind Leigh that she knew this fact of Duncan's will very well. "I'll get the papers and bring them to your office, Leigh."

"Thanks. Oh—and congratulations, by the way."

Mercy frowned. "For what?"

"For trading up. Or, at least, not losing ground."

"Leigh, what're you talking about?"

"Why, I'm talking about you becoming Mr. Ross's personal assistant." Leigh's pale blue eyes were coolly amused and not a little speculative. "That seems to be on the agenda."

Mercy shook her head. "You've been misinformed."

"Then so has Mr. Ross. He's been telling everyone you're going to stay on and work for him. I need those papers as soon as possible, Mercy." Smiling, Leigh turned and went back into her office.

Mercy stood there for only an instant, gazing thoughtfully at nothing, then went on through the quiet lobby. But instead of going to her own office or the one that had belonged to Duncan Grant, she went directly to the big corner office occupied by Nicholas Ross.

His door was open, but he was on the phone. Mercy closed the door behind her, then sat on the arm of one of his visitor's chairs. And while she waited, she studied him.

Even sitting as he was, and behind a huge mahogany desk, he was obviously an unusually large man, and unusually powerful. His dark suit was expensive and well made, his shoulders could fill doorways, and his presence was nothing less than massive and overpowering. One glance, and anyone would want Nicholas on his or her side no matter what the fight was about.

No one would ever call Mercy a small woman, yet Nicholas made her feel absurdly delicate. He also made her feel incredibly feminine, especially when her quiet voice was contrasted by his harsh growl.

She supposed some people would be afraid of him.

Maybe most people.

Because he was so big, because he sounded so rough

and angry—even when he wasn't. And because he was ugly.

With the best will in the world, she could describe him only as ugly.

He was barely forty, but looked older. He looked, as the saying went, like ten miles of bad road. Maybe twenty. His face, tanned years ago almost to the color and consistency of old leather, was marked by several small scars he had gotten God only knew where or how, making him look even more thuggish. His cheekbones were high but flat, his brow high and wide, and his nose had most certainly been broken at least twice. There was a ludicrous dimple in his strong chin, his mouth was a straight, thin slash without any particular shape and definitely without softness or charm, and his deep-set eyes were such a light shade of brown that they were almost eerily hypnotic.

Like the eyes of a cat. Or a snake.

Mercy knew almost nothing of his background, except that it had been hard and that he had seen parts of the world tourists were warned away from. He didn't talk about himself, so what little she knew or had guessed came from observation, and from the occasional snippets of information he let slip while talking of something else. Such as when he had once said absently that the summer heat of Richmond was worse than the Kalahari. And when he had recommended to a Europe-bound client all the best places to eat in Florence.

And when he had startled her on various occasions by being fluent in French, German, Italian, and Japanese.

Wherever he had been, and whatever he had done, Nicholas Ross had turned up in Richmond about five years previously, his ugly face already worn by time and experiences and his unsettling gaze cynical. He had been obviously wealthy, though the source of his wealth remained a mystery, and he had wanted to get into investment banking.

For reasons he had never explained to anyone, Duncan Grant—who had never needed and seemingly never wanted a partner—had invited him to join the firm.

Mercy had signed on as Duncan's assistant not long after that, and even that early Nicholas was already becoming known for his uncanny instincts for seemingly risky business ventures that would prove to be wildly profitable.

He was smart and he was lucky. Or maybe he was smart enough to make his own luck. In any case, Nicholas Ross was a success.

"You're looking very serious," he said to her as he hung up the phone, his voice harsh and deep.

"I have a serious problem," she told him. "Someone keeps telling people around here that I'm going to be your personal assistant."

Heavy lids veiled his eyes as Nicholas glanced down at his immaculate blotter, and continued to half hide his gaze even after he looked at her once again. "That doesn't have to be a problem."

"Nick, we've had this discussion before."

"I know." He grimaced slightly, producing a face likely to frighten small children. "But I hate losing. You know I hate losing."

Mercy sighed. "I'll say it one more time. I will work for you, or I will sleep with you. But I will not do both. You choose."

His eyelids lifted and those pale eyes flickered. "I want both."

"No." It was said very simply, very quietly.

It was his turn to sigh. "Have I ever told you what a stubborn woman you are? Dammit, Mercy, what would be the harm? I need an assistant and you're the best I've ever seen at the job. So what if we're sleeping together? We've managed to be discreet for nearly a year. The sky hasn't fallen in, and our clients haven't turned up at the door foaming at the mouth because you spend an occasional night at my place or I sleep over at yours. Nobody could even imagine you might be promoted or get a raise for any reason other than solid good work. So why the hell not?"

"I'm not going to sleep with my boss. Period. Full stop. End of statement. How much plainer do I have to be?"

"That's plain enough," he growled, clearly annoyed.

Mercy shrugged. She was actually getting quite good at pretending to be indifferent. "Hey, if a personal assistant is more vital to you, just say the word. I'll pack up the stuff I've left at your place and tear up my résumé."

He grunted. "You would too."

"Well, of course I would. Good lovers may be scarce, but good jobs are almost impossible to come by—and the latter pays the rent. Look, stop giving me a hard time about this, will you? You think I'm looking forward to being on the job market again?" Her family background held wealth, but Mercy always had and always would make her own way in the world.

Instead of replying to her hypothetical question, Nicholas rose from his chair and came around the desk to her.

"There's no lock on that door," she warned, but made no further protest when he pulled her to her feet and then into his arms.

He was always careful with her, always consciously gentle—or so it seemed to Mercy. It was the trait of a physically powerful man who knew only too well his strength could hurt and damage, and it never failed to move her in some way she couldn't explain even to herself.

He kissed her with astonishing skill, his hard mouth so sensual that her knees instantly went weak. Her arms slid up around his neck and held on. Even after a year and countless hours spent mindless in his bed, the hunger he roused in her was sharp-edged and intense, demanding satisfaction. It was not something she could fight, not even something she could manage, but, rather, an elemental force that overwhelmed her.

And it irritated Mercy no end that she was never the one to pull back, never the one to regain control easily and swiftly.

He was always able to.

Always—damn him.

Raising his head and smiling very faintly as he looked down at her, Nicholas unlocked her arms from around his neck and eased her down on the arm of the chair behind her. "So sure you could turn your back on my bed, love?"

He had always called her that when they were alone like this, ever since the stormy spring evening nearly a year before when he had offered her a ride home, and they had somehow—to this day, Mercy wasn't sure just how it had happened—wound up naked on the rug in front of her fireplace.

He called her love, but she didn't deceive herself into thinking it meant anything. Nicholas Ross was a hard, abrupt, and rather secretive man with very strong physical appetites, and a "relationship" was clearly not something he wanted in his life. Just a woman in his bed three or four nights a week, with no ties or promises.

Mercy had learned to play the game just the way he liked.

So, when she caught her breath, she made herself say dryly, "It would naturally be a severe blow, but I think I could manage."

He let out a bark of a laugh and stepped back to half sit on the edge of his desk. Crossing his arms over his broad chest, he stared at her. "You're not going to back down on this, are you?"

"Afraid not."

"So once Duncan's estate is settled and the bank back to normal, you'll resign?"

"That is the plan." She shrugged. "Look, you know I'm not doing this just to make things harder for you or the bank. There are some lines I won't cross, and sleeping with my boss is one of them."

"I'm your boss *now,*" he reminded her.

"No, you're my boss's partner. Until Duncan's estate is settled and the future of the bank decided, I still work for him. It may be splitting hairs, but that's the way I see it."

Nicholas frowned. "Suppose Rachel decides to keep her interest. You could stay on here as her representative. Then she'd be your boss, not me."

Mercy was a little surprised. "I hadn't thought of that. But, anyway, it isn't likely, is it? You've always seemed so determined to buy her out. Aren't you?"

His frown deepened. "Yes, I'm still determined. But if she's anything like Duncan, she has a mind of her own. Is she like him? I haven't spent enough time with her to know."

"She's like him in some ways." Mercy considered the matter. "Smart, intuitive, creative. Like Duncan, she's capable of flashes of inspiration. Problem is, Rachel's carting around a lot of baggage right now, most of it painful. Until she sorts through that, there's really no telling what her decision about the bank will be."

"Your brother's death?"

Mercy nodded. "She's coping with that as well as the

loss of her parents—or will be whenever that frozen shell of hers shatters. She needs time, Nick."

"I don't know how much time I can give her." He spoke absently, his gaze abstracted and his face curiously immobile.

Mercy felt a tingle of uneasiness, but said lightly, "I wasn't aware you had some kind of deadline in mind."

Those hypnotic eyes focused on her, unreadable, and after an instant he smiled slightly. "I don't. I'm just naturally impatient. You should know that by now."

What Mercy knew was just the opposite, that he had the patience of a hunting cougar, perfectly capable of hunkering down in utter stillness and waiting as long as it took to get what he wanted.

He always got what he wanted.

What she didn't know was if he had deliberately lied just now or if he honestly had no idea that he had given away that character trait of patience. Either way, it made her uneasiness increase.

Reluctant to question him, she got to her feet and changed the subject. "I have to get some papers out of Duncan's safe before Leigh has a fit, so I'd better go. Anything you need me to do?"

Before Nicholas could answer, there was a soft knock followed instantly by Leigh peering around the door. She had been so quick that if they had been doing anything indiscreet, they would have been caught. But if she had hoped for that, the office manager hid her disappointment well.

She smiled brightly. "Sorry to interrupt—but, Mercy, I really need those papers."

"I'll get them now, Leigh."

"Good. Thanks. Sorry again." She retreated, closing the door quietly.

"Yes, there is something I need you to do," Nicholas said. "I need you to have a lock put on that door."

"Oh, no!" Mercy turned away, adding over her shoulder, "Then she'd know she was right to suspect sinful things going on in here. See you later." She heard Nicholas laugh as she left his office, but thought the sound didn't hold much amusement.

And that bothered her more than anything.

It was Friday afternoon when Rachel decided to go into Richmond. She was planning to do a bit of shopping, more to get out of the house than because there was anything she wanted or needed. Her restlessness had not abated; if anything, it had only gotten stronger. And her vacillation between selling out and returning to New York or staying here was really beginning to bother her.

She got into her mother's Mercedes sedan and drove down to the front gate, which was standing open because Darby's workmen had been hauling attic furniture from the house since early morning.

Rachel turned toward Richmond, and her car began to pick up speed as it moved down a long slope. She reached absently to change the radio station. When she glanced back up at the virtually deserted road, she felt a shock as she once again saw the blond man.

He was standing at the bottom of the slope, still a quarter-mile away, but Rachel knew it was the man she had seen before. Sunlight glinted off his silvery hair, and his lean face was turned toward her. He was just off the road, near a big oak tree and the corner of the brick wall that surrounded much of the Grant estate.

Without arguing with herself, Rachel stepped on the

brake, determined not to let him slip away this time. She had to see him, talk to him, had to find out who he was—

The brake pedal resisted for an instant, and then went easily all the way to the floorboard.

The emergency brake proved equally useless, and the gearshift refused to budge.

She couldn't stop the car.

In the space of only heartbeats, Rachel knew that her only choice was to somehow get off the road. Just beyond the bottom of the slope was a traffic light, always busy; she couldn't take the chance of getting through it without hitting another car or a pedestrian.

She waited until the blond man flashed by on her right, then she wrenched the steering wheel to the right, praying desperately that she could avoid the trees.

There was no curb to provide even a nominal barrier, and the heavy sedan barely slowed as it plowed through the spring flowers, weeds, and bushes filling what was essentially an empty lot. Still, Rachel thought she might make it.

Until the rear of the sedan began to fishtail, and she lost control.

Seconds later, the car crashed headlong into an old oak tree.

In those first confused moments, Rachel's mind seemed to function at half speed while her heart pounded in triple time. She found herself sitting behind the wheel, dazed, the air bag deflating now that it had done its job. The car horn was wailing stridently, and the hood was crumpled back almost to the windshield.

Rachel was surprised to be alive and apparently undamaged.

The passenger door was wrenched open suddenly, and a handsome blond man with intense violet eyes leaned in to stare at her. "Rachel, my God, are you all right?" he demanded.

The shock of the accident was forgotten. Her stunned gaze searched that face, as familiar to her as her own, and she was barely aware of whispering, "My God. Thomas."

Then everything went black.

THREE

In the hospital, where paramedics had taken her, the doctor who examined Rachel was not happy. He could find no serious injury barring a slight bump on the side of her head where she had apparently hit the window frame of the car, yet she had remained unconscious long enough to raise grave concerns. Rachel tried to explain that the cause had been emotional shock rather than physical, but apparently only she had seen Thomas.

He had vanished once again.

When she had awakened in the ambulance, the paramedic treating her insisted that there had been no blond man at the scene of the accident.

Rachel didn't want to sound like a lunatic by insisting on the reappearance of her long-dead fiancé, so she finally just submitted when the doctor ordered tests and an overnight stay to keep her under observation.

She was ruefully aware that her father's generous endowment to the hospital—and her own possible future interest—was largely responsible for the doctor's caution.

It was more than two hours before she was in a private room and could call the house to inform Fiona and her uncle, and ask that Graham be called so he could find out about the car. She was fine, she told the anxious housekeeper. There was no need for anyone to come to the hospital, because she'd be home in the morning anyway. She just wanted to rest.

But when the silence of the room closed around her, Rachel began to wish she had asked for visitors. Anything to distract her from her muddled thoughts.

Thomas? How could it have been him? He was dead. He had been dead for nearly ten years. And yet . . . it was no ghost that had leaned into her car, no ghost's voice that had called her by name and demanded to know if she was all right. No ghost, but a real flesh-and-blood man. She had even felt the heat of his body, caught the scent of aftershave.

Think it through.

It couldn't have been Thomas, surely it couldn't have. Because if he had been alive all this time, and had let her go on believing him dead . . . No, the man she had loved would never be so cruel.

Unless he hadn't been able to tell her the truth?

He had often been somewhat mysterious about his trips out of the country, so much so that it had bothered her. Yet whenever she had expressed that worry, he had merely laughed and told her she was imagining things. He was a pilot who worked for a shipping company, and he hauled cargo. Normal stuff, he told her. Supplies and equipment.

Yet something in his eyes had made Rachel wonder.

Mercy had often said that her brother loved intrigue

and invented it in his own life, that that was why he sometimes seemed mysterious about his activities, but Rachel had not been reassured. She had been certain that he was sometimes in danger, and with a young woman's flair for drama, she had imagined that danger to involve guns and bullets even though there had been no evidence at all to support that.

Now, with an older woman's rationality, Rachel found it difficult to think of any reason Thomas might have faked his own death, any reason he would have needed to stay away for nearly a decade from those who loved him. It just didn't make sense.

But if it hadn't been Thomas she had seen, alive or dead, then who was this man that might have been his twin? He knew her, or at least knew her name. Three times he had been nearby, seemingly watching her, only to vanish before she could touch him, speak to him. Who was he? What had brought him into her life, and why did he stand back as though uncertain or wary of approaching her?

That didn't make sense either.

She was still arguing with herself about an hour later when a hasty knock at the door heralded Graham's arrival. He was carrying a vase filled with her favorite yellow roses and looked very much upset.

"Rachel—my God, are you all right?"

Odd that he used the exact same words the stranger had.

"I'm fine, Graham. A little bump on the head and an overly cautious doctor, that's all. Lovely flowers, but you didn't have to."

He set the vase on the table by her bed and stood staring down at her with a frown. "From what Fiona told me on the phone, I expected to find broken bones."

Rachel smiled. "By now you should know how Fiona exaggerates."

"I do. But I also checked on your car. After seeing it, I expected worse than broken bones."

"I'm fine, really. The air bag worked like a charm. Remind me to send a note of thanks to whoever invented the things."

"I'm more interested in what caused the accident." He drew a chair close to the bed and sat down, still frowning. "How did you lose control? The police say there were no skid marks."

"I didn't lose control. Well, I mean, I didn't until the car started to slide all over the place on the grass. I had to steer it into that empty lot because I had no brakes."

"What? You mean they were just gone?"

For the first time, Rachel thought about something other than Thomas, and a shiver of remembered panic crept up her spine. "The pedal felt a little spongy for an instant, then went all the way to the floor. I guess the brake line was somehow broken."

"I don't see how." Graham shook his head. "But I'll have the car towed to a good garage and checked out bumper to bumper. And I'll arrange for another car for you. You don't want to drive Duncan's Rolls, do you?"

Rachel grimaced. "Hardly."

"Didn't think so." He smiled. "Any preferences?"

"Anything but a sports car. I hate them."

"So that's why you never want to ride in my 'Vette."

"That's why," she agreed.

"I'll keep that in mind." Graham's faint smile died, and he added very seriously, "You're sure you're all right?"

"I'm sure." *Just losing my mind, that's all.* "The doctor wants me here for observation because I was . . . unconscious for a little while. But I'm okay. I'll be able to go home in the morning."

"Then I'll come by and pick you up—not in the 'Vette." He got to his feet. "In the meantime, I should go and let you rest."

Rachel wanted to object, because she really didn't want to be left alone with her bewildered thoughts. But she also didn't want to explain to Graham that she had once again seen Thomas's ghost or his twin, and he would certainly wonder if she expressed an unusual desire for his company.

So she merely said, "Will you do me another favor?"

"Of course I will."

"Stop by the house and reassure Fiona and Cam? Tell them I'm fine and I'll see them in the morning?"

"I'll do that."

"Thanks."

"Don't mention it." He hesitated, then briefly touched her hand. "See you in the morning."

She nodded, and held on to her smile until the door swung shut behind him. Then she sighed and turned her gaze to the uninspiring ceiling.

It was going to be a long night.

It was probably after midnight when Rachel half woke from a drugged sleep. The doctor had insisted on the sedative once he'd found no evidence of concussion, saying she needed a solid night's rest. But now she wanted to be awake and the drug was fighting her. She didn't know why she wanted to be awake, not at first. It was very quiet, and the room was dimly lit by the panel light above the head of her bed.

Then he moved out of the shadows near the door and came toward the bed, and Rachel felt her heart leap.

He came to the side of the bed and stood looking down at her for a moment, his face grave. She made a little sound, wordless but urgent, and reached out a wavering hand to him. And when he took her hand in his, the warmth of his flesh touching hers was so solid, so real that it was shocking.

"Who . . . ?" It was all she could get out, and Rachel concentrated fiercely on fighting the drug that was trying to drag her back toward unconsciousness.

He bent down, closer to her, and for a moment Rachel could only stare at that familiar face. Then her heart clenched in pain.

"I'm sorry," he murmured.

His eyes were blue.

Rachel wanted to cry. She thought she might have, but the drug in her system finally won the struggle, and the familiar face of a stranger grew hazy and then disappeared into the dark peace of sleep.

In the bright light of day, the sedative cleared from her system, her nighttime visitor definitely seemed ghostlike at best, and a total figment of her drugged imagination at worst.

Except that she knew he had been there.

She couldn't explain the certainty, but didn't doubt it. The blond man had been in her hospital room last night. He had held her hand, and he had said he was sorry. And his eyes had not been violet as she had thought at the scene of her accident, but pale blue. Despite the dim light of her room last night, she was sure of that.

He was not Thomas.

In one sense, that fact was a relief; at least now she could stop agonizing over whether Thomas had been alive all the time she had believed him dead. He hadn't lied to her, hadn't been cruel enough to hide himself from her.

He had, quite simply, died in a tragic plane crash before his thirtieth birthday.

No, this was another man entirely. A man at least a few years younger than Thomas would have been, maybe thirty-five at most. But the resemblance was certainly uncanny. It made her seriously ask herself if maybe everyone really did have a twin somewhere in the world.

So. There was a stranger who looked like Thomas, a man who knew her name and who had seemingly been watching her for at least several days. The question was—why?

That question remained in Rachel's mind after she went home and all through the weekend, while Fiona fussed over her and Cam exclaimed, and the phone rang with worried inquiries from concerned friends—this surprising her, since she had not realized so many people still thought of her as a friend after she had spent so many years away from Richmond.

She found herself going often to her bedroom window, where there was a view of the front gate, her gaze searching for sunlight glinting off blond hair. But she didn't see what she looked for. Who she looked for. And without information only he could supply, there was no way for her to know who he was and why he had come into her life as he had.

By Monday afternoon Rachel had reached the point of wondering if she should take out an ad in the newspapers asking the mysterious blond man to give her a call. She didn't, but the thought was definitely tempting.

No one seemed to notice her preoccupation over the

weekend, or if they did, chalked it up to her brush with near death. Graham was the only one to comment on Monday afternoon when she went to his office to sign yet another stack of legal documents.

"You're very quiet today," he said, leaning back in his chair to study her thoughtfully. "Aftereffects of the crash?"

"Probably." She made her voice reassuring. "I don't know, maybe everybody should crash their car into an oak tree at least once. It sort of puts things into perspective for you."

"What kinds of things?"

Her shoulders lifted and fell. "What really matters. Graham, I don't think I want to sell the house after all. Even to Cam."

He didn't seem surprised. "What about the business?"

"I haven't decided about that yet. But the house . . . Mom and Dad loved it so much, and they're very much there in spirit." Despite control, her voice quivered. "I started cleaning out their bedrooms yesterday, finally going through everything, and I couldn't believe how close to them it made me feel. When I thought of Mom's letters and her collection of lace handkerchiefs being packed away, and all the books Dad loved going into storage because I don't have room for them in my apartment in New York . . . it just hit me what I was thinking of doing."

She hadn't actually begun cleaning out their bedrooms. What she had done was take two steps into her dad's room and then sit in a chair, crying for the better part of an hour. But the result had been the same. She couldn't bear the thought of selling out.

Graham smiled. "Well, there's enough money to maintain the house, no question. Would you move back to Richmond and commute to New York? Keep the apartment in Manhattan and visit here on weekends? Or do your design work out of the house?"

Rachel sighed. "I haven't made those decisions yet—except there's no way I could work totally out of the house and keep my job. To make a name for yourself in the fashion industry, you have to be where it's happening—and that means New York."

"So that's still important to you? It's one of the things the accident put into perspective?"

She thought about it, nodding slowly. "It's not fame I'm after. It's not even success, really. It's . . . being creative the only way I know how. It's the excitement I feel whenever I see an idea actually taking shape in a sketch and then in fabric and on a model."

"You could have that here in Richmond," he said neutrally. "Open a boutique, maybe, with one-of-a-kind designs. The label of Rachel Grant, a Richmond exclusive. I'd say most of the ladies around here would eat it up. In time, New York could come knocking on *your* door."

Even as he spoke, Rachel knew it could work, could be a huge success. She was only surprised she hadn't thought of it before then.

"It's a possibility," she said slowly.

Graham nodded. "Definitely something to think about. I mean, if you're going to keep the house, it'd be a shame to have it go unoccupied for long stretches. Living here, working here. Makes sense to me." And it would keep her in Richmond, which was what he wanted.

She smiled at him. "You should have stayed with trial work, Graham. You can be very persuasive when you want to be."

"That's why I stopped criminal trial work." He smiled slightly in return. "I was able to sway a jury to believe my client was innocent when he was actually guilty as hell.

Didn't much like the way that made me feel, so I switched to corporate law."

"I never knew that."

He shrugged. "I didn't run my car into an oak tree, but what happened did put things into perspective for me. I've found life often forces us to make choices, whether we think we're ready for them or not."

"I'm beginning to think you're right about that." Her voice was somewhat rueful. "When I came back here, it seemed there were nothing but choices to make, and I didn't want to make them. Yet, somehow, every time I've had to choose, it's been easier than I expected. More simple and clear-cut."

"Maybe you're getting back on balance. You've had a hell of a rough year, Rachel, don't forget that. Give yourself time. There's no decision you absolutely have to make now, no choice so imperative that it won't wait a few weeks. As with the house, you'll know the right choice when it hits you."

"I suppose you're right."

"Of course."

She laughed and got to her feet. "I'll let the whole situation simmer for a while and see what happens. Satisfied?"

"For the moment." He rose as well, smiling. "How's the car?"

"Drives like a dream, thanks. I meant to ask if it's a rental or leased?"

"Leased. Let me know if you want to buy it."

"Okay." If she lived in Richmond on a permanent basis, she would need to own a car, something she had not needed in New York. Then there would be insurance, and a tag, and maintenance . . . responsibilities. Ties to this place. If she kept the house—and she was fairly certain she would—that would be the biggest tie of all. She felt a tinge of uneasiness but pushed that reaction aside.

"Rachel?"

She looked at Graham, saw his frown, and realized that she must have flinched or otherwise betrayed discomfort. "It's nothing. For a minute there, I let the . . . weight of choices overwhelm me. But you're right. There's nothing I have to decide right this minute. Which reminds me—"

"I'll tell Nicholas you need more time to decide about the business."

"Thanks. I'll see you later, Graham."

"You bet."

Rachel left his office and drove her leased sedan home without incident. Except that she couldn't stop scanning her surroundings in search of the blond stranger. She didn't see him.

That newspaper ad began to seem more inviting.

When she went into the house, it was to discover that Fiona was upset because Darby's workmen had been "tramping" up and down the stairs all day, getting in her way, and Cam wanted to talk to her about buying a rosewood wardrobe that had been found in the attic even though Darby was desperate to have it for her shop, and Darby needed to check with Rachel because she had a list of requested pieces from clients.

Rachel dealt with each of them patiently, soothing, answering, or making a decision—whatever was called for. Fiona was promised fewer difficulties caused by workmen, Cam was promised the rosewood wardrobe, and Darby's list was gone over and selected items agreed upon. Then Rachel retreated to her father's study so she could be alone for a little while.

It was a room she had always loved, a fairly small room off a side hall on the first floor, where her father had spent much of his time when he was home. It was one of the few rooms in the house not furnished with delicate antiques—though the huge Regency table that had served as his desk was certainly an exquisite piece. The remaining furniture consisted of big, comfortable, overstuffed chairs and a sofa that faced the marble fireplace, as well as big, solid end tables and occasional tables. The floor was hardwood, but covered with a lovely rug in muted shades of blue and burgundy, and bookshelves lined the wall between the two large windows.

Rachel had already been through all the business papers her father had kept in this room, but she was still in the process of sorting through his remaining personal papers. He had been quite a letter writer, especially in his younger years, and Rachel was loath to throw away his correspondence without reading it just to make sure nothing important was discarded by accident.

She was sitting at the desk bemusedly reading a letter to her father from a rather well-known sixties actor, when the door opened and Fiona stepped in, a peculiar expression on her face.

"Miss Rachel . . ."

"What is it, Fiona? Darby said she'd speak to her guys, so they should stay out of your way now. Is that it? Or is there another problem?"

"No. That is—I don't know. There's a—a gentleman here to see you." The housekeeper's voice was as odd as her expression, a little shaky and more than a little hesitant.

"Oh? Who is he?"

"He says his name is Delafield, Miss Rachel. Adam Delafield. He says."

Rachel frowned at the housekeeper. "Did he say what it was about?"

"Something about your father, he said."

"All right. Show him in." Since her parents had died, she had been getting calls and visits from people they had known, and in particular from people who had been helped in some way by her father.

"Miss Rachel—" Fiona hesitated, then turned away, muttering something under her breath. And crossing herself.

So Rachel probably should have expected her visitor to present something of a shock. But she didn't. And when the blond man walked into the room a few moments later, she could only stare at him in astonishment.

"Hello," he said, his voice low and curiously compelling. "I'm Adam Delafield. It's nice to finally meet you, Rachel."

His eyes were definitely blue.

He was tall and athletic in appearance, with wide shoulders and an easy way of moving that spoke of an active life. His lean face wore a tan that had obviously come from time spent outdoors over the years. He was dressed casually in dark slacks and a black leather jacket worn over an open-necked white shirt, and looked perfectly at ease.

He also looked, amazingly, incredibly, heartbreakingly, like Thomas.

Of all the questions swirling around in Rachel's mind, the first one to find voice was "Who are you?"

He smiled slightly. "I just told you."

She got up and went toward him, stopping when she could rest her hands on the back of a chair, keeping it between them as a barrier. "You told me your name. But *who are you*? Why have you been watching me? Why did you leave the accident and—and come to my hospital room, and how do you know my name?" *And how is it that you look so much like him?*

"Lot of questions." His smile remained. "Can we sit down while I try to answer them?"

Rachel hesitated, then gestured for him to sit on the sofa while she chose the chair across from it. She couldn't take her eyes off his face, and even as he began speaking in a voice that was—surely it was!—eerily like Thomas's, she realized that he was not as at ease as he appeared. There was tension in him; she could feel it. And those blue eyes held a muted intensity that stirred a new and wordless uneasiness in her.

"My name, as I said, is Adam Delafield." He spoke slowly, consideringly, and his gaze was intent on her. "And the simple answer to all your questions is that I knew your father."

"How did you know him?"

"He invested money in a . . . project of mine."

Rachel frowned, trying to take in what he was saying, to separate his words from the overwhelming confusion of his looks. "I don't recall seeing your name on any of Dad's financial records."

"No, you wouldn't have. The investment wasn't through the bank. He used personal money and there were no records of the transaction."

Her frown deepened. "I know Dad occasionally invested his own money in ventures he considered too risky for the bank, but no records? A handshake deal? How could he report his profits or losses if there was no paperwork?"

"In my case, he didn't expect either profit or loss. The deal was simple, a turnaround of the money. He invested a considerable sum, which I was to repay within ten years."

"Interest free? That sounds like a loan rather than an investment. And a pretty good deal for you."

Adam Delafield nodded. "An excellent deal for me. But he called it an investment because he was sure we would do business together in the future. That was a little more than five years ago. I expect to be in a position to pay off the . . . loan—within the next six months."

"And that's why you showed up here? Why you watched me from a distance for days?"

"You make me sound like a stalker." His voice was light, but that intensity lingered and lent the words shadows. He sighed. "Rachel—I hope you don't mind, but Duncan talked about you and I got into the habit of thinking of you as if I knew you."

She hesitated, then shrugged. "No, I don't mind."

"Thanks. Rachel, I just wasn't sure how to approach you. I intended to introduce myself to you earlier, right after Duncan and your mother were killed, but you had already gone back to New York, and until the estate was settled, or nearly so, you weren't expected back. I didn't want to intrude on your grief. And—I knew about the resemblance."

Taken aback, she said, "You did?"

He nodded. "Duncan commented on it, even showed me a photograph of Thomas Sheridan. So I knew my appearance would probably come as a shock to you. I didn't want to upset you, that's why I hesitated to just come up and knock on the door. At the same time, the investment Duncan made in my project was substantial, and since I knew there were no documents, and that he wouldn't have mentioned it in his will, and possibly not even in his personal papers, I had to see you and explain the situation."

She thought it said something about this man's character that he insisted she know about a part of her inheritance she would never have missed; she couldn't help wondering how many people would have just kept the money and their silence. But all she said was "It doesn't really sound like Dad, investing money with no records. He must have trusted you a great deal."

Adam looked down at his clasped hands. "He was very kind to me at a point in my life when kindness meant more than money. And he had faith in my future, something I didn't have myself. I don't know why he trusted me, but he did. I'll always be as grateful to him for that trust as for the money that put me back on my feet."

Rachel was moved despite both uneasiness and fascination. *Dear God, he looks so much like Thomas!* And sounded like him. She clasped her hands together and made herself concentrate. "How did you know Dad? I mean, how did you meet him?"

"It's a bit involved." He raised his gaze to her face and smiled faintly. "He came out to California, where I'm from, more than five years ago on a business trip. I had, the week before, called up an old friend to ask for help. The friend, as it turned out, was away in Europe. His partner, as it turned out, was Duncan Grant."

"Nicholas Ross?" That surprised her, although she couldn't have said exactly why.

"Yes. We'd known each other a long time and Nick . . . sort of owed me a favor. Anyway, when I couldn't reach him, I spoke briefly to Duncan. I found out when he came out to San Francisco the next week that he had called Nick and asked about me. To this day I don't know what Nick told him, but he came out to California specifically to see me. He listened to my problems and my plans, and offered me the money I needed on the spot.

"Over the next three or four years I flew out here

several times to see him. To let him know how his investment was doing. How I was doing. We'd have lunch, maybe even do a flyover of the city in that little plane he was so proud of. And then I'd go back to California."

Rachel flinched a little as she thought of the sleek twin-engine plane her father had loved—and that had taken both her parents to their deaths. Adam obviously saw her reaction.

"I'm sorry. I didn't mean to cause you any pain, Rachel."

"No, it's just . . . I don't like to think about that plane, that's all." Planes had taken all the people she loved. She conjured a smile. "So you know Nicholas. Didn't you assume he'd tell me about Dad's investment?"

Adam shook his head. "No, I knew he'd leave it to me. Nick isn't exactly the most candid of men, you know. I mean, he isn't apt to discuss other people's business."

"Or even his own," Rachel observed dryly.

"Very true." Adam's eyes grew even more intense when he smiled at her, and it made her feel strange. *He isn't Thomas. He isn't! No matter how much he looks like him.* But those logical reminders did nothing to curb her growing desire to reach out and touch him.

Unwilling to let a silence fall between them, she said, "Why did you leave the scene on Friday when I hit that tree? The paramedics told me only the highway patrol was there near the car when they arrived."

"You should have asked the highway patrol about me," he told her with a touch of amusement. "When they reached the scene, they made everyone else stand back. You were in expert care and there didn't seem to be anything I could do, so I left when I heard the ambulance coming."

She half nodded, then said, "Why did you come to my

room at the hospital so late? You did, didn't you? I didn't imagine it?"

"No, you didn't imagine it." He hesitated. "I just wanted to make sure you were all right. Didn't expect you to wake up, but you were obviously groggy and went back to sleep almost at once, so I didn't stay."

"You came late. After visiting hours." That still bothered her.

"There were some things I had to take care of first," he said rather vaguely, looking briefly down at his hands in a way that shuttered his gaze for a moment. "It was late when I finished up and got to the hospital. To be honest, I snuck in."

She thought his smile was very disarming. "I see. All right—Adam. I suppose all this makes sense." *But it doesn't, none of it does.*

"But you still have your doubts?"

"Well, let's just say it surprises me that Dad would have done business the way you say he did. However, you didn't have to come and tell me all this, and I can't think of any devious reason why you would have. And I imagine Nicholas will vouch for you."

A flicker of some emotion Rachel couldn't read crossed his handsome face, but he merely said, "I'm sure he will. In the meantime, I just want to assure you that Duncan's investment will be repaid as promised. By the end of the year, I believe."

Realizing suddenly that she had no idea, she said, "I suppose I should ask what kind of business Dad invested in."

"It was more a project than a business, initially. I had dreamed up an electronic gadget that would improve most manufacturing facilities. I had to get the design patented, a prototype built, and try to sell it. It was so successful that I was able to start my own electronic design and engineering firm. All possible due to the investment Duncan made."

"I'm sure he was pleased with your success. Dad loved to see people achieve their dreams." Rachel started to rise to her feet. "How much was the investment, by the way?"

Matter-of-factly, Adam replied, "Three million dollars."

FOUR

Rachel sat back down. "Three million dollars?"

He nodded.

"You're telling me that my father invested three million dollars of his own money on a handshake?"

Patient, Adam said, "I've already told you that, yes."

"You didn't tell me it was three million dollars." She was incredulous. "Adam, I've seen Dad's bank records going back years. There was no unexplained withdrawal anywhere near that size, not five years ago and not ever. Every penny has been accounted for."

"I don't know what to tell you. Except—as I remember, he transferred the funds to my bank from a Swiss bank account."

She blinked. "He what? He doesn't have a Swiss bank account."

"He did five years ago. I was sitting in the room, admittedly a bit numb, but I remember the call clearly. He definitely called Geneva."

Rachel had passed bewilderment; now she felt distinctly unnerved, and not only because the image of her long-dead fiancé was sitting across from her. What would an honest businessman want with a Swiss bank account? And why had no sign of such a thing come to light during all the months countless experts had combed through Duncan Grant's financial records?

It naturally occurred to her that she was hearing this from a virtual stranger, and that she had every reason to doubt what he was telling her. Except that he seemed about to hand her three million dollars, and she couldn't imagine how that could be part of some tangled deception. And—he looked like Thomas. He looked so damned much like Thomas.

"Rachel? Are you all right?"

"No, I'm not."

He hesitated, then said reassuringly, "I'm sure there's no reason for you to be concerned. Duncan may have routed some of his funds through Geneva temporarily for some tax reason. If the account still existed, you surely would have found some record of it among his papers."

"Would I? I found no record of a three-million-dollar investment, so I would say nothing's certain where my father is concerned."

Adam hesitated once again before saying, "He wouldn't have wanted you to miss getting part of your inheritance, so I'm sure he would have left some kind of word for you if he had money . . . put aside somewhere you wouldn't expect it to be."

"You mean if he had money hidden somewhere."

"I didn't want to put it that way," he murmured.

"My father," she told him fiercely, "was an honest man. He earned every nickel he had. Every last one. There was no reason for him to hide money."

"I'm sure you're right." Adam shook his head. "Look, Rachel, I'm sorry I've upset you. It wasn't my intention to do that. I just wanted to let you know that Duncan's investment will be repaid this year. You might want to talk to whoever advises you financially. That's a pretty large chunk of money."

"No kidding." It was Rachel's turn to shake her head. "And how do I explain it? How will *you* explain it?"

"Repayment of a personal loan," he said promptly. "It started my business, so I've had to be fairly specific in my own paperwork, but since the repayment is coming out of clear and already taxed personal profit, I don't expect there'll be many questions."

Obviously, his "dreamed-up" design and new company had proven to be enormously successful if he could repay three million dollars from his personal bank account. "Simple for you, but I know enough about finance to be fairly certain that if I can't prove that loan was made to you out of already taxed earnings, I'm going to have problems. Somehow, I doubt that's the way Dad planned it."

"So do I," Adam agreed with a slight frown. "Which means he must have left some record somewhere, if only a notation about making a personal loan and where the funds came from. Have you gone through all his personal papers?"

"Not all of them, not yet."

"There you go. Until you do and nothing turns up, let's not borrow trouble."

Rachel managed a smile, even though too many questions remained unanswered. "I guess you're right. Besides, an hour ago this money didn't even exist for me. Anything realized from it is more than I expected."

"That sounds like a sensible way of looking at it." Adam got to his feet. "And now, since I've taken up enough of your time, I'll be going."

Rachel got to her feet as well, and hoped her voice didn't sound as anxious to him as it did to her when she asked "Back to California?"

"No, not yet. I plan to stay in Richmond another week or two. I'll be at the Sheraton if you . . . need to get in touch." He took a step toward her and held out his hand.

Rachel hesitated only an instant before giving him her hand, and as braced for it as she was, the touch of him was still a little shocking. *He isn't Thomas. He isn't.* But that certainty didn't have the power to change what she felt. She gazed up into his eyes and felt stirrings of sensations she hadn't experienced in a long, long time.

This is wrong. I don't know him. I know only what he looks like.

"I realize I'm a stranger to you," he said abruptly, still holding her hand, "but—I'd like to see you again, Rachel. May I call you, say in a day or two? We could have dinner, see a movie. Something casual."

He isn't Thomas.

"I'd like that." She hadn't planned to say it until the words came out, but once they did, she didn't regret them.

"Good." He smiled at her and squeezed her hand gently, then released it. "I'll see myself out. It was very nice meeting you, Rachel—at last."

"And it was nice finding out you weren't a ghost or a figment of my imagination," she told him, keeping it light.

He had a nice laugh.

When she was alone in the study, Rachel sat in the chair and stared across the room at nothing, thoughts and emotions swirling within her and her hand still tingling from the touch of his.

"My God," she murmured.

"Three million dollars?"

Rachel nodded, gazing across his desk at Graham's surprised expression. "That's what the man said."

"Duncan lent this man three million dollars on a handshake?"

"Uh-huh."

"I don't believe it."

"Startled me too," she murmured.

"No, I mean I flat-out don't believe it. Rachel, that's not the way Duncan did business. It'd be insane to risk that kind of money with absolutely no written promise of repayment. What if this man—Delafield, you said his name was?"

"Adam Delafield."

Graham made a note on the legal pad on his blotter. "What if he denied getting the money? Or simply decided not to repay it? Duncan would have had no recourse, no legal means of demanding the debt be repaid."

Calmly, Rachel said, "Obviously, Dad thought he could trust this man. And the proof of his good judgment came to see me yesterday. If he hadn't, I never would have known about the loan—not unless something turns up in Dad's private papers, anyway. All he had to do was sit on the money and keep silent. But he came to tell me the debt will be repaid in the next six months or so."

Graham shook his head. "There's something fishy about it."

"Well, if you can figure out some way a con artist

would benefit by promising to pay me three million dollars, let me know. I couldn't think of a damned thing."

"Did he ask you for anything? Anything at all?"

I'd like to see you again, Rachel.

She shook her head. "No."

Graham drummed his fingers on the legal pad. "And you say you saw him watching you before he came to the house? That he was the man you mistook on that street corner for Thomas? And that you saw him just before your car's brakes went out?"

"I told you why. He wasn't sure how to approach me, especially since he looks so much like Thomas." Despite her own uneasiness, Rachel smiled. "Graham, you're so suspicious. Why can't Adam Delafield just be an honest man trying to repay a loan? Why does there have to be more to it?"

Graham reached to open the top drawer of his desk and drew out a sheaf of papers. "I got this just a couple of hours ago. Since you'd already called to say you were dropping by, I decided to wait until you got here to discuss it."

"Discuss what?"

"This is the mechanic's report on the Mercedes. The brake line didn't fail, Rachel. It was cut."

She didn't even blink for a moment, but then drew a deep breath. "Cut. You mean—deliberately?"

"That's what it looks like. The mechanic says it would be difficult to prove in court, that it's *possible* the line could have been cut accidentally, but he knows his job and he believes it was no accident."

"You're saying someone wanted to—to hurt me? To cause an accident?"

"I'm saying we should both cultivate a little healthy

distrust, especially where strangers are concerned." Graham's voice was deliberate.

Rachel leaned back in her chair and stared at him. "You think it was Adam?"

"I think it's a damned suspicious coincidence that he turns up mysteriously in your life with a convenient resemblance to your dead fiancé, and a few days later your car smashes into a tree."

She felt a chill, but even so had to object. "What would he have to gain? Graham, he *told* me about the money he owes Dad. Why would he have done that if he wanted to renege on the debt?"

"Rachel, you have only this man's word for it that a debt exists."

"But why would he—"

"Think about it. What better way to ingratiate himself into your life than by claiming that your father helped him when he was down on his luck. That he's so grateful your father's *investment* let him turn his life around. *And* by telling you he's going to pay you three million dollars by the end of the year."

"What could he hope to gain by lying about those things?"

"You're an heiress," Graham reminded her bluntly. "Worth a hell of a lot more than three million dollars."

"So he cut the brake line on my car? That is what you're implying?"

"What I'm *saying* is that his story is damned suspicious, especially following what looks very much like a manufactured accident. Rachel, given where the accident happened—had to happen—the chances were good you wouldn't be driving very fast. It wasn't likely to be a serious crash. He could have planned it that way."

"But why?"

"As a distraction, a diversion of your attention. Or mine."

After a moment, Rachel shook her head. "That's too Machiavellian for me, Graham. A possibility only a lawyer could consider."

He didn't smile. If anything, Graham's grimness increased as he slowly realized something. The crash might have put "things" into perspective for Rachel, but something else had happened since then. She was . . . waking up. Coming out of the deep freeze where Thomas's death had left her. Her features were more animated than he could remember seeing them, her smile quicker, and even her voice held more life.

It was a subtle change—but it was a definite change. A hint of more changes to come. And there was only one reason for it that he could think of.

Adam Delafield.

If Graham had been a man given to shouting and throwing things, he would have done so then. All his patience. All his undemanding, understanding friendship, his help and concern for Rachel all these months, and none of it had so much as chipped her frozen serenity. Then came Adam Delafield, looking, apparently, like Thomas Sheridan's twin—and Rachel was thawing.

Keeping his voice level, Graham said, "There have been more involved plans to gain a fortune, Rachel. Plenty of them."

She stared at him for a moment, then shook her head. "No, I don't believe that he's—what? Trying to sweep me off my feet? Marry me before I discover he's a con artist?"

"It's been done before."

Rachel couldn't help but laugh. "That's absurd! Graham, I'm not an idiot. Nor am I so trusting that I'd give anyone power over me unless I was absolutely certain that power wouldn't be misused."

"How's he supposed to know that? Until he gets to know you, I mean."

"And I thought *my* imagination was working overtime when I was so sure I'd seen Thomas." She shook her head again, this time bemusedly. "Yours is really overactive, you know that?"

Graham's mouth firmed stubbornly. "Maybe so, but humor me. I'm going to have him checked out, Rachel. His background. Find out if there's really a company out in California."

Her first impulse was to tell him not to, but Rachel knew it would be the sensible thing to do. And since she had just claimed she wasn't foolish, she could hardly object to a sensible and responsible precaution. *Because he's not Thomas, after all.*

"Fine," she said. "And you might want to check first with Nicholas, since they're old friends."

If Graham had expected an argument, it didn't show; he merely nodded. "I'll get right on it. But in the meantime, do me a favor? Park your car in secure places and stay away from Adam Delafield?"

"I'll be careful," Rachel promised. Which was not, of course, quite what Graham had asked for, but he didn't realize that until she was gone.

Swearing softly, he reached for his phone.

It was almost midnight on Tuesday night when Mercy's pillow moved under her, and she murmured a sleepy complaint.

"Sorry, love, but I can't stay tonight." Nicholas eased away from her and slid from the bed.

"Why not?" She winced when he turned on the lamp on her nightstand, then rolled on her side and blinked owlishly.

"Just some things I need to take care of at my place."

"At this hour?" Mercy raised her head and propped it on one hand, watching as he got dressed. She enjoyed watching him dress. Or undress, for that matter. He had an incredible body, so powerfully muscled there was almost no give to his flesh at all. At the same time, he didn't look like those weight lifters with their exaggerated physiques. He was strong in ways they couldn't begin to match, and his muscles were not for show, but for use. Hard use.

Or so Mercy guessed. She guessed he had needed to be strong more than once in his past, probably for his very survival. The several long scars marking his back, chest, and rib cage told that story.

When she had asked, he had said only that he'd been in "a fight or two" in his past, offering no further details. Wary of asking for more than he wanted to give, she had not brought up the subject again. But his silence only encouraged the sometimes incredible tales she made up to account for his various marks and traits and abilities. It was not an unpleasant occupation.

But wearing a bit thin after five years of knowing him and a year of physical intimacy.

Replying to her plaintive question, Nicholas said, "I'm a night owl, you know that. I work best this time of night." He sat on the edge of the bed and began to put on his socks and shoes.

"You could have warned me earlier. I put out a steak to thaw."

Mercy did not cook for Nicholas since he was perfectly able to cook for himself; in fact, he tended to fix breakfast for them both whenever he stayed over at her apartment or she stayed over at his. And, being a very large man with a correspondingly large appetite, he favored substantial breakfasts such as steak and eggs.

"Mmm. Leave it in the refrigerator and we can have it next time. Okay?"

"Sure." It was, strictly speaking, his steak, anyway—bought and paid for. At least once a week he arrived bearing a bag of groceries, always replacing what he had eaten at Mercy's place, and she had never objected. It was just one more way he had of keeping their relationship on a carefully balanced footing, with neither of them beholden to the other.

Dressed now except for the jacket he had left in her living room, he half turned to look down at her consideringly. "Or . . . I could come back in a couple of hours."

Mercy didn't know quite what she was supposed to say to that; it wasn't a suggestion he had ever made before. So she shrugged and murmured, "Suit yourself. You have a key."

He looked at her a moment longer, his ugly face unreadable, then nodded and got to his feet. "Go back to sleep, Mercy." He turned off the lamp, plunging the room into darkness.

Like a cat, he could see easily in the dark.

Mercy lay back on her pillow, listening to the very faint sounds of him leaving the bedroom and then, moments later, the apartment. She didn't go back to sleep for a long time.

In its heyday, it had been known as The Tavern, a nice restaurant and bar that had served good food and good booze to most of the upper class of Richmond. Its Old

English-style sign hanging out front had been a landmark, and it had been the place to be on Saturday nights.

That was then.

Neither the neighborhood nor The Tavern had aged gracefully. Most of the surrounding stores were either vacant or else provided shelter for Richmond's population of homeless and aimless. The rest had thick steel doors and iron bars on the windows, and inside went on the quiet, desperate kinds of business that destroyed lives and souls.

The police seldom bothered to patrol the area, and the denizens had learned to take care of trouble on their own.

As for The Tavern itself, the sign out front had long ago vanished, and nobody had bothered to replace it. The interior had been trashed so many times that the current owner had finally stripped the floors down to the stained concrete and the furnishings to little more than scarred pool tables.

The place was incredibly dark and smoky, to say nothing of being three deep at the bar with most of the worst citizens of Richmond, but no one gave Nicholas any trouble. In fact, men gave way for him instantly and without a murmur of complaint or abuse, even the drunkest ones.

He found Adam Delafield in the back corner, occupying one of only three booths not torn out long ago to provide more room for the pool tables and the clientele—a standing man taking up less space and much less furniture than a sitting man.

"Nice place." Nicholas slid into the booth across from Adam, automatically shifting the unsteady table a bit more toward Adam to make room for himself.

Adam rescued two wobbling glasses as the table rocked, then handed one across to Nicholas. "Have a beer. You sound disgruntled."

"I am disgruntled. You dragged me out of a warm bed."

"The beer's not bad. Honest."

Nicholas sipped, then grimaced slightly. "Okay, it's not bad. But that was a very warm and comfortable bed I had to leave, Adam. Couldn't this have waited until morning?"

"You tell me. Did you get the call?"

"From Graham Becket? Yeah. Asked me if you were on the level with Rachel. If Duncan really had loaned you three million dollars."

"And you told him?"

"That you were, and Duncan had. Wasn't that what I was supposed to say?"

"I hope you managed to sound a bit more convincing, Nick."

Nicholas smiled. "Naturally. Fair warning though—Becket's a suspicious bastard at the best of times, and where Rachel's concerned, he's even more so."

Adam frowned. "Is he that protective of her?"

"He's that in love with her."

"You're sure about that?"

Nicholas shrugged. "As sure as one man can be of another man's feelings. He'd just love to slay dragons for her. Protecting her and her money from an ex-con with a fishy story would suit him right down to the ground."

Adam scowled. "Great."

"I did try to warn you this wouldn't be easy."

"I know. But I'm an optimist." Adam took a drink of his beer, still frowning.

"You'd also better know that Becket will turn up the conviction and jail time in pretty short order. I don't like the son of a bitch, but he's efficient as hell and definitely motivated. So you'd better start planning to look at Rachel with big, sad eyes while you tell her your long, sad story."

Adam grunted.

Nicholas looked at him with cynical amusement. "Pretty long limb you're crawling out on."

"It's no place I haven't been before."

"True." Nicholas studied him across the table. "And this time you've dressed for the part. That's a new look for you, isn't it?"

Adam shrugged.

Refusing to be warned off, Nicholas went on coolly. "Longer hair, more casual clothing. I seem to recall that was Thomas Sheridan's style."

"You don't say."

"You're taking a big chance, Adam."

Once again Adam shrugged, but a frown drew his brows low. "Maybe. But I don't have much choice, do I? She wouldn't have let me in the door otherwise."

"Which door are we talking about?" Nick asked gently.

Adam ignored that question. Instead, he fixed his attention on using his sweating glass to connect water rings on the scarred table, and changed the subject. "How much time do you figure I've got?"

"Before Becket rides to the rescue? A few days, maybe a week. He'll start with the dope on the company, I imagine, and think about a possible criminal record afterward."

"Shit. That isn't much time."

"No. But all you've got, so make it count."

Adam gave him a look. "Cheap advice."

"If you want the more expensive kind, you have to pay for it." Nicholas smiled.

"Yeah, yeah." Adam leaned back and continued to stare across the table at his companion. "What about you,

Nick? Just what do you mean to do if Rachel decides not to sell out?"

Wide shoulders lifted and fell in a shrug as Nicholas said indifferently, "I'll land on my feet. I always do."

The conversation broke off for a few moments as a noisy fight erupted at the center pool table and threatened to spill over into the entire room. Adam and Nicholas watched with wary interest, returning their attention to each other only when the tattooed bouncer tossed both combatants out into the street.

"You don't have much time either," Adam noted.

"No, damned little."

"Want me to encourage Rachel to sell to you?"

Nicholas laughed. "Do you plan on having so much influence over her decisions?"

"You never know."

"Take some more cheap advice. Do what you came here to do and don't fuck around along the way."

"I have to get close to her."

"You don't have to crawl into bed with her."

Adam shrugged. "There was a spark. Damned hard to ignore it."

"Do your best," Nicholas advised. "Unless you really do like being a stand-in for another man, and a dead one at that."

Adam smiled a bit wryly. "There is that. She must have been crazy about him. The way she looked at me when she thought I might be him . . ."

"She was, so they say. Never the same after he was killed." Nicholas took a sip of his beer and added almost absently, "Some people love only once, it's the way they're made."

Adam didn't reply, and after another moment of silence Nicholas pushed his barely touched glass away and slid from the booth. Pleasantly, he said, "Don't drag me out of my warm bed again, Adam. I get cranky when I lose sleep."

Just as pleasantly, Adam said, "I'll remember that. Next time."

Nicholas strode toward the door, the sea of mostly drunken men parting for him the way the Red Sea must have parted for Moses. Adam was amused by the comparison, for a less holy man than Nicholas would have been hard to imagine.

Not that he himself could afford to cast stones.

Amusement fading, Adam went back to using the base of his dewed glass to connect water rings. That occupied him for some minutes, and then he sighed and stopped. He wiped his damp fingers on his thigh and reached into the slightly open neckline of his white shirt, pulling out a small gold locket on a fine chain.

In the center of the elaborate designs on one side of the locket were the initials *RG,* and on the other side the initials *TS.*

Adam used a thumbnail to open the locket. Inside on the left was a silver St. Christopher medal, sized perfectly to fit as a photo would have. On the right side was a photo, protected by a tiny clear shield. A girl smiled radiantly. She was so hauntingly lovely that Adam's breath caught even though he had seen the picture countless times before.

It was Rachel.

The tip of his thumb gently brushed across the picture, and then he closed the locket and dropped it back inside his shirt. On a long, rough sigh, he muttered, "Goddammit."

• • •

Nicholas stood outside the bar for several minutes, his breath misting in the chilly night air. He gazed off in the direction of Mercy's apartment, even took a step that way. But then he halted, swore, and reversed direction.

He called himself a damned fool all the way to his car.

FIVE

hat?" Cameron Grant stared at his niece across the dining table. "You're going to keep the house? But I thought you were planning to go back to New York."

"I was. I changed my mind."

Rachel was still surprised at herself for the decision she had made sometime in the previous twenty-four hours. She couldn't even say what had finally tipped the balance. All she knew was that the decision had been made, and that it felt right.

It was Wednesday evening, and Rachel had spent the day helping Darby with the furniture inventories.

Obviously trying not to sound as unhappy as he was, Cameron said, "So you'll be keeping the breakfront and the Queen Anne chairs?"

Rachel smiled at him. "No, I promised them to you. They're yours. As for the rest, I'm going to let Darby continue to inventory the entire house, room by room. It needs to be done, and since she's started, she should finish."

"What about the pieces you don't plan to use, Rachel? Are you going to let her sell them to strangers?"

"All the extra stuff has been collecting dust for decades, giving no pleasure to anyone." Rachel's tone was reasonable. "There's no good reason to keep what I won't be using."

"But, Rachel—"

"Don't worry, Cam. If there are other pieces you can't bear to see sold, we'll work something out. But how much room do you have in that house of yours?" Cam had been staying here since shortly before his older brother had been killed, but home was a lovely old town house in San Francisco, currently being renovated. Since he was a moderately successful artist, he could live anywhere he chose, and the West Coast had been his home for more than twenty years.

"There's enough room for a few more big pieces. But whether I can display things or have to put them into storage for the time being isn't the point. I just can't bear to see Grant family things going to strangers, Rachel, that's all. One of us should keep them."

A little weary of the argument, she said, "Hanging on to history isn't always the best thing to do."

He hesitated, then smiled and lifted his wineglass in a small salute to her. "So, you've decided to stay in Richmond. And—what? Take Duncan's place at the bank?"

"I haven't decided whether to keep my interests in the bank, but I certainly won't be working there. I don't have Dad's gift."

"You have your own. Some kind of fashion design, then?"

She told him briefly about Graham's suggestion that

she open a boutique selling her own designs. "The idea appeals to me. I think I'll give it a shot."

"That designer you work for is not going to like losing you."

"He won't be too upset. He liked my work, but there was some friction between us."

The friction had consisted of Brian Todd's unshakable belief that he was God's gift to women of all ages, but Rachel didn't feel any impulse to confide this to her uncle.

"Your dad always said you'd come back here," Cameron said.

Rachel was surprised. "He did? Was he—were he and Mom upset that I stayed in New York all those years?" Even though Graham had reassured her, it was something about which Rachel still felt profoundly upset.

Before Cameron could answer, Fiona came into the dining room with dessert and said sourly, "They missed you. Of course they were upset."

"You were listening at the door," Cameron accused.

The housekeeper snorted. "How else am I supposed to find out what goes on around here?"

Cameron had made several attempts to charm Fiona in the months he'd been living there, but she had resisted his blandishments. Since then, the two had observed a wary, occasionally bristly, understanding.

They didn't like each other.

Rachel said, "Don't you two get started. Fiona, I know Mom and Dad missed me. But they understood why I stayed away. Didn't they?" *Tell me they understood.*

The housekeeper's face softened almost imperceptibly. "Of course. And he's right—about this, anyway. They knew you'd come back here to stay sooner or later."

Almost to herself, Rachel murmured, "I thought there'd be time enough. That I'd come back one day, and everything would be the way it was before I left. But . . . the months turned into years. And time ran out."

"They understood, Miss Rachel. Both of them. Your mother especially, I think."

It was a reassurance Rachel needed, and even if she still didn't quite believe it, the housekeeper's words gave her the first really good night's sleep she'd had since coming back home.

On Thursday morning, while Darby continued with the inventory, Rachel excused herself to drive into town. A visit to a real estate agency resulted in a list of several properties she wanted to have a look at, and though the agent had wanted to accompany her, Rachel preferred to be alone in the initial stages of choosing a location for her boutique.

It occurred to her only during the drive that "her boutique" had taken on the solidity of reality in her mind, so much so that she had a very clear idea of just what she wanted to do.

Like the decision to keep the house, the decision to open a boutique, once made, also felt very right. Whether the venture was a success or a failure, Rachel was looking forward to it—and it was exhilarating to find herself looking ahead rather than back.

She had spent too many years looking back.

The first address the agent had provided turned out to be totally unsuitable for what Rachel had in mind. The second one, however, had definite possibilities. It was a fairly small vacant store in a block-long area that already contained several small specialty stores, and foot traffic was brisk even on this weekday morning.

Standing on the sidewalk as she considered the store, Rachel didn't notice a quiet black sedan pull up to the curb behind her, so it surprised her very much to hear Nicholas Ross's harsh voice.

"Good morning, Rachel."

She jumped, but only a little. The sheer size of him was overpowering as he reached her side and loomed over her, but she managed not to back away. "Hi, Nick."

He had always made her feel wary. She hoped it didn't show.

He nodded toward the For Lease sign in the dirty window. "Is that what interests you so much?"

Rachel hesitated, then nodded. "I'm thinking about opening a boutique here in Richmond. One-of-a-kind fashion designs."

Nicholas frowned slightly. "I see. Then I take it you won't be returning to New York."

"No, not for good. I'll have to go back there eventually, of course, and pack up my apartment."

"What about the bank?"

She shook her head. "I haven't decided about that yet. It's why I haven't come to talk to you. But you can be sure I won't be trying to tell you how to run things, Nick, no matter what I decide to do. For all intents and purposes, it's your bank now."

His frown remained, and those pale eyes were unreadable as they gazed at the empty store before them. In an abrupt tone he said, "If you decide to keep your interest, you couldn't go wrong asking Mercy to manage for you."

Rachel was a little surprised. "I hadn't thought about it. I guess I assumed she'd be working for you now that Dad's gone."

"No." He looked down at her. "I've asked, but . . . Mercy knows I've never wanted an assistant. She's an asset to the bank, though, and I'd hate to lose her. She has a rare understanding of finances. If you're looking for someone to manage all your business interests, I'd put her at the top of a very short list."

Curious, Rachel said, "Where would you put Graham?" She was aware the two men didn't care for each other, but wasn't sure of the cause. Distinctly different personalities, maybe?

"Graham Becket is a fine lawyer."

She waited a moment, then said dryly, "And that says it all?"

Nicholas smiled, and it was not a charming thing. "I think so. I'd trust him with my legal affairs, but I'd want someone else giving me financial advice. It's not his specialty."

"I see. Well, thanks for the suggestion about Mercy. I'll keep it in mind."

"Do that. Can I give you a lift somewhere?"

"No, thanks. I have a leased car I'm trying out." She didn't see any reason to confide in him about the possibly sabotaged brake line. "It's over there. So thanks anyway."

"Off to look at another store, or has this one caught your fancy?"

"This one's a little small, but possible. I've just started looking, though, so no decision is imminent."

"Glad to hear it." He glanced around them. "You wouldn't know to look at it, but this neighborhood isn't the best. A higher crime rate than some of the worst parts of town."

Rachel didn't bother to tell him that she would have researched the crime rate as well as other important elements before making a decision. She merely said, "Well, maybe the third place will be the charm."

"Where is it?"

"On Queen Street. The Realtor was enthusiastic."

"I imagine so. It's pricey real estate. But a good location." He took a step back and turned toward his car. "Let me know if I can do anything to help, Rachel. I'd be happy to."

"Thanks, Nick."

She watched as he got into his car with a grace uncommon in such a big, powerful man, and moments later the black sedan had purred its way out of sight.

She was still wary of Nick.

And she had a feeling it had definitely shown.

Shrugging off a lingering unease, Rachel used the key the agency had provided to go into the store, and spent another ten minutes or so checking it out.

Naturally, her thoroughness had nothing to do with Nick's dismissal of the spot as a good prospect.

But she reached the same conclusion for different reasons, however reluctantly. The layout of the interior was wrong, would require considerable remodeling, and that was not something Rachel wanted to waste time with if at all possible.

So she got back into her car and drove to the next spot, on Queen Street. Nick had been right about this area as well; it was high-ticket real estate boasting some of the most exclusive stores in Richmond.

An area no more than two blocks long, it was designed with foot traffic in mind, with wide sidewalks and handy benches placed near the decorative and functional lampposts. Parking was handy without being intrusive, and a nearby police station was undoubtedly a deterrent to crime.

Rachel was impressed by the store she had come to see. It was slightly larger than she had planned, but temporary walls could take care of that until—hopefully—the need for expansion arose. Other than that she could see no structural problems. There was even a huge office space and storage area in the back, both of which would come in handy.

She was standing in the center of the front part of the store, jotting down a few ideas for colors and a decorating style, when a voice from the open door caught her by surprise.

"Rachel?"

Adam Delafield.

"Hello. What are you doing here?" After the first moment of surprise, her heart rate had returned to normal. Or almost.

"I was going to ask you the same thing." He came in and crossed the space between them. "I was in a store across the street, and thought I saw you come in here."

"I'm . . . thinking of starting a business. Fashions designed by me."

"So you're not going back to New York?"

Rachel realized it was a question she was going to hear a lot. "No. I don't think so. I belong in Richmond."

"Ghosts and all?"

Whether it was the cryptic note in his voice or simply the reminder, Rachel found the question a difficult one to answer casually, and confiding in this virtual stranger was impossible. So she tried to keep it light. "I don't believe in ghosts."

"Don't you?"

"Of course not."

"You thought I was Thomas Sheridan." There was something almost insolent in his voice.

"Yes, I did," she admitted. "Thomas—alive and well. Not his spirit haunting me. I never believed that."

Not for a moment. Right.

"In any case," she added, making her tone brisk, "it's a bright, sunny spring day, and there are certainly no ghosts lurking here." She turned away from him and gestured to the space around them. "What do you think? A classy store selling unique designs? The label of Rachel Grant, a Richmond exclusive."

"I think you'll be a hit. A major hit."

She looked at him, relieved that his voice was casual again but bothered by the intent way he looked at her. It made her feel self-conscious. No, more than that. It made her feel that no one else had ever really looked at her before. And that was disconcerting.

It was also a little scary.

She made a production of putting her notebook away in her shoulder bag. "Well, we'll see. Who knows? Maybe I inherited a little of Dad's business savvy."

"I wouldn't doubt it a bit." He followed her from the store and stood just behind her as she locked up.

"I have two other places to check out," she said as she turned to face him, "so—"

"Why don't you let me buy you lunch? It's after noon, and there's a really good restaurant just down the block. Do you like Italian?"

"Yes, but—I really should take a look at the other stores."

"You can do that just as well after lunch. And you have to eat."

When Rachel hesitated just a moment too long, Adam nodded slightly and a wry expression crossed his face.

"Would it help if I promise not to ask any more dumb questions about ghosts?"

"Not dumb. Just . . ."

"Just not welcome. Especially from somebody who looks like me." He smiled, but that intensity she had sensed earlier was still in him, lurking just below the surface. "I understand. Have lunch with me, Rachel, please.

I'd like to talk about a man I admired very much—to his daughter."

That was an appeal Rachel could hardly refuse, especially since she wanted to hear more about her father's relationship with this man. And he had a point. She had to eat.

"In that case, thanks. I'd love to have lunch with you."

"The restaurant is close enough to walk to. If you feel like it."

"Sounds great."

Adam offered his arm, and Rachel surprised herself by taking it. She was immediately aware of strength and leashed power, of hard muscles beneath her fingers, and other senses whispered to her of force and will. And darkness. *He isn't what he wants me to believe he is. Who he wants me to believe he is.* That knowledge was so strong that Rachel almost pulled her hand away from him. But along with wariness and uneasiness was curiosity.

Who was he, really? And what did he want from her?

Despite Graham's warning, Rachel didn't believe it was her money Adam was after. She had never thought much about intuition, but hers was alive in her now, and it insisted there was much more to this—to him—than simple greed. She was sure of it.

And he looks like Thomas. That has to mean something. Doesn't it?

Nicholas Ross sat in his long black car and gazed down the block, watching Rachel and Adam stroll along the sidewalk toward him. As far as he could tell, they were pleased to be in each other's company.

Then Rachel looked up at her companion and smiled that slow smile of hers, transforming her face into something radiant. Even at this distance, Nicholas could see Adam's reaction, see his free hand reach to cover the one resting in the crook of his arm in a gesture any other man would recognize as possessive.

"Slow down," Nicholas murmured. But nobody heard him, of course. And even if the right person had, Nicholas doubted his warning would make much of a difference.

He understood obsession.

He watched the couple until they disappeared into an Italian restaurant, the door of which was barely twenty feet from the hood of his car. Rachel hadn't appeared to notice the car, and behind the tinted windows Nicholas knew he was virtually invisible.

Adam hadn't so much as glanced this way.

Once they'd vanished into the restaurant, Nicholas started his car and pulled away from the curb. He reached for his mobile phone and punched in a number. The phone rang a long time before anybody answered.

"Yeah."

"Simon, it's Nick. I have a job for you."

In her bed that night, Rachel thought about the interlude with Adam, but she still wasn't sure what she felt about it. Adam was a charming man, no doubt about that, and all her instincts told her he had sincerely liked and respected her father. Though they hadn't talked much about Duncan Grant, now that Rachel thought about it.

They had, she realized, talked mostly about themselves.

Or had she done most of the talking, with Adam asking questions and offering little except agreement now and then?

He was not an easy man to read. There was that intensity she sensed lurking in him, a kind of force that was very much belied by his casual, almost lazy exterior. He struck her as the kind of man who would make a very good friend and a very bad enemy, and she thought he could—and would—be ruthless if the stakes were high enough.

But what were the stakes now?

He had said no more than that he had been "down on his luck" when Duncan Grant had made him the loan. No one else had believed in the design he had invented. So Rachel had no way of knowing what his life had been like then. But if he had built up a prosperous engineering and design company in less than five years, he had clearly worked hard and made all the right business decisions.

He had to be tough, that was certain; he was obviously smart.

In the course of the conversation, it had emerged that they had similar taste in books and movies, shared a love of horses and cats, preferred baseball to football, were staunch independents, loved to look at the ocean, and were vehemently opposed to AstroTurf and the designated hitter. Both liked to sleep with the windows open unless it was too hot—it was never too cold—enjoyed putting together jigsaw puzzles, and loved the sound of wind chimes.

He seemed to smile more quickly than frown, and his voice could be serious one moment and filled with amusement the next, but his blue eyes gave nothing away, and had once or twice even appeared to be shuttered, deliberately veiled with secretiveness.

Rachel couldn't deny to herself that she was attracted, but she was wary. Very wary. Because he looked so like Thomas. And because she didn't trust her own feelings—about him or anything else just then.

A week ago she had been in limbo, feeling little, refusing even to grieve for her parents. But now, suddenly, she was feeling too much. What little Adam had said about Duncan Grant during lunch had pulled the tears so close to the surface that she'd had difficulty holding them back. Twice during the remainder of the day she had found herself crying unexpectedly, once because she'd found one of her mother's old handkerchiefs in a drawer and once because she could have sworn she had caught the scent of the cologne Thomas had always worn, the kind she had bought him for his birthday when she was fifteen and that had become his signature scent.

But the scent was only another ghostly reminder of fact.

Dead. Thomas was dead. Her parents were dead.

Ghosts and all?

She had lived a long time with ghosts. One in particular. And as simple as it was to tell herself that Thomas was long dead, her heart had never been able to believe that. He had lingered in Richmond for her, his memory filling all the corners. And because she had run away rather than face those corners, his memory was still vivid.

How could she be sure that it wasn't his memory coloring her feelings for Adam? Could she trust her own mind and heart not to latch on to him eagerly because he was the nearest thing to Thomas she had found?

That was a creepy thought.

Rachel turned over in bed and told herself to stop thinking. She told herself that several times.

By the time it finally worked and she fell asleep, it was past the witching hour, and she dreamed vivid dreams in which a man wearing a mask of Thomas's face was Adam, and when he removed the mask of Adam there was another mask underneath that was Thomas again. *"I tried to reach you,"* he said urgently. *"I tried over and over. But you shut me out for so long, for so many years. Don't shut me out now, Rachel, please, it's so important. Listen. You must listen to me. . . ."*

And then somebody was laughing, and someone else was calling her name with Thomas's voice, and in the distance she could hear something else, a rustling sound that made her skin crawl.

Then she smelled something like rotten eggs, and the voice that sounded like Thomas whispered, *"Run, Rachel. Get out. Hurry. Don't trust—"*

She sat straight up in bed as the alarm buzzed insistently on her nightstand, and stared around the room with wide eyes.

Morning sunlight slanted in, brightening the room. A slight breeze lazily moved the curtains. The alarm clock buzzed.

She was awake.

Rachel turned off the alarm and got up, trying to shake off the dream. She didn't believe in signs and portents, and certainly not in the clairvoyance of dreams. What she did believe was that her uncertainty about her feelings for Adam, her confusion about two men who looked so much alike, had followed her into sleep.

That was all.

She showered and dressed, and her morning routine soon pushed the dream into the back of her mind. Breakfast, with Uncle Cam and Fiona sniping at each other. The arrival of Darby and her guys, all briskly determined to get as much accomplished as possible on this Friday.

Rachel left them to it. Though she wasn't quite sure how it had happened, she had somehow, during yesterday's lunch, invited Adam to meet her at the real estate office that morning, where more keys awaited her. There were two more stores she wanted to check out, and he was going to keep her company while she did.

Or something like that.

She didn't even bother to chide herself, especially once she reached the real estate office and saw Adam waiting for her.

He isn't Thomas. That isn't why.

"So where are we going today?" he asked when she emerged from the office with keys.

"Two more stores. One on Evans, and the other on Claiborne. Unless you know the city better than I think you do, I'll drive."

"Fine by me," he said agreeably.

They left his rental car parked there, where it would remain until they returned the keys later, and were quickly on their way to the first of the two addresses. As the day before, Adam was a pleasant companion, casual and humorous, keeping her mind occupied with unimportant things. He told her a funny story about the room service waiter he'd had the night before, and another about a hotel message system that had suddenly gone nuts and notified him every ten minutes for more than an hour that he had a call from someone in Cairo.

"I gather you don't know anybody in Cairo?"

"Not the one in Egypt, no. The hotel finally pulled the plug on their system and sent me champagne as an apology. I decided to save it for later. In case I want to celebrate something."

Rachel let that pass. "Good idea. Let's see . . . I think the first address is just ahead. . . ."

It was, and they didn't have to get out of the car. The store was obviously tiny, and the seedy pawnshop next door argued against the sort of upscale image Rachel had in mind.

"I don't think so," she said.

"No, I'd agree. Onward."

More casual conversation occupied them for another five minutes, until they reached the second address.

"Possible." Rachel stood beside the car and studied the storefront. It was just about the right size, and the neighborhood was a good one. The only drawback she could see was that the store, with parking on one side and a narrow street on the other, seemed isolated.

"Which could be a good thing," Adam suggested when she brought that up. "Make you look even more exclusive."

"Umm. Let's take a look inside."

The key stuck a bit, but finally turned with a faint click, and they went into the store. It was a very plain space, virtually unfinished, with concrete floors and white block walls, and their footsteps echoed hollowly. An interior wall held a single door, which presumably led to either office or storage space in the back.

"Not much personality," Adam noted.

"No, but that could be—" Rachel caught a faint whiff of an odor like rotten eggs, and a chill chased up and down her spine. It was what she had smelled in her dream. "Do you smell something?"

Even before he spoke, Adam was grabbing her hand. "Gas. Let's get out of here. *Move,* Rachel."

He hadn't shouted, and didn't seem to move hastily, yet Adam had her outside the store in seconds.

Seconds later, the whole world seemed to blow up.

SIX

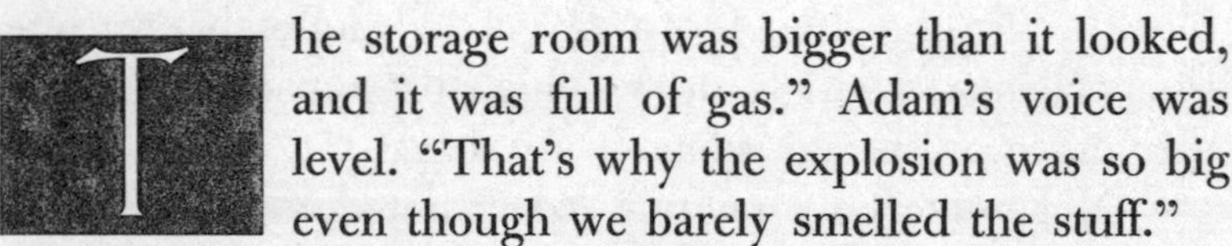

The storage room was bigger than it looked, and it was full of gas." Adam's voice was level. "That's why the explosion was so big even though we barely smelled the stuff."

Rachel winced as the paramedic stuck a small Band-Aid on the cut on her cheek. As hard as she tried, she couldn't quite keep her voice as steady as his. "Will there be enough of the building left for them to figure out what caused the spark?"

Before Adam could reply to that, a plainclothes cop approached them, notebook in hand. "Miss Grant? If you're up to it, I'd like to ask you a few questions now."

He had talked to Adam before, while Rachel was being checked out in the paramedics' van.

"I'm fine," she said, but she was grateful for Adam's quick hand helping her out of the van, and glad he kept an arm around her shoulders. She felt more than a little shaky, and she would undoubtedly be stiff and sore tomorrow from all the bruises, since she and Adam had been thrown to the pavement by the force of the explosion.

Fire department personnel were still milling around, but the explosion had been so ferocious that there had actually been little fire. There was also little left of the store, except for a few yards of the side walls and a very large heap of rubble from the collapsed roof.

"I have Mr. Delafield's statement," Detective James said. "It's pretty clear. Did you see or hear anything unusual, Miss Grant? Before the explosion?"

"No."

"Did you notice anyone lurking around the store, or walking away quickly?"

"No." She frowned, the idea occurring to her for the first time with a sharp chill. "You don't think it was an accident?"

The detective shrugged. "Well, Miss Grant, we've had some arson in this area, and several times the target was a vacant store. That's the most likely answer. We think a valve was opened, and that doesn't happen by accident."

"What about the spark?"

"There are some fairly easy tricks to set up a delayed spark, and most arsonists know them all. We'll find enough evidence to be sure of just how he did it." He shook his head. "Bad luck that you two happened to be looking at the store today."

"Yes." Her voice was hollow. "Very bad luck."

Adam's arm tightened around her.

"I'm going to give you one of my cards," Detective James said, "so you can call me if you think of anything else. You might have seen something you don't remember right now—a person or thing out of place, something like that. Give me a call if you do."

She accepted the card. "I will."

Adam asked, "May we go now?"

"Sure. I have your numbers if I need to get in touch."

Rachel took one last glance at the smoldering ruin, then walked with Adam back to her car, which had narrowly escaped getting a huge dent when a chunk of concrete had fallen near it. She didn't object when Adam took her to the passenger side, and even managed a smile when he spoke.

"This time I'll drive."

He turned the heater on when he got in, and Rachel realized only then that she was shivering.

"I'm all right," she said.

"You're in shock." Adam's tone was quite pleasant, but there was a note underneath that sounded almost savage.

She glanced at him, hearing the latter and wondering at it. "Accidents happen. We were just in the wrong place at the wrong time."

"Yeah—but this was no accident. Some sorry bastard took the idea of playing with matches way too far. A few more seconds . . ."

"We got out," she reminded him. "Whole and pretty much unharmed."

"Yeah." But he was obviously unconvinced of that. He drove only a couple of blocks, pulling over to the curb in front of a coffee shop. "I'll be right back."

"Okay." Rachel watched him get out and shut the door, then turned her gaze forward and her attention to the worried questions in her mind.

Obviously, the explosion had been no accident. But there was no reason for her to assume she had been the target. People committed arson with depressing frequency, and that cop had even said it had happened several times in the area recently.

So it *was* just bad luck that she had stopped by that day to look at the store.

Nothing more than that.

Besides, how could she have been a target? No one had known where she would be today except the Realtor, and since that very nice lady had pulled the addresses out of her file only that morning, there had hardly been time for lethal plans—even if she had been so inclined.

Which was, of course, ridiculous.

Still, Rachel was uneasy. The cut brake line loomed much larger now with this second "accident" following so soon after it.

She didn't know what to think. Or what to believe. All she really knew was that she was very glad Adam had been with her. She doubted she would have reacted so quickly to the gas if she'd been alone. And though it had all happened too fast for her to be sure, she had the hazy idea that he had shielded her as they'd fallen, his thick leather jacket withstanding some flying debris that would have easily torn through her linen blazer.

He had probably saved her life.

And since he had been with her every minute from the time she'd gotten the addresses, he had certainly not been the one to rig the explosion.

The relief of that was overwhelming.

Adam returned to the car just then and handed her a steaming cup. "Tea. Hot and sweet. Drink it, Rachel."

"Good thing I like tea," she murmured, sipping.

He smiled suddenly. "Am I being high-handed? Sorry. I'm not usually a bully, I promise you. Just worried at the moment."

"I'm fine. Really." She did her best to sound convincing despite her awareness that only her death grip on the cup was keeping her hands from shaking visibly.

He looked at her steadily for a moment, then nodded and put the car in gear. "Okay. But I don't want you driving today, so I'll take you home."

"Your car—"

"I'll call a cab to take me back to the real estate office, and I'll turn the keys in. It's no problem, Rachel."

She decided not to argue with him. For one thing, she was pretty sure he'd made up his mind. For another, it was pleasant to let herself drift while someone else made the decisions for a while.

She drank her tea.

They were almost at her house, when Adam spoke abruptly. "I get the feeling something's worrying you about that explosion. Am I wrong?"

Rachel hesitated, but reminded herself that he couldn't possibly have had anything to do with the explosion. "That car accident I had last week. The mechanic thinks the brake line was cut."

Adam shot her a quick, hard look. "Are you saying somebody's trying to hurt you?"

"I don't know. Hurt me, scare me. Maybe. I just can't think of a reason why anybody would want to do either."

"Scare you? You could have been killed today, Rachel."

She flinched a little, and stared at her half-finished tea. "You heard that cop. There's been arson in the area. Besides, nobody could have known I'd be there just then. Nobody."

"That makes sense," he said slowly. "Not even the Realtor could have known for sure which store we'd check out first. It took some time for the gas to build up, time to set up some gadget to cause a spark. We were inside no more than a couple of minutes before we smelled the gas."

"So—it couldn't have had anything to do with me."

"I don't believe in coincidence," he said.

"In this case, you'll have to. It can't be anything else." She was arguing with herself as well as him.

"Maybe. Just promise me you'll be careful from now on, Rachel. Very careful."

"You bet," she said lightly, and watched the tea slosh around inside her cup.

"I'd like to know why the hell I had to hear about this from the police, Rachel." Graham was definitely upset, and didn't try to hide it.

Rachel sat on the edge of her bed with a sigh. She'd just been about to go soak in a hot tub in a hopeful attempt to ward off soreness tomorrow, having finally escaped the anxious attention of Fiona and Cam. Adam had remained just long enough for his cab to arrive.

"I'm sorry, Graham. I would have called as soon as I had a chance to catch my breath. But why did the police call you?"

"They always call me whenever anything happens involving the Grant family. Are you all right?"

"I'm fine." She was getting tired of saying it, especially since it wasn't true. "Although, if it hadn't been for Adam, I wouldn't be."

"So he was Johnny on the spot again."

"He probably saved my life, Graham. I wouldn't have moved fast enough to get out of there, not without him."

"I don't trust him, Rachel. And I sure as hell don't like this explosion coming barely a week after your car's brake lines were cut."

"It was just a bizarre accident. No one could have known I'd be at that particular store at that particular moment." She kept repeating that fact like a mantra.

"Delafield was always with you? He didn't excuse himself for a few minutes at any point?"

"No."

Graham was silent for a moment, then repeated, "I don't trust him."

"You checked him out, didn't you? Like you said you would?" She rubbed her forehead slowly and thought longingly of a bath and peace.

Again, Graham hesitated. "I did. The company exists. Delafield Design. It was founded about five years ago. It *appears* to be successful."

"Then he told me the truth."

"Maybe. Or maybe he just told you some of the truth. His background information is too damned sketchy for my taste. I'm going to keep digging."

Rachel sighed. "Fine. You do that. In the meantime, I'm going to go soak a few bruises away. Good-bye, Graham." She hung up without waiting for a response.

She was accustomed to Graham's caution, knew it came from affection and concern, and sincerely valued his opinions—but this time he was taking things too far. She could trust Adam.

He'd saved her life, hadn't he?

Mercy hung up the phone and gazed across the kitchen at Nicholas, who was clearing up the remains of the Chinese takeout they'd had for dinner. "You heard?"

"Your half of the conversation, yeah. So Rachel's all right?"

"I think so. What do you know about this Adam Delafield she says probably saved her life?"

Nicholas dumped several empty cartons in the trash

and turned to look at her. "We knew each other a long time ago."

"That's what Rachel said. That you two were old friends." She left it there, but watched him steadily from her stool at the breakfast bar.

Nicholas came to the bar and poured fresh wine for both of them. "It isn't a long story, love. About ten years ago Adam worked for a design firm I did some business with."

"Had you known him before that?"

Nicholas shrugged massive shoulders. "As a matter of fact, I had. We first met about fifteen years ago. He was in college. We had some mutual interests, and a mutual friend introduced us."

Mercy smiled wryly. "You'd think I'd learn."

"Learn what?"

"Not to ask questions about your past."

His brows rose in surprise, carving deep furrows in his forehead. "There's just nothing to say that would interest you, love."

"I have my doubts about that, but never mind. What do you think about this explosion?"

"That they're damned lucky they got out in time."

"Don't you think there's something strange going on? I mean, a week ago Rachel practically wraps her car around a tree, and today she's nearly blown to smithereens. She went twenty-nine years without so much as a sprained ankle—and now this? Am I the only one who thinks this is something more than just a bad week?"

Nicholas sipped his wine for a moment, studying her with one of his more enigmatic gazes. "What are you suggesting?"

"I don't know." Mercy shrugged helplessly. "I can't imagine anyone wanting to hurt Rachel, can you?"

"No."

"Nick, something's going on."

"Two violent accidents in one week is a bizarre coincidence, I admit. But how could it be more than that?"

Mercy hesitated, then said, "Rachel wrecked her car because the brake lines had been cut. Deliberately."

"How do you know that?" Nicholas was intent, but not frowning.

"Rachel told me. Graham's gone all suspicious of your pal Adam, but so far he isn't convincing Rachel, especially after today. But somebody cut that brake line. Somebody wanted to hurt Rachel. Or scare her."

"Scare her? What would be the point?"

"To make her go back to New York, maybe. How should I know?"

Nicholas shook his head. "The explosion might have been arson, but it doesn't appear to have been aimed at anyone in particular. Rachel and Adam were just in the wrong place at the wrong time. As for the cut brake lines—even the best mechanic can make a mistake, and brake lines have been known to fail without helping hands. There's no solid evidence either occurrence was anything more than an accident, love."

Mercy knew when she'd lost an argument, especially with this man. She sighed. "Okay, okay. But I'm worried."

"You told Rachel to be careful. What else can you do?"

"Worry." She smiled.

He came around the bar and lifted her easily off the stool. "I can think of a few better things to occupy your attention."

As always, she felt engulfed in his embrace, blissfully wrapped in warmth and strength. "I'm certainly open to suggestion," she murmured, tilting her head back to smile up at him.

"Good." He lifted her completely off her feet with an ease that never failed to astonish her, and carried her through the sparsely furnished apartment toward his bedroom.

Mercy spared a passing moment to consider the bland color scheme and minimalist decor, and sighed. "You've got to get more furniture."

"Why?"

He had a point. He never entertained here that she knew of, and there were enough chairs—and a big enough bed—for two, so what did it matter?

"Never mind," she said. "The next time I'm out shopping I'll find you a plant or two, and maybe a rug. . . ."

When the phone on his nightstand rang a couple of hours later, Nicholas reached over so quickly that he got the receiver in hand before the first ring finished. "Yeah?"

Half asleep, Mercy heard only his side of the brief conversation, but it was enough to bring her fully awake.

"You fucked up," Nicholas said. His voice was low. It was also unpleasant. He listened for a moment, then added, "I'll call you tomorrow." And replaced the receiver in its cradle.

"Trouble?" She made sure her voice was drowsy.

"Nothing I can't handle. Tomorrow." Nicholas shifted slightly and put a hand under her chin to tilt her face up. "Are you going to sleep all evening?"

"I was just resting my eyes," she explained.

"Are they rested?"

"I think so."

He kissed her, taking his time about it. One big hand

was wrapped gently around her throat, while the other one pushed the covers down and began a leisurely wandering.

Mercy tried her best not to purr out loud.

"How would you like to spend the whole weekend in here with me?" he murmured, his mouth replacing his hand on her throat.

She heard an odd sound, and thought it was probably her, purring. She cleared her throat. "What? The whole weekend? In bed?"

"Why not?" His mouth moved lower.

Mercy clutched a handful of sheet at her hip. "Um . . . it sounds . . . very hedonistic." The words were followed by another of those throaty murmurs, and she felt a vague embarrassment. Damn the man, did he *have* to reduce her to incoherent sounds?

His laugh against her skin was a caressing rumble. "I like that word. Shall we be hedonists?"

She let go of the sheet and clutched at him. "Nick, for God's sake—stop *talking.*"

With another laugh, he did.

Rachel was in her father's study on Saturday morning, when a still-unnerved Fiona announced Adam and quickly retreated, crossing herself once again.

"Hello," Rachel said. "I didn't expect to see you today."

"I don't want to make a nuisance of myself," he said, coming toward her. "But I thought maybe I could take you to lunch?"

She had been working at the drafting table and sent a surprised look at her watch. "It's nearly noon? I had no idea." After a virtually sleepless night it had taken her hours and another hot bath to work most of the stiffness and soreness out of her body; her unsettled thoughts and emotions had been far less easy to tame, and only fierce concentration on this work had steadied her somewhat. But she knew her control was uncertain at best.

"Looks like you've been busy." He nodded toward the sketches on the table. "Designs for the new store?"

"Yes."

"So you're going forward with the scheme?"

"Of course."

He shifted a bit restlessly and jammed his hands into the pockets of his jacket. "I guess it'd be useless to ask you to put off moving on that for a while?"

"Until?"

"Until the police have the fire marshal's report on the explosion. Until I can nose around a bit, ask some questions."

Rachel frowned at him. "Ask who what kind of questions?"

"I'm not entirely sure. Yet. But I know I'd like to talk to the mechanic who examined your car. Maybe to your lawyer."

"Why him?"

"You come home to settle your parents' estate and things start happening. Maybe there's no connection—and maybe there is. Maybe something your father was involved in has survived him."

"My father had no enemies."

"Rachel, every rich man has enemies."

She shook her head, but instead of arguing, said, "I don't think you want to talk to Graham. He . . . wouldn't be very forthcoming."

"Most lawyers aren't. But I'm sure he has your best interests at heart."

"Adam, I appreciate your concern, but—"

"But it isn't any of my business?"

She hesitated. "I wasn't going to say that. It's just . . . I don't need a watchdog. Or a bloodhound, for that matter. I don't believe anyone's trying to hurt me. Just accidents, that's all."

"Rachel, I know I'm a virtual stranger to you, and there's no reason on earth why you should listen to me. Except one."

"Which is?"

"I'm asking you to."

After a moment, Rachel moved away from him to lean against the edge of her father's desk. She was still shaky, and hoped he couldn't see it. "Okay. I'm listening."

Instead of coming toward her, he respected the distance she had put between them and remained by her drafting table. "Look, I don't know if there's someone out there who's a threat to you. All I do know is that both of us will feel better when we eliminate the possibility. And the only way to do that is to find a few answers."

She shook her head slightly. "Suppose the mechanic tells you he's positive the brake line was cut. What then?"

"Then we try to find out who had access to the car between the last time it was safely driven and when you got in."

"And if the fire marshal's report says the explosion was arson?"

"Then we try to find out who was seen near the building yesterday morning before we arrived."

"But that won't tell us if I was meant to be a target."

"It will if we find the arsonist."

"Isn't that for the police to do?"

"The police have a city to take care of. We can focus entirely on you."

Rachel shook her head again. "Adam, I'm not a cop. Or any kind of investigator."

"I know that. I'm not either. But I know how to find answers. All I'm asking is that you let me try."

"I thought you were going back to California."

"Not for a while." He looked at her steadily. "A staff I trust is running the company for me. Anything I have to do I can do by phone and fax, or with my laptop. Right now this is more important to me."

Rachel asked the question before she could stop herself. "Why?"

"I could say it's because you're the daughter of the man I owe everything to."

"You could. Would it be true?" At that moment, she forgot about being sore and shaky and afraid.

"Partly."

Rachel shied away from pressing for anything further. She wasn't sure she wanted to know the answer.

"All right, I'll accept that. For now."

"And you'll let me try to find out what's going on?"

She smiled briefly. "I get the feeling I couldn't stop you if I tried. But you can forget about talking to Graham. He wouldn't tell you anything about Dad's business. Or mine, for that matter."

Adam frowned. "Have you gone through Duncan's personal papers yet?"

Rachel glanced over her shoulder at the huge desk. "I barely made a start. A few letters so far. There's an awful lot packed into this desk. I think Dad kept every scrap of paper he wrote a note on. And I haven't even gotten that far with the little desk in his bedroom."

Slowly, Adam said, "I know you want to go forward with your plans for the store, Rachel. And I know it's

. . . less painful to postpone going through your father's things. But it needs to be done."

"You're so sure the answer's there? That my father made an enemy so vicious that now he's after me?"

"I think we have to rule it out. Rachel, none of us ever knows all the secrets of the people we're close to. I'm absolutely positive your father was an honorable man, and if he ever broke the law, it would come as a shock to me. But he was a wealthy man who dealt with a wide range of people. It isn't beyond the realm of possibility that he got involved in something that became dangerous. That he might have made an enemy."

Reluctantly, Rachel nodded. "I accept that. But an enemy coming after me now? I can't believe that."

"The explosion—"

"A random arsonist. You heard what the police said."

Before she could continue, the phone on her father's desk rang. With a slight smile of apology, Rachel went around to sit in the swivel chair and answer the call.

"Hello?"

"Miss Grant?"

"Yes?"

"Miss Grant, this is Sharon Wilkins, from the real estate office. I just wanted to call you and say how horrified we are about that explosion."

"A random arsonist," Rachel said lightly. "None of you could have known it was going to happen, Sharon. It's just a shame the building's gone now."

"Yes—but at least it was insured." The agent's voice became brisk. "Miss Grant, I didn't want to bother you, on a Saturday and all, but I did want to assure you that if you do lease a property we're representing, we'll make sure security is part of the package."

"Thanks, Sharon. As a matter of fact, I've made up my

mind. I want to lease the store on Queen Street." She was aware of Adam moving restlessly, but didn't look at him. "So if you could get the papers ready?"

"Absolutely. I can have everything ready for your signature by Monday afternoon."

"Great."

"I'll see you then. Oh—and, Miss Grant?"

"Yes?"

"Did your friend find you?"

"My friend?"

"Yes. He called here just after you left yesterday morning, very eager to talk to you."

Rachel felt a slow chill crawl up her spine. "So—you told him what stores I was going to be looking at? The addresses?"

"Well, yes." Sharon's voice became anxious. "I just assumed— He knew all about your plans for a boutique, and I assumed he was somehow working with you. If I did the wrong thing—"

"No." Rachel cleared her throat. "No, of course not. And, yes—he found me. I'll see you Monday, Sharon."

Gently, she hung up the phone.

"Rachel?"

She looked at Adam, vaguely surprised to find that he had come around the desk and knelt beside her chair. "The strangest thing."

"Someone knew where you'd be yesterday? Is that what she told you?" His voice was grim.

"Yes. Someone called the real estate office. A man. He knew about the boutique idea. So she told him."

"So that explosion could have been meant for you."

Rachel drew a breath.

And for the first time, she really believed it.

It was very possible that someone wanted her dead.

SEVEN

dam wanted to take her to lunch, but Rachel was too shaken by the phone call, and he didn't press her. Instead, Fiona brought soup and sandwiches to the library. Rachel hardly touched the meal, but she was able to get the shakes under control by the time she pushed her plate away.

"Stop watching me," she told him. "I'm fine."

"I wasn't watching you, I was looking at you." He smiled slightly. "Don't ask me to stop doing that. And you're not fine. You wouldn't be human if you weren't scared and worried."

"I just can't quite get my mind around the idea that someone might want to kill me."

"We still don't know that for sure," he said, now playing devil's advocate. "Whoever called the real estate office may have really wanted to see you. Maybe he got there after the explosion, and didn't try to approach you in all the confusion."

"I don't know who it would have been."

"How about Graham Becket?"

Instantly, Rachel shook her head. "He wouldn't have told Sharon he was my friend. He would have said he was my attorney." She smiled. "He likes the sound of it."

Adam leaned his forearms on the desk they were using as a dining table. "Can you think of anyone else? Any reason why someone would have wanted to find you yesterday?"

"No. No one who knew about the plans for the boutique. That's where the list gets really short."

"Me," he said.

"Yes, but—logically—you were with me the whole time. Graham knows. My uncle Cam. Nicholas Ross. Any of them could have told someone else, but why would they?"

"Maybe we'd better ask."

Rachel grimaced. "Why don't you ask Nick? I mean, since you two are friends. He unnerves me."

"I can deal with Nick," Adam said.

"I'll ask Cam later. And call Graham."

Reluctantly, Adam said, "Do you suspect any of them?"

She didn't immediately say no. Instead, she replied with a carefully maintained detachment. "I have a will. Or, rather, a trust. It was updated after Mom and Dad were killed. If I were to die anytime soon, childless, Cam would get the house and contents. Nick would get my shares in the bank. Graham would get a relatively small bequest, some beach property. Is any of that enough to kill for?"

Adam reached across the desk and took her hand. "I don't think that's it, Rachel. This all started when you came home to Richmond to settle your father's estate. I think we have to look there first."

She looked down at his hand and, almost absently, said, "It's taken months to sort out Dad's business affairs at the bank. Sorting out his personal affairs could take just as long."

"I'm not going anywhere."

"You know, you don't have to feel obligated to do this. To watch over me. No matter what Dad did for you, he wouldn't expect—"

"Rachel."

She looked up and met his gaze. That was very different from Thomas, that gaze. The color of his eyes, their intensity. There was something in them that made her breath catch in the back of her throat.

His fingers tightened around hers. "Tell me not to say it. Tell me you're not ready to hear it."

Nobody had ever looked at her like that before. Not even Thomas. For just an instant, she hesitated, almost not breathing. But then she leaned back in her chair and very gently pulled her hand from his grasp. Her heart was pounding, and she didn't know if it was excitement or terror. "I'm not ready. Adam, we barely know each other—"

"I know all I need to know." But he was smiling faintly, that naked look in his eyes gone now. Or hidden. "But I also know you need time."

"Yes. It's an understatement to say there's a lot going on in my life right now. The timing is—"

"Lousy. Yeah, I know. Rachel, listen to me. I won't push. I learned a long time ago how to be patient. And I am not going to let anything happen to you. All right?"

She nodded slowly, conscious that her heart was still thudding against her ribs, that it was still difficult to catch her breath. "All right."

"Good. Now—why don't I get out of here and leave you alone. We need to start asking those questions."

"Right," she murmured. "Questions."

"Did I tell anyone about your plans to open a boutique?" Graham raised a surprised brow. "Until I heard about the explosion, I hadn't even been aware that you were serious enough about the idea to be looking at property. Why would I have told anyone?"

"It was just a question, Graham." She kept her voice casual, but gazed steadily across the desk at him. For this, she had wanted to be face-to-face, and so had driven into town after Adam had left. Graham was always in his office on Saturday afternoons. "Somebody called the real estate office just after I left there yesterday morning, looking for me. Somebody who knew I was thinking of opening a boutique. So I just wondered if you'd told anyone."

"No."

"And you weren't looking for me yourself?" She knew he hadn't been but asked anyway.

"No. I think I would have mentioned it when we talked after the explosion. Of course, since you hung up on me—"

"I didn't do that."

"As good as. I tried to call you around lunchtime. Fiona said you were shut up in Duncan's library with Adam Delafield."

Rachel had let the housekeeper take that call when the phone had rung partway through their meal. She had still been too upset to talk to anyone, and knew Fiona would have told her if the call had been important. Unfortunately, Fiona had always had a soft spot for Graham and was,

Rachel sometimes thought, a tad too willing to tell him everything that went on in the Grant household.

"We had lunch."

"It obviously wouldn't do me any good to ask you again to stay away from him until I get the background information on him."

"That wasn't a question. But the answer is no."

Graham scowled. "I don't trust him, Rachel."

"You've said that before. But, so far, you haven't shown me any reason not to trust him." She kept her voice quiet and even, knowing that Graham's concern was sincere. "Graham, he probably saved my life. Dad trusted him enough to lend him three million dollars on a handshake—"

"Or so he says."

"And I like him," she finished defiantly.

Graham's face closed down into its lawyerly expression of detachment. "Which, of course, has nothing to do with the fact that he could be Thomas Sheridan's twin."

That wasn't something Rachel wanted to hear, but she managed to meet his eyes steadily. "I don't know if it does or not. But I'd like the chance to find out."

"And the fact that during the week after he appeared in your life you had two rather violent close calls doesn't bother you?"

"Of course it bothers me." Rachel kept her voice matter-of-fact, reluctant to encourage Graham in any way to overreact. "In fact, it should relieve you to know that Adam is just as concerned. He thinks Dad may have made an enemy who has some reason to want me out of the way."

Clearly hesitant to agree with Adam, Graham said, "Rich men do make enemies. But even if that were true, I can't imagine why it would carry over to you."

"I can't either." Rachel frowned. "Unless it has something to do with the bank. I haven't decided what to do about my shares yet. Maybe somebody's trying to . . . encourage me to sell out."

"You suspect Nick Ross?"

Rachel barely hesitated before shaking her head. "Not really. He has enough control at the bank to do virtually whatever he wants, with or without my shares. I've told him I won't interfere, and I meant it. I think he knows that. As a matter of fact, he told me that if I intended to keep my shares, he'd advise me to hire Mercy to manage them for me."

"I don't see who else would benefit if you gave up your shares."

"Graham, it's just a possibility. That's all I have right now, possibilities. I can't be sure of anything. I don't know, for a fact, that either of those two . . . violent close calls were specifically intended to injure me. The brake line *could* have failed by accident, and the arson of that building *could* have been completely random. I just don't know."

"You know enough to be careful."

"That's more or less what Adam said."

Again Graham didn't appear thrilled to be in agreement with Adam. "It's common sense, Rachel. You shouldn't even have driven into town alone today. And where's your car parked? In the secure lot, or—"

"Out front," she murmured.

Graham picked up his phone and called a cab. "Leave the keys to the lease here. I'll get another car sent out to you. And when I do, promise me you won't leave it in *any* unsecured area."

Rachel pushed the car keys across the desk to him. "All right."

"Will you also promise me you'll try to stick close to home for a while? Until we know more?"

She avoided the promise by saying, "What do you expect to know? More about Adam's background?"

"Among other things."

"What other things?"

"I intend to go through my copies of Duncan's business papers. Contracts and the like."

"You've been all through those to settle the estate."

"Yes, but I wasn't looking for any reason someone might want you out of the way. This time I will."

Rachel nodded and stood up. "Okay. You do that. I'm due to sign a lease on the store on Queen Street Monday."

"Bring it to me before you sign."

She grimaced slightly, but nodded again. "In the meantime, I'm going to start going through Dad's personal papers. Maybe I'll turn up something."

"Just be careful, Rachel, all right?"

"You bet."

When he was alone again, Graham sat for a long time in his silent office, gazing at nothing. Then he reached for his phone.

When the car pulled over to the curb, Adam moved out of the shadows and got into the passenger side.

"Did we *have* to meet so late?" the driver complained. "I should be at home in bed. And why this shitty neighborhood? Jesus, I don't dare turn off the engine or I'll find my tires slashed. Or missing."

"Will you stop bitching, Mike, and show me what you've got?"

Mike reached inside his dark raincoat and pulled out a small plastic bag. "Here. And if they find it missing from the evidence locker before I can get it back, my job is history. When you call in a favor, you don't mess around, do you?"

Adam ignored the question. "This is what the fire marshal found?"

"That's it. Arson for damn sure."

Instead of turning on the dome light, Adam removed a penlight from inside his jacket and used that to slowly examine the charred bits of metal and melted plastic inside the bag.

"Any suspects?"

Mike shook his head. "Nah. The other arsons in the area were started with plain old gasoline and a match. What's left of this thing shows a lot more imagination, according to the experts. And a lot more expertise. State-of-the-art sparking mechanism, says our guy. And probably on some kind of timer. But those bits and pieces don't match up with any unsolved explosions or arsons in the computer."

Adam grunted.

"You see something different? I mean, I know you're some kind of electrical wizard and all."

"No," Adam said. "I don't see anything different." He turned off the penlight. "Guess there's no chance of me keeping this for a while."

"Hey, pal, I don't owe you *that* big."

Adam returned the bag to him. "No problem. But I would . . . appreciate a copy of the fire marshal's report."

Mike groaned. "Christ, you're gonna get me fired."

"Just a copy. You can get it."

"Yeah, yeah. I'll see what I can do."

"Thanks, Mike."

Mike peered through the gloom at Adam. "You want to tell me what all this is about?"

"I'm just keeping an eye on a friend, that's all."

"Rachel Grant? That's some friend, pal. Most any man in Richmond would just love to be keeping an eye on her."

Adam shifted slightly in his seat, but all he said was "Anybody suspicious of this on her account?"

"You mean does anybody think your girl was meant to end up on a slab?"

"Something like that."

"Not that I've heard. She was just in the wrong place at the wrong time, is the thinking. Why? You know something we don't?"

"No. Just wondering."

Mike grunted. "If it comes to that, I would have thought you were a more likely target for an *accidental* death than Rachel Grant. You've made more than your fair share of enemies."

"Yeah. But not in Richmond."

"Oh, I think you might have one or two even here."

Adam turned his head to stare at him. "Oh?"

"Yeah. Saw an old . . . friend of yours the other day."

"Who?"

"Max Galloway."

"Son of a bitch."

"He's all of that. And a loose cannon into the bargain. I don't pretend to know what he's doing in Richmond, but you can bet your last dollar it's nothing good."

"Can you find out?"

"Only if he breaks the law, draws attention to himself. He isn't likely to do that. The Richmond cops don't know him. Except for me, of course, because I used to work in California."

"Maybe you'd better warn them."

"Yeah. Maybe I will. And you watch your back, Adam. Galloway never made it a secret that he hated your guts. Maybe he followed you here to finally do something about it."

Adam didn't say anything to that, and when he opened the car door, the dome light showed no change in his calm expression. "Thanks for giving me a look at the evidence, Mike. I'll wait for your call about the fire marshal's report."

"Give me a few days."

"Right." Adam got out of the car and shut the door.

Mike didn't waste any time in leaving the neighborhood.

Adam turned up the collar of his jacket, conscious of the chilly mist that was drifting in, and began walking slowly along the littered sidewalk. Blocks away from The Tavern, the area was desolate, mostly deserted. The only sounds were the rustle of trash skittering over the pavement and his own quiet footsteps.

Max Galloway.

Patterns of fate? Threads of destiny? How else to explain it?

And how long had that violent enemy been in Richmond? Maybe waiting. Maybe watching.

Maybe acting.

Rachel.

Automatically, his hand lifted to touch the slight bulge of the locket beneath his shirt. Its presence did nothing to reassure him.

Max Galloway.

Rachel.

Jesus.

Adam quickened his pace.

• • •

Rachel came out of her bathroom on Sunday morning and stopped dead in her bedroom. For just a moment she could have sworn she had once again caught the elusive scent of the cologne Thomas had always worn. But even as she sniffed, it was gone.

Oh, of course it was gone. Because it hadn't been there at all.

Just my imagination.

She sat down at her dressing table and began brushing her hair, an unseeing gaze fixed on the mirror. With that imagined scent had come a rush of memories, and she had no choice but to endure them. Thomas, teasing her because it turned out the men's cologne she had fallen in love with was what the TV commercials insisted women dreamed of their men wearing when they came home from the sea. It was not something *he* would have chosen to wear, but he had worn it for her. He had always worn it.

Thomas hiding little notes and presents for her, here in the house and out in the garden, laughing at her when she couldn't find one. His voice whispering words of love. His promises . . .

He wasn't very good at keeping his promises.

When that thought occurred, it felt so much a betrayal that Rachel was jerked from the daydreaming. She focused on her face in the mirror, saw her cheeks were wet. Slowly, she wiped the tears away.

He hadn't been very good at keeping his promises. And not only the last one. Thomas had more than once made a careless promise, only to find himself unable to keep it later. He had always been sincerely apologetic—she thought—but it occurred to her for the first time that the character trait might well have made him a less than perfect husband.

The realization unnerved Rachel. She got up from her vanity table and went to dress, and it wasn't until she was ready to leave the room that she saw the rose. It lay on her pillow, a single yellow rose so fresh there was still a drop of dew on a satiny petal.

Rachel's first reaction as she picked up the flower was simply one of pleasure. She loved flowers, especially yellow roses. But then she realized that there was something very strange about this. Where had it come from? The flower hadn't been there when she had gone to shower half an hour before. So who could have come in and placed it on the pillow? It was still early; Cam was a late sleeper, and Fiona was far too brusque for something like this—even if there had been a yellow rose in the garden to pick. There wasn't.

She stood there, staring at the rose, baffled and uneasy.

It was after noon on Sunday before Rachel could finally bring herself to sit down at her father's desk one more time. She would have preferred to do something else. Almost anything else. But suspecting that somebody was trying to frighten—or kill—her was even more painful than facing her father's memory.

At least, she hoped that was true.

For the first hour or so, she occupied herself by sorting through what she found in the two top drawers and placing them in reasonably neat piles atop the desk. Her father's day planner was put to one side so she could go through it at her leisure; what looked like personal correspondence was stacked together; pens, paper clips, and other standard supplies; endless scraps of paper with sometimes cryptic notes in her father's hand; quite a bit of business correspondence unrelated to the bank; stacks of business cards.

And two small notebooks detailing deposits and withdrawals.

To and from a bank in Geneva, Switzerland.

Rachel placed one of the notebooks on the blotter and began slowly to thumb through the other. Her hands were shaking.

The deposits and withdrawals went back more than twenty years. Some were fairly small. Most were large, into six and even seven figures.

Millions. Millions had gone through the accounts.

After the first shock had passed, Rachel found a legal pad and a sharpened pencil and began doing some figuring. It took some time, but she gradually realized that there was a pattern to the deposits and withdrawals.

Over the first five years there had been only deposits made, until the total reached just over ten million dollars. After that, each year there was never more than a single withdrawal, though there was sometimes more than one deposit. A million in, two hundred thousand out. Five hundred thousand in, two million out. Two hundred thousand in, a million out.

Slowly, Rachel found the matches. Each withdrawal was matched to the penny by a deposit at a later date. The account never held more than fifteen million dollars, and never held less than five.

When she looked more closely, Rachel saw that the note of each withdrawal contained a series of numbers and letters—always ending in two letters. Initials, she realized. And each set of initials for a withdrawal was matched by a set for a later deposit.

"Loans," she whispered as realization dawned.

The two notebooks contained a history of loans—or, as her father had undoubtedly called them, "investments"—made and repaid. Over the space of twenty years. With no paperwork except these simple figures kept in two little black leather notebooks.

"Rachel, that's not the way Duncan did business."

Graham had said that. And he was right. It hadn't been the way her father had done business, not for the bank. But for himself, it seemed, a handshake and these little notebooks had been enough.

And there it was—five years before, a three-million-dollar withdrawal. And the series of identifying numbers and letters ended with *AD.* It was a series not yet repeated in the notebook, because the loan had not yet been repaid.

Adam had told her the truth.

If he was who and what he claimed to be.

I trust him. Of course I do. And not because he looks like Thomas.

Her own doubts disturbed her as much as the existence of this notebook. And then another realization dawned and she bent over the notebooks and her legal pad and did more figuring.

The sum she arrived at left her feeling a bit light-headed.

Not counting the loan she assumed was Adam's, there were three loans still outstanding. One for a hundred and fifty thousand, one for one and a half million, and the last for five million. The initials were *RS, LM,* and *JW,* and the most recent loan—the largest—had been made just months before her father's death.

So there were three people who had been given loans by her father who had not yet come forward to repay them. The problem was, Rachel had no way of knowing when those loans had been set to come due. Adam had been lent his money five years ago; according to the notebooks, several other loans had run at least that long, and one for six years. For all she knew, these outstanding loans also had lengthy lives and simply weren't yet due to be repaid.

Of course, that didn't explain why those given the money hadn't sought her out, as Adam had, to promise repayment.

She knew what Graham would say, of course. That these three people were taking advantage of her father's trust, not coming forward in the hope that she would have no way of knowing what they owed.

She had no intention of telling Graham about this.

That was not as difficult a decision as Rachel had expected. It seemed to her that her father had kept this quiet and private because that was the way he had wanted it. For twenty years he had apparently helped people like Adam, people who had needed large sums of cash to achieve their dreams.

She doubted that Graham would appreciate that.

But she did.

That was an easy decision. There were several others to be made, however. By her calculations, even if the outstanding loans were not repaid, the account held upward of ten million dollars.

"Oh, wow, Dad. Now what do I do?"

It was a heartfelt question. For all she knew, her father's personal financial dealings, while undoubtedly noble, could well be illegal. She definitely knew that none of this money had been counted in his estate. Although, now that she thought about it, she vaguely remembered a phrase contained in the trust that went something like "deposits in any financial institution other than those in

Duncan and Ross Investments, Ltd., to be transferred outright to my daughter, Rachel Grant."

Something like that.

So the money was, she assumed, legally hers. That was to say if any of this was legal . . .

She definitely foresaw a confidential visit to a specialist in taxes and estates in her near future.

She pushed that aside to be dealt with later. Until her father's estate was finally settled, the problem of this money could wait. What most concerned her at the present was the question of whether any of this held the answer to why someone might want her dead.

Maybe someone *really* didn't want to repay his or her loan.

Her first thought was that only the five-million-dollar loan might be motive enough for murder. But when she thought about it as dispassionately as possible, she realized that even the smallest loan, for a mere hundred and fifty thousand, could be worth murder.

It was all a matter of perspective. And from the right perspective, killing for a hundred dollars or even less could make sense.

That was a chilling thought.

Slowly, she circled the three outstanding entries on her legal pad.

Three people, any one of whom could have decided that killing Rachel would cancel their loan.

Three people with nothing to identify them for her except initials.

Three people with nothing to lose and everything to gain by her death.

• • •

Rachel opened the big black iron gate, its hinge creaking loudly, and began to follow the path toward the woods. It was misty, the fog rising from the ground and swirling as though stirred by a restless hand.

It was very quiet.

She was happy. Around her neck she wore the locket she had given Thomas, the one containing her picture and the St. Christopher that she had hoped would keep him safe.

She followed the path, oblivious of the mist. Of the chill. Her eyes were fixed ahead on the edge of the woods, where a figure waited.

He took shape out of the mist as she neared, a tall man with fair hair gleaming in the strange light. He smiled a welcoming smile. He held out his arms to her.

Rachel laughed and ran toward him.

But then, close enough to really see him, she faltered and stopped.

His face had become a mask of cracked porcelain, the eyeholes dark and empty. And from the gaping hole of the mouth, a hoarse voice whispered, "Don't trust him, Rachel. Don't trust him."

Worms began to ooze from the eyeholes of the mask.

Rachel screamed and screamed. . . .

Adam bolted upright in bed, a cry tangled and trapped in his throat. His heart was pounding violently, and his breathing rasped audibly. He looked around, his gaze stabbing into every corner of the hotel room that was lit by dawn's gray light.

Slowly, very slowly, he lay back on his pillows, lifting his hand to grasp the locket he wore.

"Oh, God, Rachel," he whispered.

EIGHT

iona? You didn't leave a rose on my pillow yesterday morning, did you?"

The housekeeper looked blank. "A rose? Why would I do that, Miss Rachel?"

"Never mind." Rachel tried to laugh it off. "My imagination has been working overtime recently." Except that she hadn't imagined it. That rose was very real, and in a bud vase on her nightstand.

Fiona frowned, then shrugged and asked what she wanted for breakfast.

Rachel talked to Sharon at the real estate office after breakfast, and to save time had her messenger the lease agreement to Graham's office. Unless he found something wrong when he went over it, she could still sign it that day, and then the store would be hers. And during that process she wouldn't have to leave the house, which definitely appealed to her.

Whether someone was after her or not, remaining close to home for the time being seemed like a good idea.

In the meantime, with only a slight hesitation she called Adam. She considered calling Mercy, since her friend had always been the one she'd confided in, but something stopped her this time. Mercy didn't know about the loans. She knew that Adam claimed to be on the verge of repaying a private loan, but she had no idea of the extent of Duncan's private loans. And just as she had decided not to tell Graham, Rachel decided not to tell Mercy. Not until she could feel more certain of doing what her father would have wished.

But Adam, bent as he seemed to be on finding out who and what represented a threat against her and already in Duncan's confidence to the tune of three million dollars, seemed the best person in whom to confide this new information. It would have been too much to say that she trusted him completely, but Rachel's instincts told her to tell him this much, and she listened to them.

It isn't because he looks like Thomas. It isn't.

He arrived at the house within half an hour, and once again Fiona announced him and quickly retreated after crossing herself.

"Why does she always do that?" he asked, coming into the study.

"Because you look like Tom," Rachel answered as casually as she could. "It unnerves her."

Adam smiled slightly. "It unnerves her. How about you?"

Rachel, standing behind her father's desk, gazed at him. "No, it doesn't unnerve me. Now." She paused, then added honestly, "But it isn't something I can forget, Adam. You do look like Thomas."

"Is that the only reason I'm here, Rachel?"

She hesitated, then shook her head. "No."

He nodded. "Good."

Deciding that enough had been said about that, Rachel handed the two small notebooks to Adam. "Look what I found. It seems you were right about that bank account in Geneva." She sat down behind the desk and watched as he took the visitor's chair and frowned over the notebooks.

"Loans?" he guessed, looking up at her.

Rachel nodded and pushed the legal pad with all her notes across the desk.

It didn't take Adam long to see the pattern. "My God. Nearly twenty loans of varying sizes over twenty years."

"Almost all of them repaid to the penny," Rachel said. "My dad obviously had great judgment about whom he could trust. See the initials? At the end of each series of numbers. Yours are there."

Adam smiled at her. "I see. I'm glad he left you this, Rachel."

"I'm not so sure I am. Take a look at that last page of figures."

He did, and a frown quickly replaced his smile. "Three loans other than mine outstanding?"

"That's what it looks like."

"Goddammit," he muttered. "That means three people with a potential reason to want you out of the way."

"That's possible. But I've been thinking about it. Adam, what threat am I to those people? All I have are their initials, so I don't know who they are. And even if I did, there's nothing legally binding about this setup, not that I can see. Any of those people could knock on my door and say the loans wouldn't be repaid, and there's nothing I could do about it. If it comes to that, they could claim the money was a gift."

"That's a good point." He considered it for a moment.

"Still, there could be something we don't know about all this."

"What do you mean?"

"I'm not quite sure. Except that it makes me damned uneasy that none of these people have been in touch with you since your father's death."

"Maybe their loans aren't due to be repaid."

"Maybe. And maybe they have other reasons to stay anonymous."

Rachel shook her head. "I don't know how we can find out what those reasons are. None of the initials tells me anything."

Adam put the legal pad and the notebooks on the desk. "You found the notebooks in this desk?"

"Yes."

"Did you find anything else? Anything that might give us some clue as to who these people are?"

"I don't know, Adam. About a ream's worth of scrap paper, all of it with notes in Dad's hand. I haven't gone through it all yet."

"Maybe we'll find an answer there. Or at least a hint." He looked at her steadily. "I'll help."

"It could take all day. And then there are two more drawers here I haven't even opened, and the secretary in his bedroom . . . Adam, what if your company needs to find you?"

"I have a pager. Rachel, I want to help. Let me. Please."

Rachel wasn't entirely sure that spending the better part of a day in Adam's company was the wisest thing to do. But it was what she wanted to do.

"I'd welcome the company," she said.

• • •

"Do I expect to have total control of the bank? I have that now. No, it hardly matters whether Rachel Grant sells me her shares. I have the authority to act in any way I see fit." His tone was very pleasant as he spoke on the phone.

Very pleasant. And completely ruthless.

It made goose bumps rise on Mercy's bare arms. She hadn't heard the beginning of the conversation, but came into his office in time to hear that much. It was enough to disturb her.

She shut the door behind herself and crossed the room to sit down in his visitor's chair, pretending to thumb through the papers she carried rather than listen in on the conversation.

"I told you that last week," Nicholas said. "No. No, I don't see any reason to do that. I imagine the problem will resolve itself fairly quickly."

He paused. His gaze was fixed on Mercy. She could feel it.

"I can come up with ten million."

She looked up in surprise, and felt herself flush when he smiled at her sardonically.

"No, I don't need Rachel's shares to do that. I've told you. I have the authority. Yeah. Yeah, you do that. See you there." He hung up.

"But you don't have the authority," Mercy protested. "An investment that size needs Rachel's approval. In fact, it needs the approval of the board."

Nicholas smiled. "Love, do you intend working for me as my assistant?"

"You know I don't."

"Has Rachel hired you to manage her interests?"

"The subject hasn't come up. I'm not even sure she means to keep her shares."

Softly, he said, "Then don't concern yourself with whatever decisions I make in running the bank."

He had never warned her off quite so bluntly before, and coming now, this warning served only to make her more worried. He was up to something. She could sense it. She just didn't know what was going on.

"I don't mean to meddle in your business, Nick."

"I know you don't, love."

"It's just—ten million dollars is a hell of a lot of money. Even for a bank this size."

"I know what I'm doing, Mercy."

His record with the bank bore that out, so all she could do was nod. "I know."

He smiled, then nodded toward the papers forgotten in her grasp. "Are those for me?"

She got up and handed them to him across the desk. "Some things you need to look over and sign—"

Nicholas grasped her wrist. It was a warm, strong, inescapable hold. "Sure you don't want to work for me?" he murmured seductively. "Be right at the seat of power? Know all my secrets?"

She leaned her free hand on the desk. "I have a feeling I'll never live long enough to know all your secrets, Nick."

His eyes gleamed at her. "But it's something to strive for, surely."

"Oh, it's at the top of my list."

He let out one of those short barks of laughter so characteristic of him, and released her wrist. "Could you pander to my ego at least once, love?"

"I have a sneaking suspicion your ego is remarkably healthy as it is," she said, still leaning on the desk.

"Perhaps." He glanced down at the papers he held. "Do you need these right away? I need to go out for a while."

"They can wait until tomorrow. I didn't see an appointment on your calendar." She kept her voice casual.

"A last-minute arrangement." He got up and came around the desk, and when she turned to face him, he lifted a hand to lay alongside her neck. He bent his head and kissed her, taking his time about it and totally ignoring the unlocked door.

Then again, she thought hazily, maybe he had a sixth sense about such things. They'd never been interrupted—and he had provoked greater intimacies than this in the past.

When he finally drew back far enough to speak, he murmured huskily, "Trust me, Mercy. I really do know what I'm doing."

It took her a moment to remember what they'd been discussing. "I do. Of course I do."

"Do you?" His fingers caressed her throat. "Then why are you so worried?"

"Because— How do you know I'm worried?"

"I know."

Well, *that* was certainly unnerving. Up until then she'd thought she had a great poker face.

This time his laugh was a deep rumble. He kissed her again, then released her and stepped back. "Mind the store for a couple of hours, will you, love?"

"Of course."

But he was no sooner out the door than Mercy made an impulsive decision. With a hurried order to Leigh to mind the store, she grabbed her purse and dashed out before the office manager could do more than sputter in surprise.

Mercy wasn't at all sure she could follow him without his knowledge, but she intended to give it a damn good try. He had asked for her trust, and she had said it was given—but Mercy had lied. He seemed to her more secretive than ever these days, and she didn't like it. There had been too many cryptic telephone conversations, too many evasions, too many enigmatic gazes and inexplicable silences.

Her best friend had survived two so-called accidents, a fact Nick seemed almost totally disinterested in, even though he stood to gain by her death. And soon after the second one, he had told somebody on the phone that they had "fucked up."

Damned straight, Mercy was worried.

She had no idea if the man she loved was a man she could trust.

Fiona brought them lunch on trays since they didn't want to stop going through Duncan's private papers. But by two o'clock Adam firmly called a halt.

"My eyes are beginning to cross, and that's the third time you've rubbed yours," he told Rachel. "We need a break."

"Maybe you're right." She rubbed the back of her neck instead, finding it a bit stiff. They had moved from her father's desk to the leather sofa and big, square coffee table. Adam sat on the sofa, while Rachel had ended up sitting on the floor on the other side of the table with a big pillow to lean on.

Not because she wanted to avoid sitting beside him, but because . . . because they'd needed the entire coffee table on which to spread out papers, and it was easier to work from both sides.

That was all.

Adam got up and came around to offer her his hands.

"Come on. Why don't we go outside and take a walk or something."

She took his hands and allowed him to pull her up, wincing as her left leg protested the sudden change in position.

"Did I hurt you?"

"No, no. Just a slight cramp in my leg. It's easing off." She released his hands and stepped away, unnerved by his closeness. At such moments she was always aware of that leashed power in him, that hidden strength. It bothered her in some way she could hardly put a name to.

Realizing suddenly that she had been silent just a moment too long, she said casually, "If there's no furniture barring the way, I'll show you through a bit more of the house on our way to the back. We have a kind of informal garden, and it's a pleasant place to walk."

"Sounds good to me."

They closed the study door when they left, and Rachel locked it, sliding the key into the front pocket of her jeans.

"Have you been keeping the room locked?"

"No, just the desk. But with all those papers spread out, locking the door seems best for now."

"A sensible precaution."

They encountered a barricade in the hallway outside the formal dining room. And encountered her uncle Cameron, who was not happy.

Since he'd already met Adam, he simply acknowledged his presence with a nod, launching immediately into complaint. "Rachel, Darby says she found three rolltop desks in the basement, and she won't let me go through the contents."

Soothingly, Rachel said, "That's because I asked her just to box up the contents for now, Cam. We can go through all that later. Anything that's been down there for decades can wait a while longer."

He seemed satisfied, but said, "We don't want her throwing away something important thinking it's trash." Not as distinguished-looking as his older brother had been, Cameron carried the added burden of cupidlike features, which tended to make him look pouty even when he wasn't.

"She won't do that, Cam. She's boxing up the contents of everything she finds, no matter what. Don't worry. Darby knows what she's doing."

A crash from the basement caused her uncle to wince in horror and bolt.

"I hope," Rachel murmured.

Adam grinned at her. "Want to go see what ended up in splinters, or shall we go on to the garden?"

"I'm tired of sorting furniture and old boxes." She shrugged. "Let Darby handle it. And Uncle Cam."

"He does seem worried," Adam noted as Rachel let go of his arm so she could pick her way through the furniture barricade.

"He hates the idea of non-Grants having a say in the disposal of family things. Not the family tradition, you see. But I don't see any reason to keep most of the stuff in storage, and Darby is the fairest, most trustworthy antiques dealer I know."

"Why's he so worried about the contents?"

"Because a few days ago Darby found a diamond cocktail ring tucked away in a little drawer of an old dresser. Thirties design. I'm almost afraid to have it appraised."

Adam whistled. "So every piece is a potential treasure chest?"

"Well, to Uncle Cam. He always did love poking into corners, so this really does seem like a treasure hunt."

They emerged at last from the forest of furniture, and Adam casually took Rachel's hand. "Which way now?"

"We'll go through the sunroom," she decided, trying not to be so conscious of that warm, strong hand surrounding hers. "Fiona's already working on dinner in the kitchen, so if we go that way, she'll burn something."

"She has her own methods of letting her displeasure be known?"

"Definitely. This way."

The sunroom, a bright and plant-filled space that doubled as a breakfast room, opened onto a tile veranda. Steps led down to a lawn, from which a path paved only with stepping stones wandered off into a lush landscape of bright flowering shrubs and spring greenery.

Large trees towered to either side of the garden area, offering a sense of being closed off from the world outside. The air was mild, and heavily scented from all the flowers.

"Nice," Adam commented as they began strolling along the path.

"Most of the homes in this neighborhood have more formal gardens than we do. But this was designed two hundred years ago, and so far everybody's kept it casual. I mean to as well."

"I like it." They strolled for a few minutes in silence, and then Adam said abruptly, "Tell me about Thomas Sheridan."

Startled, Rachel stopped on the path and stared up at him. "Thomas? Why?"

"I'd just like to know."

"You said Dad talked about him."

"He did. But he wasn't in love with Sheridan. You were."

Rachel pulled to free her hand. "I don't want to—"

"Rachel." His free hand lifted and touched her cheek,

making her go still. "I said I wouldn't push, and I won't. But I . . . I need to hear you talk about him."

"Why?"

"Because he was so important to you. Because I look like him, and I need to know that *you* know I'm not him."

She turned and continued walking slowly. But she pulled her hand gently from his, breaking the connection and making them both conscious of the loss. "All right. What do you want to know?"

"Whatever you feel comfortable telling me."

"I loved him from the time I was ten years old. Is that what you want to hear?"

Adam's voice remained steady. "If it's the truth."

"It is." She drew a breath. "He was out of high school when I started—there were ten years between us—but I wore his ring for four years, and never dated anyone else. We got engaged when I turned eighteen, but Tom insisted I go to college for at least a year before we married.

"So I did. But I lived at home, and we saw each other every weekend." She paused. "I didn't like his job."

"He was a pilot, wasn't he?"

"Yes. He flew cargo planes for a company based here in Richmond. It wasn't usually dangerous work. He said."

"You didn't believe that?"

Rachel shrugged, and her voice was a bit tense. "I had a romantic imagination. So I imagined things. Once or twice I got the feeling there had been close calls, just from something he'd said. But he'd only laugh and tell me not to worry. I did, of course. Worry. I gave him the locket on his twenty-ninth birthday."

"The locket?"

Rachel nodded. "A small gold locket. I had our initials engraved on the outside, and a St. Christopher put inside. To protect him. He had my picture put inside as well."

She paused. "Neither one protected him very well. His plane vanished just a few months later."

They walked in silence a few minutes, and then Adam said quietly, "Did you bury your heart with him, Rachel?"

"I thought I had."

They stopped, and when she turned to face him his hand reached up to touch her cheek again. This time it lingered. "Did you?"

There was a long silence so intense that even the sounds of the garden seemed to have stilled. Then Rachel took a jerky step away from him, that instinctive retreat making her words unnecessary. But she said them anyway. "I don't know. I just don't know, Adam."

A little flatly, he said, "And I look so much like him."

"It isn't something that's going to go away," she reminded him. "You look like Thomas. But Thomas is dead. And I know that."

"But you haven't said good-bye to him, have you, Rachel?"

He didn't wait for a reply, but reached for her hand, tucked it into the crook of his arm, and began walking along the path once more. For several minutes, they walked in silence.

"Adam?"

"Yes?"

"For a long, long time, I never really believed he was gone. For . . . for years I woke up from dreams about him. He was always trying to tell me something, and I could never quite hear him. I finally realized he was trying to say good-bye. And one day the dreams just stopped."

Adam looked down at her, his face without expression. Then he said, "It's all right, Rachel. I understand."

"Do you?" She shook her head a little. "I'm not so sure I do."

Adam didn't respond to that. But a moment later, as they rounded a bend in the path, he stopped suddenly. "What's that?"

She gave him a curious look. "There's a path through the woods to the river. That gate is the way out of the garden."

Adam stared at tall black wrought-iron gates, at the winding path beyond. His voice sounded strange even to him when he said, "I didn't know it was here."

"No, you wouldn't have seen it except from here—or from the river. Adam, is something wrong?"

"No. No, of course not." He got hold of himself, and walked on, putting the gate behind him.

They completed the circuit of the garden in silence, and it wasn't until they'd almost reached the house again that Rachel spoke.

"You aren't a stand-in for a dead man, Adam."

"I'm glad."

"You don't believe me?"

He hesitated. "I don't believe you've said good-bye to him yet, Rachel. Until you do, you can't be sure."

She didn't reply to that. But she didn't remove her hand from his arm, not even when they went inside and a truculent Fiona met them at the door of the sunroom.

"Mr. Graham has been waiting in the front parlor these fifteen minutes and more, Miss Rachel!"

Mildly, she said, "I'm sure he didn't mind, Fiona."

The housekeeper snorted, shot Adam a dark look, and stomped away.

"Makes a lot of noise for such a little thing," he observed.

Rachel couldn't help but smile, but all she said was "If we go this way, we can avoid the furniture blockade."

They did, and shortly afterward walked through the

double doors of the front parlor with Rachel's hand still tucked into the crook of Adam's arm.

Graham didn't like what he saw.

"You two haven't met officially," Rachel said. "Graham, this is—"

"The man who lied to you," Graham snapped.

NINE

Mercy was more than a little worried to find that Nicholas was heading for a decidedly bad part of town.

It hadn't been easy, keeping her small car behind his without making it obvious he was being followed, and as they left the heavier traffic behind, she had to drop farther back to avoid discovery. So she was barely within sight when he finally pulled over to the curb at what looked like a deserted warehouse.

She pulled her car to the curb and killed the engine quickly.

For about ten minutes, nothing happened. Then a tall man who seemed roughly dressed from where Mercy was sitting appeared seemingly out of the shadows of the building and got into Nick's car.

Mercy would have given a year's salary to be a fly in that car.

The meeting lasted no more than five minutes. The

stranger got out of the car and melted once more into the shadows. Nicholas's car pulled away from the curb and went on.

Mercy followed.

"What are you up to?" she muttered to herself, her gaze fixed on that big black car. "Dammit, Nick, what are you up to?"

His actions for the next hour offered Mercy no clue. He met twice more with unsavory-looking men who appeared and disappeared into shadow. These meetings were a bit longer, but still were clearly furtive in nature.

Frustrated, Mercy followed him to yet another seemingly deserted warehouse and parked half a block back from him. This time Nicholas left his car and headed for the warehouse. He didn't look to the left or right.

Mercy didn't actually see him open a door; he just appeared to vanish into the shadows as all his grungy pals had done.

She drummed her fingers on the steering wheel and debated getting out and going to look for him.

The passenger door opened suddenly.

"Hello, love. I hope I didn't make it too difficult for you to keep up."

"What did he lie about?" Rachel asked quietly.

"The man's a convicted felon, Rachel." Graham's voice was heavy with satisfaction. "He served five years in prison."

"Well, since I never asked him if he'd been in prison, I don't see that he lied about it, Graham."

"Rachel, for God's sake!"

"Well, I don't."

Adam looked down at Rachel with a slight smile. He

led her to the sofa facing the fireplace, and when she sat down, he went to the hearth opposite where Graham stood and faced the other man.

"Tell her the rest," Adam said.

For the first time, Graham looked a bit discomfited. "I don't know what you mean."

"Sure you do. Tell her what my crime was, and where I served my time." Adam shoved his hands into the pockets of his pants and lounged back against the mantel.

The physical contrast between the two men was a stark one. Graham, inarguably good-looking and elegant in his business suit, appeared curiously tame standing so near Adam. He lacked Adam's height and visible strength, but it was more than that. Less formally dressed, his hair a bit shaggy, and his pose a lazy one, Adam radiated leashed intensity in the alert tilt of his head and the sharpness of his gaze, and his slight smile was not so much polite as it was inherently dangerous.

For the first time, Rachel saw a man who might well have spent time in a cage.

She looked at Graham, hiding a sudden anxiety. "Well?"

Reluctantly, Graham said, "He was in prison in South America."

"And my crime?" Adam prompted softly.

Through gritted teeth Graham said, "Crimes against the state."

Adam looked at Rachel through shuttered eyes. "That's a nice little euphemism used by tinpot dictators after they've successfully instigated a coup. A blanket charge to throw over any perceived enemy of the new regime. That's what was happening in San Cristo, about a week after I arrived. Since I was there to help close down an American-owned business that the new regime promptly nationalized, and since I spoke out against them, I was perceived as an enemy of the state."

He paused. "The *trial* lasted about five minutes. The sentence was life. I got out early only because the tinpot dictator got himself shot almost five years later, and there was a new regime. One that didn't consider me an enemy of the state." He turned his gaze to Graham. "And I think that's all you need to know, Becket."

"I agree," Rachel said.

Graham frowned at her. "Rachel—"

"Did you bring the lease by for me to sign?"

"Yes."

"Is everything in order? All the I's dotted and T's crossed?"

He sighed. "Yes."

"Then I'll sign it now. And you can drop it off at the agency on your way back to town. I don't want to take up any more of your time." She kept her voice quiet, unwilling to get into any discussion with Graham that would lead to her defending Adam.

Graham shot Adam a look and opened his briefcase on the coffee table to get the lease. "Rachel, listen to me. No matter what his story of the imprisonment is, the fact is that I can't find out anything about his background beyond a few sketchy facts. You know only what he's telling you, and it could all be a pack of lies designed to win your trust."

Rachel signed the lease and handed it back to him. "Thank you for going over this, Graham. As for the rest—I've always depended on you for advice. So what do you advise?"

"Don't trust him."

She looked at Adam, leaning silently against the mantel, then returned her gaze to Graham. "I'll have to make up my own mind about that, Graham."

"Rachel—"

"Well, what else do you expect me to say? He landed in a South American prison through actions that neither of us would consider wrong. Once he got out, he convinced a man we both respected to give him a loan in order to start his own company, and five years later that company is thriving, the loan about to be repaid in full—"

"He says," Graham interrupted.

Adam watched and listened in silence, offering nothing.

Rachel shook her head. "All right—he says. You haven't offered any evidence that he's lying, or even any reason why he would. So far, in fact, you haven't given me any reason at all not to trust Adam, aside from your suspicions. I don't happen to share them."

"Because he looks like Thomas. Don't you see, Rachel? He walked into your life looking like Thomas, and you've given him the benefit of every doubt because of that."

Is that really it? Is that why I trust him? Rachel hesitated, then shook her head. "I think you've said enough, Graham. You can show yourself out."

Graham looked at her for a moment, wondering dimly if she had yet realized what was happening to her. He did. And it was a bitter thing to Graham to see her waking up, coming out of the state that Tom's death had left her in, and to know that where he himself had failed, another man had succeeded.

He hesitated only an instant, knowing also that nothing he could say just then would change what was happening. Not unless he could find evidence that Adam Delafield was not who and what he claimed to be. Graham shot another look at Adam, then gathered up his briefcase and strode from the room.

Still lounging back against the mantel, Adam said quietly, "You were pretty hard on him."

"Was I? Maybe."

"He seems to have your best interests at heart."

"Even so." Rachel looked at him steadily. "I'm sorry."

"About what?"

"Graham's attitude. And . . . about what happened to you. It must have been terrible."

Adam came to the sofa and sat down a couple of feet away, turning toward her. "I want to tell you about it."

"You don't have to."

"I know. But I want to." He smiled slightly. "The way I told your father."

Rachel nodded. "All right."

"I was working as an electrical designer at an engineering company in California." Adam spoke slowly. "In that work, I developed a more efficient version of an electrical component already in wide use. It was sort of like inventing a better mousetrap. There was a built-in demand for the gadget, a huge one. Both the company and I stood to make a lot of money."

Rachel nodded again, and waited.

"What I didn't know at the time was that my superior in the company wanted to take the credit—and the money—for himself. All unsuspecting, I gave him my diagrams to look over. The next day I was handed plane tickets and told to get down to San Cristo, close down our manufacturing plant, and get our people out of there before the rumbles of a coup became reality."

"Why was there a plant down there?"

"Cheap labor. And God knows what kind of tax breaks and kickbacks they'd been granted from the old regime. In any case, there was a plant running three shifts, and dozens of American supervisors and office personnel. I had to get them out."

"You must have been very young for such an assignment."

"I was twenty-five. But I'd traveled a great deal during my college years, I could fly a plane, and I spoke Spanish like a native. At the time, it made perfect sense to me that I was the one to go."

"I see." *Another pilot. Like Dad. And like Thomas.*

Adam shrugged. "Getting the others out was a major headache, but nothing I couldn't handle. The company had sent two planes, one for the people, and a cargo plane for all the equipment I could get out."

She frowned. "This was—ten years ago?"

"Not quite. It was in November of eighty-eight."

Six months after Tom's plane had vanished somewhere in South America. Rachel sighed. "So you got everybody out?"

"Yeah. But my superior had been insistent that I be the last man out, and that I do a final check of the plant to make sure nothing valuable had been left behind. Hell, I could practically smell the army coming, and I still went back there." He paused. "I was barely able to get off a call to the cargo plane and tell the pilot to get out before they grabbed me."

"So the new leader wasn't too happy with you."

"Not much, no. He could have used a lot of the equipment I'd managed to get out of the country. So, he gave me a five-minute trial and sentenced me to life at one of his country clubs."

Rachel winced. "It must have been horrible."

"It wasn't fun." He smiled faintly, but his eyes were still shuttered and he didn't offer details.

Rachel decided not to ask. Instead, she asked another question. "But didn't anyone here try to get you out? An American citizen being held like that on trumped-up charges—"

Adam shook his head. "I had no family. When the president of the company tried to find out what had happened to me, the new dictator in San Cristo claimed I'd been killed. He even had a body to ship home—conveniently burned beyond recognition. Seems the plant caught fire, and I didn't get out in time. Terrible accident." He paused, then added, "There's a grave in California, a nice headstone all paid for by the company. And my name on it."

Rachel shivered. "You mean still?"

"Oh, I went through the official process of having myself declared legally alive again. But nobody got around to digging up that poor bastard and finding out who he was. Another enemy of the state, I guess."

"My God."

Adam lifted a hand as though to touch her, then let it fall. "When I got home, I found out that my former superior had made a fortune on the gadget I'd invented, him and the company. There was no proof, of course, just my word against his—and five years later, nobody believed me. Nobody wanted to believe me.

"They offered me a job, but I couldn't take it. To prevent me from suing for five years' back pay, they offered a cash settlement—which I did take. It wasn't enough to start my own company, but it was enough to live on while I drew up the plans for a new design I'd dreamed up in prison. That was about the time I called looking for Nick, and talked to Duncan Grant instead. You know the rest."

"How did you know Nick?" Rachel asked. "I've wondered."

"We met while I was in college. I was bumming around in Europe the summer after my sophomore year. Nick was"—Adam eyed her thoughtfully for a moment, clearly hesitant, then sighed—"I gather you didn't know he had done some intelligence work for the government?"

Rachel blinked. "I certainly didn't."

"He'll skin me if he finds out I told you. I don't know if he likes to keep his past murky or if he feels he should because of the government work. Whichever it is, I've learned to respect his wishes. So, for Christ's sake, don't tell him I told you about the cloak-and-dagger stuff."

"How did he get involved in something like that?"

"You'd have to ask him. All I know is that during that particular summer, he was involved in a . . . situation in Rome. Don't ask me for the details. I'm still hazy on them, and I was there. The only thing I can tell you for certain is that totally by accident I found myself caught up in an international incident involving a Turk, two Frenchmen, an Italian, and Nick. And everybody had a gun but me."

Rachel didn't know whether to laugh or gasp. "What happened?"

"I got shot." He smiled. "It wasn't too serious, but it so happened if I hadn't stopped the bullet, Nick would have been in deep, deep trouble. Somehow, he managed to finish his assignment successfully, and get a wounded American back home without arousing too many questions."

"And after that he owed you a favor."

"A big one." Adam shrugged. "We kept in touch for the next few years, while I finished college and started working with the company. Saw each other a few times.

But it wasn't until after the San Cristo trouble that I called him to collect on the favor."

"And got Dad instead."

"And got Duncan instead."

Rachel shook her head. "That's . . . quite a story."

"I'm sure Graham Becket would say it's all lies. I know he's suspicious of me. But he couldn't find anything much in my background because there isn't anything to find, Rachel."

"I know."

"How can you?"

"Because Dad trusted you. And because I do."

Once again Adam lifted a hand and touched her face gently. His own face was very still, revealing nothing of what he was feeling. "Don't trust so quickly, Rachel."

"How can I not?"

His hand fell, and his smile was a bit strained. "It might be better for us both if you didn't."

"Why?"

Adam shook his head. "Never mind. Would you like to return to Duncan's scraps of paper? We still have some time today, and we need to find those answers."

Rachel wasn't at all sure she liked the way this conversation was ending, but Adam was already getting up, and she had little choice but to follow suit. It bothered her, though.

It bothered her that Adam wasn't quite comfortable with her trust.

"Okay, I admit it was wrong." Mercy felt like a scolded little girl and Nicholas hadn't even said anything yet. He just sat there behind his desk, staring at her. She wanted to throw something at him. Other than his unpleasant smile and sardonic comment when he'd surprised her in the car, all he'd said was a brief order to meet him back at the bank.

So, there she was. And there he was.

And things were not looking good.

"I'm sorry, Nick. Is that what you want to hear?"

"I want to hear a reason, Mercy. Just what the bloody hell do you think you were doing?"

"My curiosity got the better of me. You were being so damned cryptic and—and I just wanted to find out what you were up to."

"It didn't occur to you to ask?"

She sat up straighter. "You would have told me?"

"No." He smiled for the first time. "But you might have made the attempt before resorting to TV-private-eye tactics."

"Dammit, Nick!" She scowled at him.

"Mercy, I asked you to trust me. You said you did."

"Yeah, well—I do. Almost."

"Almost is not good enough." His pale eyes were very serious now. "Either you trust me, or you don't. If you trust me, then believe that I know what I'm doing."

"Nick, I believe you know what you're doing. I just want to know what that is."

"I'm not going to tell you."

"Why not?" she almost wailed.

Nicholas smiled again, but his eyes remained grave. "Because you have a lousy poker face, love. And I can't afford to risk the chance that the wrong person is a better card player than you are."

"Well, if that isn't cryptic, I don't know what is." She glared at him. "Just tell me this—are you up to something illegal?"

"Would it surprise you if I said yes?" He sounded honestly curious.

Mercy thought about it. "I don't know. For a good enough reason, I think you'd go to just about any lengths. Maybe even breaking the law. Is that what you're doing?"

"No. As a matter of fact, I'm playing strictly by the rules." Now he sounded mocking.

Mercy wasn't reassured. "How about the law?"

"The law is on my side."

She had a feeling he had somehow evaded her question, but she wasn't sure exactly how. She sighed. "And I'm supposed to just accept that."

"I wish you would, yes."

She hesitated, then blurted out, "Just tell me you aren't doing anything that might hurt Rachel."

Nicholas leaned back in his chair and laced his fingers together over his flat middle. "I am not doing anything that might hurt Rachel." His voice was level, every word precisely pronounced. He wasn't smiling any longer.

"I'm sorry."

"Why? You said you didn't quite trust me. Now I know what you think I'm capable of."

This was going from bad to worse. He was angry.

He was very angry.

"I didn't say you were. I *asked* if you were."

"Somehow, I don't get the distinction."

On the defensive and floundering, Mercy said, "Well, there is one. To me. I'm not saying you'd deliberately hurt Rachel. But some of these deals of yours are incredibly complex, and the results might not be good for her interests."

"Oh, I see. It's her *interests* you're worried about. I thought I was being accused of blowing up a building with her in it."

"Nick, for God's sake! I never even thought—"

"Didn't you?"

She stared at him and, very quietly, said, "No. Not that. Never that."

"You just thought I was the sort of ruthless bastard who'd take advantage of her."

After a moment, Mercy got to her feet. "Look, this isn't getting us anywhere. You're mad and I'm getting mad. I'm going to go to my office and finish up for the day. Then I'm going home."

"Good idea," he said flatly.

She turned around and left the office, closing the door with exquisite quiet behind her.

Nick stared after her. Then, softly, he said, "Shit."

Adam sat back and raked a hand through his hair. "Okay, so we think most of this is not going to help us a bit."

Rachel nodded, then reached out to tap three small scraps of paper lying alone before them. "These are the only ones that look even remotely helpful. And we're not sure they mean anything. Just the same initials."

Written on small, irregularly sized pieces of paper in Duncan Grant's neat hand, the notes were as cryptic as any clue ever left to a puzzle.

Only the initials printed there offered a possible connection to what Rachel had found in the notebooks.

RS called.
Wants my opinion
on the new design.

LM called from TX.
Return call soonest.

JW called.
Have to put him off.
Must consider what to do.

"They look like just ordinary notes to himself," Adam mused. "What to do about phone calls, or what they were about. He doesn't say whether he means to offer an opinion on the new design mentioned in the first note. In the second, he means to return the call, no subject noted, but we can assume LM lives or works in Texas. And in the third he seems . . . hesitant, or reluctant."

Rachel looked at the notebook open at her elbow. "If it's the same JW, he's the one who got the big loan. Five million."

"The initials don't mean anything to you?"

She shook her head. "No. We don't even know if this JW is local. LM is apparently in Texas, you were in California. Dad traveled a lot, so these people could be from anywhere in the world."

"This is not narrowing the field," Adam muttered.

"No kidding."

He sighed. "Well, we haven't delved into the other desk drawers yet. Or that secretary upstairs. Maybe we'll find more scraps of paper that make these mean something."

"Maybe." Rachel started to say something else, but then Fiona opened the door and stuck her head in.

"Supper in ten minutes, Miss Rachel." She sent a hostile look toward Adam. "I suppose *he's* invited?"

"Yes, he is," Rachel replied serenely. "Set another place, please, Fiona."

"I don't want to wear out my welcome," Adam said when the housekeeper had withdrawn, muttering.

"You won't." She smiled at him. "You've been helping me all day. The least I can do is feed you."

"I'd love to stay, but I'll leave right after we eat. You need to get some rest this evening, Rachel. Put all this out of your mind. Curl up with a good book or something."

"That could be a plan."

"In the meantime," he said, "is there a copier around?"

"In that cabinet over there. It pulls out. Why?"

"If it's all right with you, I'm going to make copies of these notes, and the relevant pages of the notebooks. I'd like to go over them again tonight, think about them. You should put the originals in a safe place."

"I have a safe in my room."

"Sounds good. May I?"

"Of course." While he was making the copies, Rachel gathered up the scraps of paper they had decided were irrelevant and put them in a file box. "I'll keep these a bit longer. Until we're sure."

"That's probably wise." He handed her the original notes, notebooks, and one copy of each. "I made you copies too, just in case." He folded his set of copies and went to put that in the pocket of his jacket, which he'd left lying over a chair.

"I'll take this stuff up to my room. And show you where you can wash up before supper."

"Will Fiona examine my fingernails?"

"She just might."

Adam followed her from the room, chuckling.

She showed him to the upstairs guest bathroom across the hall from her bedroom, and then went into her room to put the notes and notebooks away and make use of her own bathroom.

It had been so long since she'd used her safe—hidden

in a conventional way behind a painting on one wall—she had almost forgotten the combination, but a minute of thought brought it to mind. There was nothing in the safe at the moment. She had never cared much for jewelry, and so had only a few basic gold pieces she kept in a jewelry box on her dresser. Her mother's jewelry was in a vault at the bank.

She put the notes and notebooks away, then went into her bathroom to wash up. As she stood before the vanity running a brush through her hair, she found herself thinking about Adam and his behavior today.

In the garden he had been so intense. Asking her to talk about Thomas. Asking if she had buried her heart with him.

He wouldn't be a stand-in for a dead man; she understood that. He knew that she had not yet said good-bye to Tom.

Rachel put down the brush and went to the doorway of the bathroom, gazing into her bedroom without really looking at anything there. She thought that nearly five years in a hellish South American prison would have changed any man. But how had it changed Adam? He had gone in an idealistic young man, unaware that he was about to be betrayed, his design and years of his life stolen from him. How had he come out?

What else had he lost there?

"Ready to go down?" He stood in the doorway of the bedroom, smiling at her.

"I'm ready," she said, and went to join him.

TEN

It was still well before midnight, but The Tavern was fairly crowded on this Monday night, and at least half the patrons were well on their way to getting falling-down drunk. Even so, the drunkest of them made way when Nicholas walked through.

He found Adam sitting in one of the booths, two beers sweating on the rickety table before him.

Joining him, Nicholas said, "Becket called me late this afternoon, breathing fire. He can't believe the ex-con story didn't wash with Rachel. So she bought your version?"

Adam nodded.

"Well, just so you know, Becket is hell-bent on finding something damaging in your past. Can he?"

"Not if you did your job."

"I always do my job."

"Then I'm clean."

Nicholas picked up his glass and sipped the beer for a

moment. "Okay. We'll assume he comes up with zip. It won't stop him, Adam. In fact, it won't hold him for long. He sees Rachel slipping away from him. And he does not want to let her go."

"Maybe I can use that to distract him."

"Maybe. Dangerous, though. Jealousy can be a violent thing."

"You mean if he can't have her, no man can?" Adam frowned. "Would he go that far?"

"I honestly don't know."

"I'll have to stick close to her."

Nicholas smiled wryly. "Like you haven't been up till now?"

"I know what I'm doing."

"Do you?"

"Yes." Adam met those pale eyes unflinchingly. "I know what I'm doing, Nick."

"You planned carefully, didn't you?" Nicholas looked at him thoughtfully, unsmiling. "From the very beginning. Including putting me where I'd do you the most good."

"I just made a suggestion," Adam said lightly. "We both know nobody's going to *put* you anywhere you don't want to be."

"Richmond wasn't even on my long list."

"Maybe not, but it all worked out. Didn't it?"

"For me? Sure. For you?"

"It will. Eventually."

"But what will it cost you?"

Adam shrugged, and his voice roughened. "Like I said. I know what I'm doing."

Nick accepted that with a nod. "Well, it's your hand to play out. In the meantime, on *my* side of the table, things are getting tight. Without Rachel's shares, I can't control enough of the bank's assets to make Jordan Walsh eager to do business with me."

"If she knew what you were doing—"

Nicholas shook his head. "No. No way. We play this out without involving her. Without involving . . . anyone else. If we go down, we go down alone."

Adam nodded slowly. "I agreed to that from the start."

"So—I have to find a way around having control of Rachel's shares."

"What are you doing right now?"

"Bluffing."

"And if Walsh calls the bluff?"

"Damned if I know," Nicholas said. "I'll figure out something."

There was a moment of silence, and then Adam drew a sheaf of papers from inside his jacket. "Take a look at this."

Nicholas bent forward over the table, squinting in the dim light to study the copies Adam had made earlier at Rachel's. "JW," he said softly. "Unless you believe in coincidence—Jordan Walsh."

"That was my take. If so, he was on the hook to Duncan for five million."

Nicholas looked over the remaining copies, including the ones from the notebooks. He shook his head. "I knew Duncan was handing out money, but I had no idea it was this extensive."

"Neither did I. He left Rachel with a hell of a financial headache."

"Maybe not. When all his papers have been gone through, you may discover that he planned carefully to make sure she wasn't harmed by this. I never met a smarter man about finances."

"We'll see. There's still plenty to go through at the house."

"And Rachel is welcoming your help?"

"I think so. I was invited back for tomorrow."

Nicholas sat back and looked at him for a moment, then tapped the papers on the scarred table between them. "You do realize that Walsh is just a possibility? That any one of these three people could have enough to hide to want to make these loans disappear?"

"I know that. But you have to admit, finding initials matching Walsh's name tells us we're on the right track."

"I hate to admit anything. And there is one huge question about this, if the five-million loan was made to Walsh."

"Why."

Nicholas nodded. "Why. Duncan wouldn't have done business with the man. Especially not a handshake deal."

"So?"

"So there's more to this than we know about. Maybe a lot more."

"And in the meantime, someone wants Rachel out of the way."

"So it seems."

Adam scowled at him. "I'm not happy about that, Nick."

"Do you think I am?"

"For all I know—"

"Don't even finish that sentence."

After a moment, Adam nodded. "Okay, okay. I'm a little tense about the subject."

"No shit."

"Look, keeping Rachel occupied in going through Duncan's private papers is also keeping her close to home, and right now that house looks like the only haven she's got. So she's safe—and out of the way. But she's leased the property on Queen Street, and she's going to want to get to work on her boutique. She'll be out in the open, Nick. And that means trouble."

"I know, I know."

"We're running out of time."

"Then we'll have to pick up the pace, won't we?"

Adam said, "There's something else."

"Oh, great. What?"

"Max Galloway's in Richmond."

Nicholas said softly, "Son of a bitch."

"Yeah."

"A wild card." Nicholas shook his head in disgust. "Are you ever involved in *anything* where a wild card doesn't turn up?"

"Not so you'd notice."

"This is getting old, Adam."

"Tell me about it. And don't shoot the messenger. I didn't invite the bastard to visit, you know."

"Any idea why he's here?"

"We haven't talked. But I'd be willing to lay you good odds that he's here to even the score."

"I don't suppose you could ask him to wait his turn. Maybe put off revenge until next year?"

Adam laughed shortly. "Not likely. As long as I watch my back, though, he shouldn't be able to get close. Sneaking up from behind is his favorite tactic."

Nicholas sighed. "Okay. So that's another complication in an already dizzying situation."

"Agreed."

"I'll see what I can do. In the meantime, you be sure and watch your back."

Adam nodded. "Yeah." He paused, then added absently, "By the way, I was supposed to ask you if you told anybody about Rachel's plans for the boutique. You didn't, did you?"

"Not a soul. So unless Becket did—or somebody at the house, I suppose—you've got a very short list of people who could have mentioned it to that real estate agent. Always assuming, of course, that it *was* mentioned, and she didn't say so just to cover her ass."

"I hadn't even thought about that."

"That's your trouble, Adam. You assume people tell you the truth."

"And you assume they lie."

Nicholas smiled. "That assumption, my friend, has saved my skin many times. And yours, once or twice."

"It's a hell of a way to live, Nick."

"Don't waste any time feeling sorry for me. My life is just the way I want it."

"I'm glad. Mine could use some work."

"Then after we get this situation taken care of, work on it."

"More cheap advice."

"Which is the easiest kind to take." Nicholas pushed his half-finished beer away and slid out of the booth.

"One more thing," Adam said casually.

"Yeah?"

Adam cleared his throat and sent Nick a somewhat guarded look. "In the course of my confession earlier today, I sort of mentioned that you'd done some work for the government."

"Oh, you did, did you?"

"Sorry. I guess I got caught up in the narrative."

"Don't get caught up again," Nicholas warned grimly.

"I won't. And I doubt Rachel would say anything about it, except to you or me."

"Sometimes," Nicholas said, "I wish you'd never stepped in front of that bullet in Rome."

"I imagine so."

"Just be careful, will you?"

"I will. You too."

"Always." Nicholas turned and walked back through the bar, along the wide path drunken men made for him.

The warm day had become a chilly night. Nicholas stood outside The Tavern and let out a long breath, watching it turn to mist. A crash from behind him in the bar made him look over his shoulder briefly, but he didn't go back inside to find out what had happened.

Despite his propensity for stopping bullets meant for other people, Adam was more than capable of taking care of himself.

But the deck was stacked against them this time. They were running out of time. And, as usual, there was a wild card in the game.

Max Galloway.

Nicholas swore, watching his baleful words turn to mist. Then he walked slowly to his car. He got in and started the engine, but for a long while just sat gazing off in the direction of Mercy's apartment, his hand idle on the gearshift.

"I'm a fool."

He pulled away from the curb, and at the corner hesitated again.

Then he turned the car toward Mercy's apartment.

"I'm a goddamned idiot."

• • •

It was still a little before midnight, but Mercy was nevertheless surprised to look through the peephole and find Nicholas at her door—considering the way they'd said good-bye at the office. But she opened the door and stood looking at him, wondering if she would ever be able to read his face. Not tonight, that was for sure.

"Hi."

"Hi. May I come in?"

"Sure you want to? I mean, I might accuse you of trying to blow up my best friend."

"Not without evidence, I hope."

She stepped back and gestured for him to come in, but kept her face expressionless. She hoped. Since she hadn't been expecting him, or company of any kind, she was already dressed for bed in a long, football-jersey-style sleepshirt, which she felt put her at a distinct disadvantage.

But at least she wasn't wearing her damned fuzzy pig slippers.

"I was having a glass of wine," she told him. "Want one?"

"Please."

She left him in the living room, returning a couple of minutes later with the glasses to find he'd loosened his tie but hadn't removed his jacket, and had not sat down. Definitely not the usual drill. Nicholas never seemed to take their relationship for granted, but they had reached a level of ease with each other, and he usually made himself at home in her apartment.

Then again, they'd never gotten as angry with each other as they had that day.

She handed him his glass and then curled up in the big armchair at a right angle to the fireplace, leaving the sofa for him. "Have a seat."

He did, and sipped his wine. He didn't take his eyes

off her. "I suppose I should apologize," he said. "But I'll be damned if I know why."

"If you don't know, it wouldn't be worth much."

"I got mad. I had reason. I wasn't the only one at fault, Mercy. You had no business following me."

"Granted. I apologized for that."

"And then asked me if I was trying to kill Rachel."

"That's not what I asked. And I won't apologize for it," Mercy said steadily. "You ask for my trust and offer nothing. I've known you for five years, Nick, and I don't have a clue what you're about outside the walls of the bank. Are you trustworthy in business? Absolutely. Honest? I'd have to say yes. Good with finances? No question. Enigmatic and secretive as hell? You bet. Do I know your favorite color? No. The music you like? No. Whether you would do something not in Rachel's best interests *for a good enough reason*? No. I don't know that, Nick. So I asked."

"You never asked before," he said. "Not about my favorite color, or the music I like. Or what I'm about outside the walls of the bank. It didn't seem important to you, Mercy. You didn't ask, I didn't answer."

"You didn't want me to ask."

He was silent for a moment, his gaze now fixed on the wineglass that he rolled back and forth slowly between his palms. "Maybe."

"Maybe? Be honest, Nick. You weren't about to let me get that close."

"Is that what you think?"

"I think it's obvious."

He set his wineglass down on the table and got to his feet. Then he crossed the space between them and went down on one knee beside her chair, his arms reaching for her. "I want you as close as I can get you," he said, his voice low, almost harsh.

Mercy wasn't at all sure she would have protested, but in any case she wasn't given time to say a word. He was kissing her, his arms so tight around her that it was almost painful. She supposed he must have taken her glass away from her, or maybe she'd dropped it, but either way her hands were free, and her fingers were tangled in his hair.

Against her mouth he murmured huskily, "My favorite color is green."

Mercy tried to catch her breath when his lips left hers, and she tipped her head back when he began to explore her throat. "It is?"

"I love classical music, especially piano concertos."

"Do . . . you?"

"And I can't think of a good enough reason to do anything that would hurt Rachel."

She tightened her fingers in his hair and tugged until he drew back and looked at her.

"Good," she whispered.

Nicholas picked her up and carried her to the bedroom.

"You are a wonderful lover," Mercy observed a long time later.

"I know."

She grinned at him. "Modest, aren't you?"

Raised on an elbow beside her with his free hand lying on her stomach, Nicholas smiled slightly. "I figured out by the time I was sixteen that if I wanted women, I'd have to be good enough in bed for them to look past this ugly mug of mine."

That startled her. She was wary of asking, but raised her brows in a questioning expression.

Surprising her again by answering readily, Nicholas said, "When you're a teenage boy enslaved by your hormones, you'll do just about anything to get laid. Girls my age wouldn't look twice, not even on a bet. But I was lucky. There was an older woman in my neighborhood who was interested in things other than looks. She wanted a young lover, I needed a teacher. It lasted about a year. She taught me how to please a woman, and gave me confidence in myself. I'll always be grateful to her."

Mercy reached up a hand and slid her fingers into his dark hair. It was his one beauty, thick and shining, a little longer than was fashionable, incredibly sensuous and silky to the touch. "I imagine there have been quite a few women since your teacher."

"A few. I'm forty, Mercy. And I've been on my own since I was seventeen. There's a lot of road behind me."

"No relationships? Just women along the way?"

"More or less. I've never lived with a woman. Never fathered a child as far as I know. Until I came to Richmond, I'd never spent more than a year in any one place."

"You never wanted a family?"

"I never thought I'd have one." He shrugged, and his voice was not quite careless when he said, "I'm a realist, love. Being good in bed is one thing, but the prospect of spending thirty or forty years staring at this mug across a breakfast table is enough to daunt any woman. And that's okay. I don't mind being alone. Sometimes I even prefer it."

"Do you?"

He smiled. "One thing my life has taught me is to live day to day. And night to night. Tonight I have you. A beautiful, warm, giving woman beside me in bed. Some men have passed through their entire lives never knowing that."

Mercy wondered why her throat was hurting, why it was difficult to hold her voice steady. "We've never talked like this before. You've never talked like this before."

"You never asked, love." He caught her hand against the side of his face and pressed his lips to her palm.

Somewhat fiercely, she said, "You're damned sexy, in case you didn't know that."

He chuckled, the bedroom rumble of the laugh much softer than his usual harsh one. "I'm glad you think so."

"And I've looked at your face across many a breakfast table. It hasn't bothered me so far."

"I'm glad of that too." He leaned down and kissed her, his lips playing lightly with hers in a teasing seduction that instantly sent her senses whirling and her entire body throbbing.

Mercy put her other hand up and pulled at his hard shoulders until she could feel his weight on her. He was wonderfully heavy.

And he definitely knew how to please a woman, how to touch and taste and caress, how to bring her body alive. More than knowledge, though, was infinite patience and empathy. He had very quickly learned all Mercy's most sensitive spots, learned to read her responses and build her desire until she burned in his arms.

But for the first time, Mercy didn't allow herself to be merely a passive lover, accepting his astonishing skill and the control it demanded of him. She didn't want him to feel that he had to give some extraordinary performance, that he had to remain detached, critical of what he was doing, striving to be the perfect lover. She wanted a mutual passion.

And she knew how to get it.

He wasn't the only one who had learned from a lover. Mercy had paid attention as well.

Her fingers and lips found the most sensitive spots on his hard body, and she used all the skill and passion at her command to arouse him past his ability to control what he felt, to push him beyond his detachment. She used the fire in herself to make him burn.

She had the dim awareness that what she was doing was dangerous, that Nicholas with his control in splinters just might be more than she or any woman could handle. But she didn't care.

For once, just this once, he was going to be as ensnared by her as she was by him.

"God, Mercy, what are you doing to me?" His voice was hoarse, almost gone, and his fingers bit into her shoulders.

"Making love to you," she murmured huskily. "You don't want me to stop, do you?" Her lips moved slowly down his hard stomach.

He groaned. "Christ, no."

Mercy had learned a lot. And by the time his control shattered and his heavy body covered hers, she was so wildly aroused herself, she could only hold him and cry out in a pleasure so intense she wasn't sure she would survive it.

And didn't care.

The lamp on her nightstand burned low, but Nicholas didn't bother to turn it off. He didn't want to let go of her long enough to move.

They were on their sides facing away from the light, curled up back to front. Spooning, he thought it was called. Mercy's silky back pressed against his chest, her warm bottom curved into his loins. His arms were wrapped around her.

She was sleeping.

Careful not to wake her, he rubbed his cheek against her hair and breathed in the sweet scent. He loved the way she smelled. Her hair, her skin. He wanted to absorb the smell of her, make it his own.

Make a memory.

Something had changed tonight. He had been so careful, and still it had happened. She had made it happen, had made him lose control. So now she knew.

She had to know.

It was only a matter of time now. Maybe not tomorrow or next week, but it was inevitable. He had known that from their first night together.

He rubbed his cheek gently against her hair and listened to the soft sounds of her breathing.

Making another memory.

It was very quiet.

All she heard was that soft rustling sound, the sound that made her skin crawl and terrified without definition.

Rachel walked on.

She didn't know where she was going.

She was in a building, one with many hallways and rooms, and doors that were locked. She tried some of the doors, but most remained stubbornly closed. Then one opened for her, and she blinked in surprise.

Just a brick wall with a mask hanging on it.

Rachel closed the door and walked on. She passed by a room that held odd lights and shadows, and when she paused to look in, she found more masks. Hanging on the walls. Dangling from the ceiling.

Rachel walked on.

Another room she looked into had windows covered with brown paper, blocking the light.

She went on, and around the next corner there was a door that seemed to have a great deal of light behind it. At first Rachel thought it was locked, but she tugged and tugged, and finally it opened.

For a moment, she was blinded by all the light pouring from the room. That's all there was—light.

"Rachel."

She took a step back.

"Rachel." He stepped out of the light, smiling at her.

Adam. Happily, she held out a hand to him.

He took off Adam's face, and it was Thomas.

Rachel's hand fell, and she took another step back, suddenly frightened.

"Don't trust him, Rachel." Thomas took off his face, and it was Adam again.

"Don't trust him."

The Thomas mask fell to the floor, and when she looked down at it, it was horribly broken, the ragged edges dripping blood. . . .

Rachel woke up with a cry tearing free of her throat. Her heart was thundering, her breathing so hoarse that each gasp stabbed her.

She sat there, her knees drawn up and her arms wrapped around them, shivering, staring around at the morning-bright room, trying to reassure herself that it had been only a dream.

Slowly, her fear and panic faded, but anxicty lingered. She had never in her life dreamed like this. Masks.

Thomas and Adam, seemingly interchangeable, one or both of them warning her not to trust . . . someone.

Who?

Was it only her own subconscious warning her to be very sure of her feelings for both men—the living and the dead?

Or was it a different kind of warning?

ELEVEN

hen Rachel came back into her bedroom after her shower, she paused while getting dressed and gazed at the yellow rose in the bud vase on her nightstand. It should have been wilting at least a little, she thought.

It wasn't.

She reached out and touched a silky petal, then withdrew her hand and stared at her fingers. On two of them were crystal drops. As if the flower were so fresh, it still held morning dew.

Rachel sank down on the side of her bed and stared at the rose. Flowers didn't just appear out of nowhere and then freshen themselves every night. So there had to be an explanation.

Except she couldn't think of one.

Even if there had been nothing else, Rachel would have been unsettled. Added to her dream, it was profoundly disturbing.

"Don't trust him, Rachel."

Dreams were seldom straightforward, instead presenting symbols and signs that had to be interpreted based on what was going on in one's life at that moment. She knew that. So what was her subconscious trying to tell her? Not to trust Adam? Or not to trust her growing feelings for him?

Rachel didn't know, and not knowing was painful.

She finished dressing and went down to breakfast, pleased to find that Mercy had stopped by, as she sometimes did. Their lives had been so busy that they had not had much time to talk lately, but during the past weeks Mercy had made it a habit to stop by once every few days for coffee and conversation.

On this morning, Mercy was a bit preoccupied, but she did note a change in her friend. "Bad night?" she asked as she joined Rachel at the table.

Rachel grimaced. "Does it show?"

"Yes," Mercy replied slowly. "It does."

"Just unsettling dreams," Rachel said.

"About?"

Rachel hesitated, then shrugged. "Tom. Adam."

"You still dream about Tom?"

"I hadn't for a long time. But lately . . ."

"Since Adam came?"

Rachel nodded. "I guess my subconscious is trying to work out how I feel about them both. Adam's coming over this morning, so you may see him, Mercy. Be warned. He's the image of Tom."

"Maybe that's it," Mercy murmured.

"What?"

"Why you're different."

"I didn't know I was."

Mercy smiled. "Look in the mirror. It isn't a drastic

change, but this morning you look a lot like that girl I knew as a teenager. Your whole face seems more alive somehow. Expressive of what you're feeling."

Rachel knew that Tom's death had changed her. What she had not realized was that Adam's arrival had wrought another change. "And you think it's because Adam looks like Tom?"

"Isn't it possible? You lost the love of your life, and ten years later his double shows up. I can only imagine that he would be easy to love."

Rachel gave herself a moment, sipping her coffee, then spoke slowly. "I can't deny that Adam looking so much like Tom might have influenced me in the beginning."

"Might have?"

"All right—did. But, Mercy, I know he isn't Tom. He looks like him, even sounds like him, but there's something in Adam I never saw or sensed in Tom."

"What?"

"A toughness. A danger. Tom was always more careless and carefree than anything else. Friendly, charming. You never got the feeling that Tom could be dangerous, that there was anything especially powerful or tough inside him." Rachel shrugged. "He loved fast cars and fast planes, and he laughed more than he frowned. He'd make promises blithely, with every intention of keeping them, but somehow . . ."

"Somehow they always got broken."

A little hesitantly, Rachel looked at Tom's sister. "He always tried to keep his promises, I know that."

Mercy smiled. "Of course he did. He was my brother, Rachel, and I loved him. But he was a lot like our father. His charm took him through life, and it succeeded so well for him that he never really had to work at anything. Never had to fight for anything that mattered to him."

"You've never said anything like that before."

"You weren't ready to hear it." Mercy shook her head. "He loved you, and I like to believe he would have made you a good husband, but those fast cars and fast planes would have kept him away from you a lot. Just the way they've kept Dad away from Mom."

Rachel had been vaguely aware of Tom and Mercy's parents as a child, and had gotten to know them a bit better during her engagement to Tom, but she had never really considered them as a couple. Thinking about it now, she realized that Alex Sheridan traveled a great deal and was seldom home, and that Ruth Sheridan—like her own mother had—occupied her time with charities and other social duties and responsibilities. To all appearances, it seemed a content marriage, just as her own parents' marriage had seemed content. On the surface.

"I never thought," she said slowly.

Mercy's smile held a touch of ruefulness. "Charming men have a way of discouraging thought."

Rachel looked at her. "Is that why you've tended to date men who were—"

"Not charming?" Mercy laughed. "I guess you could say that. I learned to value other qualities more." Then she sobered and gazed at her friend steadily. "The point is that you can't believe you're being disloyal to Tom because Adam has come into your life. Whether anything develops between you or not, Tom shouldn't be part of the equation. He had his share of faults, just like the rest of us, and you have no way of knowing—really knowing—if the two of you would have been happy together. But even that isn't important. He's gone, Rachel. Let him go."

Rachel managed a smile. "That's easy for you to say. You haven't met Adam yet."

"Looks can be deceptive, as the man said. At least, I

think it was a man. Anyway, just keep reminding yourself that Adam is not Tom. Sooner or later you're bound to get them separated."

"Umm. I hope you're right."

"I am. Which entitles me to ask one nosy question."

"That being?"

"Why is Adam Delafield coming over this morning?"

Rachel's hesitation was brief. "To help me go through Dad's private papers."

Mercy raised an eyebrow. "Oh? Rache, I hate to sound too much like Graham Becket, but is that a good idea?"

"I don't know," Rachel replied frankly. "Yesterday I would have said I trusted him. In fact, I did say it. Today . . . I just don't know."

"Then maybe you should ask him not to come. Give yourself a little more time to make up your mind about him. With everything that's happened to you recently, it would probably be a good idea."

Rachel shook her head. "No. Dad trusted him, Mercy. He trusted him enough to lend him a lot of money on a handshake."

"You're sure of that?"

"Reasonably sure. Maybe as sure as I'll ever be. In any case, I can't see how his helping me would be a mistake on my part."

"You hope."

Rachel sighed. "Yeah. I hope."

There didn't seem to be much to say after that, and in a few minutes Mercy took her leave. She was preoccupied once again as she walked toward her car, but that abstraction vanished as she watched a strange car pull up beside her own—and the living image of her dead brother get out.

"My God," she whispered. Until that moment "he looks like Tom" had been a statement she only vaguely understood, but now Rachel's confusion became all too clear.

He saw her, saw her shock, and came toward her slowly. His expression was as enigmatic as Nick's had ever been, and that veiled look sat oddly, she thought, on her brother's open face. The disparity freed her from the paralysis of astonishment.

"My God," she repeated.

He stopped an arm's length away and slid his hands into the pockets of his jacket. "You're Mercy Sheridan," he said. "Rachel described you."

Tom's voice. Yet not quite. "And she described you. But I didn't . . . quite believe her."

"I'm sorry," he said. "I know it must be a shock."

"You could say that. You could certainly say that." Mercy shook her head, her eyes fixed on his face. "You really could almost be his twin."

"So I've been told."

"No wonder Rachel is . . ." She didn't finish that sentence, and if there was any reaction from Adam, it was so subtle, she missed it. Mercy drew a breath. "Well. I would say it's nice to meet you, but you'll have to let me get used to the idea."

"I understand."

She wondered if he did. "Rachel's expecting you. And I have to get to work. So—I guess I'll see you again."

"I hope so," he said, the words conventional and his tone light. He stepped back onto the walkway and watched her until she reached her car and got in. Then he turned and headed toward the house.

Mercy had a lot on her mind these days, but the shock of Adam's appearance stayed with her all the way to the bank. And she wasn't sure which bothered her more. That Adam looked so much like her dead brother, or that his familiar face held a secretiveness Tom's had never displayed.

"Here's something." Rachel was at her father's desk, going through the contents of the bottom drawer while Adam sat on the sofa with the contents of the other remaining desk drawer spread out on the coffee table before him. "Another scrap of paper with a name and phone number, and the notation *call about JW.* Those were the initials beside that largest loan." She kept her tone casual, just as she had since he had arrived.

"Is it a Richmond number?" Adam asked.

"There's no area code, so it must be."

"What's the name?"

"John Elliot. Doesn't ring a bell with me."

Adam came to the desk and looked at the paper for a moment, then reached for the phone. "One way to find out."

He punched the number, listened for a few moments with his brows rising, then gave his and Rachel's names and her number and asked that the call be returned to either of them as soon as possible.

"Voice mail?" Rachel asked as he hung up.

"Yeah." He frowned. "John Elliot is out of town for an unspecified length of time. Rachel, he's a private investigator."

She leaned back slowly in the desk chair and stared at him. "So Dad wanted this JW investigated?"

"Looks like it."

"But the bank has an investigator on retainer. Why would Dad use another one?"

"Maybe because this was one of his private loans."

Rachel shook her head. "There's no date on the note.

We have no way of knowing if this JW was investigated before or after Dad lent him the money. Or even at all. It could be a plan he was never able to put into motion. Until John Elliot gets his messages and calls us . . ."

"We just have another question."

Rachel took the note and said, "So I guess we just copy this, put a copy in the file with the rest of our bits and pieces—and keep looking while we wait for Elliot to call."

Adam perched on the corner of the desk. "You sound discouraged."

"Well, it's like putting together a jigsaw puzzle when we don't know what the picture is supposed to be. *And* half the pieces are missing. I'm afraid I'm going to look right at something vitally important and not realize it. Why the hell did Dad have to be so cryptic?"

"He was a very . . . discreet man." Adam smiled.

"To a fault."

"If you want to put off finishing this, Rachel—"

"No, no. It has to be done."

"Yes, but not necessarily today. I know this is hard for you, and not just because we're putting together a jigsaw puzzle. Maybe we need to take a break. Why don't I buy you lunch, and then maybe we can take a closer look at that store you leased yesterday."

Rachel smiled slightly. "You're not going to let me off the leash, are you?"

He grimaced. "That obvious?"

"That you don't want me leaving this house by myself? Oh, yes, it's fairly obvious." *But is it for my safety, Adam? Or for yours?*

"Rachel, until we know more than we do now, it's better to be safe than sorry. That explosion last Friday was too close for comfort."

"I know, but, Adam, the mechanic admitted the cut brake line *could* have happened accidentally. And even though the police said the explosion was definitely arson, it's happened more than once in that neighborhood in the past months, and nobody in the area saw anything."

"We still don't know who called the agent looking for you," he reminded her.

"I know. And I mean to be careful. But I won't be a prisoner. Even in my own house."

He nodded. "Okay. But that aside, I still want to take you to lunch, and I'd like to hear your plans for the store. You're not going to abandon me today just to prove a point, are you?"

"Of course not." Rachel looked at him, wishing, for the first time that he didn't look like Tom. But he did, and because he did, how could she trust the instincts telling her she could trust him?

"Good. Then why don't you go grab a jacket and tell Fiona we're leaving, and I'll straighten up in here."

"Okay. I won't be a minute."

"Take your time."

When he was alone in the study, Adam hesitated, then picked up the phone and quickly punched a number. When the call was answered briefly, he said merely, "We're leaving," and hung up.

He quickly gathered up the scattered papers on the coffee table and put them into a box where they were keeping the items that didn't mean anything to either of them. He locked the file with the new note and copies of the other notes and notebooks in the top center desk drawer.

He was about to close the desk drawer Rachel had been slowly emptying when something down at the very bottom caught his attention. It looked like the corner of another small black notebook.

When Adam dug it out, that was exactly what it was. But this one was filled with numbers more cryptic than anything they'd yet found. And something that looked to him like some kind of code.

Adam hesitated, then swore under his breath and put the notebook into the inside pocket of his jacket, then locked up the drawer.

When Rachel came downstairs, he was waiting in the foyer, lounging back against the newel post and watching two of Darby's men wrestle with a rather fine barrister bookcase. It was taking up much of the hallway leading toward the rear of the house.

Darby appeared with her ever-present clipboard, and Rachel said, "We're going out for a while. If you need anything while I'm gone, just ask Fiona."

"And hope she's feeling charitable?"

"I've spoken to her. She promised to be polite and helpful."

"Uh-huh. Well, we'll see."

A few minutes later, as they headed toward Richmond in Adam's rental car, he said, "So Fiona's rough on other people as well, huh? I thought it was just me."

"No, she's pretty democratic in her dislikes. Actually, though, she's just slow to trust and hates change. But she's been with my family a long time."

"I gathered as much."

There was a short silence, and to Rachel it felt a bit strained. If Adam had noticed her reserve, he hadn't commented, but she couldn't get last night's dream and her doubts about him out of her mind. She cast about for something to say to break the silence. "We'll have to go by Graham's office before going to the store. He called last night and said he got the keys from the agency when he took the signed lease by."

Adam frowned slightly. "Rachel, I think you should arrange to have security in that store right away. A top-notch alarm system for sure, maybe even a security service to make regular patrols."

"That's what Graham said."

"It's a sensible idea."

"I know. I'll call and make the arrangements tomorrow. But I also have to arrange for some preliminary remodeling. At night we can lock everything up, but security won't be very tight with workmen coming in and out during the daytime."

Adam frowned, but didn't comment.

Rachel wondered what disturbed him. The possible threat to her safety? Or something else? She wished she had the courage to ask.

When she spoke again as they reached the restaurant, it was to change the subject. "Have you talked to Nick lately?"

"I asked him if he'd told anyone about your plans for the boutique. Did you ask your uncle Cam, by the way?"

"Yes. He'd forgotten I'd even mentioned the plans. All he has on his mind these days is furniture. What about Nick?"

"Didn't tell a soul."

"Then it really is a short list of people who knew."

"Unless . . ."

"Unless?"

"Unless the agent added that part when she realized you were upset. So she wouldn't sound so irresponsible in telling a stranger where you'd be."

"I never thought of that." She sighed. "Why is nothing ever as simple as you think it is?"

Adam didn't answer until he'd parked the car and come around to open her door. Then he said, "To keep us on our toes, maybe?" He was smiling, but his eyes weren't.

"As good a reason as any, I guess."

"Come on," he said, offering his arm. "Let's forget all about it for an hour or so."

"That I definitely agree with," Rachel said so cheerfully that she almost convinced herself.

The phone conversation was brief.

"You wanted to know where they went."

"Yes."

"A restaurant first. Then a quick stop at the lawyer's office. She went in, he didn't."

"And from there?"

"Looks like they're heading to the store."

"All right."

"Do you want me to—"

"I want you to follow your orders."

"Right."

"And this time don't fuck up."

"I'm surprised Becket didn't insist on coming along," Adam commented as Rachel unlocked the front door of the store and they went inside.

"He did make a suggestion."

"That he come along?"

"It might be a good idea, he said. Just to look the place over and hear about all my plans. So he could advise me about business permits and so on."

"Which you're perfectly capable of finding out on your own."

"Exactly what I told him."

Adam looked at the big empty space surrounding them. "Still, this is quite an undertaking. Maybe he *could* advise you."

"You're more charitable about him than he is about you." Rachel kept her voice casual.

"I'm a nice guy."

Are you? Are you really? "And not a suspicious lawyer."

"I guess it's an occupational hazard for him."

"Definitely more charitable than Graham." Rachel shook her head, then said, "I want to go check out the back. I didn't take more than a quick look last time."

"Hold on a second." Adam slipped around her, moving quickly enough to catch her off guard, and went through the door into the back areas of the building.

By the time Adam reappeared, Rachel had managed to remind herself that all kinds of appearances could be deceptive. Maybe Adam really was worried about her safety.

Or maybe he just wanted her to think so.

God, I hate this!

"Satisfied?" she asked lightly.

Equally lightly, he said, "Just because you're paranoid doesn't mean someone isn't out to get you. Being careful never hurts."

"What did you cxpect to find back there?"

"A clear space and a locked rear door. Which is what I found."

"You do realize this place doesn't even have gas heat? It's electric."

"I realize it now—after seeing the furnace in the back."

"May I go back there now?"

"Yes, ma'am."

They were, she thought, both being polite. Very polite.

"I need to get a rough estimate of the space back there."

He followed her this time. "So you can get the work started?"

"That's the idea." She stood beside a tall stepladder left behind by the previous occupant, opened the small notebook she'd brought along, and used one of the steps as a makeshift desk.

While he watched, she paced off the dimensions of the office space, then did the same in the storage area behind it, and recorded the rough measurements in her notebook. "Plenty of space."

"I'd say so."

She looked at him quickly, the hair on the nape of her neck stirring suddenly. "What's wrong?"

Adam was looking slowly around. "Nothing."

"There is something. I can hear it in your voice."

He shook his head. "I thought I heard something, but I guess not. Are you about done?"

Rachel closed the notebook and put it in her shoulder bag. "I have enough to get started with."

"Then let's go." He took her hand, and she could feel his tension as they walked through the big, echoing space of the store.

Because he thought something might happen? Or because he knew something would? As Graham had pointed out to her earlier, just because Adam was with her when something happened didn't necessarily acquit him of being responsible, as Rachel had assumed. He could, Graham had suggested, be working with a partner.

The suggestion made Rachel feel a bit sick.

When they stood outside on the sidewalk and Rachel

had locked the door behind them, she realized she'd been almost holding her breath. It sounded a little shaky when she let it go.

He looked down at her. "I'm sorry, Rachel—I didn't mean to worry you. I guess I'm just jumpy."

She shook her head, too relieved that nothing had happened to hide it. "I'll have a good security system installed tomorrow, and find out when I can get a contractor in to inspect the place from end to end."

"Good idea."

They had to walk about half a block to Adam's car. But they were no more than twenty feet from the store when the sudden roar of an engine jerked both of them around.

It was a huge black car, the windows tinted dark, and it was coming straight for them.

Fast.

For what seemed like an eternity, Rachel stared, frozen, at the car bearing down on them. She saw it shear off a decorative lamppost as it jumped the curb and roared onto the sidewalk toward them.

Fast.

So terribly fast.

A hard arm locked around her middle.

Rachel felt herself yanked off her feet, and then the car was gone from her vision and only the ungodly roar of its laboring engine filled her ears. Adam had literally swept her out of the path of that juggernaut.

Then they were on the hard pavement, the momentum rolling them over and over, and the engine of the black car screamed.

Rachel felt the hot breath of its passing.

• • •

The paramedics treated Rachel for a sprained wrist and one ugly abrasion just below her elbow. They said she was in shock.

She agreed with that assessment.

Once again, Adam's thick leather jacket had protected him somewhat, even though he had taken the brunt of the punishment in trying to shield Rachel. But he, too, had been treated, for several abrasions on his hands and a scrape along one cheek.

They were both lucky, the paramedics said.

The cops said the same thing, and were very unhappy to find that none of the witnesses to the scene could tell them much.

"A big black car," one of the cops said to Adam while Rachel was being patched up. "Tinted windows, no way to see the driver. And nobody got a license plate." He eyed the shattered lamppost and what was left of a bench the car had taken out before leaving the sidewalk, and shook his head. "Damned thing must have been a tank."

"It was big and heavy, no question," Adam said. "I didn't get the make or model. It just happened too damned fast."

"Do you think it was deliberate? Was the car driven onto the sidewalk in an attempt to get you two?" It seemed an automatic question; this officer seemed to have no awareness of Rachel's previous close calls.

Adam hesitated, then shrugged. "Like I said, it all happened too fast to be sure of anything. It could have been a drunk driver, I suppose, or somebody who just lost control." He didn't mention that laboring engine, a sound he suspected would linger in his memory for a long, long time.

And in Rachel's, no doubt.

He saw one of the paramedics helping her out of their

van, and said quickly to the cop, "I need to get Miss Grant home. You know how to get in touch if there are any more questions."

"Sure, go ahead."

"She's in shock," the paramedic told Adam flatly when he reached them. "But she won't go to the hospital. Keep her warm and get something hot inside her."

Adam hesitated, on the point of overruling Rachel. But then she looked up at him with pleading eyes, and there was no way he could withstand that. He took off his jacket and put it around her shoulders, then took her to his car and put her inside. He turned up the heat, full blast.

And he got her away from there.

"More hot tea?" she murmured when he pulled over in front of a café five minutes later.

"I think so. Unless you'd rather have something else?"

"No. Tea's fine."

Adam didn't want to leave her for a minute, but her pallor and the darkness of her eyes bothered him. And she looked so small with his jacket enveloping her.

He brought the hot, sweet tea back quickly, and put the cup into Rachel's hands.

"Thank you," she said politely.

"Drink it, Rachel."

Obedient, she sipped.

She didn't say anything else until they were almost at her house, and when she did speak, her voice was unnaturally steady. "In case you're wondering, I believe it now."

He looked at her quickly and saw a single tear fall.

"Rachel . . ."

"Someone wants me dead." She drew a breath, and a tremor shook her voice. "Someone really wants me dead."

TWELVE

"Listen to me, Rachel. I am not going to let them succeed."

She sniffed, then murmured, "That's twice you've saved my life. How can I ever thank you for that?"

He didn't like the way she sounded. Almost mechanical. "Don't," he said. "Just . . . don't."

"We have to find out who it is, Adam. We have to finish going through Dad's papers."

"Yes. But not today."

Rachel was silent while he parked the car near the house and came around to help her out. For a moment, she stood there, looking at the house, and then she said, "I won't be a prisoner."

"I know. Come on." He put an arm around her and took her into the house.

He saw her safely into the anxious care of Fiona and Darby, both of whom seemed to know exactly what Rachel needed. They took her upstairs at once, Darby saying something about a hot bath and Fiona promising hot soup.

Adam briefly explained the day's events to Cameron, who was appalled, then promised he'd return the following day to check on Rachel. Then he drove back to Richmond, to Duncan and Ross Investments.

As he strode rapidly through the lobby and toward the offices, Adam thought one or two people had the idea of asking him his business, but he didn't give anyone the chance. He went into Nick's office and closed the door behind him.

Behind his desk, Nick immediately looked up and asked, "How is she?"

Adam wasn't surprised by his knowledge. "Shaken. Scared. It's a miracle she isn't dead."

"You're why she isn't dead, according to what I heard."

Adam waved that off. "Have you found Galloway?"

Nicholas eyed him somewhat warily. "I have a few possibles. Why?"

Adam came forward and put his hands on Nick's desk, leaning toward the other man. "Because I want to talk to him."

"Adam—"

"I have to know. I have to know if it's Galloway."

"And if it is?"

"Then I have to make damned sure he doesn't kill Rachel trying to get to me."

"And you propose to do that how?"

Adam laughed shortly. "Break his neck?"

"The law frowns on that."

"I don't really care."

"For Rachel's sake, you'd better." Nicholas paused a

moment and watched that sink in, then went on calmly. "I agree, we need to have a little talk with him."

"We?"

"Well," Nicholas said, rising, "your hands already look pretty beat up. Mine are nice and fresh. Let's go."

"He left his jacket," Rachel murmured.

"I'm sure he'll be back for it tomorrow," Darby said. She removed the tray from Rachel's lap and added, "You should try to rest. I'll be glad to sit with you—"

"No, Darby, you've already done enough. I'm okay, really. The bath helped, and so did the soup. I'll probably be able to sleep in a little while. You go on home."

"Sure?"

Rachel smiled. "See you tomorrow."

But when she was alone in her bedroom, Rachel felt the shakes start up all over again. She was bundled in a thick robe as well as pajamas, but still she shivered. She was already so sore that getting comfortable in bed was impossible, so finally she got up and took a couple of aspirin from her bathroom medicine cabinet.

That didn't help the shakes.

She went to the chair where Darby had left Adam's jacket and sat down there, using it as a blanket. It smelled of him, and she inhaled slowly, glad that whatever cologne or aftershave he used was not what Tom had worn. Very glad.

The shakes stopped after a little while despite the insistent inner voice reminding Rachel once again that just because Adam had been with her, just because he had seemingly saved her life once more, she still couldn't be sure he wasn't involved in this.

No. How can I believe that? He could have been killed as well, and surely that makes him innocent? Surely . . .

A few minutes later, she found the notebook in the inner pocket.

And recognized her father's handwriting immediately.

The shakes came back.

Max Galloway had a long history of dealing with his victims by remote control. Call someone and give an order; plant evidence to be found eventually; set explosives to go off when he was far away.

He seldom stood close. Rarely looked them in the eye.

Which was one reason he hated Adam Delafield.

Another reason was that he really hated getting slammed against a hard tile wall.

"I'm not going to ask again, Max." Adam's voice was quite gentle, in stark contrast to the hands threatening to make Max's next breath an arduous challenge.

Max sent one glance past Adam's shoulder, and wasn't reassured. Nicholas seemed indolent as he leaned against the closed door of the dingy men's room. He held the gun with indifference.

But it was a big gun.

"All right," Max gasped, coughing once in an effort to get those iron fingers around his throat to loosen.

They loosened. A bit.

"Talk," Adam said. "You followed me from San Francisco."

"Hell, what did you expect?" Max allowed his honest indignation to surface. "Jesus Christ, Adam, you fucking ruined my life! I've got a price on my head because of you."

"You went renegade, Max. You almost blew up two

square blocks of the city. Did you expect me to just let you do that?"

"It wasn't any of your business, Adam! You were out, how many times did I hear you say it? Just wanted to run your company and be left alone. So I left you alone! Your company wasn't in that area, so—"

Adam tightened his fingers, and Max choked.

Easing off just a bit, Adam said, "I'm not here to listen to you try to justify wholesale murder, Max. All I'm interested in right now is what you've done in Richmond."

"Nothing," Max said sullenly.

"Oh, no? You didn't try to blow up a building with me in it?"

Max looked bewildered. "Somebody try to blow you up, Adam? You just make friends everywhere, don't you?"

Adam applied a bit of judicious pressure, and Max choked again. "You're saying you didn't call the real estate office trying to find Rachel and me? Get there ahead of us and set a timer?"

Max coughed. "It wasn't me, goddammit! I haven't been in town long enough to be able to lay my hands on—my usual supplies. Especially not with this fucking price on my head!"

Adam glanced at Nicholas, who lifted a brow and shrugged.

Returning his attention to Max, Adam said, "But you were driving that car today, weren't you?"

"Car? What car?" This time his bewilderment wasn't convincing.

Adam slammed him against the wall again, making it perfectly obvious that he didn't care if he cracked Max's skull open.

Max groaned. "*Shit.* Okay, okay."

"It was you?"

"Yeah, it was me. I saw you with the girl and—it just seemed like a good idea at the time."

"Bullshit. You came here planning to get me."

"Well, yeah," Max said. "But not with a car. That was a great car too, and I had to ditch it right after."

"Another black mark against me?" Adam asked dryly.

"I really liked that car, Adam."

"How were you planning to get me?"

Vaguely, Max said, "I hadn't decided. Something painful."

Adam glanced at Nicholas, who was smiling slightly, then looked back at Max and tried not to smile himself. It wasn't that Max wasn't dangerous; he was definitely that. But he also possessed a kind of cockeyed charm that had more than once saved his skin.

Still, Adam wasn't about to let him off that easily. And remembering what had happened to Rachel today made his fingers tighten on Max's throat once more. "You made a big mistake today, Max. I wasn't alone when you aimed that car at me. Because of you, the lady got hurt. That makes me very unhappy, Max."

"Stop talking to him," Nicholas advised calmly. "Just kill him."

When he was allowed to breathe again, Max muttered, "I know the good cop-bad cop routine."

"Yeah," Adam said. "But you also know we aren't cops. And neither one of us is very good. Now, give me one convincing reason why I shouldn't collect that bounty—which is, as I recall, for your carcass dead or alive."

"You don't want to kill me, Adam."

"That's up to you. But I'll sure as hell turn your ass in."

Max groaned. "Might as well kill me. You know they will."

"That," Adam said, "is not my problem."

"Wait! I have something that might be worth listening to."

"I doubt it."

"I swear, Adam!"

"Then let's hear it."

Cagey, Max said, "You'll let me go? Give me a head start before you call out the dogs? That's all I'm asking, Adam."

"That depends on what you have to say, Max."

"I say kill him," Nicholas offered, supremely indifferent. "If you let him go, he'll just turn up somewhere else and pull another stunt like today."

"No, I won't, I swear."

"But you want to get even, Max," Adam reminded him. "I ruined your life, remember?"

"Yeah, but if you let me go now, you'll sort of be giving it back to me. And I'd appreciate that, Adam. We'd be all square."

"Now, do you really expect me to believe that?"

"I wish you would," Max said earnestly.

Nicholas let out a short laugh, which Adam knew was more amused than it sounded. It sounded derisive, and Max flinched.

"Adam, I swear I'll get out of your life and stay out. I swear."

"Let's hear what you have to say, Max."

Max cleared his throat. "If you could let go of me, it'd be easier."

"No."

"Well, okay. I just thought—"

Adam tightened his fingers for a moment, then eased off. "Max, pretend you're talking for your life. Because you are."

"Right. Right. You know I've sort of been watching you. Not every day, just sometimes."

Adam merely nodded, not admitting that Max's greatest talent—an ability to blend into his surroundings—had prevented Adam from noticing the surveillance.

"Well, I saw something else while I was watching you."

Nicholas barked suddenly, "Spit it out, goddammit!"

Max jumped. "Okay! Somebody else has been following you. I saw two different guys at different times."

"Following just me?"

"Well—you and the girl."

Adam stared at him. "Who were they?"

"One looked like a crook," Max answered. "Scruffy as hell. The other one . . . I dunno. Too polished to be a crook or a cop. Maybe a spook. Hard to say. They stayed well back. Knew what they were doing, both of them. It didn't look like a hit, Adam, honest. Surveillance."

Adam glanced at Nicholas, then looked back at Max. "What did the polished one look like?"

"Well, big, blond. Built sort of like you. As a matter of fact, he reminded me of you a bit. Way he moved, I guess, like he wouldn't have made a sound. I never got a good look at his face, Adam, he kept to the shadows mostly."

"Okay, Max. You just bought yourself a head start. Twenty-four hours. Got it? Twenty-four hours and you better be out of here." He let go of Max's throat and stepped back.

"I'm leaving right now, Adam, I swear." Max didn't even bother to straighten his crumpled shirt. He sidled away from Adam and studiously avoided Nick's gaze as he hurried out the door Nick held open for him.

Adam flexed his hands, which were in even worse

shape than they'd been earlier, and went to one of the stained sinks to hold them under cold running water.

Closing the door behind Max, Nicholas thumbed the safety on and put the gun inside the waistband of his pants at the small of his back, where it was concealed by his jacket. "I told you to let me," he said.

"You were more effective just standing there holding that gun."

"Do you think Max is on his way out of town?"

"I think so, but I'll stay alert just in case he has a brave moment."

"He'd be less trouble all around if you turned him in, Adam."

"I know. But he's right. They'd kill him."

"Which is, as you said, not your problem."

Adam shrugged. Changing the subject, he said, "I'm surprised nobody came banging on the door while we were in here."

"I'm not. Every soul in the bar saw us drag Max back here. Nobody was going to risk getting in the middle of that. Not in a place like this."

"I suppose." Adam dried his hands gingerly on a paper towel. "The scruffy one's Simon, right?"

"Nobody'd ever call him polished, so we can assume so."

"Then who the hell is the other one?"

"You never saw him?"

"No. I saw Simon, but I was looking for him." He tossed the paper towel toward an overflowing trash can and turned to stare at Nicholas. "Goddammit, I was hoping it was just Max. Just me."

Nicholas shook his head. "The odds always favored Rachel being a target, you know that."

"I'm not liking the odds very much, Nick. That explosion was meant to kill her, not frighten her. I told you about the timer. The police don't have a clue, but I recognized it. It's the same kind of thing Walsh used before. Designed to leave nothing alive."

"Then we'll have courtroom evidence against him. If I can maneuver him into the net."

"I just don't get his motive for going after Rachel. Even if he did owe Duncan five million, there's no way she could have gone after it. She doesn't know what we suspect, doesn't even know who the JW in her father's notebook is. So how does she threaten him? How could he even imagine that she could threaten him?"

"I don't know."

"Shit. Let's get out of here." Adam didn't say anything else until they'd made their way back through the bar and into Nicholas's car.

It was nearly midnight; it had taken them hours to find Max.

As Nicholas started the car, Adam said suddenly, "My jacket."

"You haven't been wearing one."

"I left it at Rachel's." He paused, then repeated hollowly, "I left it at Rachel's."

Wednesday morning was bright and sunny, so Adam wasn't too surprised when Fiona told him Rachel was out in the garden. But he was surprised when the housekeeper politely showed him as far as the sunroom.

Either Fiona was mellowing toward him, or she was having a really good day.

Adam didn't push his luck by questioning. He just thanked her and went on into the garden in search of Rachel.

He found her near the center, sitting on a teak bench as she gazed absently into a koi pond, where bright flashes of color spoke of active fish. Adam paused for a moment before announcing himself, watching her. She looked none the worse for her close call the day before, but her long-sleeved silk blouse hid both the abrasion on her arm and most of the elastic bandage wound about her sprained wrist.

Even as he watched, she lifted that wrist and used her right hand to massage it gently, wincing.

"Are you going to tell Rachel she wasn't the target?"

"I don't think so. We know she's still in danger. She needs to believe it too. If I tell her that car was aimed at me, she'll go back to doubting that explosion was meant for her. She won't see any reason to be cautious."

"And explaining why you were a target would lead to so many questions, wouldn't it, Adam?"

Questions. God.

Adam walked slowly to Rachel and said, "Good morning."

She looked up at him, and the wariness in her eyes went through him like a bullet. "Hi. I didn't know if you were coming by."

"I didn't even get the chance to say good-bye yesterday, much less make plans. You were obviously in good hands with Fiona and Darby."

"Yes, I was."

She hadn't invited him to sit down, but he did anyway, in a chair at a right angle to her bench. "How are you?"

"Okay. A little sore." She glanced at his hands and frowned. "I didn't know your hands were that bad."

"They look worse than they feel." Since he had iced them the night before, there was little swelling. But they were sore from numerous abrasions and bruises, and still stiff as hell.

"I know you were protecting me when we hit the pavement. Otherwise, I'd be a real mess."

"Rachel—"

"I just want to thank you. I have to." Once again it was said mechanically, with more resolution than anything else.

He drew a breath. "You found the notebook, didn't you? In my jacket?"

She was staring at the fish, her profile still. "Yes."

"Rachel, I saw it in the bottom drawer of your father's desk just before we left the house yesterday. I was going to tell you about it."

"Were you?"

"Of course I was."

"All right."

That wariness again. It tore at him.

"Rachel, you said you trusted me."

"And you told me it might be better for both of us if I didn't trust so quickly."

"I was wrong. You have to trust someone. Trust me. You have to know I'm not trying to hurt you."

She turned her head and looked at him for a long while. Her eyes remained wary. "I believe you've saved my life twice. How can I not trust you?"

Adam wished it weren't a question. He reached over and covered her hands with one of his. "Rachel, I shouldn't have taken the notebook and not told you about it. I'm sorry. But, I swear, with everything that happened later, I simply forgot all about it."

"All right. Did you look in the notebook, Adam?" Her voice was steady.

"Just a glance. Numbers. And what looked like some kind of code."

"His own private code. He taught it to me when I was a child, and we used it in notes to each other. It was a kind of game. I still use it myself whenever I need to take notes."

"You can read the entries?"

Rachel nodded. "Yes."

"And?"

"And it's what we've been looking for, Adam. It's the journal Dad kept detailing his private loans. The recipients are identified."

"All of them?"

"All of them."

If Mercy expected things to be different between her and Nicholas after the greater intimacy of Monday night, she was not disappointed. But she was disappointed—and frustrated—to find that the difference did not appear to be a positive one.

She had a strong feeling that Nick was cautiously withdrawing, that he regretted even the tiny step they had taken from a casual relationship to something closer.

He'd been gone when she woke up the previous morning—which had given her the chance to stop by Rachel's—and he'd busied himself for most of the day in his office, not even taking a break for lunch. Then Adam Delafield had stalked into the bank, looking as if he wanted to take something major apart with his bare hands, and they had left together just moments later.

Mercy didn't find out about Rachel's latest brush with death until she had called her last evening. Rachel had sounded shaky enough, so Mercy didn't mention Adam's arrival at the bank or his subsequent disappearance with Nicholas.

But she wondered. Jesus, what was going on?

And when Nicholas showed up at his usual early hour today, she wondered even more. He was perfectly pleasant as he greeted the few staff members there so early, then shut himself in his office once again. The lights on Mercy's phone told her he was on his private line for much of the morning, and when she ventured to stick her head into his office once and ask if he wanted coffee, she was waved off with no more than an absent smile.

She had an uneasy hunch that he and Adam had gone hunting the driver of a black car last night, though she had no way of knowing whether they had been successful. And while it relieved her to believe neither of them wanted to hurt Rachel, she couldn't get past the idea that both men knew a lot more about the situation than they were willing to admit—at least to the women in their lives.

And despite telling Nicholas she didn't mean to meddle in his private affairs, she couldn't just sit by and wait for him to deign to tell her what was going on.

If he ever did.

Not that she had any intention of following him again. No, that wouldn't get her anywhere. Besides, Mercy's strength wasn't in TV-private-eye tactics, as Nicholas had so mockingly called them.

Her strength was in finances.

If this involved Nicholas, Adam, and Rachel, then the common denominator was obviously Duncan Grant. And what Nicholas either didn't know or chose to ignore was Mercy's familiarity with most areas of Duncan's life.

Since she had been executive assistant to the senior partner of the bank for five years, Mercy not only had all the computer access codes to bank records, but also access to at least some of Duncan's private records. And none of that had been cleared from the computer because Mercy had not yet been told to do so.

Nicholas wasn't the only one who could be secretive.

Mercy made sure Leigh and the rest of the staff were occupied, then shut herself in her own office and got down to work.

If there were answers in numbers, she'd find them.

Sooner or later.

"He kept pretty complete notes," Rachel said.

On the other side of her father's desk in the visitor's chair, Adam said, "Oh? How complete?"

Rachel looked at him for a moment, then began to read aloud from the small black notebook open on the blotter before her. " 'He strikes me as a fine young man with an exceptionally bright future ahead of him. The betrayal of his former employers coupled with his unjust imprisonment has left him wary and disinclined to believe anyone would help him without expecting something in return. I also believe he has placed himself in dangerous situations since he was released from prison several months ago, possibly in an attempt to exert control over his life, but more probably because his own experience left him with a keen understanding of cruelty and injustice.' "

Adam was looking down at his hands. "I had no idea he had given me so much thought."

"Was he right? About the dangerous situations?"

Adam finally met her gaze, and smiled faintly. "Let's just say I could have taken fewer chances along the way."

Rachel nodded, accepting that for the moment. She was more relieved than she wanted to show that Duncan Grant had indeed lent Adam Delafield all that money five years ago, that he had recorded the loan and his impressions of the man in his notebook. But even with that reassurance, the wariness she felt toward Adam wouldn't quite go away.

He was hiding something. Every time he looked at her, she could feel that intensity in him, and though she wasn't sure what it meant, she had the uneasy feeling that Adam definitely wanted something of her. That he had always wanted something of her.

She just didn't know what that was.

Returning her attention to the notebook, she said, "I don't think we need to concern ourselves with most of this. All the loans except these last three have been repaid. We have to start there, don't we?"

"I'd say so."

"Okay." She drew forward a legal pad, turned to the right page in the notebook, and spoke aloud as she began translating the notes onto the legal pad. "RS, lent a hundred and fifty thousand dollars, is—Robert Sherman. He's apparently from Kansas City, where he has a small graphics design business. His partner left him in the lurch, and that's why he needed the cash to reinvest in the business, get some new equipment and whatnot. According to his notes, Dad gave him the money—outright."

That surprised Adam. "Outright? No repayment?"

"No. He told Sherman that when he was a success in years to come, to pass on the favor." Rachel looked at Adam with a slight frown. "You know, I wouldn't be surprised if he'd done that more than once with some of the smaller amounts. I'll have to check on that later. In the meantime . . ."

She found the next entry that interested them. "LM, lent one and a half million, is Lori Mitchell. She lives in a small town in Oregon, where the loan helped her start her own newspaper. Seems her father had known Dad, and that's why she turned to him for help when the local banks refused her loan application. The loan from Dad isn't due to be repaid for another three years. That may be why she hasn't contacted me—if she even knows Dad was killed. He notes here that he told her to concentrate on getting her paper going and not waste time keeping in touch with him."

"Oregon," Adam said. "We can check, just to make sure she's where she's supposed to be. But I think we can probably cross her off the list."

Rachel made a note, then turned a couple of pages of the notebook and began translating again. "JW, lent five million dollars, is—Jordan Walsh. It says he lives in D.C." She glanced up at Adam. "Close enough."

"I'd say so. What does it say in Duncan's notes?"

"Let's see. . . . The money was lent to start a business, though what kind isn't mentioned. Dad was hesitant, but he was asked as a personal favor to lend the money."

"Asked by whom?"

"Doesn't say."

"What does it say *exactly,* Rachel?"

She glanced at him again, then slowly translated aloud, " 'Walsh is very persuasive, and the company he means to start could help countless people. Still, I'm not entirely convinced this is the best way to finance his efforts. But as a personal favor to an old friend, I am willing to take the risk.' " She looked at Adam. "That's it."

"Nothing more?"

"Not here." She thumbed through the remaining pages slowly. "I don't see his name come up again."

"When is the loan to be repaid?"

"Doesn't say. But . . ."

"What?"

"Dad transferred the money to Walsh just a couple of

months before he and Mom were killed. It was the last loan he made."

"And one of the largest."

"Yes."

Adam frowned. "Then I'd say we need to find out a bit more about Jordan Walsh."

"How?"

"Nick can probably help us."

"And what do we tell him?"

"Rachel, he knows about the explosion. He knows about yesterday. It won't surprise him to hear we're going through Duncan's papers looking for an answer." He paused. "You said you didn't suspect Nick. If he isn't a suspect, then maybe he can help us."

"All right."

"Why don't I go and talk to him? After what happened yesterday, you could probably use a quiet day. Stay in, maybe work on the floor plan of your new boutique. Forget the rest of this for a while."

While you do what, Adam? Talk to Nick? Or something else?

Rachel looked down at the notebook, hating her own suspicions.

Adam got up and came around the desk. He took her uninjured hand and pulled her gently to her feet, then reached for her other hand as well. Looking at the elastic bandage wrapping her wrist and hand, he said, "Until we know absolutely that you're safe, you shouldn't be out alone. You've already been hurt enough. If something else happened to you, I don't think I could stand it."

She wanted to believe that. He was looking at her, that intensity unshuttered, explicit hunger in his eyes, and Rachel found it hard to breathe suddenly. "Adam—"

"Oh, I know. You don't quite trust me, do you, Rachel, in spite of saying you do. So much is happening right now, and I'm still a stranger. A stranger who looks like a dead man." There was a tinge of bitterness in his voice. "Jesus, Rachel."

"What do you want me to say? That it doesn't matter? I wish I could, Adam. I really wish I could. But I can't. Not yet. I'm sorry."

"Do you think that helps?"

"I think I don't want to talk about this anymore. Not now."

Adam stared down at her for a moment, then swore beneath his breath. "I'm not Thomas Sheridan, Rachel."

"I know that."

"Do you? Maybe what you need is proof."

Rachel opened her mouth to ask him what he was talking about, but before she could make a sound, she had her answer.

His head bent, and his mouth touched hers. Softly, gently, as if he feared to damage something unspeakably fragile. His mouth was warm and hard, and disturbingly unfamiliar.

She let her eyes drift closed, mesmerized by the butterfly sensations of his lips caressing hers. The heat came slowly, welling up from some core she hardly recognized, rising inside her, swelling until it filled all the places in her that had been cold and dark and empty. She felt a tremor ripple through her body.

He felt it too.

In a moment, she was gathered against him, surrounded by powerful arms, held in an inescapable embrace. Yet still his kiss remained feather light and tentative, his mouth toying gently with hers. Until finally Rachel heard a wordless plea escape her, and her arms slid up around his neck.

His arms tightened around her, and his mouth slanted across hers, finally taking what she offered him.

It shook Rachel as she'd never been shaken before. When she had last felt real desire, it had been the tremulous, yearning passion of a girl for the man she trusted implicitly, the man she had known virtually all her life. Safe in Tom's arms, she had felt no uncertainty, no fear, no anticipation of pain or loss.

In Tom's arms, she had been totally, completely innocent.

Ten years later, grief and loss and pain had taught Rachel there was no safety in loving or being loved. And maybe that sharper awareness of how fleeting and uncertain life could be opened the floodgates containing a passion she had not known herself capable of feeling.

Maybe it was that.

Or maybe it was Adam.

The only thing she knew for certain was that it had nothing to do with Thomas Sheridan.

Adam kissed her in a way she understood not from experience but only because comprehension sprang from primitive instinct. And she responded with the same all-consuming hunger, the same need to possess, to mark as her own the man who belonged to her.

And it was she who cried out in disappointment when he wrenched his mouth from hers.

"Rachel . . ." His forehead pressed against hers, and his ragged breathing was warm on her face. "Christ, Rachel—"

"Don't stop," she murmured, touching his face with shaking fingers when he drew back just a little and stared down at her.

"I have to." His voice harshened. "I won't win like

this, Rachel. I won't take you away from Thomas simply because I can carry you off to my bed—and he can't."

Her hands fell away from him. "You think—"

"I think this is a decision you have to make, and not in the heat of desire. I want you. But I have to be sure it's me you want. You have to be sure. Or it'll destroy both of us."

Adam released her and stepped back. His face was still, his eyes once more shuttered. "I'll go and talk to Nick."

He left her there, staring after him.

THIRTEEN

After Adam left, it was a long time before Rachel could get her thoughts organized. And, even then, they didn't make much sense. She felt shaky, and wasn't sure if it was aftereffects of yesterday's brush with death or what had just happened.

A brush with . . . something else.

Too restless to just sit, needing desperately to be busy, Rachel locked up her father's desk and left the study. Lunchtime was still more than an hour away, and she wasn't sure what she intended to do, but when she reached the foyer, she encountered Darby.

"Hi. I was just looking for you."

"What's up?"

"Well, I was going through that lovely little mahogany secretary—the one that you said used to be in one of the upstairs bedrooms? And I found something I thought you should see."

"I thought you were going to just box up whatever you found when you cleaned out drawers."

"Oh, I am. That's what I've been doing, in fact. But since this has your name on it—literally—I thought I'd better give it to you."

"What?"

Darby pulled a small blue envelope from her clipboard and handed it to Rachel. "I suppose there's no telling how long it was in that drawer—"

"At least . . . ten years."

"Ten years? How do you know that?"

"Because this is Tom's handwriting." She stared at the envelope, at her name scrawled in Tom's sprawling hand, hardly surprised that she remembered his writing so vividly.

"Tom? Tom Sheridan?" Darby looked concerned. "Jeez, maybe I should have just dropped it in the box with the rest of the stuff. I had no idea it'd bring back bad memories, Rachel, I'm sorry."

"No, it's all right." Rachel smiled at her friend. "Good memories, not bad ones. Tom used to leave me little notes and presents hidden in the house. I always suspected I'd never found them all, but he'd never confirm that when I teased him to tell me."

Darby hesitated, then asked, "Are you going to read it? Should I go away and leave you alone?"

Alone with my dead lover. Rachel wasn't surprised that Darby would expect her to be upset; what surprised her was that all she felt was a slightly wistful sadness that hardly hurt at all.

"Of course I'm going to read it. And, no, there's no reason why you should go away and leave me alone." Rachel opened the envelope and withdrew a folded sheet of blue notepaper, which contained only a few words sprawling over the page.

Look in your jewelry box, Rachel.

She showed it to Darby, smiling. "He must have left me a present there. I seem to remember finding one or two over the years."

"Romantic." Darby was smiling as well.

"Yes, he was. Or maybe just playful. I never was quite sure."

Darby chuckled. "Well, I'll keep an eye out for more of his notes to you. And whatever else he may have left for you."

Rachel put the note back into the envelope and slid both into her pocket. "That would be a good idea. In the meantime—could you use some help? I'm not in the mood to do nothing today."

"Sure, if you feel up to it. Do you? With all the bruises you collected yesterday—"

"Moving around a little will do me good. Besides, if I go ahead and start cleaning out drawers, you can get finished faster."

"In that case, you're on. We have more stuff from the basement parked out in the hallway near the kitchen, if you're interested. I had just started to go through the drawers, when I found the note."

Rachel was interested, and a few minutes later was sitting on a borrowed dining room chair while she emptied the drawers of a tallboy. Darby left her to it, retreating once more to the basement to continue her tagging.

Rachel didn't really know what had prompted her to help Darby, when she had resisted doing so before. Maybe it had been Tom's letter, with the implicit promise of more hidden in the house. More from him—and perhaps from others. Not that Rachel believed the answer to why someone apparently wanted her dead was hidden in some drawer last closed years ago. But given her father's secrecy about the private loans, it was possible that useful information could be found.

Then again, maybe she just wanted her hands and thoughts occupied.

By the time Fiona announced lunch, Rachel had filled one cardboard box with a variety of trash from drawer liners to old church bulletins, used greeting cards and crumpled stationery, and had another half-filled with yellowed linens and yards of unused material. And that was only from the tallboy.

She went upstairs to wash her dusty hands before the meal, pausing to run a brush through her hair and then pausing again as she came back through her bedroom. The rose on her nightstand looked as fresh as it had that morning. As it did every morning.

She wondered what Adam would make of that. She didn't know what to make of it, and every time she considered it, her mind shied away. *It's as if someone places a fresh rose in the vase while I sleep, so fresh there's still dew on the petals. . . .*

"I'm losing my mind," Rachel murmured, and it seemed as good an explanation as any.

She sighed and pulled Tom's note from her pocket. A note from a long-dead lover. A rose that wouldn't wilt. Definitely the stuff of madness.

She carried the note to the little desk near the window and opened the top drawer to place it inside. Then she stopped, aware of a niggling unease. There was something not quite right here, she thought. Something that was . . . something that shouldn't be . . .

She opened the drawer farther and looked at the neat stack of stationery and envelopes, the small notecards. Small blue notecards. Slowly, she compared Tom's note to what lay in the drawer. The stationery was the same. There was nothing wrong with that. Except for one thing. This was stationery she had brought with her from New York.

Ten years ago, there had been none like it in the house.

Look in your jewelry box, Rachel.

Rachel found herself crossing the room to her dresser without thought, but when she stood before the closed leather jewelry box, she went still. Absurd. It was, of course, absurd to think she'd find anything inside. She'd had the box open only yesterday, after all. There was nothing unexpected in there, certainly nothing Tom could have left for her. Not ten years ago.

Not even yesterday.

Drawing a breath, she reached out and opened the box. There was nothing new in the top tray. Her familiar jewelry, nothing more, the everyday things she often wore. She lifted that tray out and set it aside. In the second compartment was also her jewelry, pieces less often worn. A few gold chains, some simple earrings, and—

A delicate gold identification bracelet that had not—surely had not—been there the day before.

Rachel lifted it out slowly. Her name was etched in script on the front. On the back, also in flowing letters, was another inscription.

To my beautiful Rachel
Happy, Happy Birthday
All my love, Tom
August 16, 1988

A birthday present. Except that her birthday had fallen three months after Tom's plane had disappeared. And this was a gift she had never received.

Until now.

Ghosts.

She turned quickly, the bracelet clutched in her hand, and stared around the room. It looked just the same as always. Pretty and neat—and empty of anyone except her.

"Tom?" she whispered.

She listened, her senses straining, but there was nothing to hear.

Of course there was nothing to hear.

Rachel returned the bracelet to the jewelry box and replaced the top tray, telling herself that this, too, could be explained. Tom could have brought stationery from outside the house, the similarity to what she owned now mere coincidence. She had been so in shock and numbed by grief after Tom's death that she could have missed a gift already left for her to find. Could have overlooked it in the bottom tray. Of course she could have.

But for ten years?

Maybe she really was losing her mind.

For the rest of the day, Rachel pretended that nothing out of the ordinary had occurred. She went back to going through the furniture that Darby and her men had brought up from the basement, and it was nearly four that afternoon when Fiona summoned her to the study, where Graham waited for her.

"Rachel, are you all right? Why the hell didn't you call me?"

For just a moment, she wondered how on earth he had found out, but then she realized what he must be referring to. Leaving the study door open behind her, she came into the room and perched on the arm of a chair near her father's desk. "I'm sorry, Graham. I was so shaken up, I just didn't think about it. How did you hear?"

He thrust a folded newspaper toward her. "This."

It was a brief article on an inside page and below the fold. A couple was injured slightly when a car came up onto the sidewalk and nearly struck them. The driver fled the scene of the crime. Her name and Adam's, but virtually nothing else.

Rachel shook her head and handed the paper back to him. "Well, at least they didn't make a big deal about it."

"Is that a bandage on your hand?"

"It's just a sprained wrist, Graham. I'm fine. A bit sore today, but I'll recover. Thanks to Adam."

Graham took a couple of steps away and turned to face her, leaning back against her father's desk. "It's always thanks to him, isn't it, Rachel?"

"I would have been killed if he hadn't been there."

"Yeah? Maybe it wouldn't have happened at all if he hadn't been there."

"You're still convinced he's the one who's trying to hurt me? Just your suspicions, Graham? Or something more?"

He drew a breath. "Rachel, there's something fishy about this."

"I know you think so."

"All this started when he came to Richmond. And he's

always *there,* Johnny on the spot, ready to be your hero. These *accidents* always just miss you."

"Would you rather they didn't?" she snapped, her own doubts and worries suddenly raw on the surface.

"That's not what I'm saying, and you know it. Rachel . . . a man comes to you. He's ready—he says—to repay a huge loan your father gave him—he says. He looks amazingly like the fiancé you lost ten years ago. And he keeps playing hero and saving you from death, in the best melodramatic tradition."

"Thanks a lot," she said dryly.

"You know what I mean. It's a con, Rachel. He's after your money."

"Graham, for God's sake, you found the information yourself. He has a company doing well out in California."

"That doesn't mean it couldn't do better with more money to spread around."

She shook her head. "You're wrong."

"I don't think so, Rachel."

She didn't know why she didn't tell him about the notebooks and journal they'd found. Maybe because she wanted to keep her father's secret. Or maybe because she didn't want to defend Adam to Graham.

"I trust Adam," she said instead, the declaration slow and firm and hiding her doubts.

"Do you? Then ask him why he's been out of the country more often than in during the last five years. Ask him if he can run that company of his by remote control, because he sure as hell hasn't spent much time there."

"You're still checking his background? Graham—"

"I won't apologize for it, Rachel. Your father would turn in his grave if I didn't do my best to look out for you. And I'm telling you, there's something strange about a man who takes regular trips to places they warn the tourists to stay away from."

"I believe he has placed himself in dangerous situations since his release from prison. . . ."

She crossed her arms and stared at him. "Graham, I know you have my best interests at heart. And I appreciate your concern, I really do. But I am almost thirty years old, and I can manage my own life. Whatever is between Adam and me is between *us.* Stay out of it, please."

His mouth hardened. "I see."

"I wish I believed you did."

"Oh, no, I see well enough. I see more than you do. Tell him to dye his hair black, Rachel, and then see how you feel about him."

"I am not mistaking my feelings because he looks like Tom."

"Aren't you?"

"No. Maybe I did at first, but not anymore. Tom's dead." *Even if he is still giving me presents . . .* "And Adam is alive. And I know the difference."

"Rachel—"

She drew a deep breath to steady her voice. "If that's all you came to say, Graham, then I wish you'd go. I am really sorry you and I don't agree about Adam, but you have to realize that nothing you could say would change my feelings for him."

Slowly, Graham said, "Yes. I see that."

Without another word, he turned and left the room.

Rachel was dimly aware of the angry sounds of his powerful Corvette roaring away from the house, but she didn't really listen. Graham's anger barely touched her.

"Nothing you could say would change my feelings for him," she whispered in realization.

How ironic, she thought dimly, that on the day she

had discovered a lost gift from Tom she had also discovered she was beginning to love another man. A man she still wasn't sure she trusted.

"It doesn't tell us much that's new," Nicholas said.

"I know." Adam shrugged. "But at least now we see that Walsh did owe Duncan five million. And that Duncan wasn't easy in his mind about the loan. That jibes with what he told me."

"And no word yet from that P.I.?"

"No. I checked, and he's still out of town. He doesn't have regular office help, and his landlady doesn't care where he is because he paid for the month before he left."

"So we have no way of knowing if he did any looking into Jordan Walsh's dealings."

"Not as far as I can see. I, uh, checked the office. His filing system is something of a mystery, but I couldn't find anything on Duncan or Walsh. That doesn't mean it wasn't there. I didn't have a lot of time."

"Did you find out if he had a security system before you picked his lock?"

"I took a chance."

Nicholas shook his head and leaned back in his desk chair. "I just know I'm going to be bailing your ass out of jail before this is over."

"Think positive. Are you any closer with Walsh?"

"Maybe. Finessing that guy is a lot like dancing with a tiger. One wrong step and the music stops for good."

"Rachel is going to ask me questions about him. I'm supposed to be finding out the answers from you."

"Tell her only as much as you have to—but keep it vague. Because we don't know why Walsh would come after her, and we don't know for sure that the loan Duncan made him has anything to do with it. The ultimate answer may still lie among Duncan's private papers."

Adam sighed. "Well, there may be more information, but I think it's doubtful. What else would he have?"

"A copy of the P.I.'s report, if he made one?"

"That's a big if."

"Granted. But possible."

Adam nodded. "I'll go back to Rachel's tomorrow."

"Yeah, well, get some sleep tonight, will you? No offense, friend, but you're looking a little ragged around the edges. You won't be any good to Rachel if you don't shut it down for a few hours."

"I will."

If the dreams will let me.

"She has more lives than a cat."

"It's that watchdog of hers. Get him out of the way, and—"

"Never mind Delafield. I'm getting sick of this bullshit."

"She's going through her father's papers. Do you really want to take the chance that she won't find something?"

"I'm telling you, he didn't know."

"And I'm telling you, he might have. Duncan Grant was no fool. If he knew, he would have left information or evidence behind. The risk of her finding and understanding it is too great."

"I've taken bigger chances."

"Well, I'm not willing to take this one. I've worked too long and too hard to see this thing fall apart now because of Rachel Grant. And I'm telling you to take care of the problem."

• • •

Rachel was back inside the house with all the hallways and doors, and she didn't like it.

She wished she could find a safe place and just wait, but an overpowering urge she didn't understand kept her moving. The hallways were illuminated only by sconces on the walls, and as she walked deeper into the house, the sconces became wrought iron and held candles, and they were fastened to walls of rough stone.

It was getting cold, cold and damp.

Dimly, Rachel could hear sounds, sounds she didn't want to listen to. Something was hurt. Something was hurt, and it groaned and whimpered its pain. As badly as Rachel wanted to escape the sounds, they grew louder as she approached a door at the end of the hallway.

It was a cold metal door, massive in size. A heavy padlock secured it. And there was a small access opening in the door, fastened only by a sliding bolt.

The sounds came from inside.

Groans. Whimpers. And something else, something terrible.

Rachel wanted to turn around and leave. She wanted to run.

She wanted badly to run.

Completely against her will, she saw her trembling hand stretch slowly out toward the small access door. She could hear her own breathing, rapid and frightened, and beyond that the sounds from inside the cell.

"No," she whispered, "I don't want to see. I don't want to know."

"Open the door, Rachel." Tom's voice.

"No."

"Open it and look inside."

"I don't want to."

"You have to."

"No."

"You have to know where he's been, Rachel. You have to understand."

"Please . . ."

"Open the door."

She saw her fingers hesitate, then grasp the bolt and slowly draw it back until she could open the access door.

"Don't make me."

"Open the door."

Almost sobbing, she opened the access door.

And cried out.

They had hung him from a heavy beam across the ceiling, his wrists lashed together and stretched above his head, bearing his entire weight. His back was to the door, and he was stripped to the waist. Two men stood on either side of him, and one of them held a whip.

That was the other sound Rachel had heard.

As she stared in horror, the man with the whip used the entire strength of his arm to bring the whip across the back of his victim. A back already crisscrossed with bloody welts.

A muffled groan.

Rachel beat her hands on the door, crying out, "No! Stop! Stop hurting him!"

One of the two men turned his face toward the door, but his face was a featureless mask, and his laugh was hollow.

The man with the whip turned a matching mask toward her, then reached over and slowly turned his victim until he was facing the door.

"No!" Rachel screamed.

The Adam mask the tortured man wore was horribly crushed and bloody, almost unrecognizable. Scarlet dripped from underneath the mask, painting ghastly tracks down his throat and over his bruised chest.

"No! Adam!"

One of the torturers laughed and reached out to his victim, his fingers curling into the eyeholes and the mouth hole of the mask as he jerked it away from the face beneath.

"Look! Look what we've done to him!"

But Rachel couldn't look. She covered her face with her hands and screamed and screamed. . . .

The screams were only whimpers, but Rachel's throat ached as though she had been crying out in agony for hours.

She turned on the lamp on her nightstand and sat huddled against the headboard of her bed, shivering. It took a long time for her heartbeat to slow to its normal cadence, and even longer for the shivering to stop.

It was two o'clock in the morning.

The thought of going back to sleep was too awful to contemplate.

Rachel got up and took a long, hot shower. It eased the lingering stiffness in her body and warmed her up so that when she got out, she felt almost human.

And the only person in the world awake at this hour.

The house was silent, and she wasn't willing to risk waking Cam and Fiona by going downstairs. But it was a long time until morning. And she really didn't want to think about that dream.

She turned on her television to CNN, the volume low, then looked around her room for something else to occupy her mind for a few hours. She found her father's datebook, and it took her a moment to remember that she'd brought it up days before, meaning to go through it when she had time.

Now she had time.

She curled up in a chair and began looking through the last year of her father's life. All his appointments, professional and private. Notes he'd jotted while on the phone. Addresses and phone numbers.

It was hard for Rachel to turn the pages, to see his last days play out before her. She cried a little, her emotions closer to the surface than they had been in a long time. And then she got to the day of his death.

And went cold.

"Oh, my God," she whispered.

When he heard the knock on the door of his room, Adam was only mildly surprised, even though it was four A.M. Room service had delivered coffee and rolls an hour before, and all Adam thought as he went to glance through the security spyhole was that somebody downstairs was bored and had come to collect the tray.

It wasn't room service.

Adam started to open the door, then stopped. He quickly unfastened the chain from around his neck and slid it and the locket into the front pocket of his pants. Not long out of the shower, the pants were all he was wearing.

Then he opened the door. "Rachel, what in God's name are you doing out this time of night? And alone, dammit—"

"Sorry if I woke you," she murmured.

He didn't like the stillness of her eyes. "I was up. Come in."

She did. "I remembered your room number, and—" She gasped.

Realizing his back was to her as he closed the door, Adam turned around quickly. "Rachel—"

"My God," she whispered.

"It wasn't as bad as it looks." He got a shirt from the closet and shrugged into it, leaving it unbuttoned. "Just scars, and those will fade away until they're hardly visible. Eventually."

"How could they do that to you?"

He said lightly, "They were the bad guys."

"Oh, Adam . . ."

He took her hand and led her to the sofa in the small sitting area. "Here, sit down. Good thing the coffee's still hot. Your hand's like ice."

She sat there, her eyes never leaving him, and when he fixed the coffee the way she liked it, she accepted the cup and wrapped her hands around it. "I don't understand people like that."

"Good." He smiled.

"They did that to you . . . for five years?"

"No, most of it came in the first few months. After that they got bored with me. Besides, given the methods of the new government, there were plenty of prisoners coming in every day. I became a very small and unimportant target." He sat down in the chair across from her, not daring to get any closer.

"But why? Why did they want to hurt you like that?"

Adam shook his head. "It was a brutal regime. All they knew was violence. They wanted to make sure I didn't have any information that could benefit them. And . . . I had to be punished."

"For what?"

"For doing what I'd been sent there to do. Getting those people and that equipment out of the country."

"It was your job."

"I never said they were fair, Rachel."

"I'm sorry. I'm so sorry."

"It was a long time ago. I healed."

"Did you?"

He managed another smile. "More or less. Rachel, what are you doing here? To come into the city this time of night, alone . . . What were you thinking?"

She seemed to shake off her horror. Adam was glad. But he was also wary.

"I was thinking I needed to ask you something," Rachel said.

"Something that couldn't wait until morning?"

"Yes."

"Why didn't you just call me?"

"I needed to see your face when I asked. When you answered."

That watchful stillness was back in her eyes. It made him feel cold. He was afraid this was going to be bad. "Okay. You're here. What's your question?"

Rachel leaned forward to set her cup on the coffee table between them. Her gaze never left his face. "Why didn't you tell me you were with Dad the day he died?"

He'd been right.

It was bad.

FOURTEEN

How did you find out?" Adam kept his voice level.

"Dad's datebook."

"And he'd noted a lunch appointment with me just a couple of hours before he and your mother got in that plane."

"Yes." Rachel shook her head. "Why didn't you tell me you were with him?"

Adam drew a breath and let it out slowly. "Because . . . it might have led you to ask other questions I wasn't ready to answer. I didn't want to say anything until we had proof."

"Proof? Proof of what? And who is 'we'?"

Adam answered the last question. "Nick and me."

"Nick was with Dad that day?"

"No. But he believed me when I went to him and told him what I suspected. What I knew. So we've been working together. Looking for proof."

Rachel sat back on the sofa and stared at him. "Proof of what?"

"Proof that the plane crash wasn't an accident."

"Dad's plane? You're saying you think somebody deliberately rigged it to crash?" She felt an icy chill sweep over her. "That somebody wanted to kill them?"

"That somebody wanted to kill Duncan. Your mother wasn't scheduled to fly with him that day. I don't know why she was on the plane."

"She . . . sometimes went with him when she was in the mood," Rachel murmured. "Adam—the FAA concluded that an electrical spark ignited fumes. That it was an accident."

"I know."

"Then why do you think it wasn't?"

"Because I was there, Rachel. At the airport when he took off, waiting for my own flight back home. Because I was able to see the wreckage a few days later, and I found something. The FAA investigator should have found the same thing, because it was fairly obvious. But his report stated that the crash was an accident. Maybe because he was inept, or maybe because he was corrupt. I don't know—yet. But I found enough to convince me that Duncan's plane was brought down deliberately."

"What? What did you find?"

Adam leaned forward, elbows on his knees, and looked at her steadily. "I know electronics. And even more than most pilots, I know what electronics are found on a plane. What I found didn't belong there. The explosion destroyed most of it, but there were a few pieces of a device that must have been fixed to the altimeter. A kind of timer. That, and a package of explosives hidden near the fuel tank, must have caused the plane to explode when it reached a certain altitude."

"But you don't know that for sure."

"I'm sure, Rachel. In my own mind I'm positive. And those pieces I found are being kept safe by your father's mechanic out at the airport. He agrees with me. And he'll testify. When we have more evidence."

"Why didn't you go to the police?"

Adam hesitated. "Because while I could prove the plane was brought down, I was also fairly certain that the guilty party couldn't be identified by what's left of that timer. Going to the police would just alert him that he was under suspicion, and we'd never get him. I thought Nick and I stood a better chance on our own. It . . . isn't the first time we've done this sort of thing, and I trust us more than I trust the cops."

Rachel was trying to let it sink in, let it make sense to her. "Why would anyone want Dad dead?"

"That's something we haven't been able to find out." Adam paused, then said, "At lunch that day, Duncan seemed preoccupied, unusually distant. So I asked him if anything was wrong. He said it was nothing, just that he was somewhat troubled by something he'd found out about a recent business venture—with a man named Walsh."

"Jordan Walsh?"

"We think so. It's the only clue Duncan offered, the only trail we had to follow."

"Then—you knew about him before we found Dad's journal?"

"We've been concentrating on him for months. The note about the loan just gave us a more concrete reason to suspect him."

"Adam, even if you had only suspicions, surely the police would be better able to investigate than you two. They must have more resources."

"Maybe. But sometimes belief counts for more. Rachel, Jordan Walsh has ties to the underworld. The police suspect, but can't prove, that he was involved in more than a dozen murders during the past few years. They suspect, but can't prove, that he ran a multimillion-dollar money-laundering operation for a New York crime syndicate.

"And even though the police would no doubt investigate him on your father's behalf, we don't have enough proof to give their investigation the weight it deserves. If we go to them now, they'll just have another unsolved homicide on their books—and Walsh will know we're on to him."

"Adam, I don't understand this. Jordan Walsh doesn't sound like the kind of man my father would do business with."

He nodded. "We think the same thing. It's the most puzzling question in all this. One thing—Walsh was operating out of D.C. when your father lent him that money, and his public reputation is clean. If Duncan had asked around, he wouldn't have necessarily heard anything negative, not unless he dug really deep. And that note in his journal, about doing a favor for an old friend, might also explain it."

"You mean he might not have investigated Walsh until something made him uneasy after he'd already lent the money?"

"Could be. He never asked Nick about Walsh, but that was very much in keeping with how he handled his private loans." Adam paused, then went on. "Except in my case, when he was aware Nick had known me for years. But he might have used a P.I. unconnected with the bank—like that John Elliot we saw named in his notes—to investigate if he became uneasy."

Adam shrugged. "But we won't know that unless and until we hear from Elliot. Assuming he knows anything."

"So all we know is that Dad loaned Walsh money at the request of an old friend."

"Yes."

"Who? What friend?"

"I have no idea. Have you?"

Rachel thought about it, but none of the names flitting through her head made sense. "Dad had lots of old friends. Here, in D.C.—all around the world. It's a long list, Adam."

"I was afraid of that."

Slowly, Rachel said, "But no matter who it was who recommended the loan, you believe that Jordan Walsh is responsible for Dad's death."

"Yes."

"And . . . the attempts against me?"

"It seems likely. We haven't been able to find another answer, Rachel."

"I don't understand that. I didn't even know about Walsh until I found Dad's journal. And even then, how could I be a threat to him? You can't take a notebook to court and demand repayment of a debt."

"I know. We—haven't been able to come up with an answer for that either. All we can be reasonably sure of is that somehow you pose a threat to someone. Walsh seems most likely, but we don't know for sure. But he turned up in Richmond just after you came home. And things started happening."

Rachel was silent for a moment, then said, "How have you and Nick been investigating this?"

"Cautiously. I had to return to California shortly after the funeral, and with the work involved in settling Duncan's estate, Nick pretty much had his hands full. But in the course of that, he went through all the bank's records, which told us that whatever dealings Duncan had had with Walsh had either been in the very early stages, or were very private. From my experience with him, we knew he made private loans and investments." Adam paused. "What we didn't have was access to Duncan's private records."

Rachel drew a breath. "I see."

"Rachel—"

"That was your job, I take it. To cozy up to me and get access to Dad's papers."

"That's not the way it was."

"Oh, no? Are you saying it wasn't your . . . assignment to tell me about your private loan from Dad and so encourage me to go through all his papers probably sooner than I otherwise would have? That it wasn't your job to talk to me, and help me, and just possibly find the evidence you wanted?"

"Rachel—"

"Wasn't it?"

"You make it sound very cold-blooded."

That was answer enough.

She nodded slowly. "It is cold-blooded." Astonishingly to her, she was able to keep her voice calm, even reflective. "But I guess I can't be too upset about it, huh? After all, you and Nick were just trying to . . . avenge my father's death."

"And protect you."

"It started with Dad."

"I owe him a great deal, Rachel. So does Nick."

"And you didn't owe me anything. I understand that."

Her voice must not have been as calm as she'd thought, because he flinched.

"Rachel, please. I never wanted to hurt you. And I never lied to you. What happened between us—"

"Nothing happened between us, Adam."

A muscle in his jaw tightened. "You know better than that."

"No, I don't." A little laugh escaped her. "In a way, Graham was right. It was all a con. So I'd trust you, and confide in you. But the goal was always Dad's papers."

"Rachel—"

She got to her feet and moved toward the door. "I think I'll go home now."

Adam was there beside her suddenly, gripping her arm and forcing her to face him. "No. You have to listen to me."

"Listen? To what, Adam? More half-truths? I don't want to hear any more of them."

He was staring down at her, a little pale. "All right, then," he said roughly. "Don't listen." His arms went around her, holding her tight against him, and his mouth covered hers.

Rachel would have said she was too hurt and angry to respond to him with desire. She would have said this man still had too many secrets he wasn't willing to share with her. She would have said she could not become the lover of a man she had known less than two weeks.

She would have been wrong.

The naked hunger she had seen before in his eyes was alive in him now, a fever she could feel burning in his entire body. He kissed her as though he were utterly certain he would never again have the chance to do so, and held her as if he expected someone to try to snatch her away from him.

That intense, overwhelming need was not only

strangely moving, it was also explosive. And Rachel had no defense against it.

Her body gave itself over to him, molding itself to him, and her arms slid up around his neck with an eagerness she was beyond trying to hide. All that mattered to her was that she give him what he needed.

What she needed.

Adam groaned against her mouth and held her even tighter for a moment. Then he eased back just a little, far enough to mutter, "Tell me you're ready for me, Rachel. Tell me you want me."

"I want you." She pushed his shirt down off his shoulders and pressed her mouth against his chest.

"Are you sure?" His voice was ragged.

"I'm sure."

He had no choice except to believe her; it was what he wanted, needed, to hear.

"Rachel . . ."

In the quiet of the hotel room and the darkness before dawn, nothing seemed to exist except the two of them. Nothing else mattered.

They were more like longtime lovers than strangers, with no awkwardness or hesitation. Each seemed attuned to the other, as though they had done this together many times. Every touch of the hands and brush of the lips was slow, deliberate, the restraint between them only intensifying the building passion until it was like a wild storm trapped beneath glass.

And the glass shattered.

Rachel pushed herself up on an elbow and looked down at Adam. "Just so you know, I'm still mad at you."

"Yeah, I had a feeling you were."

"You should have told me, Adam."

"I know. And I probably would have, days ago, but I'd given my word to Nick. He didn't think we should involve anyone else in this, or voice our suspicions until we had proof. Not even to you."

"God, he's secretive."

"He is that."

"Didn't he think I was concerned in the matter?"

"Of course. But neither one of us wanted to upset you when all we had were suspicions and speculation."

"And when somebody started trying to kill me?"

Adam reached up and brushed back a strand of her hair, his fingers lingering to stroke her cheek. "I wanted to tell you, Rachel. All along. Please believe that."

She nodded, telling herself it was all right to believe him because the alternative was too painful. "But, Adam, don't keep things from me for my own good, all right? I need to know what's going on."

"I agree. And I promise I won't keep anything else from you for your own good." His hand slid into her hair, and he pulled her down far enough for him to kiss her.

Rachel had the dim realization that he had somehow hedged on that promise, and it bothered her. But she pushed worry aside for the moment, unwilling to disturb the fragile peace between them. It had been a long time since she had felt physically close to someone, and she needed that, needed to feel wanted. She relaxed against him for a moment, then lifted her head and said, "I wasn't finished talking."

"Weren't you?" He shifted them slightly until he was raised above her, then pushed the sheet down so that he could see her. "I was."

She felt just the slightest bit self-conscious when he looked at her with a fixed intensity and absorption as tangible as a touch. "Do you realize what time it is? The sun's coming up."

His mouth trailed over the slope of one breast. "Is it? I hadn't noticed."

Rachel caught her breath as he toyed gently with her nipple. She could feel that incredible heat welling up, building again inside her, spreading outward from his mouth on her like molten ripples in a pool. Her fingers slid into his hair, and she held his head to her breast, astonished anew by what he could make her feel.

"Hadn't noticed what?" she murmured, willing to pay whatever price was demanded of her for this.

The sun was well up, bright light slanting through the narrow opening of the drapes, when Rachel stirred again. "I should probably call home. I didn't leave Fiona a note or anything."

"Tell her you probably won't be home for lunch."

"Won't I?"

"Not if I can persuade you to stay here with me. Room service isn't bad at all."

She had to climb across him to use the phone on the nightstand, and all during her brief conversation with Fiona, he distracted her by tracing the line of her spine with first a finger and then his lips.

"Where are you getting the energy?" she demanded when the call was finished and his exploration continued.

"I have no idea. Your skin is like silk."

Rachel felt her own energy rebuilding, and did a little exploring of her own.

She found more scars.

"Don't," Adam said unsteadily when quick tears welled up in her eyes. "I'm okay, Rachel. Now I'm okay."

Nevertheless, she tried to make it up to him, to offer him all the comfort and sweet passion at her command. Whatever brutality he had suffered at the hands of those cruel men, she wanted him to be very sure that there would be memories for him now of beauty and pleasure.

By the time they finally forced themselves from bed for a shower and room service, there was something in Adam's face Rachel had never seen before, a kind of contentment and peace. It was almost as if he had found something for which he'd been searching a very long time, something he had given up all hope of finding. He looked at her constantly, touched her often. Even his voice was different, lower and softer, like rough velvet.

Rachel didn't know what it meant, and it unnerved her more than a little, but she didn't question. For now it was enough to just be with him, to believe that whatever else he wanted of her, desire was real.

"It won't do any good to keep avoiding the subject," she told him finally as they finished with the brunch they'd ordered.

"What subject is that? We've been talking almost nonstop. I figured we'd covered everything."

"You know better."

Reluctantly, he nodded. "Okay, maybe I do. The world intrudes, doesn't it?"

Rachel pushed her chair back from the little table in the corner but didn't get up. "It has to. At least until we can stop whoever killed Mom and Dad."

Restless, Adam said, "You never talk about her."

"We weren't close, I'm afraid. It was nothing major, just very different personalities. Adam, you can't keep putting it off."

"Okay, you're right. So let's talk about it."

"What's being done to get evidence against Walsh?"

He grimaced. "Right to the point. And the answer is—it's a little complicated. Nick has let it be known, through various . . . connections he has in the city, that he might be willing to make a substantial investment if guaranteed a high rate of return."

"Meaning a risky venture. An illegal one?"

"That's the idea. And Walsh is nibbling at the bait."

"Does he think he's dealing with Nick personally, or the bank?"

"The bank. Nick's running a huge bluff at the moment, claiming he can control most of the bank's assets." Adam shrugged. "The original plan was based on our assumption that you intended to sell your interests to Nick. That way, he could have controlled what money he needed to without having to explain himself to the board."

"If he'd told me—"

"I know. I brought that up a couple of times. But he was determined not to involve you. He hasn't said, but I have a hunch he's backing his bluff with at least some of his own money."

"So . . . if Walsh takes the bait, he'll come to Nick with some kind of phony investment, but what he'll really have planned is—what?"

"Another money-laundering scheme, we think. Turning dirty money to clean is a very important cog in the mob's wheel."

Rachel frowned. "Okay. But how does that help Nick find evidence that Walsh rigged the plane to crash? Or that he's the one trying to kill me?"

"If Nick can win Walsh's trust, there's a chance he can get inside the operation and find the evidence we need. He's done this sort of thing before, and he's good at it."

Rachel was still frowning. "But doesn't something like

that tend to take months, even years—assuming it works at all?"

"Sometimes."

"And it's dangerous."

"Very," Adam replied steadily.

She drew a breath. "And our only other option?"

"Hope we find something more among Duncan's papers." Adam shook his head. "If we knew why you're still a threat to Walsh, we'd have more of the answers. But that part just doesn't make any sense."

"And you're convinced it's Walsh who's tried to kill me?"

"Rachel, I had a friend with the police here get me a look at the evidence the fire marshal found after that store exploded. It was a state-of-the-art sparking device on a timer that triggered the explosion. And it came from the same hand that built the device on your father's plane."

"You're sure?"

"I know electronics. I'm sure."

Rachel didn't doubt him. And his certainty made her feel cold. "Then we have to go back to the house. We have to finish going through Dad's papers."

"Yes." He reached across the table between them, and when she put her hand in his, he held it strongly. "And you have to be careful, Rachel. Very careful."

"Not only me. Adam, you've been getting in his way. What if he decides that he can't get to me until he gets you first?"

"Don't worry about me. I'm always careful."

"Really? Dad thought you put yourself into dangerous situations deliberately. And you admitted yourself that you hadn't always chosen the safe path."

"I will this time." His fingers tightened around hers. "I have a lot to live for."

Rachel wished she could believe Adam would be cautious. But she had a feeling it was not in his nature to stand back and let things happen. She let the subject drop for the time being as they left the hotel and drove back to her house in Adam's rented car.

"That's one more leased car I'll have to have them pick up," Rachel noted wryly about her own abandoned car.

"Because you parked it outside the hotel in plain view. These people build bombs, Rachel. I don't want you getting into any car you're not absolutely sure has been in a secure place."

"I know, I know. I should have just taken a taxi."

"Maybe you should make that a habit until this is over."

It made sense. It also made Rachel feel trapped.

"I hate this."

"I know. I'm sorry." He paused while they got out of his car in her driveway, then added steadily, "Maybe you should go away somewhere."

Rachel looked at him. "Is that what you want me to do?"

He hesitated, then swore. "No. I'm not sure we could keep you safe somewhere else, even with real iron bars. The only way to stop this is to stop Walsh."

"My thoughts exactly."

He smiled. "You wouldn't have gone anyway."

"No. I don't think it would solve anything." She took his arm. "Come on. Let's go look for some answers."

Peace reigned inside the house; after so many days of furniture being shifted from attic and basement, Darby and her crew were working in her store today. And Cameron was out in the garden, painting.

"Thank God," Rachel said when Fiona informed her of this. "He's hardly touched his paints since Mom and

Dad were killed. If he's painting, things are definitely looking up."

Fiona, who gave no sign at all that she knew Rachel had left the house in the middle of the night to go to a man's hotel room, sniffed and said, "Maybe he'll be going back to San Francisco now."

Rachel smiled at her. "This is his home too, Fiona."

The housekeeper sniffed again. "If you say so, Miss Rachel."

"We'll be in Dad's study."

"Shall I bring coffee?"

"A little later."

Fiona nodded, sent Adam a look he couldn't interpret to save his life, and left them.

"Is she making a wax doll in my image?" he wanted to know as they went into the study.

"I doubt it."

"You *doubt* it?"

At her father's desk, Rachel turned and smiled at him. "I very much doubt it."

Adam went to her and surrounded her face with his hands. He kissed her, taking his time. Then, huskily, he said, "Do you have any idea what it does to me when you smile at me like that?"

Rachel blinked. "No. Like what?"

Instead of answering, he kissed her again. Or maybe that was an answer.

When Rachel was finally able to catch her breath, she'd forgotten what they were talking about. "Didn't we come in here to do something?" she asked idly.

Reluctantly, Adam removed her arms from his neck and guided her gently back to sit in the desk chair. "Yes. Look for evidence."

"Right. Right." She looked at the desk for a moment,

then shook her head bemusedly. "You have the strangest effect on me."

He touched her cheek with caressing fingers. "Likewise."

She caught his hand and held it firmly. "Adam, if you keep doing things like that, I won't be able to concentrate."

He sighed. "Likewise."

"Look—why don't I go upstairs and get started on the secretary in Dad's bedroom while you finish up in here?"

"I guess that would be best. But I don't have to like it."

Rachel didn't like it either, but she left him and went upstairs to her father's bedroom.

She'd scarcely been in the room since coming home, and for a moment, as she stood in the doorway, Rachel could hardly bear it.

It even smelled like him.

Then she squared her shoulders and spoke aloud. "Okay, Dad. I need to know all your secrets. And I need to know them quick."

She moved toward the secretary by the window.

FIFTEEN

By Thursday afternoon, Mercy had spent so many hours staring at her computer screen that she had a throbbing headache. Her search had to be meticulous; it was incredibly time-consuming. Duncan had stored a great deal of information in his various files; the problem was there was no rhyme or reason to his private system.

He had also installed virtually every appointment-keeping and information-organizing software program on the market, and with his love of high-tech toys, he'd used them all—indiscriminately. And since he tended to go back and make changes or just add notations to old files, not even the dates last worked on were any help.

So Mercy had been reduced to simply wading through years and years worth of files.

Duncan clearly had no use for the delete command.

When she wasn't frowning over apparently useless information such as accounts long since dead and notes of appointments ten years in the past, Mercy managed to do her usual work at the bank. Not that there was much left for her to do.

Until the last week or so, Nicholas had supplemented her final chores for Duncan with some for him, obviously hoping she'd find herself working for him in a smooth transition—and give up her objections to that. But recently, especially in the last few days, he had taken to spending much of his time closeted in his office, either on the phone or else doing work he didn't explain to anyone in the bank. And when he wasn't in his office, he wasn't in the bank, period.

He wasn't using Mercy as his assistant.

In fact, he was barely speaking to her.

That wouldn't have bothered Mercy so much, except for one thing. While he had, in the past, become so involved in a project that he had shut himself in his office and worked long hours, he had still made sure they spent three or four nights a week together.

But he hadn't been to her place, or invited her to his, in days—and showed no signs of planning to.

As she shut down the files she'd been searching through on Thursday afternoon and rubbed her stiff neck, Mercy figured she had a couple of choices. She could wait Nick out, holding strictly to the careful guidelines they had established for their no-relationship relationship, asking no questions and making no demands, pretending it didn't matter to her if he didn't feel like getting laid at the moment.

Or she could break a couple of their rules and force the issue.

The first option was safer. That way, she wouldn't look like a lovesick fool if this was Nick's way of easing out of the relationship. The second option was a lot riskier, especially if he had merely withdrawn from her temporarily because she'd gotten too close the last time they were together. If she pushed now, he could decide he wanted out for good.

But one thing Mercy knew was that she did not like being in limbo. So she left her office and went to his.

And he wasn't there.

"Nothing worse than getting all worked up for a confrontation that doesn't happen," she muttered to herself.

"Looking for me?" Nicholas came into the office behind her.

She jumped. "Jeez. Don't creep up on people like that."

His brows rose, but Nicholas merely shut the door behind them and went to his desk. "Sorry. I thought I was just walking into my office." He was terribly polite.

This was not going the way Mercy had planned.

She went to his visitor's chair, but put her hands on the back of it rather than sitting down. "I noticed Jordan Walsh came to see you this morning," she said. Which was not at all what she'd planned to say, dammit.

"He had an appointment, yes."

"The bank isn't going to do business with him, surely? Nick, I've been hearing things about him in the past few months. People in the financial community are beginning to talk, and what they're saying is that he can't be trusted at best—and is a criminal at worst." She just couldn't seem to say what she'd come in to say.

"Listening to gossip, Mercy?"

"It's more than gossip."

Nicholas shrugged. "Sometimes the bank backs risky investments. And risky people."

"Not Jordan Walsh's kind of risky."

"I know what I'm doing."

"Do you?" Mercy looked at his expressionless face and enigmatic eyes, and felt so frustrated she could have screamed. "And it's none of my business."

"And," Nick said with that terrible politeness, "it's none of your business."

Mercy drew a breath and nodded. "Okay. I'm through for the day." *In more ways than one.* "I guess you aren't interested in dinner."

"I have a few more calls to make."

"Fine." She managed a smile, and knew it looked as false as it felt. "See you, Nick." And walked out of his office.

He stared after her for a moment, not moving until he heard a sharp sound and realized that the pencil in his hand had snapped raggedly in half. Then, hardly aware of speaking aloud, he muttered, "Christ, what's wrong with me . . ."

"Nothing." Rachel shook her head and looked at Adam, who had joined her upstairs about an hour before. It was almost impossible to concentrate when she looked at him, but she tried her best. "Plenty of notes and old letters, but nothing to help us."

"Then we depend on Nick," Adam said.

Rachel slowly returned a stack of unused stationery to one of the drawers, frowning. "Adam, it doesn't make sense."

"Which part?" he asked wryly.

"Dad. Except for his private records, his estate was in meticulous order."

"So his private records should be as well?"

"Well . . . yes. He knew I'd have to deal with all this stuff. He knew I'd be the one to go through his desk downstairs and this one, and that I'd find the notebooks and the journal. There should be more paperwork."

"Okay. Where would it be?"

"That's the problem. I don't know. The safes here in the house have all been checked. The safety deposit boxes at the bank. And now both the desks Dad used. There isn't anyplace else, not that I know of."

"If you're right about the records, there must be."

Rachel shook her head, then frowned again. "Maybe we're looking for the wrong thing."

"Papers?"

"Yes. Maybe we should be looking for a key. Maybe to a safe deposit box other than those at the bank."

Adam looked around the bedroom, which was filled with massive mahogany furniture—and a great many drawers. "A key. Great."

"And not just in here." Rachel sighed. "This is a big house."

"But would Duncan have made you look for it? I mean, shouldn't anything you needed to know be readily available, or at least easily found?"

"I would have thought so. All his business records were."

Adam saw her rub the back of her neck wearily, and came to pull her up from the chair. "Enough. Let's go walk in the garden for a little while before it gets dark, and then I'm going back to town and leaving you to get some rest."

Rachel slid her arms up around his neck and leaned into him, feeling her body respond instantly to the closeness of his. When she was near him like this, all she was aware of was how much closer she wanted to be. "Suddenly, I'm not tired at all," she told him.

Adam wrapped his arms around her and held her for a

moment, and that enveloping embrace moved her oddly. Once again, just as in the hours before dawn, she had the feeling that he thought she was going to be taken away from him.

"Adam?"

He eased back just far enough to look down at her, his eyes intense. Then he kissed her, one hand sliding up her back to the nape of her neck.

Rachel lost herself in him. She forgot about questions and puzzles and doubts, and threats to her life. She forgot about everything but the way he made her feel.

Adam made a rough sound and muttered, "You are not making it easy for me to leave."

Rachel looked up at him. "You could stay."

He touched her cheek lightly. "If I do, you won't get any rest. And I know damned well I won't."

"We might not sleep much," she agreed, "but there's a lot to be said for pillow talk."

He smiled, but it looked a little strained. "Definitely not making it easy for me. Rachel, you still have a sprained wrist and several bruises—"

"I think you counted them last night. Didn't you count them?"

Adam cleared his throat. "You might not feel it right now, but after that car almost ran us down, your body needs a chance to recover."

"I feel fine."

He rested his forehead against hers and sighed. "Why are you making me be the grown-up?"

Rachel couldn't help laughing, but her question was more than a little serious when she asked, "Am I being shameless?"

He kissed her once, hard. "You're being wonderful. I

want to take you to bed right now and stay there for at least a week—never doubt that."

"But . . ."

"But you've been through a hell of a lot in the last few weeks. And it isn't over. We can't know the worst isn't yet to come."

It was Rachel's turn to sigh. "Well, if you're going to be practical about it . . ." Still, she knew he was right. Too many restless, dream-filled nights had come before last night's almost entirely sleepless and active night. She was exhausted, and she was willing to bet he was as well.

"I'll come back tomorrow, Rachel. Bright and early."

Repeating something he had said earlier in the day, she said, "I guess that would be best. But I don't have to like it."

The walk in the garden was peaceful, the leave-taking a while later something else entirely, and Rachel was left with a long evening stretching ahead and way too many emotions and worries running through her mind.

Adam found Simon parked just down the block, where he had a clear view of the front gate of the Grant estate, and Nick's scruffy private investigator gave him a somewhat jaundiced look when Adam pulled up beside him.

"Make me obvious, why don't you?" he said.

Adam ignored the complaint. "Anything?"

"Nah, not since you and the lady got here. Incoming, that is. Cameron Grant left a while ago."

Adam nodded. "I want you to watch this place, and I mean carefully. Rachel shouldn't be leaving, but if she does, stick close."

"Like white on rice."

"You have a partner, right?"

"Yeah. He's always on watch here, while I follow the lady whenever she leaves. Right now he's watching the river side of the property. Nobody goes in without one of us seeing 'em."

"And relief?"

"Two shifts, twelve hours on and twelve off. One follows the lady, the other one stays here, always. The other two are good, don't worry about that. Nick pays for the best."

"None of you kept us from nearly being blown up that day," Adam retorted. "Or being almost run down by a car."

Simon looked both sheepish and defiant. "I was supposed to follow and look out for dangers, yes—but how could I know that store was rigged to blow? I didn't have time to check it out before you two went in. As for the car, the fucking thing came out of nowhere. I didn't have time to do anything, I swear. Besides—you were there. Nick said you had great reflexes, and he was right. The lady hardly got a scratch."

Adam gave him a look, then said calmly, "If the lady gets even that much on your watch, my friend, you'll answer to me. And I won't just dock your pay."

Simon returned the stare and nodded slowly. "Nick also said you were a lot tougher than you look, and since you look tough enough, I should keep it in mind. Okay, I got you. We'll keep a close eye on the lady."

"And if you see anything suspicious—anything, no matter how vague—call me at once. You have my pager number?"

"Yeah. And your number at the hotel. I'll call."

"Be sure you do. Very sure."

• • •

"You'll be in for supper?" Fiona came into the foyer to ask Rachel.

"Yes. Where's Cam?"

"Said he had a date. I didn't ask how much he was paying her."

Rachel laughed. "For heaven's sake, Fiona. He knows plenty of people here in Richmond, and that includes a few ladies who enjoy his company. I'm glad he's getting out."

Fiona sniffed. "At least he isn't underfoot, going through cabinets and drawers until a body'd think he was looking for secret treasure."

"Well, considering some of the things we've found in the furniture so far, you can hardly say he's wasting his time."

"I suppose. I'll just be glad when all this is done and past, and we've the house to ourselves again, Miss Rachel."

"It won't be much longer, Fiona."

The housekeeper sniffed again. "It's already been too long. You should get some rest tonight—assuming everybody'll leave you alone long enough, that is."

Rachel smiled. "I'm fine."

"I know." Fiona paused, then added in a different tone, "Or at least you will be. Now."

Rachel was too startled to respond until the housekeeper had turned back toward the kitchen, but then managed to say, "Fiona? It isn't because he looks like Tom."

Fiona paused for just a moment and looked at Rachel. "I don't know that it matters much whether or not that's the reason, Miss Rachel. You're alive again after ten years of just . . . walking through life. As much as he loved life, Mr. Tom would surely say that was a wonderful thing."

"And Adam?"

"If he loves you, he'll agree."

Rachel didn't respond to that, but as the housekeeper retreated to the kitchen and left her alone again, she couldn't help but think about a couple of things that made that statement sound hollow. Adam hadn't mentioned love. And he had more than once made it clear that he did not consider his resemblance to Tom a good thing.

Except, of course, that it had gotten him more easily and quickly into her house, her life. Her trust. Adam might not like the resemblance, but he had been ruthless enough to use it for his own ends.

Rachel couldn't help wondering if he was still doing that.

And what did she really feel? In a way, Tom's death had encased both her heart and her sexuality in ice, and that ice had remained through all the years of study and work. She had been so young when she lost him and all her dreams of them together; her very youth had encouraged her to cling to those dreams, to prefer them to the reality of going on without Tom.

For a long time, she had felt disloyal to Tom even in dating casually, and by the time those feelings had naturally and inevitably faded somewhat, work had been her focus and her outlet.

By that point, she had thought it easier just to maintain the status quo, especially while she'd been living and working in New York. Work had demanded all her time and energy, she hadn't had to face and deal with the ghosts in her life, and so she had been able to keep herself in an emotional limbo. Until she had come home.

But now she was home. And whether Adam was responsible or not, the ice had cracked, even shattered. The barrier between her and her own feelings had been removed. Everything she felt was stronger, sharper, and seemed to originate from someplace deeper inside her, a place untapped and even untouched for most of her life.

Her anger at Adam had come from there. So did her doubts and her passion.

So did her love.

For so much of her life she had believed that what she had felt for Tom had been the deepest, most powerful feeling she would ever know. Her commitment to him had been absolute, without hesitation or question, and the agony of his death had nearly destroyed her.

But recovery from a devastating loss was not all that had happened to her in ten years. There was also the transition from child to woman. And the development of her creative urges and abilities. And her independence.

The girl who had loved Thomas Sheridan for so long and so absolutely no longer existed.

What she felt now, for Adam, was so much more than she had ever expected to feel for anyone in her life. Far from simple adoration, it was a complex jumble of excitement and fear, growing love and paralyzing doubts, dreams and anxieties, passion and uncertainty, trust—and distrust.

And her physical response to him was so strong that it seemed to push everything else aside. Her body felt different, curiously alive and sensitized. An unfamiliar hunger lurked just below the surface and ambushed her unexpectedly whenever she looked at him or touched him. The mere sound of his voice made everything inside her go still in listening, and his slow smile made her want to smile in return.

But that was her. Her feelings.

Except for his undeniable desire for her, she really had

no idea what Adam thought or felt. He was still too good at hiding from her anything he did not want her to know.

She knew he had secrets left to tell, that there were still details in his past and quite possibly his present that he wasn't ready to share with her. That he might never be willing to really talk to her about what he had endured in that brutal prison.

She also knew that if she had seen the scars on his back without the warning of her dream, she probably would have pressed him to talk to her about it, which would have been a mistake. As it was, her dream had shown her a barbarity so clear and detailed that she had not been able to bear even the idea of learning more. Not now, at least. Probably not for a long time.

You have to know where he's been, Rachel. You have to understand.

For the first time, the full import of her dream hit Rachel.

His scars. How could she have known about his scars, dreamed about them?

Oh, she might have guessed that Adam had been mistreated in that prison, but the bloodied welts she had seen crisscrossing his back in the dream—and still saw, too vividly, when she let herself—closely matched the pale but visible scars he bore in reality.

Maybe even perfectly matched.

You have to know where he's been, Rachel. You have to understand.

It had been Tom's voice she had heard, subtly different from Adam's.

"I'm just tired, that's all," she said, her own voice startling her in the silence of the house. "Imagining things."

Tom's voice in her dreams. A note from him. A yellow

rose on her nightstand. A gift delayed by a decade and a death.

"I don't believe in ghosts," Rachel heard herself say, firmly this time. But even as she did, a faint chill made gooseflesh rise on her arms as she recalled that terrible awakening ten years ago, and Tom's anguished appearance at the foot of her bed.

She had not dreamed that.

"Miss Rachel?"

Fiona's voice startled her, and Rachel was thankful to be pulled from her unsettling thoughts. "Yes?"

The housekeeper didn't seem particularly surprised to find Rachel still standing in the foyer, then Rachel realized that only a few moments had passed since their earlier conversation.

"I forgot to tell you before. Miss Lloyd left a note for you on the table by the basement door. A list of pieces your uncle has asked for."

Rachel nodded. "Thanks, Fiona. I'll take a look at it." She hesitated, then added, "Has Darby finished going through the stored furniture?"

"Not quite. There's still a part of the basement left. She's moved out what you wanted sold and what's been taken to be repaired, and tagged what's been gone over and added to the inventory. The rest she said she'd get to next week."

"I think I'll go down to the basement for a little while. I haven't been down there in years." Anything to get her mind off other things.

"Be careful on the stairs," Fiona warned automatically, as she always did.

"Yes, I will." Left alone again, Rachel headed for the basement, her thoughts taking a welcome new turn.

Her uncle Cameron had always been the artistic

brother, uninterested in business; he hadn't wanted to be bothered by practical things, so he had a business manager who took care of his various investments. As far as Rachel could remember, her father and uncle had never even talked about business of any kind, and as for Cameron recommending that his brother lend someone five million dollars—the idea was absurd.

And that aside, he couldn't possibly be the "old friend" to whom Duncan had referred in his journal; the brothers had gotten along well enough, but neither would have called the other an old friend.

An old bastard, maybe, but not an old friend.

Cam's list was on a table beside the basement door, and Rachel scanned it quickly. A few items, none of which interested her particularly except to wonder idly where on earth Cam intended to put everything.

Leaving the list on the table, she opened the basement door and flipped on the lights as she started down the steps. The musty smell of basements everywhere wafted up to meet her, and for a moment she stopped on the steps, horribly reminded of the dream and Adam's prison.

She had to stand there, holding tightly to the railing, and tell herself several times that it had only been a dream, that this was not a prison she was descending into, not a place where people were trapped and tortured. It was just a basement, a space dug out of the earth to provide storage for a family.

Slowly, she continued down the stairs, and by the time she reached the bottom, her panic had faded. Bright fluorescent lights illuminated even the corners of the huge space, and underneath their cool glare there was nothing that resembled a prison, just the refuse of generations, furniture and boxes full of things ultimately cast off as broken, out of fashion, or simply no longer wanted.

From the steps she could see a more methodical, spaced arrangement of the things nearest her, and knew it was Darby's work. Farther away, toward the north side, it looked much more chaotic to her, with chairs piled atop tables, wardrobes pushed up against chests, and little room in which to move among the pieces.

Rachel walked away from the stairs, along an aisle with tagged furniture on either side, toward the north end of the basement. She looked at a few things in passing, noting that each had been beautifully polished and/or cleaned, and marveled at how much Darby had accomplished.

By the time she reached the north end, she had become absorbed in looking at what there was to see. She'd known there was a lot down there, but she was surprised at how many beautiful pieces a careful inventory had unearthed.

No wonder Darby was so thrilled.

Rachel couldn't move very far into the section that had not yet been inventoried. She could see boxes and trunks, yet couldn't get to them because of all the heavy pieces of furniture in the way. And the furniture was turned this way and that, some facing outward, some inward, and some even lying on their sides or backs.

The only way to get to most of the pieces was to do as Darby had done: Move one thing at a time.

"I wouldn't even know what I was looking for," Rachel muttered.

"Rachel? What the hell are you doing down here?"

Cameron was standing near the bottom of the stairs, staring across the room at her.

SIXTEEN

This, Mercy told herself, was a mistake. A big mistake.

She stared at the door for a full minute, gathering her nerve, drew a deep breath, and knocked. Mistake or not, she refused to spend yet another evening pacing in her apartment and asking herself whether she should force the issue or wait.

She really hated waiting.

Nicholas opened the door, holding a glass in one hand, and for a moment just looked at her.

"I need to talk to you, Nick."

He nodded slowly and opened the door wider, gesturing for her to come in. "I've been expecting you," he said.

That surprised Mercy somewhat, especially given the tense scene at the bank only a few hours before. She came into his apartment, eyeing him uncertainly as he closed the door. He looked, she thought, as if he had had a very, very bad day. Coat and tie discarded, white shirt untucked and half unbuttoned, the sleeves rolled up loosely. His hair looked as if he'd run his fingers through it more than once, and there was something almost . . . numbed about his face.

"Maybe this isn't such a good time," she said slowly.

Nicholas crossed his sparse living room to the corner wet bar and splashed more whiskey into his glass. "For some discussions, there's no such thing as a good time," he said coolly. "Drink, Mercy?"

"No thanks." She hesitated. "How many does that make for you?"

"I have no idea. It's a new bottle." Which was now half empty. He turned back to her and lifted the glass in a mocking toast. "Don't worry. I'm not driving anywhere tonight."

In all the years Mercy had known him, she had never seen him even finish a drink of whiskey, much less consume several. It was scaring her to see him like this; for all his coolness and seeming detachment, he was curiously out of control. "Nick, this isn't like you."

"Maybe you don't know me as well as you think you do."

She shook her head. "What is it? What's wrong?"

"Just say what you came here to say, all right? Not that you have to."

"What do you mean by that?" Mercy didn't have a clue what he was talking about.

He shrugged, swallowed half his drink, and went to sprawl in a big armchair by the cold fireplace. "I mean, it isn't like I'm going to be surprised. I've been expecting it."

"Expecting what?"

He lifted his glass in another mocking toast and said matter-of-factly, "Expecting you to tell me it's over."

It was definitely not what she had expected.

After the first moment of surprise, Mercy dropped her shoulder bag on the sofa, shrugged out of her jacket, and moved across the room to sit down on the big hassock in front of his chair. In the same matter-of-fact tone she said, "How long have you been expecting it?"

"Oh . . . from the beginning." He was staring at his drink rather than at her. "Since the day after our first night together, I suppose."

"Why?"

"You want a list? Because I'm an ugly bastard and you're a beautiful woman who can have any man she wants. Because I'm prickly as hell, with a foul temper and worse moods, and I'm no picnic even on my best days. Because there's eleven years between us in age and a few lifetimes in experience. Because even the best lover in the world can't make a woman's heart respond to him the way her body will."

Nicholas shrugged and finished his drink in one swallow. "I tried, God knows. Tried not to crowd you, not to ask too much of you. But I knew it was only a matter of time. The other night . . . I knew everything had changed. After that, I couldn't hide the way I felt from you. Couldn't be casual anymore. What I felt wasn't something you wanted. So . . ." He looked at her at last, his pale eyes wearing a hard sheen. "So I was expecting you."

Mercy drew a shaky breath. "Well, as a matter of fact, that wasn't what I came here to say."

"No?"

"No. I came here to ask if—if I was right in believing that *you* wanted it to be over."

He leaned his head back against the chair, heavy lids dropping to veil his eyes. "And now you know. The answer is no." His voice was still cool and matter-of-fact.

Mercy wasn't about to leave it there. "Then why do you keep pushing me away? Shutting me out?"

"Have I been doing that?"

"You know damned well you have."

"If you're talking about bank business—"

"This isn't about the bank. This is about us. You know everything about me, don't you, Nick? All my favorite things, the way I feel about politics and religion. Where I shop, and who my doctor is, and where I get my car fixed. You know where I come from, who I am."

"So?"

"So I don't have a clue who you are. I told you that the other night. And you let me see a little bit. And the next day you were miles away again. So far out of my reach I couldn't even touch you. So I figured you just didn't want me even that close ever again."

"It isn't a question of what I want." For the first time, his voice roughened. "It's a question of what I can survive."

"I don't understand."

"I know you don't." His smile was twisted. "Let's put it this way. When it *is* over between us, I will survive losing you. I'll even survive losing the pieces of myself you'll take with you, the pieces you . . . own despite everything I've tried to do to keep myself intact. But I couldn't survive much more than that."

Mercy was having a difficult time believing this. Her heart was thudding and her hands were cold, and she was very, very afraid she might be hearing only what she wanted to hear. So she drew a deep breath and asked the one question that mattered to her.

"Do you love me, Nick?"

He closed his eyes, his face very still except for the muscle that moved suddenly in his jaw.

And the glass in his hand shattered under the force of his grip.

"My God, Nick—"

When she pried his fingers open, she found only one cut, and though it bled profusely, it didn't seem dangerously deep. With her efficient nature kicking into gear, she wrapped his hand in a clean dish towel, then found gauze, bandages, and antiseptic in his medicine cabinet. Sitting on the edge of the hassock with his hand across her lap, she carefully cleaned the wound and bandaged his hand.

Through it all, Nicholas sat silent, his gaze fixed on her. He seemed to feel no pain, obediently flexing his fingers when she asked him to but not moving otherwise.

Mercy cleared up most of the broken glass by simply gathering it into the dish towel, which she laid aside on the bare coffee table with the bandages and antiseptic. She could feel his eyes on her, but hardly knew what to say to him. Finally, she found an ounce of lightness somewhere and said, "You didn't have to slice your hand open to avoid the question, Nick. A simple no would have been enough."

"Of course I love you, Mercy." His voice was very quiet. "I've always loved you."

She looked at him then, and felt her heart catch at the utter desolation in his face. "Nick—"

"I hadn't planned to stay so long in Richmond, you know. Before you came to work for the bank, I was out of the country more often than in. But then you came. I took one look at you when Duncan introduced you as his new assistant, and I knew I'd be staying for good. Whether you ever wanted me or not, I couldn't walk away from you."

Mercy slipped to her knees between the hassock and the chair, her body leaning into his, almost between his thighs as she reached up to touch his face. "Nick . . ."

"I don't want your pity, goddammit," he said thickly. "Don't do that to me."

"It isn't pity." She slid her fingers into his hair and pulled his head toward her. "You stupid man. I love you."

His breath rasped and his fingers bit into her waist for a moment. "Mercy, don't say that unless—"

"Unless I mean it? Do you want me to show you my diary entry from nearly five years ago? *Started work at the bank today. I like my boss. But when I shook hands with his partner . . . God, it happened so fast. How can it happen so fast? How can I love a man I don't even know?*" Her lips feathered across his cheek toward his mouth. "I love you, Nick."

His arms went around her and held her with a strength just this side of painful, and his mouth slanted across hers wildly. For the first time, he held back nothing of himself or his need for her, and Mercy was almost crying when he gathered her up and carried her to his bed.

After the first surprised moment, Rachel moved back across the basement toward the stairs and her uncle. "I thought you'd gone out," she said.

"I went off without my sketch pad, and Kathie wants a sketch," he said more or less automatically.

"I don't have it," Rachel said lightly, assuming he referred to his date that night.

He frowned. "I know that. The basement door was open. I wondered who was down here. Are you looking for something, Rachel?"

"No. I wanted to see how much progress Darby had made." She paused, then heard herself ask, "What are you looking for, Cam?"

"Me? I told you. Just came back to get my sketch pad."

Rachel got to the bottom of the stairs and stood there, looking up at him gravely. "That isn't what I meant. What are you looking for in the furniture, Cam?"

"I don't know what you're talking about."

Cam turned and went back up the stairs.

Rachel followed. She found him in the living room, which was his favorite place in the house. He had poured himself a scotch, and was standing by the cold fireplace, gazing up at the painting of his brother that hung above it.

The painting was his own work.

"We didn't like each other very much," Cam said when she came in. "You knew that?"

"I knew you were very different."

"That's one way of putting it. Another is that we were encouraged to compete in a way that wasn't healthy for either of us."

"Brothers often are."

"Yes." His mouth twisted. "But our father—your grandfather—was a master of the game. He started when we were young, and he never let up. I was pushed into sports because Duncan excelled at them, and never mind that I wasn't athletic. Duncan was tortured with art and music lessons despite the fact that he loathed them."

Rachel came farther into the room and sat on the arm of a chair, watching him. "I had no idea. Dad never spoke of anything like that—and I never knew Grandfather."

"No, he died not long after you were born."

Rachel nodded, and waited.

"He was one of those people who thrive on conflict. Everything had to be a struggle, a battle of wills. He made our mother miserable, browbeat the servants, alienated the rest of the family. Life with him was . . . hard.

"Duncan and I were pushed all the time. And our father blew hot and cold with both of us, promising things he never delivered, threatening punishments. Full of praise one day and scathing criticism the next. It was like living in a mine field, never knowing when the next step would cost an arm or a leg, or some other piece of yourself."

"It sounds horrible."

"It was." He leaned a shoulder against the mantel and gazed at her steadily. "And it only got worse as we grew up. We both had to fight for our identity, to struggle against his domination. Leaving home for college gave us our first taste of independence. First Duncan, then me. But we had to come back here because he commanded it. And neither of us was strong enough to win that battle."

"Cam, why are you telling me this?" Rachel felt uncomfortable, keenly aware that she was learning things her own father had not chosen to tell her in his lifetime.

"So you'll understand."

"Understand what?"

Cameron hesitated, then drew a deep breath. "From the time we were old enough to understand, our father talked about how he meant to leave his fortune when he died. That was the carrot he held out in front of us, and the stick he beat us with. When one of us was in his good graces, he was promised the entire fortune, everything—the other was taunted that he'd be left out in the cold. It went on for years. And he even went so far as to have two different wills drawn up. One promised everything to Duncan, the other promised everything to me."

"That isn't how he left his estate," Rachel said slowly.

Cameron's smile was brief. "Oh, but it is."

"You have Grant property. Real estate, stocks. They came from your father."

"No. They came from Duncan."

Rachel understood immediately. "Grandfather went with the will naming Dad—and Dad deeded you part of the estate."

"Half. He said he'd be damned if he'd live under our father's rule a moment longer, that those wishes and intentions meant nothing to him." Cameron shrugged. "So I got half the money, which I at least had the sense to invest, and Duncan got the other half—and built it into a major fortune."

"So Grandfather lost."

"Did he? He made my brother and me virtual strangers, Rachel. Each of us reminded the other of our father and his torments. So, not long after our father died, I moved to the West Coast. In the nearly thirty years since, I've come home only for brief visits. Until last year, when Duncan invited me to stay here while my place was being renovated."

"Did you two get any closer before he died?"

"No. But at least the old ghosts were quieter after so many years. There was a kind of peace between us. And I'm glad of that."

Rachel nodded. "I'm not sure if I should thank you for telling me all this, but I'm glad you did." She paused, then added, "I still don't understand, though, what it is you're looking for in the furniture."

Readily now, Cameron said, "One of the things our father always said, one of his promised rewards, was a large piece of property overseas. An island, in fact. He swore he owned it, that he had the deed. But when he died, it was never found."

"You're looking for the deed to an island?"

"Rachel, my father was a devious old bastard, and he loved playing games. He told us once that he'd hidden the deed here in the house. That was when we were boys, and

Duncan and I both searched for it. We never found it. Maybe it never existed. But it occurred to me that it would have been just like him to hide something important in a piece of discarded furniture."

"I see."

Cameron smiled at her. "It probably isn't here. Probably never existed. But, just once, I'd like to win one of my father's games. The promise of that keeps me looking."

"Thank you for telling me, Cam."

"I'm just sorry I didn't confide in you before." He shrugged. "But you've been busy, with a lot on your mind. Naturally, if I do find the deed, you'll be the first to know. I'd like to keep looking."

"Of course."

His expression lightened. "Thanks, Rachel. Now I think I'll go get my sketch pad and then meet Kathie for dinner. I'll probably see you tomorrow."

"Good night, Cam."

"Good night, honey."

Rachel sat there on the arm of the chair for a long time after Cameron left. She heard him go upstairs, then come down again a couple of minutes later. Heard the front door close, and his car start up outside. Heard him drive away.

She wondered why he had lied to her.

There were holes in his story, several of them. For one thing, he'd had thirty years to search the house; why was it only now important to him to get his hands on a possibly nonexistent deed? Granted, furniture was just now being moved out of the house, but Cameron had to know already how thorough Darby was, and that a deed to an island would have been useless to Darby even if she was disposed to steal it—which she wasn't.

No, the deed was probably nonexistent.

So what was Cameron really looking for?

• • •

"Do you really keep a diary?"

Mercy pushed herself up a bit so she could smile down at him. "It's more of a journal. But, yes. I'll show it to you if you like. It was the only place I could safely make a fool of myself over you."

He toyed with a strand of her dark hair. "I never guessed. Never even imagined you could feel anything for me."

"I couldn't let you know. Mysterious, enigmatic Nick, who never seemed to give me a second look—until the night he offered me a ride and we ended up stark naked on the rug in front of my fireplace. Was that planned, by the way?"

Nicholas smiled slightly. "That, love, was the most incredibly lucky night of my life. I kissed you because I had to, figuring I'd get my face slapped. But when you responded . . ."

"You thought I might be agreeable to a nice, undemanding affair?"

"I thought it was the most I could hope for."

Mercy shook her head. "And I thought it was the most you wanted from me. Just a warm body in your bed now and then. You were always so damned careful to make sure neither of us owed the other a thing."

"I didn't want you to feel any pressure."

"And didn't want to risk yourself?"

"That too."

She leaned down and kissed him, but pushed herself away when he showed definite signs of losing interest in talk. "Wait a minute."

"Why?"

"Because we aren't finished talking."

Nicholas looked at her warily. "No?"

"No. We have to reach an understanding here."

"I thought we just had."

She firmly pushed his hand away when it began roaming over her hip. "Nick, I'm serious. I walked a high wire for nearly a year trying to figure out what you wanted of me. So now I want you to tell me."

He slid a hand into her hair and pulled her down so he could kiss her. Against her mouth, he said huskily, "I want you with me for the rest of my life. I want to go to sleep with you and wake up with you—and maybe even make babies with you."

More than satisfied with the answer, Mercy smiled and murmured, "What excellent ideas. So when do we go for blood tests?"

"Are we getting married?"

"Well, I won't have babies out of wedlock. Not the way I was raised. So if you want babies, you'll have to marry me."

Nicholas surrounded her face with his hands and gazed at her for a long time. Whatever he was looking for, he found, because he smiled slowly, his eyes alight. And his ugly face wasn't ugly at all.

"I love you, Mercy."

"I love you too."

He pulled her over on top of him. "Enough to see this face across the breakfast table for the next thirty or forty years?"

"Oh, easily." She kissed his chin. "I love this face."

His arms tightened around her. "You're a remarkable woman."

"That's good. I found myself a remarkable man." She

folded her hands on his hard chest and rested her chin on them. "And speaking of how remarkable you are . . ."

He groaned, but he was also smiling. "Let me guess. That singular curiosity of yours is back at work, and you want to know once again what I'm up to."

"You love me," she said. "You must trust me."

"It's not a matter of trust, Mercy."

"Then what is it a matter of?"

He hesitated, then spoke slowly. "Experience. Habit. In some situations, the fewer people who know what's going on, the safer it is for all concerned."

"Then you're into something dangerous. I thought you were."

Again, Nicholas hesitated. "It's . . . no place I haven't been before."

"Somehow, that doesn't surprise me much." She lifted her head and looked at him gravely. "What was it—military? Or something a lot more secretive?"

"The latter. I was recruited when I was barely out of my teens, and the adventure appealed to me. Also the education. I showed an aptitude for finance, so they trained me to understand that. I was used as an investigator more than anything else, an information broker."

"But not always."

"No. There were dangerous situations. Times when I had to use a gun as well as my brain. International finance is a marketplace worth hundreds of billions of dollars, so the stakes are always high."

"Did you work for the CIA?"

"Close, but no. The people I worked for didn't list their address and number in the phone book."

"Worked for. Past tense?"

He nodded. "For years now. But I still have some connections, informants, resources."

"Which you're using now. To do what, Nick? What are you and Adam Delafield up to?"

This time Nicholas barely hesitated. He told her about Duncan's plane crash and what Adam believed had caused it. He told her whom they suspected and why, and what they planned.

It was a story that took time to tell, and when most of Mercy's questions had been answered, they were sitting up in bed drinking wine and eating cheese and crackers, with Mercy wearing his shirt and Nicholas wearing nothing.

"Well, I can see why you've been preoccupied," she said finally.

"I have had a few things on my mind."

"Nick, you're taking an awful risk. From what I've been hearing lately, Jordan Walsh is pure poison. And according to the grapevine, people who do business with him have a nasty habit of turning up dead."

"I know."

"Isn't there some other way?"

"Doesn't appear to be. As yet, the only connection we've found between Duncan and Walsh is that loan and the notes he made in his journal, and neither tells us much."

"No idea who this 'old friend' is?"

"None. Duncan had a lot of friends. A lot of old friends. You saw them at the funeral, men and women from all over the country, the world, most of them clearly devastated by his death. We had to count them all as possibles, and it's a long list. We're checking them out one by one. But so far there isn't a sign of a connection to Walsh."

Mercy brooded for a moment, then said, "Along other lines, I suppose it would be useless to ask you if Adam is working for the same people you used to work for?"

"That isn't my story." Nicholas smiled. "But let's just say that legitimate American businessmen who are smarter than most and can handle themselves in tight situations are a definite asset."

"Mmm. How honest has he been with Rachel?"

"I don't know."

Mercy eyed him.

"I swear. All I can tell you is that Adam is utterly committed to finding out who killed Duncan and his wife, and even more determined to make sure nothing happens to Rachel."

"Because of the loan Duncan made him?"

"He owes his success to Duncan, and he's a man who pays his debts. Even more, Duncan believed in him. At that point in his life the belief and trust were worth more than gold." He had briefly touched on what happened to Adam, the betrayal and prison, simply as an explanation of why Duncan had offered the loan.

"And is that why he's romancing Rachel? Because he owed Duncan?"

Nicholas smiled at her belligerent question. "No, I think the romancing is all on his own account."

Mercy stared at him. "Do you trust him, Nick?"

"Yes."

"It's odd that he looks so much like Tom."

"He didn't arrange it that way, if that's what you're asking me. No surgery, not even hair dye. He simply looks enough like your brother to be his double." Nick shrugged. "I've encountered stranger things in my life, that's all I can tell you."

"He won't hurt her, will he?"

"I don't think so. Certainly not deliberately. Mercy, I don't know all of Adam's secrets, but I know one thing. In some way I don't understand and he's never explained, he is somehow connected to Rachel. And has been for a long time, I think."

"What do you mean?"

"I'm not sure. She's always been his focus. Finding out who killed Duncan and his wife is justice and repayment of a debt, but Adam's here for much more than that. In some way he's here for Rachel. Came here for her even before we knew she'd be in danger."

"But he never met her until a couple of weeks ago."

"As far as I know."

Mercy shook her head. "This whole thing is so—I don't know. Bizarre. Almost unbelievable. That somebody brought down that plane to kill Duncan, and now is trying to kill Rachel. Why?"

"If we knew that, we'd have all the pieces of the puzzle."

"Nick, I want to help."

"No."

"Nick—"

"I don't want you involved."

"Look, I wasn't proposing to pick up a gun and go hunting, but I *was* Duncan's assistant for five years. I owe him too. And I know there's something I can do to help."

"Mercy, what we've set in motion has found its own momentum now, and I want you to stay out of it. There's nothing you can do anyway. Please—I don't want to have to worry about you."

She opened her mouth to tell him about her computer search, then changed her mind. Chances were, she wouldn't find anything anyway.

"Mercy?"

"All right. I'll stay at the bank and mind my own business. If you promise not to keep me in the dark from now on."

"I promise."

"Good. Now, do you want to put this tray on the floor? It's getting in my way."

SEVENTEEN

The long stone corridor stretched before her, but Rachel had no intention of going that way. Not this time. Not again.

She couldn't bear the thought of seeing Adam like that again.

She turned around and walked steadily, relieved when the stone walls gave way to smooth, painted Sheetrock, and the candle sconces became electrical fixtures.

"Secrets. Everybody's got secrets."

Rachel stopped, listening. The whisper had seemed to come from no particular direction—and all directions.

"Who's there?"

"Look for secrets, Rachel."

"Tom?"

"Secret things in secret places."

Frustrated, she said, "Why won't you tell me where to look? What to look for?"

"You already know."

"No, I don't. I—"

"You know. You only have to remember."

"Help me!"

"I can't."

"Tom, please!"

She saw him then as he stepped out of the shadows just ahead of her. It was Tom and yet . . . not.

"This is a house of secrets, Rachel. Don't you know that yet?"

She took a step toward him. "Whose secrets?"

He shook his head, and the faint light glinted off the polished surface of his face. His mask. "I can't hurt you."

She frowned, baffled. "Knowing who the secrets belong to will hurt me?"

"Yes."

"It's someone I trust?"

He was silent.

"Someone I love?"

"Remember about secret places, Rachel. Remember."

He backed away, out of the light.

Rachel started forward quickly. "Tom? Wait!"

But hard as she tried, she couldn't catch up to him. He was always just ahead, within sight and out of reach.

Then she realized that the Sheetrock walls had given way to stone ones again, and her steps slowed. "No. Not here. I don't want to be here."

"You have to."

"I've already looked. You made me look. I don't want to look ever again."

The door was just ahead. But there were no sounds coming from inside it, not this time. And there was no lock this time.

"Open the door, Rachel."

"What will I see?"

"What you must. Open the door."

The voice came, suddenly, from inside that room.

Slowly, she reached out for the handle and opened the door.

At first, all she saw was darkness. But then light glowed from a small central point, getting brighter until she could see him. There were no torturers now. Just him, standing in the center of the chilly room.

"Tom?"

"No. Yes."

"I don't understand."

He reached up and took off his Tom face, revealing an Adam face beneath it that was cracked and stained. An Adam mask.

And Adam's voice said, "Which one of us do you want, Rachel?"

"I . . . want you."

"Who am I?"

"Adam."

"Am I?"

"Don't do this to me! Don't play these games!"

"Games? Rachel, I would never play games with you."

What she saw wavered suddenly, like heat shimmering off pavement on a summer's day, and she heard Adam's urgent voice coming from outside the room.

"Don't listen to him, Rachel. It isn't me. Don't you understand? He wants you back."

She backed away from the open door. "What? Who?"

"Thomas Sheridan. He wants you back."

"But he's dead."

"Yes, Rachel. He's dead."

The man inside the room came toward her, arms outstretched. "Rachel. My Rachel. Come to me, darling—"

Worms squirmed from the eyeholes of his Adam mask, and blood dripped from the mouth.

Rachel turned, crying out, and ran.

Behind her, the footsteps were loud and close.

Adam jerked upright in bed, the sounds of her screams ringing in his ears, and stared around the hotel room that was bright with early morning light. Bright, and empty of any threat.

A dream. Just another dream.

"Jesus Christ," he muttered.

Rachel huddled against the headboard of her bed, hugging her drawn-up knees as she waited for the shakes to stop, for her breathing to return to normal. It took a long time.

A very long time.

When Adam showed up early that morning, he found Rachel in the sunroom with coffee and an untouched breakfast on the table. He paused in the doorway, watching her, unannounced since Fiona had merely told him where Rachel was.

She looked tired, he thought. More than that, really. Her face was too drawn and pale, her eyes too dark. Almost haunted.

It certainly was not the inexpressive face she had worn when he had first talked to her in this house. Her face had been masklike, the animated beauty she had been known for as a girl buried so that the only hints of its existence had been her slow smiles. She had appeared to feel nothing deeply. At some point in the past couple of weeks, however, Rachel had most certainly begun to feel again.

Adam wanted to believe he was responsible for that change. He just wished the face he saw when he looked in his own mirror had not been one shared by a dead man. And he wished he could take Rachel far away from all this.

As he watched Rachel, she looked down at her left wrist, flexing and turning it absently. She was no longer wearing the elastic bandage, but obviously still felt the sprain, if only a little.

Adam drew a breath and came into the room. "Good morning."

"Adam." She came out of her chair and into his arms as if it were the most natural thing on earth.

He held her tightly for a long while, then bent his head and kissed her. He couldn't hide his desire, and she was so responsive, it stole his breath and made his heart ache. There was, he thought, something almost desperate in the way she clung to him.

He framed her face in his hands and looked down at her gravely. "Are you okay?"

"Bad night." She smiled. "But I'm all right now."

"Did you get enough rest?"

"I got enough sleep," she answered, the distinction wry. "Here—have some coffee."

Adam joined her at the table and accepted the cup she fixed for him. "Thanks. Was it . . . dreams?"

"Nightmares." Rachel shrugged. "Wandering a house with endless corridors and getting . . . unpleasant surprises. I seem to return there every night. Natural, I suppose. There have been so many changes in my life in the last few months, it's no wonder my subconscious is going nuts trying to sort everything out."

He looked at her a moment, and decided not to dwell

on the subject. He didn't want to burden her with his own nightmares, or force her to relive hers just because he had the crazy idea they were both dreaming the same dreams.

A really crazy idea.

Instead, he said, "Any new ideas about where your father might have left a key for you to find?"

"Not really." She frowned suddenly, and added almost under her breath, "Secret places."

Adam felt a little chill. "Secret places?"

She shook her head. "Something from my nightmare. Secret things in secret places."

"Do you know what that means?"

"No—except that I found out a few secrets last night." She told him about the conversation with Cameron, finishing by saying, "He's looking for something, and since he lied about it, I guess it's secret."

"You said there was virtually no chance Cameron could have been the one to ask your father to lend Walsh the money. Do you still believe that?"

Rachel nodded. "I don't think his search has anything to do with the loan to Walsh—or any other. No, Cam is looking for something else. I just don't know what."

"Secret things in secret places."

"That must be why that showed up in my dreams. It was on my mind."

"So you don't believe it has anything to do with what we're looking for?"

"I don't know, Adam. That's probably one more thing my subconscious is trying to work out. So—maybe. I was also . . . told in my dream that I know the answer and I just have to remember." She smiled faintly. "So far I haven't remembered anything useful." She didn't want to go into more detail about the dreams, and most especially did not want to mention Tom's name. Not to Adam.

"Then try not to think about it." He smiled at her. "That's the kind of thing that never comes when you're trying."

"I know. It sneaks up on you later and blindsides you."

"Let's hope not." He paused, then said, "I talked to Nick a while ago. We may have gotten a break on Walsh."

"What kind of break?"

"One of Nick's contacts swears he knows someone who works for Walsh and wants out. Supposedly, this man is one of those Walsh has used to construct various explosives—like the ones that brought down Duncan's plane."

"That sounds very convenient," Rachel said.

Adam grimaced. "Yeah. Walsh may be on to us. But we have to follow the trail, Rachel. We don't have a choice."

"You think this man—if he really exists—might be the one who—"

"Built the explosive that brought down Duncan's plane? Maybe. Though something tells me that would be too easy." He shook his head. "The best we're hoping for is that he knows something that might help us."

"Is it as much of a long shot as it sounds?"

"Pretty much. But if there's anything to it, we'll find out soon enough. Nick and I are scheduled to meet with him in a couple of hours."

"I guess I'm supposed to stay inside the castle, huh?"

He reached across the table and took her hand. "It won't be much longer, I promise. One way or another, we're going to finish this."

"Don't take any reckless chances, Adam. As prisons go, this is a lot better than most."

"I'll be careful." He hesitated, then said, "Just so you

know, we've had a couple of men watching this house—and you if you leave."

She blinked. "You mean, when I went to your hotel in the middle of the night—"

"You had an escort." He smiled. "But very discreet. The one who follows you tends to hang back if I'm with you, which is why he wasn't close enough to do anything to help when that store exploded and the car tried to run us down. But he and his partner are watching the house from the front and the river. They'll see if anyone tries to sneak in."

"Almost as good as a moat." She returned his smile, hers a bit rueful. "It makes me feel a little creepy, though. Being watched."

"I thought you'd probably feel that way. It's why I didn't tell you before now. But it's necessary, Rachel. So far, none of the attempts against you have come here, but we're not sure where your car was when it was sabotaged, assuming it was. And even though this is a walled estate, the front gate stands wide open and there's easy access from the river. So we have to keep an eye on the place."

"I'm not arguing. I just want it to be over, Adam."

"I know." He squeezed her hand, then released it reluctantly. "I have to go. Nick and I have some things to go over, and we have to check out the meeting site in advance."

"Will you come back and tell me what happened?"

"Of course I will. But it may take all day, depending on whether Nick's informant is right and this guy really does want to talk."

"I'm not going anywhere," Rachel said.

• • •

The whole day stretched before her, and Rachel was more than a little restless. She didn't want to work on the plans for the boutique, and she couldn't think of where her father might have left a key for her to find. She didn't like the idea of Adam and Nick doing dangerous things outside the walls of her prison while she sat inside like some medieval maiden awaiting rescue.

With her ghosts.

She told Fiona not to bother about lunch for her since this was the housekeeper's habitual day to go to the market, and went upstairs in search of some way to occupy her time and her thoughts until Adam was safely back with her again.

Without planning to, she found herself in her mother's room, which was across the hall from her father's. This room, too, aroused memories, and Rachel was surprised by how strong they were.

The lavender scent her mother had always used.

The needlepoint pillows she had spent endless hours doing.

The costume jewelry she had loved.

The delicate gilded furniture that had suited her petite beauty and seeming fragility.

For the first time, whether because her emotions were so near the surface now or because she simply had a better understanding now of how complex people and relationships could be, Rachel was able to mourn the loss of her mother. She was able to grieve for all their differences and misunderstandings, for the distance that had grown between them from the time Rachel was a teenager. For all her regrets.

Needing to feel close to the woman she now felt she had hardly known in life, Rachel sat at her mother's dressing table and looked at all the pretty things, touched them.

She even tried on the long string of pearls her mother had often worn, and smiled wryly at herself in the mirror because pearls didn't suit her.

Finally, she began to tentatively go through her mother's things, deciding what to keep and what to pack up or give away. The clothing, which she didn't bother sorting at the moment, was easy. Most would go to a thrift shop, where others could get some use out of it, and the more formal things could be put aside for charity auctions or some such thing.

After making that decision, she then went to her mother's elegant little desk and began going through the drawers.

Somebody else had done the same thing.

She wasn't sure how she knew, but there was no doubt in her mind that since her mother's death, these drawers had been opened, their contents rifled through.

Rachel murmured, "Dad's desks were locked, and I had the keys. But Mom never bothered to lock hers."

There had been a great many strangers in the house at various times since her parents' deaths, but Rachel couldn't think of any reason why her mother's personal things would have been inspected. There was, she thought, little of interest in these drawers, and certainly nothing of any intrinsic value. Stationery not yet used. A few letters, none of which looked important. An appointment diary that held only social engagements noted with detachment. The usual drawer lint composed of paper clips and rubber bands and stamps and pens that no longer worked.

Nothing else.

Frowning, Rachel got up and went to check a few more places, finding the same rifled disorder in her mother's nightstands and tall chest of drawers. There was no question they had been searched.

For a moment, she stood in the center of her mother's bedroom, looking around. All right. Someone, for whatever reason, had searched through her mother's things. Cameron was her first thought, but it didn't make sense that he might have expected to find anything of value among her mother's personal things.

She went into her mother's dressing room/closet, to the island of drawers in the center of the room. She looked through each, carefully going through sweaters and casual shirts and frilly, scented sleepwear and underwear. None of this appeared to have been searched.

But there was also nothing to find.

Nor was there anything unusual in the built-in drawers for jewelry, or the storage areas for shoes and hats.

But in the specially designed case that held all her mother's collection of antique lace handkerchiefs, Rachel did find something unexpected.

A false bottom.

And underneath it, a bundle of letters tied up with faded blue ribbon.

Rachel carried the letters back into her mother's bedroom and sat down with them at the desk. Even before she untied the ribbon and looked at the first letter, she felt a bit queasy.

She didn't recognize the handwriting, but the scrawled signature was all too clear.

Secret things in secret places.

The first letter, dated only a few months after her own birth, began with devastating simplicity.

My darling Irene . . .

• • •

"I don't like the setup," Adam said.

"Do you think I do?" Nicholas shrugged. "But he was only willing to meet us on his terms. And that means here."

Adam looked around at the warehouse, which had been unused and deserted for a good many years. Even with the warm spring day outside, inside this place was chilly and dark and dismal.

Not to mention dangerous.

"We're sitting ducks. Look at those catwalks up there. Anybody could take potshots at us."

"There's nobody up there. I checked."

"Are you kidding? You could hide a dinosaur in this place."

"You're jumpy today."

"Damned right I am. My life is beginning to look really good, and I'll be extremely unhappy if something bad happens to mess that up."

Nicholas, who was leaning idly back against a huge but empty wooden crate in the shadows, said calmly, "Then stay out of the light."

"You have no nerves at all, do you?"

"None to speak of."

Both men kept their voices low, and despite the contentious tone of the conversation, it was obvious they were entirely comfortable with the tension of the situation. It was no place both of them hadn't been before.

But Adam was restless, and it showed. "I'm still bothered by the fact that we don't know who else has been following Rachel and me."

"Assuming Max was telling the truth."

"I think he was. I think he saw Simon for sure. We were out only during Simon's shift, so he had to be one. But the other one . . . Big, blond, casually dressed, yet somehow polished, smooth. Not a cop but maybe a spook?"

"In Max's opinion."

Impatiently, Adam said, "The point is that there's a player out there we don't have identified." Then he frowned. "Or is he somebody you just haven't told me about?"

Nicholas folded his arms across his chest. "You are jumpy. I'm not keeping anything back, Adam. You know what I know."

Adam looked at him a moment, then nodded. "Okay. Sorry."

"It could be one of Walsh's men, you know. Keeping an eye on Rachel, maybe looking for an opportunity to get at her."

"Maybe. But Walsh would almost certainly use a man he knew was loyal to him, a wiseguy. And if there's anything Max would recognize, it'd be a wiseguy."

"In that case," Nicholas said, "we'd better hope we get this settled before whoever it is has a chance to surprise us."

"Yeah."

They both heard it at the same time, the faint sound of an engine outside the warehouse.

Adam said, "You're sure your guy won't object to me being along?"

"I'm sure. Sammy owes me so much, he couldn't object if I brought the district attorney to a meet with him."

They stood there in silence, waiting, and a couple of minutes later one of the front doors creaked open and a thin, worried-looking man about Nick's age slipped into the warehouse. He came immediately to where they were waiting, his eyes darting around with profound nervousness.

"Hello, Sammy," Nicholas said.

"Nick." He looked warily at Adam. "Who's this?"

"A friend. You can trust him. Where's the one you were supposed to bring?"

"I think he might've got whacked, Nick." Sammy's voice was matter-of-fact, but underneath the calm was crawling sheer terror.

Nicholas didn't change position or alter the calm tone of his voice. "What makes you think so, Sammy?"

" 'Cause I went to pick him up like we'd planned, only he wasn't there. He lives about halfway between here and Arlington, in a real quiet neighborhood, respectable as hell. But when I cruised by his place, it was—well, there were cops all over. And the coroner's wagon." Sammy swallowed hard.

"Had he told anyone else he meant to inform against Walsh?" Adam asked sharply.

"I don't know what he told anybody else, just what he told me. Said he was scared to get out, scareder staying in, and that he knew way too much about Walsh's operations, especially here in Richmond. He figured he didn't have a chance of staying alive on his own, and maybe Nick could protect him like I said. I been talking to him, Nick, like I told you I was. Tryin' to convince him you had the juice to protect him no matter who was after his ass. He was jumping out of his skin, said he'd done something really stupid and Walsh would hunt him down on account of the evidence—"

"Evidence?" Nick's voice was also sharp.

Sammy nodded. "Said he'd stumbled across a computer disk when he was doing a job for Walsh a few weeks ago, and the idiot took it."

"With what on it?"

"Records. A shitload of records, he said. For bribes

and payoffs, bank account numbers. All the big jobs. Hits ordered and carried out. Lists of bought judges and cops—even some government people. His whole Richmond operation, and it dates back further than anybody knew. Walsh has been pulling strings in this town for years, Nick."

"He never showed his face in Richmond until a few months ago," Nick said.

"Yeah. But, man, was he here in spirit."

"Jesus Christ on a pony," Adam muttered.

Sammy nodded as if wholeheartedly agreeing. "Yeah. That stuff gets made public, and a lot of big shots besides Walsh are going down."

Nicholas said, "Do you believe he actually had evidence of this?"

"He showed me a disk, Nick, that's all I know. He said—" Sammy broke off, looking uncertain.

"What?"

"Well, when we talked last night, he said if anything was to happen to him before he could talk to you, I was to take you to a certain place, and maybe that disk would be there."

Nicholas scowled at him. "Sammy—"

"I swear, Nick. I don't have a way in to the place, which is why I couldn't get the disk myself even if I wanted to do that. But he said you could get it. He said you could get it easy. He picked the place special when I first told him about you a couple of weeks ago."

"Sammy, if you're lying to me—"

"Nick, I swear to God it's the truth. Don't I owe you my life? Didn't I swear I'd repay you someday? I said I'd be there when you called in the favor, and I'm here, Nick. You can trust me."

"I hope so, Sammy. I really hope so."

"I don't like this," Adam said. "It smells like a trap."

Sammy was offended. "No way."

"You might not know about it, Sammy," Nicholas pointed out. "He could be using you."

Sammy looked uncertain a moment, then shook his head. "No. I believe him, Nick. He was on the up-and-up."

"Okay," Nicholas said. "Where is this place, Sammy?"

Before the other two could stop him, Sammy had darted back toward the front door. "Come on. He said I was to take you there, not just tell you where it is."

"Sammy—"

But the worried little man didn't hesitate. He yanked open the door. For just a moment, he was silhouetted, the light from outside pouring through the open door.

Then a shot.

Adam and Nick reached the door as a squeal of tires outside declared the successful departure of the shooter. Sammy lay in a rapidly spreading pool of blood, and grim experience told both the other men he wouldn't last long.

"Goddammit," Adam said bitterly as they knelt beside Sammy.

"Nick . . ." Sammy reached up and grasped the lapel of Nick's jacket with bloodied fingers. "Listen—"

Nicholas bent low, his ear no more than an inch from Sammy's labored whisper.

Then Sammy's hand dropped away, a rattling sigh left his mouth, and his sightless eyes gazed into eternity.

"Well?" Adam watched as Nicholas straightened. "Did you get it?"

Nicholas looked at him with an expression that defied description, and said slowly, "Yeah. I got it."

EIGHTEEN

It took Rachel some time to read all the letters. She didn't want to read them. They hurt more than she would have thought possible. But she forced herself to because she wanted no more secrets in this house.

Why didn't you burn them, Mom?

Love letters. Love letters from her uncle to her mother. And from what had been written, it was clear they'd had an affair during the summer he had been home from college, just scant months after Rachel's birth. It didn't seem to have lasted long, only a couple of months, but it was obviously intense while it was going on.

The only relief Rachel got from reading the letters was in knowing that the affair had begun *after* her birth and not before. That was clear in what Cameron wrote; though he claimed to have been in love with Irene for years, he had not dared to speak until that summer.

No reason for either his silence before or his change of mind that summer was offered.

It was also clear from the letters that Cameron had been the supplicant, wildly begging Irene Grant to leave her husband and infant daughter, promising that he could give her a better life. She had been unhappy, married to a man who had not, apparently, needed her as she'd wanted him to.

Rachel, remembering her pretty, serene mother, also recalled arguments during her childhood when Irene had wanted Duncan to get involved in the society events she had so enjoyed—and he had despised. Rachel had not thought much about the arguments, because they had seemed low-key, with her father's refusals and her mother's frustration expressed calmly, almost more like debates than arguments. Neither had seemed particularly upset either during or afterward, and there had always been other escorts available to Rachel's mother, friends or otherwise "safe" men who could escort a married woman without causing talk.

Rachel wondered now if there had been lovers as well.

Which was a hell of a thing to wonder about your mother.

Her parents had had separate bedrooms as long as she could remember, and though she had memories of affection between them, especially during her sporadic visits home in the last ten years, she could not remember anything even remotely romantic.

Was that it? Had Irene craved the sort of romance that the plain-speaking, practical Scotsman she'd married was incapable of giving her?

Two brothers, one blunt and unromantic, the other artistic and somewhat dramatic—and handsome, in his younger years.

Two brothers, raised by a father who had pitted them against each other, pushed them to compete on every level, rewarding success and ridiculing them when they failed, setting them up to feel that what one had the other had to better.

Two brothers. And a woman who might have loved them both.

"I wish you'd kept a diary, Mom." Then again, Rachel thought as she slowly retied the blue ribbon around the letters, maybe she didn't wish that at all. It was profoundly disconcerting for her to face this window into her parents' troubled relationship, and even more so to learn that her mother had very nearly run off with her uncle.

Because it looked as though that had nearly happened.

That Irene Grant had not left her husband appeared to be, at least according to Cameron's bitter words, almost solely due to her love of social position. Duncan, as the elder son and likely heir to his father, had far greater potential than Cameron, the younger son and a struggling artist to boot.

She had apparently ended the affair shortly after her father-in-law had died, and did not change her mind when her husband deeded half his inheritance to his brother.

With only Cameron's letters to tell the story, Rachel had no idea how accurate his assessment of the situation was. He had been clearly bitter and unhappy, hugely resentful of his brother, and had accepted Irene's decision with the declaration that he would never love anyone else.

Rachel didn't know what she felt about this. She had no idea if her father had known of the affair. She had no real idea of what her mother's emotions and motivations had been.

And it had been nearly thirty years ago.

But Rachel did wonder, now, if her mother's serenity

had been natural to her personality before the affair with Cameron. Or had that tranquility, like her daughter's twenty years later, stemmed from an agonizing loss she had been unable to completely recover from?

There was, of course, no way for Rachel to know now. But wondering made her feel the loss of her mother more bitterly than she ever had before, because it seemed possible that they'd had far more in common than Rachel had ever guessed.

"I thought there'd be time," Rachel murmured to herself, gazing down at the evidence of her mother's secret soul. "I thought I'd come home one day, when it didn't hurt anymore, and we'd have time to fix all the broken things between us and be close."

But there hadn't been enough time, that plane crash stealing forever any chance Rachel might have had to repair the damaged relationships with her parents. While she had remained in New York, working long hours so she didn't have to think or feel, keeping herself in limbo because that had been less painful, they had been snatched from her life, her future.

Rachel faced that for the first time.

She had thought loss was the most painful thing of all, but now she knew there was something more painful. Regret.

When she finally got hold of herself once again, Rachel discovered that she was lying across her mother's bed, the letters thrown aside. Instinctively, she reached under the pillows for the lavender-scented handkerchief that had always been there, and not finding it made a fresh wave of grief sweep over her with a force she couldn't fight.

It was a long time before Rachel finally pulled herself off the bed. She went into her mother's bathroom and splashed cold water on her face, avoiding any glance in the mirror. She undoubtedly looked awful, though she certainly felt better. Drained, but more at peace somehow.

She returned to her mother's desk and gazed down at the letters for some time, thinking, before she finally made her decision. This was not her story. It had not affected her life while her parents had been alive, and it did not seriously change her feelings, in any negative way, for either of them now that they were gone.

It wasn't her business, all things considered. And the only surviving member of that triangle deserved his privacy.

Cameron's urgent search, undoubtedly for these letters, was clear evidence of his feelings on the matter; she had no doubt he would have destroyed them—or kept her from knowing about them, had he discovered them himself.

Rachel's first impulse was to leave them on his pillow to find when he returned from the trip he had taken today into D.C. to check out various galleries. But when she thought of both of them being painfully aware of her knowledge of the affair, it was simply not something she wanted to have to deal with.

She would never be close to Cameron, but she did not want old secrets and regrets to shadow her relationship with her uncle. There were some things a niece just didn't need to know.

With that decision made, Rachel picked up the phone and called Darby.

"Hey, pal," she said when Darby answered. "I need a favor."

"You've got it," Darby replied without hesitation.

• • •

If Nicholas had not wielded considerable influence over numerous officials within the Richmond police force because of his background and connections in law enforcement, and commanded enormous respect among its various politicians because of all the successful business ventures he had backed, he and Adam would have no doubt been forced to spend the entire day with the police answering questions about Sammy's murder. Even so, it still required a couple of hours for them to tell their story —the one they had decided to tell, at any rate—and be granted leave to be on their way.

As long as they didn't leave the city, of course.

"It's a good thing you routinely use informants to gather information for the bank," Adam commented as they finally left the warehouse and the crowd of police officers and technicians behind. "How long do you think it'll be before somebody starts to get very curious about exactly what information you wanted that would have gotten Sammy killed?"

"A few days, if we're lucky." Nicholas shrugged. "Not that it'll matter if we get our hands on that disk and it holds even a fraction of what Sammy claimed it does. We'll just go public holding a hand full of aces, and all will be forgiven."

"If we get our hands on that disk."

"You always tell me to think positive. Now it's your turn."

Adam looked at him curiously. "You really think the disk is where Sammy told you it would be. Why?"

"Because," Nicholas said, "the irony is just wonderful. And I've always believed the universe had a wicked sense of humor."

Adam was puzzled, especially since Nick had not yet told him where the disk was supposed to be. But, moments later, when the big black car turned into the parking lot beside the bank, puzzlement turned to surprise.

"You're kidding," Adam said.

"Like I said." Nick turned off the engine and smiled. "The irony is wonderful."

Rachel was just closing the basement door behind her when Fiona appeared.

"Miss Rachel, I'm going to the market now. Is there anything special you want me to get?"

"Nothing I can think of, thanks, Fiona."

The housekeeper frowned at her, but did not comment directly about swollen eyelids. "There's cold chicken and salad in the refrigerator. You need to eat, Miss Rachel."

"I will—if I get hungry." She smiled. "Don't worry about me, Fiona. I'll be fine."

Fiona sniffed. "If you say so. I'll be back in a couple of hours."

"Take your time."

Alone once again, Rachel slowly went back upstairs. She turned toward her father's room, intending to try once more to figure out where he might have hidden a key for her to find. But she stopped dead in the middle of the hallway just past her own room, staring.

A yellow rose lay on the rug at her feet.

She bent slowly and picked up the flower, turning it in her fingers as she straightened. She had glanced in her room as she passed, and the rose had been in the vase on her nightstand, as always. Now this one . . .

"If this is some kind of joke," she murmured in a shaky voice, "I'm not amused."

She hadn't expected an answer, but a glimpse of movement made her look quickly at the far end of the hallway.

The door that led up to the smallest of the three attics was there. And it was slowly opening.

If she had behaved rationally, Rachel realized a long time later, she would have turned around and gotten out of there, especially when the distant doorway remained empty. Instead, she found herself walking slowly toward it, the rose still gripped between her fingers, her heart thudding.

Just a stray breeze, probably. Darby or one of her guys had undoubtedly left the door ajar, and some stray breeze had blown it open.

That was all.

Rachel stopped in the doorway, gazing at the stairs leading upward. Then she took a step back. Ridiculous. This was ridiculous—

"Rachel . . ."

It was only a whisper of sound, so faint she could almost convince herself she had not heard it at all. Almost. Except that the hair on the back of her neck was stirring, and she knew this was not her imagination.

Drawing a deep breath, she flipped up the switch on the wall at the foot of the stairs, then slowly climbed upward. At the top of the lighted stairs, she paused, looking slowly around. This space, like the other attics and the basement, was stuffed with furniture and other cast-off items, and since nothing had yet been tagged or sorted, it was clear Darby had not yet begun her work here.

But Rachel's realization of that was distant and occupied little of her attention. She knew what she was supposed to be looking at. It was a storage chest that had, for most of her life, been in her bedroom. On one of her brief visits home after Tom's death, her mother had explained that she had moved the chest to the attic. To spare Rachel, because in it she had kept all the mementos and notes and silly little gifts from Tom.

Rachel had not been able to bring herself to sort through any of the things, not then, and not in all the years since.

Now the lid was raised invitingly, the bare lightbulb hanging directly above it seeming to spotlight the open chest, and Rachel knew without a doubt that she was being asked—commanded—to look inside.

"No." Her voice sounded to her unnaturally loud in the close silence of the attic.

"Rachel . . ." Almost inaudible, like a breath of wind.

"No." She felt her eyes sting with tears, blurring her vision, and she had to swallow hard before she could go on. "I'm sorry. But you're . . . you're gone, Tom. You've been gone a long time. And I love somebody else now."

She opened her fingers and let the rose fall to the floor.

There was a moment when the lights seemed to flicker, or something else seemed to happen, and when Rachel looked down, blinking the tears away, there was no rose. When she looked at the chest, it was closed, the layer of dust atop it undisturbed.

She stood there for a long time, listening, but heard nothing. She turned around and went back down the stairs, turning off the lights at the bottom and closing the attic door carefully.

She walked on, pausing only when she reached the door of her bedroom, and looked inside. There was no yellow rose on her nightstand, no bud vase. And when she went to open her jewelry box, there was no gold identification bracelet inside. She was afraid to look in her desk drawer, but when she did, the note from Tom was there.

On white notepaper, the kind he had used ten years ago.

Rachel sat down on her bed and murmured, "I must be a lot more tired than I thought I was."

Or perhaps she had just needed concrete things to make her face and deal with her feelings about Tom. It seemed as good an answer as any, and infinitely preferable to the notion that she was losing her mind.

After a while, Rachel got up and went downstairs. A glance at a clock surprised her; only a few minutes had passed since Fiona had left the house. Shaking her head, Rachel went into the study and looked around slowly.

Maiden in a locked castle she might be, but only she had known her father well enough to have any hope of figuring out where he might have left a key for her to find. And without that key, they might well never have all the answers they needed. She concentrated on that.

Secret things in secret places.

However secret his private loans had been, Duncan Grant would not have left even that part of his estate untended. He would have made certain that everything had been set up in such a way that when Rachel eventually and inevitably discovered what he had been doing, she would not only be unharmed financially, but would have the option of safely continuing what her father had begun so many years before.

That meant detailed records, tax information, and a clear explanation of his system.

And given his secrecy on the matter, he would have left that information where it would not be casually discovered after his death, but where Rachel *specifically* would know where to look for it once she found the notebooks and journal.

Of course, he had certainly not counted on his daughter being so distracted by attempts on her own life and the fact that she had fallen in love, so what might have seemed obvious to him eluded her now.

"Where?" Rachel muttered, looking around absently. "Where does X mark the spot? Come on, Dad, I need your help. Where did you leave it? Where would you hide a key?"

A key.

Secret things in secret places.

Her mother's handkerchiefs had hidden secret letters.

A woman would hide her secrets among treasured things put safely away; where would a man hide his secrets?

More important, where would he hide them if he expected his daughter to know where to look?

"You already know."

"No, I don't. I—"

"You know. You only have to remember."

The dream conversation came back to her vividly, and Rachel frowned as she considered it. Her subconscious nagging at her again? *Was* there something she needed to remember?

Her father.

Secrets.

Secret things in secret places.

Secret things in secret places.

"Of course. My God—why didn't I remember it before now?"

"It's our secret, Rachel. Just yours and mine."

As a small child, she had often played in her father's study, and she had been endlessly fascinated with the desk he had designed and had custom-built years before. She had loved the gleaming wood, the deep drawers, the leather desk set he had always used.

And the secret.

Rachel had to sit down on the floor in order to get far enough underneath the desk, and it took her several moments to remember which place in the kneehole to look, but eventually she found it. A small section of wood with no seams showing, so cunningly crafted it would have taken an inch-by-inch measurement—if not a total dismemberment of the desk—to determine hidden space.

Carefully, Rachel's fingertip probed, and she felt the tiny indentation. And pressed firmly.

Obediently, the secret compartment popped open. And her fingers closed over a small box hidden inside.

Adam looked over Nick's shoulder as he worked at the computer on his desk. "I still can't believe this Alan Fuller just walked into your bank a couple of weeks ago and calmly rented a safe deposit box." He shook his head. "We might well have had all the answers we needed right under our noses for two weeks."

"It was a smart thing to do," Nicholas noted absently as he began to access the information on the disk. "As long as either he or Sammy got word to me, getting the disk was easy for me, even without the renter's key. In the meantime, Walsh didn't have a clue where it was—and he's been in and out of here at least twice recently."

"I'm wondering if Walsh had Fuller's place searched before or after he was killed. If he did, and if he got his hands on the key, he'll be turning up here or sending somebody else quick."

Nicholas nodded. "If we get anything at all off this disk, we'll need to move fast."

Grim, Adam said, "Let's just hope whatever we get is worth two lives. If we don't get him for anything else, I want to burn Walsh for Fuller and Sammy."

"You and me both." Nick's skilled fingers moved lightly over the keys. "Ah."

After a moment, Adam said, "I'll be damned."

"So he was an explosives expert, just as he claimed," Nicholas noted as he read the information on the screen. "But also a computer genius. It looks like Walsh was just a bit careless with access."

"People who don't understand computers often are," Adam observed, also reading. "Look at that—Sammy was right. Lists of paid-off judges and cops, with dates and amounts. Bribes and kickbacks. Everything necessary to bust Walsh's entire operation here in Richmond."

"The D.A. is going to love us," Nick said.

"What about Duncan's death? Is there some record of that explosion?"

Nick frowned as he read. "Nothing so far. Let me go back a few more months. . . ."

In her office, Mercy worked at her own computer.

She knew Nick and Adam had gone out and that they'd returned, and she'd been unable to answer Leigh's so-casual question when the office manager had come in to ask her why Nick had made a sudden and unexpected trip downstairs to the lock boxes.

She had, of course, wondered herself, but made herself do as she'd promised Nick. She stayed in her office and asked no questions.

And worked at her computer.

It was an hour or so after Nick and Adam had returned

that she suddenly frowned and leaned toward her screen. Well, now, that was odd.

That was very odd.

The box was small and made of intricately carved wood. It had been a gift from Rachel to her father several years before. Another way Duncan had ensured she would search for what was hidden; eventually, she would have wondered what had happened to the box, because her father had loved it.

"Oh, Dad . . ."

Rachel climbed back up and into her father's chair, and put the box on top of the desk to open it. Inside, as she had expected, was a small key, obviously to a safe deposit box. And a note.

Rachel—

By now you undoubtedly know what you'll find when you use this key. Everything you'll need is there. If you choose to continue this work, I know you'll do well, and many people will benefit. But make your life your own. I love you, sweetheart.

Dad

The key to the safe deposit box was neatly labeled with the name of the bank.

Rachel shook her head over it, but she was smiling. She had no idea if her intuitions and judgments about people would prove as accurate as her father's had been, but she was willing to put them to the test.

Then her smile faded, and she looked at the key in her hand, wondering if among that information lay the connection that she and Adam—and Nick—had been searching for. The connection between Jordan Walsh and someone Duncan had known and trusted.

She wanted to leave now, to rush out to the bank and find out exactly what information awaited her in the box. But she also wanted Adam to be with her. Whether or not his meeting had been successful, he might be at the bank with Nick—

The phone rang.

Hoping it was Adam, Rachel hurried to pick up the receiver. "Hello?"

"May I speak to Rachel Grant, please?"

Rachel didn't recognize the voice. "This is she."

"Miss Grant, this is John Elliot. I got a message to call this number and speak to either you or an Adam Delafield."

For a moment, Rachel was totally blank.

"I'm a private investigator," he added.

"Oh. Oh, of course. I'm sorry, Mr. Elliot, things have been a bit hectic, and I'd forgotten. . . . The reason we called was that we wanted to ask you a question about some work you might have done for my father."

"Duncan Grant?"

"Yes. Among his papers, we found a note indicating that he might have asked you to investigate someone shortly before he was killed."

"As a matter of fact, Miss Grant, he did. But he was killed just days later, and we never finalized the arrangement."

"I see. Was it Jordan Walsh he asked you to check out?"

Immediately, Elliot said, "No, ma'am, it wasn't. He just said he was looking at a potential business problem, and wanted me to do a little digging, very quietly."

"Did he give you a name?"

"No, ma'am. He said there were a couple of things he wanted to check on himself first, and that he'd be in touch as soon as he did that. I can't be sure, of course, but from the way he talked, I got the idea it was somebody he'd trusted up till then, somebody close to him."

"I see. And that's all you can tell me?"

"I'm afraid so, Miss Grant. As I said, the arrangement was never finalized."

Not very helpful, but there was nothing Rachel could do about that.

"Thank you anyway, Mr. Elliot, for calling. I'll pass on the information to Mr. Delafield."

"I'm sorry I couldn't be more help, Miss Grant."

"So am I. Good-bye, Mr. Elliot."

"Miss Grant."

Rachel hung up the phone slowly.

And then a voice came from the doorway.

"Hello, Rachel."

Mercy opened the door of Nick's office without knocking and marched in. She saw both men look up in surprise from the computer they'd been intent on, and spoke before either of them could.

"I know you boys like the cloak-and-dagger stuff, but let's cut to the chase. Do you know about Graham Becket?"

NINETEEN

Rachel stared across the study at Graham. She felt very cold, and not only because he had a gun.

A gun pointed squarely at her.

"Graham? What's going on?"

"Haven't you figured it out yet, Rachel? I thought surely you—or your lover—would have found what you were looking for by now." His voice was the one that had been so familiar to her for so many years, quiet and pleasant.

Involuntarily, Rachel glanced down at the box on the desk.

Graham was quick. "Ah, so you have found something. A little note condemning me, perhaps? Or something more damning, maybe information Duncan managed to gather on someone else?"

"No."

"I don't believe you, Rachel. You never were a very

good liar." He came farther into the room, that gun still aimed at her. "Move away from the desk. But not too far away."

She obeyed, but heard herself offer an idiotic protest. "That's just about some information Dad left for me. About more loans he made. Like the one to Adam."

Graham looked at the note briefly, then pocketed it and the key. "Yes, I'm sure he kept meticulous records somewhere. I always suspected it. But there wasn't much of a risk of anyone finding them until you came home and started going through everything. I could have found them myself, but you had to be the one to sort his private papers. And since he'd locked up his desks and, as I recall, left the keys for you in one of the safes, I couldn't slip in here and get it done before you came back to Richmond."

"I must be very slow," she said, hearing the reluctance in her own voice. "It was you. You were the one who recommended Dad lend Jordan Walsh all that money."

His eyes flickered. "So you already know about the loan."

"We found a notebook." She hesitated. "Adam has it. So whatever you're planning won't work. He knows. And Nick knows."

"Maybe. But they don't have proof, or they would already have moved on it." He patted his pocket with his free hand. "I'll make very sure they never have proof."

"And what about me?" She swallowed. "Another exploding building? Another car playing hit-and-run?"

Graham frowned. "I had nothing to do with either of those things."

"I don't believe you, Graham."

"I can't help what you believe, Rachel."

"You tried to have me killed."

His frown remained. "The cut brake line was meant only to scare you, to send you back to New York."

"And the rest?"

"I told you. I didn't have anything to do with the rest."

"Then it was your boss. Jordan Walsh." And that certainly seemed to touch a nerve.

"Walsh is not my boss," Graham said shortly. "But he's a powerful man, Rachel, a man you don't say no to. You must see that."

"And he told you to kill me?"

A nerve throbbed beside Graham's mouth, but the gun never wavered. "He told me to deal with the problem. His people couldn't seem to—I'm sorry, Rachel. This isn't the way I wanted it to end. If it hadn't been for Delafield—"

"What does Adam have to do with it?"

A little sound escaped Graham, a sound that was a laugh but held no amusement. "Not a goddamned thing, Rachel."

She drew a breath. "Graham, I don't understand this. How would it harm you—or Walsh, for that matter—for that loan to come to light? Or for me to know you asked Dad to make it to Walsh?"

"The loan wasn't the problem. With Duncan gone and that loan made on a handshake, there was no way the money could ever be collected. But I made a mistake in giving in to Walsh and recommending he go to Duncan in the first place. The money was for a legitimate business, you know, a nice, respectable front Walsh could have used in years to come. It all would have worked out if only Duncan hadn't seen Walsh here in Richmond, somewhere he shouldn't have been. He got suspicious."

"Until then, he'd accepted your recommendation of Walsh."

"Of course. I was an old and valued friend as well as

his attorney. And Walsh had such a good cover story, you see. About all the good he was going to be able to do with that money. But then he blew it. He put Duncan on guard, made him start wondering."

Slowly, trying to understand, Rachel said, "And any investigation of Walsh would have turned up information that you had also been involved in illegal activities."

"It was a concern. Duncan could have ruined me with that information. And it would have focused way too much light on Walsh's activities here in Richmond."

Rachel felt queasy. "Your reputation as a fine, upstanding attorney meant more to you than other people's lives. More than the life of a man who'd called you friend for fifteen years."

"I'm glad I never had to make that decision," Graham said, almost thoughtful.

Rachel stared at him. "You sabotaged Dad's plane."

"As a matter of fact, I didn't. I wouldn't know the first thing about how to bring a plane down. No, that was a fortuitous accident."

"The plane was brought down, Graham. It was made to crash."

For the first time, he looked uncertain, but the expression quickly passed. "Well, perhaps Walsh acted without telling me. In any case, we were safe after that. Until you came home. I really am sorry, Rachel. You should have stayed in New York."

Getting a little tired of his meaningless apologies, Rachel said steadily, "Well, I didn't do that, Graham. So what are you going to do with me now? A bullet would look a bit suspicious, don't you think? Especially with Adam and Nick working to get Walsh."

Graham shook his head. "Rachel, how could you even imagine that I could kill you like that?"

She wasn't reassured. "No?"

"No. We're just going to take a little walk, that's all."

"Where?"

"The river." He smiled. "It's such a pity you never learned to swim."

It was the most chilling thing she'd ever heard in her life.

Rachel knew without a doubt that Graham could—and would—push her into the river. A river that had sometimes refused to give up its dead.

"Let's go," he said, gesturing toward the door.

A little desperately, she said, "Don't you think that my death coming so soon after Mom and Dad's will make people wonder?"

"Not really. Their deaths were tragic, but that crash was ruled an accident. Everyone knows it was an accident. You, on the other hand, have been terribly despondent about the new burdens that have fallen onto your fragile shoulders. I mean, everyone knows you never really recovered from Thomas Sheridan's death, and now you've lost your parents in a senseless accident—another plane crash. The estate so complex, all the details overwhelming. And the double of your dead lover showing up on top of everything. Well, who could be surprised that it all just got to be too much? Especially after I spread the word about how depressed you've been, how you cried in my office and talked about suicide. It's such a pity I didn't take you seriously."

"What about Adam?"

"Oh, he might try rattling a few cages, making some noise. But he won't have any proof. If he gets too bothersome, Walsh will take care of him."

"You bastard."

"Start walking, Rachel."

"If you think I'm going to just tamely walk to the river with that gun in my back—"

"Rachel, understand something. I've gone too far to turn back now. If I have to, I'll knock you over the head and carry you to the river. It's your choice. On your feet or slung over my shoulder. But make up your mind. I intend to be long gone by the time Fiona returns from the market."

Habits, Rachel thought, could sometimes be used as weapons. He had known Fiona's regular market day and had waited, knowing it was his best chance of catching Rachel alone in the house.

Panic was a mild word to describe what she felt, but even with that fear and horror running through her mind, she remembered something. She wasn't entirely alone.

There were guardian dragons outside the gates. One watching in front—and one watching from the river.

The only question was, could either of them help her before Graham managed to kill her.

"Let's go, Rachel." He smiled. "And do try to remember that I can pull this trigger before you could throw anything at me—and certainly before you could run away. I don't think a bullet hole would matter too much after you'd been in the river awhile."

She had an awful feeling he was right.

"I hate to sound like a bad TV movie, but you'll never get away with this." She moved toward the door.

"Oh, I think I will. No, don't bother looking back at me. Just keep heading for the back of the house, Rachel."

Help didn't come from the river.

Rachel was near the foot of the stairs, moving as slowly as she dared, when the front door suddenly burst open and a total stranger came flying in. Almost literally flying.

He landed on the rug, outstretched hands holding a businesslike automatic, and his command was shouted.

"Move, Rachel!"

Things happened very fast after that. Rachel darted toward the stairs, which was the only direction she could move in. Graham whirled toward the newcomer, his gun leveling.

"Drop it, Becket!"

Two shots sounded so close together that they seemed one.

Rachel looked back over her shoulder and saw Graham stagger back against the wall at the foot of the stairs, scarlet blooming on the upper arm of his jacket. But it wasn't his gun hand that hung useless.

And the man on the rug was still, his gun in limp fingers.

Rachel didn't hesitate; she ran up the stairs as fast as she could. She knew this house better than Graham ever could, and if she could just get upstairs with a few seconds' grace, there was a good chance she could elude him —at least for a while.

"Rachel!"

She reached the top just as another shot rang out, and wood chips flew from the banister beside her.

"Stop, Rachel! The next one goes in your back."

She didn't make a conscious decision to stop; she was willing to take her chances and keep running. But suddenly she felt as if she moved through water. There was resistance in the very air, an odd impression of something tangible slowing her forward momentum until she stopped moving.

She turned to watch Graham come the rest of the way up the stairs toward her. Again, she felt that curious sensation, and it compelled her to begin backing away, step by slow step.

She felt strangely calm.

"Don't make me shoot you, Rachel." He reached the top of the stairs and paused. "We're going back down, and we're walking to the river."

"You're bleeding, Graham," she observed with a detachment that astonished her. "And that other man is hurt as well. What do you mean to do about him?"

"A watchdog Nick or Delafield hired to stand guard, I suppose? He's dead meat. I'll throw him in the river. Let's go, Rachel."

She was waiting for something. And she didn't know what.

"Rachel—" He took a step toward her.

Footsteps pounded on the walk outside.

From the open front door, Adam yelled, "Becket!"

Graham started to turn.

For just an instant, Rachel thought her eyes were playing tricks on her. They had to be. Because out of a shadowy area near the top of the stairs, Adam appeared, and moved toward Graham.

And then she realized it wasn't Adam.

There was no way of knowing what Graham felt behind him. Maybe he felt powerful, furious hands or maybe, like Rachel, he merely felt the sensation of an irresistible force compelling him onward. All Rachel knew for sure was that utter and complete terror showed briefly on his face before he pitched forward and fell.

Rachel closed her eyes as the horrible sounds of Graham's heavy body crashing down the stairs seemed to fill the house. When the sounds finally stopped, she opened her eyes slowly, looking at the top of the stairs.

There was nothing there.

"Rachel!" Adam came up the stairs two at a time, his face pale and eyes almost wild. He had a gun, which he hastily stuck inside his belt at the small of his back as he reached her, so that he could put his hands on her shoulders. "Are you all right? Did he hurt you?"

"No. No, I'm . . . fine." She looked up at him. "Did you see? Did you see him?"

"Yes," Adam said. "I saw him." And then he pulled her into his arms.

As it turned out, Graham had been wrong about Simon being dead meat. He wasn't happy, and he was in a great deal of pain, but he was very much alive when the paramedics wheeled him out.

That made Rachel feel better. She didn't know how she would have been able to bear it if a man had died trying to protect her.

As for the man who intended to kill her, he was not as lucky as Simon. Then again, maybe he was lucky. The fall broke Graham's neck.

Which, Adam said viciously, would save the state a bundle and had probably made those in hell happy to see a new face.

Rachel didn't know how she felt about any of this yet. She was numb about part of it, about Graham's massive betrayal and the incredible violence that had occurred here today. Yet there was a definite relief in the knowledge that it was over now, that finally her life could return to normal.

And with that relief she found her mind dwelling instead on what she had seen at the top of the stairs.

Tom?

It was absurd, of course. Like the rose and the notepaper, the odd trip to the attic and the gift Tom had never given her, it had only been her imagination. Some trick of the light . . .

Except that Adam had seen him too.

Rachel couldn't help remembering waking up on that early morning a decade before to see Tom standing at the foot of her bed. And she knew, she was absolutely certain in her own mind, that she had not dreamed that.

He had come to her once in a moment of anguished farewell.

Had he come to her again today, knowing somehow that she was in danger and needed him?

Adam had seen him. And Nick might have seen him, since he'd been right behind Adam as they rushed into the house.

They had all seen . . . a dead man.

Rachel definitely didn't know how she felt about that. On top of the emotions she had worked through, her feelings about Adam and Tom, her imagination working overtime, and the nightmares filled with tangled symbolism that had haunted her nights, to believe that Tom had actually come back to help her . . .

For the first time, she had to wonder if it had been more than the voice of her own subconscious in those dreams and nightmares, if Tom had actually used that means to reach out to her, to try to help her, and warn her.

And question her feelings about Adam.

That was unnerving, to think that the first love of her life might be observing from some betweenworld, frowning over her choice of lovers.

"I'm imagining things," she muttered to herself. "Still imagining things. That's just not the way it works."

Or was it? Did the dead watch over the living?

"Here, Rachel—Fiona sent this in." Mercy carried a

tray into the study, where Rachel was curled up on the couch, wrapped in an afghan Adam had put around her.

"She shouldn't have bothered. She's as shaken up as I've ever seen her," Rachel commented, a little surprised by her own steady voice.

"Well, she needs to be busy." Mercy put the tray on the coffee table and sat down beside Rachel. She fixed her friend a cup of tea and handed it over. "And you need this."

Rachel sipped, then smiled. "Hot and sweet. You know, I've been drinking an awful lot of this stuff in the last couple of weeks."

Mercy eyed her thoughtfully. "Is that incipient hysteria or real, honest-to-God humor?"

"The latter."

"Glad to hear it. Graham Becket isn't worth a tear or a wasted regret."

Rachel frowned. "The guys are out in the foyer still talking to the police, aren't they?"

"Oh, yeah. Graham dropped the lockbox key when he fell, but the cops are more than half convinced they ought to keep it as evidence anyway. If I were going to bet, I'd bet on Nick and Adam getting it back." Mercy fixed a cup of tea for herself.

Rachel said, "Well, while they're out there doing that, would you mind telling me how you guys showed up at just the right moment?"

"That's simple enough. Me." Mercy, who had waited in the car until the shouting was over, grinned at her friend.

"Thank you. What did you do?"

"I found a note in Duncan's personal computer files at the bank."

Rachel blinked. "I didn't know he had any."

Mercy rolled her eyes. "Did he ever. I'd have turned them over to you eventually as part of settling his estate and clearing his things out of the bank, but when I realized Nick and Adam were up to something, it occurred to me that the only common denominator was Duncan. So I started going through the files on his computer. I thought I might recognize something odd more quickly than the rest of you." She paused. "Of course, I also wanted to teach Nick a thing or two."

"Along the lines of—anything you can do I can do better?"

"Something like that." Mercy grinned again. "They were both really focused on the cloak-and-dagger aspects—which, to be fair, turned out to be where almost all the answers were. But I found one tiny little key among Duncan's files."

"What was it?"

"It was a note Duncan had made just a few weeks before his death. He'd been looking at some kind of storage property near the river, and he saw Graham come out of a seedy building—with Jordan Walsh. Something about what he saw bothered Duncan, even though he knew they knew each other. But the point was what his note told me. Nick had finally confessed about what was going on, what he and Adam were up to, and he told me who they suspected. He'd also told me they hadn't found a sign of a connection between Walsh and any of Duncan's friends. So I burst into Nick's office and asked them if they knew about Graham."

Fascinated, Rachel said, "And then?"

"When he realized that neither of the watchdogs they had guarding you had any reason at all to suspect Graham, and had in fact already let him come and go freely here, Adam went the whitest shade of pale I've ever seen and dove for the phone. In the meantime, Nick was pulling a couple of guns out of a drawer—guns in the bank! Can you believe that?—and the next thing you knew we were all in Nick's car, breaking every speed law to get here."

"My God."

Mercy chuckled. "We picked up two squad cars along the way, which turned out to be handy."

Rachel took a healthy swallow of her tea, then said, "The cloak-and-dagger aspect. So that meeting today gave them some answers?"

"Pretty much all of them, from what Nick told me on the way over here. Lots of lovely damning information about Walsh and his operations here in Richmond, all nice and neat on a computer disk. Unfortunately, though, the witness they thought they had turned out to be dead."

Rachel sighed. "With Graham gone, the witness gone —how much of this will ever come to light in court?"

"Nick thinks most of it." Mercy shrugged. "Your testimony is enough probable cause to start digging into Graham's records—and what do you want to bet that, being an anal lawyer, he kept good ones? I bet he'll hurt Walsh more than that other witness ever could. And then all those computer files the witness made copies of will give the prosecutors plenty of other places to dig. They'll get him, Rachel."

"I hope so."

"They will. And in case you're wondering, they'll make it way too hot for him to even *think* about coming after you."

Rachel smiled. "It crossed my mind that I might be stuck here in the castle for a good long while."

"Not if Adam has anything to say about it. I gather he plans to take you away somewhere for a while. Maybe on a honeymoon?"

"He hasn't said. Or asked, for that matter." Rachel eyed her friend thoughtfully, smiling a little. "How about you and Nick?"

Mercy widened her eyes innocently. "What about us?"

"Ah. I thought so."

"Rats. What gave me away?"

"Oh, just the way you talk about him."

"I gotta watch that," Mercy muttered, then grinned. "I've got a bet with Nick that Leigh will faint dead away when I walk into the bank with a wedding ring."

"It's that serious, huh?"

"I chased the man ferociously until he caught me."

Rachel smiled at her friend. "I'm glad. He unnerved me for the longest time, but I have plenty of reason to be grateful to Nick."

"He's a remarkable man." Mercy shook her head. "Secretive as hell, though. I'm going to have to cure him of that."

"I have complete faith in you."

"Thank you. So do I, as a matter of fact."

Rachel laughed. "That poor man doesn't have a chance, does he?"

Walking into the study just then, Nicholas said with perfect calm, "If you're referring to me, the answer is no."

Mercy gave him an innocent look than laughed. "What makes you think we're talking about you?"

"Just a hunch." He put a casual hand on her shoulder, then looked past her at Rachel. "Not much longer now. The cops have agreed that your statement can wait for a day or two."

"Wow," Mercy murmured. "I for one am impressed."

"Adam was . . . insistent," Nicholas said. "In any case, they're clearing out now. I know it's been a hell of a day, but you should have some peace and quiet shortly. You can put all this behind you."

Rachel hesitated, then said, "When you and Adam came in, did you see what happened to Graham?"

"Yes."

She looked at him, unsure how to phrase the question.

Nicholas smiled slightly. "There have been times in my life when I know someone helped me. There was just no other way to explain it. Maybe we all have guardian angels. Whether they exist, or are who we think they are, doesn't really matter, does it? In times of crisis, we somehow find a way to survive. It's all that's important, in the end. Survival."

"And asking no questions?"

"Sometimes, that's for the best. We don't need to know all the answers, Rachel."

Mercy looked between them curiously. "Say what?"

Nicholas glanced down at her, still smiling. "I'll tell you later."

"You bet you will."

Rachel drew a deep breath, then smiled at him. "Did I say thank you?"

"No need. We'll have a lot to talk about, but that can wait." He paused, then added seriously, "And you can feel safe in this house again, Rachel. We have men stationed outside, and this time they're both close and very aware of who the enemy is."

"Thank you."

"You'll have your life back soon," he promised her. "Walsh is about to find himself caught in a meat grinder. He'll be too worried about his own hide to come after you again."

Rachel nodded, then looked past him as Adam came into the room.

"They're gone," he announced.

"And so are we." Nicholas took Mercy's hand and drew her to her feet. "We'll go back to the bank and copy that disk, then personally deliver a copy to the D.A. Might as well get things rolling."

"Watch your back," Adam warned. "We don't know we weren't seen at the meet with Sammy."

"We'll be fine."

Mercy said to Rachel, "I'll call you tomorrow," then went out hand in hand with Nick.

"How about that?" Adam said absently.

"They'll be good together," Rachel predicted.

"I imagine so. She seems lively enough. Gave Nick hell on the way over here once he told her—" He broke off.

Calmly, Rachel said, "Once he told her about that meeting you two had today? It went badly, didn't it? Mercy said something about a witness being dead."

Adam sat down on the couch beside her. "Nick's informant was shot. Killed. But he lived long enough to tell us about the disk."

Rachel was afraid to try counting up the lives lost because Graham Becket hadn't wanted to tarnish his sterling reputation. So she pushed that aside for the moment. "Did the police let us keep the key?" she asked.

"It's in my pocket," Adam told her. "So we can go check out that safe deposit box tomorrow, if you feel up to it."

She didn't know how she would feel tomorrow, but nodded. Another question was bothering her. "Adam, when you guys burst into the house, you had a gun."

"I still have, as a matter of fact." Adam shrugged. "You're safe here, Rachel, I promise, but I mean to be very careful nevertheless. At least until Walsh is too busy to give us a second thought."

Rachel leaned forward to put her empty cup on the coffee table, then sat back and smiled slightly as she looked at him. "Since when is an electrical engineer and designer comfortable with guns?"

Adam drew a breath. "Well, I told you about meeting Nick in Rome."

"Yes."

"After that, I sort of helped him out now and then."

"But you were a college student."

"Most recruits are in college or fresh out. I wasn't that young, Rachel. Besides, they used me mostly as a courier, and there wasn't much risk involved in those assignments. A lot of foreign travel in the summers and during my breaks, but I enjoyed that."

"What about after South America? Was Dad right? Did you put yourself in dangerous situations after that?"

"Maybe." He shook his head. "At that point in my life, maybe I needed to risk to feel free. I don't know."

"And now? You still work for them, don't you?"

Readily, he said, "Until this year, until Duncan was killed, I took an assignment every few months. It was travel outside the country, a break from my work that always seemed to reenergize me. I had a solid cover as a legitimate American businessman, and I was useful. It was still mostly courier work."

"But not always."

"No. Not always."

Slowly, she said, "I know I should be grateful, in a way. Your training and experience obviously left you with good instincts and quick reflexes, and I'd be dead if not for you."

Adam shook his head, but said, "However?"

"However, if these past weeks have taught me anything, it's that sometimes life can be dangerous enough even when we don't go out looking for trouble."

He reached over and took her hand. "I know. Rachel, I'm out of that business now, and I don't mean to go back."

She looked a little troubled. "What if it's something you need?"

"All I need," he said, "is right here with me now."

Rachel managed a smile. "What about that company out in California?"

"I'm thinking . . . we need an East Coast office. And Richmond is a great place for a business. You'll sell one-of-a-kind designs in clothes, and I'll sell electronic gadgets."

Before Rachel could respond to that, Fiona appeared in the doorway and announced belligerently, "I've got supper ready and you two need to eat. Miss Rachel, you haven't had a bite since breakfast, and I don't doubt Mr. Adam hasn't either. So I don't want to hear any arguing."

She vanished from the doorway.

Adam looked at Rachel with raised brows. "Mr. Adam?"

"The ultimate sign of approval," she explained. "You're in."

He grinned, then got to his feet and grasped her hands to pull her gently up and out of the afghan cocoon. "Fiona approves of me. How about that? I thought I was going to have to buy her diamonds or something."

"Diamonds wouldn't have worked. So I'm glad you didn't waste your money."

He chuckled, then put an arm around her as they began heading for the dining room. They had to pass through the foyer, and though no evidence remained of what had happened there, Rachel knew he felt her tense a bit.

"You'll stay with me tonight?" she said.

His arm tightened around her. "I was hoping you'd ask."

TWENTY

They retired to bed not long after supper, early enough that Cameron had not come in yet, and they decided to leave it until the morning to tell him what had occurred. Both Rachel and Adam were weary, and both fell asleep long before midnight.

"Rachel. Come, Rachel."

She was instantly awake, and even as she lifted her head from Adam's shoulder and looked down at his sleeping face, Rachel realized that what she had heard had not been spoken in the room, but inside her own mind.

Her first impulse was to close her eyes and go back to sleep. But something was nagging at her, the vague sense of something left undone, unfinished. The voice in her mind, she thought, was only her subconscious prompting her once again.

She slipped out of bed, careful not to wake Adam, and found the nightgown and robe she'd discarded—or Adam had—the night before. She put them on and paused only to run her fingers through her hair, then left the bedroom, closing the door quietly behind her.

She had no idea where it was her subconscious wanted her to go, but when she glanced toward the far end of the hall, she was not surprised to see that the door to the attic was open once more.

She went down the hall. It didn't seem strange to her to be leaving the haven of a warm bed and Adam to respond to the proddings of her subconscious—which was, perhaps, the oddest thing of all. She turned on the attic lights and went up the stairs. The storage chest was open.

This time, Rachel barely hesitated. She knelt before the chest and began lifting things out one at a time. Most were the usual mementos girls kept, like theater stubs and dried flowers and love letters. Ribbons from gifts. Tom's football jersey from college. A half-finished box of Valentine's Day candy. A book of poetry he had given her.

They cost her no more than pleasant pangs of memory, which told Rachel more clearly than anything else had that she had finally left Tom in the past, where he belonged.

She took them out of the chest and looked at them, and put them aside, and when the chest was empty, she slowly put everything back.

When she picked up the book of poetry, an envelope fell out.

At first, Rachel thought it was just one of the love letters that had gotten separated from the others, but when she opened the envelope, she found something else entirely.

"I knew it was here somewhere."

She looked quickly toward the top of the stairs to find Cameron standing there. He was fully dressed, as he always was when he left his room in the morning, and he looked very tired. Almost absently, he added, "I saw the attic door open and the light on when I came out of my room, so I came to see . . . I never thought to look up here."

"This is a check written from you to Tom," Rachel said slowly. "For ten thousand dollars. And it's dated the day of his last trip."

"Yes. I gave it to him just a few minutes before he went to you to say good-bye. Remember? I was here that weekend on one of my visits. I gave him the check, but he left straight from here, didn't have a chance to deposit the money or take it home. He never carried anything but cash on trips, and when the check never turned up and you never said anything, I figured there was a chance he'd left it here somewhere."

"This is what you've been looking for? Why?"

Cameron drew a breath. "Because I didn't want you to find it. I didn't want you to know it was . . . my fault Tom was killed."

"What?"

"He had a cargo run only as far as Mexico, Rachel. I hired him to fly from there down to South America. We'd done it before, but—"

"Cam, I don't understand. Why did you hire Tom to fly to South America?"

"I had a man down there who bought emeralds for me. Raw emeralds. But it was so damned hard to get them back here without, well, without going through customs."

Even a week ago, Rachel would have been shocked to hear that. But now she felt only a little surprise, and a small wrench of disappointment. "Tom did that? He brought gems into the country for you?"

Cameron nodded, avoiding her steady gaze. "The money didn't mean anything to him, of course. He enjoyed the thrill of it. More and more with every trip, in fact. I guess the fast cars and fast planes weren't exciting enough after a while."

Remembering how Tom had been the last time she had seen him alive, Rachel could well believe that. He had been the picture of a man looking forward to enjoyment, eager to leave her despite their approaching wedding date, promising blithely and carelessly to return. And now she had a good idea of how to explain his sometimes secretive smiles as well as her own instinctive feelings that he'd been doing something dangerous.

She wondered how many others besides her uncle had found Thomas Sheridan ready and willing to bend or break a few laws just for the thrill of it.

"I'm sorry, Rachel."

Rachel returned the check to the envelope and held it out to him, smiling a little sadly. "Don't worry about it, Cam. You aren't to blame for what happened to Tom."

He stepped forward to take the envelope, his expression lightening with a relief obvious in his voice. "I stopped buying the gems after that. And if I had it to do over again—"

"Yes. I imagine Tom might make a different choice too." But would he, given the chance? Rachel wasn't sure. And that was the saddest realization of all.

Cam retreated to the stairs, but paused at the top to look back at her. "Fiona was still up when I got in last night. She told me what happened here yesterday. About Graham. I don't know what to say, Rachel."

She managed a smile. "We'll talk about it later, Cam."

"Of course." He hesitated, then went on down the stairs.

Rachel knelt there a few moments longer, her hands folded in her lap and her thoughts years away. Then she finished putting all the mementos back in the chest and closed the lid on them.

The clock on the nightstand said only eight A.M. when she slipped back into bed beside Adam. He was still sleeping deeply, but made a satisfied little sound and gathered her close even so, and she relaxed in his arms with a wonderfully content sense of homecoming.

Nothing nagged at her now. There was no sense of something left undone, and her subconscious—or whatever the voice in her head had been—was silent now.

She decided that she would retrieve Cameron's letters from the untagged secretary in the basement, which Darby had promised to make sure he was given the opportunity to search first—and burn them. It would be less painful all around, Rachel thought. And it felt like the right decision. She made a mental note to tell Darby the plans had changed, and that was her last clear thought. Without even realizing she was going to, Rachel fell asleep.

She woke a couple of hours later, alone in the bed, and was almost immediately aware of the faint sounds of Adam in the shower. She stretched languidly for a moment, smiling, then got out of bed and found her robe, which had somehow gotten itself pushed off the bed and to the floor. Their clothes from the day before also were scattered, and she grinned to herself as she moved around the room picking up her things and his, and laying them neatly on the foot of the bed.

When she heard something metallic fall from his pants pocket, she thought it was the safe deposit box key. But something gold glinted up at her from the carpet.

Rachel laid the pants aside and bent down to see what had fallen.

A locket.

She picked it up in suddenly nerveless fingers, and

slowly straightened, staring at it as it lay in her palm. It was easy to see, on one side of the locket, the initials TS. And when she turned it over . . .

The initials RG.

Rachel found her way to a chair without even realizing she was moving, and sat there, dry-mouthed, thoughts whirling.

But it couldn't be.

The locket had vanished with Tom, he'd always worn it, never took it off even to shower or sleep. He'd had it around his neck when she had last seen him, when he had come to tell her about the unexpected trip and to say good-bye to her.

How could Adam have it?

This couldn't be the same locket. The initials were the same, but that could be a coincidence, surely. Had to be.

Unless . . .

With trembling fingers, she carefully opened the locket. On one side, a St. Christopher medal.

Her picture on the other.

"Oh, my God," Rachel whispered.

"You kept me alive," Adam said.

She looked up to where he stood in the doorway of the bathroom, a towel wrapped around his lean waist and a look of terrible foreboding on his face, and what he'd said made no sense to her.

"How did you get this?" she asked.

Adam came into the room far enough to reach the chair across from hers. He did not sit down, but gripped the back of it with both hands. His knuckles showed white through taut skin, but his voice was even, calm. "Thomas Sheridan gave it to me."

Rachel shook her head. "No. No, he wouldn't have. He couldn't have."

"He did, Rachel."

"When? Where? How—how did you know him?" She drew a shaky breath. "And why in God's name didn't you tell me before now?"

He answered the last question first. "I didn't know how to tell you."

"What? Adam—"

"Rachel, I didn't know how to tell you. I still don't."

Her whirling thoughts settled, and she said slowly, "Start at the beginning. How did you know him?"

"We met . . . in South America." The words were careful, measured. "In the prison."

"I . . . don't understand. You said you were in that prison months after Tom's plane went down."

"Yes. He wasn't killed in the crash, Rachel. His plane was shot down, and he survived."

"No."

"Yes. They thought he was running guns in, weapons to help fuel what was obviously going to be a coup. The cargo line he flew for had done that sort of thing before, so it was under suspicion."

Rachel wanted to say that Tom wouldn't have done that, but she was reasonably sure he would have.

"He wasn't even carrying any cargo, according to what he told me. But they didn't know that, or chose not to believe it. They shot him down. But he didn't die."

"He was still alive months later? When you were put in that awful place?"

Adam nodded. "Barely. He'd been injured in the crash, and they—well, the guards of the old regime were no better than those who dealt with me."

Rachel bit her bottom lip, afraid to probe for details.

He hesitated, then said steadily, "I was put into a cell next to his. Given Tom's condition, his appearance, I didn't realize how alike we were myself, not then. There was a loose stone in the wall between us. Not big, barely room enough to see each other, to talk without attracting the attention of the guards. So we did.

"I think he knew he was dying. I've wondered since if he held on just long enough to do what he had to do."

Rachel swallowed hard. "What?"

"Tell someone he could trust about you. My face wasn't as—damaged—as his, so he knew I could have been his twin, even though I didn't. It must have reassured him somehow. Then again, in his condition, he probably would have talked to anybody who spoke English. He gave me the locket and made me promise that if I ever got out of that place, I'd find you and return the locket to you. Make sure you were all right. He wanted you to know that he loved you. That he was sorry he couldn't keep his promise."

Quick tears burned her eyes, and Rachel looked down at the locket in her hands. "He never could keep his promises," she murmured. She looked back at him. "You should have told me, Adam. Why didn't you tell me?"

"Why?" Adam held out a hand almost beseechingly. "Do you think I wanted to tell you that Thomas Sheridan didn't die quick and painless in a plane crash, as you'd always thought? That he lived on for months? That he suffered? That his last days were pure hell?"

Rachel flinched.

Adam nodded jerkily, his mouth twisting. "Oh, yeah, that was really something I wanted to tell you. Just like I really wanted to tell you that your name was the last word on his lips, Rachel. Of course, it was a scream, but I heard it clearly enough."

"Don't," she choked out.

He swore under his breath, hesitated, then went over

to the bed and gathered his clothes, dressing quickly, his movements automatic. Maybe he did it just to give them both a minute or two to collect themselves. Or maybe such naked words demanded the frail protection of clothing, Rachel thought dimly.

Dressed now, Adam moved back toward her, sitting down in the chair across from hers. His face was very pale, his shoulders were hunched, as though to ward off a blow. His voice was suddenly very quiet and calm. "We didn't really have much time to talk. He was in bad shape then, and fading fast. Whatever he was waiting for, after we started talking, he didn't last long. A few weeks. He was delirious at the end."

Rachel tried and failed to get a terrible image out of her head. "Oh, my God," she whispered.

It was Adam's turn to flinch. But he didn't look at her. Instead, he clasped his hands before him and stared at them. Still in that calm voice, he went on. "I was mostly alone after that, in that cell day after day and night after night, except the few times the guards had a merciful impulse and let me get some fresh air outside in a walled courtyard. There wasn't much to do except count the days. And stare at that locket."

He drew a breath. "I knew your face better than I knew my own. Years before we met. When I said you kept me alive, I wasn't kidding. You did. You were my lodestar. You represented all that was beautiful in the world outside that jail. I'd stare at your picture by the hour, open and close the locket, polish the gold."

"Adam—"

He didn't let her interrupt, just kept talking in that calm voice as if too much had been stored up inside him for too long.

"I fell in love with you before I ever heard the sound of

your voice. And with every month that passed, that love grew stronger." A rough laugh escaped him. "Oh, I know what you're thinking. It was just a picture of you, without personality, so how could I believe I loved you?"

"How could you?"

"It's nothing I can explain, but that locket was a real, tangible connection to you, Rachel. I felt it. Maybe because you'd given it to Tom in love, or maybe because he'd been so damned determined that his last message reach you. I don't know. All I do know is that when I went to sleep at night, you were in my dreams. And in my dreams I heard your voice, and felt your worries and sorrows, and knew you. I left that prison and spent time with you. Almost every night."

Slowly, Rachel said, "I was dreaming about Tom a lot in those first years."

Adam nodded. "But sometimes, in your dreams, he was just out of reach, wasn't he? Not easy to see. You spoke to him, and sometimes he answered you, but sometimes he was just there, watching. Because sometimes he was me, Rachel."

"People don't dream the same dreams," she protested.

"We did, the whole time I was in that prison. And we've been dreaming the same dreams the last couple of weeks. Do you want me to describe the house with all the rooms and hallways? The masked men? The way Tom and I kept wearing masks of each other? And that stone-walled room where they hung me up and beat me?"

Rachel was silent.

Adam went on, his voice calm again, almost detached. "The locket was a connection to you. I don't know how I was able to keep the guards from finding it, but I did, just as Tom had. And somehow, it made all the months, and finally all the years, bearable. I just kept telling myself that

I had to survive, I had to beat the bastards and live long enough to get out, because I had to find you, just as I'd promised I would. And not only for Tom's sake, but for mine as well.

"When that dictator was finally overthrown, and the first decent regime in decades took over, they opened the cell doors and told us we could go home. Even so, since I was an American, it took several weeks for me to get home."

He paused. "Then, of course, I had to face reality. As badly as I wanted to go and see you, there was no way I could, not then. I was in fairly bad shape and looked like hell, aside from being dead broke. And then there was the story I had to tell you."

Adam looked at her finally, his eyes very dark and still. "I didn't want to. It seemed to me that it wasn't something you needed to know. Thomas Sheridan was dead. Period. How he died didn't really matter. I figured you'd gone on with your life, and there was no need to distress you by hearing such terrible things from a stranger."

He shook his head. "That's what I told myself. But I barely waited long enough to settle with the company before I started looking for you. I knew where to start, of course, and it didn't take me long to find out you'd gone to New York. That you were okay, happy, I assumed. I could hardly approach you in any sense, I knew that. Especially since I'd found a picture of Thomas Sheridan by then, and knew just how like him I appeared. But I couldn't quite let go either. So I came here to Richmond. Saw this house, found out all I could about your family."

"You didn't know Nick was Dad's partner?"

Adam hesitated. "He wasn't Duncan's partner then. Rachel, it was my suggestion that Nick approach Duncan about joining the bank."

She stared at him. "Why?"

"Several reasons. I had contacted Nick almost as soon as I got out of prison, and I knew he was looking to set up in some kind of financial business, that he wanted to settle down for a while. I knew he'd be damned good at it, and that he'd be able to lighten some of your father's burdens."

"I never thought of him as burdened," Rachel murmured.

"It wasn't more than he could handle, Rachel, I just got the feeling from what I'd found out about him that taking on a junior partner might give him more time to do some of the things he seemed interested in. And I wanted someone near your family, in a position to let me know if anything happened. If anything changed."

"I see. Then later, when you called looking for Nick, it was a ruse?"

"That wasn't quite the way it happened. I'm sorry, Rachel, for lying about that. But without explaining about the locket and why I was in Richmond, it was the only way I could think to account for how I happened to get that loan from your father. In reality, I approached him openly, approached the bank, I mean. I told Duncan it was because I knew Nick, and Nick was out of Richmond at the time. The rest happened just as I said. Duncan listened to me, and offered the private loan."

"He must have been shocked that you looked so much like Tom."

"Surprised, yes. I don't think much shocked him, though." Adam shrugged. "In any case, I went back to California and got to work. I came out here once or twice a year, as I told you. And kept in touch more often with Nick."

Rachel drew a breath and kept her voice steady. "Then Mom and Dad were killed."

He nodded. "And I found the bits of that timer, realized there was more to it than a tragic plane crash. I saw you at the funeral, but I stayed back, out of sight. I thought the way I looked might be one blow more than you could take just then. Nick and I had already decided to find out what was going on. I knew it was only a matter of time until we met. But you'd told him you were going back to New York until the estate was nearly settled, and I wasn't about to introduce myself to you when you were burying your parents."

Rachel said, "After I came back to Richmond, just before my car's brakes gave way, I saw you watching me."

"Yes. I'm sorry I frightened you."

"Why didn't you approach me then?"

Adam's gaze dropped to his hands once again. "Nick had said he'd introduce us, and we'd already realized we could get access to Duncan's private papers only through you, but I wasn't ready to face you. By then I knew what everybody said, that you'd buried your heart with Tom, that you were still mourning him even after so many years."

"Is that what you thought when we did finally meet? That I was still mourning him?"

"I knew how you'd looked at me in the moments after the crash, and in the hospital, when you thought I was Tom." His gaze returned to her face, dark and grave. "Yes, I thought you were still mourning him. And I knew that my looking so much like him would only complicate that."

"I *was* still mourning him," Rachel said. She paused, seeing his face tighten and those eyes grow even bleaker. Then she said, "It had become almost a habit, I think. Something I hadn't questioned until you showed up. Then

I had to face it, because you were here and I was feeling things for you. I was so confused at first."

"I know."

She looked at the locket still lying open in her hand, and slowly closed it. "And this . . . I'm glad it helped you. I'm grateful to anything that helped you survive that place. And I'm glad you told me about Tom. But he's gone, Adam. He's been gone a long time."

"Is he? We both saw him yesterday, Rachel. We both saw what he did for you. And I was told that several times a man was spotted following us, watching. A big blond man, athletic, polished. He kept to the shadows, and walked as if he wouldn't make a sound. There's no way of knowing, of course, but it's a possibility I can't eliminate."

Steadily, she said, "Nick said maybe we all have guardian angels. And maybe they look the way we expect them to look. I don't have any other answer, Adam. All I know is that Tom is dead—and we're alive."

"You loved him."

"Yes, I loved him. I was a nineteen-year-old girl with my life ahead of me, and I thought that life was with him. But ten years changes a lot of things. It changes people. It changed me. I'm not that girl anymore, Adam. Just like you're not the young man who flew to South America to do a job. We both got through what we had to, and it changed us."

"I know."

"Do you?" Still holding the locket, Rachel left her chair and knelt beside his. She put the locket in his hand. "This belongs to you. It was yours much longer than it ever was Tom's—or mine."

He looked at the locket for a moment, then at her. "I promised—"

"You promised you'd bring it back to me. You did. And you delivered Tom's message."

He nodded, silent.

"I think we should change the initials on one side. I don't think Tom would mind."

"Rachel—"

"I love you, Adam. Don't you know that?"

He caught his breath. "I hoped."

Rachel linked her fingers together behind his neck and smiled slowly. "In case you're wondering, you are not a substitute for Tom. And I am not in any way confused about my feelings, not anymore. I love you with everything inside of me. I want to spend the rest of my life with you."

His arms went around her, tightly. "Rachel . . ."

Unnoticed by either of them, the locket slipped from his fingers.

And glinted gold in the carpet.

She looked ahead, and saw a man standing with the light behind him. She knew who he was, even though he wore no mask this time.

And this time, Tom didn't speak. But he was smiling, and his face was at peace. He spread his hands wide in a gesture taking in the both of them.

Then he turned and walked away into the light.

Rachel opened her eyes slowly, and for a moment just lay there thinking about the brief dream. She raised her head and looked down at Adam, not surprised to find him awake.

And she didn't even have to ask.

"That hasn't happened in a while," she said.

"No. I guess he thought we needed an ending." Adam smiled.

Rachel smiled and reached to touch his face, the gold of her wedding band glinting in the morning light. "Or he did."

Adam's arms went around her. "I prefer beginnings."

"So do I," Rachel said. "Oh, so do I . . ."

EPILOGUE

A year later

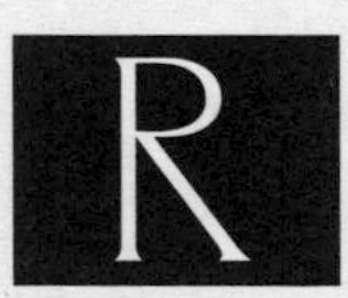

achel was surprised to be there.

She was at the garden gate, the one that opened onto the path that led through the woods and to the river.

The gate was open.

She passed through it and followed the path toward the woods, conscious of an odd sense within her. There was a tinge of sadness, but, more than that, there was a kind of joy.

When she entered the woods, she paused on the path, looking ahead to a very bright light.

"Hi."

Rachel turned her head to see Adam beside her. He reached out and took her hand, and the twining of their fingers made her smile.

"Hi. Why are we here?"

He nodded toward the bright light ahead. "One last visit, I think."